WHEN DARK CLOUDS PASS

J. A. FRANCES

WHEN DARK CLOUDS PASS

Matador
9 Priory Business Park,
Wistow Road, Kibworth Beauchamp,
Leicestershire. LE8 0RX
Tel: 0116 279 2299
Email: books@troubador.co.uk
Web: www.troubador.co.uk/matador
Twitter: @matadorbooks

ISBN 9781 785890 710

British Library Cataloguing in Publication Data.
A catalogue record for this book is available from the British Library.

Printed and bound by CPI Group (UK) Ltd, Croydon, CR0 4YY
Typeset in 11pt Minion Pro by Troubador Publishing Ltd, Leicester, UK

Matador is an imprint of Troubador Publishing Ltd

For Bea and the Family

Part I: 1904-5

ONE

Spit against the Wind

Broomburn, Lanarkshire
November 1904

The Inspector of Police sat motionless astride his bay gelding on the rim of a grassy hummock overlooking the village. Only the occasional twitch of his lip betrayed any emotion at the prospect of the day's work. He was a tall, spare figure in his early fifties, his face tanned and grooved by long years of service in the mounted branch of the Glasgow Constabulary. It was not for him to judge the rights or wrongs of any dispute; his reputation spoke for itself. Whenever civil disorder threatened, Inspector Chisholm could be relied upon to carry out his duty with ruthless efficiency.

At last his patience was rewarded. Almost imperceptibly, the inky black sky began to lighten, giving birth to a grey November dawn. Straining his eyes in the uncertain light, he could make out the gaunt black skeleton of the winding wheel silhouetted against the skyline. As the daylight grew stronger, other features appeared: engine house, colliery offices, the looming mass of the coal bings. To his right lay the gridiron streets and monotonous rows of miners' cottages; beyond them a ribbon of road twisted its way into the distance. The leaden clouds reflected a scene of brooding silence, broken only by the faint but steady gurgle from the river, the Avon Water, as it cleft and wound its way towards its tryst with the Clyde.

Chisholm reached down to pull the field glasses from his saddlebag, and slowly swept the ground in a wide arc. He had no interest in how industrialisation had spread its tentacles to gouge and despoil a once beautiful countryside; the lie of the land was merely another factor to be taken into account in laying his plans. His assistance had been requested to uphold the law in a neighbouring district, and that was all there was to it.

Replacing his binoculars, he wheeled his horse and began to trot back the mile or so across country to rejoin his command.

The crossroads where the rutted track leading to the mining community of Broomburn met the Glasgow highway was normally fairly quiet. But not that morning. A swelling din assailed his ears long before the inspector came within sight of the assembly point to confront a picture of utter confusion. The road was jammed by a seething mass of bodies – men pushing and jostling, shouting and cursing, some even coming to blows. The grass verges were littered with scattered piles of equipment, wherever they had been thrown down from passing supply carts. Here and there black helmets could be seen bobbing up and down amid this tide of humanity, as burly constables in oilskin capes, their cheeks puffed and scarlet from their exertions, strove to impose some semblance of order.

"What a herd of bloody sheep," muttered Chisholm to himself as he slowed his horse to a walk. "Christ save us from Polacks and bog Irish." But he felt no real malice. He was far more contemptuous of the Lanarkshire constabulary who had been foisted upon him and made up the bulk of his force. Thank God he had at least insisted on bringing his own team of mounted police. They may have numbered only a score, but they were a tightly knit, highly disciplined group, handpicked for their self-reliance and horsemanship. Well did they deserve the nickname of *Chisholm's Horse*. And there they were, partly hidden among a clump of trees some distance from the melee, no doubt deriving great amusement from the performance of their country cousins.

A slight movement in the lee of a ruined farm steading caught Chisholm's eye. This must be the third component of his motley band, fifteen or twenty estate workers sworn in as special constables for the occasion. These were the unknown quantity. Could they be trusted? Chisholm had his doubts. He did not want them; he had been even more vehement in his opposition to the use of civilians, but once again had been overruled. At least they had had the sense to keep away from the mayhem on the road.

The last of the open wagons were just rolling up to disgorge their loads. This human cargo had spent the night in squalid billets, before being roused, cold and hungry, to face a jolting, lurching journey to an unknown destination. Unloading the carts was proving a tricky business. It took all a driver's skill to hold his horses steady; their hooves clattered and slipped as they strove to keep a firm purchase on the wet cobbles. The carters, too, were nervous, keen to be rid of their charges and away from the scene as quickly as possible. Each was only too well aware of the reprisals that would follow if his participation in the affair ever became known in the district.

"Sir, Mr Chisholm, sir!" The high-pitched, agitated voice was barely audible above the tumult. The inspector looked over to see a fresh-faced youth struggling to extricate himself from the crowd. Once free, he came up at the run, panting deeply, his well-tailored uniform now sadly awry. Chisholm permitted himself a fleeting smile of sour satisfaction. It was his second-in-command, Sub-Inspector Dunlop.

This young man represented all that Chisholm detested in his chosen career. It was gall and wormwood to know that despite all the accolades, he stood no chance of further advancement, while this dandified sprig was destined for a smooth passage to the top. That might be the way of the world, but at least he could vent his feelings by taking the wind out of Dunlop's sails. He had quite deliberately left him to organise the arrival of men and equipment while he had gone off to reconnoitre, knowing full well his subordinate would never cope with the inevitable chaos. Judging by the bedraggled, almost tearful officer before him, he had succeeded admirably.

"It's just impossible. No one could be expected to manage this madhouse," sobbed Dunlop. "These cretins don't take any notice, no matter what you do. Most of them don't seem to understand English at all. The Poles are bad enough, but the Irish are beyond belief." His speech quickened, the words tumbling out as he regained his breath. "I should never have been faced with this. You didn't give me enough men. They had no training in riot control. Why did your horsemen and those estate workers just stand round and gape? Aren't they supposed to lend a hand?"

Chisholm listened to these excuses with growing impatience. It was all very well for Dunlop to fail to set up the march properly, he had expected no better; but for his junior to whine and try to pass the blame merely served to confirm his impression of the sub-inspector's lack of fibre. He cut short the tirade, and rounded on the hapless youth.

"Dunlop. Mister Dunlop. Do ye consider it appropriate for a police officer, an officer of rank, to chase around like a one-legged cripple in a bawdy house? Is that how they taught you to conduct yourself at yon fine college in England?" Chisholm spoke quietly, even softly, but the icy contempt in his voice cut through the younger man like a knife. "Look at you. Like a refugee from Culloden, or a tinker down on his luck. Cap not straight, two tunic buttons missing, boots filthy." He warmed to his task. "Ye dare to come up here and bellyache. What will your men think when they see their leader running to hide behind his mama's skirts? Ye've made yourself a laughing stock. You knew what had to be done. Ye were just too damned incompetent to direct the men properly."

Dunlop reeled before the onslaught. Chisholm's steely gaze betrayed not the slightest vestige of pity. But as his wrath subsided, he realised that perhaps he had gone too far. He still had need of this wretched youth, indeed his willing cooperation, if the enterprise was to be crowned with success. If the boy were to be of use, he would have to be stiffened. Destroying his confidence was not the way to achieve that.

"See here, lad," he continued gruffly. "Yon was a right farce ye made there, and no mistake. It's always the same, wet behind the ears. You thought you knew it all. Well, it's a hard knock to take, but perhaps we can still make something of you if you're prepared to try. Here's my advice. Get your men away from that mess down there. Order them to line up on both sides of the road, a couple of yards between each man. Tell them to pick up a handful of tools each, ready to give out when the time comes. Understood?"

Dunlop nodded, too choked with shame and humiliation to look up. He dare not disobey or give less than his best efforts; the full blast of Chisholm's rage would be too terrible to contemplate. All he could do was to grit his teeth and find consolation in thoughts of revenge. Surely something could be contrived. After all, his father had the ear of the chief constable.

"Good," said Chisholm. He could not resist a final jibe. "Just you concentrate on your part of the job. Leave the real professional to do the difficult bit."

The younger man stiffened, but wisely made no comment. He turned to walk back down the slope. Suddenly he stopped, as if something had occurred to him, hesitated, and then retraced his steps. "Just remembered, sir." He bit off the last word. "Mr Semple wants a word with you." He indicated with a vague sweep of his arm. "He's over yonder in the four-wheeler. Seemed quite put out when he asked me where you were."

"Put out, is he?" Chisholm's eyes glinted at the implied criticism. "Well, his neb will have to stay out of joint awhile longer. I've more important affairs to attend to."

With a sudden flick of the wrist he brought his riding crop down on the animal's rump. The horse sprang forward, taking Dunlop unawares and almost knocking him to the ground. Struggling to maintain his balance, the fledgling sub-inspector swore angrily. Sullen and resentful, he watched from a distance as Chisholm dismounted and gathered his squad round him. Then, with a final glare, he reluctantly set off to try to carry out his instructions.

Half an hour later the inspector could have been forgiven for basking in the glow of self-congratulation. The main body was now firmly caged, swept by his horsemen into the channel between the two lines of police, with the estate workers sealing the far end. As he had anticipated, the men soon quietened down. After much prodding, they began to sort themselves out into ranks, shouldering the tools passed out by the county constabulary.

Not until he was satisfied with the formation did he deign to take personal direction of the proceedings. Ramrod straight in the saddle, he slowly, even majestically, approached the column and circled round. If this was the best material the coal owners could find to break the strike, then they really must be down to the bottom of the barrel. Some, a few, had tried to seek refuge in anonymity by smearing mud on their faces. These must be local men from neighbouring pits, driven back to work by hunger and despair. Heaven help them if their identities were ever discovered; they must know they could expect no mercy from their fellow miners. Ah well, it was not his problem. His responsibility was to see them safely inside the colliery gates. Once delivered, how they fared was none of his concern.

An irate call broke in upon his train of thought. He looked up sharply towards the source of the disturbance. On the peak of the knoll a carriage was drawn up on a small sidetrack. A face appeared at the window, followed by an arm gesticulating violently. He had completely overlooked the existence of the mine owner. This was a tart reminder.

Inspector Chisholm knitted his brow, but otherwise gave no outward sign of annoyance. With great forbearance, as if indulging the wishes of a slightly wayward child, he made his way unhurriedly towards the waiting vehicle.

"Mr Semple, I believe. Good day to ye, sir."

"Good day be damned," came the testy response. "What the devil do you think you've been playing at? I've been left to kick my heels here for over an hour. And I'm not accustomed to be kept waiting, I can tell you that. Were you not informed I wanted to see you?"

The inspector gave Semple a hard look. The latter, puffed out with self-importance, hardly noticed it.

"As for your organisation," he continued, "I've never seen such a shambles in my life. These ninnies down there haven't a clue. And I was told you were good. I'm beginning to doubt it."

Chisholm had to struggle to bite back his anger. "We have had a few problems," he replied evenly, "but as you can see, we're ready to move off now."

"Long overdue." Semple refused to be placated. "Why could you not have started earlier, instead of wasting half the morning like this? Do you think we can afford to pay good wages for men to stand around doing nothing? And, forbye, why do they have to walk? Why not take the wagons right up to the pithead?"

This was too much for Chisholm. "I am in charge here," he said stiffly, "with full powers to act as I see fit." He paused, and then made an effort to answer more reasonably. After all, the fellow had a lot at stake. "If we set off before daybreak, too many things could go wrong. Your chaps are jumpy already. They'd be likely to imagine desperadoes behind every bush and turn in the road. And if we were attacked under cover of darkness, it would be well-nigh impossible to prevent the ruffians from getting in amongst us. I don't have to tell you what the result of that might be. No, it's too much of a risk."

"That's all very well," grumbled Semple. "But my company has had to lay out a pretty penny to recruit that lot, not to mention the cost of transport and lodgings for the night. I have to answer to a board of directors. Are you aware this dispute has been dragging on for over five months?"

"Perhaps if I had been called in earlier –"

"Listen." There was a new note of urgency in his voice. Or was it desperation? "If it doesn't end soon, I'll be bankrupt, finished. This pit is the key. If we can get production started here again, the others will soon come to heel. Either we crush the strike here and now, or we go under ourselves."

Chisholm could appreciate the situation. A word or two of reassurance would not go amiss. "Better an hour's delay and a safe arrival than a bungled effort. I'll get your coolies to work, never fear."

He nodded briefly to the coalmaster, touched the peak of his cap in salute and cantered back to his position at the head of the line. A final glance round, then he raised his arm and barked a word of command. The column began to shuffle forward uncertainly, as though fearful of stepping into the unknown.

* * *

Old men in the parish could still recall a golden age before man in his greed had set his hand to pillage and pollute and scar the land. Though memories were hazy and inclined to play tricks, their reminiscences were of boyhood friends long gone, and happy, dreamy days of youth spent rambling along the Avon Water, its steep banks awash with bright yellow *broom,* the springy shrub from which the village derived its name. Then it was a renowned beauty spot, the perfect setting to walk out with a sweetheart; to sit and rest and kiss and fondle, and speak of hopes and ambitions for the future. They would remember when Broomburn was only a tiny hamlet in a sea of farms, woods and moors stretching for miles in every direction, with only an occasional mill penetrating this far into the valley of the Upper Clyde to give warning that even an isolated settlement could not remain immune forever from the pressures of industrial and social change.

Now, broken in body and spirit by a lifetime of heavy, unremitting toil, those who were left were wont to forgather by the Jubilee Memorial in the Square, but only on days when the weather was fine and rheumatic limbs and wheezing chests could withstand the exertion. They had grown to manhood as the first mines were sunk; coal had provided their livelihood and left its mark upon them. Crushed bodies, diseased lungs and impaired eyesight were a constant reminder of the grim tolls exacted as the price of tunnelling in the bowels of the earth. Even so, few suspected that coalmining had a more insidious bequest for their offspring – the seeds of its own decay which slowly and stealthily, but just as surely, would sap the lifeblood of the community.

Industry had arrived late in this corner of Lanarkshire, at the tail end of a century which had seen the central belt of Scotland climb to a pinnacle of achievement as one of the chief manufacturing regions of the world. The insatiable appetite of factory, mill and ironworks demanded fuel, coal in abundance to power steam engines and smelt iron ore; and a huge, untapped wealth of quality splint coal lay conveniently to hand. The few pockets of habitation, which had hitherto clung to the old order of things, had been simply engulfed by this tidal wave.

During the first orgy of speculation in the 1860s and 1870s the coalmasters had fought each other tooth and nail. In this contest for power and profits, none had fared better than the Avon Valley Coal Company, a consortium of businessmen financed by Glasgow bankers. Shrewdly, it had evolved a strategy of buying out smaller owners as soon as their holdings began to produce coal in quantity. Among its earliest acquisitions was the Duchess Colliery, by far the largest mine in this part of the coalfield, named for the consort of the Duke of Hamilton, on whose land it stood. In its heyday in the 1880s it had been a showcase pit employing nearly five hundred men and boys, and disgorging fully three thousand tons of the finest splint coal each week to feed the iron foundries and provide warmth for the burghers of Glasgow.

But those times had long since disappeared. As the mines grew older, the lush, thick measures had petered out; now only thinner, stony, less productive seams remained. Geological faults, dampness, flooding, sagging roofs, made the winning of coal difficult, sometimes very dangerous. As the workings spread further and further from the main roadways and shafts, problems of accessibility and transport to the pitbank loomed ever larger. The Lanarkshire coalfield, already hit by competition from imported European supplies, had had to give ground to the more efficient collieries recently developed in Fife and the Lothians.

Few mine owners had had the wit to grasp the nature of the deep-seated structural malaise. But all had reacted promptly and predictably enough to short-term depressions. They whined long and loud about unfair foreign competition, they complained about the extortionate royalties exacted by the landowners, they questioned new government safety regulations which had increased their costs; then they cast the full burden of the slump onto their own employees. Wage cuts and short time working inevitably provoked resistance, but watchful owners were quick to stamp down on trade union activity before it could develop firm roots. Strikes had sometimes been successful, but all too often had resulted in humiliating defeat.

It was in the wake of a particularly damaging dispute that Robert Semple had stepped into his father's shoes as managing director of the Avon Valley Coal

Company. Young and ambitious, he was not the type to let the grass grow under his feet. In less than a year the axe had fallen on fully half of the company's works, with hundreds of miners laid off. The cowed remnants were kept in place with the threat of dismissal; any union official daring to set foot on company property was sure of a rough reception. These steps had gone far to restore the confidence of shareholders and creditors, but were hardly calculated to improve industrial relations. Sooner or later simmering discontent was bound to erupt. In the spring of 1904, following yet another pay cut, work had ground to a halt.

The board of directors had responded with a ritual condemnation of unwarranted industrial action, but Semple and his colleagues were far from displeased at the turn of events. With production at a standstill, labour costs would be saved. In the autumn, with reviving demand at the onset of colder weather, the directors had been keen to resume operations, and so had offered a few token concessions. But they were soon jolted out of their smug complacency when the terms were indignantly spurned. Through October and into November the dispute had dragged on in a war of attrition. The miners withdrew all safety cover, while management sought to tighten the screw by threatening eviction from tied houses. At last, after five months, the first chink appeared. Men, a few at least, driven to distraction by fear and want, had started to trickle back to work in some of the outlying collieries.

Buoyed up with renewed hope, Semple felt this was the decisive moment to force the issue once and for all. One sledgehammer blow at the Duchess, the kernel of all the trouble, and his problems might well be solved. The stakes were high. If this effort were to fail, the bankers would probably cut their losses and pull the rug from under him. But surely nothing could go wrong now. The whole weight of the business community had been enlisted in support, the full apparatus of law and order mobilised, the best available man brought in to see the thing through. All the same, he was consumed with anxiety as he watched the formation creep inexorably towards its destination. It was too late for second thoughts. The next hour would resolve everything.

* * *

"Aw' right, lads. It winnae be long now. Get yerselves organised and let's get stuck intae these bastards. Show them what happens to scabs in this neck o' the woods."

Hardly Bruce's address to the troops at Bannockburn, but it would have to do. Geordie Baird scanned the tattered army before him. He saw bowed heads and averted eyes, worry and dread etched on every brow. But he saw also quiet, dogged determination. The pitmen grasped their clubs firmly; their pockets bulged with stones for use as missiles. They would fight all right, fight with all the courage of despair. But would it be enough?

"You tell them, Geordie. Man, it's a grand day for a fight." Cha White's eyes gleamed with anticipation at the prospect of coming to grips with the coalmasters' lackeys. His best friend would not claim Cha possessed the brightest of intellects; but his unfailing optimism and robust cheerfulness acted as a tonic whenever Geordie had one of his rare bouts of despondency. He made an invaluable right hand man, solid and dependable.

"Are ye dressed for the occasion?" he asked, half-jokingly. "Got your padding on?"

"Aye," replied Baird. "But newspaper stuffed under our bunnets and jackets will no' gie us much protection against police batons, I'm thinking. There'll be plenty of sore heids and cracked shoulders."

"Ach, cheer up, man. Remember our pick handles are much bigger than their wee sticks. They'll never get near us. We're goin' to win this one. Show the bosses where they get off, eh?"

"I hope so, but I hae my doubts."

"C'mon, Geordie. That's no' the attitude. Never say die. We're all dependin' on you." He gave Baird a consoling clap on the back and moved on to chivvy the men into position.

Depending on him. The words echoed in Baird's ears. Why had leadership been thrust upon him? He was proud of his standing in the community as a skilled hewer, a master of his trade, but at heart he was no more than a down-to-earth working man with little formal education, no better than dozens of others down the pit. He had no aspirations to seek power, to dominate others, to lead them towards some pipe dream. Yet the day the pitmen downed tools, he had been elected as their spokesman.

During the summer things had not been too bad. Most families had coped with the loss of earnings; they were used to belt-tightening in hard times. Mining communities had a tradition of mutual aid; the marginally better off helped those less fortunate. Tradesmen, mindful of future custom, were still prepared to offer credit. If all else failed, there was always poaching or stealing potatoes.

On the chill winds of autumn, however, blew a change in mood. Just as the leaves withered and fell, so the last vestiges of enthusiasm faded and died. A pinched, vacant stare brought on by cold and slow starvation began to appear on more and more faces. There was no talk of surrender, but a resigned realisation that they could not endure much longer was self-evident. That was why, when news of the proposed strike-breaking attempt filtered through, miners from all the remaining company pits had assembled outside the Duchess for one last trial of strength.

Suddenly he felt very tired; the strains and pressures of these last months were taking an enormous toll. But it would never do to give way to adversity. He must show a brave face, whatever his innermost thoughts. The men forming up into a picket line outside the colliery entrance deserved no less.

No such doubts troubled Inspector Chisholm. He had supreme confidence in the result, but he was a sly old fox and would take no unnecessary risks. Caution and good planning – these were the guarantee of success. That was why he brought the column to a halt on the approaches to the village, a good quarter of a mile from the first houses.

"Sub-inspector Dunlop!" Chisholm beckoned to his subordinate. "I've just stopped for a minute or two to let the men catch their breath. We can employ the time profitably to continue your education. Now, as ye can see, this road leads to the mine yonder on the far side of the village. We've seen nothing amiss on the way here. What do you make of it?"

"Nothing to it, sir. The place is absolutely deserted. It's a walk-over." He could hardly keep the impatience from his voice.

"Oh, ye think so? Where are the strikers then?"

"Cowering in their hovels, if they've any sense. They've seen our strength and run for cover. These creatures are all the same, yellow to the bone. I daresay there might be a few hotheads at the colliery, but they'll be no problem. Probably bolt like rabbits at the first sight of us," he added with a sniff.

"I'm greatly obliged to ye for your valuable opinion. Perhaps I'm a trifle over careful, but it would set my mind at rest if ye just took a wee dander through the village – purely as a precaution ye understand. Take three or four constables with you and see ye look in all the side streets."

Something in the inspector's tone gave Dunlop pause for thought. As he hesitated, Chisholm spoke encouragingly.

"Off with ye then, before we all catch our deaths of cold. As ye say, there's nothing to worry about. The very sight of your uniform would send any number o' these scallywags scuttling for cover."

Dunlop gritted his teeth; he was being put down again. He called curtly to a sergeant to bring his squad and stalked away towards the murky redbrick terraces.

An eerie silence pervaded the whole village, seeping from every close and alley, every door and window. There was no sound to be heard, not even the bark of a stray dog or wail of a hungry infant. Only the crunch of heavy boots echoing on the cobbles broke the ghostly stillness. The policemen were unsettled, darting glances apprehensively in all directions. Dunlop felt prickles of sweat on his spine. A strained, high-pitched voice croaked an order to stick closely together; he scarcely recognised it as his own. He trembled at the very idea of being trapped by a mob of angry miners with no help at hand.

But perhaps they were only starting at shadows. Their progression had by now taken them as far as the village square. Another few minutes and they would be clear of this hellhole, able to report that Chisholm's fears were groundless. He stopped before the Jubilee Memorial and glanced at the inscription. Suddenly every nerve in his body stiffened; out of the corner of his eye he glimpsed the door of a house swinging open. He whirled round. Framed in the doorway was a woman, well-built and amply bosomed, her figure set off by glowing auburn tresses. Dumbfounded, Dunlop could only gape open-mouthed as she impudently swung her hips and crooked her finger beckoningly towards him.

"Come ower here, hinnie. Let's hae a good look at you."

Instinctively the sub-inspector took a step or two forward, then checked himself. Before he could gather his wits sufficiently to respond, she went on coaxingly. "Why, you're nothin' but a boy. Handsome though. Never mind, since they've let ye out o' school maybe we can manage somethin'. I'll bet your mammie never taught ye what's below a woman's skirts. Slip inside, and I'll break ye in myself."

Dunlop, beetroot with rage and humiliation at the suggestion, at last found his voice. "You shameless hussy. I'll teach you to mock your betters." He sprang forward, raising the swagger stick he carried.

The object of his venom was in no way intimidated. She merely smiled malevolently. A heavy iron refuse bin stood outside the house. In one swift motion she swooped down, lifted the lid and banged it down sharply on the rim. The effect was electrifying. One minute the square was deserted; the next it seemed full of jeering, gesticulating Amazons bearing down from all sides. Dunlop halted in mid-stride as though transfixed.

It was the sergeant, a quiet-spoken veteran near to retirement, who saved them. Calling to his four constables to form close order, he darted forward and tugged the arm of the bemused sub-inspector. "Come away, sir, for God's sake. We've got to get out of this."

Dunlop stared uncomprehendingly at him; then, as the urgency in the man's voice penetrated his dulled mind, nodded agreement. Truncheons drawn, the tiny band gave ground as they backed away towards the nearest alley.

The sergeant whispered out of the corner of his mouth. "These biddies are getting worked up to rush us. When I give the signal, turn and run like hell. It's our only chance. Ready? Now!" he yelled.

As one, all six spun round and took to their heels. The suddenness of the action gained them priceless seconds. The women, caught unawares, did not immediately grasp what was happening; then, realising that their prey might slip free, surged forward, like a torrent of angry water tumbling into a narrow channel.

In a frantic race for safety the hapless policemen sped from one street to another, round corners, through byways, with the hue and cry nipping at their heels. By sheer chance their reckless dash carried them back to the high road almost on the outskirts of Broomburn. Thankfully the way was clear; they could even glimpse the welcoming sight of Chisholm's column only a few hundred yards off. With fresh heart they redoubled their efforts to make good their escape. Dunlop turned to look back. Their tormentors had given up the hunt at the edge of the township; now they were hounded only by cries of triumph, raucous laughter and jeers of derision. To cap it all, on reaching their own lines they were greeted with snide remarks and ribald comments. Dunlop himself had to endure a sarcastic greeting from his commanding officer.

"Ye seem to have stirred up something of a hornet's nest, Mr Dunlop. Ye have a rare talent for getting yourself into a scrape."

Prudently the sub-inspector made no reply.

"See here now. Ye realise what a mistake it would have been to barge straight into the village. These creatures could have cut us to pieces from the cover of their own homes, and nary a blind thing could we have done to prevent it. In that confined space horses would be useless. Never fight on anyone else's ground if ye can possibly help it. Always keep out in the open whenever ye can. That way ye cannot be taken by surprise, and ye may deploy your own strength to best advantage."

Chisholm raised his field glasses and once more swept the ground ahead. Then he turned back to his subordinate.

"These women would be plain daft to try to charge us out here. My lads would just ride them down, crush them like fleas. No, we'll skirt round the village. That's the way to ensure a safe arrival at the mine. Now, back to your station, Mr Dunlop. And profit by your experience."

To the miners on the far side of the village, the sudden uproar caused consternation. Were the police raiding their homes? What was happening to their womenfolk? They could see nothing of what was going on. Hesitantly, some started to break ranks. The danger was all too evident; a trickle back to the village would soon become a stampede. It took all Baird's presence and strength of mind to hold the men in place. They simply dare not abandon their positions; this might be a ploy to entice them away from the gates. With the colliery unguarded, the blacklegs could slip in, and the battle lost by default.

It was touch and go, however. The pitmen could not have been restrained for long. Baird swore with relief as a group of women came running up the road towards the mine, waving and shouting. Their leader could hardly wait to blurt out the tale of how the police had been ignominiously put to flight. To the strikers it seemed to augur well for the decisive clash to come.

Geordie Baird did not share the general feeling. Worry and concern gave way to anger. Quivering with rage, he stamped up to the woman and roughly pulled her aside.

"What the hell do ye think ye're playing at, Madge Potter? Do ye think ye've achieved something wonderful, seeing off a few bobbies? Ye had us scared near half to death wi' yer hair-brained antics. It could have cost us dear had we to come and find out what was up."

"Dinnae fash yerself, Geordie. Keep the heid. We women have shown what we can do. We're no' the helpless ninnies ye suppose. We want to stand alongside you and the boys."

"Over my deid body. This is no place for you. There's goin' to be some hard knocks out here. The polis are nae respecters o' persons. They'll put the boot into anyone in their way, man or woman. Christ, can ye no' get that through yer thick head? We'll hae our hands full. There'll be no time to watch out for womenfolk. So you just go back and tell them to bide indoors till this is over. Right?"

Each glowered at the other in a silent battle of wills. At length Madge dropped her eyes and turned away without a word. Her followers trooped after her, the exhilaration of the moment now gone flat.

Daft bitch, thought Baird, with a rueful shake of his head. But he had scant time to digest this little victory, as a warning shout from down the line attracted his attention. His heart skipped a beat; involuntarily he gripped his club more tightly as the enemy hove into view, row after row appearing as though pulled along by some invisible thread. His compatriots, too, seemed mesmerised by the spectacle, like rodents before an approaching snake. Mouths dry, ashen faced, they could only stare in fascinated silence as it wove its way closer, then drew to a halt two or three hundred yards distant from the colliery. Baird's eyes narrowed as he searched out his opposite number, the police inspector they had brought all the way from Glasgow. He was not difficult to spot, the tall figure on horseback, apparently disdainful of the presence of the pitmen, for he never once spared them so much as a glance.

There was a sudden flurry of activity. The blacklegs were hustled well to the rear out of harm's way, prodded by the staves of a gang of brawny-looking characters in civilian clothes. Baird saw the inspector gesture with his arm; the uniformed officers hastened to form themselves into a wedge-shaped phalanx, batons drawn, ready for the word to advance. Another flick of the wrist sent the mounted police galloping off to the left flank; they circled round to bring themselves into line with the pickets and reined in a couple of furlongs away. Baird scowled in vexation; the odds against them, already poor, were lengthening still further. That chap down there might act as if he thought himself lord of creation, but he certainly knew his business.

Finally satisfied that his preparations were complete, the inspector deigned to turn his attention to the object of his mission. Without escort, imperturbably, almost nonchalantly, he made his way up the track towards the colliery.

"Who is in charge here?" The words rasped out imperiously. Chisholm was no fool; he was well aware that these hungry, misguided simpletons might turn on him without warning. But the risk was worth the taking. His example would hearten his own men and demoralise the opposition, if past experience stood for anything. Besides, it was his responsibility to try to avoid violence if at all possible.

"Ye can address yourself to me," said Baird, stepping a pace or two forward.

"And you might be?" queried Chisholm.

"My name disnae matter. I speak for everyone here."

"Very well. Then it is my duty to inform you – all of you," he said, raising his voice, "that this constitutes an unlawful assembly, likely to cause a breach of the peace. I must ask you to disperse immediately."

Not a soul stirred.

"You are acting in restraint of trade. I have been instructed to ensure that these employees of the Avon Coal Company are allowed free access to their place of work."

"Save yer breath, copper. We ken what you're here for. Ye know we cannae allow scabs in to take the bread from our mouths. So just you get on with it."

Chisholm nodded. "You have two minutes. After that…" He shrugged his shoulders, wheeled around and trotted back down the pathway.

At least he had gained something from this brief encounter, a sense of the mood in the opposite camp. They certainly looked drained and enfeebled by months of hardship, but nevertheless there was an air of dogged resistance. All in all, it posed an interesting tactical problem to gauge just how much pressure would have to be applied before the strikers crumbled, broke and fled. His thoughts crystallised on the fine-tuning of his plan of action. He would not squander his own men by throwing them into the initial attack. The county plodders under young Lochinvar there could have that honour. Then, if necessary, his horsemen could charge in to administer the killer punch. His mind made up, he dismounted to give his final instructions.

"Mr Dunlop, your orders are to proceed to the colliery entrance. There you are to demand immediate access to the mine. In the event of a refusal to comply, you are to press on, using such measures as you deem necessary to attain your objective. Once in possession of the area round the gates, you are to adopt a defensive position, forming a passageway to permit the workmen to pass through. The mounted officers will be held in reserve under my personal command, but will come to your assistance if required. Any questions?"

Dunlop blanched at the enormity of the task entrusted to him. How could his small force hope to win through against the opposition? But he would not give way to the rage he felt. He would not give Chisholm that satisfaction. His protest must be delivered calmly and rationally if it was to have any effect.

"Sir, we are heavily outnumbered. Surely it would make more sense for the mounted police to go in first to break up their positions. That would knock the fight out of them, or at least throw them off balance to some extent. It would give my lads an opening to stage a baton charge to the pit gates with a good chance of success."

Chisholm looked at him sharply. The boy was afraid, no doubt of that, angry and afraid. But he was learning. He had the gumption to curb his feelings and try to reason his case. Perhaps something might be made of him after all. At any rate his argument merited an answer.

"I can't afford to spread my squad too thin, have them galloping all over the place probing for weak spots. They need to be concentrated at one decisive point for maximum impact. I won't know where that is until their defences have been tested. Forbye, I can't commit them at all unless I'm certain those rascals haven't scattered tacks or spikes on the ground. That would really scupper the horses. So it's vital that I find out if the way is clear."

He lowered his voice confidentially. "I'm relying on you, you realise that? Don't let me down. This is your chance to win your spurs. I'd have given my right arm for that at your age. Now, anything else? Then move off. And good luck," he added, almost as an afterthought.

The colliers, nerves wound taut as watchsprings, waited expectantly. Geordie Baird caught his breath with suppressed excitement. Perhaps there was just a glimmer of hope. He could scarcely credit that the police were taking so much for granted, were so confident of an easy victory that they were advancing with only part of their forces, making straight for the entrance where the defenders were packed thickest. Their approach, moreover, lacked cohesion and discipline. Evidently unused to a tight, V-shaped formation, they were continually falling out of step, at times coming to a standstill as one rank cannoned into another, then having to hurry forward to make good the gaps that appeared. This was a weakness his men might be able to exploit. And there was something else, too. Yon inspector seemed to consider the pitmen unworthy of his steel, for he himself had stayed behind, evidently as a gesture of his contempt. Indeed, he had dismounted to sit on a large flat stone beside the roadway and was lighting a cigarette, as though settling down to watch the performance. Well, there would be a show all right, but perhaps not the one he anticipated.

Baird roused himself from his thoughts; high time he was making his final dispositions. He turned to the self-appointed lieutenant who stood beside him, awaiting instructions. "Cha, bring the men in closer. Pack them deeper, especially at the gates. They're goin' to try to push straight through. Bloody saps. Tell the lads on the sides to be ready for my signal to swing round and surround them. Then we'll gie the bastards laldy."

"Right ye are, Geordie. Nae problem." White caught his friend's eye, grinned with glee; then he was gone, scurrying away to carry out the assignment.

There was a flurry of movement as the ranks closed up, then stillness once more. The minutes dragged on by inches. They could only stand and wait as, like some bloated black slug, the police stumbled and lurched their way up the incline.

For Dunlop time raced by as if in tune with the thumping of his heart. Savagely he cursed his luck in finding himself in such a vulnerable position, the whipping boy at the head of the line. Christ, he had only been sent on the expedition to learn about riot control. He should have been the observer, studying the operation from the rear. It was Chisholm's responsibility; he should be the one leading from the front. But recriminations were useless now. His instructions had been to halt and deliver a final warning, but he knew his voice would betray him. If they pulled up, he might not be able to induce his men, novices as they were in this sort of work, to resume the advance. His best chance might be to keep the momentum going, trusting to luck that the miners would be intimidated by a show of strength, and would allow him unhindered passage.

He swallowed hard; it was now or never. Fixing upon the fellow a yard or two in front of the rest, he strode forward and prodded him in the chest with his swagger stick as an inducement to step aside. The result was instantaneous. There was a whirl of arms, a heavy wooden object flashed in the air. Purely by instinct Dunlop swayed to the side; the cudgel, instead of cracking his skull, caught him a glancing blow on the shoulder. He reeled, felt a searing pain, the sticky wetness of blood, but did not go down. Fury welled up within him. With a roar of anger, fists flailing, he flung himself on his adversary. Taken aback, mineworkers and police alike watched spellbound as though at the ringside of a prize-fight. The sub-inspector, young and athletic though he was, was no match for the pitman's wiriness and strength. Baird simply brushed him off like a fly, followed up with a kick in the groin and, as the youth sank to his knees in agony, steadied himself to land a vicious uppercut to the jaw.

The spell was broken. All restraint gone, the miners surged towards the hated law officers like a pack of hounds snapping round the fox at bay. Such was the speed and ferocity of the onslaught that those not clubbed down in the first rush found themselves pinned in a small circle round their prostrate commander. The old sergeant, quick on the uptake, seized the initiative. On his instructions, three or four constables lifted the stricken Dunlop, with the others ordered to form a protective shield; then, shoulder-to-shoulder, the whole group tried to cleave a path through the throng. But to no avail; the ring was just too strong.

Inspector Chisholm flicked away his half-smoked reefer. It was a nicely balanced calculation exactly when to commit his reserves. He must be certain the strikers were totally preoccupied with the struggle at the pit entrance, yet he dared not delay too long or the largest segment of his force would be lost. Experience told him it was most unlikely that sharp objects had been scattered on the ground to hinder his horsemen; the voicing of such a possibility had been merely a ruse to ensure Dunlop would carry out the role allocated to him.

Now he judged the moment had arrived. Standing on the rock, he gestured to the distant riders. Nothing more was needed. Drawing their truncheons like cavalry sabres, they trotted into line abreast; as one they broke into a canter, rapidly working up to a full-scale charge. Chisholm swung himself into the saddle and spurred his own mount on a diagonal course to join his troop just before the point of impact.

The thud of hooves speeding over the rough grassland, the huzzas of the mounted police bearing down on their prey went unheard amid the general commotion. So engrossed were the mineworkers on the task in hand that they were in amongst them before anyone could grasp the danger, bowling men over, riding them underfoot, hacking savagely with their batons. The shock was irresistible; it was like foxes let loose in a hen coop.

Baird cursed himself for a fool; he should have realised, should have taken precautions. In the forefront of the fighting round the gates, he had been as dumbstruck as everyone else by this bolt from the blue. But he was quick to recover. The miners had been thrown into disarray by the assault, some had taken to their heels to escape the carnage; but he noticed that this new foe was tiny in number. Moreover, the impetus of the onslaught had already slackened. The sheer mass of the crowd acted as a kind of sponge, soaking up the momentum; the horses were beginning to mill around, the riders to become separated from each other. If only the pitmen could readjust to the situation, regroup for a counter-attack, perhaps all was not yet lost.

Chisholm, however, was far too wily a strategist to allow his forces to be caught up in confused, close quarter fighting where they might be picked off one by one. He pulled a whistle from his tunic pocket and blew several blasts. Obedient to the recall signal, his men neatly extricated themselves from the melee and cantered off to reform. The intention was plain; they were making ready to drive head on into the crowd once more.

"Stay where ye are! Steady there, bigod!" roared Baird. "There's only a few o' them."

But it was no use; the sullen, hangdog looks told him the game was up. The victims of the first charge were there for all to see, some inert on the ground, some groaning in pain, others trying to drag themselves away. As the pounding hooves and flaring nostrils bore down a second time, panic seized the remainder; most cast aside their weapons and took to their heels. Only a few individuals had the willpower not to give way to the mass hysteria. Spontaneously they edged together against the gates to await their fate, but resolved to go down fighting.

How had it happened? How could the tables be turned so completely in such a short space of time? One moment they were on the point of a famous victory; the next almost all had fled, and now the police were closing in for the kill. It was all so unjust. His temples throbbed with a dull, aching rage. By God, at least he would give one or two of them cause to remember Geordie

Baird. As if in response, the leading rider swung his mount straight for him. Features twisted into an ugly, mocking leer, the man leaned over, stretched forward, ready to club down another easy target. Baird dodged the blow, and as the horse swept past, grabbed at the stirrup. Half-dragged along, he managed to crook his arm round the policeman's waist and, exerting all his might, yanked him from the saddle.

There was the briefest premonition of a shadowy figure looming up behind him, no time to fend off the blow to his head. His hold on the horse slackened, and as he tumbled down, its hind-leg caught him full in the stomach. Gasping for breath, retching blood, he tried to pull himself to his feet, but was again knocked flying. This time the grass was cool and soft and inviting. His mind seemed curiously detached; he felt strangely at peace with himself.

TWO

The Way of the Transgressor

"The Workman shall faithfully and diligently employ himself at the mines of the Company and guard and defend its property from spoil, waste and injury. He will be submissive to, and obey orders given to him, by those in authority at the mines. If the said Workman shall at any time refuse to perform or comply with any of the conditions of this agreement, he shall be liable to be dismissed and to forfeit all sums of money which may be due to him by the Company in the name of wages or otherwise."

Robert Semple looked up from the document he was reading to his board of directors. Over the past few days the letters and telegrams of congratulation had come pouring in; he was universally lauded as the architect of victory. True, it was Inspector Chisholm who had crushed the miners, but only as the agent summoned to carry out the owners' bidding. Now he and his men had departed, as had the estate workers and bulk of the constables. That young sub-inspector had acquitted himself well, and thankfully was making a full recovery from his injuries. Chisholm should never have placed him in the firing line without adequate support. That was an error of judgment, if nothing worse. Perhaps a hint in his report about Chisholm's high-handedness would not go amiss either.

Still, matters were proceeding satisfactorily. Production had restarted at the Duchess and would soon resume at the other pits. Only a few bored policemen were left to patrol the boundary fence and escort the labourers to and from work. Not that there was much likelihood of trouble. The villagers were thoroughly cowed, anxious about what the future might hold for them. The ringleaders, even those who had escaped from the field of battle, had been rounded up and carted off to Hamilton where they now languished in police cells, awaiting the company's pleasure. Well, they could reflect on their misdeeds a while longer. As for the others, it was for the victor to dictate to the vanquished.

"Are we agreed then, gentlemen, on the terms? Each man must affirm his readiness to be bound by this pledge before he can be considered for re-engagement."

There was a general murmur of assent, but Guthrie, the Glasgow Bank's representative on the board, ventured to demur.

"I suppose I must go along with the will of the majority, it would be churlish to be obstructive at a time like this. But for the life of me I cannot see any necessity for re-employing those who have broken their contracts by striking. They are born troublemakers who will only cause us more mischief in future. Why not simply continue with the replacements we have already brought in? They seem docile enough, grateful for the opportunity of work, and, in addition, do not expect standard wage rates – a not unimportant consideration. Housing should present no problems, once the notices of eviction have been served."

"Mr Guthrie," replied Semple, "I bow to your expertise as a financier, but with all due respect, mining is scarcely your forte. It's not as simple as you appear to believe. I have here the deputy manager's latest production report. It states that coal reaching the pithead amounts to approximately ten percent of the daily figure before the strike. Carry on like this and we'll soon be out of business. We have at present one hundred and eight-seven men at work. Our pits normally employ well over double that number. Where am I to find the remainder?"

"Advertise," said Guthrie. "There's an army of unemployed. And they'll come cheap – increase our profit margins."

Semple shook his head. "Not practicable, I'm afraid. Times have changed since the early days at the Duchess. We need experienced colliers, especially good hewers, to cope with the type of seams we're left with now. Untrained newcomers simply won't do."

He opened a manila folder and flipped through the pages. "Here's the evidence. Trucks derailed by putters who don't know how to handle them, a roof collapse because the face workers were so gormless they didn't realise the necessity for adequate supports, dozens of minor injuries and at least two near fatalities. Need I go on? You've no idea how long it takes to clear up the mess after every accident, and heaven knows what it has cost us in lost production. No, gentlemen, it was always appreciated that outside labour would only be a means to break the strike. The few local men and the Poles could be retained, but the others are more trouble than they're worth. Besides," he added, looking round the table, "we hold the whip hand. The miners we take back will have to accept the reduced rates we offered six months ago. They'll not refuse."

"Admirably put, Mr Chairman, if I may say so," piped a quavering voice from the far side. The wizened figure of Auld, now well into his eighties, was rarely seen at meetings these days, but his mind was still clear as a bell. "Your arguments are unassailable. But I was wondering about the malcontents at present remanded in custody. I am given to understand that there is a possibility they may not be brought to trial after all. Surely the likes of Baird and White are not to be re-employed. We can well do without the services of a handful of agitators."

"Hear, hear," said Guthrie and one or two others, but the managing director was equal to the situation.

"Thank you, Mr Auld. I'm glad you brought up the subject. I fully endorse your concern. My first impulse was exactly as yours, to recommend we prosecute with the full rigour of the law, to demand exemplary sentences, and to evict the families from their tenancies. But I must confess to having had second thoughts. The press and public opinion have been firmly behind us during the dispute, but that could change if we appear too harsh in exacting revenge."

"It's not revenge," interjected Guthrie. "It is merely justice. Lawbreakers must pay the penalty or we shall have anarchy."

"Very true, but we must bear in mind how we present ourselves. A poor public image is bad for business. A show of magnanimity would do no harm. We don't want to create martyrs for the gutter press to exploit. Over the piece, I think it would be safer if we took them back. It's vital that we destroy their influence over the others. Dismissal and imprisonment are scarcely likely to achieve this. In fact it could be counter-productive, simply bolstering their standing in the eyes of their following. Think of the blow to their self-esteem, the public humiliation, when they have to beg for reinstatement, sign the pledge of good behaviour. They'd never raise their heads again."

Auld nodded thoughtfully. "Yes, I can see what you're driving at," he said slowly, "but it sticks in the craw to allow these ne'er-do-wells to escape scot free. I'm sure the rest of the board agree with me."

"Ah, but here's the rub. They will not be getting off lightly. There's more than one way to skin a cat. We'll make an example of them, never fear, but at a time to suit us, in a way only pitmen would understand. They will serve as a constant reminder of the folly of industrial action. By the same token, we avoid any adverse publicity. In fact, we appear as paragons of virtue, bending over backwards to offer clemency – in effect to forgive their sins."

There was a ripple of laughter, faces lit up at the prospect; hands thumped the table in approval. He had convinced them.

"Order, please, gentlemen!" said Semple in mock admonition. " Surely this is hardly seemly behaviour for the boardroom. Am I therefore to take it that the board approves this course of action? Yes. In that case, is there any further business? No. Then I declare the meeting closed. Thank you for your attention."

He ushered his colleagues from the room, shaking each by the hand and in return receiving a few words of commendation. When all had gone, he resumed his seat at the head of the table and pressed the bell to summon his chief clerk.

"Go you and draw up two copies of this document. One is to be posted at the main entrance, the other on the Memorial in the Square. Pass the word to the colliery manager that he is to make arrangements for re-engaging the men. Inform him he is to have the Duchess back in full operation by Monday week. And I'll take no excuses for any failure on his part."

The lackey bowed obsequiously, took up the paper and left without a word, closing the door softly behind him. Semple sank back into the padded upholstery and lit a cigar, well pleased with his efforts. It had been a hard fight, the risks had been awesome; but he had come through, he had won.

* * *

The hollow ring of approaching footsteps echoed on the flagstones. The sounds grew louder, and then stopped. A key jangled in the lock, followed by a dull metallic thud as the bolt drew back. The cell door creaked on its hinges.

"Visitors for you, Baird. Look alive there."

Geordie Baird grimaced, but otherwise gave no indication of having heard. He lay motionless on the hair mattress which covered the narrow stone ledge running along the far wall of the cell. The turnkey came closer. "Get up. I ken fine you're malingering. It'll be the worse for you if ye don't," he threatened.

Another voice broke in from the background, crisp and authoritative. "All right, constable, I'll handle this. No need for you to remain."

"If ye insist, sorr," came the grudging response. "I'll be outside in the passage if ye require assistance."

The door banged once more. In the quiet that followed, Baird stirred, gingerly made an effort to push himself upright. Jesus, it was hell to move. Leaning back against the wall, he opened his eyes. At first there was only a blur, but gradually they adjusted to the gloom. Two shadowy figures swam into focus.

"How are you feeling, Baird? You certainly have been in the wars," said the taller of the two. He recognised that voice. And the familiar garb of authority, bowler hat, starched collar and dark jacket. It was McIntosh, one of the pit deputies. One of the few with any spark of humanity in him, though. What in God's name were they up to? Surely this could not be a social call to enquire after his health.

"I'm told you're on the mend now," the man was saying. "Apparently your ribs were not broken, only badly bruised. And that head wound, just concussion. You certainly are a hard nut to crack. Anyone else would have been killed in that stramash, or at least crippled for life, but you'll be as good as new in a week or so."

"It's yersel', Mr McIntosh," said Geordie stonily. "Fancy that. Come to gloat, have ye? Kick a man when he's doon, eh?"

"That's enough," McIntosh cut in harshly. "You know me better than that, Baird. I'm genuinely sorry to see you here in this condition, but you've only yourself to blame. You're a good worker, one of the best. You could have been made up to oversman or even a deputy long since, but you had to fill your head with all that nonsense about workers' rights. What a waste!"

"You widnae understand, a bosses' man like you. You've never grafted underground."

"Sticks and stones, Baird. That sort of attitude will get you nowhere. Always tilting at windmills. Will you never learn? But I'm not here to rake over the past."

"Then just why are ye here?"

"To offer you, along with the others in jail, the chance of a fresh start. The company is not vindictive, whatever you may think. As a gesture of goodwill, the charges will be dropped, and you can return to work just as soon as you are fit."

"Oh aye, that's very generous. What's the catch? What do the bosses want as their pound o' flesh?"

"Tush, man. This dispute has been disastrous for everyone, you must admit. We simply wish to take steps to restore normal working arrangements which will be fair to both management and men. All we require are assurances that this type of action will not recur."

"Assurances? Now what wid that be?"

The deputy hesitated, seemed about to reply, then thought better of it. Instead he changed tack. "Here's a workmate of yours, John Archibald, come to see how you're getting on. Talk to him."

For the first time Geordie peered closely at the second man who still hung back near the door, obviously ill at ease. "Is that you, Archie? Dinnae be shy. Come into the body o' the kirk. Take a seat, an' tell us what's goin' on. They fairly keep ye in the dark in here."

With the utmost reluctance, or so it appeared, his next-door neighbour dropped onto the stool beside the bed. He found it impossible to meet Baird's eye.

"Well, man, have ye no tongue? Speak up. Gie us the news."

"What can I say, Geordie? I'm that ashamed." Archibald spoke huskily, in little more than a whisper. "I was so feart. We broke and ran like sheep, abandoned ye to this. There's nae excuse."

"It's aw' right, Archie. Naebody is blamin' you. The lads did all that could be expected. Put it out o' yer mind." He stretched out his arm in a gesture of sympathy. "How are my wife and weans? How are the chaps takin' things?"

"Good an' bad, Geordie. Kate and the family are just fine. They send ye their best. That's some woman ye have. Did ye ken she walked the five miles here the other day, but they widnae let her in? And her sae quiet, as a rule. But Mr McIntosh has arranged it so that ye can see her tomorrow."

Baird glanced up, and gave an almost imperceptible nod of thanks to the pit deputy. Then his eyes dropped back. "Go on," he said.

"Weel, nobody was killed at the pit gates, praise be. Three or four will be crippled for life. Crushed under the horses, they were. They'll never work again. God knows how their families will make ends meet. It'll be the poorhouse, likely. Some o' the rest were hurt quite bad, but they'll recover, given time. Apart from that, split heids, cuts and bruises. Maybe it's as well so many of us ran away. I suppose ye could say it's lucky the casualties were nae worse."

"Lucky!" snorted Baird. "What else?"

Archibald swallowed hard. He had been brought here to deliver a message, words that stuck in his craw. Why had McIntosh singled him out? Could he not do his own dirty work? Geordie had a fiery temper; there was no way of knowing how he would react.

"Here's the worst part, Geordie. That night, after dodgin' the bobbies on the hills, we stole back when it got dark. For the next few days we cowered like mice in our holes, afeard o' any knock at the door in case it was the boys in blue. But naebody came. Then we found out about the notice offerin' us our jobs back. Well, ye ken how we're fixed. Drownin' men clutchin' at straws. That bastard o' a colliery manager made us wait two hours before he opened the gates. Then, wi' a smug grin on his face, he tells us we have to sign a pledge no' to go on strike again and to accept the wage rates we turned down six months syne. Either that, or we could go to hell. Our families would be evicted and we would be blacklisted in every pit in Scotland. What could we dae? It was eat humble pie or starve. What choice was that? A'body signed up."

Geordie buried his face in his hands and groaned. So it had come to this – unconditional surrender. Not really surprising, but that made it none the easier to accept.

Archibald stammered on. "I dinnae know how to put this. Mr McIntosh brought me here to get you to sign as well. I asked off, but he said it was for your sake. There's nae point in makin' a martyr o' yerself. We've lost and maun just make the best o' it."

As though taking his cue, McIntosh stepped forward, slipping a folded document from an inside pocket. "Please be good enough to read this over," he said, holding it out.

Baird stared up blankly; then, as realisation dawned, angrily swept the paper aside. "Never," he shouted defiantly. "I'm no' giein' in to the bosses, no' on these terms, no' after all we've been through. Submit now and thon slimy sods will be able to ride roughshod ower us whenever they like. There's yer answer, Mr McIntosh. Go and tell them there's one man at least they cannae force back like a whipped cur."

The deputy appeared in no way put out by the outburst. "I can understand your feelings," he said mildly. "You're a bit overwrought. When you've had time to think, perhaps you'll see sense. Talk it over with your wife. I'll leave this with the desk sergeant. Should you change your mind, an officer will witness your signature and you'll be released. Simple as that. Oh, by the by, all the others in jail have accepted the terms, even your friend, White. They were discharged earlier today."

"You're a bloody liar," snarled Baird, but somehow the words lacked conviction. Deep down he knew it was true.

McIntosh made no response. Instead he turned and thumped on the door.

* * *

Another member of the Baird family chafed at his incarceration that Friday afternoon. Iain, eldest of Geordie's three children, sat glowering at the window set high in the wall. That patch of grey sky out there represented freedom, the freedom of a man to work, earn his living, to make his way in the world. But he was still held fast in this prison. There was no justice, he thought bitterly. Today was his birthday, his fourteenth. He was now of an age to leave school, but their rules insisted he stay on till the end of term. Small wonder he felt resentful, in a mood to kick over the traces.

His scowl transferred to the untouched sheet of exercise paper on his desk. Damned if he was going to scribble away like the others in the Leavers' Section. From his vantage point at the back of the classroom he looked scornfully at the rows of pupils bent industriously over their tasks, the hush broken only by the squeak of pencils on slates and scratching of nibs on paper. The room, stepped upwards in stages from front to rear, was accommodation for almost fifty children of all ages. In the well sat the dominie, perched at his high desk, intent on filling in the registers, as was his custom at the end of the week. It was all so familiar, so boring.

He squirmed in his seat, sucked his teeth in irritation, and once more stared at the clock, as though willing its hands to speed towards the welcome hour of dismissal. But there was no comfort to be had from that quarter.

His lips curled in contempt at the sight of his younger brother several rows below. Alastair was the runt of the family, mollycoddled from the day of his birth. His mother doted on him; his father had never laid a hand on him. And here he was now, the teacher's favourite, held up as a model pupil, given extra lessons after class, basking in the dominie's praise. Perhaps this was an opportunity to even up the score.

He groped in his jacket pocket. Penknife, string, rag – ah! Thrusting into the crevices of the lining, his fingers closed on a round, hard object. His eyes darted round the class. Good, no one was looking in his direction. Not that he really cared; no witness would be foolhardy enough to inform on him. Noiselessly he rose in his place, took swift aim and hurled the missile.

Few heard the thud as it unerringly struck its mark, only Iain saw the boy's head twitch forward involuntarily; no one could escape the sudden cry of anguish that reverberated round the schoolroom. A forest of started faces shot up, craning round in search of the cause of the disturbance. The schoolmaster, too, looked up sharply, taken aback like his pupils; for a few seconds he hesitated, weighing up the situation before deciding on his response. Andrew Ogilvie had been plying his trade nigh on forty years and was far too long in the tooth to be caught out in any classroom drama.

"Silence, silence there I say! Order!"

Stepping down from his chair, Ogilvie picked up the blackboard pointer and brought it crashing down on the nearest desk to enforce his bidding. Instantly he was the centre of attention; no one dared confront the all too evident wrath of the teacher. Discipline was restored; everyone waited with baited breath for the thunder to roll.

But his first concern was for the victim. Alastair sat hunched in his seat, face buried in his hands, sobbing uncontrollably. Before the class could grasp his intention, Ogilvie was at the young boy's side, whispering reassuring words to calm him down. Anxiously he scanned Alastair's head, then gently probed at the crown, parting the hair to reveal the injury.

"Shush now, laddie. It's nothing too bad, not much harm done. A wee bump for a day or so perhaps, but it won't damage all those brains you've got stuffed in there."

It was a feeble enough joke, but it had some effect. "More shock than anything else," muttered Ogilvie, half to himself. He stooped down once again. "Now then, Alastair. Have you a hankie? Blow your nose then, and dry away those tears. A lie down for a while and you'll be as right as rain. Do you think you can manage as far as my room?"

Still too choked to speak, the boy breathed in deeply and nodded twice.

"That's the stuff. But you'll need a hand to help you."

Swivelling round, he beckoned to a girl on the other side of the room. "Mary, come over here, please. Now listen carefully. I want you to help your brother to the staffroom. He is to lie down and rest on the couch. My coat is hanging on the peg behind the door. Wrap it round him. And put a cushion behind his head. When you've done that, see if you can find a clean cloth in the press. Go into the playground and soak it at the well. Wring it out, then dab it gently on the bruise. See here – on the top of his head. It'll help the swelling go down. Can you remember all that?"

"Yes, sir, I think so."

"Good girl. Now let's get him on his feet. Put his arm round your shoulder and take his weight. That's dandy. Don't rush him now. Let him take his time."

He stepped over to the door, held it open and ushered brother and sister out. It closed behind them, very softly, with a faint but emphatic click. For a moment or two he stood with his hand on the knob, as though collecting his thoughts, before turning decisively towards the class. A serious incident had occurred, a child harmed in this challenge to his authority. Grim-faced, he addressed the pupils, his voice low but hard as granite.

"That was a cruel and mean attack. It disgusts me that any scholar of mine could be capable of such wanton callousness. An innocent boy, not yet ten years old, has been struck on the head by some object and severely injured. It would be too much to expect the culprit to admit to his crime, but if that person is sufficiently stricken with remorse at the result of his action, then I am waiting." He paused, then added: "In the event of a confession I might, perhaps, be able to take a more lenient view, put it down to thoughtlessness rather than outright viciousness."

In the deathly hush no one dared look him in the face.

"No, I thought not. Then the perpetrator is a coward as well. So be it. I must take other measures to establish his identity … Iain Baird, step down in front of the class, if you please. Quick as you like!"

It was Iain's turn to jump with surprise. How could Ogilvie possibly know? No one had seen him, he was certain. Reluctantly he dragged himself to his feet, but made no further move to obey the order. Instead he folded his arms in a deliberate gesture of defiance.

"Do you hear me, sir?" the master repeated ominously.

"It's no' fair," Iain began to bluster. "Ye're aye pickin' on me. I get the blame for a'thing that happens in this bluidy place. Ye hate me, a'ways have done, just because I'm no' one o' yer wee pets. Ye didnae see who threw that bool, naebody saw. Weel, ye're no' goin' to get me this time. I'll no' take a leatherin' frae you again. Touch me and I'll hammer ye back. I'm warnin' ye now."

"Hold your tongue," said Ogilvie harshly. "That's quite enough. You stand condemned out of your own mouth. No mention has been made of a marble. How could you know, unless you threw it yourself? Forbye, I was already fairly certain you were the culprit. From the location of your brother's injury, it must have come from somewhere in your vicinity. Also, you pretended to carry on with your work as though nothing had happened. Just a little too obvious, don't you think? The evidence may be circumstantial, but this is not a court of law. We both know you are the guilty party. The motives behind this miserable deed are incomprehensible to me, but that is no matter. Your action cannot be allowed to go unpunished. You were offered a chance to own up, and thereby do something to mitigate the offence, but you refused to take it. No doubt you felt safe from discovery. But that is not the case. Now will you do as I say? Or must you be fetched?"

The class thrilled to the spectacle, breathlessly anticipating the next act. Such entertainment was a rare event, and therefore to be savoured to the full while it lasted. But in the end there could be only one outcome. The schoolmaster was not a man to be denied; his steady, penetrating gaze never wavered. It was Iain who finally gave way, shuffling uneasily as though in search of some bolt hole. But there was no way out. He might be able to handle Ogilvie, though he was far from confident of that. As his temper cooled, he realised there was no alternative; he had to take whatever punishment was dished out. But he could make it look good, enhance his daredevil reputation in front of the others. With as much bravado as he could muster, he tossed his head disdainfully, gave a sardonic snort and swaggered noisily down the steps.

Ogilvie could afford to ignore this posturing. "At last, Baird. You've decided to see reason. Stand just there," he said, indicating with his finger. "Hold out your hands, one palm over the other."

"Nae need to spell out the drill. I've been here before."

The tawse, a two foot long strip of leather split at one end, hung from the side of the high desk. It was the schoolmaster's symbol of power, the ultimate weapon in enforcing his authority. Rarely was it taken from its hook; Ogilvie was no flogger. Only the most serious of misdemeanours could induce him to resort to corporal punishment. This was manifestly such an occasion. The class, silent as the grave, craned forward expectantly, determined to miss nothing. Three times the belt swung high in the air over the dominie's shoulder; thrice it descended with awesome speed and whiplash effect.

"Change hands."

Once more the dose was repeated. Iain winced at every stroke, but his hands remained steady; beads of sweat appeared on his face, but no sound escaped his lips.

"Return to your place."

Iain smiled thinly and walked away. He had passed his sternest test yet. Few could have survived that ordeal without blubbing. Only after he had sat down did he permit himself to thrust his hands under his armpits.

* * *

The desk sergeant hummed tunelessly to himself as he wrote up an entry in his ledger. He heard the footfall as someone came in by the public entrance, but paid it no heed. There was a pause, then a polite cough. He frowned, but otherwise chose to ignore the distraction.

"Excuse me. I'm sorry to trouble you, but I was asked to come here."

It was a female voice, respectful, even deferential, but with a hint of firmness which demanded attention. He looked up irritably.

"Can ye no' see I'm busy? Is it asking too much for ye to wait a minute while I finish this?" He sighed heavily. "Well, get on wi' it. State your business."

The woman was flustered by his abrasiveness, but quickly recovered, outwardly at least. Intuitively she grasped that it would do no good to allow herself to be upset by petty officialdom.

"I was told you have my husband in custody here."

"Oh aye, and who might he be?"

"George Baird. I have permission to visit him. Here is the note."

The sergeant glanced at the letter, then turned back to the woman with renewed interest. Undoubtedly working class, but respectable. No gloves of course, but she wore a coat, admittedly old but still neat and presentable. And a hat, years out of fashion, but it set her off well. Most people in her situation had to make do with a shawl. Not bad looking either, if he was any judge. Certainly she was well above average in height, but not too tall; slim, but not skin and bones. Willowy, that was the word. Her complexion still retained some of the bloom of youth, though the wrinkles and crowsfeet gave ample warning that the ravages of time could not be held at bay for much longer. In her late thirties, he would say, and far better preserved than most. She coloured before his scrutiny. He was willing to bet she had rarely, if ever, seen the inside of a police station; he could sense her distaste for the experience.

"Baird, ye don't say? The striker." His tone became more conciliatory. "Weel, ye've a verra brave man there, but a bluidy fool for a' that. I hope ye manage to talk some sense into him." He shouted into the inner office. "MacAnespie! Hurry up, laddie." A pimply-faced clerk appeared. "Take Mistress Baird doon to the cells. Ye've to leave them together for a while. Mind an' lock the door ahint ye. We cannae have them waltzing out. Then ye can bring me a cup o' tea and a scone."

"Right ye are, sergeant." In a single, practised movement the youth flipped up a section of the counter on its hinges and swung back the wicket gate beneath. "This way, hen."

Kate Baird hesitated; God knew what terrors lurked beyond. But she had to go through with it. Screwing up her courage, head held high, she swept through with as much dignity as she could muster.

"It's this door here. Watch the steps, they're a bit steep."

It was as she had always imagined the descent to hell; all that was lacking was the fiery furnace. She shrank from the forbidding stone walls, the subterranean passage, the hideous glare from the electric bulbs naked in their sockets, the heavy, shuttered doors on either side, the dank, musty smell. Awesome visions preyed on her mind; it took all her strength of will to fight the urge to turn and flee. Only the thought of Geordie, and what he must be undergoing, sustained her. Thank God the journey was a short one; the policeman had stopped, was fumbling with his keys.

"Here we are. This one's your husband's."

Trembling, she watched as the cell was unlocked. Her guide stood aside and gestured. With faltering steps she entered. Immediately the door clanged shut behind her. She felt a sudden panic, as if being entombed. Mercifully the sensation passed. Her eyes blinked hard as they strove to adjust to the half-light.

"Geordie? Geordie, are ye there?" It was no more than a hoarse whisper.

"Ower here." The reply was even lower, barely audible.

In an instant she was beside him, kneeling on the stone flags, cradling his head against her bosom. Tears of anguish and relief flooded out. It was as though the dam, so carefully built up over the past months, had suddenly cracked under the strain.

"Oh, my poor, dear man. What have they done to you? God in heaven, how ye must have suffered."

Gently he broke away from her embrace. "Wheesht, lassie. There's nae need to greet. We're no' deid yet."

"But ye're in pain, I can see that. And there's nothin' I can do to ease it," she sobbed.

Wincing from the discomfort, he managed to lever himself into a sitting position. "That's better. Now I can get a proper look at ye." He took her hands in his. "Listen, Kate, there really isnae any need to get yersel' intae a fluster. There's no' much wrong wi' me. A few aches and pains, but I can get around if I take things easy. Come on now, put away the waterworks and tell us about how things are goin' at home."

"We're managing just fine, Geordie." Brave words, but they did not quite ring true. Realising her error, she hastily sought to convince him. "The neighbours cannae dae enough for us. And the bairns send ye their best – Alastair and Mary, and Iain. Can I tell them they'll see their faither soon?"

Her eyes met his in a mute appeal. The plea struck a nerve. For the first time he felt a stab of guilt. So preoccupied had he been with leading the fight for a fair deal at work that he had never stopped to consider the effects on his wife. Kate, borne down by the unequal struggle to keep the family from sliding into destitution, was plainly near the end of her tether. Had he the right to carry principle so far when it meant suffering for those dependent on him? And yet, what was the alternative? He was on the horns of a dilemma with no way out, short of craven submission. And he could not bring himself to do that. Take away his self-respect and there was nothing left. Surely Kate would see that.

"Lass, it would be pointless tryin' to pretend to you. I've nae idea how long it'll be afore they let me go. Like as not, they'll be goin' to charge me. Causin' an affray or some such thing. They'll be out to make an example o' somebody, and there are nae prizes for guessin' who. I'm sorry, but that's it straight."

"No, it is not, George Baird." She raised her voice defiantly. "And fine you know it. You could be out o' here this very day. All charges dropped, and the chance of a fresh start at the pit."

His face clouded angrily. So she was forcing him to choose. "What do ye mean? Has yon bastard, McIntosh, gotten to ye as well? I might hae known it. That's the only reason they let ye in here. To get me to give in. And ye fell for it."

She blanched at the fury of his accusation. "Dinnae be sore wi' me. I thought it for the best. It's true Mr McIntosh came to the house last night. He had Cha White wi' him. But he really seemed concerned for ye. He insisted that the only way out was for you to accept the terms and go back. Otherwise it would be a long jail sentence. Pride was a fine thing, but ye had to think o' yer wife and bairns. The mine would let bygones be bygones, wipe the slate clean, if ye would only meet them halfway."

"And what did Cha have to say?"

"No' very much, truth to tell. Most o' the time he couldna bring himself to look at me, far less speak. But in the end he agreed wi' Mr McIntosh. The fight was lost and there was nae use greetin' ower spilt milk. We had to consider the future and get back to work."

As the words sank in, the spirit of resistance died within him. Even the faithful Cha had deserted; there was no more to be said. With a supreme effort of will he hoisted himself to his feet, and then slowly and unsteadily began to pace the room. She marvelled at his determination as he forced one leg in front of the other. The physical pain must have been excruciating, but Kate knew it was nothing to the struggle taking place in his head. Wisely she held her peace, waiting for him to reach a decision. Finally he groaned, a choking, strangulated sound, and pounded on the door with his huge fists.

"What is it, Geordie? Are ye sore afflicted?" she asked anxiously.

"Dinnae fash yersel', Kate." The next words seemed to be dredged from his very soul. "Ye've won. I canna stand against ye all. I'll sign their bloody paper. Though Christ help us. We'll a' live to rue this day. You mark my words."

* * *

Baird was willing to see reason. No sooner had the news been carried upstairs than the machinery of bureaucracy whirled into life. So often creaking and slothful, it could act with almost unseemly haste when so disposed. Half-marched, half-dragged between two burly constables to the charge room, his attestation was witnessed by the station sergeant and his formal discharge read to him. The whole procedure was over in minutes. But that was not quite all. Officialdom had a hard face and a stony heart; he was a reprobate and must be made to realise it. The sergeant simply pointed to the exit in a curt gesture of dismissal, and his acolytes looked on impassively as Baird hirpled out, supported only by his wife's arms, the final degradation.

The winter's afternoon was far advanced before the couple found themselves clear of the town on the Broomburn road. Already the daylight was beginning to fade, giving way before the snell moorland haar that came swooping down from the surrounding hills. Traffic was sparse at this time of day, only the odd trap or cart; none bothered to stop. Hardly a word had been exchanged between the two since quitting the police station. Geordie had at once shaken himself free from Kate, insisting on hobbling along unaided. It was an affront to his dignity to be seen thus in public, dependent on a woman's frail strength. Tentatively she had made the offer of her coat to keep out the worst of the chill wind; brusquely he had spurned it. Now, cut to the quick at his apparent hostility, she could bear the tension no longer.

"Geordie, let's rest awhile. You're about done in. There's sure to be a cart along presently. Maybe we could cadge a lift."

He grunted acquiescence and stomped over to the roadside. There he leaned against a stone dyke, breathing heavily. Kate followed hopefully. Perhaps his black mood was easing at last.

"Please dinnae be in the huff wi' me. If ye're angry, say so, and let's be done wi' it. It's no' like you to bear grudges. If ye blame me for forcing you into signin' the form, then it's my fault. Punish me if ye must, but at least talk to me."

"Kate, no blame lies wi' you. And I'm sorry. I had nae right to take it out on you. I know ye acted for the best. But you're just a woman and have nae idea just how clever the bosses have been. There isnae a drop o' decency among the lot o' them. They'll use anything they can to get the better of ye. You were just a tool to them."

Bitter memories stirred within him "I've stood up to them a' my life, fought for the rights o' honest toil. And where has it got me? Where has it got any workin' folk? Naewhere. They use their money and power to set man against man, bend the laws to suit their ain interests. My grandfaither was a crofter in Argyll. He and his forebears won the soil by the sweat o' their brows, turned wasteland into bonnie, fertile fields. And for what? Rack-rented by lairds who claimed the land belonged to them, and then crushed, tossed aside like an empty fag packet when they found something better for their profits. He was uprooted, evicted at a moment's notice, his hoose burnt about his ears to make sure he didna come back. Just to make way for sheep. Sheep! They think more o' animals than human beings. He had to bring his family to the slums o' Glasgow and graft as a machine minder in the mills. Cooped up fourteen hours a day when before he was free as a bird. Then there was a big slump in the cotton trade just afore I was born. So he was turned off, an' finished his days in penury. Where's the dignity in that?"

"I ken, Geordie. But the past is done." She felt she had to say something.

"Is it? Then what about my faither? He was young enough to move, turn his hand to something new. The pits were just startin' then. He helped open up the Duchess seam. Then the black spit got him, ruined his lungs. You saw him cough his life away, a shadow o' the proud man I once kent. And now there's me. No' a better hewer will ye find in the coalfield, but for how much longer? Like enough I'll hae to carry on till an accident sees me off, or I lose my strength bit by bit till I cannae lift a pick down by. Then I'll become one o' these miserable old codgers ye see in the Square. Hardly a pleasant prospect, is it?"

Kate's heart went out to him; her man was in desperate need of comfort, but words seemed pitifully inadequate. She took his hand, stroked it and intertwined her fingers in his. He gave no sign of having noticed her action; his ranting had not yet run its course.

"Ye know, once there was a time, oh, near enough a hundred year syne, when miners could walk tall, when there was such a thing as an independent collier, a golden age when men worked beside masters on equal terms. There was respect then. It was the comin' o' the coal and iron companies that spelled disaster for the skilled tradesman. They bought up a' the small owners, brought in steam pumps, windin' engines and the like, and dug deeper, always deeper, and to hell wi' the dangers. Any protest, an' they stymied us by bringin' in scabs and the bobbies. The new age o' the collier serf, that's about the size o' it now."

He stopped abruptly. The outpouring dried up as suddenly as it had begun. Kate caught her breath, on a knife-edge between hope and fear. Then his lips puckered into a wan smile. She could have cried with relief; the worst was over. Eyes shining, she threw her arms round his neck and kissed him full on the mouth. He gave way to her embrace, slowly at first, then, casting despondency to the winds, swept her off her feet in a huge bear hug. She had to thump on his back to be set down again. They both laughed.

"You think I've been makin' a fool o' myself. Mebbie you're right at that. But I had to get it off my chest. I feel better for it. Thanks for listenin' to my whines, pet."

"Oh Geordie, praise be. It does me glad to see ye more like ye used to be. What's done is done. It's the future that counts now. If we can a' pull thegither, then we can face whatever lies ahead. Ye mind the old saying, the darkest hour before the dawn?"

"Aye, Kate, I suppose so. Thank God for yer good sense to keep us on the right road."

She smiled fondly, and then became thoughtful. Now that her husband had seemingly got the bitterness out of his system, perhaps it was time to broach another subject that had been gnawing away at her. He seemed receptive; she decided to strike while the iron was hot.

"Geordie, perhaps this isnae the best time, but we've never talked about the weans for a long while."

"Weans? What are ye drivin' at?"

"I mean, what with the strike and that, we havnae really considered their future. What's to become o' them when they leave school? What kind o' work will they turn to?"

"What's up wi' ye now, Kate? He stared at her, just a little puzzled. "There's nothin' to say. Iain follows me doon the pit in the New Year, and so will Alastair when his turn comes. As for Mary, there's plenty for girls round the village, or further afield if she's so minded. Ach, I see what you're gettin' at. We'll make sure she doesnae stray too far so that she can get back to help ye in the house."

"That's not the point, an' fine you ken it, Geordie Baird. I can manage perfectly well without Mary."

"Well, what then?"

She did not answer immediately. It was a delicate matter. Geordie would be sure to object to her proposal.

"I agree that Iain should be a pitman. It's the work for which he's fitted. He's got the build and, forbye, he's never shown any interest in anything else. It'll do him good to have his faither at his elbow. He's had his own way for far too long."

"Och, ye're a touch hard on him, Kate. I know he's a wee bit wild at times, but that's only to be expected, growin' up. He's a man now, no' a boy any longer. A few months as my putter will knock the rough edges off him, nae doubt o' that."

"I hope so, Geordie. Anyhow, that's him settled. Now what about Mary? We maun face the fact she'll never be anything more than a plodder at school, but she's got a gift for practical things like cookin' and sewin'. Domestic service would suit her very well, but I'd hate to see her end up as a skivvy to some jumped-up shopkeeper. No, we'll hae to make sure she sets her sights high, finds a place wi' real prospects for advancement. Some grand house where she could start as a maid, get hersel' trained, and work her way up. Who knows, she might be a cook or housekeeper to a lord one day."

"You and your ideas. Do ye no' think she'll just get married to a village lad and hae a family o' her own?"

"Very likely, but the experience will do her no harm. Set her standards to keep."

"Well, Mary's your department. If ye really feel that's in her best interests, we'll no' stand in her road. Never let it be said that I kept her tied to yer apron strings. But it'll no' be for a year or two yet."

"It's never too early to start planning. And that's especially the case wi' Alastair."

"Alastair? Havers, woman! He's just a wee laddie. It'll be ages afore he's done wi' the school. What are ye on about?"

"I don't want him to go down the mine." She had not meant to put it quite so baldly, but it was out at last. She rushed on: "He's too weak. You know his health will never be good. The dust would kill him in six months."

"I dinnae believe that for a minute. Ye always were inclined to spoil him, makin' him wear chest warmers an' caps, and keepin' him indoors whenever it even looked like rain. Small wonder the other bairns laugh at him. If ye take my advice, ye'll stop smotherin' him and let him stand on his ain two feet. Fresh air, plenty o' exercise – that's the way to build him up. The Bairds have never been weaklings, and neither will Alastair."

"No, Geordie, he'll never be really strong. It would lie heavy on my conscience to let him go underground. Besides, there's nae earthly reason why he should. He's bright, good at his letters, forever bringin' books home. It's amazin' some o' the stuff he comes out wi'. Our youngest has a future ahead o' him. Let's gie him the chance to make somethin' o' himself."

"Now haud it right there. That's as far as ye go." Baird's hackles began to rise. This was a dangerous new twist, one he did not like at all.

"But Geordie, let me explain."

"Nae buts, Kate. I suppose ye've got a notion o' sending him on to some grand college. That means money for train fares, and books an' fees. Where would we find the siller? No' to mention the loss o' any earnings he might be bringin' in. The other two will be payin' their way. Why should he be any different? I'll hae nae favouritism in this family. What will book learnin' do for him? He'll gie himself airs and graces, even as he takes the bread from our table. Like as no', he'll become a bosses' poodle, pissing on his own class. That I'll not have. The Bairds are miners, and so will he be. And that's final."

"Alastair would never turn away from his own," said Kate quietly. "I know him too well for any doubts on that score. Still, since ye feel so strongly, we'll say no more about it."

"That's fine, then. So long as it's clearly understood." He cocked his ear. "Wheesht, now, there's somethin' coming."

Through the gathering dusk the creak and rumble of approaching wheels could clearly be heard. Presently a heavy wagon loomed into sight.

"I thought as much. And I ken the driver. It's yon fairmer from Greengates, the one I howked tatties for. He'll gie us a lift. Come on."

Kate bowed her head as the cart pulled up. Let him think he had won. She was far too shrewd to press him further at this stage. But no matter how long it took to wear down Geordie's opposition, no matter what financial sacrifices had to be shouldered, she was determined that Alastair should receive the start in life he deserved.

THREE

Bread of Adversity

February 1905

Iain Baird fumbled his way along the cross-heading towards its junction with the mothergate. Even with a miner's lamp in front of him, he could make out practically nothing of what lay ahead; the dim glow from the lantern was swallowed up within inches by the all-pervasive blackness. Bloody useless encumbrances, he thought savagely. Here, at the lowest level of the mine, the owners would never dream of installing electric lighting. That was a luxury found only in the main roadways. Underground for six weeks now, and still he found it an uphill struggle to adjust to his surroundings. Once outside the immediate vicinity of his workplace it was all too easy to lose all sense of direction in the maze of shafts and tunnels.

The passageway abounded with hidden perils for the unwary: rough-hewn walls, with many a jutting outcrop; the roof low and uneven, in some places barely five feet high; the ground underfoot broken and irregular, here and there laced with pools of stagnant water. More than once he cracked his knee or banged his head as he stumbled over loose debris. Often he had to press himself to one side to avoid heavy tubs of coal coming in the opposite direction; putters made no allowance for anyone unfortunate enough to be in their path. Though barely two hours into the foreshift, his clothes were impregnated with dust, his face caked with grime and sweat. There might be snow lying in the fields above; down here, more than a thousand feet below the surface, it was like an oven. His body ached all over. Coal mining seemed far from the glamorous prospect he had once imagined.

What made things worse was the expectation he would start as a hewer beside his father. Disillusionment had been swift and brutal. He was not even made a hand putter, driving the hutches to and from the main roadway, or a haulier, leading the ponies along the tramways to the pit bottom. No, he was nothing but a colliery lad, doing odd jobs, running errands, clearing away rubbish, filling creels – a dogsbody to be kicked around. The novelty of pit life was wearing thin, enthusiasm turning to discontent.

Hurry up wi' these props, ye idle wee de'il: his father's admonition still rankled. Heaven help him if he made a mistake or took too long about the business; any holdup in the coal cutting meant loss of earnings for the piece worker. It would be a swearing for him, if nothing worse… Christ! He had come too far, completely missed the timber store in the dark. Cursing his luck, he retraced his steps, creeping along till he found his objective. It was little more than a large cavity cut into the wall. He stooped down and groped round for the wood. His fingers grasped a billet. Strange, it felt soft and squelchy. And what was that pong? Fuck, it was shit! Someone had been using it as a shitehouse. In disgust he snatched back his soiled hand and tried to wipe it clean. That was the final straw. Angrily he aimed a kick at the pile. The whole stack tumbled over with a loud crash.

"And just what the hell do ye think you're about?"

Iain nearly jumped in alarm. The rough voice was directly behind him; he had no idea anyone was so close. But before he had time to react, he found himself pitching forward onto the props. There he sprawled, floundering amongst the logs.

"Get up! Rouse yersel', ye bugger o' hell. I'll gie ye what for!"

Still dazed, Iain felt himself grabbed by the collar and jerked to his feet. The man's face, twisted with rage, was very close to his, the reek of his breath pungent with menace. It was McNair, oversman of the section; a huge brute of a man with a temper to match. No one with any sense tangled with the likes of him. And now Iain was helpless in his grasp. The youngster shuddered at the thought of what might happen next.

"And who have we here, eh? I might have guessed it. Baird's spawn. Another troublemaker. Blood follows blood, nae doot o' it. Weel, son, I've had my eye on you. Ye're a lazy wee sod. By rights I ought to splatter you across the wall. But I'm a tolerant sort o' chap, so I'll restrain myself. Just this once. Naebody falls foul o' me a second time. Ye'd do well to bear that in mind. In the meantime, get down on yer hunkers and restack that wood properly."

Contemptuously he flung the boy from him. Iain tottered, but managed to avoid falling. He backed away, half-hangdog, half-defiant.

"Well, what are ye waitin' for? Perhaps ye'd like that thrashin'. Just say the word."

"I've got work to do for my faither. I'm late already," he mumbled sullenly.

"Wrong, sonny. Ye've got work for me first. I'm the gaffer hereabouts. Yer faither will just have to wait. Now, get on wi' it afore I kick yer arse in."

With an ill grace Iain knelt to carry out the oversman's bidding. McNair was a hard taskmaster, constantly finding fault, before eventually tiring of the situation. "Now ye can look out yer wood and be off. Mind an' tell yer auld man why Hamish McNair kept ye."

"Maybe I'll dae just that," muttered Iain to himself "Maybe he'll come lookin' for you." Laboriously he began to collect billets, cradling them in his arm. Yon bastard of an overseer would be repaid, and with interest, but that would keep; his immediate concern was to deflect the wrath surely awaiting him on his return to the coalface. A glimmer of an idea came into his head. By the time he reached the gallery leading to his father's workplace he had his story pat.

Geordie Baird paced up and down the confines of his stall, like a bear caged in a pound too small for its bulk. Inwardly seething, at last he could contain himself no longer. "Where the hell has he gotten to, Malkie?" he growled at his putter. "See if I dinnae gie that son o' mine a real larrupin' when he gets back. Somethin' he'll remember for a month o' Sundays. Sittin' down on the job, or up tae some mischief, I'll be bound. And here's me no' able to cut another peck o' coal, a' for want o' a few bits o' wood. His mother was right, I have been too soft wi' him. Weel, that's about to change. I tell ye, Malkie –" He broke off in mid-sentence; there was a faint rustle in the passageway outside. "Is that you skulkin' out there, Iain? Get yer miserable carcass in here."

So his presence had been detected. Iain had hoped for a few minutes to steel himself for the confrontation, but apparently this was to be denied him. Reluctantly he dragged himself forward at his father's call, his earlier confidence turned to doubt. The old man sounded in a fearful bait, likely as not to hit out first and ask questions afterwards.

"At bloody last! Have ye been on a conducted tour o' the whole mine, or did ye just feel like a quiet kip somewhere? Do ye realise how long I've been left here tae twiddle my thumbs? Time means money in our game, as I intend to show ye." He lurched towards Iain, tugging at the buckle of his belt.

"Haud on, faither. Bide a minute now," protested Iain, holding up his hand. "Hear me out. It was McNair, he was to blame."

Mention of the name stopped Geordie in his tracks. "McNair, ye say? What the hell are ye on about? Explain yersel' and be quick about it."

Breathing a little more easily, Iain launched into the tale he had spun for himself. "Ye see, it was like this. I was collectin' the props at the storehole, just as ye told me, when along comes this big bastard, knocks the wood out o' my arms and starts swearin' at me. As if that wisnae enough, he gies a great muckle kick and sends the whole stack fleein'. Then he grabs me, shakes me till my heid was spinnin' and accuses me o' knocking them ower on purpose. He threatened to gie me a real goin' over unless I put them back right. Well, what else could I dae, wi' him glowerin' at me. Ye can guess how long that took, wi' me near blind in the dark. Then he just ups and walks away laughin'."

"Did he now?"

"Aye. He telt me to remind you that he's the gaffer in this neck o' the wood, an' that there was nae room for your airs and graces in the pit. It seemed as though he's really after your guts. Is there somethin' between the pair o' you?"

Geordie flinched angrily. "That's none o' your business," he spat. For a moment he stood irresolute, then decisively renotched his belt. "I'll speak to you later. There's been more than enough time wasted already. Malkie, see that there's an empty hutch ready for the coal. Iain, bring some o' thae props and wedge them in to support yon pillars."

Iain was careful not to smirk as he carried out his father's bidding. So there was some grudge between them. That might come in useful one day, if he could ferret out what it was.

"There ye are, faither," he said, knocking the final piece of wood into place. "Ye can get on wi' yer hewin' now."

"Watch yersel', ye cheeky wee cub. Dinnae tell me what to do. Ye might still get that hammerin'. Stand back out o' the road, and be quick wi' the sprags when I call for them."

Geordie dropped to his knees and, crouching forward, lightly ran his hand along the base of the seam. With a grunt of satisfaction he rolled over onto his side and manoeuvred his body into as comfortable a working position as the restricted space would permit. Only when he was quite settled did he call for his pick. Carefully hefting the tool, he swung it behind his head and drove a succession of powerful, rhythmical blows into the underlying fireclay. From time to time he paused to allow his two helpers to sweep aside the debris and wedge in sprags or props; there must be no chance of any premature collapse of the wall. After fifteen minutes of vigorous digging he called a halt and scrambled to his feet. The layer of coal now appeared suspended over a neat, rectangular hole, the wooden billets jammed in the gap like so many matchsticks in the mouth of a turnip lantern.

The next step was crucial; this was the real test of the hewer's skill and nerve. Baird was not to be rushed. He peered closely at the roofline, searching out the most suitable places to drive in his spikes. Stepping back, he indicated several spots; Malkie held a triangle of iron to each in turn while Geordie's heavy mallet sank them in halfway. Then it was Iain's task to pull aside the props. Finally the spikes were knocked home. As the reverberations died away, there was an eerie lull. Iain and Malkie exchanged glances. Had their efforts been in vain? There was a sudden crack, like the snap of an overwound watch spring. Fissures began to spread over the surface, hairline at first, but visibly growing ever wider. The air was filled with a tearing, rending, piercing roar; the ground shook beneath their feet. Instinctively all three sprang backwards, only just in time, as the whole section of wall plunged towards them.

Not till the dust had settled could they be certain of the outcome. But there was no cause for concern; the coal had splintered into a dozen blocks, a near perfect execution of the miner's craft. Now the hewer could afford to relax, leaning on his pick while his minions strained to carry the pieces to the nearby tram, for onward passage to the pitbank.

"That'll be the tub about full now," he said, as the last of the coal was cleared. His putter nodded, too puffed to speak. "Right ye are, Malkie. Off ye go then. See that my token's in the hutch, or the banksman will be creditin' it to one o' his cronies. Me an' Iain will have the next load ready when ye get back."

Twice the cycle was repeated before Baird was prepared to allow a brief respite. "That's well ower a ton and a half, maybe close on two tons. No' too bad for a mornin's graft, especially since near half o' it was wasted," he said, with a meaningful look at his son. "Anyhow, awa' and get yer piece, baith o' ye. We've another ton tae win afore this shift's over."

Truth to tell, Geordie felt in dire need of the break. Not that he would admit it to a living soul, and certainly not to those two young pups; any sniff of weakness and they would be snapping at his heels. But there was no denying a period of idleness fairly softened up a man. Here he was, over two months since the end of the strike, and still not fully readjusted to the routine. He flexed his shoulders and arched his back, then vigorously set to rubbing elbow and knee joints, one after the other. It was a kind of ritual into which he had slipped over the past weeks. It did offer some relief, however temporary.

Now he could think of food. He reached for the battered tin box containing his meal – bread with a scrape of dripping, a hunk of cheese, together with a flask of cold tea to wash it down. Uninspiring stuff, but it filled his belly and he was used to it. These days he usually ate alone. It was not that he deliberately avoided his fellow hewers, but there seemed little point in seeking their company. In his present state of mind he had little time for banter or small talk. No, solitude suited him best. However, on this occasion it appeared he was not to be allowed his privacy. Someone was approaching up the passage. If this was Cha White come to jolly him out of his mood, then Cha would get short shrift. But it was Iain's head which poked round the corner.

"Mind if I join ye, faither?"

Geordie was mildly surprised. Usually the lad preferred to spend his free time with the putters and other young bucks, skylarking around and generally burning up surplus energy. Curious, but of no real moment. He confined himself to an indeterminate grunt. Taking this as assent, Iain settled himself against the wall opposite, and opened his piece box. Baird made no further comment. If Iain had something on his mind, then he could spit it out; Geordie was not about to help him.

"Faither, I hope ye dinnae take this amiss, but there's somethin' really botherin' me."

"Aye, I thought ye didnae come here just for the pleasure o' my company."

"Ye do believe me, don't ye? I mean when I telt you I was stopped by that brute, McNair. Just to gie him a chance to shove a Baird around."

Geordie stiffened, then slowly nodded his head. "Aye, I suppose so."

"Well then, why did ye no' say ye wid do somethin' about it? He wants sortin' out for what he did. I ken fine the pair o' ye hate each other's guts. Ye've got an excuse now. A' the pitmen would be behind you. He's no' exactly popular, the way he chucks his weight around. If ye do nothin', a'body will think ye're scared o' him. That's no' true, is it? Ye dinnae want him to boast about how he put one over the Bairds?"

"That's enough! That's mair than enough, ye ignorant wee whelp. Ye've gone too far this time." Geordie was livid with rage. For a moment it looked as if he would strike the boy, but then he thought better of it. His fist was raised, but he let it fall to his side.

"Now just you listen to me for a change," he hissed, struggling to contain his temper. "I'm no' over proud o' what's gone on in this pit lately, but I think it's about time ye woke up to the facts o' life. So I'm goin' to put you wise to a few things, things that are really none o' your business. But they might just help ye grow up."

He swallowed hard, giving himself a chance to cool down and collect his thoughts. It did not come easy to divulge bittersweet memories, confess innermost feelings, especially to a callow youth who would probably not understand in any case. However, he was committed now.

"You're right enough. Hamish McNair and me don't get on, never have had, and that's a fact. We were rivals, ye might say, but I a'ways had the beating o' him. As a laddie I could outjump and outfight him. Then, when we were putters, I could shift the hutches far quicker than he could. And when it came tae the hewin', he was nae match for me. At one time he even had a notion for yer mother, but she chose me. He could never forgive that. That's probably why he started to suck up to the bosses. Well, he got his reward, got himself made up, but deep down he kent I was still the better man. Whatever else he did, he aye took care to keep his distance. He knew fine I would thrash him if he tried anything on."

"But don't ye see that's exactly what he's done? Here's the perfect chance to put him in his place once and for all."

Geordie shook his head. "Have ye nae brains in yer heid? The strike changed a' that. The gaffers ken fine they've got the whip hand. They're just itchin' for an excuse to be rid o' me. Gin I went for a chargehand, that would gie them a' they need. And if I was sacked, d'ye think the others would come out behind me? Nae bloody fear. They're licked, a' the spunk knocked out o' them. No' that I can blame them. Every man has his breakin' point, me included. So ye see, we maun swallow our pride, keep our heads down an' hope for better things to come. Maybe that's difficult for a youngster to take, but ye'll just hae to thole it."

Iain's face set hard. So his father would do nothing. He could hardly believe it. His boyhood idol revealed as a craven coward. "Nae chance," he spat out defiantly. "If ye winnae raise a hand to avenge a family insult, I'll just have to look for a way o' settlin' it mysel."

"I know how ye feel, Iain, believe me. But that talk's plain daft. See here now, Malkie will be gettin' a move up in a week or twa. Spare man at the hewin' in this section. How wid ye fancy takin' his place? Ye'd be my hand putter. Nae mair arsin' around at a'body's beck an' call. And another bob a week as well. What dae ye say to that?"

It was an olive branch, as close as Geordie could ever come to pleading. But it had no effect. Iain gave no sign of even having heard him. Snapping his tin shut, he jumped to his feet and stalked off without a backward glance. Geordie half rose as if to follow him, but then sank back. The young were so impetuous; he had been like that too. Only age made a man cautious. The boy was upset, upset and ashamed. He could not fault him for that. He could only hope Iain would come to his senses before he had time to do anything stupid. More trouble they could well do without.

* * *

"Haud on, lads. Ye were fair quick off yer marks when the hooter went. Nearly missed ye there in the rush."

It was the end of the haulage shift, and putters and oncost workers were streaming from the cages, anxious to be off home like the more fortunate hewers who had finished an hour earlier. Nor was the weather likely to encourage any dawdling. The morning's crisp, crunchy covering of snow had by now turned into a dirty, slimy slush underfoot. Despite the thaw, there was no respite from the bitingly cold wind sweeping across the moors, doubly chilling to those who had spent the last nine hours in the heat and sweat of the underground workings. Almost all had but a single thought, to escape from the elements into some snug haven as quickly as possible.

"Piss off, Iain," someone jeered. "Dae ye expect us to stand waitin' round here till our balls freeze aff?"

"Bide a minute. Gie's a chance to catch my breath. Ye're no' in a tearin' hurry, are ye?"

"No' in a hurry? Naw. Ye daft gowk! It's gettin' dark. We're a' cold, tired and hungry. The tea'll be on the table at hame. Is that reason enough to be goin' on wi'? Anyhow, it's no' like you to want to stay behind in this hellhole."

"That's as may be, but there's somethin' I wanted to say. Are ye game for a bit o' fun?"

Iain scanned their faces eagerly, totally unheeding of the throng scurrying and jostling their way past. There would be safety in numbers for the plan he had in mind. Though the youngest of the group of half a dozen youths, and not yet even a putter, he knew he had gained full acceptance as one of their number. Generally they were up for any lark, but on this occasion he saw only doubt and reluctance. Instinctively he turned to Jamie Anstruther. He was the acknowledged leader.

"What do you think, Jamie?"

"I'm athinkin' we'd better get out o' the yard afore the gateman comes an' locks us in. Either that or reports us to the deputy for loiterin'. We can hear what Iain has to say on the road." They hurried on, through the wrought iron gates. "All right, young yin, speak yer piece."

"Weel, if ye ask me, it's high time yon McNair got what he deserves. He's been throwin' his weight around far too much for my likin'."

"I wouldnae disagree wi' ye there, but what are ye suggestin'? That we just walk up tae him an' challenge him to a fight?"

"No, Jamie, I'm no' that stupid. But listen. He'll no' be home yet. Ye know he aye goes to the howff for a dram first. How about sneakin' down to his house and throwin' a few stones through his windaes? Naebody'll see us in the dark. It'll teach him a lesson no' to be so quick to pick on folk. Are ye on, then?"

"Aye, it has possibilities, right enough. And it wouldnae take any time at a'. Just imagine the look on his mug when he gets hame. That'd be a sight for sore eyes. Okay then, youngster, I'll go along wi' yer notion. What about the rest o' you?" Heads nodded in agreement. "Then that's settled. Let's get on wi' it."

Iain let out a whoop of glee. Punching the air and leaping like a banshee, he tore off down the hill. The others, caught up by his enthusiasm, charged after him.

Half a mile away, Iain's younger brother was also hurrying through the shadowy twilight. School had long since ended but, as usual, Alastair had remained behind. He enjoyed these sessions, helping the dominie with his classroom chores. Today, however, he had tarried later than usual. The blast of the colliery hooter had come as a rude awakening, a shrill warning that he would have to rush if he was to avoid awkward questions at home. He put on a spurt, sliding and slithering through the mire.

To some extent Alastair lived in a world of his own, his vivid imagination insulating him from the grim realities of village life. Especially stirring were tales of the past which transported him back to a much older Scotland, before the coming of mines and factories. That afternoon Mr Ogilvie had been describing the legendary deeds of the Covenanters who preached at lonely conventicles against the wickedness of their day, and whose martyrs' graves lay all around on the moors. Alastair resolved to make that his special project for the lighter evenings, to visit as many of these monuments as he could find. In the meantime he could whet his appetite by dipping into a pocket edition of *Wilson's Tales of the Borders*, lent to him by the dominie. Thrilling times indeed! Why were there no valiant acts or heroic men like those anymore?

It was as well he had books for company; otherwise the teasing of his classmates would have been hard to bear. He was mocked as the teacher's favourite, ribbed as a milksop because of the garments he was forced to wear. Still, he knew his weak chest was improving; he was prone to far fewer bouts of wheezing these days. Exercise in the fresh air was building up his strength; these long walks through the hills begun last summer had done him good. Perhaps he might manage another ramble this weekend, if the weather improved enough for his fusspot mother to allow him out. Impulsively he snatched the cap from his head and stuffed it in his pocket. If only it were so easy to be rid of these flannelette underclothes …

Crash! What was that? An almighty bang, loud and clear above the moan of the wind. There it was again, and yet again. It was the sound of breaking glass, and not far off either. He could hear shouts and rowdy laughter, quickly followed by the clatter of running feet, coming his way. Without thinking, he backed into the protective gloom of a nearby doorway, crouching motionless as a group of five or six figures swept round the corner, hardly daring to breathe as they passed within a couple of yards. Big boys all, and, despite the near darkness, he was sure he recognised his brother among them. What on earth had they been doing? Up to no good, that much was certain. Then it clicked. Of course! They had been breaking someone's windows. But this was no time to dwell on Iain's misdeeds. Already doors were being flung open, people coming out into the street. There was a growing babble of voices, surprise interspersed with anger. Were he to be found here, he might be taken as an accomplice. Visions of being hauled off to the village bobby floated before him. Instinctively he took to his heels and bolted down the nearest wynd. No matter now that he would arrive home later than ever.

Blown and panting, his small frame shaking like a leaf, he was glad to scuttle into the sanctuary of his own lane. That there would be a fearful *stooshie* went without saying. What the outcome would be was anyone's guess; but he wanted no part in the affair. It had been a close shave, but at least no one had any idea he had been anywhere near the scene. His wisest course would be to keep it to himself and feign ignorance if the subject came up. He fairly flew the final few yards to safety. Thankfully he lifted the latch on the door and disappeared inside.

Myrtle Place was yet another of the dreary terraces of company houses flung up when the mines opened. Few of its occupants realised the supreme irony of the coalmasters in naming these grim haunts after the wild flowers that had once grown there in profusion. From the outside, the dwellings were mean and dingy hovels of slowly decaying brick; but within, there was scope for a spark of individuality, a semblance of order and tidiness, though it demanded unceasing toil on the part of the womenfolk to defy the remorseless encroachment of dirt and grime. The Baird household was no exception.

The tiny lobby opened straight into the kitchen, the family's main living area. Alastair took comfort from its cheerful shabbiness: the well banked fire in the spotlessly swept hearth, with the rag rug in front nestling on the scrubbed linoleum floor; the mantelpiece with its array of *wally dug* ornaments flanking the eight-day clock; his father's worn leather armchair to one side, a clothes-horse of steaming pit garments on the other. The room was unusually quiet. Only his brother and sister were present, Mary kneeling on the rug, tending the pot on the hob, Iain lolling over the table, shovelling his food down with a spoon. Iain paid no heed to the new arrival, but Mary swivelled round to fix Alastair with an inquisitive frown.

"Where's mother and faither, then?" he said hastily, before his own latecoming could be queried.

"I like that," snorted Mary. "Look at the time on that clock. Ye should have been back lang syne. But if it's any o' your business, faither was hame ages ago, had his tea, then a wash, changed his claes, and now he's awa' out. Mither wasnae long after him. Awa' to visit a neighbour, she telt me. Satisfied?"

"Och, there's no need to be like that, Mary. I was just curious."

"Curious? Dinnae make me laugh. More to the point is where you've been till this hour. Stayed behind at the school, I suppose. Ye cannae keep away from that place. Lucky for you there's naebody in. Ye'd have caught it in the neck otherwise."

Alastair was quick to agree. "You're a sharp one, Mary. I stayed back to help Mr Ogilvie get things ready for tomorrow. There was a lot to do, and I clean forgot the time. Sorry."

"Well, there's no' much harm done," said Mary, mollified. "Dinnae stand gawpin' like that. Sit ye doon at the table. I'll get yer tea, if it's no' stone cold by now."

Alastair brightened. He slipped into his place, relieved to have escaped so lightly. Goodness knows what he might have blurted out under more rigorous questioning. A steaming bowl was set before him, a hash of potatoes mixed with slivers of onion and a few dark flecks of meat. He sniffed appreciatively, suddenly realising how hungry he was.

"There ye go then," said Mary. "Sup up." No further bidding was needed; he fell to with a will.

Iain, meantime, had spoken not a word, had hardly even bothered to look up, so intent had he been on his meal. Now, apparently he had finished. Ostentatiously banging his spoon down on the plate, he pushed it away noisily, before reaching into his shirt pocket for a half-smoked Woodbine. Scraping back his chair, he went over to the fireplace, lifted a spill to light his cigarette, then flopped into the armchair.

"What are ye on, Iain?" Mary looked at him askance. "Ye ken ye're no' supposed to smoke in here, and faither'll murder ye if he catches you in his chair."

"Weel, naebody's here to see, no' that I'd worry if they were."

Recognising the futility of further protest, she shrugged her shoulders. "It's your funeral."

Iain inhaled deeply, savouring the taste; then, half turning his head, sent a little cloud of bluish smoke billowing across the table towards Alastair. The youngster choked and spluttered.

"Dinnae dae that, Iain. Ye ken Alastair's chesty."

Iain ignored her. "So the wee man's late, eh. That's no' like mammie's boy. Not the sort of behaviour that's expected at all. So how do ye account for it, then? What mischief have ye been in? But of course that's no' your style. Mair likely sookin' up to the teacher, actin' as his wee pet as usual. You an' Ogilvie are well matched. And while you've been kissin' his arse, what dae ye suppose I've been doin'?"

"Stop it ye big lout. Can ye no' see he's red in the face?" Mary hastily fetched a tumbler of water from the scullery. "Here, drink this, Alastair."

Gratefully he took a gulp. It seemed to do the trick; the fit of coughing subsided.

"Nae idea, have ye?" continued Iain. "Well, I've been out upholdin' the family honour. Rightin' a wrong, ye might say. Teachin' folk a lesson no' to meddle wi' the Bairds. But you widnae understand that. You'll be a bosses' man yersel' afore too long. *Yes sir, please sir, three bags full sir.* That'll be your stock in trade."

Another of Iain's tirades to endure; Alastair had been through it all before. The taunts and bantering might have gone on for long enough, but just then there was a heavy tread outside the door, followed by a rasp as the latch was swung open violently. Iain sprang up as though stung; he had barely enough time to throw his cigarette onto the fire before his father burst into the room.

"So there ye are, ye stupid great sod. I thought ye'd likely be skulkin' here. Ye've been sittin' in my chair. And smokin', forbye. The place stinks o' it. But we'll let that pass. There's somethin' far more important you and me have to sort out."

"What's up, faither? I'm straight hame frae the pit. Ask Mary here."

"Dinnae gie me yer lies. Ye ken fine what it is. Hamish McNair came fleein' into the pub, breathin' fire and brimstane. He claimed a' his windaes had been stove in by a gang o' laddies, and that you were the ringleader. Do ye deny it?"

"Deny it? Of course I deny it. I'm surprised ye'd believe anythin' he says. He's just pickin' on us again. If somebody broke his windaes it wisnae me."

"You bloody fool. I warned ye only this mornin' no' to get involved. As if we hadnae enough bother. Ye did do it. I can see it in yer face."

"Aw' right. So I did do it. What's it to you?"

"You ninny. Ye havnae got the brains ye were born with. McNair was all for callin' in the bobbies then and there. Fancy a spell in clink, do ye? And he'd report it at the mine and you'd get the sack. Where do ye think ye'd get another start? To stop him I'd to eat humble pie, though I felt like smashin' his teeth. I had to ply him wi' drams till he cooled doon, promise to repair the damage and gie ye a hidin' myself. Well, that's just what I'm goin' to do. No' for what ye did, though that was bad enough, but for forcin' me to take shit from the likes o' him. So just you drop yer breeks and bend ower that table."

"Nae chance. I was only daein' what was right. He had it comin'. You widnae touch McNair. Ye'll no' touch me."

"We'll see about that. C'mere, you!"

Baird made a lunge, but Iain was too quick for him. Nimbly he jumped back out of reach, dodged round the table and, as Geordie followed, snatched up his jacket from the back of the chair and made a dash for the door. Tugging at the latch, he glanced back in anticipation of a blow from fist or boot. But there was no pursuit. His father was hirpling on one leg, clutching the other with both hands, grimacing with pain. Iain wasted no time in a second look. Slamming the door behind him, he made good his escape.

* * *

"Mrs Baird, isn't it?" The schoolmaster was somewhat nonplussed, but recovered well. There was only the briefest pause before he went on hurriedly. "This is an unexpected pleasure. Come you in. You must be near frozen."

In all honesty, visitors were few enough at any time; it was a real surprise that anyone should call on such a night, even more so that it should be a parent, a mother, unescorted and without an appointment. He felt a sense of awkwardness as he stood aside to allow Kate to enter. A respectable married woman, unchaperoned, in his house: tongues would wag freely in the village were this to become common knowledge.

"It's this way," he said, with just a hint of asperity. "In here. This is my sitting room, in the evening at least. By day it becomes the staffroom. Sorry it's in such a pickle. Bachelor quarters, you know. Please, take a seat by the fire and get some warmth back into you."

Kate made no immediate move to comply. "I see you're busy," she said nervously, glancing at the pile of exercise books open on the table. "I really mustn't keep you from your work. It was thoughtless of me to turn up on your doorstep like this. I'll come some other time, when it's more convenient."

Ogilvie thawed. Here was a curious mixture, courage, determination, and vulnerability. She really was a most presentable woman. And she was Alastair's mother. If there was something amiss, he wanted to know of it.

"You'll do no such thing. Pay no attention to my bark. I truly am most glad of the break."

"Are you sure?" Kate was still doubtful.

"Don't give it another thought. The kettle's singing on the hob and I was just about to brew a pot of tea. You'll join me in a cup. And have a slice of Dundee cake. Bide you here a minute while I fetch the caddy and cut the cake."

Kate allowed herself to be coaxed into the easy chair by the hearth. Only after Ogilvie had bustled away did she begin to unwind. At least she had not been spurned out of hand. Like most of her class, she had an ambivalent attitude towards figures of authority – awe, respect, a certain wariness. It had taken no little effort to steel herself to make this visit. Geordie must never hear of it; the very thought gave her palpitations.

Presently the rattle of crockery announced his return. "Here we are," he said, setting the tray down on the table. "Sorry to have taken so long. Not still cold, are you? You must be roasting by now in yon big heavy coat."

Kate smiled at the gentle rebuke. "Yes, it is a little warm now." She fumbled with the buttons.

"That's better. I'm sure you'll feel much more comfortable. And how is everyone at home?" continued Ogilvie, striving to put her at ease while he infused the tea. "Mr Baird? And Iain? How has he taken to the world of work?"

"My husband is in good health. And I think Iain quite likes his job. At least I have never heard him complain. But it was really Alastair I came to see you about." She leaned forward on the edge of her seat.

"Try a slice of this cake. I can thoroughly recommend it." He passed her a plate. "Yes, I guessed as much. I'm sorry if he was late home the other day. He was helping me in the schoolroom, and I'm afraid we rather forgot the time."

"No, it's nothing like that," Kate reassured him. "It's what lies ahead that troubles me. Ye see, he's aye been delicate. It's more than likely that life down the pits would be too much for him. Forbye, I think he's got a brain in his head and it would be a shame to let that go to waste. But you're in a much better position to judge, Mr Ogilvie. Has he got something, or is it just a mother's foolish fancy?"

"Not at all, Mrs Baird. Alastair does indeed show promise, way beyond his years. Put simply, if he continues to make headway at his present rate, he will be one of the best scholars ever to have come into my care. That's just between the two of us, by the way."

"I'm fair relieved to hear you say that. I know he's still a wee laddie, but I dinnae want to leave things too late. Decisions maun be made if he's to get a good start in life. That's why I barged in like this. I hope ye don't mind too much."

"On the contrary, I feel flattered. And I applaud your concern. Foresight is a quality not readily found in Broomburn. Of course it's never too early to think of the future" he went on hurriedly, sensing her embarrassment. "Alastair has a real talent for learning, but it needs to be nurtured, tended carefully, if he is to reap the full benefit. Indeed, had you not called this evening, I was intending to get in touch with you and Mr Baird on that very subject fairly soon."

"Dinnae dae that!" It was a cry of alarm. "Geordie must never hear o' it. He's determined that a' the Bairds should be miners."

"All right." Ogilvie held up a placating hand. "We'll keep the matter to ourselves for the moment. I've no doubt we can put our heads together to good effect."

Kate was mortified. "Whatever must you think of me? That was the height of rudeness. I'm so sorry. It's just that I get so worried when I think o' what might be."

"Tush, woman. Put it out of your mind. I can understand how you feel. But we must face facts. Mr Baird will have to be consulted, sooner or later. You realise that?"

"I suppose so, but I'd like to choose the time and place. It'll take a lot o' careful preparation to bring him round."

"As you wish. Now drink up your tea before it goes cold, and let's get down to brass tacks. It's early days, of course, but have you or Alastair any ideas as to a possible career? No burning ambition he's confided in you?"

"No, not really. He's never said anything. But he's a'ways got his nose in some book, and ye should hear him spouting about what he's read. Whiles ye cannae shut him up. That's why I thought he might be cut out for a dominie."

Ogilvie smiled wryly. "Is that the general view of a teacher? A know-all who can't stop talking."

"I didnae mean it like that. It's just my clumsy way o' puttin' things. What I meant to say was that Alastair looks up to you. I'm sure he would like naethin' better than to follow in your footsteps."

"Ah, Mrs Baird, I'm the product of an older, simpler way of life. In my young day it was sufficient to be a university graduate for appointment as a parish schoolmaster. Times have changed since then, I'm afraid. Society has become more complicated, not least in education. There's still scope for the *lad o' pairts* in the old Scots tradition, but nowadays there's more and more hurdles to be jumped, exams to be taken, qualifications gained. And many a pitfall for the unwary."

"But you could guide Alastair, Mr Ogilvie, couldn't ye? Maybe train him to be a teacher. I mean, that is, if it wouldnae be ower much of a burden."

"Nothing would give me greater pleasure, but it's not quite as straightforward as that. Let me try to explain. At present, the regulations would permit Alastair to be enrolled as a pupil-teacher when he reaches the statutory leaving age. But that situation could well change."

"Pupil-teacher?"

"Yes, a sort of apprentice. An indenture, a legally binding agreement, would be drawn up between the school board and the boy's lawful guardian. So you see Mr Baird would have to give his permission. Under the usual terms Alastair would be required to teach a number of hours each week to various sections of the school, after prior instruction from me, of course. In return he would receive a salary of between £10 and £20 per annum. Hardly a king's ransom, you'll agree. Are you with me so far?"

Kate nodded. "I think so."

"Good. But that's not the end of the story. At the same time he would also have to prepare himself for the leaving certificate examination, taken at seventeen or eighteen. That would mean extra tuition before and after classes, as well as personal study in the evenings. Without this qualification he could not proceed to the next stage, a two or three-year course at training college. Only after that could he be recognised as a fully-fledged schoolmaster."

"It all sounds awfully complicated."

"Well, it's a long furrow to plough, and I can't altogether recommend it."

"But if there's no other way?"

"That route involves too heavy a load for my liking. Much of the day is spent dinning the basics into the infants, hardly the most stimulating of tasks for a lively mind. Then there are the lessons to be prepared beforehand. And on top of that, time to be found for his own education. Small wonder so many fall by the wayside. It's not for the faint-hearted."

"Alastair's never been afraid of hard graft."

"Don't misunderstand me, Mrs Baird, there's no question of that. In any case, by the time Alastair's of an age, it's likely pupil-teachers will be a thing of the past. No, there's nothing for it. If he is to achieve his potential, your son must have the benefit of a secondary education, and that's simply not possible in a village school."

"But do you still think that teaching is a good idea?"

"Well, it's always been the traditional route for a bright lad to raise himself out of the labouring classes. The dominie used to be a pillar of the community, though I doubt whether he still carries the same respect. Certainly there is a fair measure of security and a steady, if unspectacular, salary. To that extent he is free from fear of want. On the other hand, it's an outlet of limited scope. Opportunities for advancement are few and far between. And, all too often, there's a sorry lack of intellectual stimulation. Deadening of the brain is an occupational hazard."

"So you're telling me it's not for Alastair?" Kate could not hide her disappointment.

"I didn't say that. But at this stage caution is advisable. Don't be in too much of a hurry to cast him into a mould. Let him have the benefit of a good, all-round education first."

"I see. And where would he get this schooling?"

"It would involve leaving Broomburn, I'm sorry to say. All I can offer here are continuation classes, which would be far beneath his abilities. The nearest secondary provision is in Hamilton. That would mean lodgings during the week or a long journey every day."

"I couldnae stomach his being away from home so young."

"Daily travel then. He could catch the train at the halt."

"Aye, that might be possible. Are there many o' these schools? I mean, what with Hamilton being such a big place."

"A fair number, six or eight I believe. You would have a choice."

"Choice! I wouldnae have a clue."

"It is rather confusing, I have to admit. Secondary institutions come in a variety of shapes and sizes. There are the new higher-grade establishments, for example. They tend to be three year colleges, preparing candidates for the intermediate certificate and entry into the lower professions, though to be fair an increasing number do now offer a full five year course."

"But you don't think all that much of them, Mr Ogilvie?"

"They haven't yet proved themselves. There are some obvious attractions, however. Run by local school boards as they are, they usually do not charge fees, though parents might be expected to make a contribution towards books. All the same, they are generally reckoned to be inferior to the old established burgh and endowed foundations. In my view that is where true secondary instruction is to be found."

"Why is that?"

"Because they are the most prestigious schools, undertaking the full range of advanced work. Their aim is to provide a passport to university and the more eminent professions. And Alastair would mix with boys from all types of background, just the thing to bring him out of himself, give him confidence to face the world."

"Suppose he still wanted to be a teacher, Mr Ogilvie. Would that be possible?"

"You don't give up easily once you have a bee in your bonnet, do you? Yes, Alastair would not be debarred from a career in education. In fact his options would be widened. He could go on to university, take his degree, and then a short training course to qualify to teach in secondary schools. That would provide much more stimulating work, higher status and better pay."

Kate sighed. "Ye make it all seem very attractive, I must admit, but there has to be a catch somewhere. How on earth would the likes of us ever be able to afford it?"

Ogilvie smiled. "I apologise if I've let my enthusiasm run away with me. Cost is an important consideration, there's no avoiding it. These schools are invariably fee paying, and the best don't come cheap. But it's not an insoluble problem. There have always been benefactors willing to give financial support to poor but deserving scholars by endowing bursaries and scholarships. These can often be sufficient to cover all expenses, both school fees and maintenance."

"These – scholarships I think you said. Are they easy to come by?"

"In the nature of things, alas no. Awards are generally based on the results of a stiff competitive examination. But that's no reason to be downhearted. Look, I've been mulling it over and I believe Alastair is capable of winning the Grierson Memorial."

Kate looked up blankly. "Grierson Memorial? What's that?"

"The name is unimportant. The point is that the holder is entitled to a free place at Fairhill Academy. The grounding provided there, in my opinion, is unsurpassed anywhere in the county. Many of its pupils have gone on to distinguish themselves in later life at the highest levels. It's a prize well worth having, I assure you."

"Do you really think he would stand a chance?"

Ogilvie nodded vigorously. "I would not have mentioned it otherwise. It would be a rare old tussle, of course, against fearsome opposition, but that's to be expected. Alastair and I would make a good team. And there would be almost two years to make ready. What do you say?"

The dominie's enthusiasm was infectious. Her imagination was stirred, dazzled by the picture of what might be. But then she drew back. The dream faded as natural caution reasserted itself.

"I'm no' sure. Perhaps we would be raising his expectations over much. I'd hate to see him disappointed. And there's his father to consider. You've given me a lot o' food for thought. It wouldnae do to make a hasty decision and regret it later. Could we talk about this again some other time?"

"Surely. Whenever you like. Only don't leave it too long. There's a deal of preparation to be done if we are to go ahead."

"I won't. And now I must be off," said Kate, rising from her chair. "It's already late and I musn't be missed at home. Thank you for all your help and advice."

Ogilvie bowed slightly in acknowledgement before showing her out. That there would be difficulties ahead, he had no doubt. In a mining district son followed father down the pit. That was the way of things, as natural as life itself. Tradition and prejudice were the scourge of academic success. But he had never shirked a challenge. And with Mrs Baird as an ally, there was at least a fighting chance. In his mind's eye he began to tick off the subjects of study which would be required for the examination.

FOUR

Waters of Affliction

March 1905

The managing director of the Avon Coal Company entered the precincts of the Duchess Colliery on foot. He might have arrived in his gleaming new motor car, like a Roman general come in triumph to enjoy the fruits of his victory, but such was not his purpose. True, time would have been saved, but he wished his visit to be as unobtrusive as possible. Besides, a breath of fresh air was most welcome after being cooped up all morning in yet another interminable board meeting.

Semple raised his cane in response to the gatekeeper's salute, and then quickened his step. His habit of suddenly materialising on snap tours of inspection endeared him to neither management nor men. On this occasion, however, he paid little heed to the hive of activity around him. Instead he made straight for the small row of administrative buildings, almost dwarfed in the shadow of enginehouse and pit bank. The office at the far end had a faded sign above the door: *Pit Deputy. Knock.* Semple turned the handle and went in.

The deputy sat at his desk, checking over a column of figures. He rose with alacrity at the sight of his employer.

"'Morning, McIntosh. Sorry about this intrusion. I can see you're busy. I hope I don't call at an inopportune moment."

"Not at all, Mr Semple. You know you are always most welcome. Let me fetch you a chair."

"Thank you, McIntosh. That's most thoughtful. Perhaps I will take the weight off my feet after my walk."

"Yes indeed. It's a fair step from Head Office. Now, was there something in particular you wished to see?"

"That appears to be yesterday's tallies you have there, if I'm not mistaken. How are we doing?"

"I've just finished the calculations. Perhaps you might care to run your eye over them. As you will note, output is not far off what it was before the strike."

Semple took the proffered sheet of paper, but barely glanced at the numbers before laying it aside.

"Quite so. McIntosh, the directors have asked me to express their recognition of the debt of gratitude owed to you, and I wish to add my own personal endorsement to that. This company would still be on its knees but for the efforts of people like yourself over the last few months."

"I only did my duty."

"Rather more than that, I fancy. Our recovery has been in no little measure due to your determination to get things moving again. Such commitment does not pass unnoticed, you may be sure of that." He paused. "However, we cannot afford to rest on our laurels. The time has come to look towards opportunities for the future. All the signs are favourable. Industry is picking up after the downturn. That means increased demand for coal and higher prices. The Avon Coal Company cannot be allowed to lag behind. We must be prepared to respond to market conditions by stepping up our operations."

"But I don't see how that's really possible. We are already near the limits of our capacity."

Semple did not reply. Instead he pushed back his chair and began to pace up and down the room, as though deep in thought.

"By the way, McIntosh," he said reflectively, "how are those malcontents shaking back to work? Baird, White and their ilk? Any signs of kicking over the traces again?"

"Not a cheep, Mr Semple. It's as quiet as the grave down by. They've learnt their lesson."

"Really? That's most gratifying. But are you sure there are no straws in the wind? No mutterings, no groups gathering in odd corners?"

"Not even a whiff, and I keep my ear close to the ground. They're all too glad of a job to think about causing trouble."

"Good. I'm relieved to hear it. Anyhow, to return to the point at issue. The answer is quite simple. We must open up a new coal face."

The pit deputy gaped in astonishment. What nonsense was this? Surely a jest. And yet Semple was not noted for a sense of humour.

"But how? Where?" he spluttered. "The Duchess is about played out. There are no fresh seams worth exploiting. And I doubt if there's anything to be gained by sinking new shafts further afield."

"Aren't you forgetting something, McIntosh? Perhaps there are no new reserves to be developed, but that doesn't mean we can't reopen an old face. There's plenty of coal still waiting to be dug out if we choose to make the effort. Here, I can show you what I had in mind. I've had a copy made of the early workings in the Duchess." He pulled a folded parchment from his coat pocket. "Clear a space on your desk so we can spread this out."

"As you wish, sir." McIntosh sounded far from convinced. The map was laid flat on the table, with a weight at each corner to hold it in place.

"Here we are," said Semple, jabbing with his finger. "Our present area of production. Now, if we were to work along those old passages and shafts, we'd be back at the old Broom seam. That was never fully cleared. It was abandoned during a slump in the market and never reopened. Think on it, man. Maybe thousands of tons just waiting to be lifted. It's an opportunity not to be missed."

"I suppose that might be so. But why ask me? Surely it's a matter for you to discuss with the colliery manager."

"I've already broached the subject with Robinson, but I'd also like the views of other senior men."

"In that case, sir, I would have to point out that it's twenty years and more since anyone has been in that part of the mine. Imagine what must have happened in the interval. There would be a risk of crushed props, buckled roadways, collapsed roofs, flooded tunnels. Especially the last, since we'd be working back towards the river. Is the effort worthwhile? We don't know what we might find."

"Exactly. And if we don't take the opportunity, we won't know what we are missing. What is there to lose? A few days' work by a handful of men? I expected a little more enthusiasm, McIntosh. You're the only one to carp at my plans."

The deputy recognised the warning sign. He had gone too far in his objections. Hastily he sought to make amends.

"I'm sorry if I gave that impression. I didn't mean to be critical. You can rely on my complete co-operation."

"Good. Then I can leave the detailed arrangements in your hands. If things work out as I hope, there could be an opening for another assistant manager." He picked up his hat, cane and gloves. "I must be off now. Oh, by the way, you might consider Baird and his cronies for our little venture. Clearing the roadway for a week or two will do them no harm. I think they deserve the chance to redeem themselves after all the trouble they've caused. Only a suggestion, of course."

Suggestion be damned! He had been given a direct order, one he would neglect at his peril. So an example was to be made of the strike leaders after all; Semple had only been biding his time. The scheme was not without merit, he had to admit, but yet he felt uneasy. The risks were dangerously high. And what of his promise to Baird that there would be no victimisation? Blast Semple and his hare-brained ideas!

An hour later the wail of the hooter roused McIntosh to his distasteful task. It was the end of the foreshift; they would be coming up now. Grim faced, he left his office to watch the cage disgorge its cargo of pitmen. He would tackle Baird on his own, he had decided. The old lion might be bruised and battered, but he was unpredictable and still capable of lashing out. It would be as well to draw his fangs first. If he proved amenable, or at least submissive, all might go smoothly. Without an example to follow, there was little chance of resistance from the others.

The crowd was passing by, shuffling along, some in groups, others singly. There was no sign of the once proud strut, the traditional hallmark of the hewer, little evidence of the exuberance that customarily signalled release from toil. Not a healthy atmosphere, the deputy thought, but perhaps he was being over sensitive. Ah, there was Baird at last, walking apart. Strange how he had distanced himself from his fellows since the strike. And there was something of a limp in his step.

"Baird! Hang on a minute."

Geordie looked up dully at the sound of his name. The pit deputy was beckoning to him. The new age of the collier serf, right enough; even a man's free time was no longer his own. He hesitated; then, shrugging his shoulders, trudged over.

"Glad to have caught you, Baird. Just wanted a word in your ear before you take yourself off home. Come into the office, will you?"

Geordie glowered, but said nothing. Breathing deeply, he followed McIntosh inside.

"God's sake, man. There's no need to look as though you've lost two bob and found a tanner. I've not called you in to find fault."

"What, then? Nothin' good, I'll be bound."

"There you go again. Always ready to see the worst in everything. Hear me out before you make up your mind."

"All right. I'm listenin'."

"That's better. I know there's been some concern about the future. Talk of lay-offs and the like. Well, rest assured that nothing could be further from the truth. We intend to expand output, not reduce it."

"Oh aye. And how's that? This seam'll no' last forever. Six months, a year maybe, and it'll be knackered."

"Possibly so, but there are other alternatives. We're about to develop a new coal face."

"And the band played! It's no' on, and fine you know it."

"Perhaps not a new face exactly. We're about to reopen an old seam."

"If ye can find one wi' any coal worth the hewin'. Anyways, why bother tellin' me?"

"Two reasons. You can let the others know their jobs are safe. Thought you might like to be the bearer of good news. Also, between you and me, there's a lot riding on this project. Success depends on the efforts of experienced men like yourself. You've been involved in this sort of thing before, none better in fact. You're the ideal choice to lead the way."

"Soft soap, is it? I'm dyin' o' curiosity. Where exactly is this treasure trove o' coal?"

"It's the old Broom face. There's tons of high quality stuff left there."

"Christ! I should have realised somethin' like this was comin'." Geordie's expression hardened; there was no trace of banter now. "Yon was a real bastard to work twenty year syne. Why do ye think it was abandoned? What sort o' state do ye imagine it's in now?"

"Hold your horses, Baird. Naturally, tests have been carried out by the mine engineer. His report indicates that conditions are stable, and tunnelling and extraction of the coal should be quite straightforward."

"Nae doot. Yon pimp would pee in his pants if Semple telt him. Damn yer tests. I ken it's too dangerous to work there. D'ye ever stop to consider the poor buggers riskin' their lives, day in, day oot, just to line Semple's pockets?"

"Spare me the sermon, Baird. If you have something relevant to say, I'll listen. But I'll tolerate no wild allegations."

"That's just fine by me, *Mister* McIntosh. I'll gie ye reasons enough."

The pitman's tone was still defiant, even provocative, but McIntosh decided against a further rebuke. "Say what you must, then," he said icily.

"First an' foremost, the Broom face was aye a wet seam. Nae wonder, right below where the Broom joins the Avon. There's a maze o' old tunnels and shafts down there. God knows how many o' them are fu' o' water. One wrong move an' we might be flooded oot, like as no' drowned in the rush. But you wouldnae concern yersel' ower much wi' that."

"Grant me patience! Utter nonsense, Baird, and I can prove it. Come round the other side of the table and study this map here. As you can see, it plainly indicates that the workings are well away from the river, and above the water table. There's scant danger of any flooding."

"Ca' that a map?" Geordie was openly contemptuous. "It's nothin' but a rough sketch. Nae mine surveyor drew that. And there's a hell o' a lot of blank spaces on it. How much is missed out, I'm wonderin'. Can ye put yer hand on yer heart and seriously tell me it's accurate?"

"I'm not here to argue the toss with you, Baird. It's a fair copy of the original. You'll just have to take my word for it."

"Aye. Suppose what ye say is true. There's still the wee problem o' diggin' back to the face. These auld passages and shafts will be filled wi' rubbish, a' the muck an' shit o' the day. Clearin' that will take time. And I wouldnae bet against findin' sagging roofs, rotten props an' twisted roads. A sure recipe for cave-ins, and de'il take the poor sods underneath."

"I can't accept that. The risks are no greater than anywhere else. It's simply a matter of exercising due care and attention. Now, you've had a fair hearing. Let that be an end to it."

Geordie shook his head. "I dinnae believe this. Nothin' I've said has made a blind bit o' difference, has it?"

"The decision is final, I'm afraid. There's nothing you or I could do to alter it. So if we could get on?"

"Is there anythin' left to say?"

"One or two practical details. Wages, for example. Time spent clearing the roadway is unproductive, and so there is no question of payment on the normal piecework basis. Half of your average earnings is the best we can do."

Baird recoiled as the implication struck home. "Half? Half!" he exploded. "How do ye expect anyone to keep body and soul thegither on that? It's starvation wages."

"Then the solution is in your own hands. The quicker you tunnel back, the quicker you'll be on piecework again. And it's not as though you'll be on your own. We've put together a good team, White, Doig, Strickland, Gow, and several others besides yourself. You can have your usual putters and oncost men to do the fetching and carrying. McNair will be in overall charge."

"So that's the shape o' things. I see it all now. Let things settle down, and then screw the strike leaders. You were always hard-nosed, but at least I thought there was a scrap o' decency in ye. Now this. What's yer promise worth now? If this isnae victimisation, what the hell is?"

The pit deputy stirred uncomfortably. The accusation struck home, puncturing his air of composure. "There was nothing I could do," he muttered lamely.

"Nothin' you could do. No, I suppose not. After all, you're only the organ grinder's monkey. Do ye think that anyone wi' a grain o' spunk would take what you've just telt me? It's slave labour, an' worse. And I'll not do it." By now Geordie had lost all restraint. "Awa' an' tell yer master that. He can go an' boil his heid. There'll be a riot if he tries it on."

"Baird, I'm not going to get involved in a shouting match. Before you do anything you might regret, consider your position. If you fail to report on Monday next, you'll be sacked. And don't imagine your friends will down tools either. There'll be no strike. Furthermore, you'll be blacklisted in every pit in Lanarkshire. You'll never work again." His voice took on a quiet urgency as he made a last appeal. "For God's sake, it's a futile gesture. Think of your family, if not yourself."

The hewer glared savagely. "A man wi'out self-respect has nothin'," he snarled. "Ye'd rob me o' that? Then damn you an' yer kind to hell. I'm gettin' out o' this."

Before McIntosh could react, he had stormed out of the office, crashing the door shut behind him. The deputy was left to sit and ponder.

* * *

"By Christ, what a rum bunch! A real rogues' gallery. And I had to be landed wi' it. Well, I suppose it takes shit to clear shit. Rouse yerselves! That cage'll no' wait forever."

Hamish McNair was his usual strident, sneering, hectoring self. His temper, uncertain at the best of times, was now on the shortest of fuses. It was common knowledge that this was a punishment detail; being placed in charge carried a stigma of its own. But at least there was little trouble to be expected from this miserable bunch of wastrels assembled at the pitbank. They hung about dejectedly, cloth caps well pulled down, hardly able to meet one another's eyes. The precaution of ordering them to clock on half an hour after the foreshift had gone down now seemed quite unnecessary. They would knuckle under. Work them till they dropped; that was the line to follow.

"Haud on a minute, though. Where's Baird? I thought there was somebody missin'. Any o' you seen him this mornin'?"

Some of the pitmen looked up furtively, a few shuffled uncomfortably, one or two shook their heads. No one spoke.

"Naebody got a tongue in their heid?" jeered McNair. His gaze flitted contemptuously over the group. "You, skulkin' over there! Aye, you wi' the plooks on yer mug. Ye're Baird's sprog. I want a word wi' you. And sharp about it, ye dummy!"

Iain scowled. With an obvious show of reluctance he slouched towards the overseer. "What's wi' you? Whatever it is, ye've got the wrong man. I've nothin' to say."

"Really?" McNair was quizzical. "We'll have to see about that." With one hand he yanked the youngster towards him; with the other he proceeded to tweak Iain's ear till he was almost doubled up with pain.

"Let go! Ye're hurting me, ye great bully."

"I'll do a sight more than that if ye dinnae jump when I tell you. Now, some information. Is yer faither comin' or not?"

"I dinnae ken. He's no likely to tell me. He was eatin' a slice o' bread an' drippin' when I left."

"That's enough, McNair. Let the laddie be. Pick on someone yer ain size for once."

The oversman twisted round, searching out the source of the intervention. It was Cha White. His face lit up malevolently; pushing Iain aside, he straightened up. The sprat could wait; here was a much bigger fish to dangle on his hook.

"Well, well, what have we here? So it's yersel', White. Ye're no' sae chirpy these days. No' often ye open yer mouth. And ye'd be well advised to keep it that way."

"Ye're no' bein' fair on the boy. It's obvious he knows nothin'. That's all I meant."

"And you're goin' to do somethin' about it? Listen, pillock. You're skatin' on very thin ice. One word from me and it's curtains for you. So dinnae poke into things that dinnae concern you."

White flushed with anger, then dropped his head and turned away.

McNair chuckled evilly. "Very wise. And Baird's finished here, you mark my words. Burnt his boats. But there's plenty of room for anyone wantin' to join him."

"Are ye goin' to tell that to Baird personally?" ventured Gow, normally a reserved, self-effacing individual with little to say.

"When I get the chance. What's it to you?"

"Oh, nothin' at all. But gie a squint ower there. That's Geordie Baird now."

Sure enough, a familiar figure had appeared round the colliery offices and was marching up the incline. McNair's eyes glittered, his mouth creased into a slow smile. Feet astride, arms folded, he planted himself in the centre of the pathway to await Baird's approach.

"That's far enough. Just where the hell do you think you're goin'?"

Geordie affected surprise. "To start work, of course. As ordered by the deputy."

"Ye'll do no such thing. Have ye any idea o' the time? Ye're ower late. We cannae stand around waitin' on your pleasure. As far as I'm concerned, ye're no longer part o' this shift. Ye'll need to see McIntosh about yer future. If ye have one, that is."

"But the cage hasnae gone down. The shift hasnae started. There's de'il a reason to black me."

"The decision's made, and there's an end o' it. The matter's out o' my hands."

Baird's expression grew ugly, the mask of appeasement dropped. "Is that so?" he rasped. "Well, you know what you can do. Away an' fuck yersel',

McNair. I'm comin' through. If ye think otherwise, then try an' stop me. I'll gie ye yer heid in yer hands to play wi'. So dinnae tempt me. Get out o' my way."

"You cannae talk to me like that," spluttered McNair.

"I just have. So if ye want to make somethin' o' it …"

The two men glowered at each other, eyeball to eyeball. For a full half minute the issue hung in the balance; then the oversman broke away.

"I've nae time to argue. We should be down by already. Everyone intae the cage. Take that glaikit look off yer face, Gow, afore I ram my fist down the back o' your throat. And you, Baird, ye've no' heard the last o' this."

Geordie laughed, a loud, raucous peel of mockery. "Whenever it suits you, McNair."

"Think ye're the big man, don't ye? Weel, try this for size. There'll be an extra hour underground this shift. And tomorrow, and the day after. Every day till we reach the face. Maybe that'll put yer gas at a peep."

Silently the pitmen herded onto the platform. McNair slammed the bar into place with an emphatic clang and nodded curtly to the engineman. The hoist began its descent, juddering and creaking in protest as it gathered speed and disappeared into the void. In the darkness of the cage Geordie felt no elation, the excitement of the moment dispelled by a gloomy premonition. The oversman would not report him to McIntosh; he was too fly for that. No, he would wait his chance; find a cast iron case to have him sacked on the spot. It had been tempting providence to cut things so fine, a stupid, senseless act of bravado. What did McNair matter anyway? He was merely a puppet on a string, dancing to his master's bidding.

The bumps and jolts and rattles of the downrush suddenly gave way to a rending, high pitched whine as the lift braked sharply, then slowly grated to a halt. There was a fleeting moment of stunned silence; then it was gone in a flurry of commotion as the colliers spilled out into the roadway, making for the shed where their tools were stored.

Cha White caught Baird by the arm. "By God he nearly had ye there, Geordie."

"And just what d'ye mean by that, Cha White?"

"Nothin', Geordie. What I really wanted to say was that we're a' proud o' the way ye stood up to thon bugger. None o' us would have had the guts for it."

"Is that so? Naebody else daft enough, ye mean. Anyhow, let it rest." He spat into the gloom beyond White. "Want something, McNair?" he called out loudly. "I ken ye're there."

Cha swivelled round in surprise; he had heard nothing. But sure enough, there was the overseer come to chivvy on the laggards.

"And what have we here?" said McNair unpleasantly. "Two ne'er-do-wells cookin' up some devilry, I'll be bound."

"Spyin' as usual, McNair? Away an' take yer crap elsewhere. I'm busy at the minute."

"You never change, Baird, do ye? Same old tune. I thought ye'd made my day by no' turnin' up, but here ye are like a bad penny. Never mind though. Since ye've decided to join us, we maun make the best use o' ye."

"Oh aye. And how's that?"

"Obvious. It's the head o' the line for you. You'll hae pride o' place. Ye should feel honoured."

"So that's the way o' it. The bum's rush for Geordie Baird. McIntosh put ye up to this. And Semple above him, nae doot. You're to see I get the dirtiest jobs. Anythin' goes wrong an' it's my neck gets chopped."

"Ye takes yer chances. Now, let's be havin' ye, if you've done gabbin'. There's work to be done."

The others had already assembled a few hundred yards down the gallery. At that point a recess in the wall marked the entrance to a tunnel, long abandoned and blocked off by an infill of rubble, splintered props and the general debris of two decades of neglect. Last week they would have passed it by without a second glance, but now it filled them with foreboding. The mood of dejection was only too evident as the three latecomers approached.

"Ready to earn yer corn now?" sneered McNair. "Gather round then, quick as ye like. *Mister* Baird here will explain all ye need to know. I'll leave ye in his capable hands." The oversman nodded meaningfully towards Geordie and ostentatiously elbowed his way through to the rear.

"Turd," muttered Baird, before turning to the group. "Right, I'll no' mince my words. It'll be a right bastard to plough through this muck, and that's a fact. Slow and sure, that's our best bet. God knows what we'll be up against. Though I seem to recall it's a straight drift down to the Broom seam. That's something, I suppose."

It was cruel, punishing toil to cleave a path through the entranceway. Every few minutes Geordie would call for quiet, listening intently for the tell-tale rustle that betokened an impending collapse, before exhorting the pitmen to redouble their efforts. For the first hour or two progress was at a snail's pace; but once the rubbish had been cleared, he was amazed to find that the abandoned mine workings had been relatively well preserved. Descending into the drift, they found only minor obstacles to delay them; the roof appeared fairly sound, many of the props were still in place and, almost unbelievably, there were few problems with water and none at all with gas. He could sense the growing optimism among the men. Grudgingly he had to admit that possibly his fears had been groundless. Perhaps that mine engineer had done his work after all.

* * *

Kate Baird hummed a Highland love lilt as she bustled about the kitchen, preparing breakfast for her two younger children. Though dreich winter still lurked outside, she felt a new spring dawning. Last night, as they lay abed, Geordie had explained it all, told her of the breakthrough to the high-grade deposits just waiting to be won. Now they could look forward to decent wages; the days of life on the breadline were almost over. Enveloping her in his arms, he had kissed and caressed and teased, leaving her body quivering and utterly submissive to his will. It was as though she was once more a twenty year old newlywed on her marriage night. And he had promised more of the same as he crushed her in a bear hug before setting off for work; her muscles still throbbed from the power of his embrace. Perhaps they could now think of rebuilding – family, home, savings – after the hardships of the last year. Perhaps Geordie might even be seduced into allowing Alastair his chance of winning that scholarship.

Cap pulled well down, jacket buttoned up to the throat, hands thrust deep into his pockets, Geordie Baird walked briskly through the shadowy village streets. Every so often a shaft of light momentarily cast its rays into the street as a door opened and another miner slipped out to fall into step behind him. That had been the pattern of the last day or so, the pitmen preferring to wait for him rather than make their way to the colliery in ones and twos. That was one in the eye for McNair. Better still, it showed he had regained his old position of pre-eminence amongst his fellows.

They swept through the colliery gates in a solid phalanx, a show of solidarity for all to see. Spirits were high; they laughed and joked, exchanging good-natured banter. As usual, McNair stood by the engine house, arms akimbo, glowering as he awaited their arrival. It was a temptation Baird could not resist.

"A guid mornin' to you, McNair. Ye look as though the wee woman kept ye on short rations last night."

"What the hell do ye mean, Baird? Ye ken fine I'm no' married."

"Then he must have meant yer wee whore," chirped Cha White.

"Naw. Naebody would gie him room space, no' even on his pay," piped another.

Strange how things had turned. Where once the men had cringed before him, now they were prepared to poke fun. Like so many mischievous schoolboys, they were taunting him, daring him to do his worst. Well, he would not give them the satisfaction of seeing him flare up in a temper. There were other ways of showing who still had the whip hand.

"Have yer wee joke. It doesnae bother me. But if ye could stop cacklin' for a minute, there are arrangements to be made afore ye go down by. As ye well know, today we start hewin' coal at the Broom."

There was an immediate chorus of ribald cheers and jeers. McNair cast his eyes upwards, refusing to be drawn. He could afford to wait till hubbub subsided.

"And I'm sure you'll be pleased to hear that help's on the way. From tomorrow there'll be another squad comin' to join ye. You'd never shift a' that coal by yerselves."

"Comin' to rob us, mair like," shouted a hewer. "We've done the hard graft an' others will get the easy pickings. How long will the work last wi 'a' thae gannets?"

There was an angry buzz of agreement. McNair shrugged. "Not my decision. I'm just the messenger boy. But you're no' being shoved off. You'll get yer fair share. Now let's get back to brass tacks. I've still to allocate a room to each hewer."

"That's no' on," said Baird flatly. "I can just about thole others havin' the benefit o' our sweat. They've a right to earn an honest crust, same as us. But no' this. You ken the system. We draw lots for the rooms. That's the way it's always been done."

"Not this time. Orders from on high. If ye dinnae like it, you ken what to do. There's plenty others ready to take yer place."

This was McNair reasserting his authority with a vengeance. He began to hand round grubby slivers of paper, each with a number pencilled on it. These represented the workplaces from which the coal would be cut. The men grumbled and cursed, but none refused to accept a number. Geordie was left to the end; after a moment's hesitation he snatched the proffered slip.

"It doesnae really matter, lads. The rooms are a' much the same. Likely we'll be stuck wi' the yins furthest in. So what? It'll just be a wee bit longer for the putters to wheel their loads. Come on, heids up and let's show the bastards they cannae grind us down."

Faces brightened; Geordie was right. It was only a petty act of spite on McNair's part. No matter how many interlopers were brought in, there was work for the present, and that was all that mattered. As he expected, Baird's station was at the far end of the gallery. The seam was thinner here, and there were traces of damp on the walls and floor, but hewing would present little problem. McNair was doomed to disappointment if his intention was to do him a mischief.

"Right, Iain, this'll do us nicely. No' the best place I've ever been in, but it'll yield a good peck o' coal afore we're finished wi' it." He glanced round at his newly appointed putter. "Dinnae hang back there. Get the tools laid out."

His son made no move to obey.

"What the de'il's up wi' ye now? Whatever it is, out wi' it, quick. There's precious little time to waste."

"I thought ye'd changed," muttered Iain woodenly. "Gone back to the faither I used to know. And now this. McNair shits on ye, and you take it like a lamb."

"God sakes, will ye no' understand? There's things ye can dae, and things ye cannae. Whiles ye can hit back at the likes o' McNair, and whiles ye must knuckle under. Or at least gie that impression. Did ye expect me to walk into yon stooge's trap? Naw. Never do what they expect. Patience, and watch for yer chance. It'll come, be sure o' it."

"Will it?" said Iain accusingly. His voice was choked. "Ye never guessed how much I looked up to you. The best faither a boy could have. I boasted about ye, hammered anyone who dared say a thing against ye."

Geordie felt a spasm of pity, but quelled it instantly. There was no room for sympathy down the pit.

"Cut out that caterwaulin'. Ye're a man now, an' this is the real world. Either get that into yer thick heid an' buckle down, or bugger off and let me find someone who'll dae a turn wi'out moanin' all day. Which is it to be?"

"I'll stay. But dinnae expect me to like it."

"Then ye'll just have to lump it. Hand ower the pick and sprags, and go you and fetch an empty hutch while I make a start here. Gin ye had some horse sense we might make a pitman o' you yet."

With that Geordie settled himself to work. He was soon into his stride, building up a rhythm as smooth as the movement of a well-oiled watch. Hole the sides of the face, undercut the seam, drive home the wedges, knock out the props, wait and hope for gravity to tear down the wall, rest while the putter filled his tub, then begin the cycle once more. The coal came away easily, almost as though in recompense for past hardships endured. Certainly the fireclay beneath was damp, oozing water in places, but that hardly mattered; he had known far worse.

The eight hours fairly flew past. He could hardly believe McNair's warning whistle so soon; only half an hour left to the end of the shift. Leaning on his pick, he surveyed his efforts with quiet satisfaction. Not a bad day's stint, not bad at all. In fact he could not recall a better one, not even when he and the Duchess were both in their prime. There was the squeak and scrunch of a hutch in the passageway. One last load, and that would do it for the day.

Once more he eased himself into position at the base of the seam. Hefting his pick, he swung it with controlled power at the underlying stratum. The head cut cleanly into the clay, then, meeting no further resistance, penetrated right up to the haft. Baird was thrown forward by the unexpected momentum. What in hell's name could that be? Exerting all his strength, he tugged and twisted and levered to pull the blade free. As the point came clear, a jet of water shot through the hole. Christ Almighty! He sprang to his feet. This was no isolated pocket of water – not with that force. Feverishly his fingers probed the coalface. Cracks, and water seeping through! That could mean only one thing. He must have broken into a flooded mine shaft. The wall could collapse at any minute – with the whole shift caught like rats in a barrel, swept aside by the rush, drowned or dashed to pulp. Seconds were precious. Thrusting his back against the seam, he braced his legs for maximum purchase. It was their only chance. If he could hold out till props could be brought, they might yet all be saved.

"Iain! Iain!" he yelled. "Quick, laddie! Get in here."

"Comin', faither." Iain darted into the room. "What's up? Why are ye standin' like that? And what's that pourin' out at yer feet?"

"Haud yer wheesht, will ye? Now listen carefully, son, and do exactly as I say. I cannae keep this position much longer. Behind me there's a flooded shaft. The wall could go at any time. Run and get some o' the chaps. Tell them to bring pit props. We might still hold it in check. Hurry now!"

Iain stared, transfixed like a rabbit caught in a sudden light. Consciousness of acute danger slowly filtered through his brain. Then blind, irrational panic took over, galvanising his limbs into action. Instinctively he turned and fled, crawling, stooping, tripping, anywhere in a desperate bid to reach safety.

The echo of running feet resonated like the hammer of coffin nails. Geordie heard his son's frenzied cries, followed by exclamations of surprise and the sounds of hurried exit further up the gallery. At least the alarm had been raised; so there was a chance they would get out in time. He redoubled his efforts, clenching his teeth and wedging his body still more firmly against the rock. But the water surged through in an ever-increasing torrent; he sensed the wall behind him crack and buckle. His legs were numbed, his last reserves of strength ebbing fast. No one would return in search of him now. So it was to end like this. He fought back the bile and bitterness rising in his throat. His lips moved falteringly, reciting a few words of a long forgotten prayer. Too late to ask for forgiveness, to wish he had led a better life. How would the family manage without him? Kate would cope, she always had. There was comfort in that.

* * *

The shrill whine of the klaxon filled the air, shattering the daily routine of village life. For this was no ordinary blast signalling the end of a shift. The long, drawn-out wail carried a stark message of its own. Mine accident! In the urgency of the moment there could be but one thought; to make for the colliery, to hear the details first-hand, to offer help and support.

Men at work in garden or allotment cast aside their tools, colliers on night shift tumbled out of bed and rushed outdoors, pulling garments about them as they ran. Wives and mothers, sisters and sweethearts, quit their tasks in kitchen and washhouse, parlour and drying green, and sallied forth, barely pausing to snatch up a shawl as they went. Idlers and gossips in the Square were swept along with the throng. Within minutes the village was all but deserted.

In the terraced house in Myrtle Place Kate Baird made no move to join this exodus. For an hour and more she had been ill at ease, unable to settle to any household chore; something was amiss, of that she was certain. Then the first screech of the siren pierced her like a dagger. Suddenly she knew. It was her husband. Some awful tragedy had befallen Geordie. She sensed his presence, reaching out to touch her, then falling back, fading away into emptiness. Her whole frame trembled, blood drained from her face, her limbs gave way. It was as much as she could do to sink into the nearest chair. As if in a dream, she stared vacantly into the gathering dusk, oblivious to the clatter of feet in the street outside, blind to the shadowy figures scudding past the window.

It was quite dark when the click of the latch roused her from lethargy. She looked up eagerly, but it was only her two younger children. The momentary flicker of hope shrivelled within her.

"Guess where we've just been," cried Mary excitedly.

"To the pit," blurted out Alastair, without giving her a chance to reply. "We were on our way home frae school when the hooter went off. A'body seemed to be rushin' there. So we ran a' the way, along wi' everyone else."

"There were hundreds o' people at the gates," Mary went on. "It looked like it was somethin' really bad, but nobody could say for certain."

"We thought you might be there," said Alastair. "There were dozens o' women. But we couldnae see you."

"So we just decided to come home. Have you heard anythin' o' what's happened?" asked Mary.

"What's that ye're sayin'? About the pit?" The babble of voices forced her attention. "No, I huvnae heard anythin'. But ye must be famished. It's long past yer teatime."

Mechanically she rose from her chair, stirred the dying embers of the fire into life, put on more coal, and lit the oil lamp. She fetched plates, bread and jam, set them on the table and began to slice the loaf.

Then came the question she dreaded. "Is there nae sign o' faither and Iain? They're usually hame by now."

Her hand shook, but she forced herself to cut steadily. "No, not yet. Like as no' they'll be helpin' out wi' whatever's wrong down by. Now tuck in and stop the palaver."

She resumed her seat and took up her vigil once more. The children, now sensitive to her mood, ate in subdued silence.

It came at last – a rasp on the door knocker. Mary was the first to react. Slipping from her place, she hurried out. In a moment she was back, followed by Cha White. Kate stared at him mutely, her eyes expressionless.

"It's Cha, come to visit us," said Mary encouragingly.

"I'm sorry to disturb ye, Kate," began White. Then his courage failed him; his voice trailed away. There was an awkward silence.

"Say hello to Cha, maw," said Mary, in an attempt to break the ice. "Ask him to sit down. I'll put the kettle on."

"That's all right, lass. Maybe you bairns would be better off in bed. I've got to have a wee chat wi' yer maw."

"No! They'll stay." It was little more than a whisper, but delivered with vehemence.

White flinched. "Are ye sure now, Kate?" he stammered.

By way of response she stretched out her arms to draw the children towards her. They came willingly, clinging to her for comfort.

"As ye please, then. Perhaps it's for the best. They'll hae to find out sooner or later." He swallowed hard before plunging on. "There's no easy way to say this. They thought it would be better comin' from someone ye knew. Brace yersel'." He choked, close to tears. "Geordie's deid. There was a flood an' he was swept away. Drowned, like as no'. But we'll never ken for certain. They widnae let us go back for him. Too dangerous, they said. So they've decided to seal the workings. That'll be his grave."

Kate unbent. "Dinnae take on, Cha. It' no' your fault." Through her own anguish she could feel for him. "Ye're no' responsible for the bad news. I had a notion already."

It was kindly meant, and White recognised the effort it must have cost. But the words were no comfort. Geordie was his best friend, they had been through thick and thin together; now he was gone, and Cha had done nothing to save him.

"Geordie was right. He spoke out about the dangers. And naebody would listen, no' the bosses, no' his mates. And he paid for our stupidity wi' his life. The only one no' to get out when the shaft flooded. Why did it have to be him? But we'll no' let it rest there. The lads are pretty fired up over this.

Ye'll get yer rights, even if it means a strike. Nothin' can bring back Geordie, but we can see ye get proper compensation."

"That's guid o' ye, Cha. And we're grateful. But we'll manage just fine."

"To be sure ye will. And there'll still be Iain's wages, of course. But dinnae let that pride o' yours get in the road. There's no question o' charity. Ye'll take what's yer due."

"Iain! My God! I never thought o' him. Did he get out safe? Is he lyin' injured somewhere? Tell me straight."

"Set yer mind at rest on that score. Aye, he got out a' right. In fact it was your youngster that raised the alarm. But for him we might all hae drowned."

"Where is he then? We've no' seen hide nor hair o' him yet."

"Aye, it's a puzzle. He was in the cage sure enough, but when we reached the top o' the shaft, he shot away like a bat out o' hell."

"Strange. But he'd be upset."

"Ach, maybe so. The bosses were in right bait, wantin' to see him. No' really surprisin', since he's probably the only witness to what actually happened."

"Why do you think that?"

"Well, he was workin' alongside Geordie. But nae doubt we'll hear a' about it soon enough. Look, Kate, I'll stay wi' ye if you like. Or I'll go if ye prefer it. Maybe the wife could look round later."

"It's very considerate o' ye, Cha, but at the moment I'd rather be alone wi' the weans. I hope ye dinnae mind."

"As ye wish. A few o' us will be round the morn to see what's to be done. I'll be off now. It's scant comfort, I ken, but we a' feel for ye at this terrible time."

"I'll see ye out, Cha," said Mary, fighting back her tears.

"Nae need, lass. Stay wi' yer mother. I'll see myself out."

They heard the snick of the catch, the creak of the hinge, then a startled oath. An instant later White was back, dragging a dishevelled figure with him.

"Here he is," cried Cha. "Skulkin' about in the street outside." He released his grasp. "Where in hell have ye been? Your mother's beside herself wi' worry. As though she hasnae had enough on her plate."

"Dinnae bother me," hissed Iain defiantly. "It's none o' your business. Ye've no right here anyway."

"That's enough of your snash," Kate upbraided him. "Cha's a guest in this house, and you'll treat him with respect. Now come over here," she added more gently, "and tell me about it."

To the astonishment of everyone in the room, Iain promptly burst into tears and flung himself at his mother's feet.

"Oh maw, it was horrible. The sight o' a' that water pourin' in. It gies me the shivers just to think on it."

Kate cradled his head on her lap. "There, there, my bonnie bairn. Hush now, ye're safe at home. Dinnae fret yersel." She spoke as softly and tenderly as to a newborn baby.

"But can ye no' understand?" Iain was nearly hysterical. "I did it. I got faither killed."

"No, no, son. Ye don't know what ye're sayin'. How can you be to blame? By all accounts ye did very well. You raised the alarm and let everyone else get out in time."

"But that's no' the point. It is my fault. I should have stayed and got help. That's what faither told me to do. But I didnae. I was that scared, I couldnae think straight. I just had to get away."

"What's that ye say?" growled White. "On yer feet, laddie. And stop blubbin', for any sake." There was no gainsaying the iron in his voice. Iain obeyed. "Now take a minute to catch yer breath, and spell out exactly what ye mean."

But already Iain was regretting his rash outburst. White's obvious disgust was like a splash of cold water, enough to set warning bells jangling in his head. A furtive look reappeared; warily he temporised.

"I dinnae ken the whole story. I only saw a wee bit o' it."

"Then tell us what ye saw."

"Weel, it's like this. I'd delivered a tram to the roadway and was on my way back when I heard faither callin' for me. I ran in, and there he was, standin' against the face wi' a gush o' water pourin' out at his feet."

"Go on."

"Well, he shouted at me to get help from the others, to fetch props an' that so we could wedge the wall."

"And what did you dae?"

"Like faither said, I hoofed it up the passage shoutin' on folk to lend a hand. But I got caught up wi' you lot jostlin' to get out, and I couldnae get back."

"You wee twister!" roared White. "That's no' what you said a minute ago. And forbye, nobody can mind o' ye sayin' yer faither was in any bother. Do ye imagine we would have left him behind had we kent? Why, I ought to kick yer arse from here to hell and back."

"Stop it, Cha!" Kate was insistent. "I'll not have the boy harmed. He's not at fault. He's just a youngster and no' able to take a man's responsibilities."

"I cannae agree wi' ye there, Kate. Down by, it's vital that each man can depend on his workmates. There's nae excuses for age or inexperience. That's the law of survival. We're only as safe as the weakest link in the chain."

"But ye'll no' take it out on Iain?" It was an entreaty this time.

"I'm sorry, Kate. I shouldnae have flared up like that. It's just that Geordie must have known what was happenin'. He deliberately chose to sacrifice his ain life to gie others a chance. The man deserves a medal. As for the rest, I feel sick, sick to the heart. I dinnae ken whether to give ye that hidin', Iain, or take it out on myself for no' goin' back to check nobody was left."

"All the same, ye'll make sure nae ill comes to him, won't ye, Cha?" Kate persisted.

"I cannae make promises. I'll do what I can to see he gets a fair crack o' the whip at work, but I tell ye, Kate, the men winnae like it, no' one bit. As for you, ye shyster, ye'd best report to McIntosh's office, first thing in the mornin'. Ye'll have some explainin' to do. Good night, Kate. I'll be in touch."

No sooner had the door closed behind Cha White than Kate turned to Iain. "Just answer me one thing, son," she said quietly. "Is there anything you could have done for your father?"

Iain could not meet her eyes. He flinched, then broke away without speaking.

"Thank you, Iain. That was all I wanted to know."

FIVE

Bitter Legacy

April 1905

T he pit deputy sat stiffly on an uncomfortable bentwood chair, faintly irritated by the clack of the typewriting machine at the far end of the room. McIntosh had firm views on such new-fangled tomfoolery, especially in the hands of a woman. But then it was all of a piece. Money was squandered on the gloss, the public face of the company, while the colliery itself was starved of investment. He was annoyed at having been summoned from the Duchess, and then left to kick his heels in some anteroom to await the board's pleasure. Did no one realise he had a mountain of work on his desk? Time had already been lost that morning. But at least his presence at the memorial service was an obligation he had been glad to perform.

Once more his attention fastened on the heavy oak door barring the way to the inner sanctum. Not one member of the board had deigned to put in an appearance at the church. Baird deserved better than that, in all conscience. Even in practical terms, boardroom representation would have been prudent; as it was, the absence of company directors had been the subject of bitter comments. Mrs Baird had greeted him politely, if distantly, when he paid his respects, but it was impossible to mistake the dark looks cast in his direction by many in the congregation. There might serious trouble in the offing, unless Semple and the others moved swiftly to defuse the situation.

Then there was his own position to consider. Daily routine was conducted by letter or telephone; if some particular problem arose, Semple himself would pay a visit to the Duchess. Boardroom involvement suggested a serious issue was at stake. And that could only mean Baird's death. The directors must be discussing the implications of the accident; surely they would be aware of the wave of sympathy for the man, the charges of negligence levied against the company. McIntosh had a clear conscience, but, as he pondered, his unease grew. Perhaps the board were simply looking to cover their backs. In that case, might not he be held solely responsible, a convenient scapegoat to deflect criticism? His dismissal might well be sufficient to satisfy public opinion. McIntosh had no illusions. Were a sacrifice to be demanded, thirty years of loyal service would be as dust in the balance.

A bell jangled on the wall behind the secretary's desk. She barely paused to glance up from her work. "They're ready for you now. Just go in."

"Much obliged, I'm sure," snapped McIntosh, nettled by her offhand manner. Had the office grapevine already condemned him to oblivion? Well, if they expected him to submit tamely, they had misjudged their man. Straightening his necktie, he strode across the room and, without bothering to knock, threw open the door.

Semple immediately rose from his place. "Come away in, McIntosh. Always delighted to see you." Advancing round the table, he grasped the deputy warmly by the hand and escorted him to a vacant seat. "Glad you could spare the time to join us. Now, what about a glass of madeira before we settle to other matters?"

"Thank you, sir, but no. I'm quite ready to answer your questions."

"Questions! Questions? My dear fellow, you're not here to be hauled over the coals. This isn't an inquisition. Quite the contrary. We merely wished the benefit of your advice."

McIntosh relaxed slightly, but was far from fully convinced. It was as well to fear the Greeks, despite the managing director's honeyed tones – or perhaps because of them! His eyes swept round the room, taking in the rich furnishings, gleaming fitments, gilt portraits gazing sternly from the walls, all redolent of power and wealth. Inexorably he was drawn back to the dozen or so directors seated round the table, sharp featured businessmen, hard as granite in the pursuit of profit. While Semple intoned the introductions, he nodded to each in turn. Their expressions told him nothing. One or two inclined their heads slightly, others seemed to stare straight through him; none offered a word of welcome. They resembled so many perching vultures, waiting to gorge themselves on some twitching victim.

"To put you in the picture, McIntosh, this meeting has been convened to deal with last week's accident – the flooding and subsequent fatality."

"I had surmised as much, Mr Semple."

"Just so. By the way, how did the service go off this morning?"

"Quite well, sir. There was a good turn out from the village. And some fulsome tributes from his workmates."

The coalmaster seemed to sense the implied rebuke, but chose to ignore it. "Splendid. A matter of regret, of course, that none of the board could manage along. But then you were present to represent us. For which service we owe you a debt of gratitude, to be sure." He smiled quizzically at the deputy, as though daring him to comment.

"Yes, yes, Mr Chairman," came a testy voice from the opposite side of the table. "That's all very well, but can we get on? We were discussing legal liability for the accident."

"By all means, Mr Guthrie. We can always depend on a banker to keep to the point."

"I'm not one to be sidetracked, as you well know, Semple. It's a simple issue. And from what I gather so far, the company bears no responsibility whatsoever."

"Hear, hear!" There was a muttered growl of agreement and vigorous nodding of heads.

"Your view appears to be popular, Mr Guthrie, and indeed its merits cannot be denied. Yet I feel all avenues should be explored before we put the issue to the vote. There may be considerations we have missed." He turned to the official. "What's your opinion, McIntosh? You were in overall charge, the man on the spot, so to speak."

"I'm well aware of my responsibilities, Mr Semple. As to my opinion, I'm no lawyer, so it's difficult to be precise. But I cannot see how a claim for negligence could be established. Baird's son was a possible witness, but his evidence is worthless. He makes contradictory statements, changes his story almost every time he is questioned. No court could accept his credibility. No, I doubt the true facts will ever emerge."

"You're sure of that?" queried Auld, the oldest director. "If so, then the incident can be considered closed. But mark my words, if blame is to be allocated, then the finger might well point towards mine officials rather than the board. Dereliction of duty is a grave charge. So consider your position well, sir."

"I do not think we need pursue this line of enquiry further," interposed Semple hastily. "We have McIntosh's assurance. And besides, he and I went into the venture very fully before it was decided to reopen the Broom face.

The mine engineer carried out thorough safety checks, or else the project would not have gone ahead. I can call him before the board, if such is your wish."

"No, no need to trouble yourself. Heaven knows there's been enough vaporing on this tinker's curse already. We'll take you at your word. Just settle the matter quietly. And now, if there's nothing else, I've other affairs demanding my attention."

"Bear with me a minute longer, Mr Auld. There is one last detail, but it requires the board's approval."

"And what's that, Semple?" asked Auld wearily, subsiding back into his chair.

"Oh, nothing of importance. The question of a gratuity for Baird's family."

"Gratuity!" ejaculated Guthrie. "Impossible! It would be taken as compensation, an admission of liability. You yourself admit we have no obligation. And you want us to reward sheer carelessness. Think where it might end, man. Paying out every time a pitman scratches his finger? We'd all soon land in Queer Street at that rate."

Semple held up a restraining hand. "Gentlemen, please," he admonished. "There's no question of damages or restitution, though I'm sure McIntosh here would claim we had a moral, if not a legal, commitment. Is that not so, McIntosh?"

"Well, the subject has certainly generated a lot of heat at the pithead. There could be trouble with the men if nothing is done. They regard Baird as something of a hero, sacrificing himself to save others. And so do I," he added, suddenly emboldened. "At least that's how it looks, insofar as I've been able to piece together what happened. It would be churlish to refuse an offering to his family."

"Exactly. That's the nub of the matter," agreed Semple. "We might attract much unfavourable publicity, especially if the press were to get hold of the story. And this is no time to provoke a strike at the colliery. On the other hand, a small gesture of compassion towards the grieving widow would do us no harm at all. Why, handled judiciously, it might even make a modest paragraph or two in the national newspapers. There would be little cost, no liability, no precedent set. What do you say, gentlemen?"

"What sum did you have in mind?" asked Merridew, the Duke's factor.

"Oh, I don't know. Make it a round figure. What say you to a hundred pounds?"

Merridew nodded. "That seems reasonable. I'm sure His Grace would give his approval. So long as it brings the benefits you imply. What about you others?" He looked round the table. No one was prepared to raise an objection.

"And you, Mr Guthrie?" probed Semple gently.

"Very well, then. Have it your own way. I take it the funds will not be at the expense of company profits."

"By no means, Mr Guthrie. Regard it as an investment. One with a very attractive rate of return."

Semple reached into the drawer beneath the table and withdrew two envelopes, one bulky, the other slim. "Just on the off chance, you understand, I had the cash made up earlier this morning. McIntosh, I believe you're the very man to act as emissary. I would be obliged if you would undertake to call on Baird's wife. This other missive is a receipt, and incidentally also a disclaimer absolving the company from any proceedings in connection with the incident. You will, of course, ensure it is signed and witnessed before discharging the settlement."

He slid the packets along the table towards McIntosh. The deputy stared at them with an expression akin to disgust. So this was why he had been summoned – a petty functionary to deliver the board's blood money.

"But suppose she refuses to accept," he ventured to demur. "Or has been advised to demand more, or even go to court."

"Then you'll just have to exercise your charm in advising her of the hopelessness of her position. You might add that, in return for her cooperation, we will refrain from exercising our legal rights to repossess her present abode. She may retain the tenancy on the existing terms."

At least that was something. But it scarcely made the task any less distasteful. He made a final appeal. "I really think it would be more appropriate for a member of the board to hand over the cash. And to extend appropriate condolences to the family."

"The matter is settled, Mr McIntosh," said Semple coldly. "We need detain you no longer. Good day."

Several hours later the mine official was still inwardly seething as he embarked on his painful task, picking his way through ill-lit streets towards

Myrtle Place. His rancour was directed against Semple; his contempt he reserved for himself. True, he had tried to evade the assignment, but it was such a puny, half-hearted gesture. His conscience gnawed like a toothache; it was a beggarly sum he carried in his pocket, the price of a man's life. The reception he faced was uncertain, to say the least; the offering might well be spurned as an insult to Baird's memory. If only he could manage somehow to sweeten the pill, add something extra to the board's pittance. Mrs Baird must be sorely in need of an alternative source of income to support her family. Perhaps there was something he could do in that direction. After all, he did have a certain standing in the community. There was a vacancy for an assistant in the local co-operative store, he recalled. Could he procure the post for her? And would she accept it? He should by rights clear the matter with the committee first, but this might be his only opportunity. He resolved to stretch a point. It was in a more hopeful frame of mind that he rapped smartly on the door.

* * *

"McNair! A word in yer ear, if ye can spare a minute."

The oversman paused in the act of locking the pit cage, and swore in exasperation. The last week had been a harrowing experience, for him as much as anyone else: making safe the workings, sealing up forever the galleries and shafts of the ill-fated Broom seam. Moreover, it was unnerving to sense the unspoken accusations, to feel the disgust, even hatred, directed against him. As though he was in any way to blame! Pit accidents were an everyday fact of life. But it was all over at last, thank Christ. The men shuffled past, anguish etched in their hollow eyes and drawn faces, all desperate to be away from that hellish place. All except one, apparently.

"Well, White, what's the beef now?" He snapped the bar into place with unnecessary force. "Or is it just tae pass the time o' day?"

"Hardly. Ye're no' exactly on my list for social chit chat. More like an exchange o' information. Official, if ye like."

"Ye don't say? And it's that important, is it? It cannae wait?"

"That's about the size o' it. I'm here to speak on behalf o' the shift. We had a meeting during the break down by."

"Oh aye," sneered McNair. "And what would that be about? Ye'd be discussin' Joe Chamberlain and tariff reform, nae doot. Or maybe the employment o' Chink labour in the African mines. Perhaps ye've a notion Semple's goin' to bring in some to the Duchess."

"A rare idea, McNair. But I'm no' risin' to yer bait. There'll be nae Chinese coolies here. No' when we've got home grown ones already. Where wid the profit be?"

"I'm in a fair hurry." The oversman abruptly dropped his bantering tone. "So say what ye must. And make it snappy."

"I'll dae that soon enough. It's about the new allocations. We'll be goin' back to the main seam, I take it?"

"All in good time, White. Ye ken the rules. You'll find out when ye report tomorrow foreshift."

"Aye, just so. But it's no' jist that. We've heard that young Iain Baird will be comin' back."

"So what? Ye cannae expect him to bide on holiday forever. A week off, wi' pay. It's never happened afore. Yon's a lucky laddie."

"No, McNair, ye've the wrong end o' the stick. What I wanted to say, what the lads have delegated me to say, is that they'll no' have him. They'll no' work wi' him underground."

"You cannae talk to me like that," gasped McNair. "It's no' for the likes o' you to pick an' choose who ye'll work wi'. It's sheer impudence on your part. Ye realise what this could mean?"

"Gie yer tongue a rest. Yer crap cuts nae ice wi' me."

McNair could only goggle at this cool defiance. His flash of anger was overtaken by alarm. He felt control of the situation slipping away. Trouble with the workforce was all very well, but not when he was in the firing line, not where he might be held accountable. Bluster gave way to pleading.

"Look, White, try an' see sense. We're both wee cogs in a big muckle machine, just doin' our jobs. Try to change it, an' ye just get chewed up. Let things rest, for a' our sakes."

"Ye dinnae get off that easy. Our minds are made up. Yon boy's a jinx and we'll no' hae him. And that goes for every man jack. So you bugger off, an' dae yer worst."

"On yer ain head be it, then. Dinnae say I didnae warn ye. But I'm takin' nae responsibility. This is far ower rich for me. Come you an' explain yerself to the deputy. He can decide."

"Lead on, then. There's a light in his windae."

McIntosh was indeed burning the midnight oil, grinding his way through the mound of accumulated paperwork on his desk. Somewhat to his surprise, though much to his relief, the visit to Kate Baird had been crowned with success. After only a token show of resistance she had accepted both the company's banknotes and his own tentative offer of a situation. And she had exercised such tact and courtesy that in no way had he felt demeaned by the experience. Semple, too, had made a point of congratulating him when he had reported back, again hinting that the possibility of an under-manager's position was not totally out of the question. All in all, perhaps as reasonable a conclusion to the affair as could be hoped.

"Come in!" The interruption was hardly welcome, but drew only a grunt of mild vexation from the pit deputy. His brow darkened at once, however, as a red faced oversman burst in, followed by an outwardly placid Cha White. This betokened squalls ahead, he could sense it. Privately, he had never cared overmuch for McNair. Promotion had puffed him up like a popinjay; he was too officious, far too inclined to abuse his petty authority. Constant bickering, trivial complaints and general ill-feeling seemed to be the order of the day in his section. And now seemingly here was yet another bone of contention – just when things were beginning to shake down again.

"Well, McNair," he said wearily, throwing down his pencil. "What ails you now?"

"It's this man here," spluttered the foreman. "I warned him. But he widnae be telt. So I'd nae option."

"You're havering, McNair. Stop talking in riddles."

"It's wilful disobedience, Mr McIntosh. Nae less. An' I bent over backwards. Warned him o' the consequences. But he widnae listen."

"Grant me patience! Is this a guessing game? What the hell has White done to put you in such a fluster?"

"Like I said, it's a conspiracy. They're threatenin' to go on strike if young Baird isnae sacked."

So that was it. Iain Baird had been cast as the scapegoat, condemned for abandoning his father. Tribal loyalties were intense; any miner breaching the code could expect no mercy. It was a tricky situation, no mistake about it; and God help him if he made a wrong move. His responsibility was to nip trouble in the bud, above all to avert any threat of industrial action. He would be held culpable for any break in production.

"Thank you, McNair. I think I have the picture now. You were quite right to bring the matter to my attention."

"Jist so, sir. Only doin' my duty."

"Quite. Well, you may rely on me to take appropriate steps. No doubt you'll want to be off home now."

The oversman flinched; he had not expected such a peremptory dismissal. "By yer leave, sir," he stammered. "I ken it's no' my place, but I must say –"

"Yes." The tone was not encouraging.

"Beggin' yer pardon, but ye don't know the half o' it. The colliery would be well rid o' this troublemaker. Make an example o' him. That'll bring the rest to their senses."

"I'm obliged for your opinion," said McIntosh icily. "I'll bear it in mind. Good night to you."

McNair made as if to volunteer another observation, but thought better of it. He contented himself with a glower of malevolence at the pitman as he left.

"And now, White," said McIntosh, "you've been very quiet this while."

"I've hardly been given the chance to do anythin' else. What wi' thon jabbergowk bummin' his load."

"Damn your eyes!" snapped the deputy. "You'll keep a civil tongue in your head. The charge is wilful disobedience. Is that not enough for you?"

Cha shrugged. "His word against mine. But nae doot you'll choose to believe him. An' likely take his advice."

"Bunkum! I run things as I see fit. And I'm not totally unaware of, let's say the climate, down by. Otherwise you'd be out on your arse long since. So just you simmer down, and let's see whether we can find a way out of this mess."

"Fine by me, Mr McIntosh. I admit that we did hae a wee bit o' a disagreement, but he's made the most o' it."

"How so?"

"I telt him we wouldnae work alongside Baird, but I never said he should be turfed out. We're no' that heartless."

95

"Oh. So what do you suggest?"

"Find him another job. Some place he can do nae harm. Where he'll no' put lives at stake."

The deputy stroked his chin reflectively. "A move might well be in the boy's interests," he mused "A spell on the surface, in less demanding work, might help him adjust. In his present state of mind he could do himself a mischief underground."

"Accidents can always happen," agreed White.

"And in these exceptional circumstances I think I may be able to square Head Office. Stop them regrading Baird – cutting his pay, I mean. The family has suffered enough already without further financial worries."

"Well, I suppose it's fair enough. I think we might be able to go along wi' that."

"Very obliging of you, I'm sure," said McIntosh drily. "I'll pass on your apologies to McNair."

"What! I wouldnae apologise tae yon b –"

"Don't press your luck, White. I'm not asking you to grovel. But wheels have to be oiled sometimes. A bit of soft soap, eh? Just try to be civil to the man."

"Aye well, maybe ye've a point. I'll no' rock the boat. If there's nothin' else, I'll be away and let ye get on. Good night to ye."

On that note they parted, each well satisfied with the outcome. What Iain Baird's feelings might be never entered their considerations.

* * *

"Chrissake, Baird! Put some beef into it. I've seen mair life on a butcher's slab. There's nae place for slap dash ways up here, ye ken. No' like yer cushy life down by."

Iain clenched his fists. It was his tormentor again, clumping on the sleepers as he hobbled up on his wooden leg, the legacy of some long forgotten accident. McNair had been bad enough, but this overlooker seemed the devil incarnate, with darting eyes that missed nothing and a biting tongue that cut like a whiplash. He yearned to launch himself at this tyrant of the grading shed, to smash that leering face to a red pulp. But ... he knew it would never happen. As though by way of solace he tugged violently at the catch of his hutch, freeing the cradle, before jerking it over to send its cargo of stone and rubble crashing down on the slag heap below.

"So it's got a temper, has it? Maybe we can change that afore ye're finished here. They tell me ye were a demon at the puttin', so it's only natural to make use o' yer rare talent. A kind o' step up, ye might say, plyin' yer trade in the midden." He laughed raucously at his own witticism. "Nothin' to say for yerself? A' weel, there's the hooter. Far be it for me to keep ye from yer social engagements."

Social engagements! Iain curled his lip. That bastard certainly knew how to turn the knife. Only two or three short weeks ago he would have made hay on a Saturday afternoon, run with the crowd, let off steam after the fag of work. Now he was shunned by his fellows: demoted, stripped of his status underground, packed off to the surface in disgrace. Even here he was allocated the most menial of tasks. Not for him to tip the hoppers or grade the coal or even load the railway wagons. No, he was just the rubbish man, dumping the shit on the slag heap.

And life was scarcely any better at home. There was a frostiness that chilled him to the marrow; hardly a word was spoken when he was in the house. His brother and sister seemed to shrink from him; their fear and disgust were only too obvious. Worst of all was the hurt in his mother's eye, an expression of silent accusation that was almost unbearable. And it was all so unjust, so totally unfair. He was not to blame. Anyone else would have done the same.

 He aimed a vicious kick at a stone as he trudged away. The solid contact was vaguely satisfying, piercing the fog of his self-pity. No point in just moping; that would solve nothing. If only there was a way to fight back. There had to be some means to repay those who had wronged him. A wheen of broken windows would make them sit up – McIntosh, White and their ilk. But how much would he manage before the alarm was raised? And if he was caught in the act … No, that game was just too risky. It would have to be something a deal less obvious.

That left the colliery. Christ! He felt a surge of glee. If he could pull off a stroke at the pit – like tamper with some piece of machinery – then that would strike at the whole community, hit them where it hurt most. Any damage would take time to repair, with inevitable loss of earnings. There was nothing to be managed during the day, of course. But under cover of darkness, now there was a different kettle of fish – especially when there was no nightshift on hand. That meant Saturday – tonight!

His heartbeat quickened. The gates would be locked, but entry presented no problems; there were any number of gaps in the perimeter fence. The night watchman was old and crippled; fat chance of him poking his head out of doors on a snell night. Once inside the grounds, the whole mine was his oyster. But there could be only one choice. The engine house! It drew him like a magnet. That was the hub of the entire workings. Damage the winding gear and it would be days, perhaps weeks, before it was back in operation. And he knew just how to tackle the job. Not for him to hurl a handful of sand into the cylinder box or set about the cogs with a sledgehammer. There was a much better way. He would simply blow it up! That would create the impact he craved, no question of it. The blast would rouse the whole district; from Semple himself to the lowest waif they would come flocking to the scene. It should be easy enough to blend into the crowd, there to savour the fruits of his handiwork whilst posing as an innocent onlooker.

He ran over the materials he would require. Shot and fuse and matches, of course. And a miner's lamp to see what he was doing. Explosives were kept under secure lock and key at the mine, and could only be issued by an official. But that was not a setback. Since each hewer had to pay for what he used, it was rare for any surplus to be returned. More often than not it was carried home, to be used up on a future occasion. And Iain was well aware of his father's store, stuffed away in a tin box in the small shed outside the scullery. There still remained the task of packing the shot and fitting the fuse, but he had watched the operation before; it all seemed straightforward enough. Even a small charge, fixed in the right place, would surely wreck the winding mechanism beyond repair. His eyes glittered with excitement at the prospect.

* * *

Kate paced restlessly up and down the confines of her kitchen. She could not settle in her chair by the fire, far less bring herself to go to bed. The hour was late; and not a sign of Iain yet. The boy was a law unto himself, but it was rare for him to miss a meal. Now both his dinner and supper had long since burnt into a congealed mess. Something was surely amiss. Fretful, anxious, and not a little guilt ridden, her mind was prey to all manner of fears. Suddenly she stiffened. There was a faint rustling in the yard outside. She peered out of the window, rubbed the glass, but could make nothing of the inky blackness. There it was again, more distinct – the creak of the outhouse door, a muttered curse, then the crash of objects knocked to the ground. There was the flicker of a match, and in that instant she recognised her son. To that extent it was a relief. But what on earth was he doing? Snatching up the oil lamp, she wrenched open the latch.

"Iain, is that you, laddie? D'ye ken the time? It's past eleven o'clock. Where have you been? And why are ye barging about in there?"

The boy whirled round, clutching an old tin biscuit box tightly to his chest. Kate's suspicions were now thoroughly aroused. Stepping into the shed, she stared in horror through the glimmer of the lamp. She had forgotten the very existence of that box, but did not need to be reminded of its contents.

"Iain, that tin belongs to your faither. You've no business with it."

"Well, he'll no' be wantin' it now. I – I mean I was just lookin' for a place to keep some things. There's nae harm in that, surely?"

"Put it back where you found it." Kate tried to stay calm, though her heart was racing. "It's dangerous even to touch. There's blasting powder and the likes in it. I never approved of your faither keeping such things at home. And since he's gone there's even less excuse."

"But I could get rid o' it for you. It would be nae bother."

"Very kind of you, I'm sure, but it's my responsibility. I think I'd prefer to see it gets back safe to the pit mysel'."

"No, ye cannae do that!" It was almost a howl of protest.

"God sakes! Iain, what nonsense is this? What would you do with explosives?" A sudden thought made her blood run cold. "Are ye mad? You could kill someone." She grasped his arm beseechingly. "You dinnae know how to set a charge. Ye might blow yourself up. I'll no' let you do it."

"Out o' my way. It's somethin' I have to dae."

She only clung to him more forcefully.

"Let go, damn ye! I'm warnin' you."

There was the briefest of tussles before Iain threw off his mother's despairing grasp. Kate reeled backwards, striking her head against a protruding bracket. Her body began to shake convulsively; blood oozed from a gash in her scalp. Scarcely aware of what she was doing, she lurched into the yard and managed to stagger the few steps to the refuge of her kitchen.

The familiar surroundings eased her numbed senses, helped clear her befuddled mind. Then the reality of the nightmare struck home. Iain was gone – hell-bent on some madcap scheme! The consequences she hardly dared envisage. Sheer desperation gave her the strength of will to pull her wits together, try to think constructively. Her puny efforts had failed miserably, but she could not just admit defeat. If only there was somewhere she could find help … Mr McIntosh! She could think of no one else who might prevent a disaster. Mercifully he lived only a few streets away, in one of the end houses reserved for colliery officials. Winding her shawl about her, she hirpled away into the night. Within minutes she was beating frantically on his door.

"All right! Enough! I can hear you. Stop that devilish din. I'm coming as fast as I can." The door was unbolted. "Is there no rest for a man? What's the bother now?" McIntosh peered into the shadows. "What on earth –? Good Lord, it's Mrs Baird. But come in. You look fair knocked up."

"There's no time. It might be too late already."

"Tush, woman. First things first. Trust me." Gently he drew her inside. "Why, you're shaking like a leaf. And that's blood on your shawl. Sit you down and let's have a closer look."

"No, it's nothing. I must go."

"You'll do no such thing. I insist." Deftly he slipped the garment from her head, then grimaced at the dark stain of coagulating blood. "Beth!" he shouted up the stairs. "Lend a hand here. Some lint and iodine. And a dash o' whisky."

"But don't ye see, Mr McIntosh?" Kate protested. "It's Iain. He's gone daft. Got hold o' blasting powder. Run off wi' it, God knows where."

McIntosh started violently, but the oath of alarm and dismay died on his lips. The woman was obviously close to breakdown; it would do no good to push her over the edge.

"Aye, just so." He contrived to contain his feelings. "I had a notion it was something of the kind. How long since you saw him last?"

"I – I hardly know. Maybe quarter of an hour."

"Then there's still a chance. He's probably made for the mine."

"But why do you suppose that?"

"Stands to reason. Whatever he's up to, he'll not want to be seen. Too many prying eyes around in the village. And I doubt he's made for Semple's house. Bide here while I get dressed. I've my bicycle in the yard. I might be able to head him off."

"That's awful good o' ye. I cannae thank you enough. But – you'll go easy on him? He doesnae realise what he's doing."

"Mrs Baird, I'll do what I can. If he's caught before any damage is done, I may be able to keep the police out of it. More I can't promise. Now, rest yourself and let my wife tend your injuries."

* * *

Iain kicked at the door in anger and disgust. It had never occurred to him that the building might be bolted and shuttered. He swore bitterly as he lit his lamp and set himself to examine the lock. The mechanism was massive enough, but old and rusty, with signs of rot in the surrounding wood. A determined assault with some heavy object might smash it open. And as luck would have it, there were a number of pit props stacked against the wall. He hefted a five foot beam; solid yet manageable, it would serve as a battering ram. Then, pacing out his run, he turned, cradled the billet in his arms and lunged forward. The door shook under the violence of the impact but did not give way. He redoubled his efforts; again and again hammer blows crashed against the lock. Under such a fusillade it gradually weakened, till finally, amid a fearful rendering and splintering, it sheared off completely. The door swung free on its hinges. Snatching up the lamp and his precious box, Iain paused on the threshold. The racket had been enough to wake the dead, but now there was nothing, only the low moan of the wind. Reassured, he slipped into the building.

McIntosh swung down from his bicycle at the pit entrance. Flushed and blown from furious pedalling, he fumbled for his key to unlock the wicket. There seemed no purpose in knocking up the gatekeeper; it was doubtful if the old fool had heard anything. Once inside the gate he hesitated, uncertain as to his best course of action. The young ass might be anywhere; finding him would be a tall order. As he pondered, trying to decide on the most likely target, his ears picked up the faint boom of a distant thud, then several more at brief intervals. Someone trying to break into the winding house; it could be nothing else. Buoyed with fresh hope, the deputy remounted and fairly flew on.

In his search for a suitable place to plant his charge Iain explored the mass of cogs and rods, shafts, belts and pulleys which linked the beam engine with the winding wheel far above. The spluttering lamp cast weird shadows, but there was sufficient illumination for his purpose. Setting down the box, he knelt beside it and carefully began to withdraw the tubes of black powder. Engrossed in his task, he had no inkling of the footfall in the doorway. But terror clutched at his heart as the room was suddenly engulfed in a flood of light. He froze, half-blinded by the dazzle, rooted to the spot by this bolt from the blue.

"That's a braw bit of handiwork. You must be fair proud of your efforts." The ringing sneer was enough to chill the spine. "But you'll never make a shotfirer, laddie. Not if you go about the business like that. Best leave things you don't understand well alone."

Iain could only goggle helplessly, as though at some apparition, as the pit deputy strode towards him; he watched numbly as the charges were deftly retrieved, repacked in the tin and the lid closed with a decisive snap. Then he felt hands on his collar dragging him to his feet.

"Idiot! Try explaining your way out of this one. Caught red-handed. And likely you'd have botched it anyway and we'd be scraping you off the wall. You really take the biscuit, and then some."

"But how did ye know?" Iain found his voice at last. "How could ye guess? I told naebody I was comin' here."

"Hold your tongue. You're in no position to ask questions. Do I need to spell it out? It's my plain duty to hand you over to police custody. You'd be prosecuted for criminal damage. You could spend years in prison. With hard labour, I don't doubt."

Iain blinked at him apprehensively. "It was just a wee bit o' a joke," he protested feebly. "Surely I wouldnae get the jail for that?"

"Joke, you say! I'd be much surprised if the court saw it that light. What kind of a specimen are you? Instead of being a comfort and support, you do your damnedest to heap shame and disgrace on your family. But I'll tell you what I'm prepared to do. I'll undertake to keep the police out of it. Not for your sake, mind, not to save your miserable hide. It's for your mother, never forget that.

After all she's had to endure, I'll not have her good name besmirched by you."

A flicker of relief danced in the boy's eyes; the ghost of a smirk twitched on the corner of his mouth. McIntosh smiled sourly.

"Don't build your hopes. You called the tune, so you'll pay the piper all the same." His voice grated harshly. "You're finished here at the Duchess. As of this moment. And if I find you on colliery property again, I'll give you in charge."

"Sacked?" croaked Iain, almost in disbelief. "What's to become of me? What'll I dae? There's nae other work to be had round here."

"That's your problem. You're getting off lightly as it is. But I'll put it about that you gave notice, left of your own accord. That way there'll be no black mark against you. That's all I can do. Now get out of my sight before I forget myself and give you the hiding you deserve. You're not fit for human society."

* * *

Alastair tossed and turned, then woke with a start. So it was not just a bad dream. The gentle, insistent tugging at his bed clothes was only too real. Rubbing the sleep from his eyes, he sat up to confront the shadow crouched at his cot.

"Mary? Is that you? What's up? It cannae be morning yet."

"Thank God. I thought ye'd never wake. Dead to the world, that's you."

"Ye didnae get me up just to tell me that?"

"No, of course no'. But there's something wrong. And it's got me fair worried."

"What d'ye mean?"

"Somethin' woke me up. I heard maw pacing up and down the kitchen. It went on an' on. I couldnae get back to sleep. Then she went out into the yard. There was a bit o' a dunt, like somethin' falling over."

"What was it?"

"I couldnae make it out, but I heard her come back. Then she went out again."

"What did ye do then?"

"I waited and listened for a while. Then I took a peek downstairs. There was nae sign o' her. And when I looked at the clock it was near midnight.

She's been gone for ages. And that's no' all. Iain isnae in his bed either."

Alastair jerked round towards the dim outline across the attic room.

"What should we dae?" It was Mary who posed the question. Generally she took charge, but this went far beyond her capacity to handle.

"Well," said Alastair slowly, "we've no idea where she might be. And there'll be nobody to ask at this time o' night."

"But we cannae just do nothing."

"We could maybe knock up the bobby, but I doubt he'll no' thank us for that. Or yon Mr McIntosh. That might be a better notion. Mother speaks well o' him. Let's bide another half hour. If she's no' back by then, we'll go for help."

They spoke in whispers, speculating on what might have happened, clinging to each other in the gnawing uncertainty. The minutes dragged past. The time was all but up when they heard footsteps in the yard. With a cry of relief, the pair almost flung themselves down the stairs, wrenched open the door and dashed outside into Kate's astonished arms.

"Where on earth have ye been, maw?" sobbed Mary. "We thought ye'd had an accident. Lying somewhere injured, maybe even –" She left the last word unsaid.

"Just as well you came back when ye did," blurted Alastair. "We were just about to look for you."

"Never mind about that," said Mary hastily. She was beginning to recover some composure. "You must be fair done in, maw. Come away and sit by the fire. Alastair, red up and put on more coal. I'll fill the kettle. A cup of tea will do you good."

"Thank ye, lass. I am a bit weary, I'll not deny it."

"But where could ye have gone this late at night?" persisted Alastair. "And did ye ken Iain's never been home."

"Wheesht, Alastair," warned Mary. "Let her get her breath back."

"No, no, I'm fine now. And I can see ye must have been worried. I just didnae think you would wake and find the house empty."

"Aye well, ye're back safe and sound. That's the main thing. Just you rest while we get things ready. Alastair, take maw's shawl and hang it up."

"That's a bandage you've got on!" cried Alastair in alarm, as Kate fumbled with her headscarf. "You are hurt! Is it bad?"

"Dinnae be silly. It's only a wee scratch. I banged my heid in the dark, that's all. No need to fuss. Now what about that cuppa ye promised?"

Kate eased herself into the fireside chair. Heavy-lidded from sheer exhaustion, oblivious to the bustle around her, she felt an irresistible drowsiness. Her head drooped, within moments she had dozed off. Indeed, some minutes later Mary had to shake her mother's arm quite firmly to rouse her.

"Wakey, wakey! Tea's ready. You take a sip of this. It's just how ye like it."

Kate smiled. "I must have dropped off. Sorry." The two children watched as she cradled the cup in both hands, savouring its warmth and aroma, before putting it to her lips and drinking deeply.

"Eh, but that's grand," she sighed gratefully. "I needed that."

"Can ye tell us what happened now?" Alastair could contain himself no longer.

"A'ways the impatient one, aren't ye?" chided Kate gently. "But I do owe the pair o' ye an explanation."

"More tea first?" Without waiting for a reply Mary refilled the cup.

"That's fine, hinnie. Truth to tell, there's no' much to it. I was a bit upset, what wi' Iain and that. No' a sight nor sound o' him. I jaloused that something must have happened. So I took the notion to go round and ask Mr McIntosh, see if he could think o' anything. He's a good man, that. Couldnae do enough to help. He even promised to find Iain himself. I saw him ride off on his bicycle. In the pitch dark and middle o' the night! It was his wife who dressed my cut. She wanted me to stay there till news came, but I said I had to get back."

"Ye're safe home now," said Mary comfortingly. "And ye've nae idea how glad we are o' that."

"Aye, that's so," agreed Alastair. "But wherever can Iain be? He's never been this late."

"That's enough now, weans," said Kate. "I'm thankful for the tea, but it's long past your bedtimes. Up the stairs wi' the pair o' you. Iain will be back afore long, I've nae doubt."

Mary scrambled to her feet … then gasped with horror, pointed and screamed. Startled almost out of her wits, Kate and Alastair could only follow her trembling finger. There, framed in the window, was a leering apparition. The face disappeared and an instant later the door crashed open.

"My, what a touchin' wee scene we have here." The voice was harsh and mocking. "Glad to hear ye all missed me. Fair warms my heart, so it does. But I'm here now. One happy family again."

"Name o' God!" cried Kate. "Iain! What a fright. Ye near gave us heart failure. Never do a thing like that again."

Iain shrugged his shoulders dismissively. "Man, that's a rare heat. Just the job to thaw out a body on a cauld night outside." He slammed the latch shut and swaggered into the room. "But then you'd ken all about that."

"What do ye mean? You're no' making sense," protested Kate. "It's you that owes us an explanation. Stayin' out till this hour. Drivin' us sick wi' worry."

"Explanation!" snarled Iain. "That's rich, even from you. Who are ye tryin' to kid? You ken fine where I've been. Naebody else could have set McIntosh on me. He wisnae just out for an evenin' stroll. You clyped to that bastard. Shopped yin o' your own to the bosses. How could ye do it?"

"No, Iain. You've got the wrong end of the stick. It wisnae that way at all. I was concerned for you. I only wanted to help. It was to protect you – from yourself. Don't ye see?"

"Help me? You did that a' right. You knew I was goin' to the mine. You went and told McIntosh. He found me. And sacked me on the spot. That's how much you helped me."

"But laddie, ye werena yourself. You had a tin o' powder. There was nae tellin' what you might do. Blow yourself up, like as no'. I couldnae live wi' that."

"Thanks for nothin'!"

"I ken you're upset. But losing your job is no' the end of the world. You'll see things different once you've calmed doon. We can talk things over in the mornin', when ye can think straight. You need some rest now. Why no' get off to bed."

"Save the pap. I'm no' a bairn to be mollycoddled. No' any more. I'll make my own decisions. In fact I've already made up my mind."

"Just so, son. As ye please. But will it no' keep?"

"No, it won't. We'll have it out here and now. I'm out o' a job, thanks to you. And there'll be nothin' for me round here. Trust McIntosh for that. I'll have to leave. Glesga maybe. Or abroad. I've always had a hankerin' to see the world. But it'll take time to find a billet. So you'll need to come up wi' the goods."

"Money, ye mean? You know fine how we're fixed. I might manage to scrape up some siller, a few shillings maybe, but that'd be all. You'd no' go far on that."

"Damned right! It's gold sovs I'm after."

"For any's sake! It's deluded ye are. Think I can conjure up gold out o' thin air? I'm no' a magician."

"No? Have ye not overlooked somethin'? A wee detail that's slipped yer mind?"

"What on earth dae ye mean?"

"Do I have to spell it out? The money ye got for faither. The payoff ye took. Surely I'm entitled to my share. And I'm for havin' it now."

"So ye've tumbled to that. Well, forbye anything else, I'd hardly keep it here in the house. It's in the Post Office. And they're not likely to open on the Sabbath, no' for you or anyone else."

"I'm not daft. I can wait till Monday. But cheer up. Ye'll be rid o' me for good. Dinnae pretend that widnae please ye. And I'll get my due. Call it a return for what ye did. Fair do's? We can part wi' no hard feelings."

Kate contrived to hide her disgust. "And what sum did ye have in mind. Five pounds? Ten pounds maybe?"

"Yer arse! I might have expected ye'd try it on. Fob me off wi' a pittance. But it'll no' do. I've seen your Post Office book. And I want half. Fifty pounds. Ye owe me that."

"You'd stoop to raking through other folks' property?"

"It's a family matter. Ye'd nae right to keep it a secret."

Deathly pale, Kate rose from her seat. "I've tried to reason with you, tried to make allowances for my own flesh and blood, but, God help me, you're deranged. You've no' the gumption to fetch for yourself. Maybe I cannae stop you leaving. But you winnae see a brass farthing. I'm not goin' to waste money on a fool's errand."

"You'll gie me what's mine," growled Iain menacingly, "or else –"

"Or nothing." Kate was openly contemptuous. "Ye'd fritter away every penny in a week. A fine tribute to your father's memory. The sum is little enough as it is. It's the future for this family, so it's not going to be squandered. The money's already spoken for."

"Spoken for? How?"

"You can like it or lump it. But you might as well know now. It's set aside for Alastair's schooling. He deserves the chance to make something of himself. He'll do us proud. Can you say that?"

"Alastair! That milksop. I might have guessed. Nothin' but the best for him. Always lookin' down yer nose at me. Why, I've a good mind to –"

Snatching the poker from the grate, he drew back his arm like a coiled snake about to strike. His face twisted into a hideous rage, but Kate's scornful gaze never flinched.

"Go on, you coward. Hit a defenceless woman. Finish off what you started outside in the dark. Your father must be turning in his grave with shame. That his son could fall so low."

For a moment time stood still. Then with a strangulated cry, a diminutive form hurled itself at the elder boy, grabbing for the weapon. It was a gesture as brave as it was futile. Iain shook off his assailant with no more trouble than swatting a fly. A single swipe sufficed to knock him spinning across the room. Alastair collapsed in a heap, sobbing. Mary rushed to his aid.

But the distraction had served its purpose. Iain took a step towards his mother, then stopped, irresolute. Finally, with a roar of frustration, he brought the poker crashing down on the mantelpiece, raining blow after blow at the ornaments on the shelf, sending the fragments of pottery cascading to the floor. As if warming to his orgy of devilment, he proceeded to sweep the plates from the dresser. As a parting shot he hurled the poker at the kitchen window; the pane disintegrated with an almighty crack. At the door he surveyed his litany of destruction.

"Something to mind me by. Ye think ye're done wi' me. But I'll no' be cheated." He spat out his derision. "Fuck ye all. One day I'll be back, be sure o' it."

SIX

New horizons

Glasgow. October 1905

The bedraggled, half-starved youth shivered in the raw autumn night. There was little shelter to be had on the edge of the waste ground where slum housing was being demolished, but at least the dark shadow gave him concealment, while providing a perfect view of the bright lights of the tavern. He blew on his hands and stamped his feet in a vain endeavour to inject a little warmth into his body. In the distance he heard the chime of a clock. They would be coming out soon, leaving comfort and conviviality to stagger homewards.

It was money for old rope – or so he had been told. The trick was to lurk near a public house, watch for anyone obviously the worse for wear, follow at a discreet distance; then rush up, knock the man over, rifle his pockets and make off before the victim could respond. But somehow it rarely seemed to work out like that. On occasion there was an opportunity to relieve a workman of the remnants of his Friday pay packet, but these were few and far between. Most targets had little more than a few pennies after an evening's carousing. Some were not too drunk to resist or raise the alarm, and often he had had to take to his heels to avoid capture. Once or twice he had evaded the clutches of the law only by the skin of his teeth. How long before his luck finally ran out?

The last months had brought mixed fortunes for Iain Baird. It had taken him three days to reach Glasgow, taking refuge in outhouses and byres by night, tramping the highways and byways by day, cadging lifts whenever he could, only to discover that the Second City of the Empire was in the icy grip of a trade depression. The evidence was there in stark reality – thousands thrown out of work, left to the charity of soup kitchens and the poor law. As for his vague idea of a life at sea, no one would take him on, not the meanest tramp steamer, not even a humble *puffer* plying its trade up and down the coast. In times of heavy unemployment only the most experienced had any chance of a berth.

Still, there were jobs to be had – if only in the sweatshops of the most menial and ill-paid trades. An opening for a bottle washer in an East End lemonade plant meant long hours for only twelve shillings a week, but steady work for all that – at least so long as the season lasted. And one of his fellow operatives had volunteered to find him a billet. It was no more than a shared room in an overcrowded tenement, but beggars could not be choosers. Thus he had drifted along through the spring and summer. But everything suddenly changed when he found himself paid off at the end of August.

A bleak autumn followed, with only an occasional day's hire – billboard carrier, road sweeper, casual labour of the lowest kind. His fast diminishing resources inevitably led to arrears of rent. His landlord's good-natured geniality had given way to scowling enmity, veiled hints replaced by open threats. In desperation he had turned to thieving.

The sound of voices roused him from his despondency. The street opposite was no longer deserted. It was beginning to fill with people, in ones and twos at first, then larger groups, hurrying along towards some unknown destination. Even the denizens of the alehouse came tumbling out as if determined not to miss whatever was going on. Curiosity got the better of him, drawing him from his hiding place to join the swelling throng. Only then did he become aware of a dull red glow spreading across the night sky.

"What's up?" he asked, to no one in particular.

"Fire!" cried someone behind him.

"Aye. Doon by the river. Near the wharves," said another.

"They say it's a textile works. Out o' control," added a third.

Iain allowed himself to be swept along. A crowd offered new possibilities. Perhaps he might manage to dip a pocket or two in the crush. At least there would be a bit of excitement.

The pace quickened, and suddenly there it was. Rounding a corner, he took in the whole scene at a glance. The road sloped sharply downhill, with the mill in open ground at its far end. The conflagration had by now taken a firm hold; tongues of flame licked from the windows and roof of the building, fusillades of sparks shot high into the sky, the acrid stench of thick smoke filled the air. Harassed policemen were trying to push the onlookers back to a safe distance, but they appeared far too few in number to make any real impact. Beyond them, tiny figures were making vain attempts to tackle the blaze. Even at a distance, the heat was stifling.

This was getting too close for comfort. High time he was about his business. It should be easy as pie. Everyone had eyes only for the fire – or for their own safety. Iain moved into the thick of the crowd. Ah, here was a likely mark. Good quality coat, slight bulge in one pocket. A furtive look round, then gently slip in his fingers.

"Watch out, Jackie!" yelled a voice. "Yon de'il's trying to rob ye. Grab the bugger!"

Iain snatched back his hand as though stung. Instinctively he swivelled round and, ducking the clumsy effort to seize him, head-butted his assailant in the stomach. Then he was off, running like the wind, down side streets, through alleyways, in a desperate attempt to throw off any chase. At last, blown and panting, he stopped to catch his breath. He could hear nothing; all was quiet as the grave. A high stone wall loomed up ahead. Above it, a red glare was clearly visible. Jesus! This must be the other side of the mill; in his flight he had skirted right round it. A few street lights cast isolated pools of illumination. Behind the nearest lamppost he noticed a narrow side door, little more than a wicket gate, set into the stonework.

Footsteps approached. Iain shrank back into the darkness. It was a short, stout individual, in a long overcoat and bowler hat; he could see him quite clearly under the lamplight. Obviously not a worker, nor yet a toff either. He could only watch as the man halted by the gate and tested the handle; then, drawing back, fetched a kick against the lock. The door crashed back on its hinges and the figure disappeared inside. Strange, thought Iain, but it was not his concern. Shrugging his shoulders, he had turned to walk away when he heard an almighty whoosh, followed by the loud crump of an explosion. For a moment he stood rooted to the spot. Then, scarcely realising what he was doing, he gave a strangled oath, sprang forward and dashed in at the doorway.

* * *

"Lang! Adam Lang!" The call was loud and peremptory.

The reporter scowled, but otherwise gave no sign of acknowledgement.

Instead he shuffled a few papers on his battered desk and pretended to look busy. That prig of a sub-editor was getting too big for his boots. Around him, the newsroom was a hive of industry; journalists consulting notes, filing their copy, some even thumping out their contributions on typewriters. Blast! Here was the young popinjay threading his way towards the little alcove that partially hid him from view.

"Are you deaf? I've little time to waste, chasing you up. The news editor wants you in his office. Right away."

"I hear you," growled Lang. "And the name's Mister Lang, sonny. Messenger boy for the brass, and you think you're cock o' the walk."

"Look at you," sneered the youth. "Just another hack, run to seed. But I'm not here to bandy words. You've got your instructions. Don't keep him waiting."

Lang made a rude gesture towards the departing figure. Cruel, he thought, but true all the same. Once he had been an ace newshound on a national daily, his byline on many a top story, but now he was reduced to a dogsbody on a downmarket rag, handed unimportant trivia no one else wanted. He lit a cigarette and stretched back in his chair. How had the mighty fallen, he thought wryly.

It was his own fault; he was honest enough to admit it. Long hours, little exercise, pressure of deadlines, snatched meals and over-fondness for whisky had worked their ravages on mind and body. Domestic life had not helped either; marriage had proved both childless and largely loveless. Before long he had taken to staying out till all hours, either at the office or in some public house, to escape the constant nagging. And then, five years ago, the fever had carried her off; he could still see those reproachful eyes as she took her last breaths. He had been left to rattle around alone in that huge, cheerless apartment in Garnethill. No wonder he preferred the dubious companionship of the *Dispatch* office, even though there was often little enough to keep him occupied.

He sighed, and flicked his stub into the sand bucket. Better get it over with. His delay in answering the summons was finely calculated, just long enough to show he was no one's lackey, but not so glaring as to invite retribution. Unhurriedly he tramped from the room and trudged upstairs.

"At last!" said the editor testily. "What d'you call this? Took your time in getting here, didn't you?"

"Sorry, sir," replied Lang meekly. "Call of nature." He met his superior's sharp glance unflinchingly.

"Well, let that pass. I've a job for you. Right up your street."

"I'm listening."

"You'll have heard about the big fire at Murdoch's? Down by the Clyde."

"Of course. But the place will be crawling with newsmen already."

"That's as may be. There's another angle I want you to look into. A fair number of mills have gone up in smoke in the last year or two. Quite a coincidence, eh? There's been rumours of deliberate fire raising."

"So you think that's the case here?"

"Could be. You know the score. Trade is depressed. Owners can't pay their bills. So they set fire to the mill for the insurance money. I want you to nose around and see what you can sniff out."

"What? Now? While the mill's still ablaze?"

"No time like the present. Wait till tomorrow and any evidence might be destroyed. You know the *Dispatch* has always prided itself on its investigative journalism. This is a chance to sink your teeth into something really worthwhile. Quite like the old days, Lang."

He saw the doubt in Lang's eyes, the protest on his lip, and his blandishments took on a new harshness.

"Not another word, if you know what's good for you. You're not exactly indispensable. When did you last pull your weight? Your services, such as they are, would scarcely be missed. So get your tail out of here while you're still on the payroll."

Lang nodded. Further complaint would be futile; that was no idle threat. What on earth was he expected to achieve at this time of night? It was senseless. No, more than that, it was just plain dangerous. And that bastard upstairs knew it. Not worth sending a top sleuth – a washed-out old relic would do. And if by some miracle the long shot paid off, the case would be handed over to someone else, and his initial discovery conveniently forgotten. He wrenched hat and coat from the stand and thrust pencil and notebook into his pocket. At least he could travel in style. He would take one of those new motor-taxis and charge it to expenses. They could make what they liked of that. A small gesture, but it gave some comfort.

By the time he arrived on the scene police reinforcements had enabled an effective cordon to be formed. Lang flashed his press card and was admitted through the line.

"Best be careful, sir," said a constable. "Don't get too close. These flames could jump anywhere. There's some of your mates down by." He indicated a knot of pressmen.

Journalists were scribbling on their pads, photographers setting up huge, unwieldy cameras, their assistants holding aloft the phosphorescent flash equipment; the results would provide the lurid accounts and grainy images for the gratification of the Glasgow citizenry in the morning. Lang strolled over.

"Look who's here, chaps," said a voice. "Old Pot-Belly himself. Managed to drag yourself away from the bar, Adam? Come to see the fun?"

Lang ignored the quip. He caught sight of a sympathetic face. Macdonald was a fellow reporter on the *Dispatch*, one of the few still prepared to pass the time of day with him.

"How are things going, Mac?" he asked.

"Difficult," replied Macdonald. "No chance of bringing it under control. Not a prayer. Just have to wait till it burns itself out. Let's hope they can prevent it spreading."

"How did it start?"

"That's the big question. Who can tell? Plenty of material to feed the flames, though, once it got set."

"Anyone seen around at the time?"

"Not that I've heard. Oh, I see what you're getting at. Might be arson, but probably we'll never know for certain."

"Then how was it discovered?"

"Beat bobby on patrol saw something in the yard. But by the time the alarm was raised and the fire brigade arrived, the blaze was well away." He shrugged his shoulders. "And that's about it."

"Thanks for the information. I'll maybe just take a wee daunder around."

"Your funeral. I'm not going any closer. No fear of that, I can tell you."

Lang pondered. It would be madness to attempt to enter the mill. But the grounds were extensive, housing a complex of facilities beyond the main building. So far as he could make out, the flames had not yet spread in that direction. There must be other entrances at side or rear. Would they all be securely locked and chained? It was worth a look.

The circuit of the perimeter wall took longer than he had imagined; it was a good ten minutes' walk before he stumbled upon the narrow gateway – inconspicuous, but a godsend nevertheless. Good job it was next to a street light or he might have missed it. He peered at the structure; rotting woodwork and flaking paint gave evidence of long neglect. Bolted, but the mounting was flimsy. One good kick and … it flew open.

The compound within was eerie in the silence, but the glow in the night sky gave enough illumination to distinguish the blur of darker shapes across the yard. He cursed at his lack of foresight in neglecting to bring a torch. But there would be gas mantles or electric light in the buildings. Find an unlocked door and he could have a good look round. Reassured, he began to grope his way through the murk.

Then it happened! The ground seemed to erupt as though struck by lightning. There was an explosion in his ears. He felt himself sucked into the air, then pitched downwards. His head crashed against the stone setts, and then … oblivion.

* * *

A scene of utter devastation met Iain's horrified gaze. Flames, red, yellow, orange, burst from buildings; great globules of fire spewed onto the paving where they spluttered and fizzled; clouds of dense, bilious smoke swirled everywhere. The smoke stung his eyes, soaked into his lungs; it was almost impossible to breathe. Nothing could survive in there. Commonsense told him to flee, escape from the scene, yet he hesitated.

It was a chance in a thousand. A sudden gust of wind cleared the smoke sufficiently to give a momentary view of a shapeless, inert lump close to one of the burning workshops. Hardly knowing what he was doing, he snatched off his muffler, wrapped it tightly round his mouth and nose, and plunged forward. It was a human body, whether alive or dead he could not tell. Without thinking he grasped under the arms and began to drag the man back. Sweat poured down his face, his muscles ached from the effort; but doggedly he refused to give up his burden. Gasping for air, his eyes red raw, he heard a voice, gruff but not unkind: "It's all right, laddie. We've got you now. You're safe." And then he collapsed, utterly spent.

Iain came round to find himself lying on a stretcher, a blanket over him and some kind of cushion propping up his head. He tried to sit up, but fell back in a paroxysm of coughing. Immediately someone in a white coat came over and knelt beside him.

"Tak' it easy, son. Just bide there quiet. I'm goin' to slip this over yer heid, an' you're tae breathe deeply. It's ca'ed an oxygen mask and it'll help get rid o' that glaur from yer system. Ready? Now breathe – in and out, in and out. Slow and sure."

"How is the boy, orderly?" The tone was crisp and authoritative. Iain glanced up to see a tall, gaunt figure in a gleaming black uniform with a peaked cap trimmed with silver. A policeman – and a high ranking one at that.

"Well on the road to recovery, sir. Nothing much wrong with him, forbye exhaustion and smoke inhalation. We're pumping the last of it out of him now."

The officer nodded. "Good, good. We'll require to interview him, of course. Find out exactly what happened. Any idea of his identity?"

"Nothing on him, sir. And he's no' up to speaking yet."

"Well, he can at least listen. See here youngster, that was a bloody foolhardy thing you did, putting yourself in danger like that. Damned brave though. You saved a man's life, you can be proud of that. I'll send one of my men to take your statement presently. We'll need to know what you were doing and what you saw. And the press will want to get hold of you. Doubtless your picture will be in all the papers. Now I must be about my duties. Good luck to you, lad." He touched his helmet and strode off.

"Just you rest now," said the medical assistant. "Get some energy back afore ye have tae tell yer tale. But ye can tak' that mask off now. There, that's better. There'll be an ambulance in a few minutes to tak' ye to hospital. So the doctors can gie ye a final check-up."

"What happened?"

"Ye were dead lucky, if ye'll pardon the expression. A fire crew was already on its way to damp doon an' stop the fire spreadin'. When they heard the explosion they hared round tae the side entrance. They found the pair o' ye just inside the doorway. Any further in, an' both o' you would hae been goners. The firemen would never hae seen ye, far less reach ye in time."

Iain shook his head. "I dinnae remember any o' that."

"There ye are, then. By the way, that chap ye pulled out will be just fine.

Thanks to you. And his thick coat. It saved him from the worst o' the burns. Concussion an' a broken arm, that's about the size o' it. A day or two in the infirmary an' he'll be right as rain."

An ambulance man came over and exchanged a few words with the orderly. The latter turned back to Iain.

"It seems our friend is conscious. Apparently he's a newspaper reporter. An' he's asking to see his rescuer. What about it?"

"I'm no' sure about that. I dinnae want to bother him."

"Nonsense. He only wants tae thank ye. It'll only tak' a minute. It widnae do tae refuse now, would it?"

Reluctantly Iain allowed himself to be pulled upright between the two medical auxiliaries, and assisted across the street to where another stretcher was just about to be loaded into a waiting ambulance.

"Can ye hear me, Mr Lang? This is the boy that went tae yer aid in the yard."

Lang beckoned Iain to come closer. He pointed towards his waistcoat pocket and mouthed: "Card. In here. Take it."

"Is this it?"

The man nodded. "My address," he croaked. "Come and see me. Once we're both a bit better. And thank you."

Lang slumped back. The stretcher was lifted and carried into the vehicle. Iain thrust the sliver of pasteboard deep into his hip pocket. What use would it be to him? Not even worth the bother to look at it.

"Mind if I tak' a few steps, stretch my legs?" he asked.

"Aye, provided ye dinna overdo it. Ye're still weak on yer pins. Stick around though. The ambulance will be here in twa shakes o' a lamb's tail."

Iain forced himself to think clearly. There might be awkward questions, his past might be probed. Still less did he crave the limelight of publicity. Someone might recognise his photograph in a newspaper and bring accusations of theft or assault. For the moment attention was focused elsewhere. But there might be only seconds to spare. He turned on his heel, limping off in the opposite direction. No one called out after him. He reached a byway. Turn up here and … simply melt away.

* * *

Adam Lang, Esq. Journalist The Glasgow Dispatch: the words were printed in italic script. On the reverse was scrawled in faded ink: *6 Dalhousie Grove, Garnethill.*

Iain Baird studied the dog-eared card yet again, flicking it over from one side to the other. Then he stared up at the imposing terrace with its honey-hued sandstone shimmering in the pale sunlight. There were wide steps leading up to the houses, each doorway with its gleaming brass doorknob and plate. He had never visited this part of Glasgow before. It was breathtaking, just like the side of a palace.

His brow puckered into a frown, trying to decide what to do for the best. He had no money, nowhere to go. His landlord had thrown him out the previous day, keeping his few belongings in payment for the rent he owed. Since then he had wandered the streets, pausing only to snatch a few hours of fitful sleep on a bench in one of the squares. It was only on awakening that he remembered the note. There was an address: he had been asked to call. What was there to lose now? The chap was a newsman, like as not to have heard he had run off that night. Maybe he would be suspicious, perhaps even try to give him away. But he was too tired and hungry to care. Gritting his teeth, he ran up the stairs and tugged on the bell pull.

Breathing heavily, all he could do now was wait. Suddenly there was a warning rasp, and the door swung open as though of its own volition. Inside was a long passageway, the floor patterned in a diamond-shaped mosaic of coloured stone. It was all spotlessly clean and really quite awe-inspiring, a far cry from the dirt and decay of his usual haunts. At the far end a broad staircase gave access to the upper floors. Light flooded down from the huge glass dome set into the roof and through stained windows on the half-landings.

A voice came from above, echoing round the stairwell. "Come right up. Third floor. The door's open."

A rather stout, florid gentleman was there to greet the youth as he ascended the last flight of steps. One arm was in a sling, and a tight bandage encased the crown of his head. Despite his injuries he grasped Iain warmly by the hand.

"Thank you for coming. I knew you would – sooner or later. Come away ben."

He paused just inside the hall. "Wonder how the front door opened? No need to go down every time there's a ring at the door. When I pull this rod, a wire does the trick. Ingenious, isn't it?

"Aye, I suppose so."

"Forgive me. I'm forgetting my manners." His eyes narrowed as he scrutinised the boy's features closely. There was evidence of cinder scorches, now healing up. That was satisfactory, so far as it went. But what was really alarming was the worn and pinched face, almost haggard in its appearance. "You look exhausted. And haven't eaten this morning either, I'll be bound. First things first. You must rest awhile, and take some nourishment."

The journalist led the way into a gloomy, cavernous apartment. On either side of the marble chimneypiece sat a squat easy chair, the leather covering now cracked and split. A small coal fire burned in the grate. On the fender was a tumbler, water jug and half-empty bottle of whisky.

"Sit ye down now and get some warmth into your body. I'll not be long."

Iain heard him bustle away into the far recesses of the house. This must be the parlour; it had seen better days, that was obvious. The windows were still barred and shuttered; narrow ribbons of sunlight filtered in round the edges of the panelling. A flickering glow came from a gasolier suspended on a thick cord from the ceiling rose. On the far wall a grandfather clock stood sentinel, its soft tick vying with the faint hiss of the gas and plop of the mantle to pierce the stillness of the room. A film of dust overlaid almost everything; there was a dank, musty scent of neglect. But the fire was comforting; he felt himself nodding, dropping off from sheer weariness.

A hand gently shook him back into consciousness. "Sorry to spoil your beauty sleep, but the tea'll go cold otherwise."

A small folding table had been set up. His host was pouring from a teapot, adding milk, lumps of sugar, and lastly a generous measure of whisky. There was also a plate containing several thick slabs of fruitcake.

"Get this down you. And tuck into the grub."

Iain needed no second bidding. The reporter recharged his own glass, splashed in some water and sipped meditatively while his visitor fell to with a will.

"Feeling better for that?" he asked, as the last crumbs were wolfed down.

"Aye. Braw. Best feed for ages."

"Good. And now it's time we got acquainted."

"I ken who ye are, Mr Lang. Here's yer card back."

Lang smiled thoughtfully as he returned it to his waistcoat. This was final proof, not that it was really needed. "Of course. You have the advantage of me. So what do they call you?"

"The name's Iain Baird."

"Master Baird. Or would you prefer Iain? The latter I think, more friendly. Just as well you came this morning. The quacks only let me out of hospital yesterday."

"How are ye keepin' now? I meant tae ask."

"Och, it looks worse than it is. Nothing much wrong bar the arm. I'm to rest for a few days. It's thanks to you I'm here at all."

"It wisnae much I did."

"Listen. Spare me the modesty. I owe you the deepest debt of gratitude possible. You risked your life to save me. You must have been scared witless, yet you went into that hellhole just the same. The least I can do is to repay you in any way I can."

Iain hesitated, but the opening was too good to miss. "Weel, if ye could spare some siller, maybe a pound or twa, just tae tide me ower, like. Mind, I'm no' beggin', Mr Lang."

"I could certainly sub you, if that's what you really want. But money's not necessarily the answer to everything. You don't have your troubles to seek, I can see that. It sometimes helps to talk. A problem shared, as the saying goes."

"There's nothin' to tell," he protested.

"Oh, but I think there is. You made yourself scarce that night, before they could cart you off to the infirmary. You're not scared of doctors, are you? Or too shy to cope with an admiring public? Now what was it?"

"I was feart they might say I started the fire. There, that's it."

"Just because you were on hand? You weren't involved, were you?" The boy shook his head.

"Then you can forget that silly notion. But there's more to it, isn't there?" He leaned forward encouragingly. "I only want to help you. Whatever you say will not go beyond these four walls."

Iain's resistance crumbled. It was the obvious sympathy and genuine concern that struck a chord, impelling him to unburden himself. Choking back tears, the story of the last few months came tumbling out, the fruitless search for work, heartless ejection from his lodgings, even a confession that he had taken to thieving. Adam Lang listened without interruption.

"You've had a hard time of it, and no mistake. And I pass no judgment on your, let's say, activities. But you're not a Glasgow keelie."

"How d'ye ken that?"

"Elementary, as Sherlock Holmes has it."

"Who's he?"

"A character in fiction, but it's of no consequence. Your accent gives you away. Lanarkshire, isn't it? Probably round Hamilton or thereabouts. Am I right?"

"Aye. Broomburn."

"So why not go back home? Surely your family would help out?"

"I cannae go back. That's the way o' it. I worked doon the pit – just started. There was an accident. Ma faither was killed, an' they said it was my fault. The whole village turned against me. Even ma mother. I was forced oot, had tae leave."

"And were you to blame? For the accident, I mean."

"No. But mebbie I could hae done mair for faither. I just panicked when the shaft flooded. Ran for it. Left him tae die."

"Any yet you conquered your fear to save me. You came to the aid of a complete stranger. I wondered why you did it." He made up his mind. "See here, laddie. How would you like to bide here? At least till you get yourself settled. God knows, there's plenty of room in this ramshackle place."

A shadow of doubt flickered across Iain's face. Lang read it at once.

"No need to fret, not on that score. I'm not that way inclined. I'm a widower. I'm not looking for a nancy boy. This is my besetting sin." He held up the whisky glass. "So you'll accept?"

"Do ye really mean it?" It sounded too good to be true.

"Haven't I just said so? There's no need to be bashful."

"In that case … I'll tak' yer offer. And thank ye. Truth to tell, I was at my wit's end."

"Good. Tomorrow we'll see what we can do about finding you a decent situation. Something with prospects. Can't have you living a life of crime. As it happens, my late wife's brother is manager in a shipyard. It's some time since I saw him last, but perhaps I could persuade him to take you on as an apprentice. Think you might like that?"

"I could gie it a try."

"That's the ticket. Then I'll get in touch with Mr Findlay – that's his name, by the way. He's in charge of making the engines for steamships. In the meantime, if you're up to it, I'll show you round. Then you can clean up a bit and then we'll go out for a bite of dinner. There's quite a decent chophouse in Renfrew Street. It's only a few minutes' walk."

That night Iain Baird slumbered like a baby. No matter that the mattress was lumpy or the bedclothes mildewed, he was dead to the world. Packed off to bed with a hot water jar to take the chill off the sheets, he slept the clock round, undisturbed by the demons which had haunted his dreams for months. It was late the next morning before he awoke. He yawned, stretched his arms luxuriantly and pushed aside the blankets. Rising from the bed, he slipped into his trousers and padded across the room. The hallway was cold and silent. He called out, but there was no reply. His benefactor must have gone out. A number of apartments led off, he recalled, dining and drawing rooms, another bedroom, kitchen and water closet.

He wandered into the kitchen in search of provisions. A solid table of undressed pine ran down the centre of the room, filled with the debris of an untidy bachelor existence. Next to a large stone sink was the larder, a shallow cupboard filled with marble shelves and a small aperture for ventilation. But his jaw dropped as he scanned its contents. A few tins, a dish of stale cheese and a biscuit barrel, that was all. Not much of a meal, but he had made do on far worse. Clearing a space, he settled down at the table. He had just cut himself a wedge of the cheese when he heard a key in the lock.

Lang scuttled in. "So you're up at last. Foraged some scran, I see. Glad you're using your initiative. Sorry about the short commons." He grinned broadly. "There's good news. I've arranged an appointment at the shipyard this very afternoon. So we'll need to find you a new suit of clothes. We can't have you going to an interview looking like a scarecrow. I know an outfitter in Sauchiehall Street. Then we'll have a spot of lunch. So you can leave that muck. There's just time for a good scrub up before we're off."

* * *

The Corporation tram set them down at Kelvinhaugh before continuing at its usual sedate pace, grinding and jolting as it struggled up the incline. No surprise the cars were called *shooglies* by Glaswegians, but more out of affection than in exasperation. Iain fingered his stiff, shiny collar, uncomfortably tight against his neck. He felt self-conscious in the tweed Norfolk jacket with its matching cap and breeches, not to mention the woollen stockings that stretched to the knee.

"There's the yard," his companion indicated. "What d'ye think of that?"

"Grand. It's huge." The low wall topped with high spiked railings ran into the distance on both sides. He read aloud the sign in wrought iron scrolling above the main gate: "*Deuchar and Sons. Upper Clyde Shipbuilders.* That the owner?"

"Yes. But the sons are in charge now. It's a vast undertaking, right enough. Covers hundreds of acres, besides the frontage on the river. There's dozens of crafts involved, each with its own workshops. Millions of parts have to be constructed and fitted together to create a ship. It's a very complicated business. More to it than simply clamping bits of metal together, as I hope you're going to discover."

"There must be hunners of workers."

"Hundreds? More like thousands. And this is one of the smaller yards. Some are twice the size, but they lie on the lower reaches of the Clyde where there's more room for expansion."

"Ye mean there's a load o' yards like this?"

"Certainly. Thirty or forty, big and small. The Clyde *is* shipbuilding. Do you know, nearly a quarter of the world's shipping comes from these few miles of riverbank. That's more than Germany and America put together. Fair makes you proud. And you could be part of this."

"So ye think they might gie me a start?"

"There's every chance of getting you into the engineering shop. It's the biggest and most prestigious department. That's where the real top-notch work is carried out. Marine engines are the lynch pin of the whole enterprise."

"Ye ken an awfu' lot about it all."

Lang laughed. "Not everything. But it's my business to know what's going on. I'm a pressman, remember. Background information is a tool of the trade."

"That a fact?" Iain did not sound totally convinced.

"Take my word for it. But it's time we went in. I'll give in our names at the gatehouse. No doubt they'll find someone to show us the way."

It was all so confusing. Iain felt dazed by the huge complex of buildings pointed out by their guide, bewildered by the maze of railway tracks, with locomotives shunting heavy components to the next stage of construction. On the stocks stood the hulls of ships, enclosed within a latticework of scaffolding; he could only marvel at the human ants crawling over the superstructure, while giant cranes towered still higher, ferrying their loads to the waiting workers. But the enduring memory was the ear-splitting din – the roar from open furnaces, the hiss of escaping steam, the rasp of saws and whine of drills, the thud of hydraulic presses and rattle of pneumatic tools, above all the constant clash of metal on metal. It came as a relief to reach the comparative quiet of the engineering compound and find sanctuary in its outer office.

"Now Iain, you'll be seeing Mr Findlay," said Lang, as a black-coated clerk disappeared into the inner sanctum to announce their arrival. "Mind you stand up straight, address him as 'sir', answer his questions directly, and you won't go far wrong. Oh, and when we're called, I'll just go in and have a wee word first."

But apparently their host was in no hurry to greet them. Pressure of urgent business was the excuse. Would they be good enough to wait? Adam Lang smiled faintly as the news was brought to him. This was Findlay's way of putting him firmly in his place.

While they were left to kick their heels, Albert Findlay stood irresolutely by his window. He liked to look out over his domain, but it gave him no pleasure that afternoon. What the devil did the man want? He had never been here before. Indeed they had not spoken since the day of poor Belinda's funeral. He had never taken to his brother-in-law, jumped-up adventurer that he was, and the feeling had intensified over the years into something more than dislike. Warnings to his sister that she was marrying beneath her had fallen on deaf ears, and she had suffered for it. Then there was the suspicion that her premature death was, at least in part, due to Lang's neglect. And to add insult to injury, he was the beneficiary of her inheritance. How else could he afford that house in Garnethill? It was his secretary who had booked the appointment; otherwise he would have refused an interview. Irritably he touched a bell, and retreated behind his desk as the unwelcome visitor entered, firmly closing the door behind him.

"Lang. How are you?" There was no shred of warmth in his voice.

"Well, I thank you, Findlay." Their fingers barely touched in the most perfunctory of greetings.

"Sit you down. Your telephone message was rather vague. But I can spare five minutes. What can I do for you?"

Lang seemed in no hurry to begin. He looked round the office, comfortable enough with its polished oak and rows of storage drawers, the Axminster carpet and mahogany desk inlaid with leather. In all honesty it had been an effort to arrange the meeting. He was unsure of his reception, recalling all too well past snubs and insinuations from his in-laws. But he had to do something for the lad. Journalism hardly seemed to fit the bill – that was too close to home. Folk could never mind their own business; they would be forever prying into his background. In any case a position as copy boy offered little prospect for advancement. No, it might stick in the craw, but it was safer to eat humble pie here. Taking a deep breath, he composed himself to speak calmly.

"I've come to beg a favour."

"Favours, is it? And why should I oblige you?"

"Call it family connections."

Findlay snorted. "That's rich, coming from you. After the way you treated Belinda."

Lang contrived to keep his temper. "Well then, let's say it's returning a favour."

"What did you ever do for me?" The sneer was palpable.

"You'll remember, some years ago I grant you, when you first had your foot on the managerial ladder. I wrote that article about promising young men in the shipbuilding industry. Your name featured prominently. I'm sure it must have been of some assistance, getting you started on the road to your present exalted position."

"A little, perhaps." It was a grudging admission. "But what of it? You've been repaid a thousand times. Marrying into the family. Living high on the hog with Findlay money."

He ignored the slur. "I could do the same again." The journalist spoke softly, almost in a whisper.

"I doubt that very much."

"There's a rumour afoot that you're in line for a directorship, a seat on the board. Another piece lauding your achievements might help swing it for you."

"What? In the *Dispatch* – that rag? It might be different if it was the *Herald*."

"You'd be surprised who reads my rag, as you put it. So may I make my request?

Findlay temporised. "I'll listen, but I promise nothing."

"That's good enough. I'd like you to find a place for my young friend outside."

"What's he to you? A distant relative perhaps?" he asked sardonically.

"Since you must know, he's the chap who pulled me out of the fire last week."

"So that's it. I read about your escapade. Too shy to stay and take the kudos, I hear. And I'm to reward him?"

"In a manner of speaking. An indenture as an apprentice would be appreciated."

"That all? Sure you wouldn't prefer naval architect or ship designer?"

Lang brushed aside the attempt at mockery. "That won't be necessary. Perhaps in time he'll progress that far off his own bat. Surely you could indenture him as a turner or fitter."

"Impossible. There's a trade depression at the moment, as you well know. And no one to speak for the youngster."

"I can attest as to his character."

"Can you? On so short an acquaintance? But it doesn't signify. I was referring to someone in the industry – a foreman or chargehand. A senior journeyman at least. Your opinion is neither here nor there."

"But surely you could make an exception."

"Look, I'm not really involved in recruitment. That's left to lesser lights. How old is he in any case?"

"Fifteen, next month."

"That settles it. He's too young. Must be sixteen before he could be considered."

"So there's nothing you can do?"

"You're beginning to try my patience. See here, business is likely to pick up again soon. No doubt you've heard talk of Admiralty orders, now that the damned politicians have woken up to the threat from Germany. We'll probably be expanding next year. In the meantime, what about a start as a rivet boy? Not my province, of course, but a note to the foreman should do the trick. That do for you?"

"I suppose it'll have to. Better than nothing."

"There's gratitude for you. But I'll go further. If he shows promise, I'll undertake to procure an apprenticeship in some branch of engineering when he's of age. Now fetch in your young sidekick while I write a line. I'm sure the gaffer will see his way to oblige me."

He scribbled a few words, then signed the letter with a flourish. Only then did he turn his attention towards the youth for whom he was expected to provide employment.

"This is Iain Baird", said Lang by way of introduction.

The manager nodded. "Quite. Now, Baird, Mr Lang and I have been discussing the possibility of an opening for you at Deuchar's. You are at present too young for an apprenticeship, but there may be a vacancy in a riveters' squad. A satisfactory performance there could lead to a move here to the engine shop at a later date. What do you say to that?"

"Whatever you and Mr Lang think, sir." Christ knew what the job involved, but it was the only offer he was likely to get.

"Hmm. We'll take that as an acceptance then."

"Aye. And thank ye, sir."

"That's better." He rang the bell. "One more thing. I have to ask this. You're not of the Roman persuasion, are you?"

"Eh? What d'ye mean?"

"Your religion. You're of the Protestant faith? Not a Roman Catholic?"

"Och, that. Naw. I went tae Sunday school at the kirk for a year or twa when I was a wean. In Broomburn, like."

"Good. Just a formality. Though I'm not prejudiced myself, of course. It's the men. They won't have papists in the yard, not in the skilled trades anyhow." His eyes swivelled towards the clerk who had appeared in the doorway. "Inform the office boy he's to show these, ahem, gentlemen to Berth Three. They're to see the foreman."

The lackey bowed obsequiously and disappeared. Findlay made a gesture that Iain should also leave. He waited a moment, then folded the paper and handed it over.

"Here's your note, Lang. You'll remember your side of our little agreement? I trust there will be no necessity for you to call here again. And now, if you'll forgive me, I have work to conclude. Good day to you."

* * *

The bothy at the head of the slipway was tiny, roughly knocked together from brick and iron, its narrow entrance masked with a canvas screen.

"Mr McLeod?" Lang called out.

Almost immediately the curtain was pulled aside to reveal a slight, middle-aged man in shirtsleeves and waistcoat. He eyed them suspiciously.

"Aye. And who might be wantin' him?"

By way of response he received the folded slip of paper. He frowned inquisitively and read it through.

"So this young man wants to join our happy band." He looked Iain up and down appraisingly. "You've got the build for it, I'll give you that. Any experience?"

"Naw. I was a miner."

"A pitman? You don't say. From the bowels of the earth to the sky and the clouds. Now that's some journey." He guffawed at his own joke. "Do you ken anything about the work?" Iain shook his head.

" Well, it's like this. To build a ship there's any number of steps, and they all have to be carried out in a special order. Afore us come the platers. It's their job to cut and shear and bend the sheets of metal to the right shape and size. Then they punch holes along the sides before hangin' the plates on the frame o' the vessel. And that's where we come in. We close up the shell and finish the job. After that, the hull's ready for launching. Look, I'll show you, if you're interested."

McLeod slipped back inside to don jacket and bowler hat, public symbols of his status on the worksite. "Ready? Then follow me. Hope you've got a head for heights."

The wooden ladders creaked and swayed as they climbed upwards from one level to the next. God, but this was dangerous, thought Lang, so rickety and unsteady. Buffeted by what seemed like a gale, he puffed and wheezed from the unwonted exercise. Sweat poured out, instantly clammy against the chill wind. But at last they gained the uppermost deck and he could catch his breath.

"Here we are," cried McLeod cheerily. "Enjoy the view." And indeed many of the city landmarks were visible, cathedral, university, the grand buildings of the West End. Further afield, now hazy in the gathering gloom, lay the mouth of the river and foothills of the Highlands.

"Had your fill of the scenery? Then we can cut to the business. There's a riveting gang. They work in squads of four. That man's the rivet heater." He pointed to a youth stirring the contents of an open hearth with a long pair of tongs. "The bolts have to be exactly the right temperature. Too hot and they might shatter. Too cold and they winnae fit the joint properly."

Iain watched closely as a glowing white rivet was pulled from the brazier and expertly tossed into a basin of sand a score of feet away. Immediately it was retrieved and pushed into overlapping rivet holes.

McLeod followed Iain's gaze. "That's the hauder-on. He uses nippers and hammer to tap in the bolt, and then hold it steady while the other two knock it down from the other side."

Iain could appreciate the efforts of the workmen, using the controlled weight of alternate blows to flatten the rivet. The skill was not far different from that of the hewer down by.

"Like to be one o' them?" chuckled the foreman." I can see you're impressed. But all in good time. You'll start at the bottom, fetchin' and carryin' for a wheen o' gangs. Ye'll be up and down thae ladders like a monkey on a string. And woe betide you if ye bring the wrong size o' bolts from the stores. Yer arse will be black and blue. Time means money to these men. Their wages depend on the number of rivets knocked down in a day. Get the picture?"

"Aye. Clear as mud."

"Bit of a comedian, are ye? You'll need to watch that. Right, it'll be eight shillings a week. After a month or two you might get made up to rivet heater and join a squad. That'll be another couple of bob. Hours are six till five, one o'clock finish on Saturday. So ye'll be able to get to the match. Start next Monday. Suit you? Then we can get everything straightened out back at the office. Let's away down."

At least the descent was less exhausting, though scarcely less daunting. Lang heaved a sigh of relief as he stepped off the ladder.

"You'll be glad to be back on firm ground, Mr Lang. Come away in."

The foreman's lair was cramped in the extreme. A scuffed roll-top desk, a trestle table littered with papers, and two battered chairs occupied most of the space.

"Now, where are we? Ah yes, here's a scrap o' paper. I'll just jot down a few details. Then you can sign it, and you can witness the signature, Mr Lang. I like to keep a tidy ship."

"I see you've some heavy machinery on the causeway, Mr McLeod. I was wondering about its purpose."

"That'll be the hydraulic riveter. Ugly great monster. Weighs tons, and a beast to move. Generally it's used for the biggest bolts on the keel. There are some smaller pneumatic tools that one man can hold, but they're a bugger to operate. Murder on the hands – from the vibration, ye ken. The men hate them. Still, hand riveting will be around for a long time yet. See my time out, and more. Anything else?"

"I think not, thanks all the same. You've been most instructive. I'm sure this young man is grateful for the job."

"Don't mention it. Always happy to be of service. Mind, six on the dot, laddie."

"I'll see he's here on time."

"That's dandy. Now you'd best be off. Ten minutes to the whistle. Stay any longer and you'll be trampled in the rush. Or at least miss the chance of an early tram. Good day to ye."

The advice was not to be ignored. Hurrying away, they managed to secure seats on the top deck of a car heading back towards the city centre.

"Missed the crowd," chortled the reporter, glancing back at the hordes now pouring out of the gates. "Well, Iain, how do you feel about your day so far? Successful enough?"

"It is that. I've got a job an' somewhere to stay, thanks tae yer kindness. Things seem tae be on the up at last."

"Yes, and this is just the beginning. My brother-in-law has little time for me, as I expect you've noticed, but he's a man of his word. He'll keep his side of the bargain. You'll get that engineering apprenticeship."

"So I'll be a skilled man?"

"When you're time served, yes. A real aristocrat of labour, as they say. But do you want to be satisfied with that?"

"What d'ye mean?"

"You could go so much further. Become a white-collar worker in a comfortable office rather than dirty your hands on a machine. Maybe rise into management."

"And d'ye really think I could dae that?"

"Why not? But you'd have to go the extra mile to get yourself noticed and marked out for the fast track. It's not enough to learn a journeyman's skills. You need to know something of the theory behind the practice, about planning and construction. And that would involve classes in your spare time."

"What? Go back to school?" Iain was clearly dismayed at the prospect.

"Not exactly. You'd attend the Institute in the evenings. And the subjects of study would be to further your career. You'd take courses in applied mathematics and science. Perhaps a little metallurgy to appreciate the properties of metals. Certainly technical drawing to grasp blueprints. That could lead on to draughtsmanship. Then, if you show promise and pass the exams, you might even be sponsored for advanced work at the university. Think about it. That's all I ask."

His companion stared into the distance as he chewed over the implications. It was several minutes before Lang broke the silence.

"I prattle on too much, I know. Let's change the subject. I think a little celebration is in order. There's a variety show just starting at the *Empire*. Ever been to the theatre?"

"No' that I can mind."

"You'll enjoy it, I'm sure. There's a comic star. Not to everyone's taste, what with his crooked stick and pawky humour, but generally goes down well with Scots audiences."

Iain's face brightened. His ambition had been stirred, his path marked out. If it took hard work, then so be it. One day he would return to the village in triumph, a man of substance, with golden sovereigns jingling in his pocket and fine broadcloth on his back. His lips twisted into a smirk of anticipation. That would put their gas at a peep, especially that young prig of a brother.

PART II: 1911-14

SEVEN

Red Letter Days

Broomburn. July 1911

"Mary! Time to open up again. It's gone two. See to it, would ye?"

The manageress surveyed her domain as the shopgirl hurried to carry out the request, unbolting the door and switching the card in the window to indicate that Larkhall and District Co-operative Society was once more open for business. Everything was neatly in its place, the floor newly swept, marble slabs wiped down and polished, dry goods weighed and made up into brown paper bags. All was in readiness for the afternoon trade.

Kate Baird had every reason to feel a sense of quiet satisfaction. True, not a night went by that she did not shed a tear for Geordie, but it could not be denied that life had treated her kindly since that tragic day. And her good fortune had been largely due to the generosity of Mr McIntosh. An opening in the co-operative store was a highly desirable situation, safe and respectable, and he had managed to secure it for her. Then, quite unexpectedly, on her daughter's fourteenth birthday she had received a letter, typewritten on headed notepaper, formally offering Miss Baird a position as trainee at the Co-operative's branch in Broomburn, to be taken up as soon as she left school. And to cap it all, when the post of branch manager had fallen vacant, he had insisted that she apply. Her cheerful disposition, capacity for hard work and dignified efficiency were solely responsible for the preferment, so he had claimed, but she knew better. It was his patronage, pulling strings behind the scenes, which had done the trick.

Her thoughts turned to the children. Mary's stolid good sense had helped her through the depths of despair in her bereavement; she had quietly taken over most of the housework, and her wage from the shop made a real difference to the family income. But nothing lasted forever. Mary was about to be wed. It was the right time, she had to admit; the girl had just turned nineteen. She was a woman now. And she had made a sound choice

– Cha White's son, Rob. They made a good match, had been walking out for the past eighteen months and more. Kate brushed away a tear; it would be selfish not to share in the universal joy. Besides, it was not quite true to think of losing a daughter. They would both move in with her till a colliery house became available. And that might not be for some time.

There was even good news about Iain. She had been consumed with anxiety when he disappeared, and it had come as a mercy to discover, months later, that he was in good health and in steady work. A letter had arrived from his landlord in Glasgow, a Mr Lang, who was concerned that his family should at least know that he was alive and well. He had emphasised that her son knew nothing about the correspondence, and strongly advised her not to write directly to him. In the meantime he would do what he could to persuade Iain to make contact himself. Alas, the effort had apparently failed. She had not seen him for over six years, but at least she could take consolation from Mr Lang's occasional snippets of information. Apparently Iain had found a proper trade, and was even taking classes to equip himself for promotion. Kate had to smile at the thought of Iain applying himself to his studies.

And then there was Alastair, the last of her fledglings. It was hard to imagine that he might be fleeing the nest in a year or so. But for the present he was due back from school on the last day of term. He had done really well at the Academy in Hamilton, far beyond even her expectations. Gaining that scholarship had been a great achievement; she recalled the dominie calling at the house with fulsome congratulations. And it had meant she only had to find the funds for his clothes and rail fare. Things had been strange and awkward for him at first, but he had worked hard and sailed through his intermediate exams. Another year and he would take his leaving certificate – followed, hopefully, by university. Her heart swelled with pride at the prospect. Mr Ogilvie had sung the praises of his old college in Edinburgh, but Glasgow was nearer, within travelling distance. He could continue to live at home. It would keep up the link a while longer.

"Look, here's Alastair comin'," cried Mary, as she set the door ajar. A flaxen-haired youth came bounding in, throwing off his satchel as he came.

"Lord-a-mercy!" exclaimed Kate. "Whatever are ye doin' back at this time? I didnae expect ye for another hour at least."

"Start of the hols, mother. I caught the early train. Mind if I take a barley sugar stick?" Without waiting for an answer he plucked a sweet from its jar.

"Aye well, ye can pay for it. Would ye fetch me a stoop o' water? I've a fair drouth in this heat."

"Of course, maw. Anything to oblige." He was back in moments with a cup. "Here ye are. It's new drawn. And now I must be off. Have to see Mr Ogilvie this afternoon."

"You an' yer precious Mr Ogilvie. What about yer dinner?"

"I'm not hungry. I had my sandwiches on the train. But can we have an early tea? You'll remember about tonight?"

"As if I'm likely to forget! Ye've telt us often enough. Away wi' ye, then. An' mind an' take that schoolbag!"

She watched him go, her eyes dewy with tenderness. There would always be a special place for him in her heart. After the first two, she had been advised to have no more children; her health would not stand it. But she had been determined on a third. It had been a difficult pregnancy and birth; he had been lucky to survive, what with his weak chest and chronic bouts of bronchitis in the early years. Now he looked the picture of rude health. He had grown and filled out slightly, enhancing rather than spoiling those finely sculptured features. There was that air about him, hard to pin down, of innocence and vulnerability, which so stirred maternal instincts in the female breast. Already Mary had hinted that several girls had shyly expressed an interest to her. Thankfully Alastair had the sense to concentrate on his lessons.

Her mood altered. There was something else on her mind. She had brooded over it for weeks before finally reaching a decision. But what would the children make of her proposal? They would have to be consulted. And time was fast running out to bring up the subject. She heaved a sigh. It would have to be today. At teatime – that would be best.

* * *

The dominie sat at his high desk, engrossed in writing an entry in the school log. He read over the text, carefully applied the blotter to the page, and closed the book. The dull thud was the death knell on his teaching career. Village teacher for forty-five years, he had served his charges to the best of his ability; and now it was over. This final day of the session marked his retirement from the classroom. He would miss the children, even the young rascals amongst them, but not the increasing bureaucracy, the apparently insatiable demand for paperwork handed down from on high. It was time to make way for a younger man. Or it might be a woman, in this enlightened age; the school board had still to make its appointment. He looked round the room, peaceful as the graveyard, now that the pupils had been dismissed to six weeks of freedom. They had given him three cheers just before the end, and he had had to brush away a tear before gruffly calling them back to order. It was their token of appreciation, and he was proud to receive it.

There was a tap on the door, and a familiar figure entered.

"Alastair! Good of you to call. I was hoping to see something of you in the holidays." He slipped from the stool to greet him warmly.

"I'm not disturbing you, Mr Ogilvie, am I? I just thought you might like a hand to pack up."

"Not at all, Alastair. That's extremely kind of you. As it happens, there's another month before I have to vacate the premises."

"But after that …?" There was a hint of anxiety in his voice.

"Never fear, you're not going to lose me that easily. I've taken the old cottage on the far side of the village – the whitewashed house on the Strathaven road. It's ample for my needs, and there's a bit of garden besides. I might take up writing in my leisure hours. I've always fancied myself as an author."

"What would you write about?"

"Oh, probably local history. It's a subject that's always fascinated me."

"Perhaps I could help with your research?"

"Maybe so. But you need to concentrate on gaining a good group in your leaving certificate. You've a mountain of work over the next few months."

"I know." Alastair sighed. "But surely there's something I can do for you now?"

Ogilvie smiled as his plea. "Well, there's always the pictures to take down. You could help me with that. Just like old times, when you used to act as my assistant after classes."

"Aye, I really enjoyed that. And it was small recompense for all that tutoring you gave me. But for you, I would never have got to the Academy."

"Stuff and nonsense! We were a team, as I told your mother. It was reward in itself when you carried off the Grierson. Fairly put Broomburn on the educational map."

"But you gave up so much of your time, especially the whole of nearly every weekend, just to coach me for the exam."

"It was a labour of love, I assure you. And you worked your socks off. It was your ability and determination that carried you through. Anyhow, let's not dwell on the past. Tell me about Fairhill. Have you been appointed a prefect for your final year?"

"Fat chance!" Alastair chuckled. "I'm a scholarship boy, remember."

"Surely there's no stigma in that at the Academy?"

"No, perhaps not. But I'm not in the rugby fifteen. They tend to pick the big bruisers to keep control over the younger boys. I never took up rugger. Or cricket. It didn't seem fair to have to ask mother to pay for the kit. Besides, I hadn't the time for the practices, having to rush off to catch the train every day. No, I made do with hares and hounds for exercise. I'm rather good at that," he added.

"I don't doubt it," agreed Ogilvie. "You have the grace of a runner. But haven't you made friends at the Academy?"

"Fellows to talk to at school, yes. But none that you could call close. I can't really invite them back to Broomburn. So how can I accept invitations to their homes?"

Ogilvie nodded sympathetically. It was the old story. The road from village school to university carried a man only so far. It was social class, with all its trappings and prejudices, that was the fearsome barrier to be overcome.

"I know I owe you and mother a debt I can never repay," Alastair went on. "And I would do anything to avoid hurting either of you. But sometimes I feel ashamed. I've so little in common with folk here now. I don't even talk the same way as them anymore. I'm like a stranger in the village. I couldn't face living in Broomburn all my days. It would crush me. Is it so terribly wrong, thinking like that?"

The master's heart went out to his favourite pupil; the boy's emotions so closely mirrored his own at that age. It was only natural to wish to remain faithful to his origins, whilst striving to rise above them. He cleared his throat, searching for words of reassurance.

"You could never turn away from your family, Alastair. The whole purpose of education is to broaden your outlook, expand your ambitions, make whatever you can of yourself. It would be pointless otherwise. I'd be disappointed if your achievements did not exceed mine. And as for your mother, she would be saddened to see you go, but more than compensated by pride in your success. She told me as much years ago, when we were considering entering you for the Grierson."

They worked in silence for a while, Alastair clambering on desks to prise out the pins, handing down the posters to be rolled and tied with string, preparatory to being stored in the cupboard.

"I think that will do," said Ogilvie at length. "Time for a rest. Come ben to the staffroom. More comfortable there."

"I'm not the least bit tired," protested Alastair.

"No, but I am. Not so young as I used to be." He led the way through. "Sit ye down. Cup of tea?"

"Thank you, sir. But no. I'd best be getting home soon."

"Of course. But we haven't spoken about your future yet. What are your plans after you leave the Academy?"

"Well, I had hoped to go on to university, but I don't see how we can afford that. Not without gaining a bursary from somewhere."

"Ah, there's the sticking point. Are you still set on teaching?"

"Yes, that's never changed. I could go straight to training college, I know, but then I'd never qualify for secondary education."

"True. But there is another path. Have you considered a concurrent course at university? That would combine academic subjects with professional studies – a degree and teaching diploma at the same time. And you would qualify for a government grant to help with the fees and maintenance."

"Sounds great. But would it be enough?"

"Not on its own, no. But there are other possibilities. We could apply for a Carnegie award."

"Carnegie? What's that?"

"You mean who. Andrew Carnegie came from Dunfermline. He emigrated to America where he made a vast fortune in business. Wishing to benefit his native land, he bequeathed huge sums to endow colleges, libraries, even public parks, and to provide financial aid for deserving students."

"Do you think I would qualify?"

"An ideal case, I'd say. Just the type of applicant to appeal to the trustees."

"So you believe there's a chance of university after all?"

"A near certainty, if my opinion is worth anything. I'll send off for the relevant documents on your behalf."

"If you could, I'd be awfully grateful. It would be a weight off my mind. And mother's."

"It's no trouble, you know that." He left unsaid his resolve to provide a settlement for the lad. There was enough put by in savings; his pension was sufficient for his frugal needs. Why should distant relatives benefit from an inheritance?

"Well, I'll keep you no longer. No doubt we'll meet again tonight." He frowned at Alastair's startled glance; then smiled to show he was in jest. "Don't think I'm totally ignorant of what's going on. A surprise presentation, is it not? And I'm summoned to the village hall under a pretext that the board wishes to review the school accounts. I'm rather long in the tooth to be taken in by that."

Alastair grinned. After all the secrecy surrounding the preparations, he should have known better than to imagine his mentor could be deceived so easily.

* * *

The table had been laid, the oilcloth replaced with a linen coverlet, places set and dishes arranged in the centre. There were thick slices of baked gammon, cold boiled potatoes and a large bowl of salad, with a cake and chocolate biscuits to follow. Rather more than was customary in the Baird household, but Kate had decided that this was a special occasion. The kettle was on the hob, the teapot ready to receive the boiling water. Mother and daughter gossiped quietly by the fire. All that remained was for the youngest member of the family to put in an appearance.

At last a familiar footfall was heard in the yard. "There he is now," said Mary. "And no' before time."

"Wherever hae ye been?" asked Kate, as Alastair came in, a little sheepishly. "Surely no' at the school till this hour?"

"No. I went for a walk afterward and clean forgot the time. Hope I haven't kept you waiting."

"Tea was ready a good half hour ago," announced Mary primly. "And after you wantin' an early meal."

"Let the boy alone, Mary. He's said he's sorry." Kate was at pains to be conciliatory.

"That's all very well. But he disnae realise the effort we've had to make. It's no' sae easy, gettin' time off for the pair o' us on a Friday night."

"Let's no' get involved in an argument. Ye've made a lovely spread. Let's enjoy it. Alastair, awa' an' wash yer hands. Mary, would ye mash the tea?"

Mary's annoyance soon faded, especially as the others were profuse in their appreciation of the viands she had prepared. Kate sensed an undercurrent of excitement in Alastair; he was bursting to get something off his chest.

"You've some news for us, Alastair?" she asked casually, as she passed him a plate.

"Aye. I mean yes. Mr Ogilvie thinks I can go to university after all. There's grants and bursaries and awards we can apply for. He says we're bound to get help with the fees. Maybe even cover all the expenses."

"That is good news. But I never had any doubts. You're gettin' to college, grant or no grant. We would hae managed somehow."

She poured the tea. The conversation drifted on to a discussion of the evening ahead. Then Mary brought up the subject of wedding arrangements. Kate winced. By this time the cake and biscuits were nearly finished; soon they would have to get ready to leave.

"About the weddin', Mary. There is somethin' else on my mind." She swallowed hard before taking the plunge. "It would be nice if a' the family could be there."

"But we will a' be there. What are ye haverin' about?" Mary was clearly bemused.

"I mean … Iain." Hastily she continued before anyone could register a protest. "It's been that long since we've seen him. He might welcome the chance o' comin' back, at least for a wee visit. I canna bear the thought o' the family split apart like this forever. We maun try to make the effort to mend what's broken. It's our Christian duty."

There was a stunned silence, broken only by the clock ticking on the mantelpiece. Brother and sister stared at one another as if in disbelief.

"The return of the prodigal. Is that how you see it, maw?" There was real concern in Alastair's voice "Maybe it works in the Bible, but I very much doubt it in his case. Remember the night he left? That temper tantrum? We thought he was going to strike you down. Anyhow, it's simply not on. No one's heard from him for years."

"But that's where you're wrong," said Kate earnestly. "I do know about Iain. I ken where he bides, where he works. It's in Glesga. And he has changed. He's stuck in, got a good job wi' prospects. He even gangs tae night school to get mair qualifications."

"And just how dae ye ken that, maw?" demanded Mary. "Ye've never made mention o' it before."

"It's his landlord, a really nice man. He writes to me every now an' again. Though Iain kens nothing about it."

"All right," said Alastair. "So Iain's hale and hearty. What then?"

Kate drew a deep breath. "Lass, I'd like for you and Rob to invite your brother to the wedding."

"What!" Mary almost choked. "You know what Rob an' his faither think o' Iain. Folk hae long memories here. They'd hae a fit. And there'd be a riot if he turned up."

"No, they widnae." Kate was quite calm now. "You can get Rob to agree. Ye ken ye can twist him round yer little finger when ye've a mind. And we'll no let on to Cha till the weddin'. I'll make sure he doesnae cause a commotion. He'll no' want to spoil yer day, whatever he thinks."

"I'm no' sae sure. An' I dinna like it, no' one bit. But, since ye're set on it, I'll no' stand in yer way. I'll speak tae Rob."

"Guid lassie. Now, Alastair, would you deliver the invitation to Iain yersel'? He might just ignore a letter. Make him see the past is done. It's time to let bygones be bygones."

Alastair gulped. This was a tall order. Bearding the lion in his den was fraught with danger. "I'm the same as Mary. I don't think this is a good idea. He'd probably refuse to come." He saw the look of dismay and quickly changed tack. "But … if you're really determined, I'll try. Lord knows, you've done enough for me."

* * *

"Elizabeth! Are you about ready? The motor-car is at the door. We must make a start now or we'll be late."

The girl pouted, and stuck out her tongue at the mirror. It was her Uncle

Robert again, calling from the foot of the stairs. She sat at the dressing table, suffering in silence as the servant deputed to act as lady's maid brushed her hair. Clumsy ass! She grimaced as a particularly vigorous stroke seemed to tear into her scalp. The skivvy had no experience, no idea of what was involved; she would be as well doing it herself. But Aunt Maud had insisted; no person of breeding should have to perform her own toilette. She pondered over what to wear. The sky blue outfit, or the pale cream? The cream set off her complexion, the blue matched her eyes. As if it really mattered, in this dreary backwater.

"Which dress would you be wanting now, miss?" asked the maid timidly.

"That one," she decided, pointing to the blue gown. "And mind you hook me up at the back properly."

Elizabeth Lixmont simmered with resentment. Why had she been packed off at a moment's notice to spend a fortnight with relations? And the Semples, of all people! True, the Seminary had requested her parents to remove their daughter from the school. So she had been caught smoking illicit cigarettes a few times? That was just part of the smart set. As for the incident with that hysterical fool of a French mistress, dropping the dead mouse into the water jug was no more than high spirits, a trivial prank at most. Others, unfortunately, had failed to see it in that light. A bad influence, the principal had claimed, sullying the reputation of the college. There was scant sympathy at home either. Headstrong and wilful, her mother had raged, before taking to her bed with one of her migraines. Even her father had been reproachful. And so, here she was, sent as a punishment till they decided what to do with her.

She had always rather looked down on her hosts as country cousins, their company to be endured rather than enjoyed. And this visit was no exception. Her aunt was cool and distant, making it all too apparent that her niece had committed some unpardonable sin. Uncle Robert was pleasant enough, but even he appeared wary. The days simply dragged by. There had been a few dinner parties, stuffy and boring beyond belief, what with talk of business or politics or domestic affairs. The young men present on these occasions were dull and insipid, hardly worth a second glance, try as they might to engage her attention. All in all, the atmosphere had been oppressive, and it was something of a relief to be returning home the next day. The fate that might lie in store for her could not be worse than this.

It was with some diffidence that her uncle had enquired whether she would care to accompany him to a local function – a retirement presentation, which, as a leading member of the community, he could not with propriety avoid. Aunt Maud was unable to attend the event due to a slight indisposition, or so she had claimed. Her immediate inclination had been to rebuff the invitation, but second thoughts had led her to concede with a nod and smile. Uncle Robert was not such a bad old stick; and, after all, it would get her away from that sour-faced dragon for the evening.

She draped the wrap round her shoulders, set her wide-brimmed hat at a jaunty angle and opened up her parasol. Thus armed, she descended the stairs. Her uncle was there to meet her at the bottom. She flashed a winning smile of apology as she swept past. Semple followed, half-rueful, half-admiring. That young madam would go far … or end up in jail. A militant suffragette in the making, like as not. Thank goodness she was not his problem.

The church clock was striking the hour as the Argyll saloon pulled up outside the village hall. They were only just in time. An usher was waiting to conduct them to the anteroom where the platform party was assembling over a glass of sherry. Semple, as guest of honour, was the centre of attraction and model of affability, glad-handing the local worthies and complimenting the ladies on their appearance. Elizabeth simpered innocently as she was introduced, sensing the appreciation of the men and hostility of their womenfolk. Finally the chairman asked if everyone was ready and, receiving assent, led the way onto the stage. The buzz of conversation died away as the audience settled down.

As she took her place, Elizabeth surveyed the auditorium. Surprisingly enough, nearly every seat was taken; latecomers had to make do with standing room at the back. Then her eyes suddenly narrowed. Sitting at the end of the front row was a youth of about her own age, fair haired and delicately built. At that moment the boy looked up: instinctively she beamed at him, grinning broadly, and wiggled the fingers of one hand in greeting. In response he smiled vaguely and looked away in confusion. So he was shy too; she liked that. Something stirred within her; she was not sure what her feelings were. But she wanted to learn more about him. It should not be too hard to engineer an encounter later on. She turned back to try to concentrate on the proceedings.

The chairman had risen, and was explaining the reason for the absence of the man of the hour. There was a polite titter from the body of the hall as it was revealed that he had no inkling of the ceremony, and had been summoned, so he supposed, to a routine business meeting. And indeed, here he was now, prompt to the minute. There was an outburst of cheering and much stamping of feet as the dominie entered. Ogilvie appeared to be taken aback by the warmth of his reception, but contrived to compose himself as he was shown to his chair. The master of ceremonies shuffled his notes on the lectern and held up his hand for silence.

The speech that followed was the usual litany of platitudes; unstinting praise for a lifetime of devoted service, the value of education in the modern world, not least when the Empire had need of the abilities of all her subjects. It was the duty of the school system to seek out promising children and take positive action. Mr Ogilvie had shown the way, and it was up to the board to ensure the continuation of the good work. He then called upon Mr Semple to make the presentation of an engraved clock. The managing director of the Avon Valley Coal Company rose to add his few words of commendation, handed over the gift, shook hands and resumed his seat.

There was a hush of expectation as, with every show of reluctance, Ogilvie slowly made his way to the lectern. He was stunned, he claimed, and totally unprepared for such an honour. But in thanking the board for their generosity, he could not help remarking that clocks would play a much less prominent part in his life henceforth. That raised a smile or two, even a few chuckles. Then he warmed to his main theme. The *lad o' parts* was undoubtedly central to the Scottish educational tradition, but at the same time the nation had been profligate in the waste of so much of its talent. In this parish, he noted wryly, the vast majority had always disappeared into coal mining or domestic service; only the odd exception had been fortunate enough to rise above such low aspirations. He was glad to hear that this state of affairs was about to change, since the board now saw it as a responsibility to encourage higher ambitions. In conclusion he wished all well, and added that his successor could do worse than to ply his, or perhaps her, trade in Broomburn.

The applause was more muted this time; some of the listeners were frowning, unsure of the message he was trying to convey. A few of the more perceptive were even shaking their heads in disapproval. Obviously his audience had not expected this. Had he gone too far in his challenge? Chivvying his superiors to live up to their fine words was controversial, to say the least. And to imply that the villagers were set in their ways, unable to see beyond the colliery gate, was a slur on the whole community. Well, he did not care. If only a few could be jolted out of complacency or apathy, that would be reward enough.

"That's ruffled a few feathers," murmured Semple to his niece. "I fancy there won't be many staying for the social now." And indeed some of the board were already scraping back their chairs and stalking away.

"A thousand apologies." The chairman was addressing his guest of honour nervously. "I'm afraid Mr Ogilvie was, ahem, somewhat robust in his comments. I hope you haven't taken offence."

"Not at all," replied Semple. "A man has a right to express his own views. Not that it'll make a blind bit of difference. There's nothing more conservative than the working class. Give them a roof over their heads, food in their bellies, the odd pint of beer, and they're satisfied. So long as there's coal to be mined, they'll be content with their lot."

"A very charitable attitude, if I may say so, sir. Some would find his opinions gratuitously offensive. Now, may I, on behalf of the board, offer both of you some refreshment in the clubroom before you take your leave."

"Very kind of you, but I think we'll be off now. Come along Elizabeth. Good night to you, Mr Allardice."

"Oh, but it's so early," the girl protested. "I'd so like to stay a bit longer. Perhaps meet a few of the village people."

Semple gave a shrug of resignation. "Looks like I'll be taking you up on your offer after all, Allardice. As you wish, my dear, but don't blame me if you find the experience boring."

"I'm certain I shan't. It would only be manners to be polite to the teacher, for instance. There he is, near the side door, talking to that tall lady. And that rather dishy looking boy."

"Aha! So that's the way the wind blows. I'm not convinced, young lady, that it would be seemly to associate with the village youth. Whatever would your parents think?"

"Oh really, uncle! Just to say hello? What harm is there in that? And I have done you a service."

"Can't deny that, I suppose. And in return, I'm to indulge you? You know how to take an advantage, Elizabeth, that's for sure. So be it. Will you do the honours, Allardice?"

"A privilege, sir. I understand the lady is widowed, a Mrs Baird, with her younger son."

"Baird? The name rings a bell. Any relation to that troublemaker we had a few years back?"

"I believe so, sir."

"Hmm. Well, never mind. Introduce us just the same."

"Of course." He led the way across the room. "Excuse us, Ogilvie, Mrs Baird. Mr Semple would like to pay his respects."

After the usual courtesies the chairman excused himself; duty required his attendance elsewhere.

"A little pompous, is he not, Mr Ogilvie?" remarked Semple, as Allardice disappeared into the crowd. "I can well understand why you took that line in your speech. However, it's important not to let things get out of hand. There's only room for a few to reach the top. Give too many the idea they can rise above their station and society would collapse. Don't you agree?"

"I have no truck with socialism, if that is your meaning," said Ogilvie quietly. "But possibly the ladder of opportunity can support more than you imagine. As I see it, the future depends on talent and intellect, with education and career open to all who are capable. A meritocracy, if you like."

"Bravely said. Perhaps you are right. But we won't dispute the point further." He turned to Kate. "Mrs Baird, I fear we've been neglecting you. You must find all this talk tedious."

"Quite the contrary. It's most interesting."

"Really? Then that is to your credit." He smiled at Alastair. "That's a fine lad you have there. What is the badge? I don't immediately recognise the school."

"Fairhill Academy. Yes, we're very proud of him. We have hopes of sending Alastair to university next year. He certainly won't be going down the mine."

The coalmaster laughed. "One of Mr Ogilvie's protégés, I can see that. And now you must forgive me. I'm due to rejoin the others. Mr Allardice will be fretting. There's no need for you to come, Elizabeth. A pleasure to have met you all." With a nod he moved away.

"Time I was about my obligations as well," said the dominie. "I must circulate before everyone goes home. There's a lot of folk to be thanked."

"That goes for me too," added Kate. "I promised to help out with the teas. I'll leave you young people to get acquainted."

Her lips pursed into a half-smile, but there was no corresponding twinkle in her eyes. She could not resist a glance, unmistakable to Elizabeth, incomprehensible to Alastair. For an instant the girl's heart fluttered. Had her stratagem been detected? Oh well, what did it matter? Everything was working out perfectly. At last she had him to herself.

"Let's find a quiet place, somewhere we can talk," she said. "I know. By the side of the stage. There's hardly anyone there."

There was an insistent tug at his sleeve. Bewildered, he allowed himself to be drawn along.

"Now we can get to know each other better." Elizabeth plumped herself down on the low platform. "Come and sit down beside me. I won't bite."

Reluctantly, as though mesmerised, Alastair obeyed.

"How old are you?" she demanded.

"Er, sixteen, Miss Lixmont."

"How formal you are. I'm Elizabeth, to my friends. And I shall call you Alastair. What a fine, manly name. Like the noble savages of the Highland clans in the history books. It suits you."

Alastair laughed in spite of himself. "Surely that's a little over the score. I've never been to the Highlands. Though come to think of it, I did hear tell that my great-grandfather came from up north. Argyllshire, I think. He was a crofter. I never knew him, though."

"There you are then. That proves it." She rattled on. "I'm sixteen too. When's your birthday?"

"Why, February."

"Mine's October. So I'm senior to you. Nearly seventeen in fact. It's nice for the lady to be older than the man sometimes. Don't you think so?"

"I've never really thought about it." He did not quite know what to make of this barrage of questioning, but her obvious interest was very flattering, and the scent of her perfume alluring. He began to relax, acknowledging the pleasure in her companionship.

"How do you spend your time in a place like this? There can't be much to do."

"Oh, there's any amount of things. I often go for rambles on the moors. There are plenty of relics to be discovered. The story of past generations is all around, if you know how to read the signs."

"It sounds so fascinating. I'd love to do that, with you as my guide." Then she sighed. "But unfortunately I have to go back home tomorrow."

"That is a pity. But perhaps on your next visit something could be arranged."

"I'll look forward to that." She squeezed his arm gently.

"Are you still at school, Miss Elizabeth?" Alastair tried to hide his embarrassment.

"No. I've just left. My parents say I needn't bother about taking exams."

"What will you do then?"

"Oh, I expect I'll be packed off to some finishing school abroad. Trained up in the social graces, how to be a good little wife and run the home to perfection. Then I'll be pushed and prodded into society so that I can be inspected by prospective husbands."

"You make it sound like a cattle market, Miss Elizabeth."

"That's exactly what it is. How I wish I could break the bonds of convention, do something worthwhile with my life."

"Then why don't you?"

"Not as easy as all that. Oh Alastair, if only there was some Prince Charming to sweep me away from my cruel fate. But that's only a pipedream." Abruptly she changed tack. "Your mother said you might be going up to the varsity. What would you study?"

"I'd probably specialise in history, and possibly take English and Latin as well. Oh, and educational studies. I hope to qualify as a teacher."

"Helping the young to develop and grow. That's a noble ambition. You'd be achieving so much. You know, Alastair, perhaps I could turn my hand to that. Much better than simply being an adornment on someone's arm. Yes, it's something to think about."

"Glad to have been of assistance, Miss Elizabeth."

"You haven't mentioned which college you're going to attend."

"Glasgow, most likely. Maybe Edinburgh. It's not finally decided."

"I see. Then you must choose Edinburgh. That's where I live. I could show you round the sights. It's a beautiful city. And you could visit my home in Trinity. That's a nice area in the suburbs, with lovely views over the Firth of Forth." She sighed. "If only my parents could be persuaded to allow me to go to university. We might actually be in the same class. What do you say to that?"

"That would be dandy. But is there any possibility?"

"Shall I tell you a secret, Alastair?" Her eyes twinkled. "Till this evening I hated every minute of my stay here. I was even looking forward to going home. And now I'm sorry to be leaving. Can you believe that?"

Before he could gather his thoughts to answer, a beckoning voice intruded. "Elizabeth, we really must go now. The car's waiting."

The spell was broken. She jumped up and held out her hand.

"Goodbye, Alastair. It's been lovely. I'm so glad to have met you. Till the next time."

He watched her departing figure wistfully. At the doorway she waved, and was gone.

"I'd be careful, son." Kate was suddenly at his side. "I've had my eye on that one. I saw her practisin' her wiles on ye. Amusin' herself at your expense. To the likes o' her, ye're just a plaything, a rag doll to be picked up an' cast out on a whim. Best to leave well alone."

Alastair stood wondering, then with something like a groan, turned to help his mother clear away.

* * *

Kate fussed and fretted as the hour drew ever nearer, peering through the window, darting glances at the mantelpiece clock, brushing imaginary creases from her new dress, restlessly pacing the kitchen; she could not keep still for a moment.

It was the day of the wedding. The weather had been obliging, a fine, sunny, summer morning, with only a few wisps of cloud high in the sky. All the preparations were complete, or as much as they were ever likely to be. Mary was next door, having her hair dressed and veil fitted by the bridesmaid; Alastair was in the street, with strict instructions to report the instant the carriage was in sight. In a few minutes Cha and his wife would be at the sneck; how thoughtful of them to have insisted on escorting her to the kirk.

The last few days had simply disappeared in a whirl. There had been so much to do, a thousand tasks to carry out. She could never have managed without so many willing hands to help ease the burden. But it was her responsibility to ensure everything went smoothly. And it was for her to meet the cost. It was a simple matter of principle. All in all, a full ten pounds had been laid out on the festivities, money saved from her husband's compensation. Had she done the right thing? It had been set aside for Alastair's education, but Mary had a claim too. Geordie would never have been niggardly when it came to giving his daughter a good send-off; he always enjoyed a good party. After all, there was still a year or so to make up the shortfall.

There was but one issue still to be resolved. Alastair, despite his reservations, had loyally carried out her wishes. He had gone to see Iain, though with no definite result. If she'd asked him once, she had quizzed him a hundred times over every detail of that visit. How had Iain reacted to the surprise appearance of his brother? Put out, at first. But once over the initial shock, things had not gone too badly. When Alastair had let slip his expectation of going up to university, there had been no tirade of condemnation. On the contrary, Iain had smugly countered with a declaration that he might not be the only one in the family destined for higher things. What did he think of the news of Mary's impending marriage? He had shrugged his shoulders. It was bound to happen sooner or later, and Rob White was as good as anyone else.

But would he come to the wedding? That was the all-important question. Alastair had felt he was being evasive, looking for excuses, reluctant to give a firm answer. His presence might not be welcome in certain quarters, not that he was bothered by that, as he was at pains to emphasise. In short, it was Alastair's view that Iain was up to his tricks again; he would keep them in suspense, and at the end leave them standing. Look on the bright side, he had told her. At least his absence would avoid any risk of unpleasantness. But she knew better. He would be there, even at the last minute, if only out of curiosity.

"Anybody at home!" It was the Whites. Goodness, was that the time already? She hastened to admit them.

"Ready for the off, Kate?" Cha made a mock bow as he presented her with a bouquet of wild flowers. "Cannae hae a weddin' wi'out flooers. An' am

I no' the lucky one? To hae the honour o' promenading through the toun wi' a bonny lass on each arm."

"Get awa' wi' ye. Ye're an auld rogue, Cha. Bide a wee while I fix my hat."

At that moment Alastair came rushing in to announce that the trap had rounded the corner.

"Dinnae fash yersel', laddie," said Kate. "We're just away. You're in charge here now. See that Mary gets hersel' settled, and come on when ye're ready. Don't leave it ower late, though. I ken ye'll no' let us down. You're the man o' the house. Make yer faither proud o' ye." She pecked him affectionately on the cheek. "Let's be off, then. It widnae do to be the last to arrive."

The house seemed strangely silent, after all the bustle. Brother and sister found little to say; Alastair preoccupied with the responsibility of giving away the bride, Mary all of a flutter at the prospect of her new status. The hands on the clock crawled ever slower, but at last reached the point that Alastair had fixed for departure.

"Time to make a move, sis." He forced a smile. "No second thoughts? Last minute change of heart?"

They looked at each other, as if in anticipation of some grim fate, and then simultaneously broke out into a fit of giggling.

* * *

On the far side of the Square, beyond the Jubilee Memorial, lay the village hall, an ugly, squat building donated by a previous generation of coalmasters as a sop to the community. In the vestibule Kate stood in line with the others to greet guests as they arrived. Once the formalities were complete, Alastair would direct them towards a celebratory sherry or whisky, followed by an invitation to view the presents. Goodness, how her arm ached from so much handshaking. At least it was nearly over. Here came the last of the dawdlers, with the minister bringing up the rear. And the ceremony itself had passed off splendidly; everyone was saying so. Mary was in her element, aglow with pride and happiness. But there was still that niggling worry. Her eyes darted round the room once more, and she strained to peer out into the Square. Still no sign of her firstborn. He had not been in church, she was sure of that. Had Alastair been right all along? Had it been foolish to suppose he would come? She did not know whether to be upset or relieved.

"Whatever ails ye, Kate?" growled Cha White. "Ye're like a hen on hot bricks. Ye were the same in the kirk. Aye lookin' about ye. Couldna keep yer heid still for a minute."

"Sorry, Cha." Kate was contrite. "Nerves, I expect."

"Weel, try an' relax now. That's the worst o' it ower. Ye've worked wonders, woman. A'body thinks so. But you're here to enjoy yersel' tae. Come an' hae some sherry. That'll set ye straight."

The reception party started to break up. Cha handed her a glass and raised his own tumbler. "Here's tae ye, Kate. May a' yer wishes come true."

There was clink of glasses, Kate smiled ... and her expression changed. She was staring past him, at the doorway. Cha whirled round, and gaped as though he had seen an apparition.

"This is your doin', Kate." He was pale with anger. "Now I ken why ye were behavin' like that. Ye were expectin' him. You invited him."

"Wheesht, Cha. And why should I no' hae a' the family here? Has he no' the right to see his sister wed?"

"After a' he's done? I should think no'."

"Ye're no' gonnae create a scene, are ye, Cha?" She looked appealingly at him. "It would just spoil things for a'body. Especially yer son an' daughter-in-law. It is their big day."

"He's enough to ruin any occasion. Ye shouldnae have done this, Kate, no' wi'out tellin' me." He hesitated, then unbent a little. "Aw' right. Have it yer own way. I'll no' make a fuss. Just keep the bugger well away frae me."

There was no time to reply. Iain was making an entrance, bold as brass, striding towards them. He swept straight up to the newlyweds and, without a word, enveloped Mary in a bear hug and planted a noisy slurp on her cheek. Rob stood aghast at such presumption, and was too bemused to resist when, in his turn, his hand was gripped tightly in a trial of strength.

"So ma wee sister has gotten' hersel' spliced at last. Congratulations to the pair o' ye. Pity I missed the weddin' ceremony. I was really lookin' forward tae that. Blame the trains, though. A'ways late. Still, we're here now. That's the main thing. An' afore I forget, here's a wee present."

"This is a surprise," was all Mary could say, as she struggled to regain her composure. "Thank ye kindly. Rob, would ye put Iain's gift wi' the others?"

Kate, too, had recoiled at such temerity, but quickly recovered. "It's good tae see ye again, son. I'm sae pleased ye could find the time to make this a real family gatherin'. "

"No, maw, it's for me to thank you. I'm fair glad that ye thought tae ask me. Have ye a wee kiss for the prodigal son?"

Kate forced a laugh. "No' if it's like the one ye gave Mary." But she turned her face to allow him the merest brush of his lips.

"Ye've nae idea how long I've waited for that," he said softly. There still remained Cha, glowering at him. "Mr White, will ye shake my hand? Have done wi' the past?"

"Never! No' while there's breath in my body. No' tae the likes o' you. Ye've wheedled yer way in. Let that be enough. Ye'd do well to keep out o' my way while ye're here. And the sooner ye're awa' back tae wherever ye came fae, the better."

"I'm sorry ye feel like that. I really wanted tae make amends." His tone was humble, even penitent.

Just then Rob came rushing back, fuming with rage.

"Dae ye ken what he's done, Mary?" he spluttered. "Thon present, if ye can ca' it that. It's an outrage, that's what it is. Just a lump o' coal, cut intae the shape o' a miner, an' sittin' in his bath. It's an affront tae honest toil. I've thrown it under the table. It isnae fit to be seen. He deserves a kickin' for this."

"And who's gonnae dae that?" began Iain threateningly. "You?"

"See what I mean, Kate," said Cha wryly. "The leopard changin' its spots, eh?"

Kate hastily interposed. "Enough! Let's hae no more squabblin'. The photographer's waitin'. And folk will be getting' hungry. Iain, you'll be beside me."

"No, maw. I should never hae come. Ye see what they think o' me. It'll just end in a fight." He turned on his heel.

Kate hurried after him, but he was outside in the deserted yard before she managed to catch up. "Dinnae leave, no' just yet," she pleaded, laying her hand on his arm.

"It's nae good, maw," he mumbled. "Ye've put yersel' out for me. And I appreciate yer effort. But it hasnae worked. I've bent over backwards tae try an' make things up. But they winnae hae it. Ye heard what Cha White had to say. I'd best be on my way. Save any mair embarrassment."

"I ken it's difficult. Folk hae long memories. But ye've taken the first step. They'll come round. Just gie them time."

"Aye. How long?" He laughed harshly. "The only way they want me back in this place is in a box."

"Ye're hurtin', I can tell that. I just wish there was somethin' I could dae for ye."

"What have you ever done for me?" He saw the mild look of reproach, and felt a stab of guilt. "Sorry. I shouldnae have said that." He tried to make amends. "I must say ye've done Mary proud. Put on a fine show. That took a lot o' organising, I'll be bound. And cost a pretty penny. However did ye manage it?"

"Well, it is for the bride after all. And it's only once in a lifetime. There were plenty o' people to offer help. And a bit o' cash left over from the compensation money." She bit her lip in vexation as soon as the words were uttered. How stupid could she be? But it was too late now.

A strange gleam came into Iain's eyes. "Naebody could grudge her that," he said carefully. "After a' she's done for you, she deserves it. And what about Alastair? He tells me he's for the university. That'll mean a fair sum, what wi' fees an' books an' such like."

Alarm bells rang in Kate's head. She was beginning to realise where this might lead. "Well," she temporised, "there's awards and scholarships. And a grant to train as a teacher."

"But that won't cover a'thing, will it? You'll still need tae help him out."

"Ye-es. That's true, I suppose."

"Maw, I wanted tae tell ye somethin'. Did Alastair mention that I might be goin' to college as well?"

"No' exactly. He said you were vague about yer prospects."

"Weel, I've no' wasted my time these past years. I've enrolled in night classes at the Institute. And won diplomas an' certificates. Enough to qualify me to take up engineerin' at Glasgow University."

"University, ye say? That would be an achievement."

"Aye. But the point is this. I'd need tae take time off work while I was at my studies. So I wouldnae be earnin'. The yard would pay the fees an' gie me an allowance, but no' enough to cover a' the costs. So I was just thinkin' –"

"What were you thinking, Iain?"

"Ye mind years ago when I asked for some o' faither's money? What I thought was my due? You refused. And ye were quite right. I would probably just hae squandered it. But don't ye see? Things are different now." His voice took on a new enthusiasm. "It would be for a good cause – helpin' me qualify as an engineer. A few pounds would make all the difference. An' then I could repay you. Gie you a comfortable old age."

So it had come to this again. He wanted his share. Perhaps the money would be used in the way he promised; but that was open to doubt. In any case there was little enough left. It had all been set aside for Alastair. He had worked so hard; nothing must be allowed to spoil his chances.

"Iain", she began gently, "I'm very pleased at what ye've managed to achieve. Truly I am. But all this is rather sudden, would ye no' say? You must be aware how we're situated. I'm sorry, but there's no' a penny to spare."

"And that's your last word?" Anger welled within him. He sprang back, snarling with bitter frustration. "So you'll do nothin' for me. I'm to be robbed again. And I thought you understood. But scratch the surface, an' ye're the same as a' the rest. Damn ye!"

Tears in her eyes, she could only watch despairingly as he stormed off. Then a sudden thought struck her, so terrible she almost quaked in alarm. Iain would be never let this pass. Given the chance, he would have his revenge.

"It's all right, maw." Alastair had run out in search of her. "He's gone now."

Kate shook her head. "It's no' all right. Ye were right, an' I was wrong tae think that he could change. I'm just a silly auld woman. But I had tae make the effort, don't ye see that?"

"Don't take on, maw. There's only one person to blame for this. And it's certainly not you. You're kind and generous to a fault. And we wouldn't have it any other way."

She took his arm. "We canna keep folk waitin'. They'll be wantin' fed." Together they slowly walked back towards the hall. "I've been havin' second thoughts, son. Maybe Glesga isnae such a good idea. Edinburgh might suit ye better. I ken ye'll be further away, an' we'll no' see so much o' each other, but … what dae ye think, laddie?"

Wild hopes stirred within him. Was it possible after all?

EIGHT

A Parting of the Ways

Glasgow. November 1911

"Hey, you! Heid the ba'! Get yer arse over here." Iain Baird was clean through with the goal at his mercy. He looked round, hesitated, and fluffed his shot. It was only a dinnertime kickabout in the engineering yard, with rolled-up jackets for goalposts, but the apprentices took their sport seriously. Iain swore loudly in exasperation and glowered at the source of the interruption. It was the foreman, who had apparently sauntered down to take in the match.

Sullenly he tramped over. It was his break. No one had the right to deprive him of that.

"Carry on wi' your game lads. Sorry ye'll have to do without your ace forward for a while."

More mockery! He was being jibbed again about his prowess at football. It was a sore point. What he lacked in skill, he more than made up in strength and effort. And there was a real chance of breaking into the works team. He needed all the practice he could get to impress the selectors.

"What is it ye want, Mr Dawson? The hooter'll be goin' soon."

"All in good time, son. How's the man o' letters the day?"

Iain clenched his teeth, biting back the urge to retaliate. Dawson was always trying to wind him up, if not about football, then on his studies. He was not a bad gaffer at heart, not a tyrant like some; but he could never resist the temptation to ridicule the young man's attempts to better himself, not since finding out about his attendance at night school. Secrets in the workplace? A snowball in hell had a better chance! It was different with the other apprentices; he was only too ready to use his fists to steer them away from comments on that subject. As for the foreman's jests, he knew he had to try harder to ignore them.

Dawson softened. "You ken, Iain, no good will ever come o' your book learning. Ye'd do well to realise yer limits and stick to that. Or else you're in for a big disappointment. Concentrate on yer football. Who knows, maybe you'll be signed up by Rangers one day."

"And the band played! But you've surely no' spoilt the gemme just tae bandy words wi' me?"

"No, that's true. I nearly forgot. Mr Findlay wants to see you."

Iain gulped. What on earth could the great panjandrum want with him? He was not conscious of any misdemeanour, at least nothing serious enough to attract attention from the brass hats. Indeed he had never spoken to the manager since the day he had gone with Lang to be taken on as a riveter. Even his transfer to the engineering works had been arranged by means of a curt note. Then it dawned on him. There could be only one possibility. His indenture would be up next month; Adam had promised to write to his brother-in-law. So it was going to be all right! His hard graft, three or four nights a week, had paid off. A broad grin spread over his face. "I think I ken what it's about, Mr Dawson."

"Do you? Then ye ken more than me."

"Aye. You'll no' be seein' me round here much longer. I'm for the university. An engineerin' degree, like as no'. And then work in an office. Black coat, collar an' tie. Ye'll no' catch me as a common or garden journeyman."

"And ye really believe that? Grow up, laddie. You'll be in the shop, wi' mucky hands and clarty overalls like the rest. If ye have a job at all, that is. Anyhow, best no' keep the chief waiting." With a rueful shake of the head he ambled away.

Iain almost sprinted towards the main building. On this occasion there was to be no long wait in the outer office. Quivering with anticipation, he was shown in after only the briefest of delays. Findlay was standing by the window, looking out over the yard.

"Iain Baird, sir. As you requested." The clerk bowed and faded from the scene.

"Ah, Baird. Good of you to come so promptly." His face was expressionless, his voice quiet and restrained. In his hand he held an envelope. "This is a letter from your – your adviser, Mr Lang," he said, tapping it with his forefinger. "Were you aware of his intention to write?"

"Aye, sir. It's nearly the end o' my apprenticeship. We were talkin' over my options."

"Just so." He seated himself behind his desk and withdrew the enclosure. "He states that you have undertaken courses of study in your own time to further your knowledge of the theoretical aspects of shipbuilding."

"Aye, that's right. And passed the exams. I've got certificates in metallurgy, technical drawin', applied science and mathematics. I can bring them in, if ye like."

"That will not be necessary. I may say that I fully approve of an employee showing ambition and applying himself diligently to master the principles of his craft. Provided it isn't taken too far, that is."

"Thank ye kindly, sir."

"Listen, Baird, I won't beat about the bush. I had my doubts when you started here. But you have apparently proved me wrong. I've taken the trouble to check with the Institute. The principal informs me that you have a keen, enquiring mind, a desire to learn, and have achieved consistently high grades. I have also requested a report from your foreman. He is of the opinion that your work, attitude, attendance and timekeeping are all first rate. So you have obviously made the most of your stay here. And that is worthy of recognition. I am pleased to announce that you are to be awarded a special bonus of two guineas. No doubt a welcome contribution towards the forthcoming festivities, would you not say?"

"Very generous o' ye, sir." Better and better! Fancy old Dawson extolling his virtues; he would never have expected it from such a crusty old codger.

"No more than you deserve. And now to other matters – perhaps not quite so cheerful. Mr Lang goes on to speak of the possibility of sponsorship in order to pursue studies at Glasgow University. He specifically mentions the School of Naval Architecture. Well, I'm afraid your friend has rather let his enthusiasm run away with him. To put it bluntly, it's no more than a flight of fancy on his part."

Iain's eagerness began to ebb away. "That cannae be right. I am qualified for the course. I do meet the regulations. The Institute confirmed it. You can ask them."

"You may well be qualified. On paper, that is. But the fact remains that Deuchar's simply could not undertake to support you for the period necessary to gain a degree."

"But you do send folk to the university. Why not me?"

"True. But we would never contemplate more than one or two placements a year. Only the most suitable candidates, those destined for the top, would be considered. And that would be either a close relative of a member of the board or a premium apprentice."

"Premium apprentice? D'ye mean thae popinjays who talk posh and just swan about. Never stay mair than five minutes in one place. Or get their hands dirty. What dae they learn about buildin' ships?"

Findlay refused to be ruffled. "That's one way of putting it, I suppose. Not mine, of course. More accurate to say someone of good family who is prepared to pay a substantial fee to be taught all aspects of the business. Someone who could expect to progress into management. So you see it's simply impossible. Not my rules. Just the way things are."

Desperation seized him. He could not give up now. There must be a way. "What about short courses? I could go to college for a spell. Then come back for six months or so. I'd be here most o' the time. You wouldnae need to gie me an allowance. It'll take longer, but I'd get there in the end."

Findlay held up a restraining hand. "I applaud your perseverance, really I do. But it cuts no ice. Sandwich courses, day release, full-time study – it makes no difference. And in case you're thinking Lang might see you through university, I fear that would be a fool's paradise. Oh, you might be accepted, be awarded a degree. But you'd never be engaged as a marine engineer. Not at any yard on the Clyde. Nothing personal, but class will out. It's for your own good really. You'd be like a fish out of water."

Iain reeled. The finality of the judgment struck him like a whiplash. He opened his mouth, but no words would come. He was totally stunned. So it had all been for nothing. All his hopes and dreams dashed in an instant. It was so unfair! He collapsed into a chair, too numbed to protest further at the injustice.

Findlay looked at his visitor thoughtfully. In the nature of things apprentices and journeymen were normally far beneath his compass. But in this case he felt some responsibility, and had decided to make an exception to inform him personally. It was not Baird's fault he came from the wrong background. The blame was entirely down to Lang, filling the lad's head with nonsense, giving him ideas way beyond his station.

Nor had the fellow been particularly helpful in that other matter. Certainly he had written the piece as promised, and it had duly appeared in print. Much good it had done! A few lines tucked away in an inside page. Either it went unnoticed or attracted snide comments. The general consensus appeared to be that if the *Dispatch* was advocating a particular candidate, then that was the one to be avoided at all costs. He should never have agreed to the article. Still, the directorship had been a long shot, and he bore his disappointment without too much rancour.

Now, however, promotion was his for the taking. Not a seat on the board, but a good second best. The international situation was on a knife-edge, the naval arms race with Germany speeding towards a climax. Admiralty orders were accelerating; there was even talk of War Office contracts. Deuchar's, like other yards, was expanding, or rather entering into partnership with an arms consortium in response to the demand. The result would be interlocking companies, vertical integration of all facets of production – from steelmaking to armour plate, to gun manufacture, engine and boiler making, even motor transport. A new site had been built further down the Clyde, and would soon be ready to start churning out the sinews of war. It was to be named *Ibrox Ordnance*: Findlay rather liked that. Perhaps it would even rival the Beardmore empire, based on the Parkhead Forge in the East End. And he had been sounded out about the appointment as general manager. He had almost decided to accept. It was the last big chance he was likely to be offered.

The plant would have need of good, time-served men – a multitude of them. And in this climate of growth there was sure to be a labour shortage. Young Baird seemed to possess the makings of a useful subordinate. Surely he would have the sense not to spurn a reasonable offer. A consolation prize, no doubt, but with opportunities for those with the right qualities.

"See here, lad. You've had a jolt, I can appreciate that. But you have to make the best of things. There's no point in moping. You'll have heard about the new works down Govan way. They'll be looking for dependable men, especially those with a spark of initiative. You could be one of the first batch to start there in a month or two, and if you show promise I think I can safely say that you'd attain foreman status within a couple of years. That's far earlier than you'd ever manage here. And it would qualify you for a company house at a very easy rent. How would you like that?"

There was no response. Iain continued to sit motionless, as though in a trance. Findlay could not be certain whether he had been listening or not. He contrived to stifle his impatience.

"Talk it over with your Mr Lang. Let me have your answer next week." He rang the bell to summon an official. "Greig, Baird appears to be rather under the weather. He requires some assistance. Would you oblige? Inform Mr Dawson that he has been given the rest of the day off. With pay."

Iain was too stupefied to offer any resistance as he was helped to his feet and led out. He had admired Adam so much, looked on him almost as a second father. And what was the result of his blind loyalty? Five years of his life swept down the drain. Book learning counted for little unless you went to the right school. How had he allowed himself to be so misled? Bosses like Findlay would only let a man rise so far before the shutters slammed in his face.

But … on the other hand there was a debt of gratitude. He owed Lang so much, rescuing him from the gutter, providing shelter, finding him a job. He had the run of the house, a room to call his own; and not a penny accepted in rent all those years. Adam rarely interfered in his private life, asking few questions how he spent his time. He was tolerant, liberal in his views, even to the extent of turning a blind eye to the female company Iain sometimes brought home to entertain in his quarters. All the same … perhaps it was time to cut the knot and move on. That might be for the best. A hazy recollection came into his mind. What was it that Findlay had said about a company house?

* * *

New Year 1912

Adam Lang awoke with a start. What was that din, disturbing a man's rest? Damn! Those blasted church bells again, calling the faithful to evening services. Heaving himself from his armchair, he crossed to the window to draw the heavy drapes. Perhaps that would cut out some of the noise. Then, stifling a yawn, he returned to the hearth to stir the embers of the fire back into life, before banking up the grate with fresh coal from the scuttle. It was Sunday, the last day of the old year. Ne'erday was only a few short hours away. No doubt Iain would be going out to celebrate with his friends. For his part he would be quite happy to remain at home with a quiet whisky for company.

Hogmanay – a time for reflection, as well as anticipation of better days to come. He was forced to admit that he had blundered badly in taking Findlay's cooperation for granted. His brother-in-law could certainly have arranged things had he been so disposed. Probably this was his retaliation for failing to win that directorship. Iain had cut up quite rough, accusing him of responsibility for all that wasted effort. It had taken all his powers of persuasion to convince him to accept the offer of a start at the new works. Even so, he was still muttering threats to walk out and leave. He had always appreciated that the parting of the ways must inevitably come sooner or later, but surely not quite yet. Iain was no fool; he knew when he was well off. He would not risk his creature comforts till he was certain of something better. Another year or so; that was all he asked. Then he could retire, sell up, leave the smoke and rush of the big city, and settle in the clean air downriver where the pace of life was more placid.

He cast his mind back to that first meeting. He had had a hunch they would rub along together. And by and large he had been proved correct. Youth and age; the combination had worked well. In the last analysis the balance sheet was very far from being one-sided, as might have been supposed. The youngster had been like a breath of fresh air, helping to draw him from his old, sloppy ways, encouraging him towards a new lease of life. He had cut down on his heavy drinking and paid more attention to his appearance; he had lost weight and regained much of his former vigour. His career had revived; his byline had even appeared on the main news page again. Of course he was not up to dashing around like a young buck any more, but this had been recognised. He was now accorded the status of an elder statesman in the pressroom, honoured where once he had been ridiculed, his advice sought out by the younger men just starting to make their way.

There was a slight creak as a door opened across the hallway, followed by the soft padding of feet on the linoleum. So the lad was up at last! It had gone midday when he had returned from last night's drunken orgy, announcing his arrival with enough noise to wake the dead. Now he would be off to the lavatory to relieve himself, before sluicing away the remains of the hangover at the kitchen sink. Doubtless he would then put in an appearance, somewhat pale about the gills perhaps, but otherwise none the worse for wear.

Ten minutes later Iain finally presented himself, in shirtsleeves and braces, just as he had anticipated. He looked up and smiled. "Back in the land of the living, are we? Come away and sit down. Get some heat into those bones."

"Thanks. Just for a minute, though. I'm due out again soon."

"But you've had nothing to eat," Lang protested. "Surely you can stay for a bite of supper, can't you?"

"'Fraid not. I'll get somethin' up the toun."

"Well, that's a disappointment. But you'll take a wee nip afore you go? Hair of the dog? We'll not see in the New Year together."

Iain stretched over to take the proffered tumbler and allowed a small measure of whisky to be poured. They touched glasses, toasted each other with the traditional *slainte*, and sipped appreciatively.

"That's the real cratur," said Lang. "Finest single malt. So, Iain, what are your plans for Ne'erday?"

"Just the usual. I'm meetin' the mates for a few jars. Then off to see in the year at the Tron. After that, try an' wedge in at some pairty."

"But the pubs are all closed today. Tomorrow as well, since it's a public holiday."

Iain touched his nose. "Not if ye ken where to go. There's aye the back door. Once it's shut the polis cannae touch ye."

Lang chuckled. "I should have known better. Will I be seeing you again in the morning?"

"I shouldnae think so. We'll probably end up dossin' down for a few hours somewhere or other. Then it's off tae the gemme at Parkheid. There's sure to be a big crowd, so we'll need tae get there early. And we'll hae to walk, like as no.'"

"You've fairly taken to football in a big way, haven't you? You showed little interest when we first met."

"That's because I'd never been tae a big match. Now, when ye're part o' the crowd, ye feel a sense o' belonging. You can let yer emotions go. Ye're totally involved. Ye share every kick o' the ball wi' the players. And the buzz ye get when the team wins. Ye're up there in the clouds. There's nothin' to beat that."

"And if they lose?"

"That's no' very often. But if it does happen, why, it's like a personal insult. Ye feel affronted. And God help the other supporters if they start crowin.'"

"So you bask in the reflected glory of a winning team and treat defeat as an intolerable slur. And that gives you a sense of identity?"

"You could put it that way, right enough. One thing I have learned is that ye have to show who ye are. In Glesga ye're either a billy or a dan. If ye're a proddie ye follow Rangers."

"So you've no time for Catholics?"

"Time? For the likes o' them? They're no' to be trusted. It's up to us to keep them in their place. Or else they'll be stampin' a'thing wi' their papist ways. Look at Ireland. Demandin' Home Rule. Bloody cheek! That means Rome rule. We want none o' that here."

Lang threw up his hands in mock surrender. "I wish I hadn't brought up the subject. You sound like a candidate for the Orange Order."

"That might be no bad thing. At least joining it wouldnae do my prospects any harm. More help than studyin' from books."

"Surely you're not going to drag that up again?"

"No." Iain was conciliatory. "It's dead and buried as far as I'm concerned. Anyhow, I must be on my way now. Thanks for the drink."

Both stood up and shook hands, then instinctively hugged one another. Adam patted him on the shoulder as they separated. This was better. The first spark of affection for many a day.

"You'll need a bottle for your First Foot. Take one from the press. And a piece of coal. It's the custom, you know." He watched as Iain gingerly picked a small lump from the scuttle and wrapped it in his handkerchief. "Mind your overcoat. It'll be cold outside."

"No, I winnae bother. Likely I'll just lose it someplace. My jacket and muffler will do fine. Sorry to leave ye on yer own like this. Hope it's no' too quiet for ye. I should be back directly after the match. Say the back o' five." He turned to leave, but paused as an idea struck him. "Here, we could take in a show if you like. Tomorrow night. Just the two o' us."

"Aye, I'd enjoy that. Call it a date, then. Have a good time, now."

Iain found the whisky in the pantry, selected a bottle from the rack, and carried it over to his room. He crossed to the washstand. Beside the basin and ewer lay his razor, its handle inlaid with mother-of-pearl; Adam had presented him with it on his eighteenth birthday. Such a beautiful object, so perfectly balanced that the blade flew open with the merest flick of his wrist. He was not expecting trouble, but … it was wiser to take precautions. Slipping it carefully into his waistband, he donned jacket and scarf, thrust the bottle into his pocket and turned down the gas. His preparations complete, he called out a final "good night" from the front door, and skipped lightly down the stairs.

* * *

The crowd came pouring through the exits in the gathering gloom, a seething, heaving flow of humanity, expanding and filling the streets round the stadium like waters streaming over a flood plain. The home supporters were jubilant with the thrill of victory, the opposition silent and brooding, the wounds still raw after the shock of defeat.

Gradually the pressure eased as the multitude fanned out to begin the homeward journey. Like so many others around them, Iain and his companions pulled up their collars round their ears, and set off to trudge westwards towards the city centre. There was little to be said; emotions ran too deep. Their team had started so brightly, that was what made the result so hard to bear. To lose three goals was unthinkable, and yet it had happened. Anger at the score tempted the disgruntled fans to trample their banners and favours into the dirt, but pride restrained them. They would come back all the stronger next time. In the meantime it only remained to wipe the insult clean. From somewhere up ahead came the trill of a fife. Inevitably it was *The Sash*, their anthem. The tune was infectious, lifting their spirits. Men were joining in; soon the whole column was singing lustily, the familiar words ringing out in defiance.

As they marched along, their numbers steadily dwindled as the less committed fell out to make their own way home or seek out a rare tram heading for the outlying districts. Thus it was that by the time they reached the junction with the High Street and Saltmarket only a hard core of a few hundred remained, mainly young men in their late teens and early twenties, and all spoiling for a fight. From a distance came a counter chant, growing ever stronger as they drew nearer. In the roadway, blocking the way, stood a solid phalanx of the enemy, brandishing makeshift weapons. Roars of derision rang out as the two groups confronted each other, taunts and challenges exchanged as they worked themselves up into a frenzy of loathing, like dervishes preparing for an all-out assault.

Papist swine! Orange turds! Such imprecations, and far worse, were hurled to and fro for several minutes. Those who had had the forethought to come armed grasped knives and hammers and knuckledusters from their place of concealment. Others feverishly grabbed whatever came to hand – bottles, stones, anything that could be pressed into service as a makeshift weapon. Iain did not draw his razor; that was a last resort. Instead he pulled up a sapling from its kerbside plot. With the upper part snapped off, the remainder of the trunk and knob of the root made a fearsome cudgel.

Missiles were thrown, a few at first as though to test the defences; and then a veritable fusillade of stones, bricks and bottles flew through the air. The yells and war cries shrieked louder; both sides began to edge closer, winding themselves up for the final rush that would pitch them into hand-to-hand combat.

* * *

Inspector Chisholm leaned forward in the saddle, his eyes glittering as he assessed the situation. The passing years had wrought little change; he might be a little more grizzled in appearance, but his brain was as keen and calculating as ever. His troop of horse waited impassively, tucked away out of sight in the lane behind him. As reinforcements there was a squad of Glasgow's finest, ready for action, and in the rear a row of enclosed police wagons.

His instructions had been to be on hand to quell any sign of disorder in the city centre. There would be no mob rule here, not on his patch – no repetition of the Hampden Riot, less than three years previously. God knew how much damage had been done on that occasion. He had been away on leave at the time, else it would never have been allowed to develop into such a shambles. And it was not about to happen now. It wanted but a few months to his retiral. A triumph here would do very nicely to set the seal on his career.

It was time to make his move. Chisholm nudged his horse out into the middle of the street; his men obediently followed him into line. The local bobbies could be relied upon to mop up and make the arrests. He drew the long truncheon from its holster and signalled the advance: walk, trot, canter

– charge! As usual his judgment was faultless. The ruffians were totally preoccupied, their front ranks converging, just starting to grapple with each other. Only those on the fringe of the affray glimpsed the awesome peril thundering down before the mounted police were in and about them, slashing out with their batons; men were going down like ninepins, trampled underfoot in the turmoil. Blind panic spread like wildfire; in less than a minute the street was emptied, apart from the dozens who were left behind, groaning, dazed and bleeding. The police vans rolled up like so many tumbrels, and the constables began to load the bodies, tossing them in like sacks of potatoes, utterly oblivious as to the extent of their injuries.

The inspector, well to the fore, cut his way through the throng. The louts fell away before him, fleeing like headless chickens. One individual running like a hare down the Trongate caught his eye. On an impulse he made a decision. This one was his. It would do no harm to make a personal arrest, show the men he was prepared to get his hands dirty. He spurred his horse in pursuit.

Like everyone else, Iain Baird had been caught off guard by this new attack from such an unexpected quarter. But he was quick to recover. Seeing the horsemen crashing into the maul, sweeping aside all in their path like so much chaff, he had dropped his club and taken to his heels. Now he stopped to listen; his heart was pounding, his breath laboured, his muscles felt like lead. Surely he had made good his escape.

God, no! There was a galloper coming up fast; the drum of hoof beats grew louder at an alarming rate. In moments he would be run down. He choked back a stab of terror. There might still be a chance. If only he could break away, dash into an alley, he might be able to dodge in the shadows and slip away unseen. Over there! He forced his legs into one last effort and swerved towards a narrow opening. Too late! His intention had been spotted; he would never make it. A dark silhouette loomed up only a few yards away, arm upraised to strike him down. He heard a swish through the air and at the last second tried to jump aside. There was an oath from his assailant as the blow glanced off his shoulder instead of cracking his head. But it was enough. There was a searing jar of pain, his knees buckled and he tumbled headlong into the gutter. Writhing in agony, he tried to haul himself to his feet. It was no good. He sank back, and slowly began to drag himself into a doorway. There he crouched, hangdog, like a trapped animal.

Inspector Chisholm reined in, dismounted and tethered his horse to a lamppost. He approached cautiously, truncheon at the ready. "Got you, my lad. Going to come quietly?"

There was a gleam of metal as a blade flashed open.

"Ah, would you now?" Chisholm brought his baton down sharply to knock away the weapon. Just in time Iain managed to interpose his other arm to deflect the blow. For a split second the inspector was off balance. Without thinking, Iain lunged upwards under the man's guard, casting the razor in a wide sweep. He felt resistance as the edge sliced into flesh. Chisholm gasped and staggered backwards, grasping at his throat. Tiny rivulets of blood began to seep through his fingers. He sank to his knees, his eyes wide in disbelief, before slumping forward in collapse.

Iain looked on in horror, aghast at what he had done. There came shouts, and the sound of running footsteps. The deed had been witnessed; people were coming. He must get away; his very survival might depend on it. Somehow he found the strength to stagger to his feet and hirple away into the darkness of the alley, the bloodied razor still clutched in his hand.

* * *

The door clicked shut behind him. Iain leaned against it, panting as he took in huge gulps of air. His arm hung limply by his side; any attempt to move it brought excruciating pain. His head drooped; he was utterly spent. There would be a witch-hunt, no doubt about it. Even now they might be scouring the city for him. But he was safe here. There was nothing to connect him with the assault. He could lie up for a few days till he had recovered, till the hue and cry died down. After all, he was not expected at the new armaments works till next week.

It had taken well over an hour to make his way back, through byways and backstreets, studiously avoiding main thoroughfares where his appearance might arouse curiosity. Several times he had almost swooned from sheer exhaustion; towards the end it had been hell just to force one leg in front of the other. But at least it had given him time to collect his thoughts, concoct a plausible story. The razor was safely tucked away in an inside pocket. His first impulse had been to throw it away or bury it in some midden, but...

there was always the remote chance that it might be found, and somehow be traced back to him. Besides, Adam was sure to discover it was missing sooner or later, and perhaps ask awkward questions. It might be wiser to take the damned thing home, wash it thoroughly and restore it to its rightful place. Then no one would ever know.

"Iain? That you?" The voice came from the parlour. "You're helluva late. We'll need to get our skates on now if we're to make curtain up."

Christ! He had forgotten all about the theatre. There was no way he could go out again tonight.

"Iain?" Lang looked out into the hallway. "Why are you standing there like that?" He stepped closer. "God Almighty, you're white as a sheet. And you look all in. Here, let me help you before you fall down."

Iain felt himself gripped firmly round the waist and gently propelled into the sitting room and onto the settee.

"That's better. More light in here. It's your arm, isn't it? I can see it's hanging like a rag doll. Let's get your jacket and waistcoat off. Why, there's spots of blood on your clothes. How did they get there? Have you been cut?"

Iain shook his head. "I dinnae think so."

"Then how…? Never mind. Time for that later."

Lang eased the outer garments from his limbs and tossed each in turn onto a chair. Then he fetched a pair of scissors from his desk and carefully cut away the shirt.

"My God! You're whole arm is in a right mess. Nothing but a mass of bruises. You have been in the wars." He probed gingerly. "Collar bone isn't broken. Nor your shoulder blade. The wrist is pretty swollen, but I can't feel any fracture. You're lucky. You'll be black and blue for a week, but I think that's about all. Now then, let's see about getting you fixed up."

He disappeared into the kitchen before returning with a large bottle, several rolls of bandages and what appeared to be a nightshirt from the linen press. Laying the other items down on the sofa, he unscrewed the cap of the glass container. "Some liniment to help with the bruising," he explained. "It'll hurt a bit at first, but it's good for reducing the swelling."

Iain stiffened and tried to stifle a groan as the liquid was rubbed into the bruises; it stung like fire, burning into his arm.

"Now we'll need to immobilise the shoulder." He wrapped several layers of bandage round his torso, effectively binding the upper arm to his side.

"Now for the wrist. There, that should hold you. Beginning to feel a bit more comfortable?" Iain nodded his thanks.

"Good. If you can stand up a minute, we'll just slip this shirt over you. And help you over to the armchair. You need to keep warm."

Seated by the fireside, a tot of brandy was thrust into his good hand. Iain sipped the fiery spirit; the warm afterglow helped calm his nerves.

"Better? Settled now? Then I'm all ears to hear your story. That is, just if you feel up to it."

"There's no' much to tell," he said cautiously. "Me an' a few mates were walkin' back after the gemme when we were set on by a gang o' Celtic yobs. Twenty or thirty o' them. We didnae stand a chance. We were lucky to get awa' at all."

"And where was this?"

"I'm no' sure. Maybe near Bridgeton Cross."

"A dangerous part of the city. Best avoided, especially on match days. And the blood?"

"I've nae idea. Maybe yin o' the others next to me was slashed. We a' got separated in the stramash. I got clear an' came straight hame."

"I see. Well, from what you say you've been fortunate. Nothing too serious. A quiet night in, I fancy. You're in no condition to enjoy the theatre. We can always go another day. It'll be a while before you're ready to be up and about again. I'll pop round to the police station in the morning and report this incident."

Iain recoiled; he had not anticipated this turn of events. A police investigation could prove disastrous. If they put two and two together … "No, dinnae dae that," he protested, trying to keep the desperation out of his voice. "I mean, what guid would it do? Naebody saw it. We've nae idea who they were. What could the bobbies dae?"

"But some of your friends might have been seriously wounded. From your account at least one of them was stabbed."

"Maybe. But in that case surely they would go to the polis?"

"That's true enough, I suppose. Well, if you're sure, we could let it ride for a day or two and see what happens. Anyhow, we'll need to have the doctor take a peek at you tomorrow. That's the main priority."

Momentary relief turned to fresh alarm. "There's nae need for that. I feel fine now. What mair could a quack do?"

"My dear chap, I'm not a medical man. It's only commonsense to have you checked out by an expert."

"But thon sawbones is such a fussy old stick. Why bother him? I'll be right as rain after a good rest."

"You certainly have a bee in your bonnet about doctors, don't you? I seem to remember something similar when you fished me out of the fire that time. Tell you what, since you're so concerned. If there's no adverse reaction after a good night's sleep, we'll let it go at that."

"Thanks. It's no' like I'm scared o' them, ye ken," he added artfully.

Lang smiled. "Have it your own way. Now just you sit tight while I see about parcelling up these togs for the cleaners."

"No!" It was almost a howl of anguish. "That is… it's only a few spots. I could wash them in the copper."

"Nonsense. It's your good suit. It should be done properly. You would probably just ruin it." He was already folding the waistcoat neatly and laying it aside. Now he was reaching for the jacket, turning it inside out. Iain could only look on helplessly, goggle-eyed, petrified with a sudden dread.

Lang's hand touched a sticky patch on the lining. Strange! He sniffed at it. Blood! There was a dark stain on the inside pocket. But Iain had not been bleeding. There was a bulge there, too. He reached in; his fingers closed on an object. He drew it out. A razor! Iain's razor. Covered in congealed blood. In amazement he looked from the razor to Iain, a horrible suspicion forming in his mind.

"You've used this." The tone was sharp, even harsh. "Who did you cut? How bad was it?"

"I dinnae ken." Iain began to panic, close to tears. "Ye dinnae understand. I was just tryin' to keep him off. He came at me wi' a great big stick. On a great muckle horse."

"On a horse?" Lang could hardly believe his ears. "You mean to say that a Celtic supporter attacked you on horseback?"

"No! Nothin' like that." He rushed on, heedless of what he was saying. "It was the policeman. He was goin' to brain me. I didnae have time to think. I didnae mean to hurt him. It was just tae warn him off. It was an accident."

Incredulity turned to horror. "You stabbed – a policeman? Where? How badly was he injured?"

"I'm no' sure. His face maybe. It was a' over sae quick. But it's no' my fault," he wailed. "He shouldnae hae come at me like that. I couldna help it. Ye must believe that."

Lang could only stare at the whimpering wretch before him. God, what a mess! How on earth was he to handle this?

"You stay here," he said at last. "Don't stir from that chair. I must find out exactly what happened. I'll go to the pressroom. They'd know there." He crossed to the closet in the hallway, donned hat and coat, and was gone.

Iain was left alone to his thoughts. Apocalyptic visions flashed into his mind; he could feel the cold, clammy sweat on his forehead. What if the policeman had died? The awful fate that would await him. What if Adam had gone to give him up? Surely his friend would not betray him. But he could not be certain. He might be caught here, like a rat in a trap. Escape was the only answer – now, before it was too late. It was agony, and it seemed like an age to dress himself with only one good arm. But he managed it eventually. Hobbling to the front door, he saw that the key to the mortise lock was missing. It had been bolted – from the outside. He was a prisoner. Shaken and crushed, Iain retreated to the parlour. The window offered no hope, not here on the third floor, forty or fifty feet above the ground. There was nothing for it but to wait, anxiety gnawing at his very soul.

It seemed like an eternity before Lang returned. He heard the scrape in the lock, then the thud of the bolt's release. He felt his blood run cold; his limbs turned to jelly. There was the sound of footsteps approaching. He sat, rooted to the spot, hardly daring to breathe. Adam entered the room – alone. Iain swayed, and nearly passed out with relief.

"Well, you've really cooked your goose this time." There was no disguising the bitterness in his voice. "The man you claim attacked you was a senior officer. All hell has broken loose over it. Fortunately for you he survived. It was touch and go for a while, but he'll pull through. Otherwise it would be a hanging matter. As it is, you'd be lucky to get away with ten years, at hard labour. I doubt any court would accept a plea of self-defence. You slashed him in the throat. The only reason he didn't bleed to death was that there was a doctor nearby. He managed to staunch the blood till they could get him to hospital. That, and the strap of his helmet. That's what protected him from a deep gash. Had the main artery been cut, then nothing could have saved him. He would have been a goner in seconds."

"Thank God for that."

"Yes, thank God. Though I fancy your concern is more out of regard for your own neck."

Iain ignored the jibe. "Does anyone else know?" he asked huskily.

"Not as yet, no. I gave out that I had called to pick up some papers for my next article. I didn't have to ask about the latest news. Everyone in the office was full of it. Only too keen to spout all the lurid details."

"So what are you goin' to do now?" He looked up in mute appeal. This was the crunch; his whole future hung in the balance.

"By rights I should hand you over to the authorities. I have a clear duty to inform the law what I know of this miserable affair. But... I couldn't bring myself to take responsibility for putting you away in some vile jail. At the same time you're not going to get off scot-free. My conscience wouldn't allow that. I couldn't live with myself seeing you every day as though nothing had happened. I used to think I could help cure you of that temper of yours. Fool that I was. You'll never improve." He paused, before delivering final judgement. "So I think that the best course is for us to go our separate ways. My debt to you is cancelled. Be out of this house by the end of the week."

Iain could only bow his head in submission. He knew he could have expected far worse. He would not languish in prison; his life was not to be forever blighted. His spirits began to revive. A steady, secure job awaited him; new lodgings should not be too difficult to find. There was money in his Post Office account, enough to tide him over for a few weeks. He no longer had any need of Lang. By way of thanks he scowled darkly as he left the room.

NINE

Hopes and Dreams

Edinburgh. October 1912

"aymarket! Haymarket Station!"

The flaxen-haired youth in the corner seat had been dozing, but now the shouts and sudden activity roused him from his reverie. He started, then jumped to his feet, belatedly realising that this was his stop. Steadying himself, he made a lunge for the trunk on the overhead rack. It swung down onto the seat, and in an instant he had dragged it out, only just in time before a porter slammed the door shut. Passengers streamed past him towards the stairs leading to the booking hall and exit. A whistle sounded, the wheels of the locomotive spun, then gripped; and in a cloud of smoke and steam the train began to disappear into the jaws of the tunnel just beyond the end of the platform.

Alastair Baird felt for his pocket book; there was a slip of paper inside with the instructions he had been given. The directions were clear enough. Straight out of the station, then turn sharp right into Dalry Road. Cross over, and it was the first opening on the left. Dalry *Colonies*: such a strange name for rows of terraced houses. He was looking for Bright Terrace. His aunt – no, his great-aunt – lived in Number 18. He wondered what she was like; they had never met. Indeed it was only a few weeks ago that his mother had recalled the existence of a half-forgotten relation living in Edinburgh. She had been fretting over where he would find suitable lodgings when she suddenly remembered Aunt Chrissie. It had taken some time to track down the address, but the search had been successful, and she had written. The reply was satisfactory: her aunt had not forgotten the young girl she had dangled on her knee. Better still, she had a spare room and might be prepared to provide accommodation for a relative as a special favour. But it must be on a business footing: fifteen shillings a week for board and laundry, to be paid termly in advance. Thus matters had been arranged, and the terms gratefully accepted.

His fingers rustled the two five pound notes he was to hand over for his upkeep. He jingled the coins in his pocket – two sovereigns and another pound in silver. In an inside pocket he carried letters of admission to the university and confirmation of fee grants from the Education Department and Carnegie Trust. Last of all there was a cheque for ten pounds from Mr Ogilvie. He had tried to resist such generosity, but his old mentor had been insistent, threatening to take offence if the gift was rejected. All in all, once all necessary expenses had been settled, he reckoned there would be nearly twenty pounds a year to live on – far more than he had envisaged. Perhaps he might even manage to repay some of the debt he owed to his mother.

Set on the western fringe of the city, Dalry was a busy, bustling neighbourhood, with its main thoroughfare flanked by high tenements and shop frontages. Near its junction with the Haymarket, however, stood a side street of superior terraced housing. This was his destination. He could not fail to be impressed by the ingenuity, and yet simplicity, of the design. Built on two storeys, with an attic on top, each dwelling had its own entrance, together with a small garden, on opposite sides of the building; access to the upper flats was up a stone staircase with wrought iron balustrade.

The place was far from silent. What seemed like hordes of children were at play, with a number of street games – peevers, skipping, tig, gird and cleat – all going on at the same time. No doubt they were taking the opportunity to let off steam after the welcome release from school. There were few women about, but doubtless most would be indoors preparing the evening meal. Bright Terrace was the third row of houses on the left, opposite Argyll Terrace. Number 18 must be at the far end of the terrace, along the narrow footpath between the gardens. He reached the gate at the foot of the stairs giving access to the last two houses, climbed the steps and set down his case on the landing. On the far side, behind the wall that ran along the boundary of the settlement, was a huge railway goods yard. Several shunting engines were at work, beavering away with their wagons like so many black beetles.

"Are ye going to stop there, gawping at the trains all day?"

Alastair whipped round as though stung. His face reddened with embarrassment. On the threshold stood an elderly woman, not five feet tall; her eyes glinted behind large horn-rimmed spectacles, giving her an owl-like expression.

"Sorry," he stammered. "Aunt Chrissie? I'm Alastair. Your nephew. Great-nephew, I should say."

"Aye, Kate's laddie. I jaloused that one. Well, come away in. Wipe your feet on the mat."

She led the way through an inner door, its upper panel of patterned glass, and along a short lobby. Alastair could not help noting that she walked with a pronounced limp. Her left leg was rigid; she had to swing it from the hip.

"That's the parlour." She indicated a door on the right. "It's seldom used. Only on special occasions. So don't go in there without an invitation."

"No – no, of course not." Alastair was a little taken aback. This was hardly the most promising of welcomes.

"I believe in plain speaking. There's no shilly-shallying here, not in Chrissie Marshall's house. We're respectable folk, Donald and I. Normally we'd never entertain the idea of a lodger, but – you're family, however remote. We may as well get things straight if you're to bide here. Back by ten at night. No tobacco or strong drink. I won't have them in the house. And strictly no visitors. Is that understood?"

"Perfectly. I've no objections." This really was laying down the law.

"I should think not." She took a brass object from a hook on the hallstand. "This is your key to the front door. See you don't lose it."

"Thank you, Aunt Chrissie." He clipped it to the fob on his pocket book. "It'll be quite safe here."

"Good. Can we get on now?"

Facing them, at the end of the passage, another door gave access to a wooden staircase curving round and upwards. "You're up there. You'll have plenty o' peace and quiet for your books. The water closet is here, below the stairs. And that's the kitchen on the right. You'll take your meals with us. Now I'll show you to your room. Mind and don't bump against my good paintwork."

She had to grasp the banister to heave herself up one step at a time. He guessed that his aunt must be in some discomfort, but not a murmur of protest escaped her lips. A real feisty spirit there, he thought wryly. And heaven help him if he dared to offer any assistance.

The attic room was clean but spare, the floor covered with dull, indeterminate linoleum, enlivened with a splash of colour from tiny rag rugs in front of the fireplace and single bed. There was a deal wardrobe, a small table and chair, and a worn armchair which had probably seen better days downstairs. Little enough, but luxury compared with home. From the dormer window, beyond the dreary expanse of the railway tracks, Edinburgh Castle sat proudly on its high rock, clearly visible above the far roofline. This was more like it – the Athens of the North people raved about.

"Aye, it is a grand view." She broke in on his thoughts. "But if we could get back to the practicalities? As ye see, you've gas for heat and light. It's a separate meter. Here, in this cupboard. You'll need to feed it wi' pennies or a shilling. So it'll be up to you how much you use. There's a sink and tap in the lumber-room next door. You can wash there. Supper is at six o'clock. Now, is there anything else you need to know?"

Alastair shook his head. "No, I think you've covered about everything. Oh, yes." He felt in his pocket. "Here you are. The rent for this term – ten pounds. Perhaps you'd like to take care of it now?" Was it his imagination, or was there the ghost of a gleam behind those glasses?

"Just as ye like." She carefully folded the two banknotes and slipped them into her apron. "I'll make out the receipt and let you have it at the supper table."

"Then I can send it off to mother. That will set her mind at rest."

"So you're Kate's youngest." Having settled the main business, she was inclined to indulge a mild curiosity. "Aye, ye have the look o' a Baird. Maybe a bit more delicate than most. Though it's thirty years or more since I saw any of them last. How is your mother?"

"Well enough. She gets a few aches and pains from time to time."

"Age comes wi' its own afflictions, right enough. Married a miner, didn't she? Thought she might have done better for herself."

Alastair decided it would be wiser to ignore the barb. "Yes. Geordie. But he was killed in a pit accident, oh, over seven years ago."

"I didnae know that. Well, we mustn't speak ill of the dead. It's a dangerous calling, and no mistake. Thank goodness I had the sense to get a man wi' a collar and tie job. No chance of him being injured or worse at work. You probably saw him on your way here."

"Saw him? I can't think how."

"He's the booking clerk at the railway station, is my Donald. He'll be in presently. So how does your mother cope?"

"She's manageress at the co-op in Broomburn. And my sister and her husband stay with us. That brings in a little more."

"Still it must have been difficult," she mused, half to herself. "And yet she's managed to send you to the varsity." For the first time there was a tinge of approval in her voice. "See you stick in at your studies. Make something of yourself. I'll away now. Six sharp, mind."

Alastair was left to unpack. His mother had insisted on a trip to Glasgow to kit him out, brushing aside all protests about the cost. With something like a sigh he began to transfer garments to hangers or drawers in the wardrobe, leaving space at the bottom for his spare pair of boots. The task did not take long; soon there were only two items left. He lifted out the framed photograph of his mother and father in their Sunday best, kissed it, and set it at one end of the tiny mantelpiece. Last of all came a small, padded blue box; he ran his fingers over the rich velvet covering before placing it at the opposite end. Somewhere a clock chimed the hour. He heard a murmur of voices below. The man of the house had evidently returned. There was no time for any ablutions. Straightening his tie, he hastily went down the stairs.

A thin, spare figure in the livery of the North British Railway Company was hovering by the kitchen door. The Dundreary whiskers and sad eyes served only to accentuate the despondency in his posture. Wordlessly he stretched out a hand; the fingers were cold and clammy to the touch. Donald Marshall was probably in his mid-fifties, Alastair estimated, several years younger than his wife. An anonymous mouse of a man, what his mother would have dismissed as a wee *bauchle.*

"Now then," came a voice from within, "don't stand around like a pair o' haddies. Supper's ready. I'm dishing up now. See and wash your hands afore you sit down."

It came as no surprise that Aunt Chrissie intoned the brief grace. Alastair made a brave attempt at conversation, but receiving only monosyllables in reply, soon gave it up as a bad job. The food itself, though plain, was substantial enough – herring in oatmeal, boiled potatoes, garden peas. He had not realised how hungry he was, and fell to with a will. The meal was eaten in near silence. It was not until the plates had been cleared and his aunt had poured herself a second cup of tea that she deigned to break the oppressive hush.

"It's the church soiree the night. I don't suppose you'll be wanting to go, Donald."

"I've had a hard day, Chrissie. You go on your own. No doubt there'll be lanternslides on *Light into Darkest Africa*, or some such thing. You'd enjoy that."

"It's a temperance evening," she replied primly. "A lecture on the evils of the demon drink. You might learn something if you took more of an interest."

"Aye, maybe. But some other time."

"Lazy lump! I don't want to find you frowsting in front of the fire when I get back."

"As a matter of fact I thought I might take young Alastair here out for a walk. Show him the lie of the land, so he can get his bearings."

"What? At this time o' night? It's nearly dark. And there's the dishes to do."

She drained her cup, donned coat, hat and gloves, picked up her bag and prepared to leave. At the door she turned. "Mind what I said," she admonished. Then she was gone.

Her husband blew into his cheeks with relief. "My wife has many fine qualities. But she can be a bit overpowering at times. Come on. Stick the dishes in the sink. They can wait till later. We'll go out for a wee daunder. I could do wi' a breath of air. I'll just away and change out of these togs." He disappeared into what Alastair took to be the couple's bedroom.

Ten minutes later they found themselves at the foot of the street. "That's the kirk up there." In the pale gleam of a street lamp Alastair could just make out the steps, portico and dome of a solid edifice breaching the line of the high tenements. "They'll be in the hall underneath. We'll go the other way."

He turned right towards Haymarket, and then crossed the main road. For a minute Alastair thought they must be returning to the station and wondered why. But he stopped at the building on the corner and pointed to a sign above the doorway.

"There's been a howff here for centuries. It used to be a coaching inn for travellers. I sometimes manage to pop in now and again. Shall we? My treat."

"But I thought you were going to show me the sights?"

"Well, this is one o' them. And I can tell you about the others from the comfort of a seat in the snug."

Alastair laughed, and followed him in. He supposed there was no harm in it. Not quite so taciturn as he had thought, was his Uncle Donald – at least on the occasions when he could escape from his domineering wife.

"Nip an' a pint, Alastair?"

"No whisky, please, Uncle Donald. I'm not used to it."

"No problem. And the name's Donald. Though you'd better carry on wi' the uncle bit in the house."

"Won't Aunt Chrissie object to our going into public houses? She seemed very much against it."

"What she doesnae ken won't hurt her. A man's entitled to a bit o' pleasure. Now, grab a seat while I get them in."

The bar was crowded with workers on their way home and evening revellers preparing for a night out, but one table was emptying and Alastair was quick enough to secure a couple of chairs. It was several minutes before his companion returned.

"Goad, but it was a fight to get through back there." He pushed a glass towards Alastair. "Wire into that." He took a long pull at his own beer. "That's better. Now I can begin to enjoy myself. Care for a fag?" He shook two Woodbines from a carton and stuck one between his lips.

Alastair waved away the proffered cigarette. "Thanks, but I won't if it's all the same to you."

Donald shrugged. "You really should, you know," he said, striking a match. "They're good for you. Help you relax, calm the nerves."

Alastair tried to ignore the wreath of smoke swirling upwards. "Have you been long at Bright Terrace, unc – I mean Donald."

"You could say so," he replied, taking a sip of his whisky. "Over twenty-five years. Ever since I came to work at the station here. Your aunt is very proud that we're house owners. It's not rented, ye ken. We got a loan from the building society. It's only just been paid off."

"Something to be proud of."

"Aye. So long as it's not taken ower far. Your aunt thinks it puts us a cut above the neighbours. That's why she has so little to do wi' them. And as for those that bide in the tenement closes further up the street, they're beyond the pale. She can barely acknowledge that they exist. She's got her own wee clique o' like-minded bodies at the church, and that's about it."

"Surely it's not as bad as that?"

"Don't you believe it. She rants and raves if I say I'm going out of an evening. I have to sneak out here for the odd pint. It's the snob in her. That, and the accident."

"Accident?"

"It was a long time ago. But she's never really got over it. Kind o' soured her, ye might say. You'll have noticed that she walks with a limp. Well, she used to work in the Edinburgh Cookery School in Atholl Crescent – that's just along by towards Princes Street. One day she fell off a stepladder and broke her leg. It was never set right, and there was no money for another operation."

"I'm truly sorry about that."

"Aye, well. Better not to mention it, even out of sympathy. She'll not thank you for it. She lost her job at the dough school as well. That's probably why she married me. At least she could depend on a safe, steady wage packet."

"I'm sure that's not the only reason. Have you been blessed with children?"

Donald winced. "No. She was thirty before we were wed." He sighed and stared moodily into his glass.

"Can I get you another drink?" asked Alastair at length, more out of a desire to overcome the awkwardness than anything else.

"What was that? Eh, no. Another time. Best be getting back. Don't want to have her sitting at home, waiting for us." He stood up and fumbled in his pocket. "Here, suck one of these." He handed Alastair a peppermint. "If she smells the drink on our breath we'll never hear the last of it."

They had to push their way through the crush. At the doorway, Donald looked round to check his nephew was close behind. "We'll need to step lively now. She's not due back yet, but you never know wi' her. And there's still the dishes to do."

Alastair did not know whether to be alarmed or amused as his uncle hurried across the road. It was an effort to keep up. "Steady on, there. Do you have to rush? I'll help you wash up."

"No, it's no trouble. You take yourself off to bed. Get an early night. I can manage fine." They turned into the footpath.

Suddenly Donald stopped and pointed up at the landing. "Look. There's no light on in the lobby. She's not back yet. So it's all right." He shot a glance at his young companion. "You won't mention any of this to her, will you?"

"I'll simply say that you told me about the district, if she asks."

Truth to tell, Alastair was not sorry to bid his host goodnight and retire to his room. Uncle Donald was certainly a rum customer. What a miserable existence he must lead. It was impossible not to feel for him. He found a match to light the gas mantle. The attic was suffused in a soft glow. He took up the blue box and opened it. There it lay, glistening on its bed of watered silk. His gold medal. Dux of Fairhill Academy. And his mother and Mr Ogilvie had been there to see him receive it. He snapped the lid shut. Could he match that achievement at university? Whatever else, it would not be from want of effort.

* * *

The lecture hall was crowded. Alastair had fully intended to arrive in plenty of time for this, his first university class, but had been waylaid yet again. Aunt Chrissie had developed an unfortunate habit of inducing him carry out any little errands she might require. And that morning had been no exception. Of all the days to run out of milk for the breakfast porridge… It had been a desperate rush, but he had made it. Thankfully he would not suffer the embarrassment of having to apologise for latecoming.

Nearly every seat was taken. It came as something of a surprise to see so many students, even more so that nearly half of them were young women. No, that was not quite true. There was a sprinkling of older ladies, no doubt uncertificated teachers taking time out to gain their *parchment*. For a moment his heart skipped a beat. He had often wondered whether Elizabeth Lixmont might fulfil her half promise, but a quick scan revealed nothing – no one even vaguely resembling her, not the slightest gesture of recognition from any of the benches. It had been only a pipedream to imagine she might be here. But there was no time to dwell on that now. The wall clock indicated that it was just on the hour. There were a few vacant places at the back; he fairly bounded up the steps. Just like up in the gods, he thought, as he settled himself down.

The lecturer bustled in, his black robe fluttering behind him – no less a person than the Professor of Education himself, Alexander Darroch, a distinguished writer on educational affairs. He set out his notes, looked up from the lectern, and the auditorium fell into an expectant silence. In welcoming the class, he wished to congratulate the new entrants to the profession and remind them of the awesome responsibility that fell to their lot, to form young minds and prepare the next generation for its place in society. He hoped he was not being overmodest when he asserted that his subject was at the core of all the instruction they would receive. Only the study of educational thinkers and reformers could give purpose and meaning to classroom activities.

He was warming to his theme when there was a loud rap on the door. He broke off in mid-sentence and, frowning at the unwelcome intrusion, testily snapped: "Come in!"

A young lady waltzed in, dressed in a bright morning gown, mink stole and floral hat. In one hand she carried a parasol and in the other a shiny leather writing case.

The professor was far from impressed. "Well! Can I help you?" he demanded.

From his perch high at the back of the room Alastair went rigid with astonishment. It was her, after all! Miss Elizabeth! How could he ever forget that image of radiance?

"Please excuse me. Is this Professor Darroch's class?" she simpered.

"It is. State your business. And quickly, if you please."

"I'm so sorry to be late. But it's such a huge building that I lost my way and had to ask for directions – several times."

"Do you mean to say that you are a student?"

"Yes, I have enrolled for the course."

"Indeed! Then you have several lessons to learn. The first is that punctuality is of the essence. Latecoming can never be tolerated. The second is that a more sober dress is required, as befits your calling."

"Yes, I do understand. I'll try to remember in future," she added demurely.

"Very good. Find yourself a place." She turned and shrugged helplessly. "Oh, I see. Perhaps those in the front row could move a little closer. There you are. Now perhaps we might resume."

Elizabeth wedged into the space created. "Thank you. Please forgive me for having been such a nuisance." She smiled coyly and lowered her eyes.

Professor Darroch twitched his nostrils and cleared his throat. He seemed about to say more, but evidently thought better of it. Instead he consulted his notes, and in a minute or two was in full stride again, outlining the content of the course of lectures he planned to deliver that term.

Alastair sat as though in a dream. She had turned up. But would she remember him? Or even if she did, would she want anything to do with him? But what if she had joined the class just to meet him again? Hopes and fears chased each other like waves dashing themselves onto the shore. He scarcely heard what was being said, far less rouse himself to take notes.

At last the professor brought his discourse to a conclusion. Gathering up his papers, he bade the class good morning and whisked out. Mechanically Alastair rose with the others and began to shuffle down the gangway, his eyes never leaving Elizabeth. She, too, had left her seat, but instead of making for the door she stepped forward on to the lecturer's dais, the better to survey the crowd of slowly departing students. Spotting Alastair, she gave a little jump and waved excitedly.

"I knew you'd be here," she cried in triumph as he shyly approached. "Bet you thought I wouldn't come. But I always keep my promises. Aren't you pleased?"

"Of course. Just a little surprised, Miss Elizabeth. Especially at your entrance."

"Oh, never mind about that. He's just a fussy old fiddlestick. And it's Elizabeth. We're fellow students now. Let's find somewhere we can talk. You don't have another class, do you? No. Good. I know a cosy little teashop. It's just round the corner, on South Bridge. Would you be a dear and carry my valise?" She slipped her arm into his. Alastair felt like he was walking on air.

The tearoom was fairly quiet at that hour and they were able to find a table for two, partly screened by a trellis of bamboo and ferns. "Not quite up to the standards of Princes Street," grinned Elizabeth. "But it's pleasant enough and does a simply scrumptious cream bun. I always feel ravenous by this time. Don't you? … Yes, we'll have a pot of tea and a plate of your delicious cakes." The hovering waitress gave a loud sniff as she departed with the order.

Elizabeth smiled fondly and laid her hand on his. "Let me get a good look at you now. Yes, you've filled out a bit more. And grown your hair longer. I like that. Makes you more handsome than ever."

Alastair blushed. "Go on. You can't mean it."

"Oh, but I do. Don't you find me just the tiniest bit attractive?" Her eyes seemed to melt into him.

"You're the most stunning girl I've ever seen in my life. I can't believe why you could be interested in the likes of me."

"Why not? You've heaps more spunk than the chinless wonders my parents keep trying to palm off on me."

The waitress returned with a tray and noisily began to arrange the tea things on the table. It was impossible to talk amid such a clatter.

"Mean old cat!" exclaimed Elizabeth as soon as they were left alone. "Did you see the dirty look she gave us?" She saw the shocked expression on his face and went on more gently: "You mustn't take on so. We girls are tougher than you might think. Forget the sugar and spice and all that tosh. Shall I be mother and pour? Don't stand on ceremony. Tuck into the cakes."

"Thanks." He helped himself to a small fruit slice.

"Fly cemetery, eh? That your favourite? I'll have the cream puff."

"So you managed to make it to university after all, Miss – Elizabeth I should say? I didn't notice you at any of the freshers' meetings. And I did look out for you."

"That was sweet of you," she replied, licking a spot of cream from her lips. "I didn't get back home till last week. I've been in Switzerland for the last year. They packed me off to finishing school there. I hated every second of it."

"How terrible. Did you really suffer so much?"

"Well, perhaps it wasn't that bad. I gave as good as I got. In the end the people there were glad to see the back of me."

"And your parents raised no objection to you coming here?"

"Don't you believe it. They were dead set against it. Mama nearly had a fit when I told her I was going to take up teacher training. Accused me of letting the family down. She was horrified at the idea I might become a bluestocking. But I just kept on till I wore them down. Eventually the pater came round. He was forced to admit that the discipline could be good for me, might even help bring me to my senses. In the end mama said she washed her hands of the whole affair since it was clear I would never make a proper match."

"That was very brave of you, to insist on the right to shape your own future."

"Not really. Not if you know how to go about it. Fathers generally have a soft spot for an only daughter. So it's usually not too difficult to twist him round my little finger. Anyway, give him his due, he was as good as his word. He had to pull a few strings to get me in, especially without the proper qualifications. Being a lawyer and on the board of the Merchant Company has its uses after all. I don't know quite how he managed it, but – well, here I am." She leaned over and squeezed his arm. "What about you? Have you done much history hunting on the moors? Like you told me last time."

Alastair laughed. "Not much chance of that, I'm sorry to say. Too busy slogging away for my leaving certificate."

"Well, we can make up for that now. We could explore Edinburgh together."

"I'd like that. But what about everything else? Will there be any spare time?"

"There you go again. We can make time. All work and no play, you know. There's always the weekends. But perhaps you don't want to go out with me?"

"You know that's not true," he protested hotly. "I'd be the luckiest man alive. It's just that others have made sacrifices for me. I wouldn't want to let them down."

"I'm sorry." All of a sudden she was contrite. "I shouldn't have said that. I was only teasing. And I do understand. But you mustn't push yourself too hard. You'll only make yourself ill."

He nodded, acknowledging the wisdom in her advice. "Yes, you're right, of course. There is a balance to be struck. I'm sure you'll keep me straight, Elizabeth."

"I'll do my best. Tell me, how did you get on last week? Did you make lots of new friends? Join any varsity clubs?"

"Hardly," he chuckled. "I still know scarcely anyone. There were one or two things that seemed quite interesting. I did look in to see what the Philosophical Society and History Forum were offering. But I found it all, well, rather overpowering. To tell you the truth I felt a bit out of place"

"It's because you're too shy, Alastair. You need taken out of yourself. Maybe I can help there. College life is more than just work, you know.

There's bags of things you can do to make the most of it."

"Well, I did intend to get involved with the Hares and Hounds. I enjoy running. And I did consider joining the Student Union. But it's a guinea subscription. A bit too rich for my pocket."

"Student Union!" she snorted. "I should think not. How can they call it that when women are excluded? It's nothing but a bastion of male privilege. Something should be done about it. Pandering to every prejudice the way it does. It's disgusting."

"It's surely not as bad as that. Ladies are sometimes allowed in – for debates and concerts and suchlike."

"So what? You call that fair? We can't be members in our own right. And hell could freeze over before they'd let us into the bar."

"I don't think I'd like to see you drinking in a bar."

"You are an old stick in the mud, aren't you?" she chortled. "Perhaps that's part of the attraction. But women do deserve more rights. You do appreciate that, don't you?"

"You sound like one of those suffragists. Up to a point, I suppose. But I'm not sure how far it should go."

"Then we'll need to educate you. But all in good time." She took up his hand, intertwined their fingers and gazed into his eyes. "You do believe me, don't you? That I'm not doing this just to spite my parents? I really do want to become a teacher, and I'm going to work jolly hard at it. We'd make a good team. You're serious, I'm a bit slapdash. Opposites attract. It'll be cosy, sitting together, side-by-side, working away, learning from each other. Like Queen Victoria and Prince Albert."

Alastair stared back, lost for words. She was making all the running. Was it simply friendship she was proposing, or something deeper? His mother's admonition flashed through his mind. But he did not care. It would be wonderful if they could work and study together.

* * *

"Have you seen Elizabeth?"

Edward Lixmont sighed, and reluctantly laid aside his paper. He had little enough time to himself. Was it so unreasonable to expect solitude to enjoy a golden half hour between church and Sunday lunch? Obviously it was, at least where his wife was concerned. She swept into the morning room like a draught of cold air.

"She didn't attend the service again, Edward. You should do more to keep up standards."

"Should I? Why don't you speak to her?" He was not particularly religious, but it did no harm to put in an appearance at a fashionable church. However, he drew the line at dragging his offspring through the tedium. They were old enough to make up their own minds.

"You know she never listens to me. There would only be another argument. Then she'd flounce off. Look at what happened last week. She refused a dinner party for her birthday. Just because we wouldn't invite this – this follower who seems to have sprung from nowhere. I mean, he might be an adventurer – or worse. She should never have been allowed to go to that college. It's your fault."

"That's hardly fair. You agreed with me that it would give her something to do."

"Only because I couldn't think of an alternative. But now this – making undesirable acquaintances. She should be locked away for her own good."

"Like banishing her to that place in Switzerland? Is that your answer to everything? We've tried your way. It would only make her more rebellious than ever."

"So you give in to her? Is that why you allowed Elizabeth to ask him here, today, to Sunday lunch? How can you bear to have this upstart sitting at your own table?"

"Be reasonable, Hilda." Lixmont fully shared her concern, but it would be folly to show it. "You must admit that Elizabeth has quietened down recently. She seems to be taking things a lot more seriously. I've even found her studying in her room of an evening. There's some beneficial influence working away on her. Could well be this fellow."

"You think so?" she said ominously. "Well, I've discovered a thing or two. You remember that spat I had with her – over the dinner party?"

"How could I forget?" He shuddered at the recollection. "The slanging match could be heard all over the house."

"Never mind that. The point is that she let out that she had met him before – when she stayed with Maud and Robert last year. I wrote to Maud and she got the story out of Robert."

"Well, so what?"

"It turns out he's penniless. No family at all. His father was a coalminer, would you believe? Worse, a firebrand, a socialist agitator. He was responsible for provoking a strike. Robert's business was nearly ruined."

"Semple always was prone to exaggeration. Sins of the father, eh? Is that your opinion? If the boy has picked himself up by his bootstraps, then that's to his credit."

"You can't seriously believe that," she spluttered. "You're far too liberal in your views. People will talk, you know. Things are expected of a man in your position. Especially if you hope to get on."

Lixmont pursed his lips. Hilda was full of airs and graces. A scion of the Midlothian gentry, she had always claimed a distant relationship with the Dundas family. So distant as to be almost out of sight, but it would never do to say so openly. As his wife so often reminded him, they had used their stranglehold over the legal system to gain control of Scotland. But that had been during the corrupt and venal eighteenth century. Such an opportunity was hardly likely to present itself in this democratic age. Still, she did have a point. Already a successful KC in the Court of Session, his prospects for the Bench were set fair, and even elevation to law lord was not out of the question, in the fullness of time.

"And if you're not bothered about your own career, think of Hugh. What would they say in the regiment if they knew about his sister?"

"You fuss too much, Hilda. I don't think it will come to that. Things will settle down. Let's try to keep calm about it."

"And that's all you have to say? Can you tell me where your daughter is now?"

"I believe she's gone to the tram terminus at Stanley Road to meet the chap. They'll be back in a minute. No, there's the gate." He stood up and looked out the window. "They're coming up the path. Try to remember your manners, my dear. You are the hostess."

His wife gave him a withering glare. But it was too late to make an escape. Two figures appeared in the doorway. She turned to fix them with a glassy smile.

"There you are, Elizabeth," said her father breezily. "We were just wondering how long you would be. Won't you introduce your friend?"

"Of course, daddy. This is Alastair. Alastair Baird."

The young man stepped forward. "Thank you for inviting me to lunch, Mrs Lixmont. Please accept a small token of my appreciation." He held out a bunch of flowers. "They're not up to much, I'm afraid."

"Er, how kind," stammered Hilda, momentarily taken aback. "Elizabeth, perhaps you might ask Agnes to put them in water."

Lixmont extended his hand in greeting. "You are most welcome. We were very pleased to have this opportunity to meet you."

"Glad to make your acquaintance, sir. Elizabeth has told me so much about you both."

"Nothing very flattering, I'll warrant," he replied with a laugh, ignoring the icy glance from his wife. As a lawyer he had a shrewd eye for character. And first impressions were distinctly favourable. Certainly the boy was a little shy, a touch nervous. Who wouldn't be, under the circumstances? But he carried himself well, with a firm handshake and frank, open face. Not the sort of person to take advantage of his daughter, if he was any judge.

"I understand you are from Lanarkshire, Mr Baird," he continued. "Have you found comfortable lodgings in the city?"

"Yes, well enough. I board with my great-aunt and her husband at Dalry."

"Dalry?" interjected Hilda. "Surely that's a rough, disreputable district?"

"Not quite so bad as that. Though I must admit that the sights and smells do have something of a reputation. The high tenements can seem oppressive till you get accustomed to them. But I'm quite sure the people are as honest and hardworking as anywhere."

The boom of the luncheon gong reverberated throughout the house. Saved by the bell, thought Lixmont. "Shall we go in?" he said hurriedly, before his wife could make a riposte. "My dear, would you lead the way?"

Hilda, however, was not to be denied. As soon as they were seated she turned to Alastair. "Mr Baird, it is our custom never to touch alcohol on the Sabbath. So I'm afraid there is no wine with the meal." She indicated the glass tumblers and jugs of water. "I hope you don't mind."

"Not at all, Mrs Lixmont. I rarely touch strong drink myself. And I've only ever tasted wine a few times in my life."

Her husband gasped. It was news to him. He particularly enjoyed a glass of claret with his Sunday roast. So this was Hilda's revenge for young Baird's presence at lunch. She met his stare of disbelief with equanimity.

Over the soup the sniping was renewed. "I gather your father was a coalman."

"A miner, yes. I'm very proud of him. He was the finest hewer in the pit. Everyone in the village looked up to him. And he sacrificed his own life to save others."

"Bravely spoken." Lixmont tapped the table in appreciation. It was right that a son should stand up for his father.

Hilda was not prepared to allow her prey to wriggle off so easily. "You say he was admired. Was that because he was a trade union agitator? Inciting his fellow workers to break their contracts? Bringing on all the suffering that that entailed?"

"No! It wasn't like that at all." The cry was wrung from the heart. In an instant Alastair had recovered himself, shamefaced. "Please forgive me. I should not have raised my voice. It's just that the coalmasters had reduced wages to a pittance. They were on starvation rates. It was sheer desperation. There was nothing else they could do."

"Very understandable." Lixmont was first to react. It was high time to put an end to this bickering and soothe things over before there was a disaster. "It does you credit, the way you defended your father. And now, I think we should steer the conversation into safer waters."

The remainder of the meal proceeded much more smoothly. Lixmont, at any rate, accounted it something of a success. The master of the house had asserted his authority. His spouse assumed an injured silence; his daughter seemed to have little to say for herself. He held the stage. Employing all his wiles as an advocate, he began to induce the lad to talk about his work at college and ambitions for the future, before returning to the thorny issue of his family background. He was in his element, conducting an examination of a reluctant witness, one to be won over with a gentle approach. Skilfully the story of his mother's battle against adversity was teased out, along with the solid worth of his sister, and even the mention of an older brother who had gone away. It was a simple tale, movingly told. No one at the table could fail to be affected by it.

Elizabeth was smiling fondly. Things were going better than expected. There had been no need to spring to Alastair's aid. He was doing so well on his own. She had always been confident of her father's attitude, but you never knew with mama. Certainly she was playing up quite well now, after the initial hostilities. Her attitude seemed to be changing; at least there were no more silly interruptions. Dare she hope, but was there a flicker of sympathy in her mother's expression?

She had, of course, heard most of it already, in bits and pieces as she had probed away at his reserve. But it was surprising how he always tended to sheer off whenever his brother was mentioned. Iain was his name and he lived in Glasgow, so she had been told. Obviously the black sheep of the family; she had deduced that much. Apparently he had once been the doyen of all the girls, but in some way had been connected with his father's death. After that the whole community had turned against him, and forced him to leave. According to Alastair he was his own worst enemy, a real tartar when roused. And that was as far as he would go. This was intriguing. He sounded a real rogue. She wondered if she would ever get to meet him.

"Mama, do you think we might skip coffee?" The last course had been cleared away. Elizabeth had achieved her objective. Alastair had clearly made an impact. Leave it like that for the time being. "I promised to show Alastair round the area. I thought we might walk as far as Newhaven. The fisher folks' cottages, you know, so quaint and pretty. Then I can see him off at the tram stop."

"Very well, dear. I've no objection. Don't be too long, though."

Taking his departure, Alastair again apologised for his conduct, but Lixmont made light of it. He had no cause to reproach himself. Hilda went so far as to offer her hand and hint that he would not be unwelcome if he cared to call again.

"Well, Hilda, what did you make of him?" said her husband, after the pair had left.

"He could never be socially acceptable, Edward. I mean he's got neither breeding nor money. Or any real prospects. A head teacher's salary is about the most he can expect. It's scarcely the standard of living to which Elizabeth would aspire. At the same time, there is something about him … At least he knows which cutlery to use."

"I don't think there's much to worry about. At the moment he's a steadying influence. That's what she needs. But it won't last. He's a bit too staid for her. Sooner or later she'll want to spread her wings. Then she'll tire of him. I give it a year at most. Maybe less."

"I suppose I'll have to accept your judgment. I do hope you're right."

"And in the meantime?"

"I dare say we could make space in the library. They could do their work there. It would let us keep an eye on them."

"I'm glad you see it that way. And now I think I'll have a brandy with my coffee. If the drinks ban had been lifted, that is."

TEN

A World to Gain

Glasgow. November 1912

"Your proposals are completely unacceptable. *Scientific management?* Do you know what you are saying, Mr Rodgers? You plan to replace the workshop with the assembly line, bring in automation at the expense of experience and craft. Why, it amounts to no less than the deskilling of the entire work process. Where is the pride in a man's efforts there? And as for your so-called system of *premium bonus*, it's nothing more than payment by results. It would cause endless trouble. There would be constant friction, disrupting production, rather than speeding it up."

"Gee, I'm real sorry that you feel like that, Mr Findlay." The much younger man sitting opposite appeared unfazed by the general manager's tirade. He spoke in a soft New England drawl that Findlay found intensely irritating. "But perhaps I haven't explained myself properly. I'm not here to impose anything. Nothing will be done without your agreement. I've simply been asked to explore possible means of improving productivity. Increased profits are in everyone's interests, would you not agree, Mr Findlay? And it is the twentieth century. There's no room for inefficiency in this day and age. We can't permit ourselves to stand in the way of progress, let our competitors steal a march on us, now can we?"

Albert Findlay barely managed to suppress a snort. He glowered across his desk at this smooth talking interloper. His eyes had certainly been opened as to modern management practices over the last months, ever since he had taken up the reins at the new works. They had given him a grand office, sumptuous compared with his previous quarters, but it was still a gilded cage for all that. His subordinates had been appointed with little regard for his wishes – youngsters, straight out of university. That they considered him a dinosaur he knew full well. And now this – this Yankee snake oil salesman, barely half his age, had been sent to coerce him into accepting some new-fangled tomfoolery. Consultant indeed! For two pins he would summon the scriveners from the outer office and have this jackanapes slung out on his ear. The bell was to hand. But he made no move towards it. He could not rid himself of this unwelcome visitor quite so easily. The consequences might be unpleasant … for himself.

He swivelled round towards the picture window which overlooked the whole enclosure. The enterprise sprawled out over more than thirty acres: shops for forging gun barrels, jackets and mountings, armour plate rolling mills, even its own power station – all that was necessary for the manufacture of naval ordnance. The latest class of super-dreadnoughts would require massive 13.5 inch guns as their main armament, and plans were afoot for diversification into aircraft production. Heaven knew what the expense would be for these new projects. A fortune had already been invested in capital expenditure, and Deuchar's could not have laid out more than a tiny proportion of this. The land would be mortgaged to the hilt, and the arms conglomerate had acquired a hefty slice of company equity in return for the loans they had made. The owners were no longer masters in their own house. They would do as they were told; there was no alternative. If the combine pulled the plug, the firm would be finished – sunk in a sea of debt. Then, with the sharks circling to feast on the remains, what would be his fate? Cast up on the rocks, like as not. He sighed resignedly as he turned back to try to come to terms with this brash young American.

"Very well, Mr Rodgers," he said, rather more amenably. "As you say, perhaps we can reach some common ground. Just so long as you do not expect us to move too far, too fast. One step at a time, eh? Old habits die hard."

"Now you're talkin', Mr Findlay. I kinda figured we could put our heads together, come to an accommodation on this one. You know your own people best. How should we go about handlin' the business? I'd welcome your input."

"Thank you. Well now, for a start it's vital to keep the foremen onside. They're our non-commissioned officers, so to speak, the backbone of the business, maintaining discipline and ensuring work rate on the shop floor. It would put their noses out of joint if part of their authority were to be usurped by clerks going round with clipboards and stopwatches. Also, if you don't mind me mentioning it, I wouldn't go all the way to the payment system you describe. Keep the present piece rates. The men at least understand them. Then award a bonus for production above the norm. The incentive of extra wages could work wonders in overcoming opposition."

"You mean walk before you run? Waal, I guess that makes sense – at least in the short term. Anything else?"

"Yes. Before you do anything we'll need to square the ASE."

"ASE?"

"Amalgamated Society of Engineers. That's the major trade union in the works. They've real muscle, and they're not afraid to use it. They'll battle tooth and nail to defend craft privileges. We could stir up a hornet's nest by acting precipitately. Alienate the union, and where would your productivity gains be? They're quite capable of closing down the entire works – for months if they've a mind."

"Gosh. We sure as hell don't want that."

"Fortunately I've had dealings with the district organiser – that's the local fulltime official. Buntin, his name is. I think we could bring him on board with a few inducements. The main thing is to guarantee that the skilled trades would retain their status and not be replaced by semi-skilled machinists."

"I see. I didn't realise that you British were so soft on the unions. In my experience they're just troublemakers. We make short shrift of them back in the US of A."

Findlay bridled. This was going too far. "If possible, we prefer to work with the unions, rather than fight or ignore them," he said primly.

"Okay, okay. So maybe I was a little hasty. Let's not fall out over a trifle. I was counting on going right to the workforce. Could we not hold a general meeting? Then we could take the proposals direct to the men, convince them of the benefits of the scheme."

"I must counsel caution. They don't like surprises. You cannot simply spring major changes at the drop of a hat. That's not the way. As I said, I'll deal with Buntin. Get him to endorse our plans from the union perspective. I'm sure he could be persuaded to say a few appropriate words at a joint assembly. And, if you'll allow me a further suggestion, it might be an idea to drop a hint to one or two sympathetic bodies on the shop floor before the meeting. Butter them up. Ask them to sow the seed, spread the word in advance. About the benefits they could expect, that is."

"Yep. I get the drift. Lay the trail. I like it."

"Well, there's still a wrinkle or two left in the old dog."

"Mr Findlay, you're a man after my own heart. I guess you got somebody in mind."

"I hope so. There is one chap who might fit the bill nicely. Why not see what you think? We could pay a casual visit to the turning shop. A quick nod and a wink in passing, and no one any the wiser. We've just time before the hooter. It's only a half shift on Saturday."

The shop foreman, after recovering from his initial fluster, was only too pleased to welcome the general manager and his distinguished guest, and to conduct them on a tour of inspection. They passed up and down the rows, occasionally pausing to watch the men at work on their lathes. Many straightened up from their benches as the party approached, some merely curious, while bolder spirits stared back defiantly at the intrusion. Others affected not to notice and bent even closer over their machines. Amongst the latter was a strapping fellow with a bushy moustache. A slight rise of Findlay's eyebrow was enough to inform his companion that he was the object of their visit.

"Thank you, Mr Dunn," said Findlay, turning to the foreman. "We mustn't trespass further on your hospitality. I'm sure you have many calls upon your time. We'll manage on our own now."

The two visitors made no attempt to move on after their guide had departed. They appeared to be taking a close interest in this particular workman. That turning was a highly skilled craft there could be no doubt. A cylinder of solid metal had been clamped into place so that when the lathe was powered up it rotated at high speed. Then the cutting edge of a jig was applied to the work piece to remove surplus material. It was obvious that a thread was being cut down the length of the steel tube. Once that had been completed, sections of the thread were then removed to obtain a smooth finish. Every so often the machine was shut down to clear away the waste and allow callipers to measure the accuracy of the cut.

At one of these pauses Rodgers ventured to speak. "Mind tellin' me what you're making?" he inquired. "I can see it's a very delicate piece of work."

"Screw for the breech of a four-point-seven," the man replied shortly, without looking up.

"Say, why does the thread not go all the way round? Sorry if it seems a stupid question. But I really would like to learn the reason."

The turner flexed his back muscles and drew himself upright to face this tiresome inquisitor. "It's so that the plug can be closed and tightened in only a quarter-turn. Means the gun can be fired quicker. Anything else?"

"No. Well, yes, if you can spare a minute or two. I'd be interested in finding out more about your work. Anywhere quiet we can go? We won't keep you long."

There was a dark scowl and a flicker of resistance, before a grudging acquiescence. "If ye insist. Ye can go ower there, in the piece room. That's where we tak' our work when it's finished. I've just about done here. I'll just unscrew this an' be wi' ye in a jiffy."

"That'll be fine. By the way, would you object to tellin' me your name? Mine's Rodgers."

"Baird. Iain Baird." He took the proffered hand warily.

With a nod the two men walked over to the door indicated. A brief gesture from Findlay to the clerk at the writing desk ensured that they would not be disturbed. The place was almost stacked out with turned components, the fruits of the morning's work, all neatly labelled and awaiting removal to the fitting shed. Presently they heard the clump of boots on the wooden floor.

"Hope I huvnae kept ye waitin'. Had to see that the chargehand booked the piece. Otherwise I wouldnae get paid for it. Now what was it ye were after?"

"Boy, I sure admired the way you handled that machine. Real skill there. I'd bet there's not many could outdo you on a lathe."

"Skip the crap. You didna come here for that."

Rodgers laughed. "Smart young feller. Sharp as a needle. I like that. We'll cut to the chase then. Let me ask you a straight question. You're on piecework, right? How much did you make last week?"

"What's that to you? Thirty-eight an' six, if ye must know."

"Thirty-eight shillings and six pennies. That's good money, but you could do better. Suppose I show you how you could earn at least another twelve shillings. That would amount to over two pounds and ten shillings a week. And no increase in the hours either."

"Aye. That'll be right. And just what would I hae to do for it? Break my back?"

"Not at all. No more effort would be required. See here, I guess you've got your head screwed on the right way. You must be aware of all the bottlenecks, the stoppages and delays. Surely you get riled when for some reason or other you can't get on with the job? Not your fault, but you're the one losing out."

Iain wondered where all this was leading. But some sort of response was obviously expected. "Is there a point to a' this?" he demanded.

"Bear with me a minute. The turners, for instance, are constantly leaving their benches – to sharpen tools, pick up materials, and carry their pieces back. Not to mention the breaks just to yap and look over what their neighbours are doing. Think of what could be achieved if each man stayed at his workplace all the time."

"And how would a' the other things get done, then?"

"Isn't it obvious? Labourers could do the fetching and carrying. Surely you wouldn't object to having your tools sharpened for you? And it would not be too taxing to devise a system for recording work that avoids a long trail to a filing clerk. Time is money. And that includes your wages."

"Ye might have a point," Iain conceded reluctantly. "But this could be the thin edge o' the wedge. Ye cannae hae skilled men replaced by machinists."

"There's no question of that." Rodgers was quick to reassure him. "Look, as you well know, the main skill is in setting up the jigs. The actual cutting and drilling could be done by anyone. Ideally, the turner would take responsibility for a number of lathes, fixing them up, and then supervising the machine minders. Think how production would soar. And, along with it, the earnings of the top men. As much as three – maybe even four – pounds a week. Now that's real spondulics."

"I'm still no' sure. Ye paint a fine picture, but there'll be a catch somewhere."

Rodgers glanced meaningfully towards Findlay. The older man obligingly took his cue. "Baird, we've singled you out because you're not hidebound like so many of the others. You must realise that old-fashioned methods are no longer acceptable. Major changes are inevitable, and the company needs younger, progressive men to see them through. Mr Dunn, of course, has rendered sterling service over many years, but he's getting on and I doubt he'd be up to the challenge. Now this is strictly confidential and must not be repeated; but it has been decided to pension him off. That would create a vacancy here in the turning shop. And I'd warrant it would not be too difficult to work out his likely successor. It would mean a considerable increase in salary, together with a company house." He paused to allow the message to sink in.

Iain started. Promotion was actually being thrust at him, and long before he could normally have expected to be considered. But he was cautious. There was a price to be exacted; he could almost sniff it in the air.

Findlay breathed deeply before going on. The hook had been baited. Would Baird swallow it?

"It would be helpful if we had some support from the shop floor to advance our cause. You know how the men would probably react to any attempt to impose changes to their routine. Now if someone were to have a quiet word in the ear of possible sympathisers, perhaps emphasise the real benefits – such as higher wages …"

"A works meeting is to be held on Monday next," Rodgers interposed. "Naturally we would wish any expression of opinion to go the right way. The ASE has been assured that there will be no change to the status of its members, and has agreed to approve our programme. However, it would carry additional weight if someone, a journeyman fitter or turner say, was to speak up from the body of the meeting on behalf of progress. Might just tilt the balance. I'm sure you understand."

So that was it. He was being bribed to become a bosses' lackey. The offer was tempting, he could not deny it. But … could any of them be trusted to keep their side of the bargain?

As he wrestled with his emotions, Findlay spoke again. "Think about it over the weekend. That's all we ask. I've no doubt you'll come to the right decision. Good day to you, Baird. We'll find our own way out."

* * *

An hour later a rather flustered young man dropped onto a park bench in Glasgow Green, glad at least to rid himself of the burden of the parcels he carried. He was still in his working clothes; there had been no time to return to his lodgings and change. It was a fine autumn day; but the clear sky and bright sunshine did little to lighten Iain Baird's spirits. He had dashed away as soon as the horn had sounded, anxious to avoid the curiosity of his workmates. But that did not solve his problem. What the hell was he to do at the meeting on Monday?

Morag was late. And he was left here to twiddle his thumbs. But she would have her own way. Before leaving for work that morning he had received strict instructions. The results – a crusty loaf, cheese, boiled ham, tomatoes and apples – lay in paper bags on the seat beside him. To wash them down, two bottles of beer were growing warm in his coat pocket. There had also been a visit to the Post Office, to withdraw a substantial sum of money – twelve pounds, no less. He tapped his inside pocket to reassure himself it was still there. It was Lang who had insisted on saving for the future, and she had encouraged him to carry on with the habit. Over the years he had managed to put aside nigh on fifty pounds. Strange coincidence, that. Almost the exact sum he should have had from his father's inheritance.

He took out his pocket watch. Likely it would be the train; it was a fair journey from the sewing machine factory in Clydebank where she worked. She deserved a good telling-off for making him rush, but … he could never be sure of winning an argument. He was used to girls who knew their place, hung on his every word, fell in with his every wish. But Morag Mackay was different – a real handful, with a mind of her own. He swore softly as he snapped the lid shut.

Perhaps that was what had attracted him. That, and her stunning looks. Golden, flowing locks; bold, determined features; deep, smouldering eyes; a firm, heaving bosom atop a trim waist – enough to turn any man. And a flash of those creamy white legs and thighs could drive him wild. A potent weapon indeed, and she knew just how to use it, turning her favours on and off like a tap. Then there was that temper of hers. She could change from a warm, purring cat to a wild, snarling animal in an instant. She knew what she wanted, and usually got it. She had sized him up the first time he entered the house, decided this was the man for her, and set out to snare him. So craftily had she spun her web that he had been lured in and trapped like a fly before he even realised what was afoot.

He knew he should be flattered, but there was a downside. It was obvious she considered this a lasting relationship, and was quick to assert her proprietorial rights. Woe betide him if his roving eye caught an appreciative smile from another female; that blistering tongue could curl round him like a whiplash. There would be no more playing the field for him, he thought ruefully, not while she was around. It was a battle of wills; and it would be a rare old tussle to tame this filly.

Still, over the piece, the last nine or ten months had been good for him; there was no getting away from it. He had really landed on his feet after Lang had thrown him out. The *stooshie* over that policeman had soon died down; the authorities were baffled, the public lost interest, the press condemned yet another example of mindless thuggery and moved on. And he had only been homeless for a couple of days. On his very first morning at the Ordnance he had run into Peter Mackay, a fellow apprentice back at Deuchar's. A casual comment that he was looking for new digs had struck gold. Peter had told him that his widowed mother might be interested; in fact he had been quite insistent that Iain accompany him after work to the flat in Partick, see what he thought. So he had moved in that very evening.

Mrs Mackay was the mothering sort, and had taken to him at once. In fact she could not do enough to make him comfortable. Nor could the daughter, as things turned out. Her mother appeared pleased, rather than annoyed or upset, that the new lodger had taken a shine to Morag, and gave an immediate blessing to the pair of them walking out together. And far from chaperoning them, she obligingly would go and visit her sister to allow them time to themselves, as she put it. Their lovemaking proved fierce and passionate. Morag had a lusty appetite, physical and demanding; many a bout would leave him totally exhausted. But she was a wily vixen – quite capable of leading him on, then rebuffing his advances. She would only submit when it suited her.

It was at her suggestion that they had spent the last weekend down the Clyde at Rothesay, posing as newly-weds. And truly it had been an event to remember. There could be no complaints on that score. But there was a price to pay. At the end she had sprung her proposal. Now it was to be put into effect. Not for the first time he wondered if he was doing the right thing. Would she be wearing that ring again? She always refused to say how she had come by it. Was there just a faint jingle of wedding bells in the distance? It had better not be. Iain Baird was not ready for the chains of marriage. Perhaps in the fullness of time …

He sat and pondered, heedless of the soft scrunch of approaching footsteps on the gravel; he did not even look up as the young woman drew close. She took in the scene at a glance, smiled to herself, and deftly stepped to the side. Creeping up behind the unsuspecting figure, she suddenly clapped her hands over his eyes.

"What the –? Bugger o' hell!" He swung round angrily. "Oh, it's you. What d'ye think ye're playin' at?"

"Dinnae get yersel' in a tizzy. It was only my wee joke. Ye were in such a dwam. I thought you would be pleased to see me."

"Aye, well. Dinnae dae anythin' like that again. Or I'll no' be answerable."

"My, my, the wee man is in a grumpy mood. And on sic a fine day. Lost a tanner an' found a farthin', have ye? A hard time at work, maybe?"

"What makes ye say that? No – no, it's nothin'."

"That's dandy, then. Let it go at that. Here, you're neglectin' yer manners. My throat's like parchment. I could fair go a drink. What did ye bring to offer a lady?"

Her bubbly high spirits were infectious. He could not resist a grin. "Beer – a man's drink," he replied, pulling the bottles from his pockets and removing the stoppers. "What kept ye?"

"Weel, I had tae stop off an' tidy myself up a bit. And by the looks o' things, you could be daein' wi' a dicht yersel'. Still in yer workin' claes, I see," she sniffed. "We cannae go an' meet the house factor lookin' like towrags."

"That's right! Blame me. How could I go an' change, what wi' a' these messages ye sent me on?"

"Och, perhaps ye're no' too bad. After we've eaten, ye can dunk my hanky in the well and gie yer face a wipe. That'll hae to do." She sat down beside him and began to rummage in the bags.

"I see you've got that ring on again," he said, half-accusingly, as she handed over a lump of bread and cheese.

"Ye ken what we agreed. It's got to look respectable. Otherwise there's nae chance o' getting' a decent hoose. They wouldnae let it to a couple who werena married, no' for a' the tea in China. Do you want us tae bide wi' my maw forever?"

"It does a turn. I've nae complaints."

"No wonder! Waited on hand and foot like that. You might be happy, but I'm no'. It's high time we had a place to ca' wir own. An' we couldnae dae better than this. New tenement in a nice part o' Govan. Fine big room and kitchen. And a separate bedroom wi' an indoor cludgie. We were lucky to get the offer."

"Ye seem to have made yer mind up. Got it all worked out, haven't ye?"

"Well, dearest, I have been round to the flat. You were too lazy to come.

Remember? And ye left me to deal wi' the factor. But he'll need to see you this time. You have to sign the missives."

"Missives? What's that?"

"I've already telt ye. It's the legal agreement for a twelve month lease. You have to be the registered tenant. Though God knows why. Ye're a right chump."

"Watch it! You can go too far."

"Never mind that. Have ye got the money on you?"

"Aye. A pair o' five pun' notes and twa sovereigns. But it's a hell o' a lot o' rent for a year."

"It's no' for a year. Ye ken that. Ye have to pay six months up front. Then there's the deposit as well. That's in case o' breakages. Forbye that, there's the rates, as well as gas and electric bills."

"Is there nae end tae a' this? It's plain daylight robbery." A thought seemed to strike him. "Here, could we no' just tak' it for the six months? I've a notion somethin' might crop up soon. An' a deal cheaper too. Fancy livin' in a company property?"

"How's that? I thought ye widnae qualify for ages yet."

"Aha! But that was then. I ken different now. Like as no', I'll be made up to foreman by the end o' the year."

"I knew it! Somethin' happened at yer work this mornin'. And ye didnae exactly seem ower the moon about it. There's mair in this than meets the eye. Come on, out wi' it, man."

"Jesus Christ! Will ye never be satisfied? A'ways tryin' to ferret out every last detail. A' right, then. Anythin' to stop yer naggin'."

"Bosh! Get on wi' it."

"That's just what I'm doin'." He made an effort to suppress his irritation. "Look, it was just afore lousin' time. We had a visit from the big cheese himself, auld Findlay. That was strange enough. It disnae happen very often. An' he had a fella wi' him – a Johnny foreigner. Sounded like a Yankee. Some kind o' an expert come to see the works."

"So what of it? Get to the point."

"I'd get there a' the quicker if ye widnae interrupt. Anyhow, they stop by my machine and the Yank asks me for a word – in private, like. So I take them outside to the piece room. Well, it was nae skin off my nose. Then he goes on about the slackness in the works, how men like me could earn a lot more if we could increase production. And then Findlay steps in an' more or less says that the foreman's job wid be mine if I spoke out in favour o' new work practices at a meetin' on Monday."

"I see. And what did you make of it all?"

He shrugged his shoulders. "Some of his ideas seemed fair enough. And I'd do well out o' it."

"So you're going to play along?"

"Why no'? I dinnae see much chance o' advancement any other way."

"Then ye're a mug!" Her voice rang loud and clear. "So you would betray yer class? Be a monkey for the organ grinders?"

Iain was stung. "If that's what it takes," he growled. "Grow up, lass. Life's like that. It's everyone for himself. There's no' a man on the shop floor wouldnae dae the same to me. Class solidarity? It disnae exist. Dog eat dog, mair like. And devil take the hindmost."

" My God, nae wonder they picked on you. They've got you taped. They didnae find your bench by accident. But stop a minute an' think about what ye're really lettin' yerself in for – before ye dae somethin' ye'll come to regret a' yer days."

"And just what do you ken about it?" he jeered.

"Maybe more than you think. They tried it on at Clydebank last year. Singer's was out on strike for three weeks. Solid – all twelve thousand o' us. Or had you forgotten about that?"

"No. You've telt me about it often enough. A braw struggle. What happened in the end? Remind me."

"You ken very well. It was victimisation. The bosses threatened to close the Kilbowie works, transfer the business overseas if we stayed out."

"So you went back?"

"Aye, I cannae deny it. There was nae option. No' after they sent out postcards askin' us to vote an' accept the majority decision. Or else."

"And after the strike?"

"There's nae need to rub it in. The leaders were sacked, of course. The gaffers picked out the activists an' they were blacklisted. As for the rest o' us, there were layoffs for days, even weeks at a time. They said it was due to slack trade. But really it was to punish us, keep us in our place."

"That's exactly what I'm sayin'. The bosses are too strong. Stand up tae them and ye get crushed. I'm no' proud. I'll tak' the crumbs frae the rich man's table. And the higher ye go, the mair ye get. I learnt that lesson lang syne."

"No!" cried Morag, grasping his arm. "Ye cannae stoop that low. Things werena as black as ye make out. It started wi' just a handfu' o' women cabinet polishers. But then it spread like wildfire to the whole factory. The workers at Singer's supported each other, regardless o' their jobs or status. We fought the bosses together, no' squabbled wi' each other. It wisnae wee groups tryin' to protect their place in the peckin' order. It was for a puckle o' women. Their fight was our fight. If the bosses got away wi' it wi' them, then we were a' at risk. Aye, we went back, but no' afore we gied them a fright."

It was an impassioned speech and made an impression. Could there possibly be something in what she was saying?

"And ye really thought it was worth it?"

"Of course. We made mistakes, but we can learn from them. Divide an' rule, that's how they beat us. Industrial solidarity, that's the way forward. Then there's no' tellin' what we might achieve."

Iain was still dubious. "Easier said than done. Skilled men wouldnae gie up hard won privileges."

"I didnae say it would be easy. Nothin' worthwhile ever is. Look, at least dinnae gie in wi' out a fight. Do ye want foremen standin' over ye, settin' the pace o' work at the speed o' the fastest? They might gie ye a bonus for higher output, but then they'll expect it a' the time. And their next dodge will be to cut the piece rates. You'll graft a' the harder, and end up wi' less to show for it."

"But suppose I'm the foreman?"

"Are ye really sae sure o' that? It's easy to find an excuse to rat on a promise once they've got what they want out o' you. Even if they do make you up, ye'll have production targets to meet, wi' yer job on the line if ye fail to meet them. You'd need to be a slave driver, crackin' the whip. Are ye capable o' that?"

"If that's what it takes."

"Ye'd be hated by the men. Oh, some would toady up to you, right enough. But for all decent folk ye'd be an outcast. Ye'd be rejected by yer ain class. And the bosses would look down their noses at ye. Do you want that? I ken I couldnae stomach it."

Iain gritted his teeth. "I'm no' gonnae be a journeyman a' my life." He spat out the words. "I'm better than that."

"Of course you are," agreed Morag consolingly. "You'll get on, never fear. But not that way. Be a leader of men – your fellow workers."

"You mean – as a union official? I hadnae thought o' that. But …"

"What? I'm no' talkin' about thae oily bastards. Claim tae represent yer interests? When was the last time they got their hands dirty? What about the cosy wee arrangements they make wi' the bosses? You might as well be a foreman as join that lot," she added contemptuously.

"What, then?"

"There's strength in numbers. D'ye ken where power really lies? In the workplace, wi' the rank and file. Only they dinnae realise it. They need to be shown the way. And that's where you come in. Back at Singer's some o' us joined an industrial union. It was open to a'body that wanted to join. A' the workers were equal, and there was nae petty demarcation disputes. We just fixed on getting' a fair deal for all. You could be a part o' that."

"Socialist claptrap," muttered Iain.

"Aye, maybe. But maybe it's the future. At least think it over. Promise me ye winnae dae anythin' daft on Monday. Please!"

Iain grunted. Whether in acceptance or rejection Morag could not be certain. But for the moment she was content to let the matter drop.

"We'd best be off. The factor won't want to be kept waitin', no' on a Saturday afternoon." She flounced to her feet. "Once that's over we can hae a good time. You can buy me high tea an' we'll take in a show at the *Variety*. Maw's spendin' the weekend wi' her sister again. And Peter will be out carousing. I've made sure o' that. We'll hae the place tae ourselves. That suit you?"

"It'll dae." He grinned ruefully. "Better than listenin' tae yer sermons, anyway."

"Ye're no' still worried, are ye?"

"Naw. Except – maybe that ring. Ye're no' set on plannin' somethin', are ye?"

"Certainly not. I'm quite happy tae be yer bidie-in." She smiled blandly. "Come along, silly." Linking her arm in his, she propelled him towards the nearest tram stop.

★ ★ ★

"Thank you, Mr Buntin."

Albert Findlay rose from his seat on the makeshift platform, giving the trade union official a nod of appreciation. He had arranged the meeting for the last half hour of the shift and agreed compensation for the loss of production. That should put the men in a reasonable frame of mind – being paid to stand and listen rather than work. And indeed things seemed to be going as well as he had dared hope. Rodgers had waxed eloquently on the benefits to the workforce, laying stress on the steep rise in wages to be accrued from greater efficiency. Buntin had been a little more circumspect, but that was to be expected. Still, he had come up with the all-important stamp of approval, accepting assurances that there was no threat to the status of his members. All in all, Findlay could not have asked for more.

He beamed as he looked over the sea of faces. There was little outward sign of enthusiasm, but the mention of increased pay had certainly caught their interest. Should he call for a show of hands? Catch them on the hop, so to speak. Now if only young Baird would play up … Ah, there he was, near the front on the left. He managed to catch Iain's eye and gave an encouraging smile, before turning back to address the assembly.

"Gentlemen, you have heard from Mr Rodgers, an acknowledged expert in the field, and from Mr Buntin, your own representative. Both have emphasised the advantages to be gained from the implementation of very limited alterations – improvements I should say – in the turning and fitting shops. No employee will lose out from these changes. Everyone will benefit from higher levels of productivity. But it is only fair that you also should be given the opportunity to make your views heard. I promise that all comments or suggestions will receive serious consideration. Now if anyone has an opinion …"

He looked meaningfully at Iain again. The journeyman could not meet his gaze. He was obviously ill at ease, fidgeting nervously, his brow furrowed, his cheeks flushed. It was some moments before he could steel himself to raise his arm.

Slight though the movement was, Findlay was quick to pounce on it. "Aha, I see a colleague who wishes to make a point. Make way for him, you men. Step up to the platform, young man, so that everyone can hear you clearly."

Iain felt himself the centre of attraction as Findlay gestured him onto the stage. It might as well have been the scaffold, judging by the extreme reluctance with which he obeyed.

"Come away, now. No need to be backward. Mr Baird, is it not? You have the floor, my friend. Say your piece."

The crowd of workers could only stare in surprise. Many registered blank amazement, others craned their necks in wonder; some of his workmates scowled darkly in sudden suspicion. Iain Baird had never been slow in grousing at delays and bottlenecks that slowed up the work. Now his interview with the bosses on Saturday took on a new meaning. Was this a setup by management? A devious ploy, with Baird cast as the Judas, ready to betray his comrades?

Every eye was upon him. His mind went numb, his mouth dry as dust; he could not think of a thing to say. But Morag had prepared him well – in her own way. Even during copulation, in the gaps between the grunts and sobs and squeals of ecstasy, she had harped on about the evils of speedups and price cutting, together with a host of other devices by which the downtrodden workers were exploited by grasping capitalists. How the hell she knew so much he could not fathom. It seemed to drive her like a spitfire, to new heights of orgasm. It was as though she had a mission to infuse her will into his very being. The experience had left him gasping, shaking both body and soul. But it was the best sex he had ever had. And the information had stayed with him, the gist of it at any rate. The jumble of memories from the last two days gradually began to filter back into his consciousness.

"My name is Iain Baird," he heard himself stutter. "I'm just an ordinary sort o' bloke. A turner, no' long qualified. So I've still a lot to learn. But I do ken one thing. What you've been listenin' to is just … just a pack o' lies."

There, he had done it now. He sensed, rather than heard, the collective intake of breath. He risked a quick glance behind him. Findlay and Rodgers and Buntin were staring at one another in disbelief, jaws agape with incredulity. But he had committed himself. There was nothing for it but to plunge on.

"They're no' interested in your welfare. A' they care about is their profits. Oh, they might try to sweeten the pill wi' a wee bribe, but that's nothin' to what they'll make from your hard graft. The pace o' work will be speeded up, what wi' bonus clerks standin' ower ye, timin' every move ye make. Even when ye go tae the cludgie. Deskillin' o' labour, that's about the size o' it. Job satisfaction? Increased pay? Dinnae make me laugh. It's the thin edge o' the wedge. Gie in now and ye'll be a wage slave tied tae the machine afore ye know it."

He paused for breath. The men were hanging on his every word, he could see that. A sensation of exhilaration, of sheer, naked power, shot through him. His voice rang out anew, strong and confident.

"Shall I tell ye about their tricks to get ye to go along wi' what they want? Like the bonus system they've just offered. Knock yer pan in an' they'll gie ye a wee bit more, but it'll be peanuts compared wi' what they make. Ye'd be lucky to get a fraction o' the extra profits produced by your labour. Then there's the dodges they huvnae mentioned. No' yet, anyhow. They'll say they have to reduce the piece rates because the market's fallen. The buyers winnae meet the price 'cos the competition's cheaper. But it's the workers that'll suffer, no' the company. They'll threaten short time workin' or lay-offs unless you accept. Then there's what they cry 'quality control'. They'll reject some o' your work as no' up tae scratch. So you'll no' get paid for it. But they'll sell it on a' the same. An' then you'll hae to graft even harder to make up what ye've missed. D'ye really want a' that?"

There was a growl of agreement, then a mighty roar of "No!" Fists were waved; the meeting broke up in disarray. The workers had evidently heard enough; to a man they simply turned their backs and streamed away. The trio on the rostrum, speechless with indignation and growing rage, at last stirred into life. Rodgers glowered at Iain, then at Findlay; he snorted and strode away, knowing his plans, and perhaps his reputation, lay in ruins. Buntin glared at this young upstart as he stalked past, his carefully negotiated arrangement now in tatters. Findlay was angriest of all; a bright red spot dimpled each of his cheeks. He was only too aware he would be held fully to account if the new schedules were not enforced.

Iain stood alone on the stage, limp from the exertion, his head aching from the strain. The burst of adrenalin was ebbing fast, leaving in its wake a dreadful realisation. Morag had cast a spell on him, and they would make him pay for it – sacked and blacklisted, if nothing worse. Now the hooter was sounding, the workforce surging out of the gates; he scarcely heard the murmurs of praise from some of the men as they passed. There was a persistent tug at his arm, dragging him back to reality. A gaunt, middle aged man had stepped onto the platform. He was trying to say something. Iain had to make an effort to focus his attention.

"That was some speech ye made there," he heard the man say. "Nailed yer flag to the mast good and proper, I would say. Time you an' me had a wee chat. But no' here. I ken a quiet howff. You look in need o' a good hauf."

Iain squinted cautiously at the newcomer. His face was vaguely familiar. Now what was his name? Stan Robertson – that was it. But he was a fitter. Worked in another shop entirely. What the hell did he want? But he was in no mood to argue.

"Why no'? I've nothin' to lose now."

He followed the older man out of the yard. Not another word was exchanged until they were ensconced in the snug bar of a nearby alehouse. Robertson pointed towards a table in the far corner, half hidden by a recess, while he went for the drinks. Iain shrugged and took the seat indicated. What difference did it make where they sat?

A shot of whisky and tankard of beer appeared on the table. "Here, get that down you." Robertson slipped into the chair opposite.

Iain tossed down the nip in a single gulp. "Man, that was guid." He blinked in surprise. "You no' drinkin'?"

"No. Not yet. Maybe after our business. By the by, you can set yer mind at rest about getting' turfed out. They'll no' dare sack ye. The hero o' the hour victimised? It would provoke a strike. An' they'll no' thole that, no' wi' all the orders on their books."

"How do ye ken that? I wish I could share yer confidence."

The man ignored the interruption. "There'll be nae comeback from Buntin either. He's probably exceeded his authority in makin' that agreement. We've a few sympathetic bodies amongst the high-ups in the union that can put the mockers on him if need be."

"We? Who's the we?"

"All in good time, lad. We'll get to that presently." He looked thoughtfully at Iain. "We've had our eye on ye for some time. Ye didnae realise that, did ye? You were an apprentice at Deuchar's, took night school classes in yer ain time. That's good. It shows initiative. Ye're no' slow in makin' yer views felt.

And, so it seems, ye can make a speech."

Iain gasped. "How dae ye ken a' that?"

Robertson smiled sourly. "You'd be surprised just how much we do know. We had you tagged as a bosses' stooge, do anythin' to get on. What did they offer you to stand up and support the scheme?"

"How could you possibly …?" He slumped back. "Foreman o' the turnin' shop."

"Thought as much. Well, you'll no' be offered that now. I'll no' ask what made you change your mind. But they'll see you as a bad lot. And treat you accordingly. First to be laid off in a slump, last to be taken back. You'll stay a humble journeyman for the rest of your days. Unless …"

"Unless what?"

"Unless you're willin' to join us. It'll be a hard shift. But we're bound to win in the end. That's for sure. Then you'll have a taste of real power."

"But who are ye?"

"We're socialists. The Socialist Labour Party, if ye want the full name."

"Labour? Ye mean like thae gowks on the toun council, or standin' for parliament?"

"Socialists? Them?" His tone oozed contempt. "They're no' real socialists. They're just reformists, if that. Tinker a wee bit here an' there wi' the machinery o' the capitalist state. Be sucked in by it, mair like. They'll aye be bought off wi' a few baubles. We've nae time for them. What we need is a revolution. That's the only way forward. Tear down the whole rotten fabric an' start again. No more masters and men, rich and poor. Those that toil wi' the sweat o' their brow should reap the rewards. And the first step is to get workers' control o' the workplace."

Iain stared. The man must be mad. Or a fanatic.

"But how would we achieve that? The bosses are too strong. How many o' ye are there? It cannae be a lot. I've never heard the name afore. Nor has anyone else I ken."

"True enough. We are few in number. That's because we're fussy about who we let in. But there are other groups as well. And dinnae forget, socialists are no' just in Scotland, or even Britain. It's a worldwide organisation. Ever heard o' the Industrial Workers o' the World? Or the Knights o' Labour? They're frae America. They're for workers' control, just like us. Then there's syndicalists in France and Europe. We've links wi' a' them, ready for action when the time comes. They exist all right, no matter what the lackeys o' the capitalist press say. And they're growing stronger by the day."

"But I still dinnae see how ye could do it," Iain protested.

"No? Then let me tell you. A general strike, that's the way. If everyone came out at the same time, that would bring the government to its knees. Where would the upper classes be wi'out our labour? Why, the state would collapse."

"But ye'd never get all the workers to cooperate. They'll only protect their ain interests against other workers. Ye cannae expect skilled men to accept the same wages as floor sweepers."

"Then it's our job to change things. We wait and watch till the time is ripe. We argue and persuade on the shop floor and at the factory gate. We spread the gospel o' socialism. We take advantage of workers' grievances. We take the lead in stirrin' up industrial action. We build up trust and followers. And when the day comes – we strike."

"You talk about time and day. It's a' moonshine. When will it ever come?"

"Listen," snapped Robertson with sudden intensity, "and mark my words. There are storm clouds ahead. There's a war brewin'. And it'll be on a scale that's never been seen before. Armies of millions. The mass destructive power of modern technology. Countries will be ravaged, casualties counted in hundreds of thousands. D'ye think entire populations would put up with that for long?"

"But does it have to happen? It's – it's unbelievable. No one could want that."

"I'd bet on it, all the same – and within the next five years. Look, there's an arms race going on. Right? Why do you think the Ordnance is bursting at the seams? And there's hundreds – no, thousands – of other factories churning out the same for every major power. D'ye imagine it's just for show? Sooner or later the military will be tempted to try out their new toys. Europe's already divided into two armed camps – wi' Germany and the Kaiser as the number one threat. The whole continent is a tinderbox just waitin' for the spark to blow it apart. Remember last year – Morocco? It nearly happened then. Sometime, someone will slip up. All it takes is a miscalculation, a misread signal, and we'll slide intae the abyss. And once started, it'll be impossible to stop."

"My God!" Iain was aghast at the prospect. Despite his scepticism he was impressed. At least it explained something of what was going on.

"And the war will no' be between peoples. They've nae quarrel wi' each other. It's the rulers that'll be to blame: them an' their puppet politicians. Oh, they'll dress it up. Call it a fight for democracy, or to preserve the national way of life. They'll blacken the other side and say it was forced on them. Did ye ken that the crowned heads o' Britain, Germany and Russia are cousins? So it's just a family argument. But it'll be the ordinary folk that bear the brunt. They'll march off to war singin' an' dancin' – the propaganda machine will take care o' that. But it canna hide the truth forever. When the effects really begin to bite, then you'll see a change. War weariness, demands for peace, protests, riots. Soldiers will mutiny, refuse to fight any more, turn their guns on the oppressors. An' that means the downfall o' the whole stinkin' order."

Iain goggled at the enormity of the picture being painted. "So you're sayin' that revolution is inevitable."

"Got it in one. Though a wee helpin' hand wouldnae go amiss. It'll be our job to speak out against the war, hold demonstrations, organise strikes. Armies an' navies cannae fight wi'out weapons and ammunition. As our support grows we can take over, factory by factory, an' smash the whole system. Get rid o' the warmongers, sweep them intae the dustbin o' history. Then we can build an international socialist world, wi' fairness and justice for all. Are ye wi' us?"

Iain was taken aback. The question was so sudden, so direct. But an immediate answer was obviously expected. Should he throw in his lot with a bunch of extremists? He was far from fully convinced, but the thing was at least conceivable. Events might just pan out as Robertson had described. Swallowing his doubts, he nodded acceptance.

They shook hands. "So be it. Mind, it'll be no bed of roses. There'll be many a hardship to be endured afore the Promised Land is reached. Now, let's deal wi' practicalities. The first task is to complete your education."

"Education? But I've already got qualifications."

"Aye. Technical subjects. Nae doubt they'll come in handy when we take over. No, it's your political education that's lackin'. Marxism – that's what ye have to learn. You'll attend classes and familiarise yerself wi' the prescribed texts. You could also go an' listen to the speakers in Glasgow Green of a Sunday. I'm sure you might manage that."

"I suppose so. If ye think it necessary."

"Good. Then I'll away an' fetch a couple o' drams. We've a new member to toast."

ELEVEN

The Price of Wisdom

Edinburgh.February 1913

Alastair was disconsolate. She had arrived late at the teashop, only to tell him that he was to be disappointed yet again. For the third Saturday in a row the promised ramble through the Edinburgh by-ways would have to be postponed. Had she grown tired of him? She always protested that her feelings towards him remained unchanged; it was just that the cause had need of her. Somehow the assurances did not quite ring true.

It had all started before Christmas, with the big suffrage pageant. Elizabeth had always had a thing about women's rights, but in a vague, generalised sort of way. It was the address by the suffragist leader, Dr Elsie Inglis, which had really set her off. She had dragged him along out of curiosity to hear the speeches, and he could still picture how her jaw had set as she listened with rapt attention. At the end she had been full of it, could not wait to join the crusade.

Matters had really gone downhill during the vacation. He had been away in Broomburn. On his return in January, he found that Elizabeth had joined the Women's Suffrage Union; in fact it appeared she was thick as thieves with the university group. She had apparently made great friends with one of its leading lights, a Miss Annabel Smart. Now he had a rival for Elizabeth's attention. She was torn between them, but it was an uneven contest.

There was real hurt in his eyes. Elizabeth felt a pang of guilt. It was so beastly to have to treat him like this. But she dare not weaken; not now she had a calling which demanded all her energies. Deep down, she had always known that teaching was not for her. She had been prepared to give it her best shot, but the regime and the grind soon began to pall. She shuddered at the prospect of what lay ahead. Confronting a mob of unruly urchins, ragged and dirty, with runny noses, impetigo and lice, and God knew what other ghastly habits and ailments. It was enough to make the flesh creep.

Then there was the other side of their relationship – or lack of it. She felt a growing sense of disillusionment, even frustration. If only he would show he had red blood in his veins. Instead, he seemed content to hold hands and peck at her chastely. They behaved more like brother and sister than ardent lovers. And he had the gall to complain about her moods! Bourgeois respectability might be the summit of his ambitions; it held absolutely no attraction for her. But nor need it any longer. She would devote every breath in her body to the quest. That was all that mattered. Should she make a clean break, here and now? But he looked so wretched. She hesitated, but only for a moment.

"Alastair, dearest, I have to be off now. But I was thinking. How would you like to come and see me?"

His expression brightened at once. This was something new. She had never extended an invitation before – quite the reverse. She had always been at pains to keep him away.

"I mean, we're only going to hand out leaflets. And I'm to make a short speech at the start. It's the first time they've asked me to take on the responsibility," she added proudly.

"You must be pleased about that. Where does it take place?"

"Oh, not far. Up by the McEwan Hall – the open space at the front. We can catch the Southside shoppers, visitors to the Royal Infirmary, and people on their way to Princes Street. There'll be a fair crowd around at that time of day."

"And just when might that be?"

"It's fixed for noon. So if you could be there by then. It'll only take half an hour or so. I'll have to report back, of course, but I've nothing on afterwards. We could have a bite together. And go on that hike after all. Would you like that?"

He nodded vigorously. Things were looking up again.

An hour later he was not so sure. Midday had come and gone, with no sign of her yet. There was little pleasure in hanging around, cooling his heels; the chill February air soon made its presence felt, even though the sun was shining. That, however, was not what really bothered him. Elizabeth had stipulated the graduation building, but had she realised what lay just beyond it? Teviot House – the Student Union! At lunchtime it would be heaving – especially with rugger types, sinking a pint or two before their afternoon game. And they were no respecters of persons. Was she aware of the risk? He almost hoped she would not come.

Damn! Was this her now? A taxi-cab was swinging into Teviot Place, pulling up not twenty paces from where he stood. Three young ladies stepped out. Two immediately began to unfurl a banner; the third carried a speaking trumpet. It was Elizabeth, all right. He gave a little wave, but there was no answering gesture. The taxi made no attempt to move off. And the engine was left running. How very odd! A flash of sunlight danced on the metal tube as Elizabeth raised it to her lips.

"We are here today to make an appeal to your sense of decency. Women are classed with paupers, felons and lunatics as being unfit to exercise the franchise. Is this fair, I ask you? Is this part of the grand British tradition of democracy? We have already made progress in the struggle for human dignity. In matters of education, in the medical profession, in the sphere of local government – in all of these, much has been achieved. But there still remains much more to be done. Women can never gain full equality as citizens of the Empire until they are granted the vote. Will you stand with us in this great enterprise?"

Her voice rang true and clear, with no hint of uncertainty or hesitation. She did not lack self-confidence, that was for sure. And not a little courage either. He could never have brought himself to such bravado. And yet it sounded so glib. How long had she spent rehearsing that speech in advance?

People were stopping to stare; soon quite a sizeable little audience had gathered. They were listening indulgently, as though prepared to humour a somewhat wayward child.

"One reason why I am a convinced suffragist is that mothers, even as wage earners, take the greater share of responsibility in the upbringing of children. Should they not, therefore, have the means to make their voice heard, to enable them to do justice to the rising generation?"

"How many kids have you got?" shouted a wag.

"None," yelled another. "That's what she needs. Gie her somethin' worthwhile to do."

"I could help out there," cried a third. "She looks ripe for the pluckin'." He was rewarded with a coarse laugh from some of the bystanders.

Oh, no! The hecklers were warming up. Was the mood beginning to change? Elizabeth flushed, but was not to be put out.

"I was about to say, before the gentleman over there made his most valuable contribution …"

Several missiles flew over – a banana skin or two, a few apple cores. Fortunately they fell short or missed their mark. Alastair jerked round. This was what he had feared. Students were pouring out of the Union, streaming down the steps, fanning out, edging forward.

"We must not overlook the victims of sweated labour …"

She was gamely trying to carry on. Surely she must realise the danger. They were like a swarm of angry wasps, out to defend their territory. Her words were lost amid the jeers and catcalls. As if that were not enough, some broke into a ribald drinking song. Would they content themselves with chanting obscenities, until the suffragists gave up and withdrew? Not if he knew their stamp. They were too enraged. There would be a rush in a minute to drive off the intruders, if nothing worse.

"Grab the banner!" It was a signal for half a dozen in the forefront to surge forward. Instinctively the girls drew together, backing against the car, faces set, but obviously determined to resist. Alastair saw Elizabeth use her loud-hailer to good effect, dashing it against the head of an assailant. One of her companions kicked another in the groin. Then it was pandemonium, a wild scrum wrestling for possession of the trophy. That was enough for Alastair. Galvanised into action, he hurled himself at the nearest attacker, bowling him over with the sheer momentum of the impact. In an instant he was on his feet again. A student was trying to grapple with Elizabeth. Drawing back his fist, he let fly, straight from the shoulder. A spasm of agony shot up his arm, but there was no time to heed the pain. The man reeled away, clutching his face. The others wavered and drew back, momentarily stunned by the unexpected intervention. But it would not be long before they recovered. There was not a second to lose.

"Into the cab!" His voice was shrill with the urgency of the situation. "Sharp now!" He found himself dragging open the door, thrusting the half-protesting Elizabeth inside. "Now you two," he rasped at the others. "Leave it! There's no time." The girls, wide-eyed with fright, dropped their burden into the gutter and hastened to obey. "Cabbie, get moving! For all our sakes! Go!"

There was a crash of gears, a screech of wheels, and they were away. Alastair had to jump onto the running board and cling on for dear life. To be left behind did not bear thinking about. He managed to inch forward and find a refuge of sorts in the luggage compartment, crouching down while hanging onto the straps with his good hand. The taxi fairly shot into the main road, twisting and weaving as it went. A carthorse shied in the traces as the drayman had to pull up fiercely. There was a shower of sparks as a tram shuddered to a halt, missing a collision by inches. Then they were clear, streaking away towards Tollcross.

Alastair winced with every bump and jolt. His body was shivering from exposure, his limbs cramped from the uncomfortable position. But at last the vehicle began to slow down, and pulled over to the kerb. Thank goodness the ordeal was over. Then he gawped in astonishment. Once cap and goggles were removed … Good God! It was another woman. Was there no end to the surprises?

"Care to join us now, Alastair?" Elizabeth was leaning out of her window.

"Are you all right, Elizabeth?" He pulled himself upright. "I mean, did any of the brutes harm you?"

"No, all serene. It was fun though, wasn't it?" Her eyes were bright with excitement.

"Fun? I wouldn't put it quite like that."

"No? Well, perhaps not. A bit more hairy than we had anticipated, I have to admit. And you rode in to the rescue like a knight in shining armour. I knew you would. But – your arm, hanging down like that. You're hurt."

"It's nothing, really. I've just barked my knuckles."

"Rather more than that, by the looks of things. Anyhow, you must let us take care of you. It's the least we can do. Get in." She waited till he was settled beside her, then tapped on the glass. "Ella, you can drive on now. Change of plan, though. We've another passenger."

She nuzzled up against him, arm round his waist, head resting on his chest. It was that perfume again, working its spell. He blushed with embarrassment. God knew what the others thought, squirming in their seats opposite, pretending to be interested in the passing scene outside. Wait a minute, though. Could this be a smokescreen? A ploy to avoid awkward questions? What was that remark she had let slip? He had to know for certain.

"Elizabeth, just now you implied that you had been expecting trouble. Was that so? Or – or was that the point of the whole affair? To kick up a shindig? Was it all a publicity stunt? Tell me I'm wrong."

There was no reply. But she squeezed him a little tighter. He pushed her away, gently but firmly, so he could confront her, face to face.

"Elizabeth, will you at least promise that you'll never get involved in anything like this again. It's sheer madness. You could have been badly injured. You might not be so lucky another time. Please? For me?"

She smiled wistfully and slowly shook her head. "I'm sorry," she said quietly. "I can't do that."

* * *

May 1913

A thin, grey haar drifted over the city, rolling in from the Forth, obscuring the setting sun. Typical Edinburgh weather, thought Elizabeth to herself – Scotch mist in May. But nothing could dampen her spirits as she picked her way across Bruntsfield Links towards the acres of stately tenements on the Marchmont side. This had been the test – an examination of her mettle. Everything had gone so swimmingly; she smiled in recollection at how easy it had been to drop the bottle of corrosive fluid into the gleaming red pillar-box. This, she had been told, was part of the campaign of secret arson, or *Scottish outrages* as the hostile press had dubbed it. Now she was on the way to report her success. No doubt watchful eyes had weighed her every move. Surely there was no fault to be found with her performance.

Recruitment into the ranks of the militant suffragettes had come as something of a surprise – though it was rather flattering to have been singled out for special attention. She had accepted the invitation to take tea with one of the Pankhurst zealots out of curiosity; she had been overwhelmed by the sheer force of the woman's charm and personality. The encounter had left her convinced by the arguments, dazzled by the prospects. Peaceful persuasion would never work; nothing would ever be achieved unless parliament could be coerced into passing legislation. And that meant war to the knife. Was she prepared to engage herself heart and soul as a soldier in a righteous crusade? Without hesitation she had begged for an opportunity to prove her worth. But apparently the plans to launch a fresh campaign in Scotland were not yet complete. For the moment she was to continue her activities with the Suffrage Union. No one must know of her new allegiance. She would be contacted when they had need of her. Two days ago the summons had finally arrived: she was now on active service.

Spottiswoode Street – this was the place. She consulted the scribbled note once more, and rang the bell of the number she had been given. No sooner had the front door opened than she skipped down the tiled hallway and ascended the broad staircase. They were on the first floor landing, waiting for her; she was almost overwhelmed by the effusiveness of the greeting. Handshakes, hugs and kisses – she was swept inside. Introductions were effected. There were four of them – Ethel, Dorothea, Liz and Fanny. A couple of faces seemed familiar. Of course! Their pictures had been plastered all over the papers; she was in the presence of two of the most renowned firebrands who had endured penal servitude for their exploits – and then forced the authorities to release them by going on hunger strike. Elizabeth could only simper as the compliments showered down from such exalted company. But best of all was when Ethel looked her over and said quietly: "You'll do." She blushed with pleasure.

"Now, ladies, to business. We've a lot to get through." Ethel was clearly in charge of proceedings. "We've asked you here tonight, Elizabeth, to go over the arrangements for our next action. We're all agreed. We'd like you to be involved."

There was a chorus of affirmation. Elizabeth beamed with happiness. She had been accepted. "Anything," she breathed. "I mean I'll help out in any way you like."

"That's the ticket. You've graduated with flying colours today. We've no qualms about you being one of the team."

"Thank you. I'll try to live up to your confidence."

"We know you will. Fanny and I will be taking part. You'll make up the third, Elizabeth. This is going to be earth shattering, make no mistake about that. It'll be more momentous than burning down the stand at Ayr racecourse or the cricket pavilion in Perth. They'll feel the shockwaves in London."

"What is it?" asked Elizabeth, just a little too eagerly. Instantly she regretted the blunder. "Sorry," she mumbled lamely.

Ethel nodded in acknowledgement and looked round the little group.

"We are going to blow up the Royal Observatory," she pronounced slowly. "On Blackford Hill. And it's fixed for tomorrow night."

Elizabeth gasped. This was enough to take anyone's breath away. The enormity of it was staggering.

"Yes. Ambitious, isn't it?" Dorothea was addressing her now. "But it's a just reprisal for acts of state terrorism against the movement. Our own dear leader, Mrs Pankhurst, has been given three years in prison on a trumped up charge of criminal conspiracy. Three years! She will bear incarceration with fortitude, as always, but think of the effects on her health. Scandalous! It cannot be tolerated."

"That's so," added Liz. "Don't forget that only last week our dear friend, Arabella Scott, was imprisoned for attempted arson at Kelso racetrack. And an old woman of sixty-five, who had taken no active part, was sentenced to three months as an accomplice. Infamous!"

"Well remembered, Liz." Dorothea took up the baton again. "If such are attempts to browbeat us into submission, then they have seriously miscalculated. Violence will be met with violence. We will never give up. Not till final victory."

"So now you know, Elizabeth." Ethel smiled reassuringly. "What do you have to say? Give us your opinion."

"I – I was a little taken aback at first. But I'm quite recovered now. I fully support everything that's been said. And I'm ready to undertake whatever you wish of me."

"Good. We'll get to the details presently. But there's something else first." Ethel gave the faintest of nudges to the small, disarming figure sitting beside her on the settee.

This was Fanny's cue. She wrinkled with distaste, but it had to be done. "Elizabeth, dear," she began, "you are one of us now. We are your dearest friends, closer to you than your own family. We give ourselves for you. You must do the same for us." She swallowed hard. "There's no easy way to put this. In a war sacrifices have to be made. Someone – someone must be prepared to be caught, allow herself be charged with destroying the Observatory. There's good reason, believe me. The publicity of a trial will resound throughout the realm. It will even rival the Pankhursts' appearances in the dock."

"There is another matter." There was just a tinge of impatience in Ethel's voice. "You are aware how force feeding is damaging the government. Not a popular policy for a so-called Liberal administration. So they've come up with a way round it." She was brisk and business-like now. "A new law has just been passed. They can release hunger strikers under licence, and return them to prison when their health recovers. It's already being called the *Cat and Mouse Act*. We need to find out how to work this to our advantage. So we need a volunteer. Will you be our first *mouse*, Elizabeth?"

Elizabeth was stunned. This was a bolt from the blue. What were they asking of her? To comply would transform her existence. It might even ruin her life. Was it too much to demand? *Get a grip on yourself, girl.* The sensation of panic cleared. Too late to back out now, suffer their silent contempt.

"I said I would do anything. And I stick by that. I'm more than willing to remain on the scene until the police arrive and give myself up."

Ethel came over and pecked her on the cheek. "Bless you, Elizabeth. Bless you for your commitment. But we want the police to have to work for their quarry. Make it too easy for them and they might smell a rat. The obvious course is to leave a clue behind – our calling card, so to speak. Have you anything – maybe a trinket or piece of jewellery – that would point to your identity? Something that might be dropped by accident?"

Elizabeth thought for a moment. "Why, yes. I've a pocket watch – a cheap, ugly monstrosity that I never wear. It was a presentation from the Bible class. The case has my full name engraved on it. And the church as well, as I recall."

"Sounds ideal. Try to damage the clasp so that it will look like it fell off when you brushed against something."

The discussion moved on to the following night's activity. Point after point, detail after detail; it all became a blur in the mind. Elizabeth felt her attention wandering. Had she the strength to survive incarceration? She could almost taste the bile rising in her stomach as she pictured the horrors of force feeding, the tube sliding down her throat as she choked and retched. She thought of her parents. How would they react? Mama would disown her, never speak to her again. At least daddy would try to understand. But he would be hurt, wounded to the core. His career would surely suffer, what with a jailbird for a daughter. As for Alastair, she could visualise his anguish at the news. But there was nothing she could do about it now.

* * *

"Mind out for the loose stones." The whispered warning hissed in her ear – too late. Her boot scraped on the damp scree; an instant later her foot gave way. She was tumbling backwards; then arms were gripping her shoulders, pushing her upright.

"You were nearly away there. Lucky I was right behind. Otherwise you might have broken the jar. And then where would we have been? For God's sake, watch where you're going."

Elizabeth seethed with silent indignation at the injustice of Ethel's rebuke. How was she to blame when she could scarcely make out the hand in front of her face? The sky was clear, but the moon had not yet risen. And the glimmer of twinkling starlight was not much help. If anything, it only served to intensify the inky blackness of trees and bushes, sentinels of foreboding looming up on either side of the steep track. They did have electric torches with them, but their use was strictly limited. Not in the open, Ethel had insisted. Only when actually laying the charges.

It was well after midnight before they had left their base, the house of a sympathiser in the Grange. Her parents had been duped into thinking she was to spend the night at the home of a fellow student; they would be working late together, preparing for the end of term examinations. It went against the grain to have to tell lies, but, after all, it was for the greater good. Thus she had stilled her conscience as she helped to check and pack the equipment.

Donning dark clothes and hats, they had set off on their journey. Rather than take the direct route by Observatory Road, it had been decided to approach from the west, up and over Blackford Hill. Longer but safer, that was the explanation. At such a late hour there was little likelihood of a dog walker about, still less the possibility of courting couples. And work at the Observatory would surely be over for the night. True, several of the staff lived nearby in the grounds, but hopefully all would be a-bed by the time they arrived. There was really nothing to worry about – so long as they were careful.

"Almost there," said Fanny brightly, ever the peacemaker. "Not far to go now."

The older women put on a spurt. Elizabeth followed, rather more slowly. She had the heaviest load, an earthenware crock filled with gunpowder, secured in the haversack on her back. She had begged for the honour, fool that she was. Up ahead she could just make out two silhouettes against the skyline; that must be the summit. She forced herself to lengthen her stride – anything to avoid another cutting remark. All of a sudden there was a shaft of pearly light, bathing the whole hillside in a deathly gleam. The moon was at last making its appearance, a creamy white orb climbing above the horizon.

"Would you look at that?" whistled Fanny. "It's beautiful."

Elizabeth could now clearly distinguish the outline of the Observatory across the open ground. Rising proudly above the complex of buildings were its twin towers, the domes sheathed in copper, glistening dully in the moonlight.

"Yes," Ethel agreed. "All ripe for the plucking. Remember I said I was counting on this? And up it comes – right on cue. That should make our task a little easier. And not a soul knows we're here," she chuckled. "Apart from Dorothea and Liz, that is."

Elizabeth stiffened. What was that? *Not a soul knows.* The words touched a raw nerve. Hastily she sought to reassure herself. It had been a tiny indiscretion, no more. It was just that someone else did know. And she was responsible. Should she confess, here and now? It would only demean her in their eyes. In any case it would never come to light, she was sure of that. And in a few hours it would not matter anyway.

She had not meant to do it, of course. But there had been a prior arrangement to call on Annabel Smart earlier that evening, on Suffrage Union business. That had been her first mistake, as she had quickly recognised. Her friend was far too shrewd not to notice that she had appeared preoccupied, her mind elsewhere. But the fatal slip had been to hint that she might be unavailable for forthcoming activities. Bit by bit, with rapier like thrusts, Annabel's relentless probing had stripped away her feeble defences, till she had the whole story. Then she had damned her for an idiot. Her life could be ruined, her health destroyed. There had been rumours of hunger and thirst strikes. Was she ready for that? They had parted on the worst of terms. But no suffragist would ever betray one of the sisterhood; she was safe on that score. And she had not revealed the identity of her companions; that was something of a comfort.

Ethel was going over the final instructions. "There are two telescopes, remember. Ours is the one on this side. So there'll be no need to creep past the staff quarters. Just a pity there isn't time to deal with them both. But it can't be helped. Use the trees for cover wherever you can. Now – good luck and God speed."

Noiselessly they glided across the grass, moving as quickly as the encumbrance of packs and heavy walking skirts would permit, flitting from tree to tree through the ghostly glow; occasionally they halted, to catch their breath and check for any sign of danger. In minutes they were crouching at the base of the tower.

"Made it," purred Fanny. "And no barking dogs. That was my main worry."

"Quiet!" snapped Ethel in an undertone. "No unnecessary talking. Spread out and try to find a window."

They crept forward, hugging the contours of the tower. Suddenly Ethel held out a restraining hand. A ray of torchlight penetrated the gloom – only for an instant, but it was enough. What luck! A casement window, and no more than waist height. Stave in a small panel, stretch in a hand, unbolt the catch – and they were in! Ethel clambered over the sill. Then the sacks were passed through, before the others joined her.

"This is where we really need the glim." Ethel flicked over the switch. "Couldn't be better – the photography room. There's the central pillar. The reflector is two storeys above us." She indicated a circular staircase. "That's our way up. Unpack the explosives, Elizabeth. And take off your footwear, both of you. We don't want any noise. Stocking soles only."

Elizabeth grunted as she lifted out the pot. Ethel twisted off the cork stopper, replacing it with a rubber one, this time with a hole in the centre.

"That's for the fuse. You can carry it up to the top now. Careful as you go. We can't afford accidents at this stage."

Elizabeth could feel the beads of sweat as she slowly climbed the spiral steps, the jar clutched to her stomach. Ethel was at her elbow, pointing the light to illuminate the way.

"Just there," she ordered. "At the top of the stairs."

Elizabeth was only too glad to lay down her burden. She stared round in amazement; before her was the huge bulk of the reflector, stretching upwards towards the great dome.

Ethel had no time to be impressed. "Got the detonator ready, Fanny?" The third member of the group had been uncoiling rolls of line from her bag as she followed them up. "Give it here." Taking a clasp knife from her coat pocket, she cut and trimmed the cord, before inserting the end firmly into the hole. "There, it's a bomb now."

Hastily they retraced their steps to the ground floor. "There's still the evidence to plant." Trust Ethel to forget nothing. "Shove the panama bag beside the pillar. Can't have the papers being destroyed in the blast. They might just think it was some other organisation. And here's a tin of biscuits. Give them the impression we had time for a snack. Elizabeth, mind the watch. Drop it outside the window. So it'll be the first thing they find."

Elizabeth drew out the fateful object; it felt heavy as lead. A moment's hesitation, then she pitched it onto the gravel path. There was a faint clink as it landed. But to her it resounded like the clang of a cell door.

"Done it? Good. Fanny, rest the end of the coil on the window ledge. On with your boots now, quick as you like. Then outside, the pair of you."

Ethel swept the torch round for a final look. Satisfied, she tucked it into her belt and pulled herself through the casement.

"Damn!" she exclaimed. "I've cut myself. Must be a nail or bit of glass." She peered at the wound. "Only a nick. Nothing to worry about. Hand me the box of lucifers, Fanny."

Dashing away the drops of blood on her wrist, she extracted a match and struck it. Cupping her hands, she waited till the flame burned steadily before applying it to the fuse. The thin, waxed rope took immediately, sending out a shower of sparks. Ethel straightened up and tossed the matchbox into the shrubbery nearby.

"Let's get out of here. We've fifteen minutes. I want to be well clear by then."

They hurried off, back the way they had come. Ethel and Fanny could barely suppress the intoxication of the moment. But for Elizabeth it had turned to ashes. What had she to savour? After all, she was to be the sacrificial victim. Her head began to throb as she scuttled after the others.

* * *

Haggard and listless, Elizabeth took her place at the dinner table. She had no appetite, could not stomach the thought of food. The headache was still there, despite the powders she had taken. Her hair was a mess, her face unmade; she could not be bothered to change her dress. Mama was looking askance at her, but mercifully forbearing to comment. It was only at her mother's insistence that she had ventured downstairs at all. *How long now before they came for her?*

Arriving home that morning, she had complained of a migraine. Well, that was true enough. Lack of sleep, she supposed. Or was it the stress and strain of the night's work, coupled with anticipation of her fate? Maybe it was all of them. But the mission had been a success; surely that was all that mattered. The bomb had gone off; they had heard the distant crump from the bottom of the hill. The Observatory had been wrecked; the noise had sent them scurrying back to the safety of their bolthole. Liz and Dorothea had stayed up, of course, eager to learn the result; Ethel and Fanny had been only too willing to describe every detail. Their excited chatter had scuppered any chance of snatching a few hours' rest.

She had declared that she felt too ill to attend college that day. Perhaps it would be for the best if she were to cut classes, and take to her bed. Mama had frowned and pursed her lips, but had made no objection. Daddy, departing for his chambers, had smiled sympathetically and kissed her on the forehead. She had been only too glad to escape to her room and throw herself down, fully clothed, on the coverlet. Why bother to get undressed when they would soon be here? For hours she had lain there – waiting. Every jangle of the doorbell had sent a shiver down her spine, sending her pulse racing, intensifying the pounding in her head. But it was always a false alarm. Surely they must have discovered the watch by now.

Course followed course; Elizabeth pushed away every plate untouched. It was as though she was in a reverie – always staring moodily towards the door. After the soup, fish and quail had been rejected, Hilda could contain herself no longer.

"You little madam! Just what do you think your game is? Slouching there with a face like a wet fish. You come into dinner looking as though you've been dragged through a garden hedge. You turn up your nose at the food. You've hardly spoken a word. No consideration for anyone else. That's your trouble."

Her daughter blinked at her. "I – I'm sorry," she mumbled. "It's just that I'm not hungry. And I still do have that headache."

"Fiddlesticks!" Her mother was not to be appeased. "You've been skulking in your room all day. Thank goodness we have no guests here tonight, that's all I can say."

Elizabeth flushed with sudden anger. "Sorry if I've disgraced the family again. Another blot on the escutcheon? That's all you care about. I didn't want to come down in the first place. You made me. Remember?" She was almost shouting.

Lixmont hastened to intervene, before open warfare broke out. "Hilda, my dear, Elizabeth appears to be in some distress. Perhaps she could be excused. Then, if she's not better, I'll send for the doctor in the morning."

"No, Edward." Hilda was firm. "You mollycoddle the girl far too much. I can't make her eat. But I can make her mend her manners. She can sit there till we've finished."

Lixmont grunted with exasperation. His wife was on her high horse again. "Well," he temporised. "Perhaps – perhaps, Elizabeth, you could stay and take coffee with us. It might help revive you."

He thought he had handled that rather neatly. No, not quite. The row had been stifled, but only to be replaced by a strained silence. His daughter had slumped back, her eyes vacant once more, the momentary rage quite gone; his wife was scowling at him with disfavour.

"By the by, Hilda, I nearly forgot. There's something I've been meaning to tell you. A snippet of news I picked up. Would you like to hear it?"

"If you must."

"I had it from Archie Knox. You remember Archie – the newspaper editor? I bumped into him at lunch."

"Yes, yes. Get on with it," said Hilda testily.

"Well then – it's the suffragettes. They're up to their old tricks again."

"That lot? No wonder they're called hyenas in petticoats. Where was it this time?"

"Here. In Edinburgh – in our own fair city."

"More letter-box devilment, I suppose?"

"No. Not this time. Rather more ambitious. An attempt to blow up the Royal Observatory. It took place last night."

Aha, that had stirred their interest; he knew it would. Hilda was all ears; even Elizabeth seemed to be perking up.

"What happened?"

"According to Archie, there were two or three of them. They broke in through a window and planted a casket of gunpowder, cool as you like. Then they lit the fuse and skipped off."

"And no one heard a thing?"

"That's just it. The Professor of Astronomy – he has lodgings on the premises, you know – swore he heard a loud noise at about two in the morning. Well, he looked out, saw nothing and went back to bed. Apparently he thought it was just a door banging. The discovery was eventually made by a porter when he came to open up. Bet he got a shock – everything open already." He chuckled at his own witticism.

"Hardly a laughing matter, Edward. Was there much harm done?"

"Sorry, Hilda. No. That's the curious thing. At first sight it looked bad. Windows blown out, floors collapsed, ceiling plaster all over the shop. But in actual fact nothing vital was damaged. The reflector went almost unscathed, and the delicate machinery was still in working order. In fact the total loss amounted to only about a hundred pounds."

Elizabeth's jaw sagged. All that effort for next to nothing. And she was to suffer imprisonment for it. She desperately wanted to ask the question, but her lips would not move. Why had it failed?

"As I said, the explosive seems to have been gunpowder. Either the charge was too small or it was packed too loosely. And they parked it in the wrong place. It was too open, so the blast spread upwards and outwards. A more confined area would have served their purpose much better."

So Ethel was not so infallible after all. How would she react when she read the press report?

"Was any evidence left behind?" her mother was asking.

"Not much. A bag with papers spouting *Votes for Women*. A tin of currant biscuits – God knows what that was all about. And a matchbox with bloodstains on it. One of them must have cut herself."

"Anything else?" It was a tiny, disembodied voice, almost inaudible.

"No. Not that I've heard of. Were you expecting something in particular?"

Elizabeth's head jerked up in alarm. It took her a moment to realise that this was meant as a joke. So the timepiece had not been found. Had it been covered in rubble? Or destroyed in the blast? Or were the police keeping it a secret until they had her in custody?

Clang – a lang – a lang – a lang. The noise startled them all. The front doorbell had been pulled with unwonted ferocity, the urgency of its message echoing through the house.

Lixmont was first to recover. "Someone's in a desperate hurry," he growled.

"What on earth –?" ejaculated Hilda. "Who can possibly be calling at this time of night?"

Elizabeth froze rigid, her face white with terror. So the ring had closed round her at last. At least the ordeal of waiting was over. Should she sell herself dearly, force them to drag her out, kicking and screaming? No, not that way. Daddy would suffer enough humiliation as it was. Go quietly, with as much dignity as she could muster? Yes, that would be the best course. Hold her head high, show utter contempt for the minions of the law. She screwed herself up to face the inevitable.

She heard scurrying footsteps, the main door unlatched and drawn back; there was the sound of muffled voices. The maid appeared in the doorway.

"Excuse me, mum, it's –"

A figure darted past, almost knocking her aside in the rush. Elizabeth gasped. Alastair? She could scarcely believe her eyes. What was he doing here?

"Come away in. This is a pleasant surprise." Her father was as urbane as ever. Or was there just a hint of asperity in his voice? "It's a fair while since we've had the pleasure of your company. Come and sit yourself down."

"No, no," panted the unexpected visitor. "I shouldn't stay. Honestly." He remembered his manners. "Sorry to have disturbed your evening meal, sir. It's just that there's – there's something I have to return. It belongs to Elizabeth. She left it behind." He laid a round, metal object on the table. The pewter casing was faded and scuffed. But there was no mistaking what it was. A watch – a ladies pocket watch.

Hilda picked it up by its short chain, wrinkling her nose with distaste as though holding a dead mouse by the tail. "I remember this. It was from the church, a year or two back. Look, there's the inscription. I never knew you wore this, Elizabeth. You always claimed it was cheap and nasty." She passed it to her husband and turned towards Alastair. "I'm sure Elizabeth is grateful to have it back," she sniffed. "But surely there was no need for such haste. After all, the matter is of little consequence. And there are more convenient times to call."

"Never mind about that, Hilda." Lixmont fixed Alastair with a penetrating, though not unkind, gaze. "How came the watch into your possession?" he inquired softly.

"I – I found it?"

"Where?"

Alastair swallowed hard, but there was no going back now. He had wrestled with his conscience all day, agonising over what he should do. The easiest option would simply have been to keep the damn thing – hide or destroy it. Then again, it was her property; honesty dictated its return. To slip it back when they were alone would present little problem. But that would solve nothing. Not when the underlying issue had assumed such frightening proportions.

"Outside the Royal Observatory. At five o'clock this morning."

It hit home like a bombshell. There was a sharp intake of breath, followed by a pregnant silence. Shock slowly turned to horror as her parents digested the implications.

Elizabeth's eyes had been riveted on the fateful object, as though mesmerised by a ghost come back to haunt her. Now they swivelled towards Alastair, bewilderment turning to rage. The significance of his words became all too apparent. The meddling fool! Why could he not leave well alone? She rose to her feet, white-lipped with fury. Alastair shrank back, despite himself. If looks could kill …

"Judas!" she spat venomously. "You've betrayed me. You've spoiled everything." She advanced towards him. "I'm ruined. They'll never trust me again. And it's all your fault. Oh, you –" Words failed her. All self-control gone, she fell on him, punching, gouging, scratching. It took all Alastair's strength to fend her off.

"I'm sorry, Elizabeth. Truly I am. Please listen," he pleaded. "I did it for your sake. You must understand. There was no other way. I had to tell them." He was close to tears himself.

But she was not to be placated. Near to hysteria, she twisted herself free. "I hate you. I never want to see you again," she screeched, and fled sobbing from the room. Moments later a door slammed on the floor above.

There was a deathly silence as they goggled helplessly at one another. It was Lixmont who at last broke the silence. "Not a very edifying spectacle," he commented drily. "At least she hasn't run out into the street." Then he seized command of the situation. "Hilda, go upstairs and attend to your daughter. Make sure she doesn't do anything foolish. Young man, sit down at the table. You've a deal of explaining to do."

His wife seemed about to demur, but catching the expression on his face, wisely decided against it. She left without a word.

Lixmont crossed to the sideboard and returned with a decanter and siphon. "You look as though you could do with a drink." He splashed whisky and soda into two glasses. "Here, get this down you. And then I want to hear the story – all of it. Leave nothing out."

The golden liquid gave Alastair warmth and comfort, helping to calm his frayed nerves. Elizabeth's father smiled encouragingly at him.

"Are you up to it now, my boy?"

"Yes, I think so sir. Thank you." He paused to gather his thoughts. "Well sir, I must tell you at the outset that I had no idea Elizabeth had thrown in with the militants until last night."

"So how did you find out? Obviously not from Elizabeth."

"No. I was working late in the university reading room. Annabel Smart turned up just before closing time. She was in a bad way, really distraught. She said she had been looking for me all over the place. Apparently Elizabeth had visited her earlier and somehow let the cat out of the bag – the plan to blow up the Observatory, I mean, and Elizabeth's part in it. It seems she tried to argue Elizabeth out of it, but there was no stopping her. Annabel begged me to do something. I was her last chance. She insisted it was out of the question to inform the authorities. Some code of honour, I expect."

"I see. And who is this – Annabel Smart?"

"One of the university suffragists. I don't particularly like her, but she's no extremist. She thinks violent methods are counter-productive. In fact it was Miss Smart who brought Elizabeth into the movement in the first place."

"How long ago was this?"

"Maybe six months. Before last Christmas anyhow. Annabel reckons she must have become disillusioned at the lack of progress with the Suffrage Union – that's the organisation she originally joined. So it made her a prime target for the fanatics. They probably recruited her in secret and filled her head with nonsense. Annabel admitted she hadn't an earthly about what was going on."

"But why pick on Elizabeth? What made her so special?"

"I've been thinking about that, sir. It must have been that incident back in February."

"What incident?"

"The stramash when some suffragists challenged a mob of students up by the McEwan Hall."

Light dawned on Lixmont. "I heard about that. So it was Elizabeth? It never occurred to me that my daughter might be one of the young ladies involved. Strange, is it not?" he mused. "The closer you are to people, the less you really know about them." He became the lawyer once more. "The timepiece. How does that fit into the picture?"

"That's just it. That's the key. It was meant to look as if it was dropped by accident. But it wasn't. It was left on purpose to point the finger at Elizabeth. She was the pawn in their scheme. They wanted the publicity of a show trial."

"And she went along with that?" It seemed incredible that she could be so gullible.

"You saw her reaction for yourself. Probably they convinced her of the glory of martyrdom. She would be held up as a heroine for the cause. Or some such claptrap."

"You may be right." A sudden thought struck him. Elizabeth would not have been the only casualty. The good name of the family would be tainted, his reputation as a pillar of the community in tatters. That was why they had chosen her. He shuddered at the narrowness of the escape. "Go on," he said, trying to keep the relief from his voice. "What happened after you learned of the plan?"

"There was no time to think. I simply hared out of the building as fast as I could. I managed to catch the last tram to Morningside and reached the Observatory as it was getting dark. Then I hid behind some bushes where I could keep an eye on the main driveway. Of course I had no idea when they were coming. But I imagined it would be pretty late, to make sure no one would be around."

"And what did you hope to achieve, if and when they did arrive?"

"Try to talk Elizabeth out of it, I guess. And if that didn't work, make enough din to raise the alarm. That would have foiled their game. They would have had to make a run for it without doing anything."

"So you were prepared to risk a confrontation with desperate women?

Did you not consider the consequences? The possibility of serious injury – to yourself?"

"No. It never occurred to me."

"Hmm. Continue."

"Well, I waited and waited. But there was no sign of anyone. I might have nodded off a couple of times, but it was only for a minute. I'm sure no one could have passed without my hearing them. I was just thinking it was all a false alarm when there was an almighty bang. It nearly made me jump out of my skin. The noise was enough to wake the dead. Funny thing was that only one light went on. At least that's all I could see. Then it went off again. After that, everything was quiet. I could have kicked myself. The deed was done. And I had done nothing to prevent it. They must have come and gone some other way."

"Hardly your fault. What did you do next?"

"Well, what could I do? Pack up and skedaddle. But then I remembered the ticker. If I could somehow spot it, maybe that might get Elizabeth off the hook. It was worth trying, anyway. There was no point in trying to search in the dark. So I hung about till first light, then went up to the dome. It was a real mess – rubble and broken glass everywhere. But there it was – right in front of me, lying on the gravel. I could hardly believe my luck."

In his mind's eye Lixmont could put flesh on the bare bones of young Baird's tale. He could envisage the ordeal, crouching in his place of concealment all through the night, nerves on edge, aching muscles from the cold and damp; dropping off despite himself, waking from dread images to cruel reality. His heart went out to the lad.

"A final question." He hesitated to ask, but was curious to know. "Why the delay in coming here?"

Alastair gave a wry smile. "Well, I had to get back to my lodgings first. I knew my aunt would be up to high doh at staying out all night. Luckily I was able to spin a yarn about working late and forgetting the time – then spending the night in the coal cellar. But to answer your question, the truth is that I didn't know what to do for the best. I think I came to the right decision. It doesn't matter what Elizabeth thinks of me now."

Before Lixmont could respond, there was a footfall in the doorway. It was his wife. There was no need to look hopefully towards her. The grim features said it all.

"She's quieter now. I've given her a sedative. But she's just lying there, curled up into a ball, whimpering like a baby. And she's hugging that doll she never got round to throwing out. I think it's serious. It could be some kind of nervous breakdown. We should send for the doctor."

"I'll telephone for Dr Shawcross at once. Then I'll go up and sit with her. Alastair, you look all in. Why don't you rest in the library? We'll let you know when there's any news."

There was nothing more to be said. Fond memories came tumbling back as he crossed the hallway. He had always taken pleasure in the quiet elegance of these surroundings. They used to sit together at that desk of an evening, working away in convivial companionship. He wandered round the room, occasionally stopping at a particular volume that caught his eye, running his fingers down the spine. At last, selecting a book at random, he sank into an armchair. Despite his turmoil, a deep lassitude stole over his body; in moments he was fast asleep, overwhelmed by the weariness of utter exhaustion....

A hand was on his shoulder, shaking him awake. His eyes were bleary as he tried to focus. Elizabeth's father was bending over him.

"Back in the land of the living, eh? You were well away there. Dead to the world an hour or more."

"What? I didn't mean to –" He attempted to struggle to his feet, but was firmly pushed back.

"You just bide there." Lixmont pulled over the neighbouring wing chair.

Alastair blinked. "How – how is Elizabeth?" he faltered, recollecting why he was there.

"Good and bad. That's about the size of it. The doctor's been with her. In fact he's only just left. He says there's an excellent prospect of a full recovery She's young and strong. But it'll take time – months, perhaps longer. The long and short of it is that she has a brain fever. Hopefully it's only temporary. But the only real cure is complete rest – absolute peace and quiet. He's advised a complete change of surroundings to give the healing process every chance."

"I see. I can't help feeling that I'm partly to blame. I mean the way I sprang it on you all."

"I'm sure you had your reasons."

"Well, yes. I knew Elizabeth was – was not herself. But she might have denied everything. I had to find a means of convincing you. Catching her off guard with the watch was the only thing I could think of doing."

"You certainly achieved that. But there's no necessity to reproach yourself. You did all you possibly could. If anything, it is Mrs Lixmont and I who have been grievously at fault. In the past my wife has been perhaps a little too hard on her. I have assuredly been too indulgent. We have to find a middle road. I can only hope it's not too late. But whatever happens, we owe you a debt we can never repay."

Alastair flushed with embarrassment. "So what happens next?" he asked hurriedly.

Lixmont hesitated a moment before replying. "The doctor is arranging for a nurse to come and stay. In a week or so, if Elizabeth is up to it, we'll take a house by the coast. The sea air will do her good. After that, we might travel on the continent. I'll take leave of absence. We'll go as a family." He let Alastair digest the information. "I'm afraid, I'm very much afraid that it will be impossible to see Elizabeth for some time – some considerable time. Even after our return, it might be wise to avoid contact. We don't want to run the risk of any setback to her recovery, now do we?"

"No, of course not." Alastair's face clouded with dismay. He might have expected something like this, but it was a body blow all the same. "May I see her before I go? Only for a minute."

"Best not. She's sleeping peacefully now."

"I understand. Well, I'll be off. I've no wish to spend another night in the cellar." He smiled wanly. It was a lame effort to hide his disappointment.

Lixmont saw him out. At the door he grasped Alastair's hand in both of his. "You have performed a signal service for this family. I won't insult you by offering some recompense. But should you ever be in need, you know you can always count on our friendship. And I shall be watching your progress with interest. When the time comes to take up your career, a word in the right ear is seldom wasted."

The door closed firmly behind him – with a finality that made him wince. Was this a sign that Elizabeth was to be shut out of his life? That he was somehow part of a past that must be excised from her memory? They were trying to sugar the pill with the hint of future preferment. But that meant nothing to him. He trudged away. His spirits had never been lower.

TWELVE

The Vilest Deed

Broomburn. February 1914

S he cut a forlorn figure, hunched in the armchair in her kitchen. Still, it came as a relief to be left in solitude, alone with her thoughts and memories, if only for an hour. All that fussing and fretting over her; that was what she found most wearying. She had insisted on rising from her sickbed, spurning the offer of laudanum to deaden the pain. She would greet her son on his return home as a mother should, not as a helpless invalid, scarcely conscious of where she was. Besides, there was unfinished business to be settled. And she would need her wits about her for that.

Kate Baird knew she was dying. But it was not in her nature to accept the inevitable without a struggle. When the attacks had first started more than a year ago, she had put it down to the change of life. But then, over the last few months, they had intensified, with growing frequency and greater pain. Even at this stage she had refused to give way to the disease ravaging her body; pride would not permit her to be treated as a cripple. All that mattered was that she be spared long enough to see Alastair graduate. Sadly, she now knew that was not to be.

It had all come to a head barely a fortnight ago – a fall in the shop that had left her helpless. One minute she had been checking stock in the storeroom, the next she had collapsed in a heap. The doctor had been summoned; diagnosis had been swift and brutal. The cancer was too advanced for any treatment; all they could do was to make her as comfortable as possible. She would never walk again unaided; indeed the next seizure would probably be her last. The suggestion of a sanatorium or nursing home she had rejected out of hand. So they had carried her back to die in her bed, amid familiar surroundings.

Was it fair to place such a burden on others? She often asked herself that. Her daughter and son-in-law, along with the new baby, had moved in with the Whites, so as to give her more peace and quiet. Yet Mary was forever in to dance attendance, as often as not to spend the night on a makeshift cot by her bed. How she managed it, balancing her responsibilities, running two households, was a marvel to behold. Others played their part, of course, and she was grateful. Rob and his parents took their turns: even Mr McIntosh and Mr Ogilvie were more than willing to sit with her. But Mary was the mainstay, holding everything together. The worry was that she would wear herself out.

Her affairs were in order; she was thankful for that. Mary and her man would have the house; Mr McIntosh had promised to see to it. And he had also gone out of his way to take care of the will. Her worldly goods amounted to just on a hundred and fifty pounds – to be divided equally amongst her children. It was a tidy sum, given the circumstances. But then she had always had the knack of making one penny do the work of two. Mary's share would not come amiss, not with a growing family to support. Another fifty was reserved for Alastair – to help him through university, ease the path to his chosen career. The remainder would go to her eldest, wherever he was now. Maybe Iain had not been wrong to demand his portion all these years ago. Was it selfish of her to deny him then? Well, she could make amends now. But would it be enough? Would he come to make his peace before – before the end? Hopefully all would be resolved in the next day or so.

The house was silent as the crypt as she waited for Alastair to arrive. Pray God she had not left it too late. She had been implacable, resisting all entreaties to inform her son. His education must not be interrupted; the end of term would be time enough. Only at the last minute had she relented, and the telegram dispatched before she could change her mind. Back had come the reply that he would be home that evening. Mr McIntosh himself had taken the trap to the halt to meet the train. She glanced up at the clock. They would be back any minute. Yes, there was the clip-clop of a horse approaching, followed by the rattle of wheels and jingle of harness. She heard it pull up outside. There was a hand mirror on the small cabinet by the side of the fender; with an effort she managed to stretch over towards it.

But there was to be no opportunity to check that she was presentable. The door flew open and in dashed Alastair. There was lump in his throat; hot tears welled up in his eyes. Behind him, Mr McIntosh appeared in the doorway; he nodded benignly and tactfully withdrew, before she could even thank him.

"Maw, oh maw, why ever did you not think to tell me before this? I should have been here, beside you."

"Hush, laddie. Dinnae take on so. Calm yersel', and gie yer mother a big hug."

He leaned over, clasping her round the shoulders, pressing his cheek against hers, and then kissed her on the forehead. Dashing away his tears, he dragged a stool from under the table and set it next to the armchair. He took her hand in his, stroking the gnarled fingers as though trying to soothe away the pain. Her heart went out to him. It was all so sudden, having to grasp the finality of it all.

"There was really nothin' you could have done," she said gently. "Your studies come first. Now, did Mr McIntosh speak to you on the way back? Tell ye about the situation?"

"Aye, he did. Is there – is there no hope? No remedy we can try?"

"None. But ye're no' to get yerself upset again. I've had a guid life – better than most. Shall I tell ye somethin'? I see yer faither – more and more often. There's an image at yon window, smilin', beckonin' to me. It's that strong I can almost reach out an' touch him. He's callin' for me. It'll no' be long till we're thegither again. Dinnae greet, son. There's nothin' to be feart about."

Instinctively his grip tightened. "Surely – surely there must be something I can do. I feel so powerless."

She smiled. "No, son, just bein' here is enough. You're like a tonic. Ye ken, Alastair, you've been everythin' to me. Ye've nae idea o' the joy ye've brought – daein' so well, makin' somethin' of yourself."

Alastair flushed. "No, maw," he demurred. "You're the real star. But for you, I'd be nowhere. You made it all possible."

"Weel, we'll no' argue over it. I'm just glad o' your company. Now let's hae a wee crack – just the two o' us. What about yer studies? Are the lessons goin' well?"

"Can't complain, maw. I passed the last set of exams – quite well, actually. I got a distinction in every paper." He was loath to blow his own trumpet, but the news would please her.

Her face lit up. "Guid lad. You stick in now, ye hear me. Dinnae get yersel' distracted. No' ower me." She ruffled his hair affectionately. "The will's drawn up. Mr McIntosh is the executor. There's an equal share for each o' ye. Even –" Abruptly she changed tack. "How's that lass o' yours? Is everythin' fine and dandy now? Last summer ye were like a bear wi' a sore heid, moochin' around the place. Then ye come home at Christmas, happy as a lark. Ye never really did explain it to me."

"Elizabeth? There's little enough to tell. She had a breakdown and her parents took her away to recuperate. I never expected to see her again. But there she was, large as life, at the start of the new session. You could have knocked me down with a feather. She had made a full recovery, was determined to make a go of it again. We've been great chums ever since. And I think Mr and Mrs Lixmont have taken something of a shine to me. I'm often invited for Sunday lunch."

It was true. The miracle had happened. On the first day of the autumn term he had been amazed to find her sitting outside the lecture hall, waving to attract his attention. Afterwards they had walked through the park, hand in hand, as she poured out her heart to him. Could he ever bring himself to forgive her? Could they pick up the pieces again? Start anew? She had looked so anxious, so appealing and vulnerable. It had been a moment of sheer bliss.

Elizabeth had been determined to omit nothing. She had described the bleak, solitary walks along the shore by the Firth of Clyde. Then there had been travel on the continent. Paris, Rome, Berlin, Vienna – the sights had left her unmoved. In Austria her father had insisted on a series of visits to a famous physician – a kind of brain doctor whose treatment consisted of a host of meaningless questions. Perhaps the consultation had had some effect, though. The bouts of depression had gradually diminished. Maybe the beauty and stillness of the countryside had had something to do with it – the woods and lakes and mountains. Or possibly it had simply been the passage of time.

They had decided to return home at the end of September; by then the devils that had possessed her were well and truly exorcised. She was done with the WSPU; women's rights were to be won by persuasion alone, no matter how long the process might take. She had made up her mind to go back and finish her teacher training, even though she had missed the exams and knew she would have to repeat the year. After the initial surprise, her parents had been quite content to fall in with her wishes. Only one thing she had demanded – to be allowed to renew her friendship with him. To forbid this might bring on a relapse, she had argued. That had been enough to produce the desired effect. Her father had greeted him like a long lost son; even Mrs Lixmont had gone out of her way to be pleasant. They had slipped into the old ways; over the past few months he had never been happier.... Suddenly conscience stricken, he jerked back to reality.

His mother was looking at him quizzically. "I see," she was saying. "And how d'ye expect it to go? Dae ye see yersel' getting' married at some stage?"

"Marriage? I'd never thought about it. It's not like that. More like a close brother and sister, I'd say. I believe she really has changed, you know. She's still lively, bubbling with enthusiasm, but there's another side to her now. She's more thoughtful, mature in her outlook. We really help one another tremendously. I'm sure I wouldn't have done nearly as well as I have this year but for her support."

"Aye, well. Maybe I was a bit sharp in judging her thon time. I'd like to meet her again. Get better acquainted."

"Would you?" Alastair could not conceal his delight. "I'm sure she'd love to come."

"It would hae to be soon. There's no' much time left."

"Don't say that, maw. But I'll send a telegram in the morning. Then she could be here by Thursday. Perhaps her relatives could put her up for a day or two. The Semples – you remember?"

"Aye. That'll be grand. And – there's somethin' else ye might manage for me. Could ye arrange tae go to Glesga the morn?"

"Glasgow? I suppose so. But why?"

"Isn't it obvious? There's a body needs to be telt."

His mouth tightened; a frown wrinkled his brow. He did not relish the prospect of another encounter with his brother. "Could we not just send a cable?" he suggested.

"No, laddie, that'll no' do." She shook her head dismissively. "He might no' come. No' after the way he was treated last time. Tell him I only want to make up wi' him. Explain about the will – that he'll get his dues. I'll beg his forgiveness if I've done wrong." Tears began to roll down her cheeks. "I only want the family thegither again. Tell him that."

"Of course, maw." How could he resist such an appeal? "It was inconsiderate of me. I'll go first thing."

She dabbed at her face with a cloth, then blew her nose lustily. "Sorry about that. I'm just a daft auld biddy. The truth o' the matter is that I canna send a message. I widnae ken where to send it."

"But I thought he lodged with that journalist chap. Keeps in touch with you, doesn't he?"

"Aye, he used to. Iain's away from the hoose in Garnethill now. Mr Lang wrote and told me he'd left. He'd nae idea where he'd gone. D'ye think ye could ferret out where he bides now?"

Alastair gulped. This was a poser. But it would never do to raise objections; she would be so disheartened.

"Shouldn't give too much trouble, maw," he said, with a breeziness that belied his doubts. "I'll start at the shipyard where he worked. Deuchar's, wasn't it? If he's not still there, likely enough there'll be a forwarding address. Never fear, we'll run him down."

Would that it were so simple. A man might so easily disappear into the anonymity of the metropolis. Or depart for pastures new, and no one any the wiser. It would be a lucky shot to discover Iain's whereabouts at such short notice. Besides, even if he did trace him, what then? Could he prevail upon his brother to come back? What if he returned and then created a scene? He shuddered at the recollection of what had taken place at Mary's wedding. But ... it was his mother's dying wish. He could not, must not, let her down.

* * *

The two brothers sat opposite one another, their features little more than shadows in the dim light afforded by the solitary lamp. At this late hour there were few passengers; they had the whole compartment to themselves. But neither felt inclined to open a conversation. Barely a word had been exchanged since the mad dash to the station, just in time to tumble into the last train of the day. The gloomy silence was broken only by the creak of the carriage and rumble of the engine as it laboured slowly along the branch line.

Maybe it was as well that Iain was in an uncommunicative mood, Alastair told himself. Was it an omen to have found him so easily? His first port of call had been the shipyard, more in hope than expectation. But an obliging clerk had informed him of Iain's transfer to a sister works

– the Ibrox Ordnance. There, a quick glimpse at a page in the ledger had revealed all he needed to know. There was no point in tackling Iain at work, he had decided. It might be wiser to give him a chance to get home and have something to eat first. Possibly that would put him in a more receptive frame of mind. After spending the afternoon wandering aimlessly round an art gallery, it was after seven before he had arrived at the address. Only at that stage had he experienced a brief moment of disappointment. A young woman had answered his knock, eyeing him suspiciously. Fortunately her attitude had changed completely after he had explained the purpose of his visit. His brother had gone out, but she knew where he would be. They could go together, and he could pass on the sad news.

And thus it had proved. Iain had been blazing mad at being dragged out of an important meeting, and it had taken all her guile and perseverance to induce him to listen. Nevertheless he had remained obdurate. But she had been equally insistent. He had a duty; his mother had need of him. It might be the last time he ever saw her. The argument had swung to and fro – but gradually she had worn him down. At length, fuming, he had thrown in the towel. They were to wait while he went to see what could be arranged. Minutes later he had returned with the curt announcement that he had fixed things. He could spare a single day.

Morag Mackay – that was how she had introduced herself. The housekeeper, she had added coyly. He wondered. Whatever the nature of their relationship, Iain had certainly met his match there. Thank goodness she was on his side; without her good offices success would have been impossible. And she had not been content even then. No sooner had they gained Iain's grudging acquiescence than she was propelling them out of the building, flagging down a passing taxi-cab. They must leave without delay; tomorrow might be too late. If he never saw her again, his abiding memory would be of a golden-haired virago seeing them off at the station, standing alone, waving good bye.

A whistle sounded. The train must be approaching the wayside halt. And not before time, Iain thought to himself. He felt frozen to the marrow. There was no heating in the carriage, of course. And with only his despised kid brother for company it was enough to dampen anyone's spirits. He stamped his feet and blew on his cupped hands in a vain attempt to inject some warmth into his numbed limbs.

The tedium of the journey had afforded ample opportunity for reflection. His initial fit of pique had given way to a smouldering resentment. Why had Morag seen fit to disrupt his meeting? And just to oblige that milksop? Everything had been going so well; this was the first time he had been invited into the inner sanctum of the SLP. Clearly he was marked out for high office. His mentor, Stan Robertson, had hinted as much. And Stan was the power behind the scenes in the Socialist Labour Party. Already he had been invited to become a tutor for the Sunday study classes in Marxism. Nor had his promise as a speaker been overlooked; for nigh on a year now he had been a regular at street corners and factory gates – wherever he could find an audience to declaim the evils of capitalism. But best of all was his role in the workplace, an elected shop steward, representing the men in the turning shop at the Ordnance. Dealing with grievances, settling petty disputes, bargaining with foremen over allowances: now there was a toehold on real power.

Was all that to be put at risk? It was galling to be summoned away just as they were about to fix the plan of operation for the next pay campaign – a plan in which the Ordnance was to be allocated a leading role. Oh, Robertson and the others had mouthed platitudes when he begged to be excused: they quite understood. But he could sense the underlying scorn. So he was prepared to put family before the movement; that was hardly the stuff of revolutionaries. And to be bested by Morag in front of his brother … Whatever had induced her to take his part? Could it be that she had found some attraction there? Surely it was impossible. All the same it would not come amiss to have a word in her ear.

That could wait, however. There were more immediate concerns. Despite assurances about his reception in Broomburn, it was impossible to be certain. Still, if the business was over quickly, he might be out and away before his presence had been noted. According to Alastair, his mother was keen to patch things up. And there had been mention of a will. Fair shares all round, his brother had said. He perked up a little. Taking things by and large, the visit might prove worthwhile after all.

Amid a screech of brakes the train shuddered to a standstill. The platform stood bleak and deserted; its only illumination was a spirit lamp hanging above the sign: *For Broomburn*. They were the only souls to disembark.

"Here we are at last," said Alastair, forcing a smile. "Not long now."

"Sez you!" jeered Iain. "I suppose we've got to walk to the village – in the pitch black."

"I'm afraid so. But it's less than a mile. Do it in fifteen minutes with any luck." He peered at the track disappearing into the blackness. "No, hold on a second. There's a big motor-car over there. And there's someone getting out."

The occupant had seen them, was waving, hurrying forward. It was a figure swathed in furs against the cold. Alastair's eyes opened wide with astonishment. Surely it could not possibly be … Elizabeth? Yes, it was, by God. She had not been expected till tomorrow. But what on earth was she doing here?

She rushed up and threw her arms around his neck.

"Here, steady on," protested Alastair. "You'll have me over."

"Sorry." She released him from the bear hug. "I was just so glad to see you. Is this your brother?" She held out her hand. "Pleased to meet you. I'm Elizabeth. I've heard so much about you."

So that was his card marked, Iain could not help thinking. Still, she seemed an attractive piece. Nice firm grasp. Pretty face. What was her figure like? It was impossible to tell under all that padding. She was certainly no shrinking violet. Whatever could she see in that weakling?

Alastair was speaking to the girl again. "However could you possibly know we would be on that train?"

"Aha! Elementary, my dear boy. But let's get into the car first. I'll tell you the whole story on the way back."

The chauffeur touched his cap as he held the door open for them. Inside, the cabin was roomy and comfortable, with rugs to keep out the worst of the chill night air. The engine gunned into life and they were off.

"Well now. You wanted to know. That's easy enough. We got your wire this morning. Daddy was a real brick. He phoned the college to explain the situation, then Uncle Robert at his office to ask if I might stay. That's the colliery owner, you remember. The upshot was that Uncle Robert insisted on sending the Rolls to Glasgow so that I wouldn't have to bother with a slow train here."

"That was generous of him."

"Yes, I thought so. I was here by mid-afternoon. But I was all in a tizzy, couldn't settle till I knew how the land lay. I expected to find you at home. So

I asked my uncle if someone could drive me over. You were away, of course. But the most marvellous thing happened."

"Really? What was that?"

"Your sister was there. She invited me in to meet your mother. We had a rare old chinwag. She was so kind and gentle, inquiring after my health, then about us and the future. Never once mentioned her own illness. She told me you'd gone to Glasgow to fetch your brother. But she was never in any doubt that you'd be back within the day. Well, the least I could do was offer to pick you up. Then tears streamed down her face. And she asked me to kiss her. It was so touching."

There was a lump in her throat. Alastair squeezed her hand tightly. It was a minute or two before she felt able to continue.

"I'm sure you can guess the rest. I went back to check on the train times and get a flask of coffee and some sandwiches in case you were hungry. But I'm afraid there's none left. I shared them with the driver while we were waiting."

"Don't worry about that. We were only too glad to find you. How long have you been here?"

"Oh, not long. Only a couple of hours. There were only three trains. And you weren't on the first two."

"And no guarantee we would be on the last one either. It was sporting of you to stay on."

She shrugged her shoulders. "But you were. And I promised your mother."

The lights of the village twinkled into view. In next to no time they were there, negotiating the maze of terraced cottages, turning into Myrtle Place A face appeared momentarily at a window as the car pulled up; an instant later the door of the house was flung wide. It was Cha White. Even in the semi-darkness he looked terrible. Alastair had never seen him so grey and haggard before.

"Bide a wee, laddie." It was a curious, strangulated voice, quite unlike Cha's hearty boom. "Mary's in with her. It's bad news. I'm so sorry." He choked, then pulled himself together. "Yer maw passed on quarter of an hour ago."

Alastair stood speechless, unbelieving; then rushed in. Iain made as if to follow.

Cha held out a restraining arm. "Gie him some space," he said gruffly. "He'll take it hard." He looked quizzically at the elder brother. "Funny thing. The last word on her lips was your name. She was callin' for ye."

* * *

"Name o' the wee man! Why the hell do I hae to spend another day in this godforsaken hole? Tell me that!" Iain had been pacing the room restlessly, like a caged animal. Now he paused to flick the stub of his cigarette into the fire.

"You know very well." Alastair tried to remain patient. "Mr McIntosh thought it would not be appropriate to discuss family matters so soon. And I'll thank you not to profane," he added tersely. "Not in mother's house. Not on this day."

Iain scowled, but otherwise chose to ignore the rebuke. The young cub deserved a thick ear for his cheek, but it was hardly worth the effort. "All very well," he grumbled. "But I've business on hand. A single day, I telt them. Now it'll be the best part o' a week." He flung himself into his father's armchair and stared moodily into the flames.

Alastair breathed heavily. He had already endured one ordeal. Was he now to suffer another? His brother was evidently in one of his black moods. But at least the last rites had gone off without a hitch – cortege, service, interment and wake. The kirk had been bursting at the seams; almost the entire village had crammed into the tiny churchyard as a mark of respect. And a good many had found time to accept the invitation to the refreshments laid out in the hall afterwards. She had had a fine send-off, carried to her final resting place in a hearse drawn by plumed black horses. For once the minister had excelled himself in his eulogy, and many were the recollections of the small kindnesses she had performed. A quiet body, with a heart of gold; doing good in her own way, without creating a fuss: that seemed to be the general consensus. It was not a bad epitaph when all was said and done.

He looked round the old, familiar features, but the room seemed strange now – somehow remote and empty. It was no longer part of his life. Tomorrow would see the reading of the will, and then the house would have a new mistress. It would belong to Mary – Mary and Rob. They had tried to persuade him to stay, insisted there was always a home for him with them.

But he had only shaken his head. It was right that they should inherit; they deserved a place of their own to raise a family. It was not for him to intrude. Truth to tell, he felt glad he would soon be away. Memories were too intense.

"How the hell did ye ever manage to get in tow wi' a lass like that?" Iain broke the silence so unexpectedly it almost startled him.

"Why – why do you ask?" he stammered.

"Oh, nothin' in particular. It's just that I thought she would be far out o' your league."

Alastair forced a laugh. "So did I. I was surprised as anything when I first met her."

"So how did ye dae it?"

"Since you must know, it was at Mr Ogilvie's retiral do. She came with her uncle. We were introduced and got talking."

"That so? And then?"

"Nothing much, really. We met up again at college the following year. We're both students there."

"That all? There must be more to it than that."

"I'd rather not say."

"Come on, out wi' it. Why the big secret?"

Alastair pursed his lips. After all, what did it matter? Iain would be gone soon. "She got into a scrape when she joined the suffragettes. I was able to help her out. She's not in with them anymore."

"So that's it. Damsel in distress, eh? That would dae the trick. I sussed she had a bit o' spunk about her. Have ye bedded her yet?"

Alastair bridled. "What a filthy thought! Certainly not. We're just good friends. We enjoy each other's company."

Iain gave a knowing leer. "And friends ye'll stay – till she gets tired o' ye. Take my tip. Get what ye can while ye've got the chance."

"I assuredly will not. It's not like that."

"Expectin' to marry her then? Dae ye think ye can dig intae her old man's moneybags? He's bound to be loaded. Or maybe it's to be a job frae her uncle. That would be a nice, cushy number in the colliery office."

"You know that's not the case. I'm training to be a schoolteacher. My friendship with Elizabeth cuts no ice there." He flushed and half-turned away. Was that entirely true? It had somehow slipped out in the heat of the moment. What had Mr Lixmont hinted about easing the path?

"Aye, that's you all over. Keep to the straight and narrow. Take nae chances. Ye'll hae a nice, quiet, steady job wi' a pension at the end. D'ye want to be shrivelled up, just like yer auld pal, Ogilvie?"

Alastair was stung. "I like to think I might do a little good in the world. Be of some service to the community. What's the sum total of your contribution?"

Iain chuckled. "Mebbies mair than ye think. Just because I dinnae hae a posh accent doesnae mean I'll be stuck at the bottom o' the heap a' my days."

"I never suggested you would. But what have you done so far?"

"Oh, ye might be surprised. I'm workin' my way up. I'll be famous one o' these days. My name'll be in a' the papers."

"No doubt in the criminal pages." It was a cheap sally, instantly regretted. But it was enough to rouse Iain.

"Very funny," he snarled. "Come the revolution, I'll be up there. You can laugh. But that day's comin'."

"Revolution? Havers, man. Whatever are you on about?"

Iain was in his element now, all thoughts of discretion cast aside. He would show this stuck-up prig who was going to be top dog. "Listen. Ye mind thon meetin' ye dragged me out o'? And that business I mentioned? Well, it's a plan o' action we're cookin' up. We're gonnae hit them all over Clydeside – strikes in every factory, shipyard an' engineerin' works to show the force o' organised labour. If everythin' goes right, we'll seize control o' industry. Then we'll ca' the tune. The bosses will hae to kowtow to us. It'll bring the government tae its knees. What d'ye think o' that?"

Alastair could scarcely bring himself to believe what he was hearing. What figment of a fevered imagination could this be? Did Iain truly accept what he was saying? Or was it just empty talk, the swagger of a braggart trying to impress? It was a moment or two before he could gather his thoughts.

"Impossible," he snapped. "You're in cloud cuckoo land. Or else you're mad. You and the rest of them in whatever tomfool organisation you've joined. Try that on and you'll fall flat on your face. They'll lock you up. Or commit you to an asylum."

"Mad, am I? No. It's you that's mad. Or else a traitor to yer class. Quite happy to be a stooge for the bigwigs, aren't ye? No' a thought for the hardships o' the downtrodden masses. Bury yer heid in the sand so long as you're a' right. Can ye no' see that socialism is the only way to a fairer society? The workers o' the world will unite to take what's rightfully theirs – by force if they have tae."

"Rubbish! The working man is far too sensible to fall for that claptrap. Anyway, I've had enough of your tommyrot. I'm away out. There's folk to be visited. I have to thank them properly for this morning. I'll have my tea with Mary at the Whites. You can fend for yourself."

The door slammed, and Iain was left to his own devices. He slumped back in his chair, suddenly deflated. His brother had walked out on him. Far from being overawed, he had scoffed. But – could Alastair be right? Was he barking up the wrong tree? It was too late to change sides now; he had made his bed. He felt in his pocket for the comfort of a smoke. One thing was certain. Industrial action might win concessions, but that was about the limit. Only an earthquake could bring down the edifice. And that meant war, a conflict between nations on a scale beyond imagination. Robertson was always saying it was inevitable. But would it ever come?

He drew on the tobacco, savouring the taste. It had a soothing effect, calming his nerves, helping him to think rationally. There were consolations. Tomorrow he would be shot of Broomburn – hopefully forever. And he would not be leaving empty-handed. For the foreseeable future it was money in the pocket that gave a man real clout. In a brighter frame of mind he fell to consider how he might use his windfall.

"Anybody home?" It was a female voice, followed by a rasp on the sneck.

Iain stirred, then grunted. If this was some busybody neighbour calling to pay her respects, she would get short shrift. All that morning he had been on his best behaviour, staying in the background, responding politely to the few who had approached him, pretending not to notice the many black looks cast in his direction. And for what? It was obvious he would always be an outcast. Damned if he would put up with the niceties any longer. He considered ignoring the knock, but there it was again. With a muttered oath he heaved himself to his feet, stomped across the room and flung open the door. What the –! His eyebrows arched in surprise. There stood Elizabeth.

"Is Alastair in?"

"Naw. You've just missed him. I've nae idea where he's gone."

"Oh dear, that's a pity. I particularly wanted to see him this afternoon. I'm going back to Edinburgh first thing tomorrow. Mind if I come in and wait?"

"Suit yersel'." He turned on his heel and disappeared into the kitchen.

Elizabeth grimaced as she latched the door behind her. To be left standing on the doorstep was such boorish behaviour. He clearly lacked the social graces. All the same … she was intrigued. There was an aura of mystery about him; it drew her like a magnet. In appearance he was not unattractive. His features were less refined than Alastair, of course, but on the other hand she could sense the naked power in his physique. A man like this cared nothing for what others thought. Could she penetrate that thick hide? Find out what made him tick? It would be hard work. It might even involve flirting with danger, like bearding a lion in its den. A slight shiver ran through her as she entered the room.

He was waiting there, standing with his back to the fire. Nervously she fumbled with her coat, unbuttoning it to reveal the mourning dress she had worn to the service. He gave a low whistle of appreciation. It really did set her off to perfection, now that he saw her up close, the shimmering darkness contrasting with the paleness of her skin. She really was a picture to behold. Wasted on Alastair, he thought enviously.

"Come an' warm yerself by the fire. Here, take the easy chair. It's far more comfortable." His tone was much more cordial now. "I'm sorry if ye've had a fruitless journey. Alastair could be anywhere in the village. And he'll no' be back for his tea either."

"Oh well, can't be helped. If he doesn't come back, then I'll leave a note. But maybe he will pop in. I can stay an hour or so." She dumped her things on a kitchen chair and shook out the tresses on her hair. "Do you mind? The car's not due to pick me up till five. It's been so hectic – the last few days. We've never had a chance to get properly acquainted. We could have a wee chat. That's if you've nothing else on, of course."

"No, nothin' at all." The prospect of company no longer dismayed him – not when sitting opposite a real stunner. Peaches and cream complexion, with a figure to match. What more could a man ask? And she was flashing a radiant smile at him. But he must remember his manners. "Ye'll be wantin' some tea?"

"Later. Let's just talk first. You don't get on with Alastair, do you? Don't think much of him?"

255

For a moment he was too astounded to react. What was this? Was that whippersnapper her only topic of conversation? "I suppose his nibs has he been doin' me down."

"No. Not at all. Alastair's hardly ever spoken of you."

"But ye said that he'd told you a' about me. Mind the time we were introduced?"

"That was just a figure of speech. In all honesty he shies away from any mention of your name. All I know is that you left home years ago over a family quarrel."

"Aye. So what?"

"Care to tell me about it? I can see you're still hurting. Talking it over might help."

"Ye've one hell o' a brass neck. I'll gie ye that. If ye were a man I ken what I'd dae. Ye're ower nosy."

"It's a feminine trait." She gave a short laugh. "I only want to learn your side of the story."

Iain clenched his teeth. Could she not leave well alone? "Aw' right. Since ye're so persistent, I'll tell ye this. It was about the compensation money when paw died. I thought I should hae had a share o' it. It's all settled now. Satisfied?"

"But surely there's more to it than that? How could the argument affect your relationship with your brother? There must be something deeper." She knew she was pushing her luck, twisting the lion's tail like this. Alastair said he had a vicious temper. He might kick her out – if nothing worse.

He stared, undecided as to how to respond. Even Morag would hardly have been so brazen. Then he relaxed. Was it her scent? Or the encouraging smile? One thing he did know – he did not want her to leave.

"Aye, ye might be right at that. Ca' it childhood jealousy. Alastair was a'ways the wee pet – pampered and cosseted by his maw. He went to the posh school, paid for wi' siller that was rightfully mine. I had to fend for mysel', fight my ain way up. But I've got qualifications, just as much as him. And I won them the hard way, goin' to night school after a day's graft."

She ventured to express sympathy. "I know it hasn't been easy for you. Sibling rivalry is perfectly natural. And the baby of the family is often the one that's favoured most. Try not to hold it against Alastair – all the advantages in life he's had. He had to work hard as well. I'm sure he would like nothing better than to be friends with you. If he knew all that you'd achieved, he'd be proud of you."

"I doubt that. I doubt it very much." He was openly scornful. "Dae ye ken somethin'? He telt me I was aff my heid. Just because I believe in improvin' the lot o' the common man."

"Surely not? It's a worthy cause – one that I know Alastair supports. That's why he's training to be a teacher."

"Maybe so. But what does that count for in the grand scheme o' things? No' very much. The only way to real change is by direct action. Dae ye get my drift?"

"Direct action? I'm not sure that I do."

"Come off it, hen. Do I hae to spell it out? You an' me, we've got a lot in common. We're baith rebels agin the system."

"Now you really have lost me."

"Listen. You're keen on equality for women, aren't ye? Ye got involved wi' the militants. Got yersel' intae a bit o' bother."

Elizabeth blanched. Now it was her turn to be caught on the hop. "How – how did you know about that?"

"Yer boyfriend told me. Wisnae impressed by yer exploits either. But I am. I can admire guts. Ye're willin' to scrap for what ye believe in. Ye're no' scared o' violence in a guid cause. Well, I'm exactly the same. Only wi' me it's the front line o' the war for workers' rights. Ever heard o' Marxism?"

"No. The name's meaningless. And I think I should make clear that I've nothing to do with the WSPU anymore. I've renounced them and their ways."

"I didnae realise that. It's a shame, really, since it's the suffragettes that'll win through in the end."

"You genuinely believe that?"

"Certainly. That is unless we manage to knock down the whole stinkin' system first. Think on it. A revolution to impose a fair society. Everyone treated the same. The wealth o' the rich expropriated for the benefit o' all."

"But surely that will involve bloodshed. People won't simply hand over their possessions on a plate. They'll resist."

"So be it. If it's a war they want, it's their lookout. It's a battle for survival. Naebody messes wi' me an' gets away wi' it. Fists, boots, razors, knives – ye fight force wi' force."

She shuddered. "Razors? Knives? Would you really resort to these? Go to such extremes?"

"That'll dae!" He wagged a finger in admonition. "I've said ower much as it is." His lips twisted into a half-smile, seeking to reassure her. "Time's getting' on, and I did promise ye a cup o' char. I'll just put the kettle on the hob. The tea caddie's in the scullery. Maybe ye could fetch it through."

She was only too glad to escape, scuttling away into what was little more than a tiny annex jutting out into the backyard. It presented an unlikely refuge, but now there was a chance to compose herself, straighten her dress and calm her nerves. He had been on the verge of blowing his top. Anything might have happened. Now where was that caddie? A row of containers stood on the shelf above the sink. Which was it? Ah, that one looked a possibility. She had to stretch to grasp it.

Suddenly her body stiffened. There was a sound behind her. The tin crashed to the floor, spilling its contents. She spun round. God, he was here, framed in the doorway in the fading light. His eyes were glued on her; she could only gape mutely, helpless as a rabbit hypnotised by the glare of a snake. He said not a word; but reached out, taking her wrists, pulling her towards him. In an instant he had crushed her to him, his lips upon hers, forcing them apart, his tongue burrowing into her mouth. Their bodies entwined, swaying together, his legs straddling her, one hand in the small of her back, the other on her buttocks, thrusting her thighs into him. She had to struggle, try to push him away, but her limbs had turned to jelly. *Oh God, tell me I'm dreaming this.*

The pressure eased. She felt herself lifted off her feet, hoisted aloft, hefted in his arms. Her brain was in turmoil as she was carried through the house. Now they were in a bedroom; he was tearing at her clothes. *No, no! It isn't right.* She wanted to scream at him, but the words died in her throat. Her muscles went rigid, her eyes bulging with fear. *God in heaven. What have I done?*

THIRTEEN

Retribution

Edinburgh. June 1914

Hugh Lixmont gazed stonily out of the window as the taxi turned off the Ferry Road into the familiar leafy streets and byways of Trinity. Why the hell had he been summoned home? And at such short notice? Why emphasise that no excuses would be accepted? The telegraph message was curt – almost sinister. He had taken an early train to the city after a hasty breakfast in the mess.

For once his devil-may-care attitude had deserted him. He felt every justification in being aggrieved. There was no consideration that he might have had other commitments that weekend. As it happened, he had been due to attend a point-to-point meeting with some of the other subalterns that afternoon; there had been raised eyebrows when he had called off at the last minute. After that, the intention had been to return to town, dine and take in a show. And to round off the evening he was booked to entertain a certain young lady of his acquaintance. He wished he had telegraphed back to say he was orderly officer of the day. That would have stymied them. Being based so close to home had its disadvantages. There was a strong rumour that the battalion had been earmarked for a tour of duty in India – most probably in the spring of 1915. But that did not help his present predicament.

All the same … the cable had been so peremptory. Did his parents know something? His creditors had been pressing hard recently. Had any of them taken to dunning the pater for the money? He had had his debts paid off once before – with the strict injunction that it would be the only time. The guvnor had cut up rough, threatening to withdraw his allowance, even though it was only a measly couple of hundred a year, barely enough to cover his basic needs. Hardly surprising he fell into arrears from time to time, especially when a subaltern's pay was under a hundred. But to cancel his allowance … he baulked at the prospect. Now that would spell disaster. He would be forced to send in his papers – a humiliating end to a career that had scarcely begun. Or transfer to some other branch, like the Pay Corps or ASC. Tradesmen – beyond the pale. The only other option was a secondment abroad, in the Sirdar's army or King's African Rifles. His blood ran cold at the thought. That meant social oblivion.

The army had always been his first choice, ever since joining the OTC at school. He would have preferred one of the smarter Highland regiments, one with real social cachet like the Argylls or Black Watch, but the old man had put his foot down: the necessary £400 a year was out of the question. He had a shrewd idea that it was only his mother's persistence in espousing his cause that had allowed him a military career at all. After passing out at Sandhurst, an interview had been arranged with the colonel of the second battalion of the Stirlingshire Regiment. Not absolutely out of the top drawer, but it might have been far worse. At least its position was secure in the upper echelons of the army's pecking order.

Did his father not grasp the cost of service even at this level? Mess bills, the expense of uniform and equipment, the maintenance of a hunter – it all added up. Admittedly he had gotten into a bit of a stew over gambling debts. But that was true of all young bloods. And fillies of the other variety did not come cheap either. But these were trifles compared with the honour and prestige a military connection bestowed on the family. Surely the pater must see that.

He was still undecided as the taxi drew up and he paid off the driver. Should he brazen it out or meekly accept the inevitable homily? Probably the latter would be advisable. A strategic retreat would avoid a war of words, ending up God knew where. A slice of humble pie should deflect most of the wrath. He could trust to the mater to intercede on his behalf and ensure the bills were paid. No doubt there would be grumbles, but in the end the old boy would come round. If he played his cards right he might even manage a speedy escape, catch a later train and be in time for the racing.

He let himself in with his latch key and paused to straighten collar and tie in the hall mirror. He was in mufti, of course, flannels and hacking jacket. His mother always liked to see her strapping son in full military fig – said it made her go weak at the knees – but that would never do, not on occasions like this. Assuming what he considered to be a suitably contrite air, he marched into the morning room.

Edward Lixmont looked up from the legal reports in the morning paper.

"Hugh! Where did you spring from? This is an unexpected honour. We see so little of you these days."

"Well, you know how it is. Never a moment to call my own. But I came as soon as I had your wire."

"Wire? I sent no wire."

"No. I did." It was his mother's voice from the hallway. She must have been watching out for his arrival. Imperiously she swept into the room.

"Why on earth –?" began her husband.

Hilda cut him short. "Don't gawp like that, Edward. I telegraphed your son. This concerns the whole family, Hugh included."

"I can explain, mama –"

"Not a word, Hugh. This is about your sister. I'll thank you to close the door. We don't want any prying ears. It only leads to servants' tittle-tattle."

Now Hugh really was perplexed. But apparently his activities were not on the agenda. That was a weight off his mind.

"Be reasonable, Hilda," his father was saying. "I know Elizabeth's been off-colour recently. But was there any need to drag the lad back on that account?"

"Of course there was. I wouldn't have done so otherwise. Off-colour, you say. I think her condition goes way beyond that. So would you, if you weren't so blind."

"That's not quite fair, Hilda. I admit she's been moody and withdrawn these past few months. She's neglected her studies. More than likely it was because she wasn't fully recovered from the turn she had last year. In hindsight it was probably a mistake to have allowed her to go that funeral in February. Young Baird's mother seems to have sparked off her trouble again. My fault."

"Yes, Edward. You've hit the nail on the head. It was a mistake. But not for the reason you think."

"Whatever do you mean by that?"

"Can't you work it out? It's all there in front of you. She's been putting on weight – and it shows now. And at mealtimes – the amount she stuffs away. Last year she would hardly touch a thing. Then there's that expression on her face. It's so mournful – like she's brooding over something. And she averts her eyes whenever you look at her. Does that convey nothing to you?"

"No. Nothing beyond the fact that she's suffering the after effects of her breakdown. We were warned it was to be expected. And she's not like that all the time. Sometimes she's quite cheerful."

"You men are such chumps!" The tone was almost contemptuous. "I might also add that she's often sick – nearly every day. I can hear her throwing up in the bathroom. Has the penny dropped yet?"

"You're surely not implying –?"

"At last. Your daughter is preg – with child."

"No! I don't believe it. You're jumping to conclusions."

"There's no doubt. I've had my suspicions for some time. Last week I was able to persuade Elizabeth to go to the surgery. We went together. A little subterfuge on my part – she was in need of a tonic to buck her up. I was able to have a private word with Dr Shawcross. He carried out some tests. We had the results yesterday. She's about four months gone. And we all know where she was four months ago."

Hugh went rigid with shock. His initial relief changed to horror. This was infinitely worse than any amount of debts. If news of this ever got out he would be ruined. He could just picture the mess suddenly going silent whenever he entered, the nudges and winks and whispers behind his back. The colonel would demand his resignation. Such a stain on the regiment could never be tolerated.

He found his voice. "Who's responsible? It's that lame duck she picked up, isn't it? I'm going to thrash him within an inch of his life."

"Get a grip on yourself, Hugh." The calm authority in her voice was compelling. "Losing the rag won't help. Cool heads are required if we're to avoid a scandal. We'll get to the issue of paternity later. For the moment let's concentrate on Elizabeth."

"Does – did she know she was – was expecting?" Lixmont digested the implications. "Have you managed to speak to her?"

"Don't be silly, Edward. She must at least have wondered about her missed – I mean her time of the month. No wonder the poor girl got herself into a state. She had no idea what to do, or where to turn. She must have been hoping against hope it would go away."

"So what do we do now? I couldn't bear just to turn her out. How could we disown her?"

"There's no question of that, Edward. So far as I am concerned, it was forced on her against her will. She needs charity and compassion, not blame or censure."

"Could we not get rid of the baby?" suggested Hugh. "I've heard there's ways of doing that."

"Abortion?" Hilda was mortified. "Never. And I'm astonished you could even consider it? Have you thought of the dangers? Your sister might even die."

"I agree. The notion is outrageous. Quite unworthy of you, boy."

Hugh gulped. His mother was staring at him, and his father looked decidedly angry. "Sorry. I didn't think."

"You rarely do," snapped Lixmont. "Besides, it's illegal. No hospital would carry out the operation. As for backstreet abortionists …" He shuddered in disgust. "No. I can think of only one way out. Marriage is the logical answer. The lad is not without honour. Once he's been fully acquainted with the facts, I'm sure he would play up to his responsibilities."

Hilda frowned. "That may well be the case. But the match would never work. And you know it. He would not be socially acceptable. Can you imagine the awkward questions? He would simply become a hanger-on, dependent on the family for his keep. Is that to be the reward for his depravity? No, I won't have it, Edward."

"What, then? I can't see anything else."

"There is another option," she said slowly. "I had a long talk with Elizabeth last night when you were at your club. She flatly refused to admit who the father was, or how and when it took place. But otherwise she is prepared to see sense and accept my proposal as the only way."

"Well, then. What is it?"

"Elizabeth must have her child. And the baby sent for adoption."

"What, here? In Edinburgh? Then everyone will know."

"No," said his wife patiently. "Not here. Allow me to explain. When my suspicions were first aroused, I began to make discreet enquiries. Are you aware of the existence of private institutions – nursing homes – that cater for a certain clientele? Very expensive, of course, but they can arrange everything. There's a place in Argyllshire, very secluded, that comes highly recommended. It can accommodate Elizabeth, give her proper care, and there are doctors and midwives on hand for the confinement. The child will be taken away almost immediately – to a good home, I have been assured of that. Then, after a period of recuperation to build up her strength, she can return and resume her normal life. We will give out that she has been invited to spend a long vacation with relatives – in Ireland, say. If all goes well, she could be back with us in six months. And no one will be any the wiser."

"Sounds ideal." Hugh was enthusiastic. "You are clever, mama. It's the perfect answer."

His father was more circumspect. "Did Elizabeth agree to this of her own free will, Hilda? You did not press her?"

"Not in the least. I simply explained that it would be for the best. She took the point. To tell the truth, I think she's relieved."

"Very well, then. I suppose there's little alternative. Let's hope the skeleton never rattles its cage. When does Elizabeth leave?"

"Today. This very afternoon. She's upstairs packing at the minute. You and I will accompany her, Edward. In fact I'll require you to chauffeur the motor. There's no convenient railway station, and we can't take the risk of a servant knowing where she is. It's a fair journey, so the sooner we get started, the better. I've ordered an early lunch."

"A moment, Hilda. Won't you have to notify the nursing home?"

"I already have. I telegraphed yesterday. At the same time as I sent for Hugh."

"You seem to have thought of everything." It was hard to keep the irony out of his voice.

"Of course. No reflection on you, Edward, but cases like this need a woman's touch. Men lack the necessary finesse."

Before he could frame a suitable response, Hugh intervened. "Here, I say. Aren't you forgetting something? What about the scoundrel responsible for all this? Is he to escape scot-free?"

"The viper we've been nursing in our bosom? No, Hugh, I had not forgotten. He betrayed our trust. He violated Elizabeth. For that he will pay in full measure. You may be sure of it."

"Hold on, you two. Can we be certain young Baird was the culprit? There's no actual evidence."

Hilda glared at him. "That's the pettifogging lawyer in you, Edward – always quibbling. You're clutching at straws. Who else could it have been? She refused to name him out of a mistaken sense of loyalty. Or shame."

Lixmont fell silent. The lad had always shown himself to be honest and upright – and he was generally a shrewd judge of character. Then he shook his head dismissively. It could have been no one else. Baird must have lost control in the heat of the moment.

"You want me to go and horsewhip the bounder?"

Hilda pursed her lips. Trust Hugh to think of charging in like a bull in a china shop. "No, son, I do not. That course of action would hardly be suitable. Nor can we have the law on him, richly though he deserves it. The attendant publicity – it would destroy the family."

"What, then?" said her husband. "You've something up your sleeve, haven't you?"

"Well, yes. An idea had occurred. He robbed Elizabeth of her maidenhood. It's only right we should deprive him of something – of his most cherished dream. Send him back to the gutter where he belongs."

"And just how do you propose to achieve that?"

"All in good time, Edward. We can discuss the details later. In the meantime, Hugh, I've a little errand for you. Take this letter. The address is on the envelope. He's still lodging there with his aunt."

"How do you know that, mama?"

"Oh, I have my methods. He's there, all right. You are to hand in the note. Should you encounter him, you must on no account arouse his suspicions. Make no unfriendly gesture. Can I trust you not to lose your temper and do anything foolish?"

"Very well, mama. I'll do my best."

"Good. It's an invitation to call tomorrow morning at ten. There'll be a small family gathering. That should fetch him. Pity it's the Sabbath, but it can't be helped."

Hugh's lips twisted into a sly grin of anticipation. How he would savour the look on the bastard's face when he was confronted with his wicked deed. And before that – his day was not to be wasted after all.

* * *

"Excuse me, mum. Mr Baird is here to see you."

"Thank you, Agnes. Close the door behind you. We are not to be disturbed."

A short bob of her head and the maid disappeared. Alastair was left to face the trio of figures seated at the library table. That was odd. Normally he would have been received in the morning room.

"Come forward. We won't ask you to sit down. You will not be staying long."

His sense of unease deepened. He had not expected a social call – indeed this was his first visit for some time. But the atmosphere was positively chilly. Mrs Lixmont wore an expression of frosty disdain, as though his very presence in the house was a personal affront. The younger man in the middle was glaring angrily at him. This must be Elizabeth's brother – they had never met. His aunt had mentioned the military looking gentleman who had delivered the letter. Only in Mr Lixmont did he detect a flicker of sympathy. Or was it pity?

He ventured to try to break the ice. "Good morning, Mrs Lixmont, sir. It's about Elizabeth, isn't it? I notice she's not here. Is she unwell?"

"You might say that. In fact she's had to be admitted to a nursing home."

Alastair's heart sank. So this was what it was all about. Her old trouble had flared up again. And he was held responsible. He should never have invited her to Broomburn; he admitted that. The funeral had been too much for her. She had been out of sorts ever since – moody and apathetic, quite unlike her old cheerful self. Her attitude was unpredictable, to say the least; one day she would cling to him like a raft in a storm, the next she would be offhand and distant. On occasion she appeared to be on the point of divulging some deep secret, but then she would either clam up or burst into tears. And things were definitely going from bad to worse. She had taken to absenting herself from college for days at a time. In the last week or two he had rarely seen her at all.

"Are you aware of Elizabeth's condition?" Mrs Lixmont was addressing him again.

"Only that she's not her usual self."

"She hasn't told you anything?"

"No. Though she's often upset. I know that."

"Then you have no knowledge that she is – is expecting a child?"

What was that? Alastair could only gasp, goggle-eyed. His mind went blank. The thing was inconceivable.

"Have you nothing to say?"

He could only shake his head in disbelief.

"She is four months pregnant. It could only have happened when she was staying with our relatives in Lanarkshire. And I am quite certain that nothing could have taken place under their roof. Do you deny it?"

"Deny what?"

"You took advantage of her. You abused her. You betrayed our trust when she was out of our care. You committed that act of depravity."

"No! It isn't true. I didn't. I couldn't."

"It could have been no one else. You are the guilty party."

"Come on, lad." Edward Lixmont spoke for the first time. "Own up. Make a clean breast of it."

Alastair was close to tears. To be accused of such an outrage. Defile Elizabeth? Not in a thousand years. But it had happened. Of course! It hit him like a thunderbolt. He had been puzzled at the time. But now the pieces fell into place. She had been there that afternoon, on the day of the funeral. Iain had told him. And then there was the leer on his face. He was positively gloating.

"It was my brother! It must have been him," he went on desperately. "Elizabeth came to the house while I was out visiting. He was there. She was alone with him. Ask her, Mrs Lixmont. She'll tell you the truth."

"I shall do no such thing. I'll not have her disturbed further. You dare to suggest that someone else is responsible. Why, it's beneath contempt. If anything, your feeble attempt to deflect blame is confirmation of your guilt."

"So you won't even listen to my explanation? I'll marry Elizabeth if you wish – provide for her, bring up the child as my own. But at least give me the chance to prove my innocence."

"Oh, no. You don't wriggle out of it as easily as that. By rights we should give you in charge. Rape is the most heinous of crimes. Punishable by imprisonment for life, I believe. Is that not so, Edward?"

Lixmont nodded.

"However, we do not intend to pursue that course. Not on your account, you may be sure of that. You have shown yourself to be morally corrupt. You are clearly unfit to be placed in charge of young minds. My husband will see to it that you are expelled from the university. You can never be permitted to enter the teaching profession – or any other for that matter. Your vileness – Ugh! Words fail me. Edward, please be so good as to show this person out. The air in here is tainted."

At the front door Alastair made a last, despairing effort. "Sir, I have been summoned here to be accused of a foul deed of which I had no knowledge. I have been given no opportunity to speak in my own defence. You had already convicted me in my absence. Will you not hear me out before you take action?"

"I am sorry, Baird. Truly sorry. But there is no doubt in my mind. You have given way to the basest of instincts. Once I had high hopes of you. But you have dishonoured yourself. You must live with the consequences."

Alastair reeled away, choked with emotion, half blinded in his misery. His world had collapsed about him. What future had he now? What would they think of him back in Broomburn? Ruined – his name blackened forever. Staggering like a drunkard, he lurched into the street. Churchgoers looked at him in disgust, and hastened to step out of his path.

Somehow he found himself at the foot of the brae, near the little port of Newhaven It looked so tranquil, with its neat rows of fishing smacks, almost deserted on a Sunday. There was a small lighthouse at the end of the harbour wall; he shuffled along the walkway towards it. Poor Elizabeth! How she must have suffered these past months, burning with shame at the time bomb ticking away inside her. And all down to that unspeakable cur. Should he go and challenge his brother? Sadly he shook his head. Appeal to his better nature? Iain would simply laugh in his face.

He stared despondently at the ships plying up and down the Firth of Forth. The sea was calm as a millpond, the ripples making scarcely a splash against the rocks. It would be so easy … He recoiled in horror at the very thought. That was no answer. No answer at all.

* * *

Far away to the southeast, in a dusty, flyblown town in a distant land, the world of another young student lay in tatters. Why had it all gone so wrong? How could the mission have failed so miserably? He was the leader; he would be held to account. He flung himself down at a pavement café and buried his face in his hands. There had been seven to carry out the task – more than ample. Six of them had taken up position at intervals along the route of the procession. And then the plan had started to unravel. The first four had taken fright, lost their nerve, allowed the motorcade to pass unmolested. Craven poltroons! At least Ned had shown he was made of sterner stuff. But he had botched his attempt. His bomb had missed its target and exploded under a following car. Cack-handed oaf! All it had achieved was to alert the authorities. There would be no further opportunity. Even now the police and soldiers might be searching for him. He should get away; find a hiding place before it was too late. But why bother? It was all over. He was too listless, too dejected to make the effort.

From the depths of his despair he heard the honk of a motor car. He looked up. His eyes opened wide with astonishment. Surely he must be dreaming. No! Not twenty paces away stood the most magnificent, gleaming, open-topped limousine. The driver was vainly trying to manoeuvre his vehicle, but the crowds of people milling around made it impossible. There were four passengers, but he only had eyes for the two in the rear – a tall man in an imposing pale blue uniform, and a lady in an exquisite cream dress. He would never get a chance like this again. He stumbled forward into the glare of the noonday sun, tugging a revolver from his waistband. He saw the look of startled surprise change to terror. At this distance he could not miss. His finger tightened on the trigger. Two shots rang out. The man lurched sideways against his consort; he was trying to mouth something. But the words fell on deaf ears. She was already dead.

Seconds later unseen hands were upon him; dragging him to the ground, wrenching the pistol from his grasp. He put up little resistance. There was a seraphic smile on his lips. He had done it. He had struck a blow against tyranny and oppression. His act would inspire others. His name would go down in history.

PART III: 1914-16

FOURTEEN

Call to Arms

Glasgow. August 1914

"Special edition! War latest! Spesh-ull!"

It was the cry of street vendors up and down the city. Iain Baird sneered in derision. What war news? Three days had passed since the ultimatum to Germany, and how much was really known? There had been reports that the Germans were advancing through Belgium, speculation that huge Russian armies were on the move in the east. And that was about the sum of it. Was this down to the fog of ignorance? Or was it a deliberate smokescreen? *Damn the letter*! He stuffed it deeper into his pocket. There were far more important matters on hand. A meeting had been called, and he would have to hurry if he was not to miss the start.

It was hard to make sense of the march of events: it had all happened so suddenly. They were saying the Balkan murders were the opening shots of the war. But it was over a month since the assassination of the Austrian archduke and his wife. How could they be connected to the unfolding drama of the past week? Friction between Austria and Serbia was understandable: they were always squabbling in that part of the world. But why did the rest of Europe have to be dragged in? Austria, Russia, Germany, France, and now Britain – bowled over like ninepins. No one could have foretold this – not even Stan Robertson.

Then there was the reaction at home. The outburst of war fever was impossible to deny; the cheering throngs and marching bands were testament to that. But how many had allowed themselves to be swept along by the hysteria? Not all were jingoists; that was for sure. A more sombre mood could be detected, even evidence of panic. Many were rushing to stock up with provisions; banks had closed their doors to prevent a stampede to withdraw savings. There was real fear of a slump in trade, with whole industries grinding to a halt and workers thrown on the scrapheap. Hardly surprising that people were worried about the uncertainties of the future, and went in dread of unknown hardships to come.

Over by Christmas: that seemed to be the watchword on everyone's lips. Was it just wishful thinking? A short campaign, crowned in victory, would be no help at all. It would only serve to bolster the capitalist state, not weaken it. However, Lord Kitchener, the newly appointed secretary for war, was calling for volunteers to enlist for at least three years. Would the young men be forthcoming? No doubt of it, if the right-wing press was to be believed. He had himself seen the queues jostling outside the recruiting office in the Gallowgate. How long before these new recruits realised they were nothing but cannon fodder?

There was a knot of idlers outside the hall in Renfrew Street, big, brawny men who looked as though they knew how to handle themselves. Trust Robertson to take precautions to avoid any chance of disruption by a pro-war mob of hotheads. The meeting place itself was a small, poky room, filled almost to capacity with around thirty activists, mostly shop stewards like himself from various engineering works and shipbuilding yards on the Clyde. He slid into a vacant seat just as the leadership filed in from the side door. They might easily have passed as shopkeepers or clerks, the picture of respectability in sober serge suit, collar and tie. Not that the audience was dressed any differently; the Party liked its rank and file neat and tidy on formal occasions. The fuss of having to rush home and change after work had almost made him late. That – and finding the letter. He tugged at his stiff collar in irritation.

Stan Robertson lost no time in taking control of the proceedings. The party line was that Britain had been sucked into war, not because France was in danger, but because of the French commitment to Russia – a country with a system of government even more despotic than Germany. Belgian neutrality was a red herring; it merely gave the British government a pretext to whip up patriotic emotion. Now was the time to turn the march of events to advantage.

"Do not allow yourselves to be deluded, comrades," Iain heard him caution. "This is not the start of the revolution. There's a long road to be travelled afore the red flag is raised over George Square."

"How long d'ye think it'll take?" someone asked.

"Difficult to estimate. Nae doubt the government will try to calm things down, say it's business as usual. For a while they'll rely on the navy to carry the load, and only send a token force to fight in Europe. The continental powers will be left to bear the brunt, smash each other up – and guess who'll be around to pick up the pieces? Very neat, eh? There's capitalism for ye. Naked self-interest and de'il take the hindmost. But they've overlooked something. This war will no' be like anythin' that's happened afore. It'll be the war to end wars."

"And it'll all be over by Christmas," piped a wit, and got a laugh. Robertson glowered, then broke into a grin.

"Not this one. Nor the next. It's like twa heavyweights sloggin' away, tryin' to hammer each other intae a pulp. Think the ruling classes will be bothered by the cost? They'll no' turn a hair at the casualty lists, nor the food shortages or war weariness. They'll just demand more and more effort from the soldiers and workers – till they reach breakin' point."

"What about Kitchener's recruiting campaign?" The question came from near the front. "He wants half a million to enlist."

"Aye. Glad ye mentioned him. He's the great empire builder – so long as its primitive tribesmen or a handfu' o' farmers that has to be tackled. Look what he did in the Sudan and South Africa. And he's daft enough to think he's been brought in to run the war single-handed. He'll try to run roughshod ower the politicians, so wi' any luck they'll soon be at each other's throats. At least he kens it'll take months – maybe years – before his *New Army*, as he ca's it, can be made halfway ready. Probably he's hopin' it'll never be needed. If so, he's much mistaken. The French are nae match for the German war machine. They'll bleat and whine about a collapse if Tommy Atkins doesnae take on more and more o' the fighting. So we'll be forced to bail them out. Half a million? One million – two million winnae be enough."

"Can ye no' give us some idea o' the timescale?" said the man next to Iain. "How long before the masses rise?"

"Well, if I'm to be pressed … I'd say a good two years. Possibly three. But no' much longer. By then the dead will be counted in hundreds of thousands. Every family in the land will suffer loss. They'll no' be able to gloss over the horrors of war then. No' a picnic, nor an adventure after all. Just hell on earth. The supply o' volunteers will dry up. The army will be desperate for reinforcements. It'll demand compulsion – conscription. The politicians will cave in. And how will the good citizens react to that?"

"They'll no' like it. They'll resist."

"Exactly. And that's where we come in. It'll be our job to sow the seeds, and then see that the shoots are well nourished. But it's no' just the mobilisation o' men for the army. Imagine how all the country's resources will need to be channelled intae the war effort, like a great muckle mincing machine. No' just munitions, but ships, uniforms, transport – everythin'. Talk about the threat o' unemployment? Why, when industry really gears up there'll be a shortage o' workers. That'll bring even more speed up o' production, more dilution o' labour. The day o' the skilled craftsman will be dead as a dodo. And it'll still no' be enough. Where'll they find the extra men? They winnae. I'm willin' to wager that they'll hae to turn to … the women. Aye, women – to dae the jobs o' time-served men."

That shook them. Never in their wildest dreams could they have anticipated this. He saw the shock, the disbelief in their faces. Could it happen? Skilled men would not stand for that – war or no war.

"Shortages o' labour will mean higher pay, I hear ye say. But no' when ye're reduced to the status o' a machine minder. And even if wages do go up, prices will rise even faster. So the cost o' living will rocket. And ye can guess who'll suffer most. Ye'll have heard about the law that's been passed to restrict freedom o' movement, impose censorship o' the press. But that's just a first step. Next it'll be to say where folk can work, how much they can earn."

"A moment, comrade." It was McManus, a shop steward of long standing, at the end of the table. "You say it'll be a year or more before real discontent rears its head. Are we to sit on our backsides till then?"

"I was just coming to that. It's up to us to exploit any signs o' grievance. We cannae afford to neglect any opportunity to stir up discontent. An anti-war movement is already starting up. The Party must make common cause wi' it."

"But ye said it was vital for the war to last as long as possible – till everyone got fed up."

"Of course, Brother McManus. But anything we can do at this stage will make little odds. The point is to establish our credentials to build up support for the future. I hear MacLean is organising an anti-war rally this Sunday. We should put in an appearance, maybe even share the platform. One or two o' ye might say a word. It would be to our advantage to make out that former differences should be forgotten – in the interests of the greater good."

"What about in the works?" It was a shop steward from Beardmore's, one of the biggest employers. "A lot o' the skilled men are actually for the war."

That was certainly true. At the Ordnance, management had been quick to seize the initiative. There were new Admiralty orders, unlimited overtime for all, as well as a promise to make up the wages of anyone volunteering for the armed forces.

"Aye, we'll need to ca' canny there for the time being. We cannae afford to put any noses out o' joint. So concentrate on other things. Emphasise the huge profits the bosses will be makin' out o' war contracts – the bloated capitalists fillin' their pockets on the backs o' the workers. Tell them they cannae afford to wait for the wage agreement to run out next year – the tuppence an hour pay claim must be met immediately. Ye could also drop a hint about a ploy to use the war as a cover to crush craft status once and for all – new machines, faster production methods, complete deskilling o' labour. Ye ken the drill. That should ruffle their feathers."

A ragged cheer went up, followed by a stamping of feet. Robertson gave a thin smile. The shop stewards had been champing at the bit. Now he had slipped the leash.

"Thank ye. I don't think there's any more to add. There's work to be done. Onwards, comrades! To victory! The triumph of socialism!"

They streamed out, the exhortation ringing in their ears. The mood was jaunty, even euphoric as they broke into little groups to chew over the message they had been given. Only Iain stood apart. Unseen, he slipped away down the backstairs. That bloody letter. Was it to be a millstone round his neck?

So his wee brother was worried about his lady friend. In the family way, was she? Well, that was just too bad. It wasn't as though he'd actually enjoyed the experience. She just lay there, limp as a lump of putty. It was like making love to a rag doll. She should have realised she was playing with fire, leading him on like that. What a waste of effort. Or was it? The family naturally assumed Alastair was responsible. And, by way of punishment, were going to ruin him, have him thrown out of college. And now his brother had the brass neck to send a begging letter, snivelling that the record be set straight.

Had that been all, he'd have laughed at the irony, and shrugged it off. But it was not. Not by a long chalk. By his own admission the rat had already clyped on him. Fortunately the parents were having none of it. Had the hussy revealed who the real father was? It was possible; but in that case it would surely go down as a feeble attempt to protect her paramour. No, on reflection, he had little to fear from that direction.

Then there was Morag. What if he took it into his head to put her wise? Would she listen? She seemed to have taken quite a shine to him that time they'd met. And the accusation that he'd fathered a child would really put her nose out of joint. She had been broody for months now, constantly bitching about the need to start a family before she was too old. Suppose Robertson got to hear of it. Christ knew how the Party would react to his dalliance with the daughter of a class enemy. One thing was certain. Alastair must be kept well away. If he ever dared show his face in Govan again …

* * *

Edinburgh. September 1914

"Baird! Slow down a minute, can't you?" Alastair looked round as a tall, gangly youth came running up. "Thought it was you. How goes it?"

It was Grove – Jack Grove. A fellow classmate – one of the better sort. They were on nodding terms, though hardly to the extent of having his hand pumped quite so vigorously, as though he were some long lost friend.

"Grove," he gasped. "What brings you back so early? It's nearly a month before classes start up again."

"Aha. That's just it. I'm not going back. It's the army for me. This is no time to be facing snotty nosed kids. It's the Boche we have to confront now. I've just called in at the Old College to let them know."

"Oh. I'd no idea. What was the reaction there?"

"Well, the place is fairly deserted at the moment, but the prof was around. I managed to barge in on him. I must say old Darroch was pretty decent about it all. Said he quite understood. In fact I was to be applauded as an example to all right thinking young men. My place would be kept open till I got back. Wished me God speed, all the best – the usual guff. It was quite embarrassing in the end."

"So you're off to join up now?"

"Yes, this very afternoon. Tell you what. There's a few of us meeting up. Why don't you come too? You'd be very welcome. We're all students. Why not serve together?"

Why not, indeed? What future had he here? Trapped in a dreary, mind numbing job – little better than a potboy. But it was all he had been able to find that summer. Maybe it was all he deserved. There had been no point in trailing back to Broomburn. There was nothing to draw him home now. As for the appeal to his brother, it had been a vain pipedream even to have made the attempt. At the same time the university appeared to be in no hurry to condemn him to his fate. As yet there had been no sign of the dreaded letter of expulsion. Was it to be a public execution? Sent down on the first day of term? The very thought preyed on his mind. Enlistment might be a godsend. To have his petty concerns swallowed up in the greater conflict would come as a welcome release.

"What d'ye say?" Grove was looking inquiringly at him.

"Sorry. I was just thinking."

"Aye, I can see that. You were miles away."

"It's just that I need to set things straight in my mind. I've often been tempted to plunge in, take the king's shilling and be done with it. But something always holds me back at the last minute. It's not that I'm a pacifist, and I don't think I'm a coward. At least no more than the next man. It's the sheer size, the complexity of the issues. It's like a runaway train – hurtling God knows where, with no one at the controls. The individual is so insignificant, so powerless to influence the outcome. I sometimes think the world has gone mad."

"Ah, maybe that's your trouble, old chap. You're too deep for your own good. I'm glad I'm no philosopher. You talk about madness. From where I'm standing, it's the Kaiser that's mad. And as for the individual – well, he does have a choice. Step in and help in the hour of his country's need. Or walk away and bury his head in the sand."

"Yes, I suppose so. But what I can't grasp is how the Great Powers could allow themselves to slide tamely into war. It must have been due to folly or negligence – on both sides. Surely with a little more forbearance the statesmen could have got together to resolve their differences. Did it have to come to this?"

"Don't ask me. I'm no expert in diplomacy or grand strategy. But does it really matter? We're in it – like it or not. No point in crying over spilt milk. It's our job to clear up the mess. Make the world a better place to live in." He glanced at his wristwatch. "Look, my appointment's in twenty minutes. Which way are you going?"

"Haymarket. Dalry Road. My digs are there."

"Good. I'll walk with you. You don't mind, do you? I'm for Melville Street myself."

"Not at all. Melville Street? I didn't know about the recruiting office there."

"There isn't one. It's chambers for a firm of lawyers. I'll tell you about it on the way."

They fell into step together. "See here, Baird. I can't pretend to understand all the ins and outs of the matter. But one thing is certain. Germany broke a treaty, and we were bound to protect Belgian neutrality. That's good enough for me."

Alastair nodded slowly. "Yes, I can't fault you there."

"So you'll not deny that the Kaiser has proved he's out to rule the roost. First he rampaged through Belgium, and now he's scything across France. Our brave lads are second to none, but there's far too few of them. Look at how they held up the weight of the German army at Mons and Le Cateau – outnumbered six to one. But gallantry can only stretch so far. With the French in full retreat, there was no option but to fall back. Now the enemy is at the gates of Paris. And if France is knocked out we'll be isolated. Having to make peace with that crackpot? Jumping whenever he calls the shots? It'll be the end for the British Empire."

Alastair pursed his lips. What could he say? Grove was right. The situation in France really did appear to be desperate – despite the gloss put on events in the press.

"That's why it's up to us to weigh in. That's the only way to throw the swine back over the Rhine. Do you want to see the triumph of German *Kultur*? Culture! They've shown up their beastly ways in Belgium all right. God knows how many thousands of refugees they've driven from their homes. Hostage taking, shooting innocent civilians, using defenceless children for bayonet practice – that's how they enforce their will. Remember what they did at Louvain? They set fire to a gem of medieval architecture, destroyed its library of priceless manuscripts. And it wasn't done in the heat of the moment. It was deliberate policy. No wonder it's called *frightfulness*. Do you imagine any civilised nation could tolerate such barbarity?"

"No, of course not. If it's all true." Alastair had his doubts. Some of the more lurid tales were simply inconceivable. Yet the weight of evidence was too great to be discounted entirely.

"The stories are true enough. You only have to listen to the tales of the Belgian refugees."

"You're not the only person to say that. It's what I'm being constantly told at work."

"Work?"

"Yes. I'm a barman at a howff back there. This is my afternoon break. I'm due back at seven. You know the one I mean. There's an army drill hall behind it. Well, it's really only a depot where detachments can be billeted for a few days before being drafted to their units. But the sergeants are often in for a 'wee refreshment', as they put it. They're forever joshing me to join up. Did you know they're paid a bounty of half a crown for each man they sign on? And the recruit only gets a shilling. Hardly surprising they come in grinning like Cheshire cats. They must be minting a small fortune."

"Do you really enjoy working in a bar?" Grove could not quite disguise a trace of repugnance. It was scarcely appropriate employment for an aspiring teacher.

Alastair caught his eye and blushed with embarrassment. "No, I don't," he said quietly. "But needs must. I have to earn my keep during the vacation. And there was nothing better to be had."

"Oh! Sorry, old man. I didn't realise." Grove was penitent. "My big mouth. Put my foot in it, haven't I?"

"Not your fault. You weren't to know. Forget all about it. Anyhow, I thought you were going to tell me about this lawyers' office. Why there?"

"Eh? Oh yes. Nearly slipped my mind. Well, there's no real mystery. You'll have heard about the new Kitchener armies. And the move to form city battalions to serve in them."

"Local worthies setting out their stall to attract recruits, you mean. Not the kind of thing you could miss."

"That's right. Lots of places have already raised their own units. They're labelling them *Pals* battalions. Glasgow has already filled two – and another one in the pipeline. Bit of a facer that Edinburgh's been left behind. No wonder the Lord Provost is fuming. He's saying the capital of Scotland can't afford to drag its heels when it should be setting the lead. So he's decided to take the bull by the horns."

"How do you know all this?"

"Don't you read the local papers? He's been shouting from the rooftops for the past week and more: *Edinburgh must fight*. Anyway, he's determined to form a top notch unit to represent the city. He's advertising for the brightest and best to come forward – men from the professions and business only. Oh, and students. The word is that they'll be in a company of their own. It's to be a service battalion of the Royal Scots – the *First of Foot*, you know. Oldest line regiment in the British army. So it'll have some pedigree. Join up for three years or the duration. They're planning to open a special recruiting office in Parliament Square."

"Then why go to Melville Street?"

"Aha, that's the rub. There's a fly in the ointment. The City Fathers haven't yet had permission from the War Office. But in the meantime the Provost has arranged for clerks at a number of legal practices to enrol potential recruits – take names and addresses and so on. Then, when the green light comes through, we can be sent for and sworn in right away. Good wheeze, eh? It'll save time later on."

"I see. And you think it'll only take a few days?"

"That's what the man said. He expects the battalion to be up to complement within a week. A thousand strong – the city's pride and joy." By now they had almost reached the Haymarket junction. "Well, here we are, old chap. I go this way." He held out his hand. "Sorry to have rabbited on so much."

Alastair was left standing on the corner. He watched as the tall figure crossed the road and disappeared from view. An image of Elizabeth swam into his thoughts. Poor girl – dumped somewhere in the wilds, alone amongst strangers. And he was responsible – at least in part. He had brought them together. He had put her at risk. Not for the first time he was stricken with remorse. If only he could atone for his misjudgement, make restitution in some way … He caught his breath; he could feel his heart racing. But his mind was made up. He turned and dashed after Grove.

* * *

Flanders, Belgium. October 1914

Lieutenant Hugh Lixmont stirred restlessly as he tried to ease his cramped limbs into a more comfortable position. It was deuced irksome, having to perch for hours on the wooden slats that served as seating – eight subalterns squeezed into a compartment barely large enough for six. How his brother officers could sleep was a mystery; all he had been able to manage were catnaps. It was an effort to tug his arm free, bring his hand close to his face so that he could squint at the luminous dial on his wristwatch. Nearly midnight – they had been travelling for over eighteen hours.

Huddled in his greatcoat against the raw chill of the autumn night, he settled back as best he could. Be grateful for small mercies, he told himself. They were making progress at last, thanks to the courtesy of the French railway system. The rank and file were up ahead in goods wagons, while the officers had the luxury of passenger coaches – but of such an inferior nature as could only have been intended for the lowest class of French peasant. Not a particularly congenial mode of transport, but infinitely better than marching on foot. His horse had long since disappeared – requisitioned along with all the other mounts to help pull supplies or gun limbers. The roan must be in a sorry state by now – if the nag still survived. More than likely it had dropped dead from exhaustion, or been blown to pieces by shellfire. Perhaps it was for the best. One less problem to worry about.

The war had been a rum affair thus far, he mused. Everyone agreed that the British Expeditionary Force was the best prepared, best trained and equipped army ever to have been sent overseas. What it lacked in numbers, it more than made up in quality – a rapier to the German scythe. Every man, regular or reservist, was a long service volunteer, armed with the superb Lee Enfield rifle, capable of fifteen aimed rounds a minute. Well, that was the target on the musketry range. Whether it could be achieved in the heat of battle was still to be tested. And therein lay the gripe. Two months on active service, and the Stirlings had yet to fire a shot in anger.

How could anyone hold them responsible for that sorry state of affairs? Mobilisation had run according to plan, smooth as clockwork – regulars recalled from their summer camp, reservists arriving at the depot by every train. It had been a monumental task to ensure the battalion was up to strength, in full battle order, ready to move within the time allotted. But they had managed it. And then, instead of embarking with the main body they had been ignored – left to kick their heels for over a week before some red-tabbed bureaucrat in Whitehall deigned to take notice and belatedly issue orders for France.

With spirits raised they had crossed the Channel – only for hopes to be dashed once more. They had arrived too late to take part in the first engagement at Mons, but just in time to head the withdrawal southwards. He scowled at the recollection of that ignominious retreat – those thirteen long, gruelling days filled with endless marching, from before dawn till late in the evening. And the battalion had suffered far less than those further back in the column – except to its pride. In all that time they had not encountered a single German, not even a troop of *Uhlans* scouting far ahead of the main force. The distant rumble of artillery was the only reminder of the existence of the foe.

As if that were not bad enough, they had also missed out at both the Marne and Aisne. It was scarcely their fault that they had failed to receive the order to turn and face the *Fritzes*; by the time the mistake was realised and rectified, the opportunity was lost. Nor had the battalion been given the chance to show what it could do when the BEF caught up with the retreating Boche. Placed in reserve, dug in to guard against a surprise attack across the river, they had twiddled their thumbs while the tide of war swung in the opposite direction, northwards towards the sea.

It had all been down to bad luck. But that was not how the rest of the army saw it. Snide comments were being made – even by fellow officers who should have known better. As for the other ranks – they had to run the gauntlet of jeers, taunts and catcalls. To cap it all, some wag had come up with the epithet, *Kaiser Bill's Own*; and the name had stuck. The men were boiling with indignation, thirsting to avenge the slur in the only way they knew how. But the damage to the regiment, the blot on its copybook, could only be erased on the field of battle.

Was that day close at hand? After so many disappointments there was good news at last. No longer were they to be relegated to the sidelines. One final gap in the line remained open – across the low-lying Flanders plain. The entire BEF was being rushed north just as fast as the railways could manage. There was scope for an advance, before the Germans could reach the area in strength. Ten divisions would be available, twice the number of the original expeditionary force, with units newly arrived from England and a whole army corps from India. Given a fair wind, the enemy would be rolled over and Brussels recaptured within days. Best of all, the Stirlings would be in the thick of the action.

The train was slowing to a crawl; he could hear the squeal of brakes. From his position in the corner Lixmont stretched out a gloved hand to rub at the grimy window. A hurricane lamp illuminated a sign: *Poperinge*. So they were in Belgium at last. He struggled to his feet, wrenching at the strap to let down the window. There was an immediate chorus of protest as an icy blast whistled into the carriage. Ignoring the groans and curses, he grinned and poked out his head. Several officials were standing in the dim light of the station platform; the colonel and adjutant alighted to be greeted by them. Presently the whole group moved off into what he took to be the waiting room.

"At the risk of stating the obvious, my boys," he chirped, still peering out, "I believe this is it. Just think. This time tomorrow … Oh look, here comes the RSM."

A tall, erect figure was bearing down – not running exactly, but covering the ground as quickly as dignity would allow.

"Good evening, Mr Logan. Or is it good morning? Any news?"

The regimental sergeant-major stamped to attention and threw out a salute. "Sah. C.O.'s compliments. Company commanders are to report to stationmaster's office. Battalion is to parade in station yard, ready to move off in fifteen minutes. Battle packs only. Kitbags to be piled. That applies to officers' valises as well. Thank you, gentlemen." He flashed another immaculate salute, about turned and was gone before anyone could think of quizzing him further.

"That's us told then, *mes enfants*. You have to hand it to the man. Fairly rattles it off. Better get our skates on, all the same." Lixmont could barely contain his excitement. Action must be imminent. That could be the only reason surplus gear was to be left behind. Stooping to retrieve his haversack from under the seat, he opened the door and swung himself down.

Men were tumbling out of the trucks, blinking in the unaccustomed light, stiff and sore after such a long confinement. Mounds of equipment appeared, dumped on the platform wherever space could be found. Harassed NCOs scurried about, bawling orders. In a trice the eerie silence had been transformed into a tumult of activity. He scanned the crowd anxiously, seeking out his own platoon, Ah, there were his Jocks – Sergeant McNab had them well in hand. Now they were being led through some kind of archway, away from the bedlam. He plunged after them. First rate man, McNab – never flustered, never ruffled. And he was a veteran of the South African War. That might prove invaluable.

By the time he caught up, McNab was in the station yard, checklist in hand, supervising the piling of kit. "Well done, sar'nt. You seem to have everything under control – as usual."

The NCO straightened up and saluted. "Aye, sir. I'll fa' the men in now – wi' your permission, sir."

"Yes. Do that. Carry on, sergeant"

Lixmont watched as the ranks were dressed. Forty men sprang to attention as one; then were stood at ease, ready to move off to their parade ground position on his word of command – whenever the rest of the battalion saw fit to put in an appearance.

"Good man, Hugh." The huge figure of his company commander appeared, just as the laggards began to stream through the station exits. *The Steamroller* – the nickname could not have been more apt. Captain Charles Crombie made a fearsome presence on the rugger field – a little past his best perhaps, but still formidable in the rucks and mauls. But now he had the appearance of a worried man; Lixmont knew him well enough to read the signs.

"Nothing amiss, is there, sir."

"Let's go over there, Hugh – out of earshot. Here, by this lamppost."

A terrible thought struck him. "You're – you're not about to say we're being stood down – again. Surely?"

"No. You can rest easy on that score. We're going into action all right. But we won't be beefing up the attack as planned. We'll be shoring up the defence."

"Defence? But that's impossible. We were assured there would only be a few cavalry brigades to sweep aside."

"So we were. But our lords and masters have obviously miscalculated. Turns out the whole ruddy area is crawling with Boche. Their Sixth Army has pushed up from the south far quicker than anyone anticipated. And there's evidence of new formations flooding in from the east. God knows where they find the manpower."

"And we're to be slap bang in the middle?"

"Exactly. Looks like another Mons in the making. Only this time there'll be no retreat. If we don't hold Fritz here, they'll grab the Channel ports, cut off our supply lines – and Bob's your uncle. It's backs to the wall stuff now, Hugh."

"I see. Death or glory, eh?"

"That's about the size of it. Look, I've a map here." He tugged a folded paper from his tunic. "Here, hold one side." It was a hastily cyclostyled print; the blurred ink made names difficult to read. "There'll be guides to show us the way. But this is the general picture. You should know – just in case I fall."

"Don't say that, sir"

"Of course I must. Now pay attention. We're here." Crombie tapped a point on the sheet. "There's Ieper, seven miles to the east. The French call it Ypres, for some reason. We take this route, skirt round the town and pick up the road again – where it's signposted for Menin. Five miles further on is this village, Ghelu –, something or other."

"Gheluvelt?"

"That's it. Glad your eyesight's better than mine. Well, half a mile or so further on is the Front. Or at least it was, last time we heard. The Boche might have had other ideas since then."

"Are we going straight into the line?"

"That's the idea. There's a crossroads. Just beyond this little hamlet – can't make out the name. No matter. We come up on the left. And we don't have too much time to get there. The relief has to take place well before dawn."

"Relief?"

"We're taking over from a unit in 7 Div. They've had a hard time of it by all accounts. Landed at Zeebrugge and had to fight their way back. They'll be … Christ Almighty! Would you look at that? Trust the colonel to cut a dash."

Colonel Rayne had just entered – astride a sleek grey. How on earth had he come by such a magnificent animal? But further speculation would have to wait. An order was barked out, and the whole compound stiffened to attention. Slowly the colonel proceeded to walk his horse up and down the ranks. Apparently satisfied with the inspection, he returned the salute. Another command sent the four rifle companies wheeling into column of march. The battalion pipers struck up, and they were off – C.O. at the head, rank and file stepping out behind, swinging through the gates, with the lanterns of a dozen guides to show them the way. *Hey, Johnnie Cope* – very appropriate. But what price the Germans being caught on the hop?

For several minutes the skirl of the pipes filled the air, and then abruptly died away. The jaunty tune had served its purpose: impress the onlookers, raise the spirits of the troops. Now it was time for the serious business. March discipline was relaxed; word was passed down to sling weapons. The men could sing if they wished; none took up the offer. To the old sweats it was simply a waste of breath. It was hard enough to keep in step over the *pavé* – the rough causeway of stone setts that passed for a high road. Less than four hours to cover more than twelve miles. Not impossible, but a fair old hike all the same.

Not till they reached the lee of the towering wall that enclosed the medieval centre of Ypres was a halt called. The old cloth town had not survived unscathed; shellfire had knocked holes in the brickwork, piles of debris blocked the canal running alongside. Cigarettes were hurriedly lit; many took the opportunity to relieve themselves into the stagnant waters. The colonel dismounted, surrendered the reins, and the horse was led away. Fresh orders were issued; companies would advance in single file along the edges of the highway. The Germans had the road targeted, well within range of their batteries. Spread out, casualties would be minimised. At the first sign of a *whizz-bang* they were to dive for cover in the roadside ditch. Ignoring his own instructions, Colonel Rayne placed himself in the centre, oblivious to any personal danger.

Progress was inevitably slower now. Lights were dimmed to no more than the merest glow. At intervals, flashes from a desultory artillery duel lit up the sky. But luck was on their side; no shells landed in their direction. All the same, the profusion of craters to be negotiated was a sobering reminder of the constant danger. At one point they passed the mangled remains of a string of packhorses – to muttered growls of rage and sympathy. Had it been human corpses there would have been far less feeling. Still, they had come this far without mishap – apart from squaddies missing their footing and pitching into the wayside sludge, from which they had to be rescued, cursing and swearing, to ribald mockery.

Dark shadows loomed up on either side of the road. This must be the village. Ahead lay the frontline. The single street was deserted. There was ample evidence of enemy fire, but some of the buildings still stood. Somewhere a dog barked. The men had fallen silent, as if overawed by the surroundings; he could sense the rise in tension. Crombie came running back with whispered instructions. There was a tiny hamlet a quarter of a mile away. Final dispositions would be made there, while the adjutant and guides went forward to make contact.

A hundred yards further on, a rough track forked to the left. At the end was the outline of what appeared to be an abandoned farmstead. Torches were extinguished; they would have to rely on starlight from now on. Men started to fidget in the ranks, nerves taut as bowstrings, keyed up like thoroughbreds before the big race. Lixmont felt a slight tremor as he gave a hushed order to load; he heard the sharp click of the clips being inserted as he fumbled for his revolver. Then Crombie was at his side again. All the arrangements were in place. They were to relieve a battalion of Gordon Highlanders. The colonel was setting up his HQ here, along with D Company in reserve. The two officers solemnly shook hands. There was no need to say more.

Drawn up into a line of skirmish, Lixmont led his platoon forward up a slight rise. Fortunately rain had dampened the earth, enough to mask the sound of their approach. Now they were on the summit of the ridge; the Front lay along the reverse slope. Where the hell were these Gordons? Were the Boche to discover what was going on … As if on cue, ghostly figures – dozens of them – seemed to swarm out of the ground, flit past, and disappear into the night.

"Sorry about the mess, old chap," murmured a voice. "No time to clear up. Good luck." Lixmont could only gape in astonishment as the man jinked away.

In less than a minute it was all over. How could they materialise like genies out of a bottle? Peering into the gloom, he could just make out the darker shadow of a depression – some kind of ditch. Crombie was already urging the men into the makeshift trench. Lixmont lowered himself over the edge and allowed himself to drop. Water! Christ! It was swirling round his leggings. And underneath – thick, cloying mud. But there was no time to think about that. There were lookouts to post, check that his Jocks were in position. He was back ten minutes later, muddied and weary, to find a tarpaulin stretched over a rough alcove cut into the side of the trench. Platoon HQ – that was

McNab's excuse. Hardly enough space, even for one, but he was glad enough to sink into the soggy refuge. Just for half an hour, he told himself.

* * *

"Sir! Wake up, Mr Lixmont. It's nearly daylight."

A face was bending over him. It was hard to focus; his eyes were rheumy, he felt groggy. The dank chill had done its work well; every bone in his body ached. Sleep had done him no good at all.

"Just you bide there a minute, sir. Gie yersel' time to latch on." Trust Sergeant McNab – fussing over him like a mother hen. "Here's Private Kerr wi' a cup o' tea for ye."

An enamelled mug was pressed into his hand. "Jist as it should be, sir. Hot an' sweet. Sorry there's nae milk. But I've put in a wee somethin' to keep oot the cold."

Lixmont nodded his thanks and sipped gratefully. Stewed beyond belief, of course, but it was still a marvel how the British soldier could conjure up a brew even under the most adverse of circumstances. Enough sugar to stand a spoon in, liberally laced with whisky: he choked at the fieriness of the liquid, then gulped down the remainder and handed back the cup.

"Feelin' better now, sir?" said McNab. "I've ordered the men to stand to. Careful how ye get up. The parapet's a bit low. Dinnae stand up tall, for Christ sake. Ye'll get yer heid shot off. But there's somethin' ye should see."

Gingerly Lixmont poked up his head. This must be some kind of drainage ditch, dug by peasant farmers God knew how long ago. Hardly ideal – it was only about four feet deep. A hurried attempt had been made to heighten the defences with logs and branches, but as a field fortification it left much to be desired. Still, it did offer some protection – infinitely superior to having to scrabble for cover out in the open. He braced himself to squint through the screen of brushwood.

Through the dawn mist he could just make out the remains of a low dyke, the outline of a few clumps of trees. Somewhere beyond were the Germans. He reached for his case, pulled out the field glasses, twiddled the eyepiece. As he did so, a pale, watery sunlight broke through the haze. Jesus Christ! Bodies! The slope was dotted with corpses – two or three dozen of them at least. So that was what the Gordon had meant. Some were recognisably human, others just bloodied fragments – torsos, limbs, even severed heads. God, it was awful! Most appeared to be German, with their grey-green uniforms, and those curiously spiked helmets. But there were also Scots amongst them. Here and there was a streak of tartan, bare knees sticking out beneath the aprons of the kilts. They must have fallen in a mad dash for this last line of defence.

"Aye sir, it's a grim sight – the butcher's bill. Nae wonder they cry it 'No Man's Land'."

Lixmont could feel the bile in the pit of his stomach. Nothing could prepare a man for this – the enormity of the carnage. Yet he must not show nerves in front of a subordinate. McNab was gesturing again, jabbing his finger.

"If ye'd just take a peek back there, sir."

His heart sank. Unbelievable! To the left the trench took a sharp dogleg – and then simply petered out! How the hell could he have missed that? There was an open space – maybe a couple of hundred yards – before the ditch picked up again. That was where A company must be. But in between … Cautiously he stretched up for a better view, heedless of the sergeant's warning growl. No, it was not totally defenceless after all: the machine gun section was feverishly making ready the battalion's two Vickers guns in a makeshift emplacement. He could only pray they would be enough to plug the hole.

"Captain coming, sir," whispered McNab. Crombie was almost bent double as he waded through the mire.

"'Morning, Hugh. Glad to see you've got your platoon on its toes. Don't expect it'll be long before Brother Boche favours us with a wake-up call."

"Yes, sir. I'm concerned about that gap on our left. If the Germans know about it, and concentrate their forces –"

"Yes, I had noticed. Can't be helped. We're spread too thin as it is. We'll just have to hope the machine guns can cope."

"I suppose so. What about all these bodies out there? They're unsettling the men. Can't we have them collected – before they really begin to stink?"

"Flag of truce, you mean? Doubt the Hun will wear that just at present. Maybe something can be arranged later on. By the by, we've had some news about the enemy in this neck of the woods. It seems they're reserve divisions of volunteers, not regular soldiers. If they only joined up at the start of the war, there'll have been no time to teach tactics. It'll be massed formations – kick and rush."

"Take cover!"

Instinctively the two officers threw themselves down, crouching into the mud, arms clasped tight over their heads. They heard the whine of an approaching shell; felt the crump as it detonated on impact, tearing up the earth behind them. Thank God for McNab and his timely warning.

"Jesus, that was close," breathed Lixmont.

"Not bad shooting," agreed Crombie. "Of course, they'll have had our range already. Here comes the morning hate."

What followed was like hell on earth. To cower helplessly in the filth and slime, not knowing whether the next moment would be their last; to hear the scream of salvo after salvo; to feel the ground shaking with the concussion; to smell the pungent, choking black smoke; to listen to the shrieks of the maimed and dying – it was an inferno. Suddenly Lixmont clapped a hand to his face; there was a burning sensation as though he had been stung. Christ! The side of his cheek had been ripped open. In desperation he groped for his handkerchief and pressed it to the gash.

And then the ordeal was over. The bombardment tailed away, leaving in its wake a deathly hush, broken only by the groans and whimpers of the wounded. Men began to stir from their cramped positions, testing their limbs, shaking themselves down, as though reluctant to believe that they had actually survived. Several bodies slumped motionless in the well of the trench. An acrid pall hung over everything.

Crombie heaved himself up, swaying slightly as he found his feet. "Hugh, you're hurt."

"It's nothing, sir. Only a scratch."

"It's probably shrapnel. See you get a dressing on that cut."

"Of course, sir. Any orders?"

"None. We've got to hold on, Hugh. It won't be long till Fritz makes his move. I know I can rely on you. Must be off now. The other platoons have to be checked. Good luck."

There was no time to watch him go. McNab was at his side, demanding his attention. "Casualty report, sir. Four deid. I'll have them covered up and laid out o' the way. Six wounded, but most o' them can still hold a rifle. Shall I order the platoon tae fix bayonets?"

"No, not yet." Time enough for that, should the enemy reach the line. In hand to hand fighting the sword bayonet could inflict fearful damage.

"Very guid, sir. Now then, ye'll be mindin' what the captain said. So if ye would be good enough …" A flask appeared in one hand, a pad in the other.

Lixmont flinched as raw spirit was dashed into the wound; before he could utter a protest the field dressing was clamped in place and secured.

"Thank you, sergeant. But there was really no need … Christ Almighty! What's that noise?"

Cautiously they peered over the parapet. The sound of voices wafted over the still air, growing stronger – thousands of them. Singing! Almost like a massed choir. *Die Wacht am Rhein* – 'Watch on the Rhine', if he could remember his schoolboy German. There they were – columns tramping into position along the foot of the ridge, swinging into line with parade ground precision. For a second he was back in the nursery, surveying his army of tin soldiers.

The assault force began to advance – rank after rank, coming on at a steady rate, shoulder to shoulder, like a sea of grey-clad marionettes. There were officers out in front, with drawn swords, waving encouragement. But for the uniforms, it might have been a scene from the history books – Waterloo perhaps, or even Blenheim. Now the pace was quickening. The Germans were finding it increasingly difficult to keep their dressing; control was being lost as the enthusiasm of the more eager got the better of them. Crombie was right. These were not seasoned troops.

His sergeant was looking enquiringly. He nodded. The Hun was about to find out the mettle of his foe, taste the fruits of long years of training. McNab was already barking out the instructions.

"Range! Five hundred yards." Backsights were slid into position.

"Present!" Bolts were eased back and locked into position. Trigger figures tightened, taking up the slack.

"Five rounds rapid – fire! Fire at will!"

Volley after volley crashed into the massed ranks, the high velocity bullets tearing through human flesh, blowing assailants away like chaff in the wind. The survivors in the first wave hesitated, faltered, only to be caught up and tossed forward again by those following behind. Lixmont found himself blazing away with his revolver, bawling at the top of his voice to target the officers. There was a click, then another. Hastily he reloaded, fired again. Damn! A misfire. The Webley had jammed. Leaving it to swing uselessly from its lanyard, he stooped to snatch up a rifle and yank an ammunition pouch from its dead owner. The endless torrent of grey was still surging towards them, heedless of losses; clambering over the bodies of fallen comrades, pressing ever closer through sheer weight of numbers. At fifty yards his Jocks were firing over open sights, using the websling of their rifles as heat shields as the barrels grew too hot to hold. Now the defenders were taking losses; the rate of fire was slackening. It was only a matter of time before the trench was overwhelmed. He tried to shout an order to fix bayonets, but his voice was lost amid the noise and confusion.

"Look, sir!"

Above the din cheers and cries could be heard. Khaki-clad figures were streaming over the crest. The colonel must have seen the danger and sent in D Company. Better still – shells started to whistle overhead, plunging into the enemy just yards away. A battery of field artillery had galloped up in the nick of time, and was making excellent gunnery practice. Thank God for the R.F.A. And thank God their opponents were raw recruits. Inexperience was their undoing. One minute the grey hordes were thrusting towards the very lip of the trench; the next the impetus was gone. Bloodlust gave way to bewilderment, indecision, sudden fear. The new arrivals lost no time in weighing in, opening up a withering fire at almost point blank range. It was the final straw. A single company of infantry, aided by half a dozen field pieces, proved just enough to tip the balance. Broken and demoralised, the attackers turned tail and fled. The Stirlings let them go. Even had they the energy, they were far too few in number to think of pursuit.

So it was over – at least for the moment. He was utterly drained. The exhilaration faded away, leaving him limp and weary. The guns had fallen silent, yet the sickly stench of death lingered. That last shot he had fired. The young soldier – little more than a boy. He had taken off the top of his head – easy as splitting a turnip. His stomach heaved: an eruption of vomit gushed over his tunic.

"Here, sir. Tak' a swig o' this." The ever dependable McNab handed him a canteen of water. The liquid was cool and comforting.

"Orders, sir?"

It was an effort to focus his thoughts. "Er, yes. Let's see. Take the roll call.

See what can be done about the dead and wounded. And – oh yes. Check the ammunition. We must be running low by now."

McNab straightened his glengarry and saluted. Lixmont waved him away. His revolver was still dangling from its cord; mechanically he thrust it back into its holster. He set himself to peer over the parapet. Christ! The scene was a hundred times worse than before. Corpses everywhere – heaps of tangled, twisted remains. It was hideous, the faces contorted in the agony of death, glassy eyes staring accusingly back at him. Angrily he forced the image from his mind. This was no time to wallow in guilt or pity.

 In an instant he was once more the detached, professional army officer, surveying a battlefield without emotion. His hands were steady as he reached for his field glasses. There was movement out there – ant-like forms rising, crawling, limping, back the way they had come, making for the sanctuary of their own lines. These could be safely ignored. But what was that? There was a flash of metal over to the left. Just there – by that shattered clump of trees. It was a small group – no more than twenty or thirty men – dashing forward, and then suddenly going to ground. Another squad was surfacing from a pile of rubble, only to dive into a shellhole. And yet another, ducking and weaving, zigzag fashion, before disappearing once more. No doubt there would be more of them following on behind. The tactics were obvious – confuse the defenders, present as difficult a target as possible. These were no greenhorns this time, but skirmishers sent forward to probe for weak points.

"Stand to! Stand to!" The lookouts had spotted the danger.

Lixmont was conscious of men cursing, heaving themselves to their feet, but refused to be distracted. What was the objective? The open space between the ditches – they must be aware of the gap. He swung his binoculars over to the left, then gulped in dismay. Hell! Where there had been a handful of craters before, now the ground was riddled with them. There was ample cover for the Germans to sneak through. And the Vickers guns were gone – wiped out, along with their crews.

"What's the situation, Hugh?" He turned, expecting to see Crombie. But it was Captain Webster of D Company.

Webster took in the look of mild surprise. "Sorry, old man. There's no easy way to put this. But Charles is dead. So is young Myles. Villiers and Green – both badly wounded. Villiers might pull through, but …" He shrugged his shoulders.

Lixmont stared in disbelief as the news sank in. Then he rallied. "It's like this, sir. If you look over yonder you'll see groups of the enemy trying to make for the hole in our defences. If they get behind us … We've got to close that gap."

"Yes, typical Boche ploy. Sacrifice untrained levies in a frontal attack to soften us up, then send in veterans to finish the job. What do you suggest?"

"I'd like to extend our front. Set up a defensive position along the line of those shellholes. If we can get there first –"

"I agree. There's not a moment to lose. Take what's left of your platoon. I'll round up the rest of C Company and send them on. At least they'll have full ammunition pouches again. I had my chaps carry extra in their packs."

"Thank you, sir … Sar'nt McNab!"

"Here, sir."

"What's our strength?"

"Fourteen. That's a' that's left fit tae bear arms. We caught a packet when they got close."

Lixmont frowned. With more than half the platoon gone, the remainder were scarcely enough for his purpose. But they would have to do. There was no time to wait for reinforcements.

"Right, sergeant. We are going to occupy the ground over there. Deny it to the enemy. Bring the men along and follow me."

Crouching low, he led the way, slithering, splashing, stumbling along the trench; then he was out into the open, sprinting for the nearest shellhole. There he paused to draw his pistol, allow the platoon to catch up; then it was off again, scrambling from crater to crater, leaving the others floundering in his wake.

He heard the shout before he saw them – the file of soldiers emerging from a dip. They had spotted him, were gesticulating. The nearest was no more than twenty paces away. He raised his revolver, took aim, squeezed the trigger. Nothing. Oh my God! He had forgotten to clean the barrel, extract the offending cartridge. Rifles were pointing straight at him. There was a flash. A searing pain ripped through his shoulder. He reeled, spun round, lurched sideways. Another blow doubled him over like a kick from a mule. His legs buckled; a mist descended over his eyes. The ground was dancing up at him, soft and enticing. He sank into it gratefully – unconscious of the slimy ooze soaking through his tunic, enveloping him like a shroud.

FIFTEEN

The Best Laid Schemes

Argyllshire. November 1914

"W hat's all this nonsense, Elizabeth?"

Hilda Lixmont was in no mood to mince her words. The telegram had been vague, hinting only at a complication, but sufficient to send her scurrying off to the nursing home. Her routine had been disrupted; she had been forced to cancel an important meeting of her Belgian refugee committee. And Edward had been obliged to make his apologies to the Lord Provost himself – just when the road to a future political career beckoned. The war had opened up new, glittering possibilities for the family. Was that to be jeopardised by an errant daughter?

Difficulties with the confinement, possibly a miscarriage or stillbirth, was a natural assumption to make. But any concern she might have felt was given short shrift immediately upon arrival. Matron's attitude had been cool, almost to the point of rudeness; it was difficult to keep mounting anger in check as the true reason for the summons was revealed. Miss Lixmont had been delivered of a healthy boy, but now she was flatly refusing to give him up for adoption. This was a grey area in law; on no account could the hospice be compromised. The parents bore the ultimate responsibility: either they persuade the girl to go through with the arrangement, or else mother and baby must leave forthwith. She seethed with indignation at this blatant attempt to absolve the management of all blame. And Edward had been about as much use as a stuffed dummy. When she had looked to him for support, he could only spread his hands helplessly. So law was not on their side? Well, that remained to be seen. In the meantime there was a little minx to be put in her place.

Elizabeth was sitting alone in the dayroom. She looked healthy enough, her father noted with relief. Perhaps a little tired and drawn, but that was only to be expected. At the same time there was a glow about her, as though bursting with pride at some great achievement. Her expression changed at the sound of her mother's voice.

"Mama? Daddy? How are you both? Aren't you going to inquire after your grandson?"

"Of course, Elizabeth." Lixmont managed a smile. "I must say you're looking well."

"That's quite enough of that, Edward. This is not a social visit. What I require from you, madam, is an explanation for your conduct."

"Conduct?"

"Don't prevaricate, girl." She subsided onto a settee. "You know full well what I mean. You agreed to an adoption. Why did you refuse to give up the child?"

Elizabeth considered. How could she make them understand? Right up to the birth she had been reconciled to the deed, even anxious to have it over and done with. It was the first sight of her baby, resting in her arms, that changed everything. The usual practice was for the newborn to be taken away immediately, but on this occasion an inexperienced member of staff, whether out of ignorance or sympathy, had brought her son, cleaned and wrapped in his swaddling clothes, back to her. The emotion flooding over her had been irresistible. Now she would never let him go.

"It's hard to describe, mama. How did you feel when Hugh was born?"

"That is hardly relevant," replied her mother icily. "There is a difference. My son was not born out of wedlock."

"Here, I say. That's going too far." Lixmont sprang to his daughter's defence.

"You think so, Edward?" Then her tone softened. "Well, perhaps. I may have spoken in haste. But at a time like this, with so many other worries … Your poor brother, lying at death's door …"

"Hugh?"

"Yes. He's been grievously wounded, fighting for his country. And it's still touch and go whether he'll survive."

"Come now, Hilda. It's not quite as bad as that. The letter we had from his colonel said he had every chance of a full recovery."

"Fiddlesticks! What would he know about Hugh's condition? I'll not rest easy till he's back home safe and sound."

"Look, mama. I really had no idea. And I'm truly sorry about Hugh. But it doesn't alter my position."

"You must see that it's quite impossible for you to bring up a child. Surely?"

"I don't see that at all. And I'm certainly not prepared to have him handed over to the baby farmers. I've heard about the way they treat the poor unfortunates abandoned to their tender mercies. How many are simply done away with when the carers get tired of them? Or when the money for their upkeep runs out?"

"Don't be silly, Elizabeth. What a thought! Foster parents are carefully vetted. Children are always sent to homes where they will be lovingly brought up."

"How do you know? The hospice will wash its hands as soon as they're carted off. Who cares whether they have a happy or a miserable childhood? And what of the mother? Not knowing anything of her child, always wondering whether she did the right thing. Well, I'm not going to end up like that. I can make provision for myself, raise my son on my own. Don't worry. I'll never darken your door with him."

"I see. And that is your last word?" Her face set hard. "Very well. It is impossible to reason with you. You have not yet reached the age of majority. You are still under our legal control. I can have the child sent away."

"Over my dead body!" It was the old Elizabeth again, ready to throw down the gauntlet. "Try it, and I'll tell all your fine friends. They'd love that. What a scandal! And you such a pillar of society."

"Oh you will, will you? Well, let me say what I think." Her head drew back, like that of a cobra about to strike. "Your mind has obviously become unhinged. Perhaps it's a recurrence of your brain fever. Maybe it would be for the best to have you shut away – for your own protection. Then you won't be able to get yourself into trouble by making scurrilous accusations."

"That's enough! More than enough!" Lixmont slapped the arm of his chair in vexation. Things were rapidly getting out of hand. "You go too far, Hilda. Wild threats like that is no answer."

"So you take your daughter's part? I might have known it. You're prepared to see the good name of the family ruined."

"No, I'm not. I'm just trying to find a way out of this mess."

"Are you? Then I'll leave it to you to talk some sense into her. But remember this. I won't have her or her child in my house. And now I'll go and wait in the car."

With that she swept majestically from the room. There was a brief exchange of voices in the hallway; then the sound of rapidly retreating footsteps. Father and daughter stared blankly at each other, before simultaneously heaving a sigh of relief.

"I'm so sorry about all this, daddy. Have I really mucked things up for the family?"

"Not at all. Your mother always was prone to exaggeration. We'll work things through, never you fear."

"You're not just saying that? Is she concerned about your practice? Or is it war work? I bet you're in the thick of it."

Lixmont chuckled. "That's my girl. Perceptive as ever."

"Not really. We do get the newspapers up here, you know. I've read all about the local schemes to help the war effort."

"Well, you know your mother. She likes to have a finger in every pie. I've lost count of the number of war committees she's joined. Mind you, I have to admit I've been co-opted onto some myself – advisory boards on the operation of various aspects of DORA in the Lothians for the most part."

"Defence of the Realm Act? You are going up in the world, daddy."

"I'm glad you think so," he grinned. "We're doing quite well. There is some profitable legal work involved. And I've been sounded out about a seat on the city council in a year or two. But that's neither here nor there. We've more important things to consider at present."

"Like poor Hugh? Do you know what happened?"

"Not much. Apparently his unit was sent to help in the defence of Ypres. He led a party to hold up the German advance, giving the rest of his battalion a chance to withdraw. According to his colonel he really distinguished himself in action. He's been recommended for an award."

"Good for him. But what about his injuries?"

"The letter was a bit hazy on that score. Hit in both shoulder and thigh, I gather. He had to have several operations, but hopefully he's now on the mend."

"I'm so glad. At least one of us has brought credit to the family."

"That's quite enough of that. You've got your whole life in front of you. So snap out of it. I'm here to listen. And to help if I can."

"You really mean that?"

"Certainly. You're a fighter, Elizabeth. And you're my daughter. I'll support you, whatever you decide."

"You realise that under no circumstances will I be parted from my son?"

"Understood. I fancy you've a notion in that pretty head of yours. So come on, out with it."

"Well, if you're really serious, daddy –"

"I am."

"Have you heard of Dr Elsie Inglis and her Scottish Women's Hospitals? She's been campaigning to send female doctors and nurses to the war zones. She's raised ever so much money, and one group has already been sent out to Serbia."

"Yes. What of it?"

"She's truly wonderful. It was hearing her speak that inspired me to join the suffrage movement. Did you know that? Now she's devoting all her energies where it really matters. I know I can't serve abroad – not with an infant – but I could train as a nurse, tend wounded soldiers back here at home."

"I see. And who would look after your child while you were at work?"

"I could find someone. I've a little money, and there would be my hospital pay. And I've been reading about the proposals to have crèches in the workplace for people like me who want to do their bit."

"Are you sure this isn't just another fad – like training to be a teacher?"

"No, it's not. Besides I was serious about teaching. I only gave up because … well, you know. Now I want to make a contribution to the war effort. Everyone else is. Why shouldn't I have the chance?"

Why not indeed? Lixmont clasped his hands together as he weighed the implications. Could this be a way out of the impasse? Whether Elizabeth's newly discovered interest in the caring profession would last was, to say the least, debatable, but it might just cover the present difficulty. Membership of the Voluntary Aid Detachments was becoming fashionable as an outlet for the patriotism of young ladies; Hilda would surely be placated if she could let it be known that her daughter had embarked on such a career – so long as it was well away from Edinburgh. It was by no means a permanent solution, but it did offer the possibility of a breathing space. For the time being it might fit the bill quite nicely.

"Suppose – just suppose I was to find you a place to live. You could have a part-time nanny for the boy, together with a girl for cooking and cleaning. I've a few contacts in Glasgow. It shouldn't be too hard to come by suitable accommodation and get you into one of the training hospitals there. I'd see to the expenses, of course. What d'you say to that?"

For a moment Elizabeth gaped open-mouthed, then burst into tears. She came over, sank onto her knees, and buried her head in his lap. "Thank you. Thank you, daddy," she sobbed. "You're the dearest, kindest daddy in the world. I don't deserve this."

"Hush now." He stroked her hair. "It's all settled. Give me a week to arrange things. Then I'll be back for you. I'll have a word with matron and explain the situation."

She looked up, smiling between the tears. "Would you care to see your grandson before you go?"

He nodded. "I'd like that just fine."

She led him down the corridor, up the stairs to her own room. There was a crib beside the bed. She lifted the sleeping infant, cradled him briefly, and then passed him over. The baby opened its eyes wide; its face lit up like a beam of sunlight. A lump came into his throat.

"Say hello to Eddie."

"Eddie?"

"Edward, silly. I called him after you."

So his grandson bore his name. He was a sturdy little chap. And yes, he thought he saw a family resemblance. His heart swelled with an unexpected joy.

"I'd best take him back now. He'll need changing soon."

"Of course. Here he is." Gently he returned the tiny bundle. "Any other names?"

"Edward Alastair. That's what it will say on the certificate."

Alastair? It was as though a ghost had stepped on his grave. He tried to keep the tremor from his voice, but failed miserably. "Is that – is that the name of the father?"

She smiled wanly, and solemnly shook her head.

* * *

Edinburgh. December 1914

He sat on the bed, savouring the old familiar surroundings for a last time. His bag was packed – shirt, socks, spare pair of boots, shaving kit – as directed. On top lay the framed photograph and little blue casket. His overcoat lay to hand, draped over the chair. The rest of his possessions were in a box in the cupboard under the eaves, there to be stored against his return.

"Are you about ready, Alastair Baird?" The call came from the foot of the stairs.

He sighed. It was his aunt again. She couldn't wait to see the back of him. Hastily he snapped the portmanteau shut and picked up his coat. Was it a wrench to leave? This had been his home for over two years, the attic room his own little world. He was far from convinced he had chosen the right path. But the die was cast. There was no going back.

She was waiting for him in the lobby. "So you're really off this time? No' another false alarm?"

"Yes, Aunt Chrissie. This is it." He tried to ignore the obvious sarcasm. "I signed up over a fortnight ago. My call-up letter arrived last week. You saw it."

"That's as may be. Ye telt me the same thing months ago. And look what happened then."

"I've already explained about that. It was all an unfortunate mix-up. The Provost didn't get approval to start recruiting till nearly the end of September. Then the law office lost our forms, so we were left out in the cold. By the time we found out it was too late. The battalion was already full."

"Sounds a bit fishy to me. Why did ye not think to ask what was going on? Or join up elsewhere if ye were really serious? God kens, there's been opportunity enough. At the very least ye might have gone back to your studies while ye were waiting. Why did ye persist in yon den o' iniquity?"

Alastair bit his lip. Would she never let up on the constant sniping, ever since the day she had discovered the nature of his employment? But there was no point in crossing swords with her. She would never accept that beggars could not be choosers, that there had simply been no other openings available.

"Surely that's all water under the bridge now. Can't we part as friends?"

"All very well for you to say that. How could you bring yerself to serve strong liquor in a public howff? Your poor mother must be turning in her grave."

"I think that's unfair," he said quietly. "But if you can't bring yourself to wish me well, I'd best be on my way."

"Aye. Away to your sodgering." She turned on her heel. "Mind and leave the key on the hallstand table."

So there was to be no reconciliation. In a way he was glad. He could walk out with his head held high. She had been happy enough at the prospect of extra rent over the summer, but circumstances had obviously changed, now that the city was beginning to attract war workers in search of accommodation. Just as well she had no suspicion of the other matter. There had been no word from the university, but perhaps it had been assumed he had done the decent thing and joined up.

Grove was already waiting impatiently at Haymarket. "Hurry up, old man. We don't want to be late." He threw a playful punch at Alastair. "We're in it now. This is the biggest day of our lives." Then his face fell a little. "I say, what's up. You look as though you've lost a bob and found a ha'penny. You're not changing your mind again, are you?"

"No, of course not. It's just that I've had a few words with my great-aunt. She thinks it'll be a damp squib like the last time."

"Fat chance! I told you there'd be another unit formed."

"I seem to remember you dashing into the bar, shrieking like a banshee."

"Heat of the moment, laddie. Didn't I show you the appeal in the paper? And didn't you promise to come to the rally in the Usher Hall? Except that I was too fly for that. Who wants to listen to a load of old fogies shouting the odds anyway? We all know what this is about. Much better wheeze to jump the gun and get straight to the recruiting office. Weren't we about the first there? Piece of cake to fill in the enrolment forms, pass the medical, be sworn in – and away before the rush started. You should be grateful to your Uncle Jack."

"Can't deny it," Alastair conceded. Actually it had not been quite so straightforward. There had been a real moment of anxiety while his future hung in the balance. The doctor had expressed concern about his chest, had hummed and hawed before finally relenting and stamping his paper A1. "But what if there's nothing ready for us?"

"You worry too much. Why did they tell us to turn up with spare togs?

So we can clean up before going home after a hard day's exercise? Army life's not like that. It's not eight till six, like in Civvy Street."

"I know that, Jack. But there could still be a hitch. I've heard of recruits having to drill in public parks. No uniforms or weapons. And no quarters arranged. Not even a tent."

"Maybe so. But not this time. Not with McCrae's battalion." Grove had no doubts. "Now there's a man of action, not some shilly-shallying politician like the Provost. He built up his own business from scratch. And he has an army background. Colonel in the Territorial Force – and a leading light in the Volunteers before that. Now he's raised his own battalion almost single-handed. Who else could have managed that? He'll have everything well in hand, you'll see. So if there's nothing else, let's get a move on. Or we'll have to fight our way through to George Street."

It was true enough. Alastair had never known such crowds before, streaming along in ever increasing numbers, slowing to a crawl as they converged on the city centre. Some were young men like themselves, carrying suitcase or kitbag – obviously fellow recruits. But the vast majority were there as well-wishers, determined to give a grand send-off to the city's pride and joy. George Street itself was almost impassable; every inch of pavement crammed with onlookers, traffic brought to a standstill as the throng spilled into the roadway.

Unabashed, Grove plunged straight into the thick of it, dragging Alastair with him. His frequent calls to make way for *McCrae's bairns* impeded rather than hastened their progress. Everyone within touching distance wanted to pump their arms, clap them on the shoulders. Ladies pressed flowers into their hands, pecked them on the cheek; some, in the excitement of the moment, clung to their necks, planted kisses full on the mouth. But at last they managed to struggle through to the meeting point outside the Assembly Rooms. Here at least some semblance of order had been established, the police presence strong enough to clear sufficient space for the battalion to muster.

"Enjoy that, old scout?" chuckled Grove as they ducked through the cordon. "What it is to be popular, eh? Everyone loves Tommy Atkins."

Alastair grimaced. "If that's the price, I can well do without it. I'll be black and blue for weeks. No good to man nor beast."

"Rubbish! You'll be right as rain in a jiffy. Better get used to it, though.

The girls will be pawing all over you once you're in uniform." He looked about him. "Anyhow, that's for later. Best get ourselves fixed up before we're posted missing. See, over there." He indicated a row of trestle tables, each with a clerk seated behind it. "That must be where we register. This one's got your initial. Mine's further on. See you in a tick. We're bound to be in the same company. That's what we were promised."

A tremendous cheer rang out. A horseman had just appeared, in full military uniform, complete with glengarry, Sam Browne belt and holster. As the rider drew nearer, Alastair could not but be impressed by his demeanour – ramrod straight in the saddle, walrus moustache, hawk-like eyes that darted everywhere. For a moment the officer's gaze settled on him; then he smiled, nodded benignly, and rode on.

"Next!" The clerk was impatient.

"Oh, sorry," said Alastair. "Didn't realise it was my turn. Who is the military gentleman on the horse?"

"Your commanding officer. Sir George McCrae. Now can we get on? Name?"

"Oh, Baird – Alastair Baird."

"Baird." He shuffled through some papers. "Ah, yes. University student. You're in A Company." He made a gesture of dismissal. "Next!"

University student! Alastair squirmed with embarrassment. Should he have insisted on giving his occupation as barman? Grove had brushed aside his feeble protestations. And how could he explain the truth of the matter? Shaken, he turned away.

"Steady on, old chap." Grove caught him by the arm. "You're going the wrong road. A Company, isn't it? Told you we wouldn't be separated, if that's what you're worried about."

He forced a rueful smile. "All pals together, eh?"

"Yes. And it'll be grand fun. You'll see." He pointed towards a placard fixed to a tall pole. "I think we go over there."

"Sorry, Jack. I was daydreaming as usual. Yes, I see what you mean."

At intervals along the cleared portion of the street billboards had been erected as rallying points for the various companies. Judging by the numbers milling round each of the standards, the assemblage was almost complete. Amid the muddle and chaos attempts were being made to impose some kind of discipline, with a handful of khaki-clad individuals barking instructions, pushing recruits into line, like so many sheepdogs nipping at the heels of their charges. Despite their exertions – and colourful language – they obviously had their work cut out. Alastair and Grove found themselves enveloped in a scrum as a group of fellow students broke ranks to greet the new arrivals.

"Jesus Christ!" An irate figure elbowed his way through the crush. "What the hell dae ye think ye're playin' at? This isnae a garden party, ye ken."

"Sorry, old cock." Grove flashed a winning smile. "And who might you be? Some kind of steward?"

"Old cock! Steward?" It was a red rag to a bull. "See these stripes. It's sar'nt to you. And dinnae ye ever forget it."

Grove affected to peer closely. "Are these stripes? Looks just like chalk marks to me."

"For heaven's sake, Jack!" Alastair tried to pull him away. "Don't provoke a confrontation. He's only doing his job."

"Hear that? Ye'd be well advised to heed yer pal. If ye've any sense, that is. I've met your type afore. Gentlemen rankers, bigod. Mair trouble than they're worth. Nae doubt ye'll be applyin' for a commission. But till that happy day we're stuck wi' each other. So we'd best get acquainted. What's yer name?"

"Grove."

"Grove, sar'nt. Ye can address me as Sergeant Harris. Spelt wi' a B. Ye get my drift? Well now, Private Grove, I'll hae my eye on ye. So you just mind what ye're about in future. And now get fell in afore I take my boot tae yer backside."

"Charming fellow," muttered Grove, as the man stalked away. "But I suppose we'd best humour him ... Hark! Something's up."

It was a renewed burst of thunderous applause. The throng was giving way; and marching towards them was the full panoply of massed pipes and drums. In an instant the atmosphere was transformed; companies straightened up, dawdlers scurried to get into line. It was as though realisation had finally dawned that they were no longer awkward civilians at a social event, but soldiers embarking on a righteous cause. The band wheeled smartly and came to attention. Sir George McCrae rode forward to take up position. A hush of anticipation descended on the gathering.

As the clock struck the appointed hour of noon the skirl of the pipes filled the air, and the battalion began to move off, shuffling along uncertainly at first, then with growing confidence and lengthening stride as the column unwound. Westward along George Street, into Charlotte Square, left again into Princes Street. The crowds along the route were ten or twelve deep, shouting themselves hoarse, waving a forest of Union Jacks and Scottish Saltires; children skipping alongside, women strewing flowers and favours on them as they passed. Who would have believed it – the staid citizenry letting their hair down to honour their own?

"This is the life, eh, Alastair?" Grove was in his element, basking in the adulation. Deftly he caught a posy and blew a kiss towards the blushing girl who had thrown it. "I could get used to this."

"Trust you." Alastair could not resist a grin: Jack's high spirits were infectious. "Wonder where we're going?"

"Do you think it might be down Leith Walk to the docks?" said the man next to him. "Maybe we're to take ship for France."

"Don't be daft," snapped Grove. "We haven't had any training yet. Most likely it'll be the Waverley Station…. See, I'm right." He pointed excitedly; the pipe band was swinging onto Waverley Bridge. "There'll be a train especially for us. Then it's off to a training camp in the countryside. Plenty of fresh air … and lots of practice in digging trenches."

"Hold your horses, Jack," said Alastair "I don't think it's the station after all."

"Oh, damn! I believe you might be right. Now why on earth would we turn into Waverley Market?"

And indeed the head of the procession had pulled up short of the station entrance, was beginning to disappear into the huge covered area that ran alongside. On this occasion, however, there was to be no trace of the usual stallholders and their wares; instead they found the vaulted cavern crammed full of tables and chairs, set for a meal. And through the air came wafting the unmistakable fragrance of – steak pie.

Grove sniffed appreciatively. "So that's it. We're only stopping off for lunch. I should have guessed as much. An army marches on its stomach, you know. We'll be off to the station afterwards. Now let's bag a table before they're all taken."

"Stand fast!" growled a voice from behind. "This isnae a free for all. You lot – ower there." Their spirits sank. It was Sergeant Harris.

Alastair, Grove and half a dozen others found themselves shepherded over to a secluded corner; Harris watched grimly as they took their places, before seating himself at the end of the table.

"Now isn't this just fine and dandy? Ye're all students? I thought as much. I've already had the pleasure o' Private Grove's acquaintance. What about the rest o' ye?" A penetrating stare fixed each in turn as they gave their names. "Just so. Fu' o' beans, I can jalouse that. But it's discipline ye need. And it's my job tae drum it intae ye. A tall order, but maybe – just maybe …"

"I say, sergeant." Grove could never stay subdued for long. "What train will we catching after lunch? I mean, where will it be taking us?"

"Train? Whatever gave ye that notion? Ye'll no' be needin' any train."

"Why ever not?"

"Ye're only going a mile up the road. Geordie Heriot's School – that's our billet."

Grove whistled. "Are you sure? You're not joking, are you?"

"Far from it, as you'll discover presently. And ye'll find Colonel McCrae is fu' o' surprises. I had the honour to serve wi' him years ago – back in the days o' the Volunteers."

"Can you tell us more about him?"

"Maybe some other time. I didnae bring ye here to chew the cud ower the colonel." He turned in his chair, as though to check that no one else was within earshot. "You lads are generally up for a lark, aren't ye? How would ye like a chance to show yer mettle?"

"You bet!" said Grove eagerly. "We're game for anything. Don't you agree, you fellows." Heads nodded in affirmation. "Tell us what's up."

"Let's just say it's a sort o' initiative test. Imagine a raid behind enemy lines at dead o' night. There's somethin' ye hae to collar and bring back safe wi'out being rumbled. Only it'll no' be the Germans to watch out for … it'll be the local bobbies. And if ye're caught, it'll no' be a prisoner of war cage … it'll be the Calton Jail." He scraped back his chair. "I'll leave ye in peace now. Enjoy yer dinner."

* * *

January 1915

It was the maid who answered the door. She peered into the wintry dusk, squinting at the shadowy figure on the step. Then recognition dawned. "Master Hugh?" Can it really be –?"

"Yes, Agnes. It's not a ghost. Now if you wouldn't mind?" She bobbed and stood aside to admit him. "Whatever happened to the porch light? Is it not working?"

"It's not that, sir. We're told no' to show lights outside."

He grunted. "I see. Are my parents at home?"

"Just the master, sir."

"Agnes! What's all this commotion?" Edward Lixmont appeared in the hallway. "Good God! It's Hugh." He swooped forward to clasp his son. "Thank God you're safe."

Hugh winced: his shoulder wound had not yet fully healed. But not a sound escaped his lips. He made an effort to compose his features as the grip was relaxed.

"Let's have a look at you." His father held him at arm's length. "You must be about all-in. Come into the morning room." He broke off. "Your leg. That's a heavy limp. Here, let me help you. Lean on my arm."

"Yes, I have to confess it does rather ache. I'll need my stick for some time yet. And the shoulder's still a bit wonky. But we're getting there."

All was as he had imagined it. The room had not changed; it was a comfort just to feel the warmth from the fire blazing merrily in the hearth, to be surrounded by the solidity of mahogany furniture, the cheerfulness of chintz upholstery. Everything was in its place – with one exception. The only discordant note came from the thick black material blocking out the window.

Lixmont followed his glance. "You've noticed. Sorry about that. But it can't be helped."

"Blackout? Agnes was telling me about it."

"I'm afraid so. It's in case the Hun pays us a visit. An attack from the air, so it's said. That's highly unlikely, in my view. I doubt they could ever come this far north. But in my capacity I have to set an example."

"Yes, I think you're pretty safe up here."

"Can I take your coat, sir?" The maid was hovering in the doorway.

"Yes, thank you, Agnes." He shrugged out of the heavy greatcoat using his one good arm, and handed it to her. "Here you are. Take my cap as well."

"Very good, sir." She glided away, closing the door softly behind her.

His father gave a little gasp of surprise. "Those pips on your shoulder. They're new, aren't they? Promotion?"

"Yes. Captain."

"My, that was quick. I'm impressed. Six months ago you were only a second lieutenant."

"Well, that's war for you. You know what they say: 'Oceans of gore, promotions galore.'"

"Do they? I've never heard that one before. Best not let your mother hear it. We don't want her upset."

"I suppose not. Do you mind if we sit down? I could do with taking the weight off my pins."

"Of course. Thoughtless of me. Come over by the fire. Get some heat into you. Whisky? Or would you prefer something else?"

"No. Whisky's fine."

He moved over to the sideboard. "You'll have to excuse us. We weren't expecting your arrival. Your mother will be sorry to have missed you. She's away at one of her meetings. But she'll be back in an hour. Could you not have said you were coming?"

"No time. It all happened in such a rush. Two days ago I was in hospital at St. Omer. Then the doctors sprang it on me. There was nothing more they could do. I might as well recuperate at home. No chance to send a wire. I only just managed to catch the leave boat. Then it's been crowded railway trains all the way home." He accepted the proffered glass. "Thanks. Bottoms up."

His father took the armchair opposite. "Here's to you."

Hugh sipped thoughtfully. "To tell the truth, I didn't want to let you know in advance. I couldn't bear to have the mater fussing all over me – bringing out the fatted calf and all that. What I need most is a bit of peace and quiet."

"Yes, I understand. Your mother can be rather overpowering at times." Suddenly his eyes widened as he caught sight of a flash of colour. "What's that?" He pointed. "The strip of red and blue above your breast pocket?"

"This?" Just the ribbon bar of the gong they gave me. It's the DSO."

"DSO? That's the Distinguished Service Order, isn't it?"

Hugh nodded. "If you're interested, I'll show you the medal sometime. I was in such a hurry I left it with the rest of my kit. It'll be sent on in a day or two."

"Yes, I'd like that. And your mother will be pleased." He whistled softly. "I say, that decoration is pretty high up, isn't it? I've heard it ranks just below the Victoria Cross. You must have done something special to earn that."

His son gave a wry smile. "Not really. In fact I acted like a bloody fool."

"Your superiors obviously don't think so. You might not be the best judge of your own actions, you know. Acts of the greatest valour can often seem like foolhardiness. Care to tell me about it? If the memories aren't too upsetting, that is."

"Not at all. In fact it might do me good to get it off my chest. But not in front of mother. I don't want to shock her. Or have to put up with inane questions."

"It'll be just between the two of us – man to man."

Hugh took another pull at his whisky. "It was our first morning in the frontline. We'd already beaten off one attack. But there was this gap, and enemy skirmishers were making straight for it. I got permission to try and plug the hole. Then I just took off, yelling for the rest of the platoon to follow on. Didn't stop to wait, or check how close they were. Well, I must have got well ahead of them; because when I came up against a party of Germans I was completely on my own. What made things worse was that I was absolutely defenceless. I only had my revolver, and that was jammed. Stupid of me. I was a sitting target. That's when I caught this. But for my platoon sergeant I would have been a goner. He brought the others up in the nick of time, killed or drove off the Fritzes, picked me up and made a fighting retreat back to battalion H.Q. Sergeant McNab. He's the one who deserved the medal."

"And did he get one?"

"No. That's the irony of it all. He went back for more wounded, and was never seen again. *Missing, presumed killed*: that's what I was told. Solid as a rock, he was. Where's the justice?"

"You're too hard on yourself, Hugh. I'd say you performed pretty courageously. And you achieved your objective, didn't you? The enemy failed to break through."

"True. We weren't overrun, but it was damned close. The line was pushed back, almost to the gates of Ypres, before the Boche ran out of steam. Just as well there were reinforcements coming up. Territorials, mostly. The regulars could never have held on by themselves."

"But you played your part. Your action probably allowed your battalion to pull back in good order."

"That's what the colonel said when he paid me a visit in hospital."

"Well, there you are. Why can't you accept the plaudits like a sensible chap?"

Hugh sighed. "You may be right. Nothing I can do about it now."

"Good man. But do go on with the rest of your story."

"Nothing much left to tell. Once I got back to the aid post the M.O. patched me up as best he could, and sent me down the line to base hospital. I had to have a couple of operations there to straighten me out. And then home to get my strength back."

"There must be more to it than that. Surely?"

His son made no response. Instead he stared moodily into the flames. How could anyone comprehend the grim reality of his ordeal? That was the stuff of nightmares. The scene at the farmhouse: stretched out on the kitchen table, held down by orderlies, his muddied, bloodied clothing cut away; the doctor bending over him, scalpel and forceps in hand, explaining there was no morphine to deaden the pain; the flickering hurricane lamp held aloft, the ground shaking from bursting shells; shock as the blade cut into his flesh, agony as the instruments poked and probed at his wounds, twisting, pulling, lacerating … He gripped his arm convulsively.

"Sorry, old fellow. I didn't mean to pry. Touched a raw nerve, haven't I?"

"It's all right, dad." He took a deep breath. The palpitations were easing as the image faded. "It's over now. Just a touch of the collywobbles."

"You're sure?"

"Quite sure. The worst of it was the uncertainty, just lying there, not knowing if I would ever regain the use of my limbs – or be sent home a cripple. At one stage they were talking about amputation. That really put the wind up me, I can tell you."

"But they decided against it?"

"Yes, thank God. That was the turning point. That's when I stopped feeling sorry for myself. The hospital staff were top-notch. They chivvied me to get better, gave me the willpower to see the thing through, however long it might take."

"And you've succeeded. It must have taken a lot of grit and determination."

"Well, I'm nearly there now. As I said, the C.O. came to see me when I was on the mend. Told me how badly the battalion had been mangled before it was pulled out of the line. It would be months before it was fit for active service again." He laughed mirthlessly. "Then he bewailed the quality of the replacements, especially some of the officers. He was genuinely concerned that stockbrokers and teachers would only lower the tone of the regiment."

"Better get used to it, I'm afraid. That's what happens when you try to raise a mass army in a hurry. Exclusivity goes out the window. But what about you? Will you return to your unit, Hugh?"

"Hard to say. I've been given a few weeks furlough. Then there's a medical board. If I pass that –" He was interrupted by a loud jangling.

"Good God! That must be your mother. She's home early. Now there's a novelty." They heard a babble of voices, then an exclamation of surprise. "I'd better go and put her wise."

Lixmont heaved himself from his chair. But before he could reach the handle, the door flew open and his wife dashed in. Hugh rose unsteadily to his feet.

"Agnes told me. Hugh! Thank God." Tears streamed down her cheeks as she fell on her son, clutching him tightly to her bosom. "You've no idea how I've wept and prayed for this moment."

"Steady on, Hilda. Don't crush the boy. He's still injured."

Reluctantly she released her embrace. "You must forgive your silly old mama," she sobbed, dabbing at her eyes. "I can still hardly believe it."

"Well, it's true enough. Here I am, hale and hearty."

"No, you're not. I can see how thin and worn you look. How you must have suffered."

"Oh, it wasn't so bad." He sought to reassure her. "And we did manage to stabilise the Front. This year we'll have the Hun on the run. You'll see."

She gave a start of anxiety. "That won't involve you, will it? You've done your part. You're not going back, are you? Leave it to others."

Her husband hastened to intervene. "You've had rather a shock, my dear. Why don't you take Hugh over to the settee? Let me pour you a sherry."

She nodded her agreement. It might brace her, help settle her nerves.

"Here you are, Hilda. By the by, your son's been promoted. And decorated. Now isn't that good news?"

"Is this true, Hugh?"

"Yes. To captain. And they gave me the DSO."

"There you are, Hilda. That's a pretty high up award. Doesn't it make you proud?

"Of course." She pecked Hugh on the cheek. "Why didn't you write and tell us?"

"Well, it only happened last month, while I was in hospital. And I'm not much one for letter writing."

"That I do know." His mother was beginning to regain her composure. "Who presented it to you? Sir John French?"

"No. The king."

Both his parents choked. "You met – the king?" Even his father was amazed. "You didn't tell me this before. What did he say?"

"Nothing, really. Just congratulations, as he pinned it on my chest. Oh, and best wishes for a speedy recovery."

"Isn't that marvellous, Hilda? Now you can tell all your friends that Hugh's been decorated by King George V in person."

His wife snorted. "Do you imagine for one moment that I would take advantage of my son's bravery?" Clearly she was back to her usual ways. "In any case, Hugh, you haven't answered my question. Have you been invalided out of the army? Or will you be taking up an administrative post here?"

"Well," Hugh temporised. "It's not quite as simple as that." He looked round, as though in search of an escape. "I say. Isn't Elizabeth at home? It must be a couple of months since – well, you know."

"Elizabeth? Your sister no longer lives here, Hugh. She saw fit to break the agreement we had."

"But – I don't quite understand. Where is she then?"

"Ask your father. He made the arrangements."

Lixmont swallowed hard. "I was meaning to tell you, son. It's like this. Elizabeth found it too much of a wrench to give up the child for adoption. And I must say I can't altogether blame her. I've seen the boy. He's a fine, manly little chap."

"You're too soft, Edward. Do you know, Hugh, she had the temerity to

316

name it after him – the crafty little hussy. But that's just typical of her. She can wind her father round her little finger."

"Be that as it may, she refused to give him up. And I had to find some other solution. She wants to do her bit for the war effort, and suggested nursing. I felt it was a reasonable idea, so I undertook to set her up in Glasgow – find her a house, get her into one of the training hospitals and engage a nanny."

"And defray the expenses, Edward."

"Yes, Hilda. A small price to pay for Elizabeth's peace of mind. And to avoid a family scandal."

"And how long will that last?" She almost sneered. "Another fad. Hospital nurse? How long will she stick at that? And she can't carry on in Glasgow forever. Sooner or later people will start to ask questions."

"Maybe so. But at least it gives us time. Anything might happen. She could meet some suitable young man – a wounded officer perhaps – who would make her a good husband. A wartime romance, followed by a quick, informal wedding? What better excuse to avoid inviting all your friends, Hilda. They could set up anywhere, and no one any the wiser."

"You're clutching at straws, Edward. As I warned you before."

"I'm not so sure. And I can think of someone who would marry her like a shot."

There was a stunned silence before the implication hit home.

"Surely you can't mean the cad responsible for this?" gasped Hugh.

"I think you owe us an explanation, Edward." His wife glowered accusingly at him. "Whenever I raise the subject, you always insist the matter is in hand. Did you carry out your promise? Have you seen to it that the scoundrel has been disgraced?"

"Well, actually – no."

Hugh stared in disbelief. "You mean to say that the beastly outsider hasn't been chucked out of university? He hasn't been packed off to the slagheap where he belongs?"

"No. Sorry to disappoint you. But it's not as easy as you imagine. I couldn't think of a way to persuade the university court without bringing Elizabeth into it. In such a serious case concrete evidence would be demanded. Vague accusations of immoral conduct simply would not do." Then he rallied. "And

I have to say that I am no longer convinced that young Baird is the culprit. Elizabeth implied as much."

"And you believed her?" Hilda was scathing. "She'd do anything to protect him."

"I know my daughter," he said firmly. "She isn't lying. It's my belief that she was taken by force – probably by his elder brother. And she was too ashamed to admit it to anyone."

"Did she tell you that?"

"Well, no. But putting two and two together … I now think we may have misjudged Alastair Baird."

"On what grounds? You're so keen on evidence, Edward." She paused. "Even if it might be true – which I do not for a moment accept – Baird is culpable. He should not have allowed Elizabeth to fall into his brother's clutches."

"Nonsense, Hilda. A man isn't his brother's keeper. On that view you should blame the Semples. She was staying with them."

"Hold on a minute. This is getting us nowhere." Hugh was perplexed. "Let me get this straight. Dad, you're saying you no longer think he is guilty. What about you, mama? Is it possible we've made a mistake?"

"Well, I – I suppose …" She tailed away.

"Yes, Hilda?"

"Oh, have it your own way. What does my opinion matter?"

Her husband took great care not to show any sign of satisfaction. He had won a concession, even though it was the merest chink in her armour.

"So what do we do now?" asked Hugh.

"Make the best of it. I don't like the situation any more than you two do. But I can think of worse matches. Look, I've made a few enquiries. Baird didn't resume his studies in the autumn. The university hasn't seen hide not hair of him. They just assumed he'd joined up. And, as it happens, that's exactly what he did. McCrae's battalion – the draper, you know. They're in training up at Heriot's School right now. Baird's an educated man. The army's crying out for officers. Right, Hugh? So there's every chance he'll be made up. If he comes through the war … well, so far as I'm concerned, he deserves a fresh start. What do you think, Hilda?"

"Really, Edward. I'm too tired to think. The whole world seems to be collapsing about our ears. The only decent thing is that Hugh is back with us. At least there's one person I can rely on." She looked beseechingly at her son.

Hugh dropped his eyes. "Sorry, mama," he said quietly. "There's no chance I'll be discharged. My wounds have nearly healed. Besides, you wouldn't want me branded as a shirker, now would you?"

"But surely –"

"Are you staying with the battalion, Hugh?"

"It's possible, dad. But I doubt it. I've no real wish to go back. Things will have changed out of all recognition. Companies filled out with clodhoppers, wet behind the ears. The mess full of strangers. No, I prefer to remember it as it was. And the colonel told me he's leaving, moving up to brigade. Well merited and all that, but still … He also gave a strong hint that the battalion might be transferred – to Egypt, of all places. We'll be bored to distraction, or go mad with sunstroke, sitting on our backsides, waiting to see if Johnny Turk will put in an appearance. Stuck in a sideshow, while the war's being won in France? Not for me, not if I can help it."

"So you do have a choice?" There was renewed hope in her voice.

"Well, yes. I have been given a few options," he conceded. "I could take over the command of the training company at the depot." He grimaced. "Putting raw recruits through their paces, trying to make soldiers of them, sending them off as new drafts every few weeks. It'll probably mean missing out on the rest of the war."

"Well, that's not so bad." His mother could have wept with relief. "Then you'll take up the offer?"

"No jolly fear. I told the C.O. as much. He agreed I would be best suited to a more active role. So he's promised to pull a few strings. There are all sorts of new formations in the pipeline – short service outfits and the like. New Army, of course, but you can't have everything. The old man thinks he can wangle me a posting. Ninth or Tenth Stirlings, he said. Second-in-command – I'd be a major. God knows how long it'll take to train up bloody civilians. But it's a chance to get back to frontline action for the final push."

"I see. And what is your opinion, Edward?"

"I think we should respect Hugh's decision. If that's where duty calls, then so be it."

Abruptly she rose and swept from the room. Her feelings were too bitter for words. Betrayed! First it was her daughter, then her husband, and now her son. But she would not give way to tears a second time. Not till she reached the solitude of her boudoir.

SIXTEEN

Stacking the Cards

Glasgow. February 1915

"Nae need to stand there gawpin', Baird. It's only the City Chambers. Are ye feart to go in by yersel'? Or maybe ye like standin' out here in the cold?"

"Oh, hullo, Stan. I didnae see ye comin'." Iain gave a rueful grin. "No, it's no' like that. I got here a bit early, and I didnae fancy the idea o' being shoved in wi' the opposition afore the meetin'. It would stick in the craw, havin' to pass the time o' day wi' thon bunch o' bloodsuckers."

"No fraternisation, eh? That's the ticket. And just who is the opposition? Bosses or union officials?"

"Both. And I dinnae ken which is worse."

"I do. Still, ye're learnin'."

"I cannae see why we're here at all," grumbled Iain as they moved off. "The meeting was supposed to be on neutral ground. Glasgow Corporation? They're hand in glove alongside the Employers' Federation."

"I wouldnae disagree. But the high heid yins in the ASE accepted the council's offer to help broker a deal. Something queer there, d'ye no' think? That's why the shop floor has to make its voice heard. That's why we called an overtime ban and formed a vigilance committee. So wherever the union officials go, we go as well. We'll no' let ourselves be sold down the river. It's either the full tuppence an hour – or a strike. And we'll let them ken it."

Together they passed through the arched doorway into the huge entrance hall. "Impressed?" chuckled Robertson.

"Naw. In fact it makes me sick."

"Thought as much. The city fathers have the cheek to claim it's a monument to civic pride. Municipal Socialism? That's a laugh. A few scraps from the rich man's table. It's nothin' but a ploy for the councillors and their friends to live high on the hog while they keep ordinary folk under their thumb."

"So after the revolution we'll knock it down?"

"Och, I wouldnae go that far. It belongs to the people. And the workers' state has to be run from somewhere. Anyway, first things first. I think our lot are over there."

He indicated a huddle of figures beside the main staircase. A handful of servitors hovered in the vicinity, obviously told off to keep a watchful eye on the visitors.

"Would ye credit it, Iain? That's what they think o' the great unwashed. We're out to wreck the place. Or else some o' us will try to pinch the silver. Oh, look. Here comes Buntin."

The district secretary of the ASE had detached himself from the rest of the delegation. Robertson studiously avoided his outstretched hand.

"Glad you could come, Stan," said the union official, with a forced attempt at bonhomie. "Just a wee word in your ear before we go in."

"Hullo, Sam. Everyone here?"

"Why, yes – I suppose so. There's the official negotiating committee – agreed with the Engineering Federation. Then there's your shop stewards – I don't know how many you saw fit to invite."

"Just as many as could get away from their work. And they're no' mine, Sam. They're the elected representatives o' the rank and file. Ye'd do well to remember that. Can we get on now? It's gone ten."

"Listen, Stan. You won't do anything daft, will you?" In his anxiety he almost plucked at Robertson's sleeve. "I mean – the employers' side aren't expecting you. I'll need to square it with them. You're just here as observers. Understood? Leave the talking to us. We don't want to give them any excuse to call off the talks, now do we?"

"I think you can rely on us to play our part. We'll do what's in the best interests o' the membership."

Buntin looked dubious at that, but forbore to press the issue further. Turning away, he beckoned to the nearest attendant.

"He seems a bit hot under the collar," murmured Iain, as the group was led upstairs.

"It's his job on the line." Robertson laughed harshly. "The bigwigs in London are no' exactly happy. They think the local officials have lost control.

Gie in to an overtime ban, kowtow to the shop floor? That'll never do. He'll be desperate to accept anythin' the bosses are prepared to offer. You'll see."

They halted outside a door of carved oak at the end of a long corridor. A brief knock and they were ushered inside. The apartment was just as Iain had imagined, the polished wood and rich furnishings reeking of power and money. Dominating the surroundings was a huge rectangular table. Half a dozen chairs had been set out for the delegation; those on the opposite side were already occupied. Iain felt a surge of revulsion at the stuffed shirts sitting there, bristling with self-importance. Five were completely unknown to him; the sixth was only too familiar – the managing director at the Ordnance, stiff-necked in wing collar and black morning suit. And not overjoyed at the intrusion, judging by the expression on his face.

"What does this mean, Mr Buntin?" Albert Findlay rose to his feet. "It was clearly understood that this was to be a private meeting, with no more than six representatives on each side. The Employers' Federation deals only with official union delegates, not a mass invasion from the shop floor."

Buntin was full of apologies. "I'm deeply sorry, Mr Findlay. These men are here purely as auditors, I do assure you." He grew even more sycophantic. "The fact is that we of the Allied Trades are confident that a framework exists for an amicable settlement. It would save time and effort if these – unofficial observers, shall we say – are allowed to report direct to the workforce on the progress that has been made."

Findlay looked round at his colleagues. There was the slightest inclination of heads. "Very well, then. As you say, it may save time. God knows these negotiations have dragged on long enough. If the official party would take their places at the table …" He laid heavy emphasis on the third word. "As for the remainder of your group, Mr Buntin …" He indicated a row of bentwood chairs against the far wall, their chipped and faded gilt strangely at odds with the rest of the room.

"No' a bad actor, auld Findlay" grinned Robertson, as he motioned Iain towards a couple of vacant seats.

"Actor?"

"Aye. Pretendin' to be put out. Buntin would never have dared spring this on him – our turnin' up out o' the blue. He'd have begged permission first. And these scabby old chairs, conveniently set out in advance – just to put us in our place. Look at that lot. They think it's a done deal. There's none o' the owners here. Nae sign o' the kingpins, like Beardmore or Weir. They've sent their hirelings to rubber stamp what's already been agreed – behind our backs."

Stan was right. There sat Findlay as chairman, mallet and gavel to hand, making a show of sifting through his bundle of documents. But he had noticed Iain, recognised him – no doubt of that. Their eyes met briefly. Findlay flushed with anger, before recovering his composure and calling the meeting to order.

Now he was launching into a speech – explaining the big picture, as he was pleased to call it. Parroting the usual claptrap: the suffering of the soldiers at the Front, their victory imperilled by the workers at home. Next came the appeal to patriotism: loyal Britons would recoil from anything which might give succour to the enemy. It was no more than the capitalist press churned out daily. Did Findlay imagine it cut any ice with them? At least his tub thumping had the merit of brevity. It did not take him long to reach the climax of his tirade.

"Gentlemen, we must have a solution. As a gesture of goodwill, the employers are willing to make a considerable sacrifice. For the sake of the war effort and a speedy resumption of full production, we are prepared to table a final offer of three farthings an hour, coupled with a substantial wartime bonus on piece rates."

Buntin had his response ready. "Mr Chairman, I'm sure that we would all agree that this is a gesture which merits serious consideration. But obviously it cannot be answered here and now."

"Aye, it can!" The interruption came from one of the shop stewards, Gallacher of Albion Motors. "It's not acceptable. The bosses are nothin' but war profiteers. They can well afford to gie us a fair shift."

The district secretary flinched at the outburst; then rallied to retrieve the situation. "I'm sure any individual has the right to his own opinion," he said primly. "But I feel certain that a ballot of the membership will provide a different answer."

"That's what you think!" Iain could contain himself no longer. "Do ye think we're taken in by yer smarmy words? Ye're nothin' but a pack o' liars. Ye spread rumours accusin' us o' helpin' the Germans. Then a government minister tells us we're a' drunkards, no' fit to put in a day's work. Negotiations? Stab in the back, more like."

In an instant there was uproar. The shop stewards were on their feet, gesticulating wildly. Iain had given voice to their feelings; now they were only too glad to vent their anger. Union officials and company directors alike were struck dumbfounded, goggle-eyed in horrified disbelief. Only Robertson remained impassive, a faint twitch playing on the corner of his mouth. The chairman, recovering his wits, banged repeatedly on his gavel for order, but his efforts were lost in the mayhem. After a minute or two he gave up in disgust, exchanged glances with his associates, gathered up his papers and, tight-lipped, led the way out through a side door.

"Now you've gone and done it!" Buntin was almost dancing with rage, jabbing his finger accusingly at Gallacher and Iain. "They would have gone to a penny an hour and ten percent on the piece rates. Now they've walked out. We'll never get a settlement."

"Get a grip on yourself, man." Robertson was openly contemptuous. "They'll be back. They need an agreement more than we do."

"That's what you say. But I'm responsible to the National Executive. I'll have to inform them. London won't be pleased about the breakdown. You may be sure I'll know where to lay the blame."

"Aye, you do that, Sam. Though I doubt they'll think much o' your excuses."

The ASE official flashed a glint of pure vitriol. "You'll pay for this – all of you." He turned on his heel. Outside the doorway they heard him snarl: "Watch where you're going, blast you." A latecomer dashed into the room.

There was a chorus of ribald greetings. The new arrival waved them aside. "I've just come from Cathcart," he announced tersely. "You'll never believe what Weir has just done."

They crowded round him, anxious to discover what was amiss. It was well known that the firm of G. & J. Weir took a hard line on workers' rights; the pump manufacturer was notorious for trying to force through innovation in production methods. It must be something serious to cause a stalwart like Arthur MacManus to turn up late.

"Gie the man some space," said Robertson. "Now, Arthur, we're all attention."

In a few crisp sentences the shop steward explained what had happened. Weir was conspiring to do down his own workforce, even as his representative sat at the negotiating table. Claiming a lack of tradesmen to complete a new Admiralty contract, he had decided to bring in foreign labour – engineers from America. And to pay them well over the odds. There were gasps of incredulity. No wonder the Cathcart men had walked out in a rage, were calling on their compatriots in other yards for support.

Instinctively they looked to Robertson. He had already digested the news. "Right. Ye ken what this means. It's the thin edge o' the wedge. If Weir gets away wi' this, the others will try it on as well. We're all in this together."

"What are we to do, Stan?"

"Just a minute. We dinnae want everyone to ken our business." He gestured towards the remaining union officials standing sheepishly in the background. "You lot – bugger off! Your kind have nae place here." They trooped out, heads bowed like so many recalcitrant schoolboys, to an accompaniment of jeers and hisses, perhaps relieved to have escaped so lightly.

"That's got rid o' them. They'll find out what's goin' on soon enough. Back to your shops – all o' ye. Tell the men what's happened. Lay it on thick about the employment o' overpaid Yanks. The only answer is to down tools – this very afternoon. That'll gie the bosses pause for thought."

"We were going to book the St. Mungo Hall for a strike meeting tomorrow," said MacManus tentatively.

"Good idea. Ye all heard that. Get delegates told off to attend – folk we can rely on, mind. Nae doubt the press will be there. Let's gie them a story worth the tellin'."

"Glad ye agree, Stan. We'll need a strike committee to coordinate everything. We cannae expect the ASE to do it."

"Especially no' Buntin," said Robertson drily. "He'll hae kittens when he hears about this." Everyone laughed. "But ye're quite right, Arthur. We will need a wee steering group. You can be chairman, Willie." He nodded towards Gallacher. "We'll get it ratified at the meeting tomorrow. Anything else? No. Away wi' ye, then. Iain, you're wi' me."

They waited while the others dispersed. The younger man was fairly brimming with excitement. "Is this the start o' it, Stan? Earlier than we thought?"

Robertson made a gesture of impatience. "Haud yer horses! It's no' about to happen. No' this time. Ye ken fine that a revolutionary situation can only exist when the people are choked and squeezed out o' their hidebound ways. And the war hasnae done that – yet."

"But surely mass action could spread to other areas."

"No, son. This is only a first step. We'll gie the bosses a dunt on the nose – no more than that. Sooner or later they'll be back wi' an improved offer. And it'll be accepted. But Clydeside will be saddled wi' a reputation for militancy. That's what we have to turn to our advantage."

"So how do we do that?"

"Patience, man. We dinnae dive off at the deep end. And that especially applies to you. Did ye see the way Findlay was eyein' ye up? If looks could kill … Your coat's on a shoogly peg. If ye werena a marked man afore, ye certainly are now. Likely he'll bide his time, wait till he's got an excuse to nail ye good and proper. See ye dinnae gie him the chance."

"If ye say so, Stan. I'll do my best."

"I only hope that's good enough. Ye've been well warned. Anyhow, we've a tram to catch. Time and tide, laddie. That's what it's all about."

* * *

Edinburgh. March 1915

Edward Lixmont pushed through the revolving door, up the stairs and into the huge expanse of the main exhibition hall, just as the clock began to chime the hour. There was a fair sprinkling of visitors to the Royal Scottish Museum on a bleak Saturday afternoon, but no immediate sign of anyone in military uniform. Perhaps the lad had been unable to get away. Or had made up his mind to have nothing more to do with the family. Well, he could hardly blame young Baird for that. Still, it would be a disappointment.

He had been in a quandary for months now. The easiest solution would have been to ignore the problem; that was what Hilda would have advised, had he seen fit to consult her. But it would be an injustice to allow the boy to go off to war, perhaps never to return, with that terrible accusation still hanging over him. In the end he had dashed off a note requesting a meeting, giving what imagined would be a convenient time and place. Chambers Street was only a short distance from Heriot's School, and discreet enquiries had established that no training exercises had been planned for that weekend. All he could do now was to hope for the best.

He resolved to wait. Settling himself on a bench facing the entrance, his attention wandered to the galleries above, high into the lofty dome. The quarter hour struck; then the half hour. There was no point in staying any longer. Disconsolate, he prepared to take his leave. Suddenly his heart skipped a beat. There he was, a flaxen haired youth in khaki tunic, threading his way past a knot of new arrivals.

It was not Alastair Baird's fault that he was late for the appointment. Promotion, however lowly, however temporary, carried responsibilities. A consignment of rifles had just been delivered, to be checked and locked away securely under the watchful eye of the quartermaster. Admittedly they were not the latest model, and there was as yet no ammunition, but things were looking up. Now at last they could drill as real soldiers. Nevertheless, the task had taken longer than expected, and it was well after two before he was free to go.

The message had been waiting for him on his return from a hike over the Pentlands. Just a business card with a time, date and place scribbled on the back, stuffed into an envelope and addressed to him. Hurrying along towards the museum, once more he tried to make sense of it. Surely the objective was not further exposure. To be drummed out of the battalion as unfit to serve would be too much to bear. Humiliation or not, there was no question of spurning the invitation. There would be news of Elizabeth. Surely he would not be denied that. He heard the chime of the half hour. What if her father had already left? He broke into a run. Bounding up the museum steps, he brushed his way through. Then he heaved a sigh of relief. Thank God he was in time.

There was an awkward silence as they confronted each other. It was the younger man who was first to break the ice. "Sorry to be so late, sir. It couldn't be helped."

"Of course. I quite understand – Alastair. The military have first call on your time. I'm only glad you were able to come." He stretched out his hand.

After a moment's hesitation Alastair took it. "It was the least I could do, sir."

"Can we talk? I believe there's a coffee shop somewhere. Would you mind?" He managed a fleeting smile. "I see you've already earned yourself a stripe."

"Yes. Though I can hardly claim to have earned it."

"Why ever so? You're too modest."

"Judge for yourself. On our first evening in barracks the sergeant presented me with a copy of the *Manual of Infantry Training*. I was to learn it straight off, because the next morning I would be in charge of drilling a section. He thought that as a teacher I should be used to giving instructions."

"But you're not yet qualified."

"That's what I told him. I was – had been – only a trainee. He insisted that was good enough. I had no choice in the matter."

"Are you sure that was all there was to it?"

Now Mr Lixmont was teasing him. His statement was true enough. For some inexplicable reason Sergeant Harris had taken a shine to him. But it was not the whole story – not by a long chalk.

The lawyer did not wait for a reply. "Shall we walk? I think I can hear the clink of tea things through that archway. You see," he went on, "I get to learn about all sorts of strange events in my line of business. Take the mystery of how McCrae's was kitted out in proper service dress so quickly. Puzzling, isn't it? Rumour has it that there was a cargo of khaki serge lying in St Leonard's railway yards, awaiting shipment to some destination in the south. But before it could be dispatched, the stuff somehow disappeared in the dead of night. Within days you lot were strutting around in brand new uniforms. Can you think of any connection?"

Alastair flushed. His guilty secret was known – suspected at least. Harris had dropped the first hint on mobilisation day. How could he refuse the invitation when Grove and the others had so gleefully accepted? Actually the operation had passed off without a hitch. Apparently both night watchmen and police officers had turned a blind eye while padlocks were smashed and the cloth removed in four lorry loads, to be transformed into battledress. Afterwards Colonel McCrae had personally singled him out. Why him, and not one of the others? Surely Grove was a more likely candidate. It made no sense.

"Don't bother to answer that. You know, Alastair, you'll never make a convincing liar. Your face will always give you away. Shall we sit over there?" He hailed a passing waitress and ordered coffee and cake.

"How – how did you find out?"

"Let's call it a lucky guess. I was aware of the broad outline, of course. McCrae was determined to have his men in uniform – by fair means or foul. It was said some students were involved. The rest was adding two and two together. You gave yourself away beautifully." He noted the crestfallen expression. "No need to reproach yourself. The deed showed initiative, and that's going to be needed in spades to win this war."

"You think so? That's what Sergeant Harris said. But it was theft, wasn't it? We all thought we'd be clapped in jail if we were caught."

"Not in a good cause. And, from what I hear, you could have blown the whole place up without anyone bothering. That sergeant of yours seems a wily old bird. He's obviously spotted leadership potential in you."

"I doubt that. Anyhow, he's not my sergeant any more. He was one of the first casualties back in January. The battalion was over strength when it was taken over by the War Office. Harris was way over age, and the colonel couldn't save him. Old comrade or no, he had to stand down. Pity about that. He taught me a lot. His replacement, funnily enough, is a serving schoolmaster. Decent enough chap, I have to admit. At least he hasn't had me reduced to the ranks – yet."

"You do yourself an injustice, Alastair. Have you ever considered that you may be hiding your light under a bushel? You could take a commission, you know. I could be of assistance. I do have certain contacts."

Baird stared in amazement. Why on earth should Elizabeth's father make such an offer? But there could be only one reply.

"Thank you all the same, but I would prefer to remain where I am. If I rise, it will be on merit, through my own efforts." Suddenly he became emboldened. "Look, Mr Lixmont, what's the point of all this? You didn't bring me here to discuss my military career. And I came in the hope of news about your daughter. I haven't heard a thing since – since that time at your house. Is there nothing you can tell me?"

Lixmont could not meet his gaze. "You are quite right, of course," he said quietly. "And I can only make a guess at the torment you must have suffered. I've been sadly at fault. I should have gotten in touch with you long before this. Procrastination on my part, I suppose." He swallowed hard. "Elizabeth is fine. And so is her baby." He made a gesture with his hand. "You've a host of questions, I know. And I'll do my best to answer them. But please bear with me. I asked you here today because –"

He broke off. The waitress was hovering. Damn the girl! Why did interruptions always happen at the most inconvenient moment?

"Shall I pour, sir?"

"Er, no. Just leave the tray. We'll help ourselves."

"Very good, sir. Enjoy your coffee." She bobbed her head and bustled away.

"Sorry about that, Alastair." He drew a deep breath. "The truth of the matter is that – is that I have a confession to make." He plunged on. "I now fully accept that the accusation against you is totally without foundation. You knew nothing of Elizabeth's condition. You are in no way responsible for it. Words cannot express my remorse at the way you have been so cruelly wronged by my family. Apologies are so inadequate. I can only try to make amends."

Alastair's jaw dropped. He could scarcely believe his ears. It was incredible. Absolved from all blame, his good name restored. Then his face clouded.

"But sir, you had me disgraced – expelled from the university. How can you go back and explain that you made a mistake?"

"Ah. Fortunately I can set your mind at rest on that score. I decided not to inform the authorities after all. Thank God I thought better of it. They believe that you, like so many others, simply abandoned your studies for the greater cause. Far from being dishonoured, you will be welcomed back."

"So – no one else knows?"

"Only the members of my family."

"And – Mrs Lixmont? Does she share your views?"

"Well – perhaps not exactly. I must admit my wife hasn't said as much. Though deep down I'm sure she realises the truth. But you know women. Once they take a stand on something, it's the very devil to shake them. She'll come round in the end."

"Yes, of course. Only – there's something puzzling me, sir. May I ask what made you change your mind?"

Lixmont shrugged. "We were too quick to condemn you out of hand. That was my failing. I should have considered all the possibilities more carefully. Afterwards I got to thinking. Your version of what might have happened made sense. And it was confirmed by Elizabeth – though that was some months later."

"Did she tell you that it was my brother who – who forced his attentions on her?"

"Not quite. And I did not press her. But it could have been no one else."

"Thank you for that." He frowned. "This must have been difficult for you. To seek me out like this, I mean."

"It was the only honourable course."

Alastair pursed his lips. "I can't blame you for believing me guilty. Things must have looked black. And I do feel at least partly responsible. I should never have put her in a position where she was left alone with my brother. If I hadn't invited her to Broomburn, none of this would have happened."

"Stuff and nonsense. You weren't to know." He smiled ruefully. "So can we let bygones be bygones? Start afresh?"

There was a vigorous nod of assent. "Nothing I'd like better, sir."

"Good. Now let's talk about Elizabeth. She has a baby boy. A fine, healthy little fellow. He's called Edward – Eddie."

"After you?" His eyes lit up. "Where is she now, sir? Can I visit her? Will she see me?"

"I'm quite sure she would be delighted to see you. But," he added more slowly, "I wonder if that would be altogether wise."

"What do you mean, sir? I only wanted to give her my best wishes. And to offer my heartfelt apologies."

"Apologies? There's absolutely no need. Quite the contrary, I should have thought. But if you insist, I'll willingly give you her address. I've set her up in Glasgow. It's a small household – just a maid and nanny. She's taken up training to become a nurse, would you believe? She's determined to do her bit for the war effort."

"And I'll wager she makes a good one. Trust Elizabeth. Once she finds a cause, she throws all her energies into it."

"True. But we must take things one step at a time. She's been through the mill. Give her a chance to rebuild her life. And with you going off with your unit at any time soon …" He left the rest unsaid.

"Yes, I see that now. You're quite right. It was thoughtless of me. Another shock is the last thing she needs. I'll do whatever you advise."

"Don't be too disappointed, Alastair. Listen, my son says the war can't go on much longer. The Hun has shot his bolt. It only wants our new armies for the final push. In a year – maybe less – you'll be home again. Then you can renew your friendship with Elizabeth. Is that too long to wait? Whatever the two of you may decide, you'll have my full support. That's a promise."

"Are you suggesting, sir, that – that Elizabeth and I might have a future?" It was a struggle to keep the disbelief from his voice.

Lixmont grinned. "I rather think I am. I haven't mentioned it yet, but she also gave her son your name. Does that not tell you anything?"

"But – but I'm not worthy of her."

"Let others be the judge of that – Elizabeth most of all. And I wouldn't worry over much about career or status. You have many estimable qualities that should carry you to the very pinnacle of your profession. I have no doubt of that."

This was mind numbing – enough to bowl anyone over. Not only had the weight been lifted from his shoulders, but a dazzling vision of the future had opened up before his eyes. And should he not return, there was hope that Elizabeth would cherish his memory. That was reward enough.

"I don't know what to say, sir."

"Then don't say anything. Let's have our coffee. And – you will think about that commission, won't you?"

* * *

Glasgow. June 1915

It was a pure accident. He had never even touched her. But what if he were called to account? His temper had got the better of him, there was no deny-ing that. On the other hand Morag was always bitching these days, whining it was high time they were properly wed – even on a Sunday morning when a working man deserved the luxury of some peace and quiet. One moment they were eyeball to eyeball, snarling insults at each other; the next she had shied away, tripped on the hearthrug, lost her balance. Then the true hor-ror – the sickening thud as her head struck the fender, the image of her still body, face white as wax, lying crumpled on the floor. A rare stab of remorse ran through him.

What if she was dead? No, that was impossible. She had come to in the ambulance, even pressed his hand and smiled forgiveness as he knelt beside her, swearing to mend his ways. And he had meant it. He would promise anything to have her safe and well again. But she had been in the hands of the doctors an awful long time now. And he had been abandoned in this dreary hospital corridor, left to his grief and misery, waiting vainly for a crumb of news.

"Excuse me."

One of the passers-by had stopped. He looked up inquiringly. There stood a gaunt, sour faced woman, dressed almost entirely in black. Some high-up official, he guessed, judging by her air of self-importance, and the amount of lace on her costume.

"No need to get up," she said primly. "And before you ask, there is no information as yet. I am here to take a statement. Purely routine, you may be assured." Without further ado she produced notebook and pencil, and perched herself at the opposite end of Iain's bench. "Now then – to begin. Can you confirm that you are the husband of Morag Mackay?"

"No. No' exactly."

"What do you mean by that?"

"My name's Baird."

"I still fail to comprehend. You accompanied the patient here. Are you a relative? Brother, perhaps?"

"Naw. She's my bidie-in. Sorry, common law wife."

There was a distinctive intake of breath. His inquisitor made a note, but forbore to comment further.

"Very well. Did you witness the occurrence?"

"'Fraid not. I was in the bedroom. But I came ben when I heard the crash."

"And you found?"

"Morag, lyin' by the fireside."

"That must have been a shock for you."

"Ye can say that again. She must have slipped while tendin' the fire. Ye see, the rug isnae fixed down. Sometimes it slides on the linoleum if ye arena careful. There's solid brass knobs at the side o' the fender. She probably cracked her heid on one o' them."

"I see. What did you do next?"

"I'm no' exactly sure. Everythin' was in a blur. I think I knocked up some o' the neighbours, and somebody had the wit to run for help. I was wi' her when the ambulance men came."

"Well, that all seems clear enough." There was a pause. "One last question. Were you and your – your partner on good terms? You didn't have an argument this morning?"

For an instant his eyes narrowed angrily. What right did the interfering old witch have to poke her nose into his business? Then he steadied himself. "Argument? I was in bed while she was up gettin' my breakfast ready." He became more effusive. "Look, we do hae tiffs from time to time. Who disnae? But nothin' serious. Surely ye're no' suggestin' –?"

"No. Certainly not. But it was my duty to ask." She closed her notepad. "You've been most helpful. I must be off now. You're welcome to stay if you wish. But it may be some time yet."

Iain grunted as he watched her hasty retreat. He had seen her off, all right. But – was she fully satisfied? Some of the neighbours must have heard: they had been at it hammer and tongs. Had anyone spoken out? He could not be sure. But in any case what did it matter? Morag would never betray him.

Poor soul! He bitterly regretted the fruits of his evil temper. But he would make it up to her. If she wanted marriage, he was prepared to tie the knot. If she demanded a child, then he would agree. Only – not just yet. Momentous events were at hand: the Party had need of all his energies. But she was a good socialist. She would understand if he explained. A better future lay just around the corner. Then she could have all she desired.

Things were beginning to fall into place, just as Robertson had predicted. The February strike had collapsed within a fortnight, with the ASE stepping in to force a settlement. And then the union leadership had promptly compounded the felony by cravenly selling out to the government. The signing of the so-called *Treasury Agreement* in March was a betrayal of hard won prerogatives – an abject surrender of the right to strike, and meek acceptance of dilution in the workplace. And in return there was only a vague promise to try to limit profiteering by employers. To say that the rank and file felt aggrieved … They were buzzing with discontent.

And that was merely the beginning. Given an inch, the capitalists would be sure to take a mile. The excuse had been the alleged shell shortage on the Western Front. Now the fiery Welsh wizard, Lloyd George himself, was rampaging around with his newly created Ministry of Munitions, determined to seize total control over workers' lives. What other meaning could be given to the imposition of penal sanctions on any form of industrial action, or the requirement to obtain a leaving certificate from an employer before seeking alternative work? And where would it all end? Conscription, both military and industrial, was on the way, if the new National Register had any purpose. Surely the masses would never stand for that. Yes, the cauldron was bubbling up nicely. A little more stirring and it would boil over.

"Would your name be Baird?" A gruff voice roused him.

"Maybe. What's it to you?"

"You're wanted. I've been sent to fetch you."

He felt his pulse quicken. So this was it. He was about to find out about Morag's condition – and quite possibly his own fate. But he was damned if he would admit to any unease in front of this lackey.

"Lead on, Macduff." He swaggered after his guide with as much nonchalance as he could command.

Together they passed along a maze of corridors, across a courtyard, through another doorway, up a flight of stairs. At the top, to the right was a sign: *Ward 16*. Beneath it a figure in a white coat was apparently deep in conversation with the snooty woman in the black dress.

"You say that this character –" The man suddenly broke off. "Thank you, porter. You may return to your other duties now." He favoured Iain with a disdainful stare. "My name is MacFarlane. Professor MacFarlane. Matron has been telling me something of the background to this case. Far be it from me to pontificate on morality, but you must understand that in strict law you are not the next of kin, and therefore have no locus here. Nevertheless, under the circumstances I am prepared to stretch a point."

"Just tell me how she is. That crack on her heid –"

"I was coming to that. The crack on her head, as you term it, is not serious. Only a mild concussion. The wound should heal quite quickly."

"Thank God for that."

"Yes. But I'm afraid it does not end there. There were more serious injuries, involving internal damage to her body. Another hour or two and she would never have survived. Even so, it was touch and go."

"Touch and go?"

"An emergency operation was imperative. Not without risk, but there was no alternative. However, the outcome was successful, and I have high hopes for a full recovery. But, I'm sorry to say she has lost her child."

"Child?" He gaped in blank incomprehension.

"Yes. Had she not told you she was pregnant?"

"No. Never."

"Well, I'd say she was about three months gone. It's possible she was not aware of her condition. Or was saving the news for a special occasion."

"Does – does she know?" It was all he could think of saying.

"The patient has been informed." It was the matron who answered. "I'm not sure how much she took in. She was still drowsy from the anaesthetic."

"Can I see her now?"

The surgeon stroked his chin thoughtfully. "Well, she is still very weak. There's a nurse by her bedside. However … a short visit might be permitted. Very well then. No more than ten minutes. Go in quietly. Your – friend is in a side ward. Sister will point out the way. I must be off on my afternoon rounds. Come along, matron."

Iain was left standing. Only now did it begin to sink in. So that was why she was so keen to get married. He had been blind, too wrapped up in his own affairs. Morag had deluded him, tricked him into spawning a brat. Well, let that pass. She had suffered for it. That was punishment enough. Pushing open the door, he marched in to make enquiry of the ward sister.

In less than a minute he found himself directed into a small, darkened room, the curtains drawn against the harsh glare of the afternoon sun. For a moment he stood with his back against the door, allowing his eyes to adjust to the subdued light. There was the silhouette of a figure sitting by the solitary bed. At the sound of his approach she rose and turned.

"Morag?"

The nurse smiled and made way for him. Suddenly her body seemed to sag; there was a little gasp of disbelief. Iain caught a muttered: "Excuse me. Other duties," as she scuttled past. What in hell was all that about? She was as jumpy as a flea. Dismissing the woman from his thoughts, he slipped into the vacant chair.

"How are ye, pet?"

Morag was lying motionless, but he could see she was fully conscious. He reached for her hand, cradled it gently.

"Ye've had a hard time o' it, I ken that. And it's a' my fault. I've treated ye like a brute. That damned temper o' mine. But it'll no' happen again. I swear it."

Her face lit up; he felt a tiny reassuring squeeze. "Hush. It's no' your fault. It was an accident." She hesitated. "Have – have they telt ye?"

"About the bairn? Aye. And I'm truly sorry. Ye must be heartbroken. But I'll make it up tae ye. There nothin' to stop us tryin' again."

"Another wean? Are ye sure? That's just what Elizabeth was sayin'."

"Elizabeth?"

"The nurse that just went out. That's her name. Funny thing, though. I had the impression she'd seen ye afore."

"Me! Havers! Ye cannae be serious. She just went out tae gie us time thegither."

"Ach, I ken fine. It's my imagination playin' tricks. She said she was fae Edinburgh. And she speaks wi' a posh accent. So I dinnae see how the pair o' ye could ever have met."

"There ye are, then."

"She's some lass, but. No' stuck up like most o' the nobs. Did ye ken that she had a wee laddie last year? Left tae bring him up on her own. And, as if that wisnae enough, she moved here to take up nursin' and dae her bit for the war effort."

"Another war widow, like as no'. Tryin' to make ends meet. There's enough o' them about."

"I dinnae think so. There was nae sign o' a wedding ring."

Something touched a chord. He stirred uncomfortably. "She didnae happen to mention her other name, did she?"

"No. But I heard someone call her Nurse Lux … Or was it Lix … something or other? I cannae quite mind. I was a bit groggy at the time. Does it matter?"

Lixmont! He nearly blurted it out. Christ! His past had come back to haunt him. This was too much to be a coincidence. And she had recognised him. Should she take it into her head to tell Morag … He had to find her, stop her somehow.

"No, of course not. Just idle curiosity." He tried to keep the strain from his voice. "I'd best be off now. The quack only gave me five minutes." He leaned over to give her a peck on the cheek. "I'll look in again the morn, after work." She smiled back gratefully. Noiselessly he stole from the room.

There was a little courtyard at the foot of the stairs leading down from the verandah at the far end of the ward. She was waiting there, sitting on a bench in the shade of the solitary tree, smoking a cigarette.

"I'm not the young innocent I used to be," she called out. "In any case you shouldn't be here. This is for hospital staff only."

"Sister said it would be all right. I told her I was just leaving, and wanted to thank ye for takin' care o' Morag."

"I knew who it was the moment I saw you. And guessed you would come looking for me. Well, here I am. No, don't come any closer," she added warningly. "Was that the real reason? Or did you come to threaten me?"

"That's no' a very nice thing to say. I really am grateful."

"And I'm supposed to believe that?" Now she was openly scornful. "All you care about is yourself."

"So what are you goin' to do?" he rasped menacingly. "If there's to be a scandal, you'll suffer far worse than me."

She met his scowl without flinching. "Oh, you can rest easy on that score. I won't say anything. Not on your account. Nor even mine. It's your common law wife I'm sorry for. She's had to endure pain enough as it is. No need to inflict more on her."

"So ye'll keep quiet?"

Elizabeth nodded. "For her sake. So long as you stay well away from me and mine. Miss Mackay will likely be moved over to the main ward tomorrow. I'm due on a training course. So with any luck our paths need never cross again." She flicked the ash from her cigarette, crushed the stub against the tree trunk. "I've work to attend to now. You can show yourself out." She rose, swished past him with a glance of utter contempt.

Iain glowered after her. He clenched his fists, took a step forward; then checked himself. After all, what did it matter? He had what he wanted.

* * *

Wiltshire, England. October 1915

"Ha-way, bonny lads. You can pack up now. Gaither roond."

It was the sergeant instructor. The newly formed 34th Division was full of

Geordies – Tyneside men, with strange ways and impossible dialect. Native Jocks were in a decided minority; only two of the division's twelve battalions hailed from north of the border. Still, it came as a welcome relief to escape from the wearisome task of hefting pick and shovel. Alastair Baird gestured to his section to pile tools.

The cosy setting and familiar surroundings of the early days had faded into distant memory. Was it really four months since they had entrained at Waverley Station, fondly believing they were bound for the Front? No such luck. Apparently there was still much to be learned before they could be considered fit for active service. But morale had never flagged; Colonel McCrae had seen to that. From brigade exercises in Yorkshire to divisional manoeuvres on Salisbury Plain, the battalion had buckled down with a will to master the minutiae of this new type of warfare.

Over the past weeks the pace of training had accelerated. They had been taught skirmishing over the Downs, advancing in line, on occasion preceded by an artillery barrage to add realism. Their feet had blistered on endless route marches, both by day and night, and woe betide any unit that arrived late or got lost. The spirit of aggression was instilled through bayonet practice, charging at sandbags, shrieking like dervishes; though it was somehow unnerving to imagine thrusting twelve and a quarter inches of tempered steel into a man's gut. And, of course, the principles of entrenchment were hammered into them on an almost daily basis; calloused hands and aching muscles were testament to that.

Surely the call to action must come soon. The colonel had honed his men to the peak of perfection, determined that the 16th Royal Scots be recognised as the best in the division. If sporting prowess was any indication, he was well on the way to achieving that distinction: no other unit could live with the Battalion XI on the football field. And at a recent parade, had not the divisional commander, old 'Inky Bill' himself, personally congratulated them on their fine turn out and magnificent spirit?

"Stand easy." The instructor held up a metal object between his thumb and forefinger. "Anyone know what this is?" It was shaped like a small pineapple, with grooves cut into the surface.

"I do, sarge. It's a Mills bomb." It was Grove, as usual. He was rewarded with a chorus of groans and jeers. Alastair shook his head. Jack never could resist an opportunity to show off. "I've been reading up about it. It's a close quarter weapon for clearing enemy positions."

The sergeant's eyes narrowed. "Carry on, lad. Tell us how to use it."

"Keep the lever pressed down whilst removing the retaining pin. Throw the bomb towards the target using a bowling action. On release, the striker will shoot down, hitting the cap and sparking the fuse. Four seconds later the detonator is set off and the grenade explodes. With obvious results."

"Bloody hell! Thanks for the lecture, professor."

Sarcasm was wasted on Grove. He gave a little bow. "We always endeavour to give satisfaction in this establishment."

"A comedian as well?" The sardonic grin hardened into a scowl. "And your name might be?"

"Grove, sar'nt. Jack Grove."

"That's better. Well now, Private Grove. Suppose you demonstrate." He spun a catch. "See that pile of rubble." He indicated a cairn of chalk, gleaming dully in the grey October afternoon. "That's a Jerry machine gun post. Your job is to blow it up? Think you can manage it?"

"Easy as pie, sarge." Nothing fazed Grove for long. He could throw a cricket ball from the boundary, right over the wicket. And the distance here was only a fraction of that.

The instructor smiled sourly, and turned to the others. "Right, take cover. Corporal, get your men into the trench." He towered over them as they tumbled into the ditch. It was only half finished: no more than four feet deep. "Look at you. Like a row of tin soldiers in a box. Where d'ye keep yer brains? When I fucking tell you to take cover, I mean it." He watched with grim satisfaction as nine heads ducked out of sight.

"Shall I jump in as well?"

"Not yet, bonny lad. Bomb first. Then funk hole. And mind you keep yer napper down." He produced a whistle. "I'll be over yonder. Wait for my signal."

Grove nodded. His grasp on the grenade tightened, but really there was nothing to it. It was almost like delivering a ball at the crease. He peered into the trench. "You fellows all right?"

Alastair twisted round. "For God's sake, Jack, be careful."

"Piece of cake, old man." He disappeared from view.

A shrill blast rang out; Baird crouched still lower. He could picture Jack drawing the pin, taking a little run up to gain momentum, swinging his arm in a wide arc …

"Ahrrgh!" It was a cry of alarm. His head jerked up involuntarily. Oh my God! Grove was dangling helplessly over the lip of the trench. He must have tripped, measured his length. He was trying to mouth something, jabbing with his finger. Christ! The bomb! Jack must have dropped it. And with the pin out –!

A trickle of debris was seeping into the trench; his eye caught the glint of metal. Instinctively he threw himself towards the object nestling amid the little pile of rubble, scooped it up, hurled it clear; the next instant he was scrabbling for his friend, reaching over the earthwork, tugging at his tunic, hauling him in head over heels. A final heave, a yelp of pain, and Grove was left sprawling. Baird dived after him, bracing himself for the shock of the explosion.

"Haw-haw-haw!" Were his ears playing tricks? It sounded like laughter. Warily he pushed himself up, peered over the parapet. It was the sergeant, grinning like a Cheshire cat.

"You dozy buggers! On yer feet! Get fell in!" Sheepishly they scrambled out of the trench. Grove was last out, wincing as he hobbled into line. "Bloody amateurs! Did you think we'd trust you wi' live grenades? It wasn't primed. It was a dummy – just like you lot." He snorted with derision. "God help me, I'm supposed to find a couple of bombers from this section. Not a hope in hell if you're all like Private Smartass there. But we'll see. You'll report to the bombing range tomorrow. Nine ack-emma. Carry on, corporal." He gave Alastair a nod. Then he was off, striding away, stopping only to retrieve the grenade.

"Right, you men. You heard the sergeant. Gather up the picks and shovels. It's two miles back to camp. So we'd best get a move on." He broke off. "Jack, what's amiss? You're hurt." Grove was on the ground, nursing his ankle.

"I'll be all right. Just give me a minute."

Baird looked dubious. "You're in pain, I can see that." He thought for a moment. "Two of you, make a chair. We'll carry him down to the track. We can cadge a lift from there."

Ignoring his protestations, Grove was hoisted up. They took it in turns, two by two, sharing the burden, sweating profusely as they stumbled over the uneven terrain. A marker post loomed ahead; the pace quickened over the last few yards. It was a relief to set the injured man down on a low wall beside the rutted roadway, and be done with his maddening quips and wisecracks.

"You chaps can cut off now. I'll stay with him."

They hesitated, exchanging glances, reluctant to leave a comrade. Baird could appreciate their concern, but there was no telling how long it might be before some vehicle appeared.

"No point in the rest of you staying. Besides, there's more chance of two of us getting a lift than ten."

They were convinced at last. Alastair watched them go, then dropped down beside Grove.

Jack pulled a face. "Well, bonny lad, I made a real pig's ear of it back there. Bombing my own trench. I'll never hear the last of it."

"Don't say that, old man. Could have happened to anyone. And you did point out where the bomb landed."

"Did I? I was in a blue funk. Didn't know what I was doing. You're the hero. You couldn't have known it was a dud. I've never seen anyone move so fast in my life."

"You think so? Truth to tell, I hardly knew what I was doing either. It just happened."

"Maybe. But I could tell that sergeant was impressed."

"Really? He didn't say anything."

"Didn't have to. But it'll get around. As for me ..." He shrugged his shoulders.

Was there a trace of bitterness there? Alastair could not help thinking that, beneath the chaffing and the banter, Jack resented his promotion. Yet he had never sought it, especially the award of a second stripe.

Grove seemed to divine his thoughts. "Sorry, Alastair. Didn't mean it like that. It's just that I feel a bit low."

"Don't take it to heart. You're a born leader. Look how you took us all in hand when we joined up. Your turn will come."

"Wish I shared your optimism. Did you know I've applied for a commission? Half a dozen times at least. Not a dicky bird. No one seems to want me. God knows what the C.O. wrote on my file. He simply doesn't rate me."

"Don't say that. I'm sure that's not the reason. Colonel McCrae is a fair man."

Grove sighed. "Well, at least we'll be off soon. Look on the bright side. Plenty of chances at the Front."

"That's the ticket. And now I'd better take a look at your leg." He knelt down and began to unwind the puttee. "A bit swollen. But there doesn't seem to be a break. All the same I think we should get the M.O. to run the rule over you."

"Don't you dare! I mean it, Alastair." There was real venom in his voice.

Baird flinched at the outburst. It seemed so out of character. Then he straightened up. "You forget yourself, I think," he said quietly.

The flush of anger faded. "Sorry. That was out of order. But I'll be fine. It's only a sprain. See, I can put weight on it." He tried to stand up, then subsided with a groan.

"There, that proves it. You do need medical attention."

"Please, Alastair. Give me a chance." Now he was pleading. "I don't want to be left behind. And even a day or two on sick parade could make all the difference."

"So that's what's bothering you. But what's to say we're off to the Front? There's been nothing official."

"No. But it's obvious, don't you see? Look at all the new equipment issued in the last few days – Lewis guns, and the like. And the colonel's just back from a week in France. Do you suppose he was there to take the air at Deauville? Or have a flutter in the casino at Calais?"

"Of course not. Nevertheless –"

"Then they've been handing out three day passes. That's embarkation leave, or I'm a Dutchman."

"All right, Jack, you've made your case. Tell you what I'm prepared to do. I'll let things stand over till tomorrow. But if you're not any better by then –"

He was interrupted by a loud honk, followed by a ragged cheer. It was a motor lorry, lurching and swaying over the rough going. And in the back, waving their arms, was the rest of his section. They must have persuaded the driver to come to the rescue. Willing hands helped Grove over the tailgate and made him comfortable on a pile of straw. He was soon in his element, making light of his misfortune, treating it all as a big joke. Alastair sat apart, saying little, pondering the consequences of the day's work.

It was later in the evening when the summons came. He was alone in the hut, trying to relax with a book. Grove had insisted in going off with the others to the wet canteen for a restorative, as he put it. But what was he to do, come the morning? There was a footstep on the gravel outside. Jack must have decided to rest his leg after all. He looked up expectantly as the door opened, then sprang to his feet. It was the RSM.

"Corporal Baird. I was told I'd find you here. Colonel McCrae would like a word. C.O.'s office. Quick as you like."

Alastair gulped. Surely the incident was not so serious as to merit the colonel's attention.

The sergeant major saw the look on his face. "Easy, lad. I don't suppose it's the end of the world. Now smarten yourself up, and get yourself over there."

Five minutes later Alastair found himself inside battalion H.Q., where he was immediately ushered into the inner sanctum. Only Colonel McCrae was in the room, warming himself by the fire. After coming to attention and saluting, he could scarcely conceal his astonishment at being waved into an easy chair, while the colonel took a seat opposite.

"Make yourself comfortable, Baird. I trust you have enjoyed your day."

So this was it. Better to take the bull by the horns. "Not exactly, sir. You see –"

"No need for excuses. I know all about it. The instructor's report is on my desk. And, let me say, it was a damned courageous act on your part."

Eh? What was that? Compliments? So he was not in trouble after all.

"Your quick thinking is very much to your credit. It confirms the impression I had already formed. I only wish your action could be recognised in some way."

"Th-thank you, sir." What else could he say?

"Don't thank me yet. I had another reason for this interview." He stroked his walrus moustache, as though uncertain how to continue. "You know, being a commanding officer is not all wine and roses. I have been given my instructions, and have no discretion in the matter. You may, or may not, be aware that there exists a severe shortage of junior officers at present. Accordingly, the Army Council has decided on a new, expanded system of officer training. Battalion commanders have been asked to nominate potential candidates, especially NCOs. I can think of no one more suitable."

Alastair gulped in astonishment. This was high praise indeed. But did he really want a commission? "I'm very grateful for your good opinion, sir," he ventured, choosing his words with care. "But surely there are others with a higher claim. I would prefer to remain where I am, go overseas with the battalion. That's why I joined up."

"I appreciate your loyalty, Baird. However, there is a wider perspective. The army is crying out for more officers. Naturally I can't force you to go, but I think you know where duty lies."

"So there's no more to be said?"

"I'm afraid not. In due course you'll be enrolled in an officer cadet unit. In the meantime I'm promoting you to lance sergeant. You'll help out with the support company till you're required."

"In Edinburgh?"

"Just so. You leave in the morning. You can collect your pass and railway warrant on the way out. Along with your stripes, of course. You'd better get them sewn on tonight. Now I'll do my damnedest to have you gazetted back to the battalion, but there can be no promises. You'll go where you're needed most. Understood?"

"Yes, sir."

"If it's any consolation, the division is not about to embark for France. I had that from the general himself. God knows when we will be moving. However, that's not your concern." He stood up abruptly, extended his hand. "Good luck, my boy. I know you'll not let us down."

Alastair took a pace backwards, saluted and about turned.

"By the by, you might send Private Grove to see me. I have my reservations, but I've decided to give him a chance. He'll be joining you tomorrow."

SEVENTEEN

Win a Skirmish…

Glasgow. November 1915

Despite its stately grandeur, the centre of the city was not unaccustomed to scenes of protest. A rallying point for socialist rallies and suffragette marches before the war, in more recent times it had become a meeting place for the peace movement and anti-conscription leagues. But rarely before had George Square witnessed such an undercurrent of seething anger. Should this test case be lost, there would be no stopping the spiralling rent increases demanded by grasping landlords, no end to the exploitation and evictions. This went far beyond traditional complaints: this struck at hearth and home. It was only to be expected that huge crowds would congregate round the courts of justice, determined to see right done.

"Time to go in, dearest. I'll be in the gallery to cheer ye on." Squeezing his arm, she gently propelled him towards the steps leading up to the courthouse. At the top he turned, gave her a wave. There was a lump in her throat; furtively she dabbed at her cheek as he disappeared inside to answer to his name.

Yet Morag Mackay felt she had never been happier. Had Iain not pledged to set a date in the New Year? Since her discharge from hospital, he had encouraged her back to health, restored her lust for life. It was at his suggestion that she had abandoned the dreary factory in Clydebank in search of something more fulfilling. The scandal of the housing shortage in Glasgow gave her the outlet she craved.

With thousands of well-paid munitions workers pouring into the city, landlords could not resist the opportunity for profit. Her involvement had begun with the plight of a widow woman in the next close: her soldier husband killed at Ypres, five young children to bring up on her own, yet served with a warrant to quit on the flimsiest of excuses – rent arrears of less than twenty shillings. Along with other local women she had helped organise resistance to the eviction order, forming a human barrier to pelt the enforcement officers with bags of flour till they fled in disarray. The very next day she had pledged her services to the Glasgow Women's Housing Association.

And now her man was in the eye of the storm himself: he was among the score of rent strikers summonsed to appear before the sheriff that morning. The sum involved was not large, easily affordable on his wages, but that was not the point: it was a matter of principle, defending class values and living standards. Iain was a champion of the people, just like the patriots of old.

There was also something else about him these days. Nurse Lixmont had told her about the chance encounter at his mother's funeral. She was a classmate of his brother, staying with relatives in the area. It was only natural that they should have met. Yet any mention of her name made him flush with embarrassment. What was there to hide? Did he imagine that she would be consumed with jealousy? Her lips puckered into a wry smile.

She moved away from the court building. Makeshift platforms had been set up in the Square to allow speakers to address the throng. It went without saying that the GWHA would have its own stand; the rest of the committee would be waiting for her there.

"Morag! Over here!" It was Mary Barbour, leader of the movement in Govan. "Round this way. Climb up by those steps."

"Is there room for me?" She clambered up, to be received with hugs and kisses. "Sorry I'm a tad late. Have I missed anything?"

"Only Helen Crawfurd's speech. It was a real corker."

"That doesnae surprise me. I thought I heard the cheering. What was it you were saying, Helen?"

"Nothing special. I told them this is a woman's fight. We're not asking for money or charity. All we want is justice."

"There you are, Morag," chuckled Mary. "Just the stuff to gie the troops, would ye not say."

"Braw. I'd nae idea there'd be so many folk here. It's *Mrs Barbour's Army*, right enough."

"What did ye expect?" snapped Agnes Dollan, another of the leading lights. "There's twenty thousand on rent strike out there. They ken what's at stake. Look at the banners. If that doesnae get the message through, then nothin' will."

Morag nodded agreement. Slogans referring to *Landlord Tyranny, Huns at Home,* even *Prussians of Partick,* were calculated to make the authorities squirm: demands for *Fair Rents, Pre-War Levels, Municipal Ownership,* would rack up pressure for reform.

"It'll certainly make them sit up," she said thoughtfully. "But will it be enough? These bloodsuckers are a devious bunch. Look at how they've changed tactics. They're no' askin' for eviction this time. It's arrestment o' wages they want."

It was true enough. The customary practice was to seek a warrant of ejectment in the Sheriff Court, enforceable forty-eight hours later. To combat this, a network of local defence committees had sprung up over the past year, so well organised that a horde of angry women could be on the spot within minutes to prevent the eviction – by force if necessary. Now one of the biggest house factors had come up with a new ploy. Choosing his quarry well – not widows or the wives of soldiers, but highly paid shipyard and munitions workers – he was crafty enough to have the summons made out for the Small Debts Court. Treat the arrears as a debt, and the sheriff could rule that the sum owed be deducted from pay by the employer. What could be neater?

"Devil take it, Morag. There's no need to believe every lie you hear." Helen Crawfurd had no misgivings. "Fat chance the bosses would do the landlords' dirty work for them. They've enough bother with their workers as it is. Forbye they know fine that putting up rents is not in their interests. It would only encourage demands for even higher wages."

"No more than the last throw o' the dice," added Mrs Ferguson. She was the main driving force north of the river. "Thon factor must be desperate. But he's backin' the wrong horse if he thinks he'll get his rents that way. The politicians in London are already in a fair sweat. They're worried about the strikes spreadin' to other cities. They'll want to put the lid on this as soon as they can."

"So you see we're bound to win through." Mary Barbour patted her arm reassuringly. "The factors will be hung out to dry – along wi' their paymasters. Now it's high time we were away in for the fun and games."

The courtroom was packed, the public benches crammed almost to overflowing. The accused had taken their places in the dock, though it was a tight squeeze to fit them all in, and were chatting quietly amongst themselves. By stark contrast the prosecution bench stood sombre and untenanted. And the sheriff had yet to make his entrance. The trial was going to be late in starting. The handful of ushers, charged with maintaining the dignity of the court, hovered uncertainly in the background, powerless to prevent ribald comments about the judge and justice system.

But at long last it appeared that the interminable waiting was over. Robed clerks were filing in, lawyers taking their places. The cry: "All rise", went up, and a gowned and bewigged figure entered, bowed and settled himself on his high chair, apparently oblivious to the ironic cheers which greeted his appearance. There was a loud call for silence, and the audience quietened down to follow the proceedings.

Sheriff Lee began with a plea for moderation. Feelings were running high, he acknowledged, and it was difficult to see how justice could be served in such an atmosphere. An adjournment might be for the best, a continuation of the case until the intentions of the government became known. Subsequent legislation might well affect his judgement. The prosecution had raised no objection. Would the defence also agree? There was a low growl from the public gallery at this blatant attempt to fob them off; then a sudden hush as the agent for the Tenants' Defence Association rose slowly to his lectern. He bobbed respectfully, and then launched into a virulent condemnation of any suggestion of postponement. His clients had already forfeited a day's pay, not to mention the loss of valuable war output. Could any further upheaval be tolerated? The case must be heard or abandoned that very day.

Morag felt her wrist grasped convulsively. Helen Crawfurd, trembling with suppressed excitement, was whispering in her ear. "That's it! It's all over bar the shouting."

"How can you tell?"

"Stands to reason. There's no way they could allow a conviction now. Watch!" she hissed.

It soon became apparent that Helen was right. In vain did the prosecution press its claim that the proprietors were also the victims of wartime inflation. Compared with the appeal to patriotism, to the need for all sections of society to make sacrifices in the country's hour of need, there was little counsel could do but bow to the inevitable and withdraw as gracefully as possible. The decision was cheered to the echo; scenes of wild jubilation soon extended to the thousands waiting outside. The owners and factors had lost in this last bid to assert legal supremacy. The sheriff's words of praise for the benevolence and forbearance of the landlords were swept away in the euphoria; he was only too thankful to beat a hasty retreat to the sanctuary of his chambers.

The defendants emerged into George Square to universal acclaim. But the plaudits did not last long; the crowd, ever fickle, was soon distracted elsewhere. Someone had jumped onto a nearby platform, his booming voice instantly audible. Iain swivelled round to catch the new attraction. John Maclean! Trust him not to miss an opportunity. They must strike while the iron was hot, he was declaiming. Communication should be made with London, summoning the government to forbid any rent increases for the duration of the war. If such a guarantee was not forthcoming within a week, then a general strike should be called. He waved his fist, as though brandishing the very telegram itself: in response he was rewarded with a deep throated roar of approval. Then the multitude began to disperse, melting away homewards, happy with the day's victory.

"That's Maclean for ye." Iain felt a tap on his shoulder. "All talk and no action. It'll be his epitaph."

"Stan! I might have known you'd be around somewhere. Dae ye have to sneak up on folk like this?"

"Och, I didnae want to spoil your moment o' glory, Iain. Forbye, it's my business to ken what's goin' on." He laughed sardonically. "There he goes – the high priest o' socialism. Away to the Post Office to send off his message – I don't think."

"I think that's a bit harsh, Stan. The man's just lost his job as a schoolmaster. And he's due to serve a spell in clink."

"More fool him." Robertson shrugged his shoulders. "It's only for five days. What's that?"

"But d'ye no' think that Maclean might have a point? This has united the masses like nothin' else in the past. It could be the start o' somethin' much bigger."

Robertson shook his head. "No, laddie, I do not. It's almost certain the government will step in and fix the rents. That's the strength o' the plutocrats – knowin' when to make a few empty concessions. What do they care if some petty bourgeois property holders get trampled underfoot? Only control of the means of production will bring down the state. Concentrate on that."

Was this a rebuke? Stan obviously considered the rent strikes a side issue.

"Ah well, what's done is done. Is that no' yer lass over there?"

Iain spun round. There she was at last, threading her way towards them.

"What a crush," she bemoaned. "I thought I'd never find you." She gave Iain a peck on the cheek, and then remembered her manners. "Mr Robertson. This is a pleasant surprise."

"Stan, please", he remonstrated, taking her outstretched hand. "You're looking bonnier than ever, Morag. Iain's a lucky man. I hear congratulations are in order."

"Thank you," she simpered. "Though I think I'm the lucky one."

"If ye say so. But I hae my doubts." He smiled, to show he spoke in jest. "Anyhow I mustn't keep you any longer. Enjoy the rest o' yer day." He touched his cap and turned away. A moment later he had disappeared from view.

"What was all that about, Iain? Has he been getting on at ye again?"

"Och, just the usual. He says the rent campaign is a red herring – a waste o' time and effort. It'll never lead to anythin' worthwhile. Takin' over the factories an' yards is what he wants. Nothin' else matters."

"I like that! Does he think he's the great panjandrum? We've struck a blow for basic rights. What has he done so far? Is he jealous, d'ye think?"

Iain grinned. "No, I widnae suppose so. Maybe he's a bit set in his ways. His gospel is the only road to socialism. He'll have nae argument about that."

"That's what worries me. Look at the way he treats you. You're just a tool to him. He'll string ye along, and then toss ye aside whenever it suits his purpose."

"Stan Robertson? He's straight as a die. And he'd always put the movement first."

"All the more reason to watch yer back."

"Really, Morag," he protested. "Just because ye dinnae like him."

"Fine, Iain." She held up her hand in mock surrender. "I've said my piece. Now what shall we do this afternoon?"

"That's more like it. What about a turn in the park? I could do wi' some fresh air after being cooped up in thon stuffy court."

"Just what I was thinking. And after that we could have a bite to eat and a dander round the West End." She took great care not to reveal her true intentions. There was a little jewellery shop just off Sauchiehall Street. It was high time he made a down payment on his promise.

* * *

London. December 1915

Whitehall Gardens was a quiet street of pleasant townhouses tucked away behind the imposing facades of the great offices of state in Westminster. Scarcely suitable for government purposes, or so it was thought; but a rapidly expanding wartime regime had to make use of whatever accommodation was available. No. 6 was typical: the residence of a man of letters, commandeered earlier in the year and allocated to the newly created Ministry of Munitions. The surroundings might be unimpressive, but the power of the department was almost limitless.

Or was it? The law might confer authority, but its application was another matter. The minister himself, Mr David Lloyd George, scowled as he pondered the issue. Efficient use of the nation's resources was vital, new working practices essential: that was obvious if victory was to be won. But not, apparently, to skilled artisans determined to cling to outmoded craft methods. It was imperative to make them see the error of their ways, to accept the introduction of less skilled workmates. But how best to proceed? It was a tricky problem. To be acclaimed as the *Welsh Wizard* was all very well, but he was only too conscious how his reputation would sink like a stone should he fail to pull some rabbit from the hat. Why, he might even be forced to resign, like Winston at the Admiralty. His jaw set hard at the prospect.

The officials round the table exchanged glances. The chief was like a bear with a sore head – obviously still piqued at his reception on Clydeside the previous week. His efforts to charm the recalcitrant workmen had ended in humiliation. And now he would be looking to throw the blame onto others. No doubt this accounted for the summons so late on New Year's Eve. His subordinates braced themselves for the inevitable recriminations.

"As you are well aware, gentlemen, I have had to fight tooth and nail every step of the way since leadership of this department was thrust upon me. War Office hostility, obstruction within the civil service, pig-headed employers, hidebound attitudes from the trade unions – I have had to deal with them all. Remember how it was the first time I walked into this very room? Nothing but a table and couple of chairs. And they even tried to take these away."

Heads nodded in dutiful agreement. It was a familiar refrain when the minister felt things were not going entirely to plan.

"And now this." His Welsh lilt became a little more strident. "Just when we were beginning to make real progress in setting industry on a proper war footing. Are we to allow our objective to be sabotaged to satisfy the vanity of radical socialists on the Clyde?" He glowered round the room.

"Of course not, sir." His three principal aides hastened to reassure him. But Lloyd George was not so readily appeased.

"All very well for you to say that," he grumbled. "But how? That's the question. It's my neck on the block," he added. "I've been badly let down."

Sir Hubert Llewellyn Smith raised his eyebrows. It was his duty to defend his department. But tact would be required. He knew his minister as well as anyone in Whitehall, ever since they had worked together at the Board of Trade.

"Sir, the situation on Clydeside is complex. You have laboured tirelessly to achieve an amicable resolution. No man could have done more. But conciliation has been met with obduracy. All attempts at negotiation have failed. Your controller of munitions in Scotland believes the labour movement has fallen into the hands of red revolutionaries."

"Weir? I've heard he's calling for industrial conscription, military discipline in the workplace. Boost production by threatening to shoot strikers? Is that what you want?"

"If I might say a word, sir?" It was Beveridge, another long standing adviser from his days at the Treasury.

"By all means. So long as you are not about to suggest another half-baked scheme."

"Not at all, sir. Weir may go too far in his views, but they are not entirely without merit. I agree with Sir Hubert. We have been over lenient in our approach. Parliament has given us the authority. We should apply the full force of the regulations. Other centres of munitions have accepted them. Why should the Clyde be an exception?"

Lloyd George stroked his moustache. The sense of the meeting seemed to be moving towards compulsion. But it went against the grain to concede the point – at least not before all options had been thoroughly explored. And he still had a bone to pick. Damned if he would allow his officials to wriggle off the hook so easily.

"Throughout my political life I have always trusted to the power of persuasion rather than the force of duress. Cooperation, not intimidation, has always been my watchword. I have always been prepared to listen, to do whatever I can to redress just grievances."

"Yes, and look at the result. The people of Glasgow complain about unfair rent increases: you freeze rents for the duration of the war. You pay them a goodwill visit: they give you the cold shoulder."

The speaker was rewarded with an icy stare. It was Rey, third in the ministry hierarchy. Too late he realised his mistake. Lloyd George rounded on him.

"And whose fault was that? Why was I not properly briefed as to the mood on Clydeside? I understood that the trade unions had everything in hand. All that was required was a brief visit to seal an agreement on dilution. Yet what did I find? The unions had lost all control over their own membership. It appears that the shop stewards rule the roost, defying any attempt to improve efficiency. Clyde Workers Committee – that's what they call their organisation. I had never even heard the name till I arrived in Glasgow. What are your minions doing up there? Don't they know what's going on?"

"Highly regrettable, Minister." Llewellyn Smith was as urbane as ever. "Nevertheless the remainder of your tour was very successful. Sheffield and Tyneside –"

"Be that as it may, the most important part was botched from start to finish. You allowed me to go naked into the lion's den." He wagged his finger accusingly. "My keynote speech was postponed for forty-eight hours. Why? No one could provide any explanation. I endeavoured to make use of the interval by going round factories to speak with the workers' representatives, yet in most cases the door was slammed in my face. Where they did condescend to receive me, I was met with nothing but personal abuse. That fellow at Parkhead –"

"David Kirkwood, sir. Chief shop steward at Beardmores," said Beveridge hastily, anxious to show that he at least had taken the trouble to familiarise himself with the report.

"Just so. He introduced me as an enemy of the workers. Told the others I was a lawyer, and that one engineer was worth a dozen like me."

"A little embarrassing, perhaps," murmured Llewellyn Smith. "But hardly worth your concern. Treat it as part of the cut and thrust of political debate."

"You think so? After all I've done to improve the lot of the common people." He managed to restrain his temper. "If that were the only slight I might agree with you. But it was only the start. I subsequently learned that by some trick the shop stewards had gained access to the admission tickets for my address on Christmas Day. So much for the hand-picked audience I was promised. I had to go cap in hand to their committee room to appeal for a fair hearing. One of their leaders was the most obnoxious man it has ever been my misfortune to encounter. He had the temerity to brandish his fist right under my nose, sneering that dilution had no chance unless it was under the direction of the CWC. He actually demanded workers' control of industry. Gallacher!" He almost spat it out. "I won't forget his name."

"A trying experience, I admit." Beveridge smiled disarmingly. "All the more to your credit that you attempted to reason with the malcontents."

"Reason?" The minister gave a hollow laugh. "Look what happened when I arrived at the St. Andrew's Hall on Christmas morning. Rarely, if ever, have I experienced such a hostile audience. It was fortunate that the balcony had been blocked with barricades, and the stage ringed with policemen. Otherwise I might have been physically assaulted. As it was, they were howling like wolves, baying for blood – three thousand of them, I was told. My speech was drowned out by constant heckling. Then one of them jumped up and tried to make a revolutionary statement. That was the final straw. There was nothing to be done but walk out. I felt mortified. Such an indignity for a minister of the crown."

"Iniquitous," agreed Llewellyn Smith. "But I trust you are not going to hold the ministry responsible for the actions of miscreants and ne'er-do-wells."

"That, to say the very least, is debatable. I should have been provided with a more moderate – more representative assembly. It was a mistake on your part to leave the arrangements to the trade unions. But what I object to most is – this." He tugged a package from an inside pocket and tossed it onto the table.

The others stared at the object in bewilderment. Then Rey reached over and smoothed it open. It was a newspaper. In bold type was the title: *Forward*.

"I was given to understand that the local press had been instructed that only the text of my speech to the munitions workers was to be reported. In particular, any mention of possible disturbances in and around the venue was to be avoided at all costs. Was that not the case?"

"I believe so, sir. The Press Bureau would have issued a statutory notice to all publications." Rey confirmed the standard procedure.

"Then how do you account for the appearance of this – journal on the streets of Glasgow today? It makes little reference to the content of my speech. Indeed it gives a detailed and, in my view, highly coloured description of the radicals and their performance. They are portrayed as some kind of folk heroes, while I am castigated as the villain of the piece. The whole thing amounts to a scurrilous attack on the work of this ministry. It reeks of sedition."

Llewellyn Smith stiffened. "I have every confidence in my officials. There has been no breakdown in communications from this end. However, I cannot answer for other agencies. The Scottish Office …"

He was interrupted by a quiet cough. "I am amazed," said Beveridge, taking up the paper, "at such a flagrant breach of the censorship regulations. Both publisher and editor must be prosecuted without delay."

"Hmm. I'm not convinced that entirely fits the bill." In an instant Lloyd George was the calculating politician once more. "Yet we cannot simply ignore the provocation. It would only give them an inflated sense of their own importance. God knows the depths of defiance that might result as a consequence." He turned to his parliamentary undersecretary, the only member of the group yet to speak. "You've been very quiet, Addison. What do you have to say?"

"Since you ask, sir, in my view it would do no harm to seek expert opinion before coming to a final decision. Obtain the latest intelligence. Listen to someone with his ear to the ground."

"Can you conjure up such a person?"

"I hope so. When first informed of your intentions, sir, I took the liberty of communicating with Glasgow. The man I had in mind took the next train. He's here now, awaiting your pleasure."

"You're not going to inflict another of Weir's dogsbodies on me, are you? I don't think I could take any more of his ranting."

"By no means. He has no direct connection with this department."

"Really? In that case we might hear some sense for a change. Wheel him in."

Dr Addison touched a bell. "By the way, his name is Dunlop."

Heads turned to scrutinise the visitor as he strode into the room. Lloyd George grunted. First impressions were distinctly favourable. A youngish man with something of a military bearing: respectful, attentive, but with an air of easy confidence. Not the type to make the mistake of trying to ingratiate himself, he decided. Military Intelligence? Police Special Branch? Either was possible. Perhaps he might pull that rabbit after all.

"Glad you were able to join us Mr Dunlop. Or should I address you by rank?"

"Just Dunlop, sir." The issue was deftly sidestepped.

Lloyd George smiled. "*Touché*. As you wish – Dunlop. You must be fatigued after such a long journey. Won't you be seated?"

"Thank you, sir. I prefer to stand."

"Very well. Have you seen this paper?" He jabbed a finger at the offending object.

The newcomer gave it a cursory glance. "Yes, sir. It's the current issue of the *Forward*. I obtained a copy just before I left Glasgow."

"What do you make of it?"

Dunlop considered his reply. "Well sir, it must be admitted that this is by no means the most pernicious example of the socialist press on Clydeside. However, its report on your visit is undoubtedly inflammatory. You would be quite within your rights to have all copies of the newspaper seized and its offices closed down – at least till it promises to mend its ways."

"What about a prosecution?"

"Not necessary. An order under the Defence of the Realm Act should suffice. It would serve as a warning shot to the militants whilst ensuring that any immediate protest should be fairly muted."

"How do you make that out?" asked Beveridge.

"If I might explain, sir. The *Forward* is the organ of the ILP – the Independent Labour Party. It is anti-war, but rejects violence as a means of resistance. As such, there is little love lost between the ILP and the extreme socialists. The BSP and SLP despise the moderates as fellow travellers, prepared to live with the capitalist system in exchange for a few token concessions."

"BSP? SLP?" queried Lloyd George.

"British Socialist Party and Socialist Labour Party. These are the real red revolutionaries. And I can assure you they would not lift a finger to save this paper."

"Really, Dunlop. The politics in your neck of the woods. So arcane, like a Byzantine intrigue. Worse than the bickering in the House of Commons." He chuckled at his own joke.

"I wouldn't know about that, sir. But divisions in the socialist movement are to our advantage. Best estimates show only a hundred or so activists trying to stir up dissent. And no more than twenty thousand in the skilled trades prepared to resist dilution."

"So Weir and his acolytes are simply scaremongering with their talk of revolution?"

Dunlop pursed his lips. "I would not go that far," he said cautiously. "There is an undercurrent of dissent on the Clyde. But at the moment it lacks a clear focus. Look at the background to the recent troubles. Opposition to the war? Anger at war profiteering? Concern at the rising cost of living? These cannot be denied. But more than anything else the unrest is motivated by a perceived threat to the status of craft workers."

"Are you certain it goes no deeper?"

"I see it like this, sir. As yet the extremists have made very limited headway in recruiting dedicated adherents. They are faced with a basic paradox. A major challenge to the authority of the state would involve building mass support for a general strike. This would involve the formation of a huge industrial union embracing all grades of worker. Yet their core is based upon artisans determined to uphold a privileged position. They would never willingly accept equality of labour. Thus far the radicals have been unable to find a means of squaring the circle."

"But could that ever happen?"

"Nothing is impossible, sir. And circumstances do alter cases. The war, for example ..."

"What about the war?"

"I was about to say that if by some mischance our coming offensive on the Western Front was to become bogged down, if the Germans were to inflict unacceptable casualties, if their submarines were to cut off our sea lanes – "

"Then the result might be civil strife. You paint a gloomy picture, young man. I fully expect 1916 to be the year of victory. Still, you may have a point. It would be prudent to prepare for all eventualities, however unlikely. Have you any suggestions?"

"I have given the matter some thought, sir. I take it that your priority is the imposition of dilution throughout the Clyde area."

"Undoubtedly. It is no exaggeration to say that the whole war effort hinges upon its successful implementation. I have tried persuasion. To no avail, I fear."

"In that case my inclination would be towards the adoption of a piecemeal approach. Stealth, rather than the heavy hand, might prove more effective."

"I'm intrigued. You have a plan?"

"I think it might be managed, sir. Not all the munitions works are equally militant. I would begin with those where the workforce appears least under the sway of the agitators. Bring them on board one by one. By isolating the most intransigent you undermine the strength of resistance. That would make the hardest nuts easier to crack."

"All very well. But how would you start the ball rolling in the first place?" Addison voiced the obvious flaw. "And what about the zealots among the shop stewards? How do you deal with them? They would hardly be willing to relinquish their influence in the workplace."

"Perhaps they might be induced to believe that their role would remain undiminished."

"A subterfuge, you mean? How would you achieve that?"

"If you were to appoint local commissioners to go round the individual works, sit down with the men's representatives –"

"Then what?"

"It would be necessary to give the impression of full consultation in devising a scheme appropriate to the particular circumstances of each shop or yard. Give a reassurance of no loss of status for the skilled men – they would become supervisors of the machine minders. Any case of grievance would go to arbitration. And there would be a promise of return to the status quo after the war."

"But surely that would give the shop stewards even more influence," protested Llewellyn Smith. "They would be practically running the whole show."

"The most important step is to have dilution accepted in principle." For the first time Dunlop permitted himself a fleeting smile. "However, that does not mean that any agreement is necessarily set in stone. Slight adjustments to working practices may be required from time to time. A gradual turning of the screw on the part of management …"

"Yes, but are you certain this will work?" Beveridge sounded dubious. "Think of the scope for confrontation. Any flashpoint could set off the whole of Clydeside."

"There is a risk. Though once in operation, concerted industrial action against dilution would be difficult to organise. And any attempt would provide a golden opportunity to deal with the hard core once and for all."

"Would that not make things worse? Martyrdom is what they seek."

"I agree that the adverse publicity of mass arrests, fines and imprisonment would probably have that effect. But that is not the path I would take."

"And how would you proceed?" Lloyd George leaned forward attentively.

"Internal exile. You have the power to direct labour. We know the identities of the ringleaders. I would have half a dozen quietly picked up and deported – well away from the Clyde where they have no following."

"And should any of them attempt to return?"

"In that case the law would impose the appropriate penalty. I doubt they would welcome imprisonment in an area where they are unknown. They would be starved of the oxygen of publicity."

Lloyd George beamed. "Well, young man, you appear to have everything worked out. You have certainly given us much food for thought." Rising to his feet he came round the table to grasp Dunlop by the hand. "I'm most grateful. Your contribution has been invaluable. And now we mustn't detain you further. You have a comfortable hotel? Good. Addison, perhaps you might show our young friend out. A safe journey back to Glasgow tomorrow.

And a prosperous New Year. Goodbye."

He resumed his seat and waited till the undersecretary had returned to his place. "Highly impressive, Addison. You are to be congratulated on finding him. What is known about the fellow?"

"Bear with me a second, sir." He consulted a small notebook. "Good county family. Commissioned into the Lanarkshire Constabulary 1904. Promoted, joined the Glasgow Force 1906. Transferred to Special Branch 1910. Liaison with Secret Service Bureau 1912. Since then –"

"All right, Addison, no need to say more. I have the picture. Still," he mused, "his obvious talents may be more usefully employed elsewhere. We must keep him in mind."

EIGHTEEN

… Lose a Battle

Glasgow. April 1916

Iain Baird trudged homewards through the backstreets of Govan. The crowd he had harangued outside the yard that afternoon had been pitifully small. Yet could he really fault the men for choosing the better part of valour and returning to work? There were rumours that martial law was about to be declared. What was certain was that nine of the leading shop stewards had been arrested. They had simply disappeared – some said under military guard to an unknown destination. Were others marked down for the same fate? Iain felt a prickle of sweat under his collar. The CWC was like a rudderless ship now. It might soon be every man for himself.

He grimaced at the change in fortunes. Had they not made the government quake? Sent Lloyd George packing with a flea in his ear? Had it all been for nothing? But of course they were only the spearhead. Victory in the class struggle depended on the support of the masses. Yet somehow this had failed to materialise. The introduction of military conscription in January should have caused uproar on Clydeside, but had been imposed with barely a whimper. As for the propaganda war … what chance did they really stand? The might of the populist press was relentless in its persecution, lambasting strikers as selfish and unpatriotic, hinting that the leadership danced to German paymasters. The voice of socialism was muted by comparison; and even that had been effectively muzzled by means of censorship and suppression, police raids and charges of sedition. The ruling class had merely to flex its muscle …

The evening twilight had almost completely faded by the time he reached Brighton Road. In a way he was glad: the gloom matched his mood, gave him a cloak of anonymity. For a moment he wondered whether he had been followed; others had spoken of being shadowed by detectives. Ah well, too late to bother about it now. What did Robertson make of it all? Come to think of it, where the hell was Stan? He had scarcely been seen for nigh on a month. Had he been lifted? Unlikely – they would have heard something. Most probably he had caught the straws in the wind, gone to ground somewhere. Small comfort in that, he thought savagely. It was hard to believe Stan Robertson could leave him in the lurch. But maybe Morag had been right about him. At least she was loyal and dependable.

He turned into the inky darkness of the close, felt his way along the unlit passage and began to clamber up the stairs. On the landing he paused to fish out his key, then twisted it in the lock and pushed the door open. Christ Almighty! He swore in surprise. The lobby was as black as pitch – not a chink of light to be seen. On the threshold he listened intently. Not a sound – only the ominous tick of the hallstand clock. The house was deserted. Surely Morag had not gone out at this hour. Then another thought struck him. Had she met with some accident? Been taken poorly again? Impulsively he made for the kitchen, felt for the switch on the wall. The room was instantly bathed in electric light.

It took a few seconds to adjust to the glare. She was sitting with her back to him, rigid as a statue. His glance took in the hearth, cold and cheerless; then turned towards the table, still bare in its oilcloth covering. Nothing had been prepared for his evening meal. He did not know whether to be angry or alarmed.

"What's the matter? How come ye're sittin' in the dark like this?" He came round the table to confront her.

She looked up. Her face was puffed; she had been crying. But now her eyes were hard as flint. "Sit yerself down." Her voice was bitter. "You've some explainin' to do."

"Oh aye." He tried to appear unconcerned as he tossed aside his cap and muffler. "Fire away. What have I done now?"

"Take a look in front of yer nose."

Jesus! Before her lay a tiny circlet of metal. It was the ring he had bought her.

"Aye, it is that serious."

"But – I dinnae understand. What the hell is this?"

"Ye don't know? Well, let me enlighten you." She gave a sour smile. "This forenoon I was up at Kelvingrove. Tenants' Association business, if ye must know. I was takin' a short cut through the park. Ye'll never guess who I happened to meet there."

"I dare say I'm goin' to find out."

"That ye are," she said grimly. "It was that nurse o' yours. Pushin' a perambulator, would ye believe. Well, of course I went over to pass the time o' day. Funny thing was that she didnae seem very pleased to see me. But she could hardly deny me a wee keek at the wean, no' when I was goin' to handsel him wi' a bit o' silver. There he was, fast asleep. Such a bonnie, cherub face. And, dae ye ken, I couldnae help thinkin' there was somethin' familiar about it." She nodded meaningfully.

Iain went white with shock. "Did – did she say anythin'?" he managed to stammer.

"No. But she took fright. Almost pushed me out o' the way. She muttered somethin' about nanny waitin' wi' his feed. Then she took off like the clappers. Gey curious, d'ye no' think? So when I got hame I started to put two and two thegither –"

"And got five," he said desperately. "It's no' my brat, if that's what ye're thinkin'. Word o' honour. Did she say it was?"

"She'd hardly admit it. But actions speak louder than words. She was ashamed. That's why she ran away. And there was a definite resemblance." The look of scorn seemed to bore into him. "Can ye deny it? Ye're like a cat on hot bricks."

"You'd be helluva jumpy if you were accused like this. Look, Morag, I'll tell ye what I ken. It should explain any likeness."

"Go on, then. Make it sound good."

"It's gospel, for God's sake. Her folks think that Alastair is the faither. After all, he went about wi' her for long enough."

"Oh aye. Very convenient. And just how dae you ken this? Did they see fit to confide in you?"

"Of course no'. It was Alastair. He wrote me a letter – it would be about the time the war started. Telt me the parents held him responsible. They were goin' to have him disgraced – chucked out o' college, or some such thing. He asked me to take the blame, let him off the hook."

"And what did you do? Dae ye still hae the letter?"

"Dinnae be daft. I tore it up. If my brother gets a body into trouble he can take the consequences. Damned cheek he had."

"And you expect me to believe that?"

"As God is my witness. Will that no' convince ye?"

Alastair – a rake and a cheat? From what she had seen he was an innocent where girls were concerned, and certainly too upright to think of passing the buck. If he had written, there could be only one reason why he had done so. And Iain had the gall to sit there, begging her to accept this cock and bull story. She was only too aware he had the rutting instinct of a polecat. Yet ... for all his faults, her heart still ached for him. He was still finding excuses to put off their wedding day. This was her chance to nail him down. Once they were married things would be different. The responsibility of fatherhood ... She picked up the ring, began to roll it between her thumb and forefinger. "Well," she said slowly, "I suppose I might –"

"Anybody home?"

She broke off in alarm. God Almighty! The call came from the hallway. Someone was in the house. For an instant Iain stiffened. Was it the police after him? But then he relaxed a little. The peelers would have made more commotion.

"Sorry," he muttered sheepishly. "Must have left the front door open. Nae need to panic. I'll see who it is."

Moments later he returned. "It's Stan Robertson. Come to see me. I'll take him ben. Ye'll no' be disturbed."

"No!" She flared up. "If Mr Robertson has anythin' to say, then I want to hear it."

"Might be as well, laddie." Robertson appeared at the doorway. "Save time later on. I left my kit in the lobby. Hope ye dinnae mind."

"'Course no', Stan. Come awa' an' make yersel' at home."

"Thanks, Iain. I'll be glad to take the weight off my feet for a minute." He dropped into the vacant place at the table. "That's better. You should take more care, the pair o' ye. You never know who might be about at night."

"Ye didnae come here just to tell us that," snapped Morag. Her nerves were starting to fray. Bad enough to have him pay a visit at the best of times. But now... Her nose wrinkled in distaste. He was unkempt, his face grey with stubble; and the whiff of stale sweat was unmistakable. This was a man on the run. And his unexpected appearance did not bode well.

"Always to the point, aren't ye, Morag? That's what I like about you. Ye're

366

right, of course. I came to gie ye the news. Brace yersel', Iain. We've been dished. Ye'll have heard about the shop stewards."

"Aye. Deported – God kens where."

"Oh, I can tell you that. It's Edinburgh. And that's no' the end o' it. Now they've got the upper hand, the capitalists and their lackeys are set on crushin' us once and for all. Fines and exile are no' enough to satisfy them. So they've decided on show trials in the High Court. For a start Muir and Gallacher are to be had up on that sedition charge."

"I didnae realise that."

Robertson shrugged. "It was always on the cards. That article they wrote: *Should the Workers Arm?* They say it was inciting disaffection, encouraging soldiers to mutiny. Who better to hang out to dry? There's always Maclean, of course. He's already banged up in Edinburgh Castle, lookin' forward to his day in court. Another audience for him to lecture. Much good it'll do him. Could be the three o' them will be put away for years."

"But surely there'll be an outcry if that happens."

"I doubt it, Iain. Everyone's runnin' scared. There's other trials in the pipeline. It's no' worth the risk."

"I see. And what about you, Stan?"

"Oh, they huvnae forgotten yours truly. Lucky I was forewarned. But the bobbies are on my tail now. Not too far behind either."

"What about Iain?" Morag was consumed by a sudden dread. "Have ye heard anythin' about him?"

Robertson shook his head. "Nary a thing, lass. He's no' on any list, as far as I ken. But dinnae let that fool ye. Even if the law isnae after him, Findlay at the Ordnance has a long memory. Sooner or later he'll want his pound o' flesh."

"Ach, I'm no' bothered about auld Findlay."

"Then ye should be. I've telt ye often enough. Never underestimate the nobs. We've lost a battle. Time for a wise man to lay low for a while."

"Sorry, Stan. Ye're right, of course. But I cannae help thinkin' we made things easy for them. We had the bosses on toast at the start o' the year. I can understand that the masses werena ready to follow us. They were bought off wi' a few trinkets. The rent strike was a false dawn, I can see that now. But the Workers' Committee could have insisted on control o' the shop floor as the price for dilution. But we didnae. Instead we shot ourselves in the foot. Yon bastard at Parkhead has a lot to answer for."

"Aye, ye might have a point there. I always did think o' Davie Kirkwood as the weak link. He never really believed in industrial unionism. Couldnae see the bigger picture. Things might have been different had he chosen no' to break ranks."

"That all ye've got to say? He was the enemy within. He near enough destroyed us."

"Och, I wouldnae go that far. He's more a fool than a knave. Vanity is his besettin' sin. The dilution commissioners were crafty – I'll gie them that. Playin' on his weakness, makin' him believe it was his scheme. They took him for a right sucker. Once they had the biggest works on Clydeside in the bag, what chance for the rest?"

"Exactly. They could afford to pick us off one by one. He went away and struck a deal behind our backs. We were left to scrabble in the dirt."

He lapsed into moody silence, recalling the growing indignities inflicted on the shop stewards once dilution had been accepted. As new demands were made of the workforce, so grievances had multiplied – only to be ignored, or casually dismissed, or become hopelessly entangled in the endless arbitration process. Had there been a deliberate intention to goad them into precipitate action? It certainly appeared so.

Robertson seemed to divine his thoughts. "I ken how ye feel, son. They've played their cards well."

"So what? The great panjandrum ca's a strike in a fit o' pique. Doesnae bother to consult anyone else first. But he expects the rest o' us to jump to attention when he chaps on the door. Bloody cheek! Nae wonder the whole thing went off at half-cock. Look at how many refused to come out. Why should they support him after he left us in the lurch? And now we have to suffer the consequences of his folly."

"Haud on, Iain. We're all a bit down at the minute. But our time will come again. This is just a setback. They cannae hide behind appeals to patriotism and sacrifice forever. There's only so much folk can take. Wait till it gets too much to bear. Then there'll be blood on the streets."

"But how much longer will that be?"

"A year. Eighteen months at most. I should be back by then."

"Back?" queried Morag.

"Well, I cannae stay here. I'll be nae good to man nor beast in clink."

"So where will ye go? England, maybe?"

"Naw, hen. A lot further away. I'm for Leith. There's a ship sailin' for Sweden the morn. I'll be on it." He sat back in his chair, savouring the blank looks of astonishment. "Thought that would surprise ye. I'll bet ye're wonderin' what's so special about Sweden. It's no' even in the war. Well, I'll tell ye. The answer is – nothin'. But it's the best way to get to Russia."

Russia? Now he had them totally foxed. Endless icy wastes, men clad in furs from head to toe; a miserable, downtrodden peasantry barely out of serfdom; famine, riots and pogroms; fearsome Cossacks mercilessly charging down peaceful protesters; a huge empire under the sway of an all-powerful autocrat: that was their picture of Russia. Who on earth would want to visit such an alien world?

Robertson chuckled. "You think I'm daft, Iain. But ye're wrong. I've never been more serious. Stop for a minute. You'll find it does make sense."

"I cannae for the life o' me see how, Stan."

"Then let me explain." He leaned forward again. "I dinnae need to remind you that imperialism is the last stage o' capitalism. And that the imperialist powers are knockin' hell out o' each other in their struggle for survival. It winnae be long afore one o' them cracks, and once that happens, the others will be dragged down as well."

"Aye, but –"

"Hear me out, son. Marx reckoned that socialism was the inevitable product of advanced capitalism. He thought Germany would probably lead the way. Russia was a backward feudal society, no' even worthy of consideration. But things have changed since his day. Have ye any idea o' the pace of industrialisation in Russia? What they've done in twenty years took us a century or more. Towns growing by leaps and bounds, peasants sucked in from the countryside in their millions. They've got some o' the biggest factories in the world – and some o' the worst conditions. Do ye realise what that means? An industrial proletariat – discontented wi' their lot, cryin' out to be organised and led."

"I see what ye're sayin', Stan. But d'ye really think Russia is ripe for the chop?"

"They'll be the first. They've suffered worse in this war than anyone else. Defeat after defeat, horrendous losses, the Germans makin' huge inroads

369

into their territory. Morale must be at rock bottom. Now if the ruling classes turn against the Tsar –"

"He and his ilk would be forced out."

"Aye. He'd be finished. Nae doubt the capitalists would be the first to jump in – declare a new regime, promise a democratic constitution. That's the bourgeoisie for ye. They'd have their day, but it widnae last long. Wi'out the support o' the workers, peasants and soldiers they would have nae authority. It wouldnae take long for the people to realise their strength, organise themselves, turn to socialism as the only way. God sakes, Iain, the proletariat could seize power within months. What's to stop them?" His voice cracked with emotion. "And I'll be there to see it happen."

Morag could not resist a snide remark. "Sounds very excitin', Mr Robertson," she said primly. "I wish ye joy o' it."

He chose to ignore the sarcasm. "Very kind o' ye, I'm sure. But I'm no' just goin' to observe. Maybe I could help out somewhere. At least I'd hope to make contacts, pick up some tips. Ye never know when it might come in useful."

"I'm sure you'll be in yer element there." She smiled sweetly.

Iain flashed a warning look. "And just where will ye be stayin' in Russia, Stan?" he asked hurriedly.

"Oh, Petrograd, of course. That's what they call the capital these days. The action's bound to start there. Ye ken, Iain," he went on, "you and I make a good team. We could both learn a lot. There's an extra berth on that ship. I'd like it if ye came wi' me."

There was a gasp of horror. Morag could scarcely believe she had heard aright.

"I mean it. Ye'll regret it for the rest o' your life if ye dinnae go. And mind what I said about Findlay. I'll no' be here to protect ye."

So this was why he had turned up like a bad penny: to steal her man away, lure him into unknown dangers, put his life at risk. Chances were that Iain might never return. She wanted to shout out, beg him not to be enticed; but all she could manage was a mute appeal.

Robertson caught her expression. "It's for the good o' the cause, lass." He turned back to Iain. "Maybe ye'd like to talk it over wi' Morag. I'll wait out in the lobby. But dinnae be long. We'll need to be off within the hour."

They were left staring bleakly at each other. Iain fidgeted uneasily, dropped his eyes: he seemed flustered, unsure of himself, torn between temptation and doubt. All she could do was bite her lips and wait. Then his brow cleared. Without a word he strode past her, into the hallway. She heard muffled voices, the sound of the door; then silence. Within a minute he was back – alone.

"I telt Stan it wisnae on. I couldnae up sticks and leave ye. My place is here – whatever the future holds."

"Thank God," she sobbed. "I thought I'd lost ye."

"Nae chance. Stan might think he kens a'thing. But Russia? I'm no' convinced. It'll be years afore it's ready for socialism. Even if he is right, what good could we do there? We cannae even speak the lingo. It's nothin' but a wild goose chase. It's here that the revolution has to be made."

"Was – was he very angry?"

"Naw. Just accepted it. Said he looked forward to bein' comrades in arms again when he came back. I ken he's upset you But he's gone now. Dry yer eyes and gie us a smile."

"I'll be fine in a jiffy. I should never hae doubted you, Iain. I'll wait as long as you like afore we're wed. Just so long as ye bide wi' me. That's all I ask." She smiled between the tears. "I could do wi' a big cuddle."

"I'll dae better than that." He held out his hands. Obediently she went to him.

* * *

May 1916

They came in the night. Shouts and banging roused him from sleep; he felt Morag slip out of bed to see what was amiss. Suddenly he sensed danger. Feverishly sweeping aside the bedclothes, he groped for his trousers.

It was at that point that they burst in – four policemen. Before he could react they were hitting out with drawn truncheons, forcing him to his knees; dimly he was aware of Morag screaming at them, trying to push through to his aid, being swatted away like some irritant fly. In desperation he made an attempt to throw off his captors, but to no avail; a single kick to the stomach had him retching in agony. Gasping for breath, he felt himself hauled upright, his arms pinned to his sides; then he was hustled out of the house, down the stairs, past startled faces peering from doorways, through the close into the street, before being thrust into a waiting conveyance. Two constables followed him in, the door slammed shut and the vehicle sped away.

Beaten and bloodied, he lay helpless in the well of the van. How long the journey lasted he had no way of knowing. His head was still spinning as the engine stopped, and he was yanked out. There was a glimpse of a building before he was hurried inside, frogmarched down a flight of steps, and along a grim corridor studded with iron doors. One stood open, ready to receive him: before he could turn to utter a protest the bolt shot home, and he was left in solitude.

In rage he kicked at the door. That scheming bastard – Findlay! He should have realised what was afoot when the envelope arrived in the post – his call-up papers. Of course it should never have happened. He was in a starred occupation, doing work of national importance; none of his workmates had been similarly served. His angry protest had been soothed with fulsome apologies; Findlay's private secretary had personally reassured him with the promise to look into what was obviously a mistake on the part of some clerk. In the meantime he was to carry on as normal; any misunderstanding would be swiftly cleared up with the military authorities. It was all part of the elaborate plot, as he now knew to his cost. The intention was that he should fail to report on time: his treatment would be all the harsher.

It seemed an age before his jailers returned, crowding into the cell, their smug, fat, grinning faces almost daring him to offer further resistance. But he knew better than to give them the excuse they craved. There was barely time for a scowl of disdain before he was dragged out, still in his nightclothes.

As they shuffled along he had the impression there was something familiar about the surroundings; once he was swept up into the light of day he was sure of it. It was a courtroom – and he had been in its dock before. Only this time there were no companions to offer support, no lawyer to plead his case, no cheering crowds in the public gallery. This time there was only a solitary figure on the high chair beyond the bench. No fancy robes this time, but there was no mistaking his identity. And there could be no doubt that Sheriff Lee would remember him as one of the rent strikers.

The magistrate fixed him with a bleak stare, then his eyes dropped to the papers on his desk. "You are Iain Baird, of Brighton Road, Govan?"

Iain glared defiantly at his interrogator.

"Come, come, man. You must answer. You know why you are here?"

"No, I dinnae. I'm the victim o' police brutality." He jabbed a finger at his head. "See that. That's what thae fuckers did tae me."

The sheriff bristled angrily. "Be careful, Baird," he growled. "Intemperate language will not be to your advantage."

"Bugger that! Ye'd nae right to send round the polis. Breakin' an' enterin', false arrest and imprisonment. D'ye call that legal?"

"I shall not warn you again, Baird. You will treat this court with respect. A warrant was issued because you failed to answer to your call-up. As for your injuries, I am informed that you resisted arrest and minimum force was necessary to restrain you."

"And ye believe that? They didnae even gie me a chance to get my breeks on. I'm still in my sark." He tugged at his cotton shift. "Nae consideration for a man's dignity," he grumbled.

"That is entirely your own fault. However, the matter is very easily resolved. You can be kitted out with clothes any right thinking person would be proud to wear."

"Oh aye. And what might they be? Khaki, I'm thinkin'?"

"Of course. The king's uniform. Nothing to be ashamed of there. Listen to me, Baird. Under the terms of the Military Service Act you are a deserter from the army. And that offence carries a very heavy penalty. However, if you are willing to be escorted to the local depot, agree to take the oath of allegiance –"

"You'll let me off? Ye must think I'm saft in the heid. But I can see through yer wee game. Ye ken ye huvnae a leg to stand on. So ye're tryin' to trick me intae volunteerin'. Well, it's no' on. I'm in a reserved occupation."

The sheriff sighed. "Unfortunately that is not the case," he said, taking up a sheet of notepaper. "I have a letter from your employer. It states that your employment has been terminated – with immediate effect. You have been dismissed on the grounds of gross misconduct. Any exemption from military service is therefore no longer applicable. It's all quite explicit, I'm afraid."

Iain curled his lip. He had expected no less: Findlay had woven his web too well.

"What d'ye say, Baird? This is a chance to wipe the slate clean. Show your loyalty by joining the colours."

He glowered back defiantly. Perhaps there was still a last throw of the dice. "I demand the right to be registered as a conscientious objector."

There was the briefest of pauses. "I see. Very well. I'll hear what you have to say. Please be brief." The tone of wearied indulgence was enough to crush any lingering hopes. But he would play it out to the end.

"That's easy done. This is a capitalist war. I've nae quarrel wi' the workers in Germany. If the ruling classes fall out wi' each other, let them fight their ain battles."

"Is that so? You have been in the employ of Ibrox Ordnance for a period of some years. Engaged in the manufacture of … munitions of war, was it not? And now, quite by chance you are stricken by conscience. How very convenient."

Now the bugger was toying with him. But he was not quite finished yet. "I'm no' a shirker, if that's what ye mean. Gie me my old job back, or let me work somewhere else. But ye'll no' turn me intae cannon fodder. I'll go to the appeal tribunal. They'll listen to me."

"Possibly – not that it matters. The opportunity to make application for exemption has expired. You should have thought of it much earlier." He cleared his throat: two officers gripped Iain's arms tightly. "In view of your intransigence, I have no alternative but to surrender you to the custody of the military authorities." He reached for his pen. "My advice to you, Baird, is to consider your position very carefully. The army may not be so forbearing." Dashing off a signature, he turned to his clerk. "Here is the authorisation. Take him down."

His escort was already there, waiting for him in the forecourt. Only three this time – a corporal and two privates. Redcaps – regimental police with their nightsticks and bulging holsters. He could only watch stonily as the formalities were completed and he became the property of the army. A jerk of the corporal's thumb, and he was bundled into their vehicle.

Moodily he contemplated the future. Short shrift would be the fate of slackers and conchies, he had no doubt. Perversely it hardened his resolve. Damned if he would allow Findlay to win. He braced himself for the worst as they turned into the Maryhill Barracks and pulled up at the gatehouse.

His reception, therefore, came all the more as a surprise. Delivered to the guardroom, he was met with curious stares, but little sign of overt hostility: some charitable soul, noticing his feet, even managed to find him a pair of boots. Not a perfect fit, and without laces, but better than nothing. Then he was whisked off again, allegedly to have his injuries tended by the M.O. So that was the ploy – trying to coax him with kindness.

His suspicions were strengthened in the doctor's surgery. A seemingly amiable old buffer in shirt sleeves and braces waved him in, sat him down, tut-tutted at his appearance, and set to work – sponging away the dried blood, disinfecting and dressing the wounds, rubbing balm into the bruises, all the time clucking over him like a mother hen. It was all done so deftly, but Iain was not fooled: the poking and prodding was to assess his fitness for military service. When asked to read the letters on a board he was sure of it. An indignant refusal produced only a bland smile. Whether he took the test or not was of little significance: there was no reason not to stamp his card A1.

Next stop was the quartermaster's stores. Behind the counter, grinning broadly, stood an NCO. But Iain only had eyes for the items of clothing, neatly piled, which lay in front of him. He knew what this meant; he could guess at the reaction when he refused to comply. But it seemed that they were determined to handle him with kid gloves. Instead of a brusque order to change, the sergeant merely commented on his nightshirt. Iain gave him a hard, calculating stare, then wavered; he was only too conscious how ridiculous he must look. Reluctantly, grudgingly he gathered up the pile, leaving behind only the cap and puttees. Obligingly the man pointed out a screen, taking care not to wink at the others until he had disappeared behind it.

Within half an hour Iain found himself back in the guardroom, a steaming bowl of Irish stew set before him. He should have scorned to touch the food, but the aroma was irresistible; only now did he realise how ravenous he was. He was just mopping up the last of the gravy when the door swung open. Everyone immediately sprang to attention; even Iain, despite himself, rose uncertainly. It was the sergeant major: the adjutant would be grateful for a short interview with the new recruit.

Captain Apperson winced as prisoner and escort were marched into his office. He was not in the best of humours; lunch in the mess would have to be postponed while he dealt with this new task foisted upon him. Did no one appreciate the mountain of paperwork on his desk? Indents and returns, requisitions and reports – the army's appetite was insatiable. Officer in charge of administration at the depot was no bed of roses. Instinctively he glanced at the empty sleeve pinned to the side of his jacket. But a return to active service was impossible. His war was over. It had ended at Loos, with the shell fragment that severed his left arm.

Still, it would never do to wallow in self-pity. The C.O. had asked him to deal with the matter, and that was that. It was a political case, apparently, to be handled delicately, and above all without attracting attention. He studied the man's features: a surly specimen to be sure, tallying with what he had already seen in the file. This would be a hard nut to crack, but it was his duty to try. However, should the fellow prove obdurate, as he very much feared …

"Your name is Baird, I believe," he said mildly. "I trust you are being well looked after. Any complaints?"

"Naw." It was almost a leer. "Apart from being knocked about by yer bully boys, that is."

"I don't think that is quite fair, Baird." A hint of tartness crept into his voice. "The army does not tolerate that sort of treatment. It is strictly forbidden by King's Regulations. Of course I can't answer for the civil power."

"What's that?

"The police. They carried out the arrest. We've had you patched up, clothed and fed you, haven't we?"

"Never mind about that. I shouldnae be here in the first place. I'm in a reserved occupation."

"I'm afraid I have no information on that score. However, I am prepared to accept that possibly there may have been some misunderstanding, and overlook your failure to report on the due date. The draft has already left for training camp, but that is easily remedied. Arrangements can be made for you to proceed there tomorrow."

"I'm no' gonnae join up. Can ye no' understand?"

This was becoming tiresome. "Why ever not? The Highland Light Infantry is one of the finest regiments in the British Army. Don't you want to do your bit for king and country?"

"I was already daein' that at the Ordnance afore I was shanghaied in the middle o' the night."

The captain fidgeted uncomfortably. This would never do. The rascal appeared to have an answer for everything. Perhaps it was time to change tack. "So you are not willing to serve in a rifle battalion. Very good, I can accept that. At the same time you must appreciate that I have no authority to offer you a discharge."

"So what happens next?"

"Not so hasty, Baird. There may be a compromise solution. You're a skilled man. Your expertise may be better suited elsewhere – in one of the specialist arms, for example."

"And what might thae be?"

"Well, consider the Army Ordnance Corps. Given your background, responsibility for ammunition and machinery might be right up your street. Another possibility is the ASC – delivering supplies. And there's always the RAMC – you could become a stretcher bearer or medical orderly. Do any of these appeal?"

"Stuff that! Ye say I'm a skilled man – ye admit it. So I should be where I'm most needed. Well, that's no' here. It's back in the munitions works."

"Face the facts, Baird." His patience was beginning to wear thin. "The army will not let you go. Make the most of what's on offer."

"I've telt ye already. I'm no' goin' for a sodger. I'd rather go tae jail."

Apperson gave it up as a bad job. The case was hopeless. "Very well," he rasped. "On your own head be it. But you will not be sent to prison. We've a special place for the awkward squad. You'll be enrolled in the Non-Combatant Corps. Maybe digging ditches will give you a taste for army life. Sar'nt major!" He turned to the warrant officer. "Get this miscreant out of my sight."

In the tiny vestibule outside the office the CSM delivered his own judgement. "Non-Combatant Corps? Nae Courage Corps, mair like." He spat contemptuously. "Think it'll be a cushy number. Stoppage o' pay if ye dinnae feel like daein' a hand's turn? Seven days CB for refusin' an order? It's France for you, my lad. Ken what that means?" He was gratified to see the blank stare. "Well, I'll tell ye. Soon as ye leave Blighty, ye're on active service. Then ye'll toe the line. Disobedience in the field is a capital offence." He drew a finger across his throat. "They'll put ye up against a wall and shoot ye. Think on that, chum."

NINETEEN

In the Trenches

Northern France. July 1916

"So here you are at last. Just in time to see the sights."

Jack Grove obligingly made room for his friend on the crowded deck. The boom across the harbour bar had been lifted to allow the little gaggle of ships to enter, and even now the escorting destroyers were turning aside, weaving away to resume the never ending watch on the Channel. A cheer went up as the warships dipped their flags in farewell.

"Thank God for the navy," said Grove as the noise subsided. "The only danger now is the Boche submarines. If one of them got in here ..." He left the rest unsaid.

His companion nodded distractedly. "You could be right." Alastair Baird shifted uncomfortably, still self-conscious in his shiny new uniform with its peaked cap, Sam Browne belt and frogged tunic. There had been a certain pleasure in placing his order at the military outfitters in Edinburgh – spending the £50 allowance granted by a sympathetic government to defray the expenses of equipping wartime officers. But that had been in private. Appearing in public, receiving salutes ... he was not so sure. Could he live up to what was expected of him?

"Shouldn't be too long now, old son." The tramp steamer which had ferried them overnight from Portsmouth was edging in towards the quayside. "All set to start earning your corn, eh? Seven and a tanner a day and all found. Who says the army isn't generous?"

"I suppose so. Ready as I'll ever be, Jack. But I still feel a bit of a fraud. I can't convince myself I'm cut out to be an officer – even a temporary one."

"That's bosh, Alastair. You're always running yourself down. Didn't you pass out near the top of the class in the training course?"

"Yes, but –"

"But nothing. Four hundred of us started out at Gailes in February. And you came in the top ten."

Baird bit his lip. How could he explain away his fears? Grove would think them irrational, damn him for a fool. In all honesty he had rather enjoyed his four months in the officer cadet battalion on the Ayrshire coast. Plenty of bull, of course, but nothing he had not endured before, and it was mildly amusing to be roundly abused by drill sergeants who were always careful to bellow 'sah' at the end – the ultimate insult. The tactical exercises and theoretical studies had been interesting, even if the relevance was not always obvious, and as Jack had pointed out, he had sailed through the exams. But what of the qualities that could not be taught? He had neither social standing nor frontline experience to justify his commission.

"Nothing to say, old man?"

"I was just thinking." He pulled a face. "I suppose there's no point in moping. Might as well get it off my chest. It's just that – that I might let the side down. I'm not like you. You're a natural – bags of confidence. Your platoon will take to you like a shot, follow you without hesitation. Officers must be superior beings – the men expect it. Where does that leave me?"

"So that's the root of the problem? I bet you've still got these rubbishy booklets they handed out. True?"

Alastair crimsoned. "In my valise."

"*Straight Tips for Subs*? *Notes for Young Officers*?" He shook his head. "Take my tip, laddie. Throw them away. Or better still, keep them for the trenches. They'll come in handy for the latrines. It's courage the men look to – not class. And you've got it in spades. Remember the grenade?"

"Not really." Grove was trying to jolly him along, and he was not ungrateful. "But I'll do my best."

"That's the ticket. Look, see that ship slipping its mooring. Our skipper's noticed it too, and he's determined to nab the berth before someone else does. God knows how long we might have been kept hanging about out here otherwise."

"Good for him," agreed Alastair. The dock basin was a tangle of masts and funnels as far as the eye could see, crowded with shipping of every shape and size – anything that could be pressed into service. Le Havre was the main entry port for the Expeditionary Force, and the demands of an ever expanding army were relentless – not least with the offensive on the Somme in full swing.

There was a slight shudder as the vessel brushed against the jetty, a low rumble as the gangway was made ready. "I'd best go below and see to the luggage," muttered Alastair.

"You'll do no such thing. Our bags are clearly labelled. Let the crew deal with them."

"Hold on, Jack. Suppose our gear were to go astray?" It was a matter of real concern. Grove could afford to replace any missing equipment: most decidedly he could not. It was amazing what an officer was expected to provide for himself: his entire grant had disappeared in a single afternoon – even with restricting himself to off-the-peg clothing and refusing apparent necessities such as riding boots and a dress sword.

"You worry too much, old chap. A gentleman doesn't hump his own belongings. And an officer deserves a few perks. Besides, you'll probably have a batman to fetch and carry for you once we reach the battalion. So you'd better get used to the idea."

A soldier-servant – polishing his boots and laying out his kit? He was not sure he could handle that.

"It's common knowledge that the Stirlings are a fairly traditional lot," Grove went on. "It even applies to some of their service battalions. There's a passable sprinkling of regular officers, I'm led to believe. So they'll want to keep up standards. Not like the rabble we joined," he grinned.

Alastair bristled. If that was Jack's idea of a joke ... Colonel McCrae had worked wonders; his battalion was keen as mustard, as well prepared as any in the new formations, and had already been in France for over six months. It would have been an honour to follow such a leader into action. But it was not to be. No doubt the colonel had made representations, but it was still a blow to find himself gazetted into the 9th Battalion of the Stirlingshire Regiment rather than the 16th Battalion of the Royal Scots.

Grove caught his look. "Sorry, Alastair. It was thoughtless of me. I'd have loved to serve with the old man. But that's behind us now. We've got to look to the future. I'm sure we'll go great guns in the Stirlings. At least they've kept us together. Brothers-in-arms, eh?"

"Too true, Jack." What else could he say? "I'm sorry I overreacted. I know you'd never run down the old battalion." It was hard to resist Grove's breezy good nature. And he had never felt the need for friendship more acutely; the ten days leave between the passing-out parade and meeting up at the Waverley Station had shown him that.

Of course he had felt duty bound to call on his Aunt Chrissie while he was in Edinburgh. But the visit exceeded even his worst fears. No offer of a bed for the night, not so much as a cup of tea: she was far too busy attending to the needs of her lodgers to fuss over an unexpected visitor. And Uncle Donald just sat grumpily in the corner, saying nothing, hardly lifting his head. It came as something of a relief to escape from such a grudging reception. Even a couple of days in a dismal hostel while he saw to his uniform were preferable to that.

Then it was on to Broomburn. In some ways this was even more of a disappointment. Mary had done her best to make him welcome, but his sister had other preoccupations, what with two lusty infants demanding attention, and a husband so exhausted by extended shifts that he only came home to eat and sleep. He had grown up in that house, but he felt an interloper. Mr Ogilvie and Mr McIntosh had greeted him warmly, but it was a shock to discover how worn and tired they both looked: the pit deputy charged with impossible production targets, his mentor recalled from retirement to take over the school once more. As for the rest of the village … there was a passing nod, a polite enquiry or two, but no more. Everyone was wrapped up in their own affairs, and he had no part in them.

"All serene then, Alastair?"

"All serene. I know I can be a bit dour. You've no idea how much you buck me up, Jack."

"All part of the service. I see they've got the gangplank down. What about nipping ashore now? That way we'll miss the scrum."

"I'm game. What's the programme? Our orders are to report to the base camp at Etaples. It's fair distance on the map."

"So we catch a train. The RTO at the railway station should be able to keep us right. Then we find out where the Stirlings are located – and Bob's your uncle. With any luck they won't bother to put us through the assault course at the Bullring. Or leave us waiting for a draft to nursemaid up to the line."

"You wish," chuckled Alastair. "Come on, then."

It was unfortunate that others were of a similar mind. Junior officers could expect no favours when it came to disembarkation: by the time they reached dry land the pier was already crowded – mounds of kitbags in their path, swarms of soldiers milling around. Trust the British Tommy to make the most of any opportunity to light up a gasper – the fug was enough to make anyone choke.

At last they managed to struggle through to the edge of the throng. "The best laid schemes, eh?" said Grove ruefully, as his comrade recovered his breath. "So much for a quick getaway. Wonder what's the best way out of here."

"Over there, I should imagine. Look beyond our mob." Further along the quayside some semblance of order had been restored. Earlier arrivals were forming up, being marched off, with a convoy of GS wagons in their wake. "Follow that lot."

"Not a bit of it, laddie. Do that and we'll be boxed in behind them. Then God knows how long we'll be at the station."

"Well, we can't go in the opposite direction. Look at the nags being unloaded from that freighter. Or hadn't you noticed?" Even as he spoke another horse appeared from the ship's hold, lifted high in the sling suspended from a crane, before being swung, legs thrashing wildly, onto the dockside, there to join the others already on the makeshift horselines.

"Can't argue there, old chap. They look likely to break loose at any minute." He snapped his fingers. "Tell you what. Let's go over by that covered area. There's bound to be another road that way."

"Are you sure?" He was far from confident, but there was no point in raising objections: Jack would never listen. "Lead on then," he sighed.

The space before them was stacked high with bales of hay and straw. "Animal fodder, Alastair. Stored here till required. No problem, though. We can cut round the side. Remember being told it was the biggest item on the army's shopping list. You'd have thought it would be ammunition."

"Not really. Not when even an infantry division needs almost six thousand horses to pull its guns and wagons. You've obviously forgotten that."

Grove snorted. "You can't expect me to make a note of every piddling little detail. I prefer to concentrate on the grand design," he added loftily. "Besides –" Suddenly he pulled up. "What the hell!"

It was an amazing sight: an alcove cut into the straw, so artfully conceived as to be almost invisible unless stumbled upon by chance. Some of the smaller bales had been pulled down into the centre to provide seating for a huddle of silent figures – military personnel certainly, but such as the two young subalterns had never witnessed before. Some were in shirtsleeves, others in ragged tunics; all looked disconsolate and forlorn. But it was their legs which drew immediate attention: iron fetters had been shackled to each man's ankles.

A sergeant came hurrying over. "Sorry, gentlemen. You can't come this way. These are prisoners under escort. We're just waiting for the dockside to clear before taking them on board."

Grove gave him a genial nod. "Of course, sergeant. We quite understand. None of our business. Winkling out a few rotten apples, I see. Mustn't be allowed to contaminate others, wouldn't you agree, Alastair? Alastair!" He looked curiously at his friend. "I say, what's up? You've gone white as a sheet. Like you've seen a ghost."

Baird swallowed hard. One of the fellows had been staring at him. It was unbelievable. But despite the grimy face and haggard appearance he knew there could be no mistake.

"Surely you're not upset by seeing a few villains? Unless you happen to know any of them?" It was a flippant remark, but seemed to touch a nerve. Alastair's face was a picture of misery.

"As a matter of fact I do," he said quietly. "One of them is my brother."

"Christ! I'm so sorry. I didn't mean –" Grove struggled to hide his confusion. "I didn't even know you had a brother."

"It's all right, Jack. I should have mentioned it before. Truth will out."

"Put my foot in it again, haven't I? Look, old man, I'll push off. Give you a chance to sort things out. Don't worry about your valise. I'll take care of it. See you at the station, eh?" He turned to the NCO. "Well, sergeant. Which way?"

"Just behind this enclosure, sir. Turn right, and follow your nose. It's half a mile or so to the main gate, but you can't miss it." He stepped back and saluted.

"Thank you, sar'nt." The salute was returned with a casual wave. "Buck up, Alastair. You're not your brother's keeper, you know. This doesn't make any difference to us."

There was comfort in that. He could trust Jack not to blab – not about something like this. By the time Grove was out of view he had regained his composure.

"You are in charge here, sergeant?"

"Yessir."

"You heard my colleague. Would it be possible to speak to my relative – only for a minute? The name is Baird. He's the well setup one, on that straw yonder – pretending not to notice us."

"Well sir, I don't rightly know. It's highly irregular." Then he softened. "Tell you what. There's a wee store shed round the corner. If you wait inside I'll have him brought over. Have to leave one of my men outside, though. No more than five minutes, mind. More than my stripes are worth to give you longer."

"Thank you, sergeant. I'm eternally grateful."

The building was not hard to find, stone built, though with obvious signs of dilapidation. The interior was dark and gloomy; he could smell the mustiness of long neglect. Overlooking the dingy window was a clerk's desk and high stool, along the walls pigeon holes for dockets and shelves for ledgers. Some kind of tallyman's hut, he concluded, fallen into disuse since the start of the war. At least it had not been crammed full of junk; there was still room to move around. He paced up and down restlessly as he pondered what on earth he was to say.

Presently there was a tap on the door. "Private Baird, sah." A shambling figure was thrust over the lintel. "Sorry about the delay. He was a bit reluctant to come. I'll be out here – just in case."

"Scouse git!" muttered Iain, as the door closed behind him.

"That's enough of that," snapped Alastair. "Remember where you are."

"My, my, the wee man. So they've made ye an officer. Couldnae resist the urge to gloat, could ye? Ye should have left well alone. Now they're bound to wonder. A black sheep in the family? Could be some awkward questions."

Alastair chose to ignore the barb. As usual, his brother was trying to twist everything to his own advantage. "Have you suffered any ill-treatment?" he asked, in an attempt to change the subject.

"What's that to you? You're one o' them now. A traitor to yer class."

"Spare me the bluster. I only wanted to know if I could help in some way."

"What could you do? You're just curious to find out how I got here." There was no response. "Thought so. Well, I'll tell ye."

"Go on, then. No doubt you'll spin some tale of woe."

"Listen, and then ye can judge. I'm the victim o' a conspiracy. Betrayed by the bosses, called up – and me in a reserved occupation, mind. Wouldnae even gie me the chance to apply for exemption as a conchie. What d'ye call that?"

"I'm sure plenty of others have been in the same position as you."

"Maybe so. But how many were forced intae uniform, shipped across tae France in secret, put to work in their so-called Non-Combatant Corps?"

"I really have no idea."

"Just because I telt them I widnae fight. Nor would I navvy for them. I'm no' a beast o' burden. So they set out to make an example o' me. D'ye ken what 'crucifixion' is?"

Alastair started at that. He was aware of the popular term for Field Punishment No.1, specified in the *Manual of Military Law*. A rough and ready retribution for malefactors: the culprit lashed to some fixed object to reflect on his misdeeds. Humiliating, but not insufferable: certainly preferable to more extreme penalties. "Unpleasant, I know, but it's only for a short period, and no more than two hours at a time."

"Ye think so?" snarled Iain. "I was staked out every day, near enough. Sometimes within range o' enemy guns. What d'ye suppose it's like wi' shells rainin' down all round ye, an' everyone else divin' for cover? Ye're shittin' yersel, I can tell you."

His brother winced. What Iain was describing was illegal – if true.

"More than flesh and blood could stand. So one night I decided to take my chances and break out. Nearly got clean away as well. But I was picked up after a couple o' days. A patrol out lookin' for somebody else. Just my luck. They carted me back, charged me wi' desertion."

Alastair gulped. This was a capital offence.

"Aye, there was a court martial, if ye can ca' it that. Only lasted about ten minutes. And nae prisoner's friend either. It was a farce."

"And the verdict?"

"Need ye ask? Guilty, of course. They let me stew for a week, then hauled me out. Sentence was confirmed. I thought my last moment had come. Then this officer steps up and says the C-in-C is pleased to commute the death penalty. Changed tae ten years penal servitude."

"At least that's something. So that's why you're here?"

"Ye expect me to be grateful? They put me in wi' thae others in some stinkin' hole, kept us there for a month afore draggin' us here in irons. We're to be handed over to the civil authorities once we get back tae Blighty. God kens where I'll end up."

"I'm truly sorry." Despite everything Alastair could not resist a tinge of sympathy. However much he deserved it, his brother was paying a heavy price.

Iain stared at him thoughtfully. "Perhaps there is somethin' you could do for me," he said softly.

"If it's in my power."

"Write to Morag. Tell her I'm safe. It's still the old address."

Alastair frowned. "Why can't you do that for yourself?"

"That might take months. At least this way she would ken sooner."

"But – what about the censorship regulations? I'm not sure it would be allowed."

"Oh well, if ye cannae be bothered –"

"Hold your horses. I meant it would be difficult, not impossible."

Officers censored each other's correspondence. Grove would oblige, if he asked it as a favour. "Shall I mention the son you fathered?" Somehow it just slipped out. He had been nettled at Iain's attitude, but that was no excuse. His lips tightened in vexation.

Iain's eyes narrowed, but the expected tirade never came. Instead he gave a thin smile. "Nae need to bother. She as good as kens already. She's seen the wean."

"But how on earth –?"

"She bumped intae yer lass in the park – pushin' a pram."

"Are you telling me it was the result of a purely chance encounter? Total strangers exchanging a few words? And she jumped to the conclusion that you were the father?"

"No' exactly. They kent each other afore. It's a long story. Leave it at that."

"I see. No doubt you're at the bottom of this somewhere. If I write, it'll be for Morag's sake, not yours. You've behaved abominably. All that pain and misery you've caused. And not a sign of remorse. Not even an admission of responsibility."

"What would be the point? Naebody would have believed me. They would think I was just protectin' my wee brother. A noble sacrifice," he added with a sneer.

Alastair spluttered with indignation. "You betrayed a trust", he hissed. "You forced yourself upon an innocent girl."

"Innocent? You must be kiddin'. She was in heat just as much as I was. Gaspin' for it, in fact." He saw his brother blench with rage, ball his fists, take a step towards him. "Gonnae hit me, are ye? An officer strikin' a private soldier. Ye can try, if ye like."

Alastair managed to check himself. "I wouldn't soil my hands on you. Guard!" he called out. The door flew open. "Get this man out of here. I've done with him."

* * *

Flanders

Major Hugh Lixmont clicked his teeth in exasperation. "Bloody marvellous, isn't it?" He was standing by the table, reading a newly arrived dispatch. "Listen to this, James. *Officers on offensive duties are to be encouraged to avoid distinctive dress. They should try to blend in with other ranks as far as is practicable. Badges of rank should be confined to epaulettes.* Have you ever heard the like?"

The adjutant coughed politely. "I was aware of the suggestion from brigade, sir."

"So what do you make of it?"

"Well, sir –"

"It's not on, you know. Officers must stand out, whatever the risk. They're the rallying point for their men. How else can they command instant obedience?"

"I presume the powers that be are concerned about losses. They want to cut down on casualty rates amongst subalterns. Only natural, I suppose."

"Damn it all, I won't have my officers skulking behind the coattails of private soldiers."

"I think we must endeavour to comply, sir." He hesitated a moment.

"Perhaps we might not have lost Moran and Robinson last week had they not been so obvious."

"That was because they were careless. Showing themselves above the parapet? Anyone doing that is just asking to have his head blown off." He glanced at his subordinate. "All right, James. I take your point."

That was the problem: the battalion was seriously under strength. While the war was being won on the rolling chalklands of Picardy, they had been stuck in the Flanders mud. Despite protests, experienced officers had been transferred to the Somme. Their replacements had been wet behind the ears – straight out of officer training. And now he had lost two of them, along with the steady drip of casualties incurred by simply manning the trenches: what the army was pleased to call *natural wastage*.

"Any sign of the new draft? Or the officers we were promised?"

The adjutant shook his head. "Not at the moment, sir. We live in hope. Any news of the colonel?"

The query was not unexpected. James would hardly have bothered to disturb him otherwise: he knew about the telephone call and was fishing for information. Only natural, he supposed: the mess must be buzzing with speculation. "Brigade couldn't be specific. But it looks like he'll be crippled for life."

"Sorry to hear that, sir. It's a real shame. The old man comes through a turn at the Front without a scratch, then goes and crocks himself in a riding accident. No justice, is there?"

Lixmont gave a brief nod. "Bizarre, I call it." The colonel would insist on his morning canter. Probably took a hedge too fast and ended up under his horse. He looked still as death when the search party carried him back.

"Yes, sir. And the battalion?"

"I wondered when you'd get round to that. I'm afraid no decision has been reached about a new C.O. So I'll be taking the battalion up the line tomorrow. You might tell the others."

It was a gesture of dismissal. The adjutant knew better than to linger; stiffening to attention, he saluted and departed. Lixmont tossed the file he was holding on top of a pile and resumed his seat. There was a whole stack of returns demanding his signature, but these could wait. Who cared how many tins of *Maconochie's* stew or *Tickler's* jam had been consumed in the last month? He had more pressing concerns. How the hell was the battalion expected to hold a frontage of over a thousand yards with four depleted companies? It was a real problem. And heaven help him if he made the wrong decision.

He gazed up at the ceiling of the farmhouse which served as the colonel's – now his – HQ. Part of the roof was missing, but a tarpaulin over the gap kept the room reasonably wind and water tight. Outbuildings and cottages provided billets for some of the battalion; the remainder had to make do with tents. However it was a bonus to have all of his command close at hand, rather than spread out over miles as sometimes happened. No civilians to get in the way either; the original inhabitants had long since disappeared. And the Front was less than twelve miles away – an easy day's march.

The irony of the situation was not lost on him. He was about to lead the battalion into position little more than a mile from where he had been wounded. In nearly two years the Front had scarcely moved. Of course there had been vast changes: a blind man could see that. An anonymous town had become a symbol of defiance, to be held at all costs. Once the surrounding area had been open countryside, only lightly touched by the hand of war; now it was a churned up morass of mud and clay, broken only by splintered trees and the debris of human habitation. Back then, there had been a single line of shallow, improvised defences; now the landscape was covered in a vast network of interconnected trenches, each six or eight feet deep, with sandbags, traverses and fire bays, protected by thick belts of barbed wire – a battle zone where soldiers eked out a precarious existence and rarely caught a glimpse of the enemy. This was not war as he understood it.

Hopefully this unsoldierly method of fighting would soon be over. The Big Push fifty miles to the south must surely force the Fritzes to withdraw troops to try to stem the advance there, thus enabling the forces at Ypres to break out from the salient. Within a few short weeks a huge pincer movement might trap the remnants of a beaten army on the Rhine. In the meantime there were orders to get out. He pulled a sheet of paper towards him and reached for his pen.

While Lixmont began to draft his instructions the adjutant made his way across the cobbled farmyard. With any luck there would be a strong mug of tea for him in the orderly room – the major could be hard going at times. A good soldier, though perhaps just a little too inclined to press military efficiency to extremes. Still, better the devil …

"Sir!" He looked round enquiringly. It was the corporal from the guard post. With him were two strangers – officers seemingly, though it was difficult to be certain. Oilskin capes, topped with steel helmets, effectively concealed their tunics, while a thick layer of mud encrusted their legs and footwear. There was a flurry of salutes.

"The sergeant sent me, sir," said the NCO. "Wi' these twa gentlemen. They say they've orders to report here."

"I see. Very good, corporal. You can trot off now." He turned to the newcomers. "You must be the new subalterns. My name is Archer-Ford. With a hyphen, I'm afraid. That's probably why they made me adjutant. And you might be?"

"Grove, sir," said the taller of the two.

"And I'm Baird," said his companion.

"Welcome to the 9th Stirlings." He gave each of them a firm handshake. "We were expecting you days ago."

"Sorry about that," said Grove. "There was a bit of a mix up at Etaples. Then we were misdirected on the journey here."

"Well, better late than never. But I say, you look as if you've been in the wars already."

Grove gave a wan smile. "That's just it. We hitched a lift in a motor lorry going up to Ypres. Trust our luck; it tumbled into a ditch a couple of miles back. So we had to walk the rest of the way. We left the driver cursing and swearing."

"And had to wade through the mud. That would account for your appearance. What about your kit?"

"Still in the lorry. We've only our haversacks and smoke helmets. If you could spare a couple of men, Baird or I could show them the place. It shouldn't take too long to lug back our valises."

"Hmm. Could be awkward. We're short-handed as it is, and everyone's pretty busy. That's because we're moving out tomorrow. Going up the line. But leave it with me. I'll see what I can do."

"Thanks awfully, sir. We're very grateful."

"Not at all. I expect you'll want to spruce up a bit before you meet the C.O. The officers' ablutions are over yonder. You'll find me in the orderly room once you've finished. Oh, by the by, we don't sport tin hats behind the lines. Fine for other ranks, but for officers it's strictly peaked caps. The C.O.

would have a fit if he saw you in battle bowlers round here. Off you go now. Don't be too long. Major Lixmont doesn't like to be kept waiting."

"Major Lixmont?" Grove was perplexed. "Our orders were to report to Colonel Weston."

"Colonel Weston has been injured. He's in hospital. We don't know when he'll be back. Major Lixmont is in temporary command. Any problem with that?"

"No. No, of course not. Come on, Alastair. Let's get ourselves cleaned up."

Captain Archer-Ford stared after them as they disappeared into the washroom. They made an odd mixture, he could not help thinking. Talk about chalk and cheese: one seemed rather bumptious, pushing himself forward, while the other hovered in the background, hardly saying anything. Grove was the type he understood: knock off the rough edges and he would make a fine junior officer. It was Baird who was the puzzle. The chap was definitely rattled about something. Windy at the prospect of his first time in the trenches? Possibly, but he didn't think so. That involuntary gasp, the flash of dismay. It was at the mention of the major's name. Now what on earth could that be about?

* * *

Company HQ was located just behind the frontline, tucked away in an angle of the support trench. *Cushy Corner*: someone with a sense of humour had chalked the name on the lintel. At least the dugout did provide a respite of sorts, where off duty subs could snatch a few hours rest on bedrolls laid on top of timber frames, and grab a bite to eat round the table in the centre. The fire trench was only a dozen yards further forward, near the tip of the salient. *Bleak Outlook*: that said it all.

He pushed aside the blanket masking the entrance. A short ramp ran down to the officers' quarters, eerily silent in the gloaming. It was the hour of the dusk stand to, with every man in position in case of a sneak attack. But he had been given permission to fall out a few minutes early, to complete his preparations. *Dominate No Man's Land*: that was the C.O.'s mantra. Few nights passed without a patrol being dispatched to reconnoitre beyond the wire, or a raiding party sent out to penetrate the enemy line and create mayhem. Cynics might argue his motive was to curry favour with his superiors, to ensure confirmation in his command of the battalion and the promotion that went with it. Be that as it may, it was undeniable that the troops responded well; morale was still high, despite the inevitable German retaliation and constant dribble of casualties. And now it was Second Lieutenant Baird's turn to show his mettle.

To be fair, there could be no complaints about having been selected to lead the raid; others had been taken before him. Still, it was puzzling that Major Lixmont should choose to regard him as a total stranger, treating him with the same aloof disdain he reserved for all junior officers – especially those who were only temporary gentlemen. Had he decided just to ignore the past? If so, was there any need to tell Grove that the girl he sat beside in class happened to be the major's sister? But Jack had been curious; he had to say something. Thank God that was as far as it went. Were he to guess at the whole story … But by morning he might be dead. Then nothing would matter.

He found a box of matches, struck a light, applied it to one of the oil lamps. Now it was possible to see properly. Laying aside his helmet, he unbuckled his Sam Browne. His greatcoat hung from its nail on the wall. Unseasonable dress for a warm night, but it would cover his tunic and hopefully spare him the worst of the scratches and tears as he scrambled under the enemy wire. He drew his pistol from its holster, unclipped the cartridge pouch and stuffed them into one of the pockets. His haversack was on the same hook; he swung it down and over to the table.

There was the sound of muttered voices outside; then the curtain was dragged open. It was the C.O. himself, followed by the adjutant. Baird instantly froze to attention.

"Stand easy, lieutenant. We've just come to wish you well. Got your men told off?"

"Yes, sir. They're making ready now." Truth to tell, he had left the selection to his platoon sergeant. Whether he fully believed the assurance they were all volunteers was another matter. They appeared enthusiastic enough at the briefing, but he had his doubts.

"Good. What time do you jump off?"

"Eleven pip-emma, sir. I've instructed Corporal McAndrew to have the men in position by ten-thirty."

"Then I won't detain you further. Remember your primary objective is to knock out the machine gun post that's been causing bother these past few days. You're also to try to bring back a Hun – alive if possible. Brigade was insistent on that point. Chuck a few bombs down any funk holes you can find, and get the hell out before the Boche wakes up. Anything to add, James?"

"Password, sir?" murmured the adjutant.

"Oh yes. 'Auld Reekie'. You might pass it up the line. We don't want an own goal on the way back."

Alastair nodded. It was a good choice. Even if the Germans learned of it, they would never be able to pronounce the words properly.

Lixmont straightened his cap, touched it with his stick. "Good luck then, Baird," he said stiffly.

The adjutant held aside the curtain for his chief to pass. "Yes, all the best, old chap." Alastair caught the wink and sly grin. A moment later the sacking swung back, and he was alone once more.

So Archer-Ford suspected something. So what? It couldn't amount to much, or else it would have been the talk of the trenches. The man was a born meddler, forever poking his nose into other people's affairs. Even the shortest of acquaintances had convinced him of that.

He sat down at the table to unstrap the canvas backpack. The woollen gloves and old tobacco tin he would need; the rest could be sent back to Broomburn, together with the letter addressed to his sister. He hesitated a moment, then reached in for the little blue casket and thumbed open the catch. Perhaps this would be his last look. He was tempted to lift out the medal, carry it with him. But what if his body was never found? Or was stripped by looters? He snapped the case shut. This way it was sure to reach Mary. Jack would see to that. Hastily he jammed the box back into the holdall.

Time was getting on. He picked up the tin, twisted off the lid, dug in his fingers, and began to apply the contents to his face. It was only common sense to smear burnt cork over exposed skin, and to insist on his men doing likewise. Lixmont might sniff at his officers done up like Christy minstrels, but any gleam in the dark could spell disaster. Satisfied, he pulled on the gloves and buttoned up his greatcoat.

Grove was waiting for him beside the sap, a narrow ditch snaking out into No Man's Land with a listening post at the far end. As officer of the watch it was his responsibility to see off the raiding party – and restrain trigger-happy sentries from opening fire on its return. But Alastair knew his friend would have come anyway. Each felt for the other's hand.

"Got everything you need, old man?" It was little more than a whisper: sound travelled a long way in the still night air.

"Yes, I think so, Jack. How are things at your end?"

"*Napoo.* The odd whiz-bang, but nothing close. With any luck Brother Boche will be safely tucked up in bed by now. Say the word and I'll have the bomb stop out of your way." This was a barbed wire gate dropped into a trench to seal it off from enemy intrusion. "Then you can crawl up the sap and surface beyond our wire."

"That was the general idea. Do it now, Jack. My lot will be here in a jiffy."

"How many are going?"

"The usual. Four men and a corporal. Here they come now." They heard laboured breathing and muted oaths as the file rounded the traverse. "By the way, Jack. The password. It's 'Auld Reekie'. That's what the major decided."

"Auld Reekie? What made the Icicle choose that?"

Alastair smiled faintly. *The Icicle.* That was what some of the subs called him – behind his back. "Maybe he wants to remind us of home."

Grove almost choked. "Him! That's rich. This war is meat and drink to him. Not bad though," he added, conceding the joke. "You should lighten up more often." He moved away to supervise the removal of the hurdle.

Baird heaved himself onto the firestep, stared out into what remained of Polygon Wood. It was not quite pitch dark; he could just about make out the ghostly skeletons of shattered trees. The German line was barely two hundred yards distant, though the sap should give cover for the first thirty or so. After that they would be out in the open, constantly in fear of a flare or star shell shedding its glow over the ground. In that case the slightest movement could mean curtains; the only chance was to freeze, hope to be taken for a post or stump. Then there were the obstacles to be negotiated before reaching the enemy wire. A daylight study of No Man's Land through a trench periscope was all very well, but actually to be there at dead of night…

"Sir, Mr Baird, sir!" It was Corporal McAndrew, obviously concerned at the delay. The men were beginning to fidget. Who could blame them?

"All right, corporal. We'll be off as soon as the bomb stop is cleared." He jumped down. A word of cheer would not come amiss – if he could think of something to say.

"Any of you from Edinburgh?" One of the men nodded. "Well, you'll be pleased that the password is 'Auld Reekie'. Mind and shout it loud on the way back."

He made the pretence of a final inspection. Two had bags of grenades strapped to their chests; the others had bayonets stuffed into their belts. All carried clubs of some description: pickaxe handles or lead piping wrapped in sackcloth. Heaven knew what other makeshift weapons lurked in their pockets. Silence would be vital for success – at least until the time came for the bombers to do their work.

"What about the wire cutters?" It would never do to forget the most essential tool.

"That'll be mysel' an' Private McDade," said the corporal. "Twa sets. Just in case."

"Very good. Well, I think that covers about everything. I've just this to say to you all. I don't know about the Germans, but by God you terrify me." Feeble enough, but it raised a snigger.

Then Grove was back. "All done and dusted, old son. I've had white marker tapes draped over the side. That's your way out and back. I'll leave a man there as a guide. You won't need a ladder to climb out. It's only about three feet."

"Thanks, Jack. I knew I could count on you." He turned to his NCO. "You heard what Mr Grove said, corporal. Take the section up. I'll join you in a minute." They stood aside to allow the squad to squeeze past and into the opening.

"Wish I was the one that was going," said Grove wistfully.

"So do I." They both stifled a laugh.

"I suppose the Icicle chose you because you used to go out with his sister. You have an unfair advantage."

"Possibly. Though I doubt his mind works like that. Rather the reverse, I should have thought."

"No need to be so touchy, Alastair. It was only a joke. If I had a sister I'd be proud to have you walk out with her."

"Even with a brother like mine."

"God's sake, laddie. So he's a bad lot and Lixmont is a snob. Forget them both and get on with your life."

It was good advice. There was nothing more to be said. He pressed Jack's arm and disappeared up the sap.

The minutes passed: every one dragged like an age. For the umpteenth time Jack Grove peered at the luminous dial on his wristwatch. Nearly an hour gone now. And still nothing. Anxiety gnawed at him. Suppose the Germans had spotted them, prepared a trap. They might already be dead or captured. But there had been no shots, no sounds of a struggle. Was that a good or a bad sign? He tried to curb his impatience. Baird would be canny, err on the side of caution. Had he not spent the afternoon glued to a trench periscope, estimating distances, taking notes? He could picture Alastair feeling his way, step by step; crawling round shellholes, dodging from one tree stump to the next, inching up to the enemy wire, praying there was no challenge. Then the point of no return; holding the strands tight while the cutters were applied, separating them back, burrowing through. After that there was no telling. Either the gods smiled, or ... He dashed the image from his mind.

High time he checked on the sentries again. His instructions had been to observe the strictest vigilance, reinforced with the promise of a court martial for anyone found nodding off at his post. But could he carry out his threat? Have a man shot on his say so? After a week in the line the men were dog-tired from lack of sleep, exhausted by the constant strain, never knowing when their last moment might come. It would be easy to make excuses, let an offender off with a warning. But it would also be a dereliction of duty. Resolved to be firm, he jumped down from his perch.

No sooner had he do so than a flurry of muffled explosions had him leaping back onto the parapet. Alastair was doing the business at last! He drew his revolver, shouted to the guards to be ready with covering fire. Two more bangs – he thought he saw the flashes. All they could do now was wait. Surely Baird would throw caution to the wind, make a mad dash back for safety before the Hun could open up. Thank God! The sound of running footsteps. Loud cries of 'Auld Reekie! Auld Reekie!' The thud of bodies hurtling into the sap. He scrambled down, felt for his electric torch, flashed it into the entrance. Three figures were stumbling towards him – the one in front roughly pushed forward by the others. The beam caught a bloodied face, eyes wide with terror. No more than a youth – in German uniform.

"Corporal McAndrew? Where's Mr Baird?"

"Just coming, sir. We left him dealin' wi' the machine gun nest. He ordered me and Daniels to bring back this specimen first."

"Well done, corporal," said a voice behind him. It was Captain Aitken, the company commander. "Best get your prisoner down to battalion HQ. I've no doubt the C.O. will be glad to see him."

There were fresh shouts, the crash of feet. Seconds later Alastair and the other three privates came tumbling through. Grove could have hugged his friend. Captain Aitken stepped forward to offer his congratulations.

"Good show, Alastair. And no casualties. Splendid news." The sudden whoosh and crump of an incoming shell made them duck. "Only to be expected, I suppose," said Aitken, straightening up. "The Boche showing his appreciation. Better sound the stand to. It might be a retaliatory raid."

They braced themselves for the expected bombardment. But in the end it was to prove a desultory affair, intermittent and poorly directed. After half an hour the shellfire died away completely. Silence descended once more.

"Might as well stand the men down, Jack. There's nothing doing here. Just a few whiz-bangs and pipsqueaks. No heavy stuff. Not like the Boche at all. Must be losing his touch."

"Yes, sir."

"Ah well, be grateful for small mercies. I'll leave you to it. Come along, Alastair."

He led the way back to the dugout. Disappearing into his own quarters for a moment, he returned with a bottle and two glasses. "Sit yourself down. Whisky?" Without waiting for a reply he half-filled the tumblers and pushed one towards Alastair. "Here, get this down you."

Alastair took a cautious sip. "I think I might have an explanation, sir."

"Really? What for?"

"The half-hearted German response. It's my belief we caught them in the middle of a changeover. Their frontline was virtually deserted, but we detected plenty of activity back in the reserve trenches. We were in and out before they knew it. It was the most God awful luck."

"I suspect there's more to it than that. But do carry on."

"Well sir, my priority was the machine gun position. I was fairly certain it would still be manned. They'd hardly leave themselves totally defenceless.

So we sneaked along the ramparts till we got close. Then we heard low voices – two of them. The emplacement juts out a bit, so their backs were to us. I sent Corporal McAndrew and Private Daniels forward." He gave an involuntary shudder as he recalled the gurgled cry, the brief scuffle. "They returned with the prisoner."

"I see. What happened next?"

"McAndrew and Daniels were detailed to escort the man back to our lines. I told the others to fan out, bombing any bunkers they came across. Then we blew up the MG, and made our way back."

"So it was a textbook operation. Neat and clean." Aitken was clearly impressed. "Bloody well done!"

"Thank you, sir. But any praise should go to the men. Their conduct was exemplary. Corporal McAndrew was a tower of strength." He could not quite blot out the image of McAndrew wiping the blood from his knife, grinning that he had slit a man's throat. Suddenly he felt deflated, inexpressibly flat and weary, desperate to avoid more questions. "If you don't mind, sir, I'd like to write my report. So if I could be excused …" He tailed away.

"Of course, Alastair. Go through to the office. You'll find a pad on my desk."

Quarter of an hour later he was back. It was hard not to notice the trembling hand, hollow eyes, sunken cheeks, taut grey lips. "I've finished my report, sir. If you'd care to read and countersign it."

"All in good time, old chap. You must be worn out. Go and lie down for a bit." There was only the slightest hesitation before Alastair allowed himself to be guided over to one of the alcoves.

For what seemed like hours he tossed and turned, unable to find the rest he craved. But at last sheer nervous exhaustion claimed him, and he fell into a troubled sleep. The next thing he knew was a hand on his shoulder, a familiar voice in his ear. It was Jack Grove.

"Sorry to disturb your beauty sleep, old man. Thought you might like to know that the Icicle is on his way up. I don't expect he'd be overjoyed to find you in your pit, snoring the day away."

There was a groan of protest; then his blanket was swiftly thrust aside. "What's that you said? What time is it?"

"Gone ten. Here, I've brought you a mug of tea. Even found some condensed milk for it."

"Thanks." He took a gulp of the sickly liquid, then struggled to his feet. "Christ! Where are my clothes? I can't let him see me like this."

"Calm down, laddie. We had to take off your jacket and loosen your tie. Just you drink your tea. I'll attend to your things."

They had only just time. Grove was tightening his Sam Browne when there was a footfall in the doorway. Both sprang to attention.

"At ease, gentlemen. If you don't mind, lieutenant, I'd like a word with Baird. I'm sure you have other duties." Grove gave Alastair a wry smile as he slipped away.

Major Lixmont laid his cap, gloves and cane on the table. "Come and sit down. I thought it was time we had a little chat – Alastair."

He almost gasped in disbelief. The C.O. had never addressed him by his Christian name before. And he had rarely seen him without the adjutant in tow.

Lixmont seemed to read his mind. "I sent Captain Archer-Ford down to brigade this morning with your prisoner. He had to go in any case to finalise the details. Kill two birds with one stone, you might say."

"Details, sir?"

"About tonight. We're to be relieved. That was the main reason for my visit. In fact the whole division is being pulled back. A spot of rest and recreation won't come amiss, eh? Give us a chance to recharge the batteries. Then it's more training and off south to join the final push on the Somme. What d'you think of that?"

"It's –it's awfully good news, sir."

"Thought you'd be pleased. You know, Alastair, I've had my eye on you this past week or so – ever since you joined the battalion. My father wrote and told me he thought you'd make a damn fine officer when you went off for cadet training."

"You knew I'd be coming?"

"Naturally. When I saw the name in the gazette I thought it more than likely. I must confess I did have my doubts about your suitability, but my father's view has been amply vindicated. You have more than justified his high opinion of you."

"Thank – thank you, sir."

"I've read your report on last night's raid. Highly impressive. Captain Aitken thinks a lot of you. And your corporal was singing your praises when I interviewed him."

"Any credit is down to the men, sir."

"You're too modest, Alastair. I've seen the MC given for less."

Military Cross! The thought of an award had never even occurred to him.

"And no doubt I'll be asked for my recommendations for promotion to full lieutenant." He let the prospect dangle.

"That's very good of you, sir." There was a moment's hesitation. "Would it be an impertinence to enquire whether Mr Lixmont mentioned anything else? About Elizabeth, I mean?"

"He did. That's why I wanted a word in private. It would appear you are no longer to be held culpable in the matter of my sister's – predicament. But I still feel you bear some responsibility for bringing her into contact with that scoundrel."

"I realise that, sir. And there's not a day I don't blame myself for leaving her with my brother."

"Well, it's all water under the bridge now. My sister is making a new life for herself. Why rake things up again?" He gave Alastair a meaningful look.

So that was it. The barely disguised offer if he gave up Elizabeth.

"Sir, it was my understanding that I would not attempt to get in touch with her until such time as I was discharged from the army. That was at Mr Lixmont's request. More than that I can't promise."

"But surely you wouldn't want her upset? The whole idea is ridiculous."

"What idea?"

"Marriage. Think of her station in life. It wouldn't work. You're too far apart. How could you ever make her happy?"

"I'd rather hear it from Elizabeth herself – from her own lips. If I survive this war, surely I'm entitled to know her feelings."

"I see. And is that your last word?"

"I'm afraid it is, sir."

"Very well." His face set hard. "You are dismissed."

TWENTY

Over the Top

The Somme. September 1916

"What's up, laddie? Mooching around on your own out here?" Jack Grove found his friend among the mounds of red rubble, all that remained of the brickwork which had once fronted the village street. "I must say you're looking a bit seedy, old chap. Not going down with something, are you?"

"No Jack." Alastair Baird made an effort at a smile. It would never do to admit to a tightness in his chest. "Just a slight chill. Nothing to make a fuss over."

"These summer colds are the very devil. Especially after all the rain we've had. You want to take more care of yourself."

"I'll bear it in mind, Jack," he said drily. Five weeks in this wasteland since moving south, and he could count on the fingers of one hand the nights he had spent in a warm billet. Tented huts were the most that could be expected; more often than not it was muddy bivouacs with the water seeping in. Small wonder sick lists were growing alarmingly.

"If you must know, I was asking myself what it's all for. People used to live here. And now they've nothing."

"That's the fortunes of war. Why worry about it?"

"See here, Jack. How far have we pushed forward? A miserable two or three miles at most. In two months! There has to be a better way."

"I've told you before, Alastair. You think too much for your own good." His eyes narrowed. "There is something else, isn't there? You're not still in the dumps because I was made up and you were passed over? Is that it? I've told you a hundred times that you're the better man, that you more than deserved a second pip for that raid. But a chap can't refuse a promotion when it's pressed on him. It's simply not done."

"I'm not jealous. I never was. I'm only sorry none of the men won any recognition."

"What did you expect? That's the Icicle all over. Making out it was nothing special. I bet it was your success that clinched the battalion for him. And you get sweet Fanny Adams. Just because he's got it in for you on account of his sister."

"No, it's not that," he said hurriedly. "You're barking up the wrong tree. What the colonel thinks of me is neither here nor there. I was thinking of poor Bobby Urquhart."

"Urquhart? Your batman? Chap from your place, I seem to recall."

"Yes. Smashed to pulp leading a string of mules up Happy Valley. I was just trying to decide what to say to his mother. He worked in the local co-op store, you know. Probably the only man in the village to be called up. The rest are all miners."

"That why you chose him?"

"More likely the other way round. He was in the first draft we picked up after Ypres. Marched right up and asked if I was looking for a soldier-servant. Stuck to me like a leech since then. And now this."

"Poor sod. What'll you write?"

"Oh, I don't know. The usual trite phrases, I suppose. About being a model soldier, always loyal and cheerful. That he fell in the line of duty and suffered no pain. How he was given a Christian burial …"

God, what was he saying? How could he spout such drivel? The incoming shell had burst right over the mule train: fifty yards further back and he would have been the one blown to kingdom come. As it was, the sight that met his eyes as the smoke cleared – the severed limbs and twisted bodies of the animals, one or two still twitching in their death throes. And young Urquhart just lying there, his breast ripped open, coughing out his lifeblood. That questioning, accusing stare: it still haunted him.

Grove seemed to read his thoughts. "It's tough, old lad. But you mustn't blame yourself."

"We didn't even bring back the body. Just pushed him into a shellhole. Not even a prayer to say goodbye."

"But the shelling, man! Your responsibility is to the living. You had to get your men away. Take my tip, Alastair. Let it go. You want to give his mother chapter and verse? Why? It would be a mercy to let her think he died a clean death. Give her some comfort. In any case it's policy to serve up pap. Your letter would never get past the censor."

Baird nodded glumly. "You're right, as always. Thank God for your commonsense, Jack."

"Forget it. I came to tell you the Icicle's back. Looking pleased as Punch, would you believe." He glanced at his watch. "There's to be an officers' meeting in the cellar of the town hall. It's about the only place still standing."

"Why bother?" Alastair sighed wearily. "Probably only more of the same. Humping supplies up Happy Valley." That was what they called the road up from Mametz: the single line of communication through which every relief, every gun and wagon, every stick of equipment had to pass, while the Germans on the heights shelled it mercilessly day and night.

"So why march us five miles away from there? And why summon our lord and master to a divisional conference?" He tapped his nose. "Something's up. You mark my words."

They trudged back in silence. Was the Big Push starting up again? Grove seemed to be implying as much. But was the battalion ready to go over the top? He doubted it. It was not the training, though that had been farcical in itself: a bare four days of manoeuvres, tramping over terrain that bore no resemblance to the actual battlefield; marching in step behind signallers and drummers, pretending to advance in concert with a creeping artillery barrage. Nor was it the two short spells in the frontline – these had been relatively uneventful. No, it was the land itself that had taken its toll: the ceaseless grind in servicing the Front, over the shell-torn, scarred mudheaps wrested from the enemy, yard by yard, since the start of July.

They were among the last to join the group assembling in the basement of the *mairie* – a score of officers gathered round a makeshift table. In the flickering shadows cast by the solitary paraffin lamp it was impossible to read faces. But there could be no doubting the note of triumph in Lieutenant-Colonel Lixmont's voice.

"Gentlemen", he began, "the decisive moment is at hand. The enemy is mortally wounded. His strength is exhausted. One more effort, and the road will be clear to Bapaume and the open country beyond. GHQ has every confidence that our forces can be on the Rhine before the onset of winter."

He grew more expansive. Intelligence had confirmed that German casualties were unsustainable, that morale was at its lowest ebb. There were inadequate reinforcements to hold the line; half-starved soldiery were surrendering in droves. All that remained was to knock on the door and the Front would collapse like a house of cards. Fresh infantry divisions were in place to achieve the breakthrough, with a cavalry corps waiting to gallop into the breach. And, to guarantee success, he hinted at an awesome new weapon to strike terror into an unsuspecting foe – the landship.

"So you see, gentlemen, nothing has been left to chance. Nothing can stand in our way. You may be wondering what part the Stirlings are to play. Well, I can answer that." He paused for effect. "We have been asked to kick off the whole show." There was a stunned reaction, broken only by a dry chuckle. "Thought that might impress you. James, perhaps you would do the honours."

The adjutant produced a wooden board which he propped up on the table. Pinned to it was a large-scale trench map, complete with contour lines and fixed points.

"Here is the current situation," said Lixmont, tapping the map. Taking up a pointer, he launched into an outline of the proposed plan of campaign.

The key to the whole German position was the Thiepval Ridge, with its fortified village and surrounding redoubts. Dominating the heights, its early capture was of the utmost importance. Accordingly it had been decided to mount the assault in two stages. The Stirlings had been entrusted with the preliminary attack to seize the lower slopes, and establish a secure base for other units to push through to the summit of the ridge itself. The operation was timed to begin at 6.20 the following morning.

There was a low whistle at that. This was cutting things fine.

"I know it's short notice. But it can't be helped. The general only decided on the battalion at the last minute."

"What about preparations for the attack, sir?" someone ventured to ask.

"Arrangements are well in hand," he reassured them. "Fresh supplies should be with us within the hour, along with guides from the engineers. It's only a two mile march, so if we set off at midnight we should arrive in plenty of time. Artillery has been laid on for our advance, so that should keep the Boche out of our hair. Any further questions? No? Good." He straightened his cap. "Company commanders to remain behind. The rest of you, dismiss. And good hunting."

They emerged into the fading light, just as a convoy of GS vehicles began to trundle into what was left of the village square. Better still, an aroma of rich beef stew wafted over the ruins, the promise of a hot supper on a chilly evening.

"I say, doesn't that smell delicious?" Grove sniffed the air in appreciation. "What d'you think of things now, Alastair?"

"I suppose we should be grateful for getting a crack at the enemy at last. A step up from being an Aunt Sally for German gunners at any rate."

"My, my. Still tetchy. What's your gripe now?"

"Nothing really. It's just that I wish we'd had the chance to have a look at the lie of the land before the attack."

"Does it really matter? The Hun will be cowering in his funk holes. We'll be on him before he knows it."

"That's just the point. I'm not sure about this creeping barrage. We've had no proper training. You'd have thought they could spare a battery of 18-pounders to simulate actual conditions. No live ammunition. Not even smoke shells. It's all on paper. If we or the artillery get out of kilter …"

"Good old Alastair. Always the Dismal Jimmy."

"Well, I've said my piece. What's your opinion?"

"It's my opinion we'd best grab some of that grub before it's all gone. Come on."

With a rueful shake of the head Alastair trailed behind. No point in admitting what was really on his mind: Jack would only accuse him of prejudice. Had Lixmont volunteered the battalion? Was he capable of sacrificing his men to further his own career? It was in a mood of grim foreboding that he joined Grove for what might be his last meal.

Despite himself, he managed to do justice to the food, and felt better for it. After that, all was bustle and activity, with no time to dwell on the future. Weapons and equipment had to be checked, ammunition and iron rations issued. With a total burden of sixty-six pounds per man, a slow jog across No Man's Land was all that could be expected; but as Captain Aitken explained at the company briefing, this was of little consequence since the bombardment would protect the advance. The battalion was to go over the top in stages, each of company strength, the first wave pushing all the way through to the final objective, a ruined farm on the hillside about half a mile away. Succeeding waves would have the task of mopping up and consolidation before moving on. Precise instructions for each platoon commander would be indicated on the battle maps to be issued on reaching the assembly trenches. Lastly, Aitken could reveal, his company had been awarded the privilege of leading the assault.

* * *

At midnight the order was given to move off. Baird could only speculate at the rate of progress over rough tracks, encumbered with extra bombs and ammunition, picks and shovels, sandbags and wire cutters, even drums of telephone cable. Fortunately the sappers who were to act as guides had laid down marker tapes at intervals along the route. Even so, it was a good hour's march before they found themselves descending into a sunken road, the gateway to the trench system. And then there followed what seemed like an eternity of plodding along a labyrinth of mud, through slimy ooze that soaked puttees and numbed feet, before finally being deposited in a communication trench just behind the frontline. Now there was nothing left but to encourage the troops to take what rest they could in what was bound to be a cold and cheerless night.

Few slept. Men huddled in small groups, smoking but saying little. Alastair tramped up and down, exchanging a few words with members of his platoon, but for the most part they were unresponsive, and he soon gave it up as a bad job. He managed to find a niche where he could squat on an upturned ammunition box with his greatcoat wrapped round him for warmth. Left alone with his thoughts, he let his mind wander. All sorts of jumbled up memories began to tumble through his brain … he dozed fitfully.

"Mr Baird. Company commander, sir." He woke with a start at the whispered warning, scrambling to his feet as Aitken loomed up.

"Just doing the rounds, Alastair. All set for the off?"

"I think so, sir."

"Good. How are your men?"

"A bit subdued. Only natural in the circumstances. But they're up for the job all right."

"That's the ticket. By the way, it seems that the gunnery wallahs have been giving the Hun a ten minute wakeup call every morning for the last week. So they'll think our barrage is just another dose of hate and stay in their dugouts. Good wheeze, eh?"

"If you say so, sir. Let's hope it's true. Any sign of the maps we've been promised?"

"Ah, yes. I was coming to that. It's been decided they're not necessary after all. The objective will be in clear sight as soon as we go over the top. A red smudge on the far slope. We're to make a beeline for it."

Alastair frowned at the news. In the fog of battle it would be easy to become disoriented, lose direction. At least a map and compass would help keep them on course.

"Less than an hour to go," Aitken went on. "The tea urn should be round presently. Nothing like a hot cuppa laced with rum to keep out the cold, eh? Well, I'd best be off now. Lots still to do." He grasped Baird's hand. "Good luck, old chap. If the artillery does its work properly it should be a walkover."

And the band played. He was not fooled by the false bonhomie. And now, as though to confirm his doubts, the air was growing dank and heavy, a fine drizzle beginning to fall. He turned up his collar. Mist and rain. That was all they needed.

The tea arrived. He was grateful to cradle the steaming mug in his hands as he sipped the contents, even though the strength of the rum left him gasping. The men were getting fidgety now, fretting over equipment, checking and rechecking weapons, winding themselves up for the ordeal to come. Dawn was breaking, to reveal the trench shrouded in fog.

Jack Grove appeared. "Would you credit it, laddie? No one was expecting this. It's a regular pea-souper. Bit of luck, though. The Fritzes won't be able to see us coming."

"Possibly." How could he make Jack understand? More than eight hundred yards to travel over uncertain terrain. Blundering forward towards the German positions. Artillery spotting would be useless – the field guns would be firing blind.

"I know what you're thinking, Alastair. But there's no need to worry. The targets will have already been laid in. All we have to do is follow the shellfire. It'll be a piece of cake."

"You really think it's that simple?"

"Trust me. Tell you what. Let's have a small wager. Last one to the Mucky Farm stands a slap-up meal. Point Blanc and Pomfritz. Deal?"

Alastair grinned in spite of himself. Who could resist such an irrepressible spirit? Aping the Tommy's mangling of the French language. White wine and chips – the staple of estaminet life. "It's a deal."

They shook hands on it, instinctively hugged one another. Then Grove was gone. He was left wondering whether either of them would live to claim the bet.

* * *

The final minutes were the worst, an agony of suppressed emotion, striving to appear calm and unconcerned. But it was his duty set an example. Should he try a word of encouragement for the nervous or faint-hearted? At least wish the men Godspeed? It was too late for that now. The order was being given, his platoon filing into position. He had barely time for a hasty check that his pistol was loaded, the whistle safe in his breast pocket, before pushing his way down the line. There was movement up ahead: that would be Grove's platoon leaving the communication trench. He gave them a minute to clear, then led his men forward.

A scaling ladder was held steady. His inner turmoil disappeared, leaving in its wake a sense of detachment, almost of being at peace with the world. Was this the fatalism of the condemned man about to ascend the scaffold? He put his foot on the first rung, climbed up and onto the parapet. Visibility was worse than ever. Without marker tapes it would have been no mean task to find the holes cut in the wire. Soldiers were emerging from the trench behind him, dressing in two ranks, four or five yards between each man, sinking noiselessly to the ground. The plan was to gain extra precious seconds by starting the assault in No Man's Land. But in these conditions …

The first salvo of shells screeched overhead, followed by the crump of overlapping explosions. As the crescendo intensified, Baird's eyes were glued to the hands of his watch as they told off the seconds, the minutes … He drew his revolver, put the whistle to his lips. The fury of the barrage slackened, there was the briefest of interludes as the guns shifted target. It was the signal to advance. He blew what he hoped was a shrill blast and plunged towards the nearest gap.

Beyond that … it was impossible to be sure of anything in the murk. Two hundred and fifty yards to the German wire, easily achieved in the time allowed, or so they had been told. But that was to ignore the sodden, unyielding clay underfoot. Even worse was the tangle of obstacles visible only at the last moment, sometimes not even then. Rusting coils of barbed wire, shellholes half filled with stagnant water, shattered trees and splintered timber: any attempt to maintain formation was doomed to failure. At one stage he stumbled into a shallow ditch, found himself treading on a bloated, putrefying mass; recoiling in horror at the realisation these were corpses, the legacy of a previous attack. The gunfire was more distant now: the advance was falling too far behind. Figures loomed dimly through the haar, to disappear once more like wraiths in the night. Men were calling out to one another, fearful of becoming lost. He blew his whistle, again and again.

"Alastair! Is that you?" It was a shout from Captain Aitken. "I'm at the Hun wire." He followed the sound of the voice. Aitken pointed to a huge hole carved out of the German entanglements. "You can get your men through this way. We must press on. There's more of a slope now. So the going should be a bit easier. At least you'll be out of this morass. I've got to see to the other platoons. Good luck. I'm relying on you."

Relying on him. He could not even keep his platoon together. It was hard not to curse in frustration. Long minutes seemed to pass as stragglers slowly responded to his ever more frantic blasts. Eventually he counted twenty men assembled: he dared not delay further. How the other platoons were faring he had no means of knowing. But for some unaccountable reason the shelling had stopped. And was it his imagination? Or had visibility improved just a little? To be caught out here in the open, without protection … He quickened the pace towards the next position.

Christ! What was that? The unmistakable chatter and rattle of machine-guns opening up. *Rat-a-tat! Rat-a-tat-a-tat!* Figures could be glimpsed falling back, turning to run. His first impulse was to dash forward to stiffen the faltering line. But his own men were hesitant, looking uncertainly at one another. What if they refused an order to continue? Was he capable of driving them on at pistol point? The renewed crackle of machine-gun fire made up his mind. Bullets were kicking up the ground, coming in their direction.

"Back to the trench!" he heard himself bellow. "Be ready with covering fire." They could make a stand there, be better able to resist a German counterattack. The day might not yet be totally lost if they could hold out till reinforcements arrived.

It was only a score of yards back to comparative safety. But the German machine-gunners were already finding the range. Several of his men went down in a single burst. One keeled over, lay writhing in agony right in his path: without thinking he found himself stooping, dragging the man by the collar, heaving him over the lip, before leaping in himself. Willing hands helped him to his feet.

The trench wall was high, well above head height. "Give me a bunk up, you chaps. I need to see what's going on." Hoisted up, he was able to peer over the parados. Despite the persistent low cloud and drizzle, the mist was definitely thinning – enough to allow him a view of the crest of the hill. There was no sign of movement. Much closer to hand lay four – no, five bodies. If only he had given the order just a few seconds earlier … But at least there was no need to risk further casualties by trying to bring them in. Shocked by his own callousness, he signalled to be let down.

"Sergeant Patterson. Is Sergeant Patterson here?"

"Aye, sir." His platoon sergeant thrust himself forward.

Thank God for that. He led him aside. "What's our strength, d'you think? How many effectives?"

"Fit to bear arms? A round dozen o' our lads, I'd say. Maybe another six or seven waifs an' strays frae the other platoons."

Hardly encouraging news. "Any other NCOs?"

"Nane o' ours. But there's a corporal frae Mr Grove's platoon." He caught the fleeting look of concern. "I believe he's a steady man, sir. Ye could do worse."

"Right." Most likely Jack was lying out there. But this was no time to dwell on his fate. "It's our job to hang on till the second wave arrives." He consulted his watch. "They should have been here by now."

"Maybe they're no' coming."

"Nonsense." But his own doubts were growing. "Perhaps you'd better send a runner back to report on the situation."

"I'll dae that, sir. Any further orders?"

"Well, it's obvious we can't defend the whole trench. So we'll need to form a redoubt. Do we still have the Lewis gun?"

"Aye, sir. But there's only a few drums o' ammo. Maist o' it is out there somewhere."

"Then we'll just have to make the most of what we have. We'll screen off a section of trench. Barricades at either end. The men still have their two hundred rounds each."

"Just so, sir. What d'ye want me to dae?"

"You'll be in charge here. Take half the men and see if you can tear down some of these revetments. Use sandbags from the parapet as well. Then get the Lewis gun set up to cover our flank. I'll work down the trench, check that it's clear, then block it off. Keep them at it, sar'nt. We may not have all that much time."

It was a harrowing task to creep along the trench, pausing at every twist and turn while a bomber went forward to toss a hand grenade round the traverse, closely followed by a rush of bayonet men to deal with any survivors. But they encountered no opposition. Not a single German – alive or dead. One bay contained the entrance to a dugout, with a long ladder stretching down into the void. To attempt a descent was unthinkable: God knew what might lurk below in a maze of rooms and tunnels. All that could be done was to launch a clutch of Mills bombs down the shaft to entomb any foe lying in wait. By now, on his estimation they had come more than fifty yards – further than his little band could hope to defend.

"Corporal," he called to Grove's NCO. "I'm going to withdraw back to where the trench is narrowest. We'll throw up a breastwork there. Get the men busy with their entrenching tools. Think you can manage it?"

The man nodded. "Sorry, sir," he muttered.

"Sorry? For what?"

"Mr Grove, sir. He was a fine officer."

"You saw him fall?"

"Aye, sir. In the first burst. Right at the wire. Captain Aitken as well. Caught in enfilade fire. They didna stand a chance."

"I see. And what about you?"

"Me, sir? I was in the second line. The man next to me was hit. Knocked me ower, fell on top o' me. Some weight he was tae. By the time I managed to crawl out it was all over. Folk were runnin' back down the hill. So I joined them," he added lamely. "What else could I dae?"

"Nothing, corporal. No blame attaches to you. What's your name?"

"Sim, sir."

"Well, Corporal Sim, put it behind you. You've another chance here. I'm going back to see how the others are getting on. I'll come and inspect as soon as I can."

So Jack was gone – never more to raise his flagging spirits with a cheery word. And how many others had perished? Probably most of the company. Should he try to pull back? It went against the grain to give up hard-won ground. He must try to save something, if only in memory of his fallen comrade.

A sudden commotion caused him to look up sharply. A flurry of missiles whistled through the air. He saw flashes, heard detonations. Jesus! Potato-mashers! Scudding round the final traverse, there was scarcely time to take in the scene of devastation. A coal-scuttle helmet appeared above the barricade, followed by a face and grey-green torso. The man was fumbling with the fuse of a stick grenade. Instinctively he raised his revolver and fired blindly. The figure jerked backwards; there was a sound of footsteps scurrying away. Gingerly he poked his head over what remained of the barrier. The bodies of three German soldiers sprawled just a few feet away, one still moaning feebly. Obviously it had been a raiding party sent to test their defences. But how long before they returned in strength? He took careful aim at the German who was still alive, squeezed the trigger. His hand was trembling as he thrust the pistol back into its holster.

"Sorry about this, sir," croaked a voice. It was his platoon sergeant, half covered in rubble, the barrel of the Lewis gun across his chest.

"Just rest easy. We'll soon have you out of this." Baird dropped to his knees, began to pull away the debris. The gun was useless, no more than a chunk of metal. He groped for the sergeant's field dressing, then drew back. There was a huge gash in the man's side. Nothing could staunch that wound. He could only watch helplessly as life drained away. A final shudder, roll of the head, and it was over. He closed the sightless eyes, then turned away, sick to the core.

"Orders, sir?" It was Corporal Sim, come to see what was amiss. Baird shook himself out of his lethargy. There were three or four men standing behind Sim.

"Good thinking, corporal. We'll need to repair our defences here. And see to the casualties. Perhaps you might detail a party to lay the dead out of the way."

"Aye, sir. I'll see to it. Beggin' yer pardon, sir, but you look a bit knocked up. Why no' take a minute to catch yer breath?"

"No time for that, corporal," he snapped. "We're all a little the worse for wear. Just you get on with it."

"Right, sir." Sim began to clamber onto the wreckage, and then visibly stiffened, staring as though in disbelief. "Sir," he called down. "I'm no' exactly sure. But I think I can see folk comin' up from our trenches."

In an instant Baird was on the firestep, squinting into the gloom. It was true: he could make out a handful of soldiers, spread out, advancing slowly in pairs, some carrying what appeared to be long poles. They approached steadily: he could pick out the brassards on their sleeves. Stretcher bearers – searching for casualties. Not the expected relief, but at least it meant succour for the wounded. Pray God the Germans did not open fire.

"Anybody there? Lieutenant Baird?" It was the M.O. What on earth was he doing out here? His place was back at the aid post. He waved his hands above his head, received a wave back in acknowledgment.

Presently the rubicund face of Captain Bentley appeared. "Is that you, Alastair? Thank the Lord you're still alive. Mind if I drop in?" He allowed himself to be helped down by Corporal Sim. Six or eight orderlies followed with their stretchers of wooden poles and canvas base. "We got your message. Any more men besides these fellows?"

"Four or five about thirty yards down the trench."

"Fetch them back."

"But why?"

"All in good time, old son. Just do it. I'll make a start here."

A nod of the head sent Sim scurrying away. Baird leaned backwards against the trench wall, breathing heavily; now the immediate danger was over the palpitations in his chest had returned – worse than ever this time. Meantime the doctor passed from man to man: a cursory examination, a note on a tag, a muttered instruction to one of the bearers, and he was off to the next case. Only once did he pause to look up curiously at the subaltern before returning to his task. The job was completed in little more than five minutes.

"Not too good, Alastair. Six dead. Another two are too far gone. I've given them morphine to ease the pain. Three pretty bad. But they've a chance if I can get them back to operate in time. The rest can travel under their own steam."

"The walking wounded, you mean?" It was little more than a hoarse whisper. "But I've still got five or six fit men."

"The orders apply to everyone, I'm afraid. That's why they sent an officer. Any isolated groups are to make their way back to our lines. The attack has been called off."

"Called off?" The strain in his voice was unmistakable. "I don't understand. What happened to the other companies? Why didn't they follow on?"

Bentley went an even deeper shade of red. "Hold your horses. It's not the colonel's fault. It seems that the general came up to observe, saw the fog, and promptly cancelled the whole thing. But by then you'd already left. Colonel Lixmont hit the roof, but the general stood his ground. Said he couldn't afford to toss away a whole battalion."

"But aren't we going to attack again? Has this all been for nothing?"

"Not today, Alastair. Fresh arrangements will have to be made. But it's all academic so far as you are concerned."

"What d'you mean?"

"You won't be taking part."

"Why not? I'm not wounded. Not even a scratch."

"That's as may be. But you're certainly not fit for active service."

"I must protest, sir."

"Don't bother. I haven't had a chance to examine you properly. But I'd say you had pneumonia. Sorry."

Part IV: 1916-18

TWENTY-ONE

Change of Circumstances

Glasgow. November 1916

Morag Mackay sat gloomily at her desk in the dingy offices of the Housing Association. God knew how many interviews she had conducted in this poky little room, as women flocked in daily with their tales of woe. Fair and fixed rents had been decreed by the government since the start of the year, yet that seemed to have little effect on the numbers desperately seeking help. Landlords were only too keen to exploit the slightest loophole in the law, and the Association was almost powerless to stop them.

And now she was about to suffer the same fate as so many others. Though it had long been on the cards, the letter that morning had still come as a shock. The lease on the flat in Brighton Road was up; the landlord was refusing to renew it. Not that she could have managed the sum due in any case; her salary was little more than a pittance, and even that was now in doubt, with funding drying up alarmingly as donations fell away. She should have taken steps earlier, she realised that. But there had been so much to do here. And what with the worry of Iain's disappearance … two months of anxious waiting, beating her head against the brick wall of officialdom, before a letter from his brother had arrived to reassure her that he was at least alive and well. Six weeks after that a postcard had informed her that he was in prison at Peterhead. Peterhead! It might as well have said Timbuktu. No prospect of paying him a visit there – if visits were permitted at all. She dashed away a tear as a knock came at the door.

"Morag, dear. Mind if I come in?" It was the Association's organiser, Mary Barbour. "I thought you'd like to be on your own for a wee while. So I've brought you some tea."

"Thank you." She accepted the cup and saucer. "You're very kind – all of you." She had already told her colleagues about the eviction.

"You know you're always welcome to come and stay with me" said Mary, as though reading her thoughts. "Just till you get settled."

Morag shook her head. "You've been a true friend. But I couldna impose on you like that. Besides, what would it solve? It would only put off the inevitable. And ye ken fine ye have to make savings here. Thanks for the offer. But there's nothin' for it. I'll need to find somewhere else tae bide – and look for another job."

Mrs Barbour pursed her lips. What Morag said was true enough. "So what will you do? They're crying out for women to work in munitions."

"That would be the last resort. I want nothin' to dae wi' their war. Makin' weapons so that men can tear each other apart? It would stick in my craw."

"At least you would have a roof over your head."

"In one o' thae hostels for single women? Bossed around by crabbit old besoms? Rules and regulations every minute o' the day? It would be worse than bein' in jail."

"Then what? Have you any idea?"

"I'm no' sure. Somethin' where I could help other folk."

"I'm glad to hear you feel that way. In that case I've a suggestion to make. It might just fit the bill."

"Anythin' ye care to name. I'd be grateful. Ye ken that."

"Well, it's like this. Maud Ritchie happened to mention that a neighbour o' hers was on the lookout for a new nanny. She's a war widow – works as a nurse up at the hospital. One child. It's a live-in position. Good wages and all found, according to Maud. Think ye might be interested?"

Morag gasped. Nannying? How would this benefit those most in need? Only the idle rich employed nannies. "But I've got no qualifications." It was all she could think of saying.

"You had no qualifications when you started here. But you've become one of my best operatives and I'll be sorry to lose you. You're efficient, show sympathy and understanding – and take no nonsense. I should say that's exactly what's needed in handling children. At least consider the opening."

She felt herself weakening. "But surely the position will be taken already." It was a feeble protest.

Mrs Barbour brushed it aside. "That's not my understanding. Maud said that the lass had only just found out. Apparently her nanny suddenly decided to up sticks to go and work in Beardmore's new factory – airships or some such thing. The point is that she's no' had the chance to advertise yet. So if we can get in first … Look, Maud told me she was going home for her dinner. Perhaps she could have a word, get something sorted out. It's surely worth a try. What d'ye say?"

Morag paused for thought. An outright refusal would be hurtful, especially in view of Mary's concern. Besides, beggars could not be choosers. "I suppose it would do nae harm to find out what's involved," she said at last.

"That's the style. You write a wee note expressing interest. I'll just go and draft a character for you. Maud won't mind delivering them."

Alone once more, something else struck her. Mary knew all about her guilt and pain. Maybe she thought child-minding might help close the chapter on the baby she had never known. It was a kindly thought. At any rate she resolved to look on the bright side. Dashing off a few lines, she addressed the envelope: *To whom it may concern*. She even managed a wry smile when Maud Ritchie came to collect her letter.

An hour later Mrs Ritchie was back, flushed with success. By good fortune the young widow had been at home, and would be grateful if Miss Mackay could call that very afternoon. It was futile to claim that she was not ready to face an interview: within minutes she found herself bundled into her coat and shooed out to a chorus of good wishes. A short tram ride and even shorter walk brought her to the address she had been given in the quiet street just off the Byres Road. She was just about to press the bell when she suddenly remembered. Who should she ask for? No one had given her a name.

The door opened as soon as she rang. A maid stood on the threshold – no more than fifteen years old, thought Morag. But the girl had rosy cheeks and looked well nourished. Not at all like the overworked and underfed skivvies that she had always imagined in most middle class households.

"Is your mistress at home? My name is Mackay."

"Yes, miss. You were expected. This way." She led Morag into a small hallway, then into a larger sitting room. "Miss Mackay, mum."

A young woman in an elegant day dress rose from an armchair. "Good afternoon. Do come in."

"Good after –" She broke off in confusion. Never once had she dreamed of this. "Nurse Lixmont!" she gasped.

"Yes. But I didn't mean to startle you. Come and sit down." She propelled her visitor into the chair opposite, then turned to the maid. "Jenny, perhaps you might bring us some tea."

Morag's head was in a spin. Then she flushed with embarrassment.

"As a matter of fact I realised who you were as soon as I read your note. I always hoped we could meet up again – if only to apologise for my rude behaviour in the park. That was inexcusable. Will you forgive me?"

"Nothin' to forgive, miss. Or is it madam? They told me you were a war widow. And I see ye wear a ring now."

There was a laugh. "Nothing like that. It's just a little deception of mine. No one has managed to drag me to the altar yet. And you wouldn't have seen the ring before." She held up her hand with the circle of gold on her finger. "It's really quite simple. The hospital doesn't allow jewellery to be worn on duty. And that other time I was wearing gloves. I've never been married. Does that shock you?"

"No, of course not. I only wanted to know what I should call you."

"I think Miss Elizabeth would be fine at home. But Mrs Lixmont in public. We must keep up appearances."

"In public? But ye'll no' be wantin' me here. No' after what Iain's done."

"Oh, so you know. Did he tell you?"

"No' exactly. But when I bumped intae ye that time at Kelvingrove I saw the resemblance. He tried to flannel his way out o' it – but I ken him too well."

"I see. Would you have come had you known it was me?"

"Never, Miss Elizabeth. I would have been too ashamed."

"I don't see why. You can't be held responsible for his actions. And Mrs Barbour has written you an excellent reference. She states that you're living by yourself. Does that mean you are separated from – your partner?"

"Iain? As good as, I suppose. He got intae a bit o' trouble. He's against the war, ye see. Widnae join up. So they've put him in clink. Ten years at hard labour."

"That must be difficult for you. I don't mean to pry, but do you still have feelings for him?"

"He's no' all bad. I ken he's done some dreadful things. And now he's payin' for them. But – aye, I do still love him. God rot me."

"Don't say that. Your honesty does you credit. Now, let's get down to brass tacks. How would you like to come and live with us?"

"But ye cannae want me to look after the wean. It would never work."

"Why ever not? Mrs Barbour has been singing your praises. She claims you have all the requisite qualities. And I would be reluctant to doubt her word. But tell you what. We could leave the decision to my son. He should have finished his afternoon nap by now. I'll just go and fetch him." Before Morag could object she had swept from the room.

There was the sound of muttered voices before she reappeared in the doorway, leading an infant by the hand. "Eddie, this is Nanny Morag. Go and say hello to her."

The boy looked up at his mother, then at the strange lady, curiosity vying with timidity. He took a few steps forward, then advanced more confidently and plucked at her skirt. As if in a trance Morag lifted him up onto her lap. He stared into her face with wide, trusting eyes, and cradled himself against her bosom. There was a lump in her throat as she put her arms round him.

"I think he likes you. And I know we're all going to get on famously. Shall we say the day after tomorrow?"

Blinded by tears she could only nod.

* * *

Edinburgh. March 1917

The war hospital stood in its own grounds, tucked away anonymously behind high walls on the southern fringe of the city. Formerly a country house hotel, it had only recently been taken over as a convalescent home to help cope with casualties flooding back from the stalemate on the Somme. Shabby genteel, he would have called it, as he surveyed what was now the officers' dayroom. In one corner a couple of subalterns were playing a desultory game of ping-pong. In another a small group was clustered round the gramophone. The tune was ragtime: *Everybody's doing it* – over and over again, till the music began to grate. Otherwise the room was almost empty.

Most people would be out of doors on a fine day such as this. They were encouraged to get out and about as much as possible; it was part of the healing process. A decent enough set, he knew, many of them only temporary gentlemen like himself, and they generally messed well enough together. At least those present had the wit to recognise when a fellow wanted to be left undisturbed. Time and again he scanned the doorway, fingering the blue armband above his elbow. Only one thing was certain. One way or another Alastair Baird would not be sporting the badge of a wounded officer much longer.

Had he gone too far at his final medical board that morning? The three military doctors had clearly taken it for granted that he would fall in with their recommendations. But the long months of recuperation had given plenty of time for reflection – at base hospital, then the sanatorium in England, and now here in Edinburgh. He could not bring himself to betray the memory of those whose lives had been wantonly sacrificed. So he had dared to spurn the offer of a home posting, demanding instead an immediate return to active service. When the senior major tried to probe his reasons, he had so far forgotten himself as to question the conduct of the war. Hardly surprising that he had been cut short, sent packing to await the board's decision. Was he to be granted his wish? Or was it to be a court martial?

At last – the inevitable summons. The mess steward was weaving his way towards him, tray in hand. Strange how the niceties must always be observed – his fate conveyed to him on a silver platter. "Are you the prisoner's escort?" he called out, only half-jokingly.

"Er, no, sir. There's a gentleman wishing to see you." He proffered the salver.

There was a brief hesitation before he accepted the card. No one had paid him a visit before, nor was he expecting anyone – except, perhaps, a brother officer come to place him under arrest. Then he read the inscription: *Sir Edward Lixmont.* Elizabeth's father! And now a knight of the realm. What on earth could he want? And how did he know he was here? It was a struggle to keep his face impassive. "Thank you. I'll come out."

A well-remembered figure stood in the hallway, apparently passing the time of day with the C.O. Possibly a little more grey about the temples, a few more lines etched on his face, but the eyes were as alert and darting as ever. He caught sight of the young officer. "Lieutenant Baird. Alastair, my boy. You've no idea how it gladdens my heart to see you safe and well."

"Thank you, sir." They shook hands. "It's awfully good of you to come. And congratulations on your knighthood. I'm sure it's well merited."

"Services to the war effort." Lixmont chuckled. "I feel rather a fraud on that score. Still, my wife likes it. And it would have been churlish to decline the honour. But never mind that. I've been having a word with Major Phelps here. He says you'll soon be off the sick list."

"That's so, sir. I had my final board earlier today."

"So I've been informed." The lawyer frowned slightly. "Shall we take a turn in the grounds? It would be a pity to waste such grand weather. Would you excuse us, major?"

"Of course, Sir Edward. I'll be in my office should you require anything further." There was a formal handshake. Then the door closed behind him.

"Come along, Alastair. You can show me the sights."

"As you wish, sir. Though there's not much to see."

"Well, at least we can walk. I could do with the exercise." They passed through the doorway and out into the sunshine. "I gather you've been resident here for some weeks now. With free rein to wander wherever the spirit takes you."

"Within reason, sir."

"Just so. The doctors obviously believe our bracing air is its own medicine. Shall we go this way?" They set off along a gravel path. "I don't suppose any of your excursions have led you down by Trinity, have they?"

Baird flushed. "I've taken the tram down to Newhaven once or twice."

The look of embarrassment did not escape Lixmont. "Reliving old times, eh? When you were a student? These were happier days before the war." He did not press the point. "Shall we stop a minute and admire the spring flowers?"

Alastair turned to face him. "I should have paid a courtesy call. And I beg your pardon if I've caused any offence. But I genuinely felt you wouldn't want to be bothered. And Mrs Lixmont – Lady Lixmont I meant to say. She didn't altogether approve of me, did she?"

"Well, perhaps not. Let that pass. And there's no need to apologise. If anything, it should be the other way round. My family owes you a grave debt. The least I can do is to take an interest in your welfare."

"I'm grateful for that, sir. But how did you know I was here? I told no one, not even my aunt. I suppose Colonel Lixmont must have been informed and passed it on to you."

"No, it wasn't that. I knew that you were in my son's battalion, of course.

He told me as much some time ago. But there was no mention that you had been subsequently wounded. Major Phelps informs me it was gas poisoning."

"That's what it said on my medical card. But the original diagnosis was pneumonia. The M.O. must have thought he was doing me a favour by saying it was a war related injury. At least it avoids any accusation that I'm trying to work my ticket."

"No one who knows you could possibly think that."

"Thank you, sir. But you still haven't told me how you found out."

"Can't you guess? Have you forgotten your visit to the Groves?"

The Groves. He gave a little start as he remembered the old lady and gentleman, holding hands as they sat together, fighting back the tears as he recounted what he knew of their son's death. They had been so dignified in their grief, so pathetically grateful that he had taken the trouble to come. Shame and guilt welled up within him. Why had they been robbed of their only child? Why was Jack gone while he had survived?

The older man seemed to grasp his anguish. "I can see I've touched a raw nerve. Let's sit on this bench and rest awhile."

Lixmont was in no hurry to resume the conversation. It was some minutes before he broke the silence. "I don't know Grove very well. But our paths sometimes cross in the line of business, and we share membership of the same club. I ran into him there last night and he happened to mention that you had called to pay your respects. It's as simple as that. Was it so very terrible?"

"I felt such a cur. Stealing away like a thief in the dark."

"What else could you have done? Your memories of young Grove would have brought comfort to them."

"You think so? How could anything I might say help fill the emptiness in their lives? And I dread having to go and see an old widow woman back in Broomburn. Her son was my batman. Blown to bits in front of me. How can I tell her that?"

"It must be hard, I know. But there's no need for the literal truth. It would only distress the old lady still more."

"That's what we're always told." There was sudden venom in his voice. "We're expected to connive at lies and deceit. For the sake of the families, it's said, to keep up civilian morale. But the fact is that it's to stifle criticism, hide the truth. So that the generals can carry on in the same old way, use the same old tactics that have been discredited time and again. What do they care how many thousands are sent to their deaths in hopeless attacks." He buried his face in his hands. "I'm sorry if I sound outspoken. You must think me terribly disloyal."

Lixmont laid a hand on his shoulder. "Perish the thought, Alastair. You've been through the mill. God knows what horrors you've had to endure. We hear so little at home."

"And you really want to know?" He stared morosely into the distance, as though wrestling with some personal dilemma. When he spoke at last, it was in a husky undertone.

"When we went into action back in September the operation was cobbled together at the last minute. Then the attack was botched – went off at half cock. There was this thick fog. We couldn't see where we were going, and when the mist started to clear the Jerry machine guns were ready for us. It was a massacre. A few of us managed to dive into a trench. My platoon was a bit behind the others, you see. Otherwise we'd have been goners as well. Then the medicos came up. That's when we found out that the attack had been called off – but too late to stop the lead company from going over the top. I was the only officer to get back."

"And you feel a sense of guilt because of it? I can understand your bitterness. You believe the generals are responsible for mismanaging the conduct of the war."

"What else can I think? We were told it was going to be a walkover. The Big Push to win the war. And look at what happened. Hundreds of thousands of casualties. Gains measured in yards, a miserable four or five miles in so many months. And they still claim it was a success. It no longer matters how far we advance, just so long as we wipe out more of the enemy than they do of us. Since we outnumber the Germans we're bound to win in the end. What kind of twisted logic is that?"

"Hmm. I take your point. Even the politicians are becoming seriously concerned about our manpower losses."

"Politicians? They're as much to blame as the general staff. Feeding us with pap about self-sacrifice in a noble cause. The war for civilisation, the downfall of Prussian militarism. Does that actually mean anything?"

"What are you trying to tell me, Alastair?"

"I suppose – I suppose I'm trying to say that I don't believe in the war any more. Not till I know what we're really fighting for. What are our terms for making peace with Germany? Can anyone tell me that?"

"I see. Have you shared your view with others?"

"No, not really. Though I blotted my copybook with the board this morning. They wanted to fob me off with a posting back to the depot. That means pushing paper or training new recruits. Sending innocents to the slaughter? I couldn't be party to that. So I told them to send me back to the Front. And I'm afraid I rather lost my temper. They didn't seem over pleased about that. I was just waiting to be put under arrest when you arrived."

"Put under arrest? I don't understand. On what charge?"

"Insubordination. Conduct unbecoming. These are court martial offences. I could be cashiered, reduced to the ranks – if nothing worse."

"So that's it. I knew there was something troubling you." He scanned the anxious face. "Listen, Alastair. I think you're making a mountain out of a molehill. A gallant young officer is wounded in action. He makes a few off the cuff remarks in private. I hardly think your superiors would wish to blow the situation out of proportion."

"I wish I could share your confidence, sir." He broke off at the scrunch of boots on the gravel. A corporal with a Red Cross armband was striding towards them. "Yes, what is it?"

"Beggin' yer pardon, sir. But the C.O. would be obliged if you would report to his office directly."

"All right. I'm coming. No need for you to wait." He waved the orderly away. "Sorry about this, sir. I'll have to go."

"Of course. I'll stay here and await your return."

"But I might not be coming back."

"Nonsense. It'll be news of the board's decision. Once we know that we can put our heads together and decide what's for the best. Cut along now. Don't keep the major waiting. And don't worry." Alastair nodded and hurried away.

Left to his own devices, Sir Edward Lixmont rose from the bench and began to pace up and down. Young Baird had been deeply disillusioned. Who could fault him for that? It had led him into a minor indiscretion. But would the army treat it as such and overlook the offence? Or must the full rigour of military law be applied in the interests of discipline? Despite his show of optimism he could not be sure. He sat down once more and took out a small notebook and pencil. Should it become necessary to prepare a plea in mitigation … He was soon engrossed in jotting down words and phrases.

Deaf to the world, he was unaware of the returning footsteps. Only the sound of a polite cough made him look up sharply. "I'm back, sir."

"I didn't hear you come. I was just making a note."

"Sorry about that, sir. You must have many calls on your time."

"Well, never mind." He slipped book and pencil into his coat pocket. Then he smiled. "Your interview didn't take long. And I observe you haven't been placed under close arrest."

"No, sir. The C.O. was brief and to the point."

"Well, sit ye down and tell me all about it. Is it good news?"

Alastair dropped onto the bench. "I don't rightly know, sir."

"What the devil do you mean by that?"

"I'm to be dismissed the service. Invalided out. Major Phelps had a telephone call."

"Ah. You didn't anticipate that outcome, did you? Did he have anything else to say?"

"Very little. I don't suppose he knows much more himself. I'm to make myself scarce as soon as the paperwork comes through. It's unlikely I'll qualify for a war pension. And any gratuity would be tiny." He forced a wry grin. "Though he did say I'd get a pound if I handed in my army greatcoat."

Lixmont chuckled. "You won't survive very long on that."

"No, sir. I'll have to find work of some description. I haven't had much chance to think about it as yet."

"Of course. But you mustn't hide your light under a bushel. You're a university man. Any profession would be proud to have you – particularly in view of your war record. You might consider the law, for example. I'll take you into my own office, get you signed up as an articled clerk."

"I'm sure it's well meant, sir. And I don't wish to seem ungrateful. It's just that somehow I don't see myself as a solicitor. I've had two years of teacher training. Perhaps I could find a post somewhere."

"That was always your chosen career, wasn't it? I should have remembered. Well, there's certainly a huge teacher shortage – especially of younger men. I've no doubt you'd soon be snapped up. And there would be no difficulty in arranging an acting certificate."

"But I wouldn't want you to pull strings on my behalf."

"No strings involved, I do assure you. It's quite common these days."

"But –"

"I won't hear another word. The only question now is to decide where you're going to ply your trade. Have you any preference as to locality?"

"No, not really." Sir Edward was nodding encouragingly. "Well, there's nothing to keep me here in Edinburgh. I don't suppose my aunt would welcome me back as a lodger. Broomburn might be an option. But to tell the truth I can't regard the village as home any more. I felt almost a total stranger last time I paid a visit."

"And you feel bad about the loss of your batman?"

"Yes, there is that. God knows how old Mrs Urquhart will take me."

"She'll be thankful that you were his officer, that he was comforted in his last moments by someone who knew him well. Go back by all means. Stay a few days. Then move on. You might consider Glasgow as a possibility." He dropped the suggestion casually, almost as an afterthought.

"Glasgow? Why there?"

"Well, there are some fine schools. You could have the pick of them. And I don't doubt," he smiled broadly, "that a certain person would be pleased to receive you."

"Elizabeth? You can't mean your daughter?" He stared in disbelief. "But I gave my word not to get in touch till the war is over."

"The war *is* over – for you." He produced a card. "This is her address."

"But she might not want to see me."

"How can you know till you've met? I'll send her word to expect you. Then there'll be no excuse. Don't leave it too long. I'd take it amiss if you let me down." He extended his hand. "Agreed?"

"Yes, sir." What else could he say?

TWENTY-TWO

The Cleft Stick

Peterhead, Aberdeenshire. April 1917

"This is the place, Mr Dunlop." The chief warder turned the key in the lock. "Not very cheery, I'm afraid, sir. Are ye sure ye really want to conduct your business in here? The governor said ye were to be given every facility."

Fraser Dunlop smiled dourly as he stepped inside. His attention was immediately caught by the long table running across the middle of the room, boxed off into compartments, and furnished with a partition of stout wire mesh to keep visitors and inmates apart. He turned to his guide. "Yes, this will suit me admirably. No doubt there will be a prison guard in attendance."

"It is the custom, sir."

"Not this time. Instruct him to remain outside." The interview would be difficult enough without the presence of an observer. That was why he had declined the prison governor's offer of his own office.

"It's no' advisable, sir. Yon's a surly brute. Always ready wi' his fists. There's nae tellin' how he might react."

"With these precautions?" Dunlop gestured towards the wire fence. "I'm certain I'll be quite safe. How long will it take to fetch the prisoner?"

"It might be a wee while. He's out on a working party at the minute."

"Is he? Well, it's of no consequence. I have some notes to look over first." There was a slim leather attaché case under his arm. "No need to stay. There must be other duties awaiting your attention."

"Aye, that's so, sir. But –"

"Well?"

"Nothin', sir." After all, it was none of his business. "I'll see ye're not disturbed."

"Thank you. That would be for the best."

Dunlop waited till the door had closed before easing himself into a chair at one of the booths. He laid his case on the desk, unstrapped it, and slid out a manila folder. Not that there was any need to consult the file; every detail was etched into his memory. It lay unopened as he pondered his chances of success.

The risks were considerable, he had to admit. It had taken all his powers of persuasion to wring a grudging permission from his superiors. Perhaps they wanted him to fail. After all, his plan for crushing unrest on the Clyde had worked only too well – and others had reaped the benefit. Little wonder he felt a sense of grievance that his career was stagnating. Lloyd George was in Downing Street, and his efforts had been forgotten. Now, while other centres of war production seethed with discontent, Glasgow was silent as the grave.

Or was it? His political masters were too complacent. Surely it had been a blunder to release the workers' leaders from jail; and the rumours that the deportees were to be allowed to return did not bode well for industrial harmony. Extreme radicals would never mend their ways, no matter what promises they might make. And over the past year much had happened to foster their ambitions. If the Irish could mount an insurrection in Dublin, then was an armed struggle on the streets of Glasgow inconceivable? If the workers of Petrograd could bring down the Tsarist government in Russia, then what might the revolutionaries at home achieve? Already they might be secretly rebuilding their organisation, gathering strength, plotting the downfall of the state. And therein lay his opportunity. If he could pinpoint the threat and nip it in the bud, then his views would be vindicated and a transfer to high office in London assured. Fall short, and his reputation would lie in shreds, his chances of further progression shattered once and for all. Everything now depended on the man he had come to see. The information on his file showed distinct promise. But would he agree to accept what was on offer?

A sudden commotion interrupted his thoughts. The door on the far side of the divide barged open to reveal a figure in prison garb struggling with his captors. It took the efforts of three warders to manhandle their charge into the seat opposite and hold him down.

Dunlop surveyed the scene with an expression of mild interest. The angry, sullen features only a yard or so away were those of a caged animal, but with any luck one that might be tamed, bent to his will. Taking a silver case from an inside pocket, he carefully selected a cigarette, struck a match to light it, and inhaled deeply. The leaf was the finest Virginia – cool and rich. As he blew out the smoke, slowly and deliberately, he noted with satisfaction the twitch of the prisoner's nostrils as he caught the aroma.

"Sit still and behave yerself, Baird," he heard one of the jailers snarl. "Or it'll be the worst for you."

"All right," he said sharply. "There's no need for that. I think our friend will calm down. You can release his arms. I'll take things from here." He made a gesture of dismissal. "Wait outside."

Iain Baird glowered after them. So the screws had been deprived of their entertainment – another ritual beating when there was no one around. Why else drag him away from the backbreaking toil at the quarry?

"Smoke?" He turned to scowl at the well-dressed stranger. Obviously a nob of some kind, judging by the way the guards jumped to his call. A lighted cigarette was pushed through the grille. He stared at the offering, instinctively wary. But the temptation was just too great. His hand reached out, took it between finger and thumb. The taste was heavenly, far superior to the occasional dog end or rollup he was able to scavenge.

"How are you getting along in here? Any complaints?"

Now he was being mocked. The evidence of victimisation should have been obvious to the most casual observer. But it would be futile to rise to the provocation. He contented himself with a sneer. "Nah! Everything's nice as ninepence. All the comforts of home."

"Glad to hear it." Dunlop chose to ignore the jibe. "But it's strange how accidents will happen in places like this. You must have walked into a fair few doors."

"Aye, that's right." He stubbed out the remains of his cigarette. "Doors that spring out at ye wherever you go."

"Just so. It's a pity, all the same. How long have you been in Peterhead? Nine months? And the sentence was ten years at hard labour, was it not?"

"So what? Ye didna come here to tell me that."

"Perhaps not. I was merely wondering how you would manage to cope in the long years ahead. The regime here is not over friendly towards conscientious objectors. Not to mention deserters from the army. You've already suffered more than your share of misfortune. And there's little prospect of remission. I'm sure you take my meaning."

"Aye. Ye want something." The bitterness in his voice was belied by a sudden narrowing of the eyes.

Dunlop smiled inwardly. "Perhaps it might be better to say we could do something for each other," he said softly.

"How? Wi' me banged up in here. Ye said it yersel'."

"True. But there are always ways and means. You may be wondering why it was you I chose to visit." He was rewarded with a hard, calculating stare. "Ah, I see you are. Well then, allow me to explain. In my line of business dozens of reports cross my desk every day. Your name happened to crop up, together with a mention of your place of birth. That was what first attracted my attention."

"Ye don't say? And why should that be?"

"Let's say it jogged my memory. I remember Broomburn well, though with little affection I must confess. There was an industrial dispute in the mines. Back in '04, it was. You would have been just a boy then. It was my task to restore the rule of law. I suppose I should be grateful that it helped launch my career. Your father was the ringleader. And look what happened to him."

The mask slipped. Iain reeled as though stung. "Dinnae dare talk about my faither like that," he hissed. The apparition was there again – the outstretched hand, that last despairing plea … He found himself trembling.

"By no means." The tone was measured, even kindly. "I had the highest regard for George Baird. He stood up for what he believed to be right. But times change and men must learn to adapt."

"My faither's been deid a long time." It had been a shock, but the vision was fading.

"I meant no disrespect, I assure you. It was simply to point out the comparison. Your father failed to grasp the folly of resorting to violence. On the other hand … it's the wise man that can profit from past mistakes – if given a second chance."

"Meaning?"

"All in good time." He was not ready to spring the trap – not just yet. "As you may imagine, I've gone through your record in some detail. And, believe it or not, come to the conclusion that you are deserving of some sympathy. I cannot, of course, condone the path you have chosen to take, but I can understand your motives."

Iain rolled his eyes.

"Why not? You were an apprentice in the shipyards, aspired to a managerial career. You even attended classes in your own time to gain the qualifications you would need. But your ambitions were thwarted. Your origins told against you. In your frustration you fell victim to the doctrines of revolutionary socialism. You became an activist and organiser, inciting strike action which would damage the war effort. And that brought you to our attention."

"So I'm meant to be impressed? Ye've done yer homework."

"Better than you might think. You don't really believe in all this socialist claptrap, do you? Brotherhood of man? Working class solidarity? It's just so much pap, isn't it? You're really after power and influence, and don't much care how you achieve it. Is that not true? At the end of the day it's every man for himself."

"Now ye're talkin' in riddles."

"Am I? What about your mentor? Stan Robertson?" He nodded sagely. "I see you recall the name. He saved his own bacon. Left you in the lurch, didn't he? It's a pity that we've never managed to track him down."

"Is this leadin' anywhere? We seem to be goin' round in circles." Suddenly he was tired of all this fencing. Stan had shown him a way out, and he had spurned the chance. His irritation got the better of him. "I'm gettin' fed up wi' your pish."

"Very well then, Baird. I'll come to the point." There was obviously nothing more to be gained by skirting round the issue. He took a deep breath. "I am in a position to obtain your release. You would be free to return to Glasgow. Go back to your old job."

"Aye. And just how would ye manage that?"

"I'll not pretend it has been easy, but my organisation is not without influence. Officially your sentence would be suspended on compassionate grounds. You could claim it was pressure from the labour movement which forced the government's hand. That would go down well with your workmates. Give you some kudos."

"Maybe so. But auld Findlay would never gie me a start. Have me blacklisted at every works on the Clyde, mair like."

"Mr Findlay is hoping to see his name in the next Honours List. He will be anxious to avoid anything which might jeopardise his chances of preferment. Quite the reverse, I should imagine. How would you like a position as charge hand, with every expectation of rapid promotion to foreman? That would entitle you to a company house."

"But I already hae a place to bide."

"Your flat was repossessed some months ago, and your – companion evicted. She is at present engaged as a live-in nanny. This is the address." He pushed a sliver of paper through the mesh. "You see how much we know."

Iain barely glanced at the handwritten scrawl. That Morag should have been reduced to working in domestic service – with someone else's child. He scowled at the thought.

"Think how she must have missed you this past year. And now you have the chance to make amends. Comfortable home, a steady income, every possibility of advancement. What more could she ask?"

"And you'd expect me to be yer pet whippet . Keep my nose clean, tell ye if I hear o' any trouble brewin'. Is that it?"

"Rather more than that, I fancy. After all, I've invested a deal of time and effort on your behalf."

"Then what?"

"Baird, at present the Clyde is relatively quiet. But I have grave doubts this will last. Most of those imprisoned for sedition last year have already been released. Others are shortly to be allowed to return from exile. It is inconceivable that their objective is no longer the overthrow of the state."

"So ye want me to snoop on them?"

"Who better? You would be welcomed with open arms."

"Suppose they gie up the notion? Think there's nae chance?"

"Then you would be of no use to me. But I am assured that plans are already afoot. Now, are you with us? Or have I been wasting my time?"

The implication was all too clear. Carry out this man's bidding, or be left to rot in this hellhole. Inside – he was finished. Poor food, unremitting labour, constant persecution would see to that. Outside … there was always a chance. Only a fool would turn down the opportunity.

"Exactly what would ye expect from me?"

"That's better. Your task will be to make contact with your former associates and offer your services. That is if they don't seek you out first."

"And report their intentions to you."

"Precisely. Except that on occasion it may be necessary to encourage more extreme action. Industrial disputes and peaceful demonstrations can always lead to mobbing and rioting, the wanton destruction of property, violent confrontation with the forces of law and order. Need I say more?"

There was the slightest inclination of Baird's head. "Naw. Ye want me to stir things up. And I can guess why." He thought for a moment. "When do I get out o' here?"

"So I can take it that you are prepared to cooperate? Excellent. You've made the right decision, Baird." His voice took on a hard edge. "Play me false and you'll be crushed like a worm. I'll have you back behind bars before you know it. After that your only way out will be in a box. I trust I make myself clear."

"Aye. Clear as shit."

"Just so long as you understand your position. Now to details. There are formalities to be observed before you can be released on licence. Also arrangements to be made regarding your employment. In due course you will receive a certificate of discharge from the prison authorities, together with a letter of appointment from Ibrox Ordnance and a railway warrant to Glasgow. On arrival you will present yourself at the main office where no doubt you will be informed of your duties in the workplace. Your contact with me will be through one of the pay clerks. He will be your handler. Any questions?"

"How long is all this gonnae take?"

"A week or so. But don't worry. I'll have a word with the governor. A transfer to light duties in the meantime, I would suggest. And you wouldn't object to some decent grub, would you? I'll see what I can do."

"What about this?" He pointed to the bruising on his face.

"I was coming to that. I think you may take it that you will not be subject to any more – mishaps, shall we say."

"Tell that to thae bastards back there. They're just waitin' to gie me another thumpin.'"

Without a word Dunlop rose from his place, crossed swiftly to the door and threw it open. As he fully expected, his guide had lingered behind. In vain Iain strove to hear snatches of the whispered conversation, but he did manage to catch a glimpse of the look of shock – or was it fear – from the chief warder before the door closed once more.

"There, I've fixed it for you. He'll pass on the message to the others. You'll not be harmed again. That satisfy you, Baird?"

"How can ye be sure o' that?" But he had no real doubts. For the time being, at least, he was under the protection of this shadowy figure – someone with the political clout to deliver on his promises, even within prison walls.

"Depend upon it. We always look after those who serve us well." He slipped the folder back into his case. "You know, Baird, I feel we are on the threshold of a fruitful relationship. I'll bid you good day. Don't forget to take that address."

Iain was left to contemplate his pact with the devil.

* * *

Glasgow

"There, he's sleeping now." The nursery door closed softly. "The wee chap really likes his bedtime story, doesn't he?"

"You can say that again. He won't go down without one. Usually nanny or I have to oblige. But she's out this evening. Thank you for stepping into the gap."

"My pleasure."

"And also for playing with him while I got his supper ready. You must be exhausted – chasing each other round the house."

"Not a bit of it. Lions and tigers – just what the doctor ordered. Do me good to get a spot of exercise."

She smiled fondly. "You two have really hit it off, haven't you? I can see Eddie has taken a shine to you already. Of course a man's influence, a father figure …" Her voice trailed away uncertainly.

There was an awkward silence. How pale and thin he looked, so vulnerable in his ill-fitting serge suit. She could have kicked herself for that slip of the tongue. Best take things more slowly. In the meantime he needed feeding up if his civilian clothes were ever to fit properly.

"You must be famished. Come into the parlour. I've laid out the tea things. Sit yourself down while I fetch the pot."

"I hope you haven't put yourself out on my behalf. Dashed cheek on my part to write and almost invite myself here. I don't know that I would, had your father not suggested it."

"You were too shy? That sounds like the old Alastair I used to know." She caught the glance of dismay. "I was only joking, silly. Now you're a hero."

"I don't know about that." He shivered in spite of himself. "It was like Dante's Inferno. Noise and confusion everywhere. You have no control. Things just happen – all round you."

Elizabeth bit her lip. Her father had warned her not to dwell on memories of the trenches. And experience in the wards had shown her how wounded soldiers could be affected long after they returned to Blighty. They were calling it shellshock – a delayed reaction to the horrors of war.

"Alastair, dearest," she said gently, "I would have been heartbroken had you not come."

"I was just so glad you bothered to reply. You've no idea what it meant to me."

Her eyes sparkled as she patted him. "You just rest here." She pointed to the settee. "I'll be back in a jiffy."

Truth to tell, he was relieved to take the weight off his feet. His exertions had left him a little winded – a slight constriction in the chest, nothing serious. It would soon pass. Before him was a low table, laden with dishes, loosely covered with a linen cloth. Curiosity impelled him to lift a corner; he whistled in amazement as the contents were revealed. Hastily he replaced the cover as the rattle of crockery announced Elizabeth's return.

"I thought we would be more comfortable in here." She laid down her tray and whipped off the cloth. "What do you think of the spread?"

"Elizabeth, I don't know what to say. I'm touched, but this would feed an army. I thought the food shortages were getting really bad now. However did you manage all this?"

"Well, it is rather a special occasion." She handed him a plate and began to pour tea. "Dad helped out a bit. The salmon and ham came from him. Only tinned, I'm afraid. Try some of the sandwiches while I slice the pie."

Alastair still seemed unconvinced. "You must have gone to a lot of effort. How did you find the time? I mean with your hospital work and all that."

"Oh, I was due a few days leave. So I decided to take them now." She flopped down beside him. "Actually, I've a confession to make. Jenny and Morag did most of the work. So you see, I can't take the credit."

"Jenny? Morag?"

"Jenny's the maid. I gave her time off to go and visit her mother. She won't be back till tomorrow morning."

"And Morag?"

"Morag Mackay. I'm led to believe the two of you are old acquaintances."

Alastair stared at her. "How on earth – ?" He was lost for words.

Elizabeth chuckled. "That was my little surprise. Quite a coincidence, isn't it? But there's no need to feel embarrassed. I've no regrets. And Eddie dotes on her."

"Well, you've certainly succeeded. I'd no idea."

"No reason why you should. I was looking for a nanny and she was sent along. I had no hesitation in taking her on."

"You must be very forgiving."

"Fiddlesticks! That's got nothing to do with it. Morag's not at fault. In fact she's suffered far more than I have. She sends her apologies by the way. Did you know her well?"

"Hardly at all. I only met her once. It was when my mother was dying. You remember I was looking for my brother to tell him, and she went out of her way to help me."

"And you returned the favour. I heard about the letter you sent her."

"It was the least I could do. How is she keeping?"

Elizabeth glanced at the clock on the mantelpiece. "Why not see for yourself? She's due back in an hour or so. Now let's eat." She began to pile food onto his plate. "I'll be in the doghouse if we let all this stuff go to waste. Tuck in."

Despite his initial misgivings, it was enticing to sit next to a dazzling hostess, to be the object of her attentions. The rich fare was delicious, the allure of her perfume intoxicating. She insisted he taste everything, emphasising the need to build up his strength as an excuse. Only when he groaned, and protested he was fit to burst, did she relent.

"Are you sure? Oh well, at least have some more tea." She refilled his cup. "Where were we? Ah yes, Morag. I expect you know she has some very decided views. But we don't let that come between us. Her latest fad is the Women's Peace Crusade. She's at one of their meetings now. What d'you think of that?"

Alastair grinned. "I seem to remember another political activist. Suffragettes, was it not?"

"Oh that! It was just a passing whim. I've grown up since then. Women are bound to get the vote, but based on their war efforts, nothing else."

"I expect you're right." He grew serious. "Listen. This might come as a shock, but I don't believe in the war any more. Not with all the wanton sacrifice, the waste of human life. In the end there will be no winners. I told your father as much."

"Daddy? What did he have to say?"

"Oh, he was mildly sympathetic. He realises the war is not going well, that we're bogged down on all fronts. But he has no answers about how to stop this insanity."

"And you have?"

"I don't say that. But I can't just stand aside and do nothing. Perhaps Morag could give me a few pointers."

"You'd join the peace movement?"

"If that's what it takes. I haven't really thought it all through yet."

"But think of the future. It could damage your career." She looked at him anxiously. "Promise me you won't do anything rash."

"Little danger of that." He gave a rueful smile. "I've got to find a career first. My army pay won't last much longer."

"But what about my father? Wasn't he helping to fix up something for you?"

"You know about that?" He pursed his lips. "I've an interview tomorrow. He must have arranged it, though I asked him not to. Quite a prestigious school, as it happens, with both primary and secondary departments."

"There you are then. Ample scope for your talents."

"If I'm offered the post. And I decide to accept it."

"You will be," she said firmly. "And the pater would be awfully hurt if you turned it down. Think about it. You'll be able to get away from that dreadful place where you're staying."

"Calton? I agree it's not much to write home about. But needs must. It's all I can afford."

"Perhaps …" For a moment she appeared lost in thought. "Tell me about Broomburn. Has anything changed?"

"Apart from the war, you mean? Not especially. My sister has three of a family now. Mr Ogilvie was pleased to see me – my old dominie, you recall. He's still soldiering on. Oh, by the way, I saw your relatives – the Semples. I was invited to take tea at the big house."

"Really? I bet you enjoyed that."

"It was rather an ordeal, I must admit. I'm afraid your aunt must have thought me something the cat dragged in."

"Yes, that would be about par for the course." She took his hand in hers. "Poor Alastair. Never mind. Now you've got me to look after you."

"You really mean that?" She nodded. Wild hope surged within him … then the moment was gone, lost in the sudden clang of the bell in the hallway.

"Damn!" Elizabeth could have wept with vexation. "It must be Morag. She's early. She must have forgotten her key. I'd better go and let her in."

Alastair was left to reflect on the turn of events. Had he misread the situation? Was she just sorry for him, or …? He heard the click of the latch, there was a moment of silence – then a cry of alarm: "Alastair!"

In an instant he was on his feet and into the lobby. "Elizabeth, what's wrong?" He could only gasp in disbelief as he confronted the scene: Elizabeth's strained, ashen face, and beyond her, standing on the doorstep – his brother!

Iain greeted his appearance with a sardonic guffaw. "Christ, I dinnae believe it. Like a pig in clover, eh? Man, I didna ken ye had it in ye."

Alastair bristled. "And just what is that supposed to mean?" He thrust himself in front of Elizabeth. "For your information, this is my first visit."

"Ye expect me to wear that? I wisnae born yesterday. I came here lookin' for my lass, and what do I find? Ye must have a cosy wee arrangement."

"That's enough of that. You'd best keep a civil tongue in your head."

"Or what? Dinnae think ye can throw yer weight around. I'm no' in the army now." His lip curled slyly. "And by the look o' things, neither are you."

"I was discharged on medical grounds. But you are a cheat and deserter. You were imprisoned for your crimes. So –"

"Aye, that's right. And before ye ask, I've no' escaped. They've let me out. So there's nae use sendin' for the bobbies." He fumbled in his jacket pocket. "Ye dinnae believe me? Here are my papers." A grubby envelope was thrust into his brother's hand.

Alastair peered at the inscription before extracting the contents. What was this? *Agreement to be of good behaviour … liability to instant recall in the event of any breach of the terms and conditions.* So the verdict had not been overturned; nor had Iain been pardoned. It was simply a release on licence.

Stuffing the sheet back into the envelope, he handed it back. "What do you want here," he demanded. "I'll not have Miss Lixmont upset."

"I didnae ken this was her house. It was Morag I came to see." He whistled softly. "So she looks after the wean. What a turn up for the books."

A sudden dread gripped Elizabeth. "You assume too much," she snapped. "What makes you think this woman is to be found here?"

"Look, I only want to talk. Where's the harm in that? I can support her. They've gied me a start back at the Ordnance. Charge hand – wi' prospects. Company hoose thrown in as well."

"Very commendable," said Alastair drily. "If true."

"It's kosher, ye can be sure o' that. She's nae need to be a skivvy anymore."

"Surely this person has the right to decide for herself," protested Elizabeth. "In any case you can see there's no one else here."

"Come off it. I'm no' daft. Maybe she's no' here at the minute. But she'll be back. There's a bench on the other side o' the road. I've a' the time in the world."

Elizabeth shrugged helplessly. "It's no use, Alastair. He'll not go away. And I'll not have Morag accosted in the street." She turned to Iain. "I suppose you'd better come in. You can wait in the kitchen."

"That's mair like it. Glad ye can see sense." He followed her into the house, leaving Alastair to bring up the rear as he brushed past.

"You can sit over there," she said, indicating a place on the far side of the kitchen table.

"Thanks, missus. There widnae be a wee cup o' tea goin' would there? I've a fair drouth in me. And maybe a wee bite to eat? I couldna help noticin' … I mean as we went by yer front room."

Elizabeth gave him a cold, dark look. "Very well," she said reluctantly. "Watch him", she told Alastair as she left the room.

Iain scowled. "A bit touchy, is she no'? Then he chuckled. "Ach, never mind. So the wee man was invalided out. What was it?"

"Pneumonia, if you must know."

"Aye, like enough. I mind ye aye were a weakling."

Alastair strove to contain his temper. "And what about you? How did you wangle your way out of your just deserts?"

"Nothin' just about it. They had nae right to call me up in the first place.

441

So they didnae hae a leg to stand on when my case came up. Scared o' public opinion, ye see. They had to let me go."

Before Alastair could respond, Elizabeth was back with a tray. She slid it along the table. "I'm sure you can pour your own tea. I hope the pot isn't too cold."

"Naw. I'm used to that. This looks dandy." He stuffed a couple of sandwiches into his mouth. "Fair tasty, these." He filled his cup, added sugar and drained it in a single gulp. "That's grand." They could only watch as he wolfed down the rest of the food.

"Satisfied?" Elizabeth could not resist a jibe. "Would you like another plateful?"

"Very kind o' ye, to be sure." Iain chose to ignore the taunt. "That filled a hole nicely." He looked round. "I must say ye do yerselves well hereabouts. A man could get to like this style o' life. Ye mind if I hae a wee peak at the wean?"

A wary look came into her eye. "I'm afraid he's fast asleep," she said hastily. "He shouldn't be disturbed."

"Just a keek round the door. I wouldnae wake him up."

"No!" She was adamant. "I will not permit it." She stood in the doorway with her arms folded.

That did it. His temper, always uncertain, boiled over. What had begun as a casual request had become a direct challenge. Spitting with fury, he jumped to his feet. "Who the hell are you to say that? I've got my rights. He's my flesh and blood."

"So you finally admit it?" said Alastair quietly. "You're the father."

Iain scarcely glanced at him. "Keep out o' this, pipsqueak. This is between me and her."

"I don't think so." Grim faced he went to stand by her side.

"Bar the door, would ye? Ye've nae chance. I'd send the pair o' ye flyin' wi' a single swipe." He came round the table towards them.

Elizabeth took a step forward. "Listen to me. Before you do something you'll regret."

"Braw words. And how would that be?"

"If you create a disturbance, I'll not hesitate to report it to the police and have you taken in charge. As for the rights you claim, they don't exist. You have always denied responsibility. So who would believe you now? My father is a lawyer, as you may be aware. He will know how to protect his family from the likes of you."

The cool, mocking tone was enough to halt him in his tracks; his fit of rage ebbed away as the stark consequences struck home. How could he be so stupid? To be arrested for breach of the peace, in circumstances such as these, would mean disaster. No doubt her father was capable of making serious trouble for him. And how would Dunlop react to his folly? His blood ran cold at the prospect.

"Sorry, missus." He dropped his hands to his side, twisting his mouth into what he hoped was an ingratiating smile. "I dinnae ken what came ower me. That paddy o' mine is forever gettin' me intae hot water. I meant nae harm. I widnae hurt a hair o' the wean's head. But if ye dinnae want me to see him, I cannae complain about that. I'll just sit here quiet till Morag comes back."

"You will not," retorted Elizabeth. "You'll take yourself off. I don't want you in my home a moment longer. The back door is behind you. You can let yourself out."

Iain hung his head. "I can see you're upset. So I'll be on my way." At the door he hesitated. "Nae need to involve the polis, is there? Or tell yer faither? I'll no' bother ye again."

"I'll have to think about that. Just go."

There was no more to be said. Shrugging his shoulders he trudged out. Alastair closed and bolted the door behind him.

"You were magnificent, Elizabeth," he said, straightening up. Then he noticed her obvious distress. "What's the matter? You're trembling. Here, let me help you." She allowed herself to be guided back to the parlour. "It's all over now. Sit yourself down and rest." He handed her his handkerchief.

"If only it were." She dabbed her eyes. "I'm so frightened of that man. What if he comes back? Promise you'll stay with me."

"Of course I'll stay till Morag comes back. Then you'll be quite safe."

She shook her head. "That's just it. I'm not sure she will be back."

"Why on earth would you think that?"

"Can't you guess? He's out there, ready to pounce. All smiles and kisses. He'll sweet-talk her into going off with him. She once told me she could never give him up. It was in her bones. If he can provide what he told us … Why would she choose to stay here?"

"Yes, but dammit …" He cast round for something to reassure her. "Eddie is the apple of her eye. How could she just walk out on him?"

"But don't you see? My Eddie can never be hers. And she wants a child of her own."

"Oh, I hadn't thought of that. But surely she wouldn't leave you in the lurch."

"You think not? He'd twist her round his little finger."

"Well, yes. Possibly," he conceded. "But at least Iain wouldn't dare touch Eddie. Did you see his release papers? He's only out on licence. Any infringement could have him back inside to complete his sentence. Do you imagine he'd risk that? No wonder he changed his tune when you spoke out."

"You could be right. But I still don't trust him."

"If it makes you feel better, I'll doss down here for the night."

She smiled at him. "Dearest Alastair, I don't know what I would do without you. Shall we go and take a look at Eddie? Then I'll be close to the two people most precious to me in the whole world."

Noiselessly they stole into the nursery; she felt for his hand as they stood over the cot. Thank God her son had not been disturbed. Yet there was still a lingering fear. What if the law gave rights to the natural father? How could she keep Eddie secure from his clutches? Now if she had the protection of marriage, with a husband as his legal guardian … Her father could arrange things. Was this why he had practically thrown Alastair at her?

"Let's go back," she whispered. "He's sound."

TWENTY-THREE

Hobson's Choice

Glasgow. November 1917

Alastair Baird was careful to close the blackout curtain behind him before slipping out by the side entrance. The hour was late; dusk had already fallen. All was silent in the schoolyard; the pupils had long since disappeared, and most of his colleagues had already departed. But he was well aware that McAlpine, the janitor, would be lurking nearby, eager to catch any breach of the regulations. Pulling up his collar against the snell autumn air, he waited a moment for his eyes to adjust to the gloom. There was a glimmer of light from the shaded street lamp by the school gate; he began to pick his way across the playground towards it.

Blast Watson! Could the man not leave him in peace? The depute rector was the bane of his life – constantly waylaying him to discuss war strategy, never failing to bemoan the poor eyesight which prevented him from joining the colours. On this occasion it had been about the capture of the Passchendaele Ridge at Ypres. He had been sorely tempted to retort that an advance of four miles through the Flanders mud in as many months scarcely constituted a glittering success. But as usual he had held his tongue. What good would it do to speak out? Watson would never be persuaded. Moreover he was in a position to make or mar a career – especially that of a new teacher on probation. How would he react to the discovery that one of his staff had joined the pacifists? And yet … was it enough to lose oneself in the anonymity of mass meetings and rallies? Not for the first time he cursed himself for lacking the courage of his convictions.

"Alastair!" A figure stepped forward into the dim yellow glow cast by the lamp.

"Morag?" He peered closely. "Is that you? Whatever are you doing here?"

"Waitin' for you. And I must say ye've taken yer time."

"Yes, I am a bit late. Sorry about that. The head of junior school wanted a word. But I don't quite understand –"

"There's somethin' I need to see ye about."

"But why here? You'll catch your death of cold. Surely you could have waited back at the house, or left a message with Elizabeth."

"Naw, I coudna stay. Iain's on foreshift the day. So he's back early. He'll be wantin' his tea."

Alastair grimaced at the mention of his brother's name. It had come as no surprise to learn that Morag had fallen for Iain's blandishments, and had agreed to keep house for him pending their nuptials. But to her credit she had insisted on being allowed to continue as Eddie's nanny during the daytime – just till a suitable replacement could be found, so he had been informed. And he had walked into the trap so artfully set for him. A child minder would be needed when Elizabeth was on night duty at the hospital. Morag's room was free, and Eddie would be over the moon. How could he refuse her plea? He had moved in within the week.

"I ken what ye're thinkin'," she went on. "But there's nae need to worry. Iain really has changed. No' even a word out o' turn these last months. And he's named the day. That's why I wanted a word wi' ye."

"Well, congratulations. I expect Elizabeth will be pleased to hear your news."

"That's just it. We dinnae want her to ken – no' just yet. We felt we should ask yer opinion about somethin' first. Could ye no' come back for a bite o' supper wi' us? I mean there'll be naebody at hame for ye. No' wi' Elizabeth an' the bairn bein' away."

"Does Iain know you're here?"

"Aye. It was his idea. He's promised to be on his best behaviour," she added hurriedly.

"But why the mystery? Can't you tell me what it's about?"

"I'd rather leave it to Iain. Please say ye'll come."

Alastair hesitated; instinct warned him to be wary. Yet what could his brother's object be? It was on the tip of his tongue to make an excuse, but … he could not simply turn her away. Not after all the help she had given, introducing him to like-minded acquaintances, encouraging him to join the No Conscription Fellowship. He looked into her pale, earnest face. It would never do to hurt her feelings by refusing the invitation. Swallowing his misgivings, he nodded assent.

"That's grand." She slipped her arm through his. "It's not far. A good plate o' stovies will soon warm ye up."

"Stovies? That reminds me of my childhood days. And the trenches, come to think of it. Bully beef hash, with onions and potatoes. Delicious."

"Hush. That's all over now. Let's talk about something else. I hear Elizabeth has gone to show off Eddie to his grandmama." She squeezed his arm. "Could be another set of wedding bells in the offing. What d'ye think?"

"God knows. I'm the last person to ask about that." Only now was he beginning to grasp the web of intrigue being spun around him.

Of course it was Sir Edward who had planned everything – with his daughter's willing connivance. Even now she would be at that swanky hotel, presumably to be reconciled with her mother. It went without saying that her parents had travelled through to Glasgow; Lady Lixmont would hardly wish the occasion to become common knowledge amongst her own social circle in the capital. Did this portend his own acceptance into the family, as Morag appeared to be suggesting? Not that he was frightened at the prospect of matrimony, he told himself. To have Elizabeth as his wife, and Eddie for a stepson, would fulfil his heart's desire. But … it was just not possible.

Morag sighed. "I just dinnae understand you, Alastair. How long have the pair o' ye been thegither? The best part o' six months. Can ye no' see she's besotted wi' ye."

"I know you mean well," he replied, after a pause. "But unfortunately it's not that simple. I'm in no position to offer marriage. I can't afford to support a family, not on my salary."

"But I thought her faither was dealin' wi' that side o' things. Did he no' come to settle the matter a week or two back? It's nane o' my business, of course –"

"Nothing's settled, since you must know." So Elizabeth had been talking. He would not allow that to alter his determination to stand on his own feet, succeed through his own efforts. To do otherwise would be to become no better than a kept man. Fortunately Sir Edward had been tactful in not pressing the issue. But no doubt he would be back.

"If ye ask me, ye're far ower straitlaced for yer ain good. Could ye no' just live as man and wife?"

Live in sin? He baulked at the proposal. It was embarrassing enough for Elizabeth to throw out the occasional hint that perhaps they might share the same bed. But for Morag to suggest a similar course of action … this really went beyond the pale. "I'm sorry," he said stiffly. "It's all or nothing with me."

"And it does ye credit, Alastair. But sometimes ye need to be practical."

"I don't agree. Call it my Presbyterian upbringing if you like. But there it is." He almost wished he was back at the Front. At least things were simpler there.

They walked on in silence, a little apart, through a maze of darkened, derelict streets, surrounded on all sides by the forbidding mass of high tenements. He was beginning to think they must have lost their way when he felt a gentle tug on his sleeve.

"I spoke out of turn, Alastair." She sounded contrite. "I ken how hard it must be for the pair o' ye. Am I forgiven?"

"Of course." He patted her shoulder. "I know you were only thinking of our best interests."

"Good o' ye to say so. But that's me all over. A'ways interfering where I'm no' wanted. I'll need tae learn to curb my tongue."

He smiled in spite of himself. "You? A shrinking violet? That'll be the day."

"Away wi' ye." She took his arm again. "Ye said ye were at a meetin'. Was it about the classes ye were hopin' to get at the big school? That would be promotion for ye, would it no'?"

He gave a short laugh. "There's no chance of that, not till next session at least. And even then it wouldn't bring in much more, if that's what you're thinking. Sorry to disappoint you. It was only the depute rector, wanting to discuss the war situation. Did you know he keeps a map of the Western Front in his office? Sticks in coloured pins to show the latest positions."

"Ye don't say? Just as well he disnae ken ye're a pacifist."

"I'm not proud of it," he muttered. "A man should stand up for his beliefs."

"But it was for a good reason. Elizabeth made ye promise. She thought it might get ye the sack if ye spoke out."

"That only makes things worse – hiding behind a woman's skirts."

"There ye go again. Will ye no' be convinced ye're doing as much as ye can? And that's more than most dae." Instinctively she reached up, gave him a peck on the cheek. "Anyhow, we're here." They had come to a halt beside the black shadow of a doorway. "Pull that bell there – top one on the left. That should wake Iain up. I'll just fish out my pass key."

The door opened to reveal the narrow passage leading into the stairwell, only marginally less murky than the street outside. At the far end was a solitary gas mantle, its globe over painted to block out most of the light. Slowly they began to climb the steps, feeling their way through the gloom. As they reached the fourth floor landing there was a sudden blaze of light; Iain was framed in an open doorway, a cigarette dangling from his lips.

"So there ye are at last. Come awa' ben." He led the way into the kitchen. "Sit yersel' down by the fire. It's a gey dreich night."

"I'll just see to the tea things," said Morag, unbuttoning her coat. "Everything's ready in the press."

Iain flicked the stub of his cigarette into the grate. "Never mind that, lass. It can wait. Ye might nip down the road for a stoup o' beer. There's no' a drop in the house. Gie the menfolk a chance for a wee chat. Remember?" He favoured her with a broad wink. "Nae need to hurry back."

"Oh, aye." She paused uncertainly. "Are ye sure ye'll be all right?"

"We'll be just fine. See if ye can fetch a hauf o' whisky while ye're at it. There might be a wee celebration when ye get back."

"No need to put yourself out on my account." Alastair felt he had to say something. The idea of Morag wandering the streets alone in the blackout was hardly gratifying.

"Oh, it's no trouble." Iain was looking meaningfully at her. "The howff's just round the corner. I could look in on auld Mrs McMinn on the way back. She'll be glad o' a bit company. Back in half an hour? That should gie ye plenty o' time for what's what."

"There ye go, laddie. That satisfy you?"

"I suppose so." Clearly there was no more to be said.

Taking a jug from the dresser, she scurried away. Iain waited till he heard the click of the front door. "Cigarette?" He took a packet of Woodbines from the mantelpiece.

"No thanks. I don't smoke."

"Just as ye please" He lit one for himself, using a spill from the fire.

"What was it you wanted to discuss? Morag said it was something to do with your wedding."

"Aye. But that can wait a minute." He blew smoke rings into the air. "I ken you and I have had our differences in the past. But it's time to bury the hatchet, now we're on the same side."

"What do you mean by that?" Alastair was incredulous. So far as he was aware, they had virtually nothing in common.

"Is it no' obvious? We both want an end to this stupid war. Morag tells me ye're goin' great guns in the NCF."

"I wouldn't go that far. I'm not a very active member."

"That's no' what Morag says. But we'll no' argue." He pulled his chair a little closer, glancing round as though afraid of being overheard. "There's talk o' conscription bein' extended. They're out to grab everybody they can now – the army's that desperate. The end o' protected occupations, medical boards to force discharged men back intae uniform. Ken anyone that might affect?" he added slyly.

Alastair ignored the barb. "It's news to me," he said coldly. "How do you come to know?"

"That the government's set to bring in a new manpower bill?" He tapped his nose. No one must ever know it was Dunlop who had supplied the information, with instructions to make good use of it.

"Suppose what you say is true," said Alastair slowly. "Why are you telling me this?

"Why? Christ, man, it's staring you in the face. We need to act afore it's too late. Show them Glasgow winnae put up wi' it. Manpower bill? *Manslaughter* bill would be a better name. We need to organise public opinion, demand total resistance. Our membership can gie a lead, but we cannae dae it all on our own. There has to be solidarity in a common cause."

"I see. And what exactly would that involve?"

"Well, we were plannin' to kick off wi' a march on the City Chambers. If the town council refused to support us, we could occupy the place till they agreed to our terms. That'll shake them up, d'ye no' think?"

"No doubt. But I'm not sure a stunt like that would be legal. You might not be bothered about breaking the law, but I am."

"Ach, ye're ower squeamish. Tippy-tappy methods will get us naewhere."

"Ah, so now we're getting to the point. What you're after is revolution. Just like in Russia."

"If that's what it takes." He grew more voluble. "*All power to the soviets.*

That's the system there, now the Bolsheviks have swept away the sham they called the Provisional Government."

"And that's what you'd have here?"

"Aye. *Dictatorship o' the proletariat*. Workers' control is how ye achieve a fair society."

"Anarchy, you mean. That's what will happen in Russia. Spare me the jargon. In any case, aren't you forgetting something? Break the terms of your parole and you risk being clapped back in jail."

Iain scowled at his brother. What Alastair was saying was true enough, but not in the way he supposed. Dunlop had a bee in his bonnet about links between extreme socialism and the wider peace movement. If there was no clear relationship already established, then he had been instructed to engineer closer connections – with dire warnings as to the consequences should he fail in his task.

"Nae chance." Bluster was his obvious weapon. "They widnae be that daft. No' wi' thirty thousand skilled men out on strike, or a mass rally in George Square, champin' at the bit to get me released."

"Really? Then you must be more misguided than I thought. People aren't interested in revolutionary socialism. They only want to get back to their normal lives. Look at your efforts to start up workers' and soldiers' councils. Every attempt fizzled out like a damp squib."

"Maybe so. But that was before the downfall o' the capitalists and their lackeys in Petrograd. There's to be another meetin' to form a council for Glasgow. This time we're out to get maximum support – a broad church wi' all shades of opinion. The ILP leaders have already promised to come. And I'd like you to be there – to represent the moderates. There'll be nae need to say anythin'. Just be on the platform. Is it too much to ask?"

"Yes – as it happens. The NCF is prepared to support peaceful opposition on all matters affecting conscription. But that's as far as it goes. I have absolutely no interest in seeking to bring down the democratically elected government."

"Democratically elected? When nae mair than half the male population has the right to vote?"

"Be that as it may, what you propose is sheer madness. And I'll have nothing to do with it."

"So ye'd turn me down? Listen to me, Alastair. I really need you there.

Suppose – just suppose the bosses at yer school got to hear about your activities. Would that alter yer decision?"

For a moment Alastair stared at him. "So it's blackmail, is it? You'd stoop that low?"

Iain shrugged his shoulders. "Nothin' personal. Sometimes the individual has to be sacrificed for the greater good. But there's still time. It's your choice."

"Do your worst. You don't intimidate me." He leapt to his feet, eyes blazing. "I won't be party to any blackguard scheme."

"Fuck off, then. There's the door. On your own head be it." He spat viciously into the fire. Damned if he would have Alastair as his best man now – whatever Morag might say.

* * *

January 1918

Once more the delegates in the City Hall burst into a lusty rendition of the *Red Flag*, hurling defiance at the warmongers of Westminster. As the echoes died away in the crowded auditorium, Iain Baird heaved a sigh of relief. Surely Dunlop could have no cause for complaint this time.

He felt a hand on his shoulder. "We did it, Iain. It worked like a dream." It was Gallacher, leader of the Clyde workers.

"That was down to you, Willie. It was your plan." He could afford to be generous. "Thon was a masterstroke – puttin' that lad up on the platform beside yon beanpole. Then askin' if he expected the wee chap to protect him frae the Germans."

"Well, he didnae exactly help his cause, did he? Fancy bein' daft enough to say the boy widnae be sent to the Front – no' till he was nineteen. Nae wonder he was howled down." Gallacher chuckled at the memory. "Sir Auckland Geddes – Director o' National Service, don't ye know. Good o' him to gie us his time. But I bet he didnae expect a reception like this. Didnae even dare mention the new manpower bill. He was only too glad to get back to London in one piece."

"Too true, Willie. But credit where it's due. You mobilised the shop stewards to pack the hall. You got the resolutions passed demandin' an immediate end to the war – or we a' down tools. You sent that stuffed shirt away wi' a flea in his ear."

"Ach, let's say it was a collective effort. And we're no' finished yet. There's still the procession to George Square. You'll be wi' me behind the banner at the front."

"Thanks all the same, Willie. But I was thinkin' I might be better employed at the back to chase up the laggards."

Gallacher nodded. "Just as ye like." He disappeared into the scrum as the hall emptied.

Iain remained in his seat. Bringing up the rear would allow him the opportunity to slip away unnoticed. Dunlop had insisted on an immediate report – a rare occurrence, showing the importance he attached to the event. This time there could be no accusations of failure. The new Military Service Bill had finally united industrial unrest with the wider anti-war protests. The government minister would tell his colleagues that Glasgow was a hotbed of sedition; surely even the hardest of taskmasters would be content with that. He glanced round. By now the place was all but deserted. Heaving himself to his feet, he quickly made his way towards the exit.

A figure rose from the back row of the stalls and stood in the gangway. With a muffler covering the lower part of his face, and cap pulled down over his forehead, it was impossible to tell whether he was friend or foe. Instinctively Iain clenched his fists, ready to deal with any attempt to block his path.

"Haud on, laddie. Can ye no' recognise an old comrade?"

Iain had been more than prepared to force his way past. Now he stopped dead in astonishment. He knew that voice. "Stan? Stan Robertson?"

"Aye. And there's nae need to gawk like a stranded haddie. I'm no' a ghost."

"But where the hell did ye spring from? We thought ye were in Russia."

"And so I was. I'm no' long back." He removed his hat, pushed down his scarf. Iain had just time to note the gaunt face and goatee beard before being enveloped in a bear hug.

"Christ, ye dinnae ken yer ain strength," he said breathlessly when he was at last released. "Ye fair ken how to gie a man a fright."

"I promised ye I'd be back. Eighteen months, was it no'?"

"Aye, but even so …" He thought hard. Robertson's surprise reappearance was an added complication. Whether it was for good or ill remained to be seen. But there was no time to think it out now. He had to get away. "It's good to see ye again, Stan. But I'm a bit pushed at the minute. There's a march to George Square. And I'll be expected."

"Then I'll no' detain ye. Tell you what, we could walk thegither. It would gie us a chance to catch up. Ye've nae objections, have ye?"

"Of course no'. Ye'd be welcome." He tried to hide his dismay. "It's just the risk. There'll be bobbies about."

"Fine I ken that. But it's dark outside. And you couldna tell who it was in here." He replaced his cap, rearranged the cloth round his chin. "Besides, the best place to lose yerself is in a crowd. Come on."

He led the way out into the Candleriggs where a rough formation had been drawn up. They were able to slip into the rear rank as the column set off.

"Now we can talk," said Robertson, out of the corner of his mouth. "Just keep yer voice low." He looked round to make sure no one was paying any attention. "As a matter of fact I've an idea I've already been rumbled. I got some hard looks when we landed at Newcastle. The docks were swarmin' wi' police – ye ken, plain clothes clods. But I managed to talk my way through. Said I was crew – and had papers to prove it. Just as well I worked my passage back on board ship. They had nae evidence to hold me, but …" He shrugged his shoulders.

"Then why take the risk?"

"Because Lenin wanted me to come back."

"You've met Lenin? The Bolshevik leader?" There was incredulity in his voice.

"Many a time. He calls me his wee Scots comrade."

"Christ! I mean –" He could still scarcely take it in.

"I was there, remember. I saw it all – from the downfall o' the Tsar to the stormin' o' the Winter Palace. And Lenin was the man who made the difference. He took the Bolsheviks by the scruff o' the neck and turned them intae the vanguard o' the proletarian revolution. I was proud to offer my services – and was accepted. The opposition was so feeble it collapsed wi' barely a whimper. So ye see a handful o' determined men can work wonders."

"And you're back to pass on the message?"

"That's the general idea. Russia is just the start o' a worldwide revolution."

"But I thought Maclean was Soviet Consul for Scotland."

"Ach, he's just a figurehead. He'll hae done his job if he distracts the reactionaries from what's really goin' on. Let him think he's the bees' knees. He can concentrate on his classes on Marxism while I get on' wi' things behind the scenes."

"So what are your plans, then?"

"All in good time, Iain. Naebody else kens I'm here yet. So dinnae let on. No' till I tell ye."

"Whatever ye say, Stan. It's just that I thought ye'd be wantin' to meet up wi' Gallacher and the others."

"Later – when I've got things fixed. I'll let ye know."

"Fine by me. But how will we keep in touch? D'ye hae a place to live? I mean if ye're lookin' for a bed for a few days –"

"Good o' ye to offer, Iain. But I'd best stay on the move. Forbye, I'm no' exactly flavour o' the month wi' your lass, no' after trying to inveigle ye to come wi' me to Russia. By the by, I see ye've managed to make an honest woman o' her."

"How did ye ken that? Oh, the ring I suppose." He twisted the circle of gold on his finger. "Aye, she dragged me to the altar, kickin' and screamin'." He tried to pass it off as a joke, but the loss of freedom still rankled.

"Sorry to have missed that. When did ye get wed?"

"Three weeks ago. Just at New Year. That's when I got the ball and chain."

"Ye dinnae sound very cheerful about it. Did ye hae to get married?"

"Nah. It's no' that. I made a promise. And she held me to it."

It was true. Morag would not be denied. That had been made abundantly clear on the night of his brother's visit. Her reaction at finding Alastair gone had only intensified into a tirade of abuse at his suggestion that they postpone the wedding. Nor did it end there. A woman scorned could bring him crashing down. And Dunlop would be merciless. He had been trapped, with little choice but to submit.

"Look, Stan, I ken ye mean well, but I'll need to be away." By this time they had reached the corner of George Square. "So if ye dinnae want to be seen –"

"All right, Iain, I can take a hint. I hear ye've moved on frae yer old address."

"How on earth dae ye ken that? I mean ye're just back."

"Oh, here an' there. It's my business to find things out. Ye've been in jail. Then they let ye out. Even gave ye a start back at the Ordnance. Now ye're a big noise in the Workers' Committee."

"Well, they couldnae keep me in. No' when they let the others out as well."

"Still, ye seem to have landed on yer feet. One thing I learned in Russia is that ye need to be ruthless to win through against the odds. There's nae room for sentiment in the class war. Any comrade who isnae up to the mark must be cast out as an enemy o' the people. That's how the Bolsheviks were able to win power. And that's how they'll stay in power. Somethin' to keep in mind. Off ye go now."

With the briefest of nods Iain hurried away, pushing himself into the thickest part of the crowd. At least no prying eyes could follow him here. But what did Robertson mean by that last remark? Was his commitment being doubted? It would be as well to take no chances. The marchers were thinning out on the far side, beginning to drift homewards. No one would notice if he scuttled away down a nearby side street.

Now he would really have to hurry if he was to keep the appointment. But even at a brisk pace it was some time before he managed to locate the address he had been given – a nondescript building in one of the alleyways behind the Trongate. The door opened immediately to his knock; a silent figure beckoned him in, pointed towards a wooden staircase. He could feel the pinpricks of sweat on his back as he trudged upwards.

"So you've deigned to honour us with your presence after all." Iain was only too conscious of the sarcasm. "My time is valuable. I'm not accustomed to being left to kick my heels."

"Sorry about that, Mr Dunlop. But it was hard to get away. There was this march to George Square after the meeting."

"I'm not interested in your excuses." He glared at Iain. "Well, man – your report."

"My report? Oh, aye. I'm sure ye'll be pleased. Everythin' went off better than expected. We gave the minister pelters. Then we passed a resolution for an immediate end to the war. There was a unanimous vote for strike action if the government refused to open negotiations wi' the Germans."

"I see." Dunlop did not seem over impressed. "And how much of that was down to you – I mean you personally."

Iain stiffened. Where was this leading? He hastened to defend himself. "I played my part. Naebody can deny me that."

"Really? Why is that?"

"I'll tell ye why. It was my suggestion to pack the hall wi' shop stewards and gie yon toff what for. It was me that persuaded the CWC to draw up resolutions against the war."

"So it was all your own work? Of course we only have your own word for that."

"What d'ye mean?" He made a show of indignation. "I'm knockin' my pan in for you."

"Are you?" Dunlop picked up a folder. "Let's examine your record since I had you sprung from jail." He flicked it open. "Quite apart from your abysmal attempts to set up the workers' council you promised, there's not much else on the credit side of the ledger. You were instructed to encourage industrial unrest – with little success."

"Ye cannae blame me for that. What chance do I have when the bosses hand out pay rises at the first hint o' a strike? Or take back sacked workers as soon as somebody cries victimisation? That's what happened wi' the women at Beardmores' last month."

"So you claim. But employers are subject to the regulations the same as anyone else."

"It's true, I tell you. They fiddle the increases as extra bonuses."

Dunlop waved away the protest. "Be that as it may, it is your responsibility to handle any local difficulties. You disappoint me, Baird. I'm beginning to think my investment may have been misplaced. Now if there's a question mark over your loyalty –"

"God's sake, sir. Dinnae say that. What else do I hae to do to convince ye?"

"A name, Baird. Give me a name. You were instructed to investigate links between the peace movement and radical socialism."

"So I have. Ye ken who the leaders are."

"And so does everyone else. Don't prevaricate, Baird. It's information about the planners and organisers I need – those lurking below the parapet, pulling the strings. These are the real authors of subversion. How much have you done to ferret them out?"

"It's no' that easy, sir."

"No? Then why were you in conversation with a man outside City Hall this evening. He joined you on the march before sloping off. Perhaps that might account for your latecoming. So if you've something worthwhile to tell me –"

"It was nothin' like that." Iain was quick to deny the implication. "Just one o' my members. There was a problem at work. I couldna just turn him away. After all I am his shop steward. And there are appearances to keep up."

"Is that all?" Dunlop looked dubious for a moment. "It must have been important to trouble you out of hours."

"Naw. Just a complaint about some o' his machine minders. I telt him I would look intae it the morn. After that we had a wee chat before he left to go home."

"And that is your explanation?" There was a brief pause. "Well, I suppose I shall have to accept it. Have you anything else to add?"

Iain breathed a little more easily. Dunlop was just fishing for information, trying to catch him out. Suddenly emboldened, he threw out his chin. "Aye. Ye sent yer minions to spy on me. I object to that."

"Spare me your observations, Baird. Do you think I would only have one operative present? The incident is now closed. We have more important matters to discuss."

Iain subsided. Dunlop was totally unfazed. Would he ever get the better of this man? "Just as ye please, sir," he said stiffly.

"That's better. Now listen carefully. One of your former associates has been flagged up. It appears likely he may attempt to return to his old haunts – if in fact he has not already done so. There was a possible sighting in Newcastle a few days ago. Our colleagues there had their suspicions, but the man disappeared before his identity could be established. It was your old friend, Robertson. I don't need to tell you the danger he might pose."

"Stan?" He managed to sound surprised, though his heart was in his mouth. "I havnae heard hide nor hair o' him in near enough two years. He would be daft to come back."

"Nevertheless we must be prepared. There is evidence he has been in Russia, even joined the Bolsheviks. No doubt his paymasters in Petrograd hope to capitalise on his experience to sow anarchy here. To have him safely under lock and key is an absolute priority. Should he attempt to make contact, you will of course notify me without delay."

"Aye, sir. I'll dae that. I'll keep my ear to the ground. If he's on Clydeside, I'll find out."

"Word to the wise, Baird. It would be in your interest to discover his whereabouts. His capture would do much to allay any doubts about you."

"I can only dae my best, sir."

"Then we'll just have to hope your best is good enough. In the meantime I need something on account."

"What d'ye mean?"

"It's very simple, Baird. Your continued employment depends on your usefulness. I must have that name, here and now. Otherwise …" He left the threat hanging.

Iain broke into a cold sweat. Dunlop was in deadly earnest, pressing him into a corner from which there was no escape. Too late to admit his encounter with Robertson: he had burnt his boats there. Besides, what did he actually know about Stan's movements or intentions? Perhaps when there was something definite to report … But for now it was vital to buy time. He swallowed hard.

"Suppose – just suppose there was this chap. Army officer, invalided out. Joined the anti-war brigade, but hides himself in the background. Covers his tracks by workin' as a school teacher. Mind you, I'm no sayin' he's the kingpin. But he could be yer link."

"Interesting. But can we be sure you're not just making this up?"

"Honest to God, sir. Ye can check it out."

"Oh, we shall. Has anyone else been informed of this man's activities? His employers, perhaps?"

"No' that I'm aware of. We dinnae want to scare him off."

"No, indeed. My sentiments entirely. Now all that remains is for you to supply the name."

Iain hesitated. But there was no going back. Dunlop was determined on his pound of flesh. He was glad now that he had never got round to informing the school authorities. This way he would have payment in full. And – happy thought – kill another bird with the same stone. What better proof of his loyalty than to sacrifice kith and kin?

"It's Baird – Alastair Baird. He's my brother."

* * *

March 1918

"Cooee! Anybody home?"

"It's Morag!" A tiny figure scrambled down from the table and rushed towards the door.

"Watch out for Eddie," called out Elizabeth. "We're just finishing breakfast."

At the threshold the toddler was swept up into Morag's arms. "My, you are excited. Must be the thought o' startin' the spring cleaning."

"Hardly." Elizabeth laughed. "I expect he wants a run in the park. But he'll need a wee nap first."

Morag set him down again. "I'll gie his face a wipe. Then put him down for half an hour. By the way I've brought in the post." She laid several letters on the table. "Come away, Eddie."

"And I must be off as well," said Alastair, draining his cup. "We don't all have the day off."

"You're welcome to stay and help. It'll be hard graft – scrubbing and polishing."

"I'd love to. But duty calls me elsewhere. My charges would be mortified if I didn't turn up for class."

"A likely story. But don't let me keep you." She began to sort through the correspondence. "No, wait. Here's a letter for you." She handed over a brown envelope. "HMSO. And it's addressed to 2nd Lieutenant A. Baird. I wonder what that can mean."

"Probably the army. Maybe they've decided to award me a war pension after all." But his face was clouded as he jabbed a finger under the flap. Why use military rank? And how did they know where to send the letter?

Elizabeth saw the change of expression as he drew out a folded sheet. "Not bad news, I hope," she said anxiously.

Alastair quickly scanned the contents. "It seems that I'm summoned for a medical review. Next week. Up at Maryhill Barracks."

"But surely that will just be to confirm that you're unfit for service."

"Don't bank on it. They'll probably say I'm sound as a bell. Pass me A1."

"But that's impossible. Not with your state of health."

"Look, Elizabeth, they haven't asked to see me since my discharge from the army. So why start now? It can only be because they've had to start scraping the bottom of the barrel."

"I suppose so. What will you do?"

"Well, I'm not going to take it lying down. I won't turn up. I'll register as a C.O. instead."

"But they won't accept that. How can you claim to be a pacifist when you've been a serving officer?"

"In that case they can do their worst. I'll not add to the senseless slaughter in the trenches."

She clutched at his arm. "There may be nothing in it. Don't go and do something silly. You've a week to think things over. At least promise me that."

"You won't get me to change my mind." Then he relented. "All right. I won't act in haste." He stuffed the letter into his pocket. "And now I really must scoot. Or I'll probably get the sack for latecoming."

A few moments later Morag came back into the room. "Is that Alastair away? He seemed in an awful hurry." She broke off. "My God! Ye're as white as a sheet. Is anythin' amiss?"

"You could say that. Alastair's had a letter telling him he's to report for a medical. He's convinced they're going to draft him back into the army."

"But they cannae dae that. No' in his condition."

"That's what I told him. Nevertheless, it seems he's to be reassessed. All we can do is hope for the best."

"Amen to that." A sudden thought struck her. "Mind you, it is queer all the same." Then she shook her head. "No, that canna be right. It must be a coincidence."

"Whatever do you mean?"

"Ach, I dinna ken if it's worth mentionin'. I thought it was Iain just bummin' his load."

"Iain? What on earth has Iain to do with it?"

"I'm no' sure. It's just that he let slip a while back that Alastair was due for a rude awakenin'. Of course I took it as his usual gripe. Nothin' would ever come o' it."

"But now you think differently?"

"I wouldnae go that far, but –"

"I don't see how his brother could possibly be connected with Alastair's call-up. Besides, aren't they both on the same side – at least so far as the war is concerned?"

"That's what I cannae understand. But he thinks that Alastair has done him a bad turn. And he'll no' pass up a chance to get his ain back."

"Even so. I could imagine him sending an anonymous letter to the school. But this …" She spread her arms expressively.

"I hope ye're no' upset – me tellin' ye about it."

"No, Morag, you were quite right. I'm very grateful." She tried to sound reassuring, though her mind was in a fog. Whatever was going on, it was too deep for her to handle alone. Impulsively she crossed to the writing table.

Morag was taken aback by the sudden movement. "What are you going to do?" she asked nervously.

"I must get in touch with my father. He'll know what's for the best. Perhaps you might take a message to the telegraph office." She dashed off a few lines. "There'll be a form to fill in. Just copy this out and send it off." She folded the slip and handed it to Morag. "You'll need some money. I'll just get it from my purse."

Once Morag had departed on her errand, it was impossible to settle to anything. All thoughts of spring cleaning cast aside, she tried to make sense of the situation. A plot to do down Alastair? It was hard to fathom. She paced up and down restlessly. The sound of sobbing came to her: Eddie had woken up, was becoming fractious. She hurried through to the nursery, lifted him from his cot, whispered words of reassurance.

Morag returned just as she was carrying him into the kitchen. "Shall I take him now?" Strong arms reached out towards her. "You look worn out. Why no' go ben and rest? I'll bring ye a nice cup o' tea."

She nodded her agreement, only too glad to slump onto the settee in the front room. At least from there she could survey the roadway while she waited for a reply. Morag brought through her tea; she sipped it gratefully. The click of the front door had her at the window, but it was only Morag taking Eddie out for his walk. She waved goodbye before returning listlessly to her seat. What if nothing could be done? Suppose her father washed his hands of the whole affair? The trill of a bicycle bell roused her from her despondency. It was the telegraph boy. She rushed to the door, looked on anxiously as he fumbled in his wallet. Her hands were trembling as she took the flimsy envelope; she had to steady herself before breaking the seal. Then relief flooded over her. Thank God! Dad was coming. He would be with her before nightfall.

Sir Edward Lixmont was as good as his word. Dusk had not yet fallen as his taxi rolled up to the front gate, and he emerged, overnight bag in hand, to be greeted by his daughter. Somewhat to her surprise, he did not dismiss Morag's story out of hand when it was tentatively mentioned to him. On the contrary, he insisted the nanny be summoned to recount every detail she could remember. Was her husband boastful, gloating at the prospect of causing harm? Or did she think it was simply bluster – a throwaway remark to relieve his feelings? At length he pronounced himself satisfied and dismissed her for the day. She would have stayed on to help out, but Sir Edward would have none of it. Morag must behave normally, leave at the usual hour – above all do nothing that might alert Iain.

Elizabeth saw her to the door, pressed her hand as a gesture of reassurance. Returning to her father, she found him writing in a small notebook. "These are murky waters," was all he would say in answer to the unasked question. "We may be in a better position when Alastair returns."

"He should be back any minute," said Elizabeth, glancing at the clock.

"Tell me about that nanny of yours. I must say I was impressed. But appearances can be deceptive. And she must have divided loyalties."

"Morag would never do anything to see either of us hurt. I'm sure of that. She's not blind to Iain's faults. It's just that she imagines she can get him to reform if she perseveres long enough. And don't forget she didn't have to tell us about Iain's threat. Surely that's a point in her favour."

"That's true enough. Well, I suppose I shall have to bow to female intuition."

"Here's Alastair now." There was the scrape of a latch key in the lock.

"I just met Morag outside." Alastair came into the room. "She seemed a bit upset about something." He caught sight of the visitor. "Good evening, sir." There was a hint of surprise in his voice. "I didn't realise you were coming."

"Sit down, Alastair. We need to have a talk."

"I hope you haven't said anything." Elizabeth propelled him towards a chair. "You promised you wouldn't."

"You've no need to worry on that score," he replied bitterly. "They already know."

"What do you mean?"

"No, I didn't tell them I was going to register as a C.O." He unbent a little. "But it was the queerest thing. When I got to the school, Watson – he's the depute rector, sir – was at the door, pumping my hand for all he was worth, congratulating me on my good fortune. It seems that a letter had just arrived saying that it was likely I would be recalled to the colours."

"How very odd," said Lixmont. "I've never heard of that before. But it could tally with something I've found out." He turned to his daughter. "When you sent me that cable I did a little sleuthing on my own account. It just so happens that an acquaintance of mine works for the Directorate of National Service. Now it is undeniable that our forces are outnumbered since Russia dropped out of the war. The Germans have been able to send massive reinforcements west. It can only be a matter of time before they launch an all-out offensive."

"That's understood, sir. But I don't see how it involves me."

"I was coming to that. It would appear that initially there were no plans to include you in the cull. It was a request from elsewhere that your name be listed for medical re-evaluation. My source couldn't – or wouldn't – reveal the origin of the request. Somewhere high up – that was all he would say."

"So there is a conspiracy against Alastair?"

"It's beginning to look that way. But our case may not be entirely hopeless. So if you wouldn't mind, Elizabeth –" He gestured towards the door.

"Of course." She was quick to take the hint. Dad was a wily old fox – he would have something up his sleeve. But it was clear he wished to tackle Alastair on his own. "I must go and see to the dinner. It'll be pot luck, I'm afraid." She gave Alastair an encouraging smile and disappeared into the kitchen.

Once they were alone Lixmont produced a hip flask from his bag. Unscrewing the cap, he poured out some liquid. "Here, get this down you."

"I don't really drink, sir."

"Nonsense. You look in need of a stiffener."

Mechanically Alastair took a sip of the whisky. "I don't know why you bothered to come. I won't change my mind."

"Now don't you get on your high horse with me. With that sort of attitude you're simply playing into their hands – whoever they may be. Just hear me out."

"I'm sorry, sir. I had no right to say that." He was genuinely contrite. "You know I have the greatest respect for you. I'll gladly listen to what you have to say. But I can make no promises."

"Fair enough. But it would be folly to refuse your medical. You simply must go. However, I have managed to wring a concession from the military authorities. They have agreed to allow you to be examined by my own physician, and to accept his findings. Now that gives us a fair wind."

"Does it?"

"Of course it does. Army surgeons might be subject to pressure which could conceivably affect their judgement as to your state of health."

"You mean that a civilian doctor would be more likely to find me unfit for service?"

"Doctor Shawcross will be scrupulously fair, you may be sure of that. But an absolute guarantee cannot be given. It was with that in mind that I have organised a fall-back position, so to speak. In the event of your recall to the army, you would not be sent overseas. An administrative post has been reserved for you at the home depot of your regiment, should the need arise."

"It's very good of you to go to so much trouble on my behalf, sir. And I am appreciative. But I will not wear uniform again. I have foresworn war. And to be responsible for sending men to their deaths is even worse than service in the frontline itself."

"I respect your sentiments, Alastair. But there comes a time when you must be realistic. I haven't told you what your duties would involve. You'd be responsible for the men's welfare – not for training or assembling drafts for the Front. My son has agreed to take you onto his staff in that capacity."

"Colonel Lixmont?" Alastair was aghast. "Back home? I thought he'd hate to be out of the firing line."

"He had little choice in the matter. His battalion was cut to pieces at Passchendaele. What was left had to be merged with the remnants of another battalion. He was junior, so lost out to the other chap. The fact that he had been wounded made the decision all the easier. He was recuperating at base hospital when he received the news."

"I see. Strange that Elizabeth never mentioned her brother."

"Well, we didn't want to bother her. In any case we knew nothing about it till Hugh walked in the front door for a spot of leave before taking up his new assignment. His mother was pleased, though."

"I can believe that. But what I can't work out is why he would be prepared to take me on. We didn't exactly see eye to eye on a certain matter."

Sir Edward coloured slightly. "I won't pretend it was easy. I had a long conversation on the telephone with my son. He was far from pleased to hear of your pacifist leanings, but I was able to bring him round in the end. He concedes that his command is severely understaffed, and could not deny that you have the requisite qualities to make yourself useful. On a personal level he also admits that perhaps he was a little hasty in his judgement of your – suitability, shall we say."

"You mean my friendship with Elizabeth?"

"Rather more than that." Hugh had growled that he couldn't care less how his sister ruined her life, just so long as he was not expected to socialise with the fellow after the war. But there was no need to mention that. "I mean that he is no longer opposed to your marriage to Elizabeth."

"Marriage? That's unfair of you, sir," he spluttered. "How many times have I said I'm in no position to support her?"

Lixmont ignored the protest. "There is something else that you may not have considered. Should you refuse to take that medical, or try to claim exemption as a C.O., then you'd probably be clapped in prison."

"I know. I'm prepared for that."

"Yes, but what about Elizabeth and young Eddie? Who'd protect them if you're in jail? I can't be here all the time. Besides, your brother is the natural father. In law he has rights which a court might uphold should he choose to make a claim. The only way to ensure he keeps his distance is for you to marry Elizabeth and adopt Eddie as your stepson."

Alastair gasped. Surely it was impossible. The thought of Iain snatching Eddie away was just too awful to contemplate.

"The first step is for you to agree to that medical. Doctor Shawcross has indicated his willingness to see you this weekend. He is even prepared to come through and conduct the examination here, if you would prefer. But will you accept?"

So that was the choice being foisted upon him. Betray his principles or abandon the two individuals most precious to him. His eyes dropped to the floor as he wrestled with his conscience. At last his head came up.

"You win." It was almost a groan. "I accept."

TWENTY-FOUR

Unfinished Business

Glasgow. May 1918

"Could do with a breath of fresh air, Hugh. What about you?"

His son dutifully followed him out onto the balcony of the private dining room. For the moment they were alone. The newlyweds had retired to the hotel's bridal suite, which had given him the opportunity to draw the reception to a close. Not that it had been a grand affair – just eight gathered round the one table. No – nine, he corrected himself. Little Eddie had strutted up and down, proud as a peacock in his pageboy outfit.

"Can't stay long, dad. Duty calls."

"Just wanted a word, son. We were glad you were able to find the time to come. I know your mother appreciates the gesture."

"The mater can be pretty persuasive. I'm just surprised she agreed to the match. How will she explain it away at her soirees and committee meetings? Surely her friends are bound to wonder."

"She hasn't confided in me. But I expect she's got it all worked out. How did she bring you round?"

"Oh, the usual, I suppose. Her grandchild needs a father if Elizabeth is to be accepted back into society. And Baird seems to be the only candidate available. Then she harped on about my failure to provide a son and heir."

"Don't take it to heart too much. Your turn will come. And there are worse things in life than to have someone like Baird for a brother-in-law."

"Not so sure about that. But there's nothing I can do about it now. At least there'll be no need to see much of him. Just as well he failed that medical. It would never do to have him spouting off in the mess on the merits of a negotiated peace. How did you pull it off with that sawbones of yours?"

"Me? How could my views carry any weight?" Lixmont feigned innocence. Privately he rather agreed with his son. It had been foolish even

468

to entertain the notion that Alastair could be trusted to keep his mouth shut. The boy was too transparent to hide his opinions. But it had been a close call, all the same. Shawcross had been in two minds, might well have passed Baird fit for light duties. It had taken all his powers of advocacy to tip the balance.

"And you expect me to believe that?" Hugh was openly sceptical.

There was the merest twitch of the lip before his father replied. "Doctor Shawcross has been the family physician for many years, as well you know. His integrity is beyond reproach. I merely asked him to carry out a consultation."

"Hell's bells! It's like trying to get blood from a stone. You lawyers are all the same. Can't you give me a hint?"

"'Fraid not. Professional ethics, and all that."

"In that case I'd best be off. Sorry I couldn't stay longer. But there's a draft going off to France tomorrow. They're badly needed to stiffen the line."

"Is the situation really so grim? All we get here are rumours."

"Well, things are far from rosy. Though the German attacks do seem to be losing impetus. That would indicate Fritz has just about shot his bolt. So, with the Americans arriving at last, there's every chance the tide could turn soon."

"Let's hope so." He felt for his son's hand. "Goodbye, Hugh. And God bless."

"Same to you, dad. Keep your pecker up. We'll win in the end, never fear."

Win in the end. The words somehow rang hollow. Gloomily he stared out over the Glasgow skyline: the city lay drab and listless as the shadows lengthened. How much longer before final victory was achieved? And at what further cost? Already people had a name for it: *The war to end wars.* One thing was certain: a conflict such as this must never be allowed to happen again.

"For God's sake, Edward! Why are you standing out here like a tailor's dummy? Don't you realise you'll catch your death of cold?" It was his wife, back after seeing off her maiden aunt.

"That you, Hilda?" He forced a smile. "Did you see Hugh on his way out?"

"I did. He wished us a safe journey home tomorrow."

"That all? Did he say anything in particular?"

"No. Why do you ask?" She peered at him suspiciously. "What have you two been up to?"

"Nothing at all. Did you manage to find a taxicab for your Aunt Matilda?"

"Yes, as it happens. The hotel porter flagged one down almost immediately."

"Can't think why you invited her to represent your side of the family. She's in her dotage – kept on falling asleep during the proceedings."

"That's precisely the reason. She'll remember the wedding, but get confused if anyone asks her about the details. Then I'll be able to step in and set the record straight. Just as well we had an excuse for sending out so few invitations."

"And what might that be?"

"That it's unpatriotic to have a large function at a time of national emergency. Thus we make a virtue out of a necessity."

"Ah. Very clever." It would never do to hint that he had sown the idea in the first place. "So that was why you wouldn't invite your sister?"

"The less she knows, the better. I'm not having Maud make snide remarks about my daughter's choice of husband. You know what she's like."

"True. But you can't keep it a secret. She's bound to find out sooner or later. Broomburn is a small place. She'll be well aware of Baird's antecedents."

"I'll think of something."

"No doubt. I suppose you've already decided how you're going to explain away the sudden appearance of a grandson. You are still planning to take him back with us to Edinburgh?"

"Of course. It's only fair to relieve Elizabeth of the burden of looking after the boy for a few days. Give her a chance to adjust to her new status. I shall have the pleasure of introducing my grandson to some of my acquaintances."

"And they won't ask any awkward questions?"

"Not if it's put the right way. This war has turned everything topsy-turvy. You can get away with just about anything if you make it sound credible – and keep a straight face."

He could not resist a grin. "Go on, then. I'm listening."

"Come inside first. It's getting chilly out here." She waited while he closed the French windows and drew the curtains before switching on the electric light. "That's much better."

He motioned her to a chair and sat down beside her. "Comfortable? You have my attention."

"Well, then. You remember how we packed Elizabeth off to that nursing home?"

"Who could forget it? You put out that she had gone to spend the summer with relatives in Ireland."

"Precisely. And then later we said that she had volunteered for war work as a nurse."

"Yes. What of it?"

"Don't you see? These are the bones of our story. Let's assume that when she was in Ireland she met and formed an attachment with a dashing young army officer – of good Anglo-Irish stock, of course."

"Oh, of course. That goes without saying."

"Do be serious, Edward. There is a whirlwind romance; marriage is proposed just as war is declared. The young man's regiment is about to embark for France, so we give our blessing and a special licence is arranged. Husband goes off to war, but is killed shortly thereafter. Elizabeth discovers she is with child. What do you think of that?"

"Well, it's an explanation of sorts, Hilda. We should have to represent the boy as being several months younger than he actually is. And what about the identity of the late lamented father?"

"Mere details, Edward." She waved away his concerns. "You'll be bemoaning the lack of official documentation next."

"It could be an issue if proof is demanded. Still, I dare say that's fairly unlikely. People will take our word for it."

"Of course they will. Don't be such a fusspot."

He shrugged his shoulders. "Do carry on. I take it that the rest of your tale is at least on nodding terms with the truth."

"You shall be the judge of that." She smiled sweetly. "Now where was I? Oh, yes. There is nothing to keep Elizabeth in Ireland once her child is born, so she returns with him to make a new life for herself. But rather than sit and mope at home, she is determined to do her bit for the war effort. With our help she settles in Glasgow and joins the VAD, nursing wounded soldiers in one of the hospitals. One day –"

"Don't tell me. I think I can guess the rest. An old acquaintance appears in her ward – a fellow student from her university days. They get on well together, relive old times. In due course he is invalided out of the army, but they continue to meet. Eventually he offers marriage and Elizabeth accepts. *Et voilà*. Is that what you were going to say?"

"More or less. What do you think?"

"Well, the story hangs together – at least on the surface. There's nothing that can be readily disproved. Some of the details need tidying up, but …" He took her hand in his. "You'd make a damned good advocate, Hilda. I wouldn't like to have you agin me in court."

She flushed with pleasure. "You know, Edward, I can read you like a book. You're wondering what made me change my mind. Actually, it's quite simple. You know I've always been a realist. There's no possibility of a society wedding. So one must bow to the inevitable, and choose the lesser of two evils."

"That's a bit harsh, Hilda. Young Baird will make her a good husband. And he has the ability to rise to the top in his career. He won't stay a classroom teacher for long."

"No doubt you'll give him a helping hand there. Did you manage to speak to him?"

"About curbing his views on the war?"

"That, and the money side of things."

"To some extent." He frowned slightly. "His conscience won't allow him to modify his attitude, but he agreed to abstain from active participation in the peace movement."

"Well, that's something. And the other?"

"Less success there, I'm afraid. He's determined to refuse financial support. Though I was able to persuade him to continue with the present arrangements till things settle down."

"But does he not realise the cost of living these days? We can't have Elizabeth and the boy going short."

"I don't think there's much danger of that. Her household allowance can always be increased. No need for him to know anything about it. Besides, I had to twist his arm to get him to the altar in the first place. If I had pressed him any further he would probably have called the whole thing off."

"I'm sure you acted for the best." She patted his arm reassuringly. "Now – about the arrangements. I've sent the nanny to give Eddie a bath and put him to bed. They've set up a cot in our dressing room."

Lixmont almost choked. "You can't do that," he stuttered. "She's our guest – Elizabeth's matron of honour. You can't treat her like a menial."

"Well, Elizabeth has no further need of her services this evening. And she did ask if there was anything she could do."

"Even so –"

"I must say I was surprised at Elizabeth's choice of bridesmaid. But perhaps it was for the best. The girl seems capable and respectable enough. I wonder if we could persuade her to come through to Edinburgh with us."

"To nanny little Eddie? I hardly think so."

"Why not?"

"Morag is a married woman. Possibly her husband would have something to say on the matter."

Before she could respond there was a knock on the door. It was the hotel undermanager. He bowed slightly to each of them in turn.

"Excuse me, madam, sir. I didn't mean to disturb you, but there is a – ahem, person downstairs. He states that his wife is one of your party. He wishes to escort her safely home through the blackout. The name is Morag Baird. He was most insistent," he added, as though to justify the intrusion.

Hilda Lixmont was the first to react. "There is no one here by that name," she snapped. "It must be a mistake. Send the man away."

"No, wait," said her husband hastily. "Tell him I'll be down directly."

The emissary bowed once more and ghosted away.

"You told me her name was Morag Mackay," she hissed as soon as the door closed.

"Well, yes." He could not quite meet her cold stare. "Mackay is her maiden name. She prefers to use it for her work."

"Rather a coincidence, isn't it? Two Mistress Bairds. Is that what you were going to tell me?"

"No. Not exactly. I know this must come as a bit of a shock, but –"

"Or were you just going to leave me in the dark? Let me see if I understand the situation aright. She is married to Baird's brother – the brute you claim is responsible for abusing Elizabeth. And now the scoundrel has the gall to turn up here."

"I would have told you, Hilda. Believe me. I just wanted to get the wedding over first. You can't hold Morag responsible for the behaviour of her husband. She has suffered as well, you know."

"And yet she tolerates his actions." She waved him away. "I'm tired, Edward. Do what you must. Though I can't think what good creating a scene will do. You'll only make a fool of yourself."

"I am not going to create a scene. I merely want a word. You'd better go and tell Morag. Explain that her husband is here."

She nodded wearily. "I hope you know what you're doing."

The hotel lobby was all but deserted as he reached the foot of the stairs – just a solitary clerk behind the desk, and a single bellboy hovering in the distance. There could be no mistaking the rough fellow lurking by an alcove. Like a fish out of water, Lixmont could not help thinking, with his shabby suit and badly knotted tie, a cloth cap grasped in his hand. So this was the cad who had violated his daughter. He fought back his anger as he crossed the floor.

"Mr Baird, I presume." He would not sully himself by offering his hand.

"What's that to you?"

"My name is Lixmont. You may have heard of me."

"What of it? I didnae come to see you. I'm here to collect the wife."

"Mrs Baird has been informed. She'll be down in a minute. I just wanted a word with you – in private."

"I cannae think why. I've nae business wi' you."

"Forgive me for being blunt. But let me ask you a question. Are you the person responsible for – for my daughter's condition?"

Iain snorted. At any other time he would have erupted with fury. But the message that Sir Edward Lixmont was coming down had given him fair warning. "So that's what this is all about. Ye shouldnae listen to my wee brother. It's a lie. And I'll have the law on anybody that says otherwise."

"So you deny that you fathered my daughter's child?"

"Certainly."

"And you have no claim upon the boy?"

"How could I have? I only met her once. At my mother's funeral."

"Are you prepared to sign a paper to that effect?"

"What is this?" He felt his blood stirring. "Is my word no' good enough? I'll hae nane o' yer lawyers' tricks." Out of the corner of his eye he saw Morag on the staircase, dressed in her overcoat and hat. "Hurry up, woman," he called out. "We're gettin' out o' here. I'm no' goin' to stand and be insulted to my face."

Fearing the worst, Morag rushed forward. "I'm so sorry, Sir Edward," she gasped. "My husband is not quite himself today." She turned on Iain. "What on earth are you doing here? For God's sake, get a grip on yerself."

"Tell him that." He glared at Lixmont. "It's his fault. Him and his wild accusations. I come here, peaceful like, to pick ye up, and this stuffed shirt turns up and gies me laldy. Now is that fair?"

"You might at least have remembered your manners."

"It's of no account, Mrs Baird," said Lixmont smoothly. "I may have overstepped the mark myself. If so, I apologise. We're very grateful for all you've done for Elizabeth. You will at least allow me to reimburse the cost of a taxi fare."

"We want nane o' your money," growled Iain. "Shanks pony will suit us fine."

"As you wish. In that case I'll bid you goodnight." He turned and walked away.

They were left to glower at each other. Morag smouldered with shame and humiliation. She was sorely tempted to lay into him there and then. But what would be the point? He would only become evasive, or fly off the handle himself.

"I should never have let ye come," he muttered at last.

"Is that why ye did? Just so that you could come round and show me up?" There was real hurt in her voice.

He felt a stab of remorse. "I wouldnae dae that. Honest, Morag. I was at a meetin'. No' far from here. Union business, if ye must ken."

"Really? Funny ye never mentioned it afore."

"It was arranged at short notice. Just a few shop stewards. I only got the call this afternoon. Ye'll never guess who sent it."

"No doubt ye're goin' to tell me."

"Aye. But outside. Let's get on the road." She allowed him to usher her through the revolving door and out into the street. There he looked round cautiously before lowering his voice. "It was Stan Robertson."

"Stan Robertson?" She was visibly shaken.

"Hush, no' sae loud. Let's get on the road. Or we'll never get hame the night."

She fell into step beside him. "But I thought we'd seen the last o' him. You said he'd disappeared again. No' a trace o' him for weeks."

"Well, he's back now. Seems he's been up in Argyllshire."

"Argyllshire? What did he expect to find there?"

"Ah, well. There ye have it. He was spyin' out the lie o' the land."

"I dinnae get it. Why would he dae that?"

Iain hesitated a moment before going on. "No' a word o' this to another soul. He was lookin' for a quiet inlet where a boat could sneak in – to land a cargo o' weapons. Guns frae Russia to arm the workers. That's why he was sent back."

There was a sharp intake of breath. "I dinna believe it. The man must be off his chump."

"It's true enough. And that's no' all. He's to find locations for trainin' camps – hidden in the woods. That's why he wanted to see me and the others. We're to sound out likely recruits – and arrange for them to go on weekend trips."

"What for?"

"So they can be shown how to fire a rifle, of course. Plenty o' scope for target practice in a remote glen."

"This is madness, Iain." Now she was genuinely horrified. "An armed rising? Ye'd never get away wi' it. Ye wouldnae stand a chance if they sent in the army."

"That's no' what Stan thinks. Things are desperate in France. It's only a matter o' time before the whole front collapses. And if the war's lost ye can guess what'll happen here. Stan wants us to be ready to lead the way."

"So ye say. And just how does he propose to dae that."

"Oh, he's got it all planned out – a revolution on Clydeside, led by a hard core of armed workers. When he gies the signal, we're to march on George Square, and seize the provost and council as hostages. Once that's done we're tae send out parties to take over the banks, railway stations, newspaper offices and ships on the Clyde. He's even hopin' that the sodgers at Maryhill Barracks will join us."

"And he expects you to trot out in front as his loyal lieutenant. God Almighty, are ye off yer heid? Ye'll just get yersel killed."

Abruptly he swung round and gripped her tightly. "You just listen to me, Morag. I ken exactly what I'm daein'. And I'll no' be the one to suffer – whatever happens. Now no' another word. There's a tram stop ower there. We'll catch the next caur. And when I get ye hame … it's an early night for you, my lass."

She felt herself stiffen, then go limp at the knees. Wonderingly she scanned his face. This was the Iain who had captured her heart. But what had he meant by that remark? Perhaps he saw through Robertson as well, was only playing along with him for form's sake. Surely he must realise that Bolshevik arms would never arrive. Even if they were sent, any ship was bound to be intercepted by one of the many naval patrols. And without weapons there could be no armed rising. In the meantime … Her whole body tingled with anticipation.

He chuckled as he released her. "It'll no' be long now. Just you contain yerself." Their lovemaking would be passionate; he would see to that. Exhaustion should induce a sound sleep, and that was vital. It would never do for her to waken and find him at the kitchen table. He had a message to compose, to hand to the pay clerk the next morning so that it would reach Dunlop without delay. How fortunate it was that Stan had let slip the address where he would be staying for the next day or two. There could be no recriminations this time. And at last he would have that bastard off his back.

*　*　*

August 1918

Ye will go and tell Miss Elizabeth, won't you? The plea rose up to haunt him as he lurched along deserted streets in the early dawn of a Sunday morning. Why was his wife so concerned for others? Had she no regard for him, and how he must be feeling?

The last twenty-four hours had been a nightmare – rushing her to hospital, waiting feverishly while the doctors battled to save her life. Now it was over. Morag was safe, though weak from loss of blood. She had suffered another miscarriage. He had been told they must never try for another child: in fact it would be advisable to abstain from relationships altogether. Deep emotions stirred within him. Now he knew what he wanted – more than anything else. A son to call his own. And now the woman he had married could never give him that.

Had he promised to deliver her message? He could not quite remember.

Perhaps he had nodded agreement. If so, he regretted giving way so readily. A warm welcome was hardly on the cards. But was there any need to risk a confrontation? Surely a note pushed through the door would serve just as well. That was the obvious solution. He could simply tell Morag there was no answer when he called. And there was no need to rush. He had the whole day to carry out the request. For the moment his only desire was rest – food and rest. Wending his way homewards, the prospect of a warm, enticing bed had never seemed more attractive.

At last, footsore and weary, he turned in at the close. Struggling up the stairs towards the top flat, an overpowering dizziness swept over him. Somehow he managed to reach his door, turn his key in the lock, push in and totter towards the bedroom: he felt his legs give way, there was a sensation of falling …

He woke with a start. Water was cascading over his head, trickling into his mouth and nostrils. "What the fuck –?"

"Glad to see you're still in the land o' the living," chuckled a voice. "I've seen better lookin' corpses."

"Who the hell –?" He sat up, rubbing the sleep from his eyes. "Stan Robertson? What in blue blazes are you doin' here?"

"Talkin' to a prize gowk. The front door was wide open. Anyone could have walked in. D'ye make a habit o' this?"

Iain ignored the jib. Instead he swung himself to his feet. "Ye didnae need to half kill me," he grumbled. "I'm drookit."

"Bollocks! A wee drop o' water winnae hurt ye. You must have had a right skinfull last night – no' botherin' to get undressed. I widnae like to be in your shoes when yer wife gets a haud o' ye. Where is she, by the way? There's nae sign of her ben the house."

"She's in hospital, since ye must ken. And that's where I've been since yesterday mornin'. There's nae chance o' getting' a drink there," he added bitterly.

For once Robertson seemed at a loss. "I'm sorry, Iain. I didnae realise. It's no' too serious, is it? I mean she'll be fine, won't she?"

"Aye, she'll survive. It was another miscarriage. So we'll never hae any weans o' our ain. That's what we were telt."

"Ye have my sympathy. But it's no' the end o' the world. There's other ways – adoption and such like. Plenty o' time to think about that later." He patted Iain on the shoulder. "There's work to be done. You go and freshen up while I put on the kettle and see if I can dig up some scran. Ye look as if ye could do wi' a feed."

Iain set about trying to make himself look presentable, at least to the extent of shaving and changing the collar on his shirt. Why had Stan turned up like some will o' the wisp? And today – of all days? Surely he must be aware that he had evaded capture by the skin of his teeth on at least three occasions over the past months. And each attempt had taken place soon after a meeting with his loyal lieutenants. He must suspect something. Yet here he was, acting as though nothing was amiss. Dunlop's men had always arrived just too late to catch their prey. Luck – or had someone tipped him off? That was another worry …

"Penny for them."

Iain spun round. "Eh? Sorry Stan. It's nothin'. Just wonderin' why ye're here."

"Does there have to be a reason? We're old friends. Come and hae yer breakfast."

A frugal meal of bread and cheese had been laid out, together with a pot of tea and tin of condensed milk. Iain ate largely in silence while Robertson babbled away about his stay in Russia. His gloom deepened. Small talk was all very well, but was hardly reassuring. There had to be a definite purpose to his visit, but apparently his mentor was in no hurry to broach the subject. At last Iain could stand the suspense no longer.

"For Christ's sake! Can ye no' get to the point?"

His visitor gave a short laugh. "Aye, I suppose it's time." He lit a cigarette and pushed the packet across the table. "Ye mind that shipload o' weapons frae Russia? Well, I'm pleased to say they're on their way at last."

"So that's what this is all about?" Iain whistled. "It's been months. We thought they'd never come."

"Ah well, I'll no' pretend it's been easy. But everything's hunky-dory now. We've fixed a spot for landin' the cargo. But there's still the problem o' storin' the guns till they're needed. I've a place in mind, but I'd like your opinion. What about comin' wi' me to gie it the once over?"

"You mean now?" Instinctively he was cautious.

"Aye. Nae time like the present."

"But – but what about Morag? She'll be expectin' me."

"It's no' that far. There and back in a few hours. She'll no' be bothered if ye're too tired to come. It'll gie her a chance to rest."

Iain wavered. If this was some ploy to lure him off the beaten track, force a confession out of him, exact some terrible retribution … But perhaps he was making too much of Stan's invitation. And an outright refusal would not go down well. If everything was above board, then his report could not fail to impress Dunlop. If not … then it would be up to him to ensure he was not taken unawares.

"I couldna come right away. I promised Morag I'd tell her employer. Morag nannies for her," he added by way of explanation. "Would that put ye out?"

"Not in the least. In fact it sounds perfect."

"How's that?"

"Think about it, man. If ye were to drop a hint that Morag might appreciate a wee visit this afternoon … Well then, it would gie ye an excuse no' to go yersel'. How long would ye need?" He glanced at the clock on the mantelpiece. "It's gone ten now. Suppose I was to meet ye at noon."

"Fine. That would gie me plenty o' time. The wifie bides up by Kelvingrove."

Robertson picked up his cap. "Then I'll meet ye at the station at Partick. We'll be takin' the train part o' the way. By the by, how is the recruitin' drive goin'? How many have ye signed up?"

Iain pulled a face. "No' that great, since ye ask. It's a slow business, gettin' the right folk. And they're no' minded to commit themselves, no' till they're sure we've got the arms stashed away."

He was rewarded with a hard stare. "Twelve noon, then. Dinnae be late."

"Ye ken ye can rely on me, Stan."

"I hope so." The words were heavy with irony. Robertson turned on his heel and stalked out.

Iain was left frowning. Stan might not suspect him of treachery, but he would not readily tolerate failure to carry out instructions. What else could he have done? The mood amongst the workforce was scarcely encouraging, not least with the news that the war was now going in favour of the Allies. Blast Robertson! He seemed to live in a world of his own – imagining that Glasgow could be another Petrograd. In all probability the guns would never arrive. And even if they did, what were the chances against fully trained soldiers? Martyrdom for the cause? Stan was welcome to it. Damned if he would dance to his tune. In the meantime there was a message to deliver. Sorting out pencil and paper, he cleared a space for himself and began to write.

Ten minutes later he was in the street, striding out towards the nearest tram stop. There were more people about now, most of them dressed in their Sunday clothes. But churchgoers held no interest for him; he was too wrapped up in his own concerns. Rounding a corner, he caught sight of a tram taking on a line of passengers. Now there was a stroke of luck – if he could catch it. Putting on a spurt, he just managed to jump on board as the vehicle moved off. Breathing heavily, he climbed the spiral staircase to the upper deck. At the top he chanced to look back: someone else was running full tilt for the car. Too far away, he thought, as he took his seat. That poor sod would never make it.

Traffic on a Sunday was light; in what seemed no time at all they were over the Clyde and heading towards Kelvinhall. If memory served him right, his destination lay off the main road, in an avenue fringed with trees. As the car screeched to a halt he swung himself down the stairs and leapt from the platform in a single bound. Out of the corner of his eye he saw another passenger rise from his seat on the lower deck. But he was in too much of a hurry to make the connection. It was the same man he had glimpsed running for the tram.

He set off at a brisk pace, looking neither to left nor right, and reached the corner of the quiet residential street within minutes. All was as he had hoped – not a soul in sight. Keeping behind the line of trees as far as possible, he stole forward till he had a clear view of his objective. There was no sign of life – just a closed door and curtained windows. Pulling up his collar, he made as if to walk past, then wheeled and threw open the garden gate. It was only a few steps to the front door. Drawing the note from his pocket, he stretched towards the letter box, and then … all of a sudden the door swung back, and there stood the mistress of the house, glowering at him.

"Sneaking up the path, were you? Up to no good, I'll be bound." Iain wilted before her anger and scorn. "I saw you skulking out there. If you're looking to commit some mischief on me or mine, then you're out of luck. You don't intimidate me. And both my husband and son are not at home."

"It's nothin' like that," he protested feebly. "I was asked to deliver a message."

"Really?"

"Aye. It's Morag. She'll no' be here the morn. She's in hospital. Just had a miscarriage."

Now it was Elizabeth's turn to reel. "What was that? Miscarriage? Is this true?"

"That's what I came to tell ye. She was taken in yesterday. Bleedin' fair bad, she was."

"But – I never knew. She never mentioned she was pregnant."

"I'm no' sure she kent herself. She was only two or three months gone. That's what the doctor said." He shrugged his shoulders. "So that's that. Nae chance o' a wean now."

Suddenly she felt sorry for him. "Is that a note you've got in your hand?"

"Aye. I kent ye widnae want to see me. So I wrote it down for ye." He handed her the folded paper. "Sorry if this puts ye out."

"Please don't give it another thought. The important thing is for Morag to get well as quickly as possible. I'm sorry I misjudged you," she added more gently. "Do you think she would appreciate a visit?"

"I'm sure she'd like that fine. I've put in the hospital and ward number."

She glanced at the note. "Then we'll go this afternoon. But what about you?"

"Oh I'll no' step on yer toes. I've been up all night. I could do wi' a few hours kip. I'll wait till this evenin'."

"Then that's settled. Thank you for letting me know."

He gave a little bob of acknowledgment and turned to leave. For some moments Elizabeth remained thoughtful in the doorway. He was really feeling this – so unhappy, yet somehow quite dignified in his grief. So he was capable of a spark of human feeling. Perhaps Morag had not made such a bad choice after all.

Iain was only too glad to quit the scene, relieved to be done with the unwelcome task. At least there could be no complaint about the outcome: Morag would have her visitor. Now he could concentrate on the business in hand. At the end of the road his pace slackened: there was plenty of time before he was due at the railway station. Like as not, Robertson would only put in an appearance at the last minute.

Somewhat to his surprise he found he was not first to arrive. Not that the fact was immediately obvious; it was not hard to miss the lone figure sitting half hidden by one of the roof pillars, apparently engrossed in reading a newspaper. Only a low growl attracted his attention as he walked past.

"Stan!" he exclaimed, turning back. "I didnae expect to see ye so soon."

"Well, I'd nothin' else on, so I thought I'd come early. Take a seat." He laid aside his *Post*. "Did ye get yer job done?"

"Piece o' cake. I managed to get her to spend some time wi' Morag this afternoon. So I'll no' be expected." It was a comfort to be able to report some success.

"That's dandy. I've bought the tickets. Ye'd better take yours." Iain read the destination before slipping the pasteboard into his pocket. "Dumbarton's no' that far," Robertson went on. "But there's a five mile tramp at the end. The walk will dae ye good. In the meantime ye'd best get yer nose intae this." He drew a folded newssheet from his pocket. "The train's no' due for half an hour."

Crafty old Stan! Who would give a second glance at two travellers catching up with events? Iain flicked through the headlines. The usual hogwash: *Allied advance on all fronts*; *Hun resistance slackening*; *Riots in German cities*. How could they print such drivel? He felt himself nodding off, the pages slipping from his grasp …

"Rouse yerself, you daft bugger!" It was Stan, shaking him awake. "Think ye're the sleeping beauty, eh? Ye've been deid to the world. It's nearly time for the train."

"Sorry, Stan. I must have dozed off."

"You've said it. Good job ye've got me to look after you. Did ye think to bring some grub for the journey?"

"Grub? No. I didna ken –"

"Then ye're goin' to get gey hungry afore we're back." He gave a mock sigh. "I suppose I'll hae to go and see if I can rustle up somethin' at the stall. Just you bide here."

He rose to his feet, looking round as though sniffing the air. Suddenly his body stiffened … The next instant he was off, sprinting like a hare.

"What the f –?" Before Iain could react he was surrounded, wrestled to the ground. He felt steel clamps on his wrists, a hood thrown over his head. There was a screech as a motor vehicle drew up; he was dragged to his feet, manhandled into it.

The van moved off, leaving him pinioned in a narrow cell. Almost at once his hands began to chafe at the tightness of the metal bands; it was an effort to breath under the mask. That bastard Dunlop! Who else? He must be responsible for this. But how did he know where to send his men? And had Robertson made good his escape? He could not help thinking his own fate might depend on the answer to that question.

The journey did not take long. It came as something of a relief to be pulled out into the open, even if he was promptly hustled into some building and up a flight of stairs.

"Good of you to drop by, Baird." The mocking tone was all too familiar. It was Dunlop – as he had expected. "You can remove that sack now," the voice continued. "And the darbies. Cuff him in front, though. We don't want him running off. Like his friend." So Stan had managed to avoid capture. His heart sank. This did not bode well for him.

He blinked as his eyes were uncovered, looked about him as the handcuffs were repositioned. Recognition dawned; this was the house he had visited before. Dunlop nodded at his guards and the two men left, closing the door behind them.

"You remember what I told you when you agreed to join the service, Baird?" I believe I said that were you to play me false, I would crush you like a worm. So how do you account for this?"

Iain felt his mouth run dry. "I can explain everythin'," he croaked. "If ye'll gie me the chance."

"Why should I? You see, I know it all already. I've had you followed – ever since that last time we failed to bag your chum. It was on the cards that he'd make contact again – sooner or later."

"Then ye'll ken I havnae seen him. This mornin' was the first time in weeks."

"True. But you agreed to meet up later in the day. You had ample opportunity to let us know. Why did you not report it?"

"How could I? I couldnae get in touch wi' yon clerk at the Ordnance on a Sunday."

"You could have come here. You've been to this address. There's always someone on duty."

"I – I didnae have time to think. And I promised to let a body ken that the wife was ill in hospital."

"So you put your wife before the interests of the service? That was unfortunate – for you."

Iain gulped, though outwardly he pretended to be mystified. "I dinnae understand."

"Then let me enlighten you. You already know that I've had you watched – day and night. It was perhaps an oversight on my part to have only one agent on duty, with instructions to stick to you like a limpet. Otherwise I might have learned of the situation earlier, and been able to make more elaborate arrangements. As it was, I was only informed by telephone from the stationmaster's office that you were in the company of an individual who matched Robertson's description. There was no time to lose. I gathered what men I could and made for the station. Regrettably they proved too few to cover all the exits. That's how your comrade was able to slip through the net – leaving you to take the consequences."

"Haud on a minute!" There was no disguising his alarm this time. "It's no' what ye think. Ye dinnae ken the whole story."

"I doubt that, Baird."

"It's true. Honest. He tell me about guns comin' frae Russia. He was goin' to show me the hidey-hole he'd picked out to stash them. I would have let ye ken once I'd seen it."

"Hmm. So he didn't reveal the location?"

"No – no' exactly. Somewhere near Dumbarton. A five mile walk from the station, he said."

"Well, that tallies with the railway ticket we found. But it scarcely gets us any further. If indeed there ever was this cargo of weapons you suggest."

"Ye dinnae believe me, sir."

"What do you think? You've let me down often enough in the past."

"I've always done my best." He tried to sound genuinely hurt.

"Really? You were warned before about your performance. Yet you chose to feed me a cock and bull story about your brother. Paying off old scores, were you?"

"I only said he might be one of the ringleaders. And you tried to get him sent back to the army."

"That's neither here nor there. He managed to wriggle out on health grounds. But at least he seems to have learnt his lesson. Unlike you."

"Maybe I did jump to conclusions. But I pointed out Robertson to ye."

"That's so. But he escaped every time. Coincidence? I don't think so. He must have been warned in advance."

"And you suppose it was me? I'd be daft to dae that. I ken where my best interests lie."

"I really wonder about that, Baird." He reached for a paperweight on his desk, hefting it in the palm of his hand as though weighing the evidence before delivering judgment. "I can't make up my mind whether you are stupid enough to believe you can get away with playing off one side against the other – or are just plain unlucky. But whichever it is, it doesn't really matter. At the moment you are of no further use to me."

The weight dropped from his grasp. Iain winced as it landed with a dull thud. "Even if I were to accept your story, you must realise that Robertson is bound to suspect you of betraying him. And no doubt he will communicate the same to his confederates. Steps must be taken to persuade him to believe otherwise. A press announcement that you have been arrested and jailed –"

"No! Ye cannae dae that." Instinctively he took a step forward. "Morag's just lost her bairn. She needs me to look after her."

"You should have thought of that earlier. Before you agreed to accompany Robertson."

"You bastard! If I were out o' these –" He brandished his chained fists.

"You'd never see your wife again. I'd see to that." Dunlop's gaze never wavered. It was Iain who shrank back, the fight draining out of him. He knew this was no idle threat. "That's better. Now calm down and listen. There'll be no trial. You'll be sent to Barlinnie under the DORA regulations. It'll only be for a month or two. Then, when things settle down, you can be quietly released. I'll square things with Findlay – tell him you're working undercover. How does that sound to you?"

"What about the wife," he muttered sullenly.

"Very well. I'll arrange for an occasional visit – so you can see her when she's better. I presume her employers will help out while she's indisposed. There'll be no question of financial hardship?"

"Aye. Like as no" It was a grudging admission.

"It's for your own good, man. You ought to feel grateful. I'm going to give you another chance. It's more than you deserve."

Iain could only shrug helplessly as the guards came in to lead him away.

TWENTY-FIVE

A Silver Lining?

November 1918

Alastair Baird stood shivering on the touchline as the rugby match neared its end. In truth he would rather not have come, but a promise to take Eddie to a game as part of his birthday treat could not be broken. It was no joke to wake up that morning with a sore throat and headache, even if a couple of aspirins had given some relief. Now the symptoms had returned with a vengeance. His whole body ached, chilled to the marrow by the swirling wind. But he refused to be a killjoy, not with his stepson jumping up and down with every kick and rush of the ball. At last the referee blew for no side, and the players trooped off to a ragged round of applause.

"Glad I was able to spot you, Baird," said a voice behind him. "The boys appreciate masters showing up on a Saturday morning to cheer them on."

It was Watson. Alastair groaned inwardly as he turned to greet the depute rector. Trust the man not to miss a house match. "Not at all, sir," he said politely. "I like to take an interest – when I can."

"That's the ticket." Watson was obviously disposed to be friendly. "And I see you've brought your son with you. How do you do, young man?" He bent down to shake the boy's hand. "Did you enjoy the game?"

"Very much, sir. It was exciting." He looked thoughtful for a moment. "I'd like to learn to play when I'm bigger."

"Excellent!" Watson almost purred with satisfaction. "It's never too early to start. How old are you?"

"I'm four, sir. It's my birthday today."

"My congratulations. No doubt you'll be joining the school in a year or so." He straightened up. "Then we can see about turning you into a rugger player."

"Plenty of time for that." Alastair forced a wan smile. "But in the

487

meantime we must be off. I promised to take this young chap to the picture palace this afternoon. He's never been before. And I believe there's a Charlie Chaplin film on view."

"Just a minute, Baird." Watson held up a restraining hand. "I've some news for you. I was going to wait till Monday, but you might as well hear it now." He paused for effect. "You'll no doubt be happy to learn that the board has decided to approve your transfer to the secondary department. And to grant you a tenured post. You've always wanted to specialise in your own subject, haven't you?"

"Ye-es. That's so," he replied slowly. "But won't that mean leaving you in the lurch?"

"I shouldn't worry too much about that. Your move isn't due to take effect till next term. And with any luck, by that time we'll have some of our younger colleagues back in the classroom."

"You really believe the war will be over so soon?"

"Why not? Look at the evidence, man. The enemy is on his last legs. The Hun can't hold out much longer, not with all his allies gone. You'll have heard about the mutiny in the navy, revolts in the cities. Hardly surprising they've sent delegates to sue for peace. It's even said the Kaiser has cut and run for some bolt hole to save his skin. But we'll have him all the same. It can only be a matter of days now, maybe even hours –" He broke off in sudden alarm. "I say, Baird, you've gone white as a sheet." Alastair had begun to sway, choking as he fought for breath. "Steady on, there. Take my arm while we get you into the clubhouse. This blasted influenza! Is there no end to it?"

Alastair could not fault Watson's solicitude as he and Eddie were ushered into armchairs on either side of a roaring fire. As the attack subsided he found a new respect for Watson's energy – bustling around, commandeering someone's motor car, bullying the owner into offering assistance to a distinguished former officer. This was really going over the score, but he was in no condition to complain. His only plea was to be driven home, rather than to hospital. Elizabeth was out at work, of course, but would be back in good time for Eddie's birthday tea. He was determined not to miss that, especially as the visit to the cinema now seemed unlikely. The maid would be at home. And Morag was due to come round to help with the celebrations.

Watson saw them off. "Take my tip, old man. Get yourself to bed as soon as you like. A tot of whisky wouldn't come amiss. Then you'll be as right as rain come Monday. You'll see."

He mouthed his thanks, then sank back on the leather seat. A tiny arm clutched his sleeve. "Don't worry about a thing, daddy. I don't mind missing the pictures. We can always go another day. I just want to see you get better."

A tear came to his eye as he ruffled his stepson's hair. Not many youngsters would be so quick on the uptake – or so understanding.

The engine hummed smoothly as the vehicle weaved its way through the midday traffic. Heads turned to stare at the burnished brass and gleaming paintwork; Alastair could not help a tinge of guilt at wondering how such an impressive machine had escaped requisition for the war effort. Influence in high places, he supposed. But he could not possibly ask about that. Fortunately their chauffeur had seen fit to devote his attention to the road ahead. Inane questions about life at the Front, or a sermon about making Germany pay, would have been too much to bear.

It took only a few minutes to reach their destination. The car drew up alongside the house – just as a familiar figure in coat and hat was unlatching the front gate.

"Look, it's Auntie Morag," called out Eddie.

The driver tweaked the bulb of his horn. Morag spun round in alarm; her astonishment was complete at the sight of Eddie scrambling out to give her a hug.

"Name o' the wee man!" She swept him up into her arms. "I didnae expect to see ye back so soon. Or in such a grand style." Her eye caught the other passenger struggling from the rear seat, clinging to the open door to keep his balance. Gently she set down her charge. "Just you run intae the house. Jenny will gie ye a biscuit and glass o' milk. I'll need to see to yer dad."

"He was taken poorly at the rugby match," said the driver, coming round from the front. "I was asked to bring him here. Shall I help him inside?"

It was Alastair who waved away the offer. "Thanks all the same. But I feel better now. We'll manage."

The man looked dubious for a moment, then nodded. After closing the passenger door, he climbed in behind the wheel and drove off.

"No need to fuss, Morag." He staggered towards her. "It's nothing. Just a touch of flu."

"We'll see about that. Here, lean on my arm." Reluctantly he allowed himself to be guided up the path, steered into the hallway. "Think ye can manage the stairs? You ought to be in bed."

"It's not that bad," he protested. "Just a tickle in the throat. I'll rest awhile downstairs. I'm not going to disappoint Eddie."

There was determination in his voice. Wisely she decided not to press the issue. "If that's what ye really want. I'll tell Jenny to light the fire in the front room. And fetch ye a blanket. Ye must keep warm."

Sweeping aside his feeble objection that coal was too precious to be wasted, she propelled him into the parlour. He felt powerless to resist as she divested him of his outdoor clothes and unlaced his boots, before draping an eiderdown round his body and stretching him out on the settee.

"Now you just bide still. Jenny's just puttin' a match to the fire. Promise ye'll rest."

"What else can I do?" He gestured helplessly. "You've got me wrapped up like an Egyptian mummy."

The afternoon dragged on. From time to time he drifted into semi-consciousness, but real sleep was impossible – aching muscles, pain behind the eyes, periodic bouts of shivering saw to that. He was fully awake when Morag looked in to mend the fire and draw the curtains. Her suggestion of tea and aspirin was met with a polite shake of the head. What good would they do? How long before Elizabeth came home? She could only shrug at his whispered appeal. Eddie would have been company for him, but perhaps it was as well to keep the boy away as much as possible. To be responsible for passing on his ailment was unthinkable – though people were saying the very young were not affected so much. Still … He dozed off again.

It was quite dark when he felt a hand on his brow. He stirred, tried to brush it aside. "You've got a bit of a temperature." It was a relief to hear Elizabeth's voice. "Morag tells me you've caught the flu. How do you feel?"

"Not too bad," he croaked. "All the better for having you back."

"Think you're up to Eddie's birthday tea? I thought we might have it in here. Much cosier."

She helped him sit up. Alastair blinked dizzily at the sudden glare of the electric light as his stepson ran into the room, closely followed by Morag and the maid with trays of sandwiches and a cake. He had no appetite, but did manage a few sips of tea while Eddie excitedly showed off his presents between mouthfuls of food.

Then came the highlight – the birthday cake itself. Elizabeth lit the four candles and watched proudly as her son blew them out. It had been an outrageous suggestion on her mother's part to pretend the boy was six months younger than his true age. Thank goodness she had dug in her heels against the proposal. As long as her husband was behind her, that was all that mattered. She smiled fondly as she passed him a sliver of cake.

Alastair gritted his teeth as he forced down a tiny morsel. It tasted like sawdust. Almost at once he felt his stomach heave; he was choking, retching, coughing up phlegm. Willing hands leapt to his aid, helping him to his feet, clapping his back, supporting him from the room. "Time you were in bed, my lad," he heard Elizabeth intone. But his abiding memory was the look of puzzled concern on Eddie's face.

An hour later Morag hovered uncertainly at the foot of the stairs. Eddie was safely tucked up in bed. Brave wee chap, so quiet and serious as she read his bedtime story. God knew what might await him in the morning. She heard the clock chime the hour. Elizabeth was taking a long time. Should she go up and knock, see if any help was required? As she hesitated, there was the sound of a door softly closing. She looked up anxiously. Elizabeth was coming down the stairs.

"He's resting quietly now," she explained, leading Morag back into the parlour. "But his breathing is shallow. And his pulse is racing. I'm afraid he might have a secondary infection." There was a catch in her voice. "Bronchial pneumonia."

"My God! That's usually –" She could not bring herself to say the word.

"Fatal? Yes it can be." Elizabeth fought back a tear. "We must just hope and pray."

Morag bit her lip. Elizabeth was bearing up well, but she could not simply abandon her to cope on her own. "I could stay the night. Gie ye the chance o' a wee break."

"But I wouldn't want to impose. You already do too much for us."

"It's nae bother. And I'd like to help."

Elizabeth pressed her arm. "You're a good friend, Morag. I don't know where we'd be without you."

"It's no more than ye did for me. When I think about –" She broke off. "Well, ye ken."

"No need to say more. Have you had any news?"

"About Iain? Aye. But this is nae time to bother about that. Will ye be sendin' for the doctor?"

"Perhaps. Let's see how he is in the morning."

"Why no' put yer feet up for half an hour. Ye look frazzled."

"I'm fine. Now what was it you were about to tell me?"

"Was I? Well, ye might as well ken. It's just that I had a card in the post this forenoon. They're goin' to let him out on Monday."

* * *

It was the day of his release. Dunlop had told him to count his blessings, but all he felt was bitterness and reproach. Why make him endure the harshest regime the jail had to offer – hard labour and few privileges? The monthly half hour visit from Morag was scant compensation for his treatment. Was it just to prove to the inmates that he was still regarded as a red revolutionary? So that word would get out to Robertson? Surely there had to be more to it than that.

He cursed himself for a fool in not checking the bundle before signing for his possessions. But the package had been securely tied, and the warders were insistent on hurrying him through the formalities. Not till he was well clear of the prison had he taken the opportunity to stop and unfasten the wrappings, only to make the discovery that his money was gone. So the screws had robbed him; he might have expected as much. More perplexing was the absence of his latch key. Was this another deliberate ploy? Unless Morag was at home he was now locked out for the day. His first instinct was to tramp back, hammer on the door, demand what was rightfully his. But then he shook his head. What would be the use? They would just laugh in his face – if nothing worse.

Not for the first time that morning Iain Baird bemoaned his misfortune. It would be just like Dunlop to have inflicted this final humiliation – if only to remind him of his place. Perhaps it was a hint that he was to be discarded, thrown on the scrapheap. But would such a fate really be so bad? Sacked from the Ordnance as war production was scaled back, evicted from his tied house as a consequence? At least he would be well out of that bastard's clutches. Almost at once he dismissed the idea. There might be a moment of rejoicing as peace was declared, but it would not take long for the hollowness of victory to sink in. Disillusion and discontent – that was the inevitable outcome. And Dunlop and his ilk would be only too well aware of it. No, his services would be required – perhaps more than ever. If the munitions works were closed down there were always the shipyards – at least until war losses were made good.

But whatever lay ahead could wait. For the time being his only desire was for the comfort of familiar surroundings, with a glass of something warming in his hand. Bugger! What if Morag was out? Chances were she had been given no warning of his discharge. In that case she would probably be at her place of work. Should he call there first? It was not so far to Hillhead. And it would only take a second to ask for the key. He decided to take the risk.

A shorter journey it might be, but it seemed endless as he trudged westwards along the main thoroughfare to the city centre, then outwards again towards Kelvingrove and the warren of residential streets beyond. He was in a foul temper; even the sight of his destination did little to change his mood. There would be no hesitation this time. He marched straight up the path and rang the doorbell with unwonted force. The door opened almost immediately. It was Morag.

"Iain! I might have kent. I was half expectin' ye."

"So they telt ye? Why are ye no' at home, then?"

"Hush!" She wagged a finger in admonition. "No' sae much noise. The doctor's here."

"Doctor?" He sounded puzzled.

"Aye. Ye'd best come in. Wipe yer boots." She led him into the kitchen, made him sit down at the table.

"So what's up?" If it was the boy who was ill …

"It's yer brother. He's been taken bad wi' the influenza." Suddenly she flared up. "It's this damned war. He's never really got over that bout o' pneumonia he caught in the trenches."

"I'm no' surprised. He a'ways did have a weak chest – even as a kid." He tried not to show his contempt, despite the image of a sickly child, the runt of the family, cosseted and favoured at his expense. "When did it start?"

"Just the other day." She frowned at the memory. "Ye could see he was feelin' poorly on Saturday. We sent for the doctor yesterday. He left some medicine, but said it probably widnae dae much good. No' since the infection got to his lungs. It was in the lap o' the gods whether he pulled through, or ..." Her voice faltered, but she refused to give way. "Miss Elizabeth went up tae the hospital to gie them the news. They let her use the phone to get in touch wi' her parents. They're both due this afternoon. And her faither is arrangin' for a private nurse."

"So it's as serious as that?" His mind was racing. Now if Alastair was to fail to recover ... "I suppose there's no' much hope," he mused.

"Dinnae say that. Alastair's a fighter. He'll no' gie up easy."

"I didnae mean –"

"Haud yer wheesht!" She quietened him with a hiss. "Here's Miss Elizabeth and the doctor now."

Iain strained his ears. He could hear snatches of muffled conversation, followed by the sound of a door opening and closing. Seconds later Elizabeth came into the room. His presence hardly seemed to register with her, even though he did rise at Morag's prompting.

"I've just seen the doctor out," she announced. "He thinks there's still a chance."

"Thank God for that," breathed Morag.

"Yes. He's very weak. But just about holding his own. And, best of all, there's no sign of heliotrope cyanosis."

"Helio – what?" It was double-dutch to her.

"The name doesn't matter. It means the patient goes blue in the face. It's nearly always fatal."

Iain shuffled awkwardly. "I'm fair sorry for yer trouble, missus. I didnae mean to butt in like this. It's just that I lost my key. So I came to borrow Morag's." His eye caught a slight movement in the doorway. "Is that yer laddie?"

A young child advanced towards the stranger, clutching a wooden railway engine. "Are you my uncle?" he asked shyly.

"I'm yer da –" He checked himself, just in time. "That's right. I'm your Uncle Iain. And you must be Eddie. That's a braw train ye've got there."

"Would you like to see it?" He held it up for inspection. "It's a birthday present."

"Yer birthday, eh? We'll need to dae somethin' about that. What wid ye like?"

Eddie had no doubts. "The picture palace," he said firmly. "My dad was going to take me when he got ill."

Iain turned to the two women. "Out of the question," snapped Morag before he could open his mouth. "I'm surprised ye could even think on it." She looked round at Elizabeth for support.

"Hold on a minute, Morag. The boy's been cooped up in this house far too long. He should have some fresh air. And we'll have our hands full. The doctor said the next few hours would be crucial." She fixed Iain with a long, hard stare. "I'm not sure I should be doing this. But needs must. His grandparents should arrive early this afternoon. Just see he's back in good time to meet them."

Morag whistled in disbelief. Had Elizabeth taken leave of her senses? But something in her expression told her it would be futile to argue. Instead she glared at Iain before bustling away to fetch coat and scarf.

"I suppose ye'll be needin' a sub," she said tartly, as she helped Eddie into his outdoor clothes.

"Aye, if ye dinnae mind." He spread his hands sheepishly. "I'm a bit short at the minute."

"Thought as much." She delved into her apron pocket and fished out a two shilling piece. "Here' ye'd best take this."

Together they went down the path. At the gate Iain paused: bold, trusting eyes gazed up at him. Suddenly there was a lump in his throat. Such a sturdy wee lad. A real chip off the old block. A wave of fierce pride surged through him.

In the distance a church bell began its peal – quickly taken up by others. People were coming out into the street, laughing and cheering, caught up in the excitement of the moment. His spirits soared. It was the end of the war.

A shaft of sunlight broke through the grey clouds. Was this an omen? Perhaps there was a brighter tomorrow after all.